MW00856827

THE COMPLETE TALES OF
JULES DE GRANDIN

VOLUME FIVE

BLACK
MOON

SEABURY QUINN

EDITED BY GEORGE A. VANDERBURGH

Night Shade Books
New York

Night Shade books may be purchased in bulk at special discounts for sales promotion, corporate gifts, fund-raising, or educational purposes. Special editions can also be created to specifications. For details, contact the Special Sales Department, Night Shade Books, 307 West 36th Street, 11th Floor, New York, NY 10018 or info@skyhorsepublishing.com.

Night Shade Books® is a registered trademark of Skyhorse Publishing, Inc.®, a Delaware corporation.

Visit our website at www.nightshadebooks.com.

10 9 8 7 6 5 4 3 2 1

Library of Congress Cataloging-in-Publication Data is available on file.

Print ISBN: 978-1-59780-985-6
Ebook ISBN: 978-1-59780-986-3

Cover illustration by Donato Giancola
Cover design by Claudia Noble

Printed in the United States of America

TABLE OF CONTENTS

Introduction—*George A. Vanderburgh and Robert E. Weinberg* vii
The Further Appearances of Jules de Grandin—*Stephen Jones* xiii

1938
Suicide Chapel (*Weird Tales*, June 1938*) 3
The Venomed Breath of Vengeance (*Weird Tales*, August 1938) 28
Black Moon (*Weird Tales*, October 1938) 49

1939
The Poltergeist of Swan Upping (*Weird Tales*, February 1939) 78
The House Where Time Stood Still (*Weird Tales*, March 1939) 108
Mansions in the Sky (*Weird Tales*, June-July 1939) .138
The House of the Three Corpses (*Weird Tales*, August 1939) 161

1942–1945
Stoneman's Memorial (*Weird Tales*, May 1942) 189
Death's Bookkeeper (*Weird Tales*, July 1944^) 212
The Green God's Ring (*Weird Tales*, January 1945) 230
Lords of the Ghostlands (*Weird Tales*, March 1945^) 251

1946
Kurban (*Weird Tales*, January 1946^) 272
The Man in Crescent Terrace (*Weird Tales*, March 1946) 294
Three in Chains (*Weird Tales*, May 1946) 313
Catspaws (*Weird Tales*, July 1946+) 334
Lottë (*Weird Tales*, September 1946) 352
Eyes in the Dark (*Weird Tales*, November 1946) 371

1947–1951
Clair de Lune (*Weird Tales*, November 1947) 389
Vampire Kith and Kin (*Weird Tales*, May 1949) 405
Conscience Maketh Cowards (*Weird Tales*, November 1949) 421
The Body-Snatchers (*Weird Tales*, November 1950) 437
The Ring of Bastet (*Weird Tales*, September 1951 455

*Cover by Margaret Brundage
^Cover by A. R. Tilburne
+Cover by Matt Fox

THE COMPLETE TALES OF Jules de Grandin is dedicated to the memory of Robert E. Weinberg, who passed away in fall of 2016. Weinberg, who edited the six-volume paperback series of de Grandin stories in the 1970s, also supplied many original issues of *Weird Tales* magazine from his personal collection so that Seabury Quinn's work could be carefully scanned and transcribed digitally. Without his knowledge of the material and his editorial guidance, as well as his passion for Quinn's work over a long period of time (when admirers of the Jules de Grandin stories were often difficult to come by), this series would not have been possible, and we owe him our deepest gratitude and respect.

Introduction

by George A. Vanderburgh and Robert E. Weinberg

W EIRD TALES, THE SELF-DESCRIBED "Unique Magazine," and one of the most influential Golden Age pulp magazines in the first half of the twentieth century, was home to a number of now-well-recognized names, including Robert Bloch, August Derleth, Robert E. Howard, H. P. Lovecraft, Clark Ashton Smith, and Manly Wade Wellman.

But among such stiff competition was another writer, more popular at the time than all of the aforementioned authors, and paid at a higher rate because of it. Over the course of ninety-two stories and a serialized novel, his most endearing character captivated pulp magazine readers for nearly three decades, during which time he received more front cover illustrations accompanying his stories than any of his fellow contributors.

The writer's name was Seabury Quinn, and his character was the French occult detective Jules de Grandin.

Perhaps you've never heard of de Grandin, his indefatigable assistant Dr. Trowbridge, or the fictional town of Harrisonville, New Jersey. Perhaps you've never even heard of Seabury Quinn (or maybe only in passing, as a historical footnote in one of the many essays and reprinted collections of Quinn's now-more-revered contemporaries). Certainly, de Grandin was not the first occult detective—Algernon Blackwood's John Silence, Hodgson's Thomas Carnacki, and Sax Rohmer's Moris Klaw preceded him—nor was he the last, as Wellman's John Thunstone, Margery Lawrence's Miles Pennoyer, and Joseph Payne Brennan's Lucius Leffing all either overlapped with the end of de Grandin's run or followed him. And without doubt de Grandin shares more than a passing resemblance to both Sir Arthur Conan Doyle's Sherlock Holmes (especially with his Dr. Watson-like sidekick) and Agatha Christie's Hercule Poirot.

Indeed, even if you were to seek out a de Grandin story, your options over the years would have been limited. Unlike Lovecraft, Smith, Wellman, Bloch, and other *Weird Tales* contributors, the publication history of the Jules de Grandin tales is spotty at best. In 1966, Arkham House printed roughly 2,000 copies of *The Phantom-Fighter*, a selection of ten early works. In the late 1970s, Popular Library published six paperback volumes of approximately thirty-five assorted tales, but they are now long out of print. In 2001, the specialty press The Battered Silicon Dispatch Box released an oversized, three-volume hardcover set of every de Grandin story (the first time all the stories had been collected), and, while still in production, the set is unavailable to the general trade.

So, given how obscure Quinn and his character might seem today, it's justifiably hard to understand how popular these stories originally were, or how frequently new ones were written. But let the numbers tell the tale: from October 1925 (when the very first de Grandin story was released) to December 1933, a roughly eight-year span, de Grandin stories appeared in an incredible sixty-two of the ninety-six issues that *Weird Tales* published, totaling well-over three-quarters of a million words. Letter after letter to the magazine's editor demanded further adventures from the supernatural detective.

If Quinn loomed large in the mind of pulp readers during the magazine's heyday, then why has his name fallen on deaf ears since? Aside from the relative unavailability of his work, the truth is that Quinn has been successfully marginalized over the years by many critics, who have often dismissed him as simply a hack writer. The de Grandin stories are routinely criticized as being of little worth, and dismissed as unimportant to the development of weird fiction. A common argument, propped up by suspiciously circular reasoning, concludes that Quinn was not the most popular writer for *Weird Tales*, just the most prolific.

These critics seem troubled that the same audience who read and appreciated the work of Lovecraft, Smith, and Howard could also enjoy the exploits of the French ghostbuster. And while it would be far from the truth to suggest that the literary merits of the de Grandin stories exceed those of some of his contemporaries' tales, Quinn was a much more skillful writer, and the adventures of his occult detective more enjoyable to read, than most critics are willing to acknowledge. In the second half of the twentieth century, as the literary value of some pulp-fiction writers began to be reconsidered, Quinn proved to be the perfect whipping boy for early advocates attempting to destigmatize weird fiction: He was the hack author who churned out formulaic prose for a quick paycheck. Anticipating charges that a literary reassessment of Lovecraft would require reevaluating the entire genre along with him, an arbitrary line was quickly drawn in the sand, and as the standard-bearer of pulp fiction's popularity, the creator of Jules de Grandin found himself on the wrong side of that line.

First and foremost, it must be understood that Quinn wrote to make money, and he was far from the archetypal "starving artist." At the same time that his Jules de Grandin stories were running in *Weird Tales*, he had a similar series of detective stories publishing in *Real Detective Tales*. Quinn was writing two continuing series at once throughout the 1920s, composing approximately twenty-five thousand words a month on a manual typewriter. Maintaining originality under such a grueling schedule would be difficult for any author, and even though the de Grandin stories follow a recognizable formula, Quinn still managed to produce one striking story after another. It should also be noted that the tendency to recycle plots and ideas for different markets was very similar to the writing practices of *Weird Tales*'s other prolific and popular writer, Robert E. Howard, who is often excused for these habits, rather than criticized for them.

Throughout his many adventures, the distinctive French detective changed little. His penchant for amusingly French exclamations was a constant through all ninety-three works, as was his taste for cigars and brandy after (and sometimes before) a hard day's work, and his crime-solving styles and methods remained remarkably consistent. From time to time, some new skill or bit of knowledge was revealed to the reader, but in most other respects the Jules de Grandin of "The Horror on the Links" was the same as the hero of the last story in the series, published twenty-five years later.

> He was a perfect example of the rare French blond type, rather under medium height, but with a military erectness of carriage that made him look several inches taller than he really was. His light-blue eyes were small and exceedingly deep-set, and would have been humorous had it not been for the curiously cold directness of their gaze. With his wide mouth, light mustache waxed at the ends in two perfectly horizontal points, and those twinkling, stock-taking eyes, he reminded me of an alert tomcat.

Thus is de Grandin described by Dr. Trowbridge in the duo's first meeting in 1925. His personal history is dribbled throughout the stories: de Grandin was born and raised in France, attended medical school, became a prominent surgeon, and in the Great War served first as a medical officer, then as a member of the intelligence service. After the war, he traveled the world in the service of French Intelligence. His age is never given, but it's generally assumed that the occult detective is in his early forties.

Samuel Trowbridge, on the other hand, is a typical conservative small-town doctor of the first half of the twentieth century (as described by Quinn, he is a cross between an honest brother of George Bernard Shaw and former Chief Justice of the United States Charles Evans Hughes). Bald and bewhiskered, most—if not all—of his life was spent in the same town. Trowbridge is old-fashioned and somewhat conservative, a member of the Knights Templar, a vestryman in the Episcopal Church, and a staunch Republican.

While the two men are dissimilar in many ways, they are also very much alike. Both are fine doctors and surgeons. Trowbridge might complain from time to time about de Grandin's wild adventures, but he always goes along with them; there is no thought, ever, of leaving de Grandin to fight his battles alone. More than any other trait, though, they are two men with one mission, and perhaps for that reason they remained friends for all of their ninety-three adventures and countless trials.

The majority of Quinn's de Grandin stories take place in or near Harrisonville, New Jersey, a fictional community that rivals (with its fiends, hauntings, ghouls, werewolves, vampires, voodoo, witchcraft, and zombies) Lovecraft's own Arkham, Massachusetts. For more recent examples of a supernatural-infested community, one need look no further than the modern version of pulp-fiction narratives . . . television. *Buffy the Vampire Slayer*'s Sunnydale, California, and *The Night Strangler*'s Seattle both reflect the structural needs of this type of supernatural narrative.

Early in the series, de Grandin is presented as Trowbridge's temporary house guest, having travelled to the United States to study both medicine and modern police techniques, but Quinn quickly realized that the series was due for a long run and recognized that too much globe-trotting would make the stories unwieldy. A familiar setting would be needed to keep the main focus of each tale on the events themselves. Harrisonville, a medium-sized town outside New York City, was completely imaginary, but served that purpose.

Most of the de Grandin stories feature beautiful girls in peril. Quinn discovered early on that Farnsworth Wright, *Weird Tales*'s editor from 1924 to 1940, believed nude women on the cover sold more copies, so when writing he was careful to always feature a scene that could translate to appropriately salacious artwork. Quinn also realized that his readers wanted adventures with love and romance as central themes, so even his most frightening tales were given happy endings (. . . of a sort).

And yet the de Grandin adventures are set apart from the stories they were published alongside by their often explicit and bloody content. Quinn predated the work of Clive Barker and the splatterpunk writers by approximately fifty years, but, using his medical background, he wrote some truly terrifying horror stories; tales like "The House of Horror" and "The House Where Time Stood Still" feature some of the most hideous descriptions of mutilated humans ever set down on paper. The victims of the mad doctor in "The House of Horror" in particular must rank near the top of the list of medical monstrosities in fiction.

Another element that set Quinn's occult detective apart from others was his pioneering use of modern science in the fight against ancient superstitions.

De Grandin fought vampires, werewolves, and even mummies in his many adventures, but oftentimes relied on the latest technology to save the day. The Frenchman put it best in a conversation with Dr. Trowbridge at the end of "The Blood-Flower":

> "And wasn't there some old legend to the effect that a werewolf could only be killed with a silver bullet?"
>
> "Ah, bah," he replied with a laugh. "What did those old legend-mongers know of the power of modern firearms? . . . When I did shoot that wolfman, my friend, I had something more powerful than superstition in my hand. *Morbleu*, but I did shoot a hole in him large enough for him to have walked through."

Quinn didn't completely abandon the use of holy water, ancient relics, and magical charms to defeat supernatural entities, but he made it clear that de Grandin understood that there was a place for modern technology as well as old folklore when it came to fighting monsters. Nor was de Grandin himself above using violence to fight his enemies. Oftentimes, the French occult investigator served as judge, jury and executioner when dealing with madmen, deranged doctors, and evil masterminds. There was little mercy in his stories for those who used dark forces.

While sex was heavily insinuated but rarely covered explicitly in the pulps, except in the most general of terms, Quinn again was willing to go where few other writers would dare. Sexual slavery, lesbianism, and even incest played roles in his writing over the years, challenging the moral values of the day.

In the end, there's no denying that the de Grandin stories are pulp fiction. Many characters are little more than assorted clichés bundled together. De Grandin is a model hero, a French expert on the occult, and never at a loss when battling the most evil of monsters. Dr. Trowbridge remains the steadfast companion, much in the Dr. Watson tradition, always doubting but inevitably following his friend's advice. Quinn wrote for the masses, and he didn't spend pages describing landscapes when there was always more action unfolding.

The Jules de Grandin stories were written as serial entertainment, with the legitimate expectation that they would not be read back to back. While all of the adventures are good fun, the best way to properly enjoy them is over an extended period of time. Plowing through one story after another will lessen their impact, and greatly cut down on the excitement and fun of reading them. One story a week, which would stretch out this entire five-volume series over two years, might be the perfect amount of time needed to fully enjoy these tales of the occult and the macabre. They might not be great literature, but they don't pretend to be. They're pulp adventures, and even after seventy-five years, the stories read well.

Additionally, though the specific aesthetic values of *Weird Tales* readers were vastly different than those of today's readers, one can see clearly see the continuing allure of these types of supernatural adventures, and the long shadow that they cast over twentieth and early twenty-first century popular culture. Sure, these stories are formulaic, but it is a recipe that continues to be popular to this day. The formula of the occult detective, the protector who stands between us and the monsters of the night, can be seen time and time again in the urban fantasy and paranormal romance categories of commercial fiction, and is prevalent in today's television and movies. Given the ubiquity and contemporary popularity of this type of narrative, it's actually not at all surprising that Seabury Quinn was the most popular contributor to *Weird Tales*.

We are proud to present the first of five volumes reprinting every Jules de Grandin story written by Seabury Quinn. Organized chronologically, as they originally appeared in *Weird Tales* magazine, this is the first time that the collected de Grandin stories have been made available in trade editions.

Each volume has been graced by tremendous artwork from renowned artist Donato Giancola, who has given Quinn's legendary character an irresistible combination of grace, cunning and timelessness. We couldn't have asked for a better way to introduce "the occult Hercule Poirot" to a new generation of readers.

Finally, if Seabury Quinn is watching from above, and closely scrutinizing the shelves of bookstores, he would undoubtedly be pleased as punch, and proud as all get-out, to find his creation, Dr. Jules de Grandin, rising once again in the minds of readers around the world, battling the forces of darkness . . . wherever, whoever, or whatever the nature of their evil might be.

When the Jaws of Darkness Open,
Only Jules de Grandin Stands in Satan's Way!

Robert E. Weinberg
Chicago, Illinois, USA

and

George A. Vanderburgh
Lake Eugenia, Ontario, Canada

23 September 2016

The Further Appearances of Jules de Grandin

by Stephen Jones

S EABURY QUINN'S PSYCHIC INVESTIGATOR Jules de Grandin and his faithful associate Dr. Trowbridge are most closely identified with the classic pulp magazine *Weird Tales*, the periodical in which all of their exploits were originally published between 1925 and 1951. However, "The Unique Magazine" was not the only place where Quinn's tales about the dapper French occult detective have appeared . . .

In this, the introduction to the fifth and final volume of *The Complete Tales of Jules de Grandin*, we will explore, chronologically, the publication history of Seabury Quinn's most memorable character outside of his appearances in *Weird Tales*.

T HE INITIAL DE GRANDIN story, "The Horror on the Links," was published in the October 1925 edition of *Weird Tales*. Just under a year later it made its first hardcover appearance in the UK anthology *More Not at Night* (1926), the second of twelve volumes in the "Not at Night" anthology series edited for the Selwyn & Blount, Ltd. imprint by British literary agent and author Christine Campbell Thomson.

The evidence suggests that Thomson had access to some of the magazine's original manuscripts, and, following a mutual copyright arrangement between the two publishers, the "Not at Night" series of anthologies became the "official" British edition of *Weird Tales* for a while (as was indicated in several volumes' preliminary pages), reprinting a selection of stories from the pulp magazine in each book.

For her next anthology in the series, You'll Need a Night Light (1927), Thomson selected the sixth de Grandin story, "The House of Horror," which had originally been published in the July 1926 issue of Weird Tales.

Although some writers, such as H. P. Lovecraft, were paid for their work by Weird Tales' London agent Charles Lavelle, and received copies of the books their work appeared in, others, like Robert E. Howard and Clark Ashton Smith, did not, and had to track down copies for themselves. It is not known whether Seabury Quinn was even aware that his stories were being reprinted in hardcover on the other side of the Atlantic.

He was, however, most probably aware of the anthology Not at Night!, published in America by Macy-Masius, Inc, in 1928. Edited with an introduction by journalist Herbert Asbury, best known for his non-fiction book The Gangs of New York (1928), the volume apparently pirated stories from the first three British editions, including Quinn's "The House of Horror" and "The Horror on the Links."

Asbury not only appears to have been a bit confused about his source material (Weird Tales is credited by him as an English publication), but he also dismissed the quality of his own book when he stated in the Introduction: "Most of the authors represented in this collection appear to be comparatively unknown in this country (Seabury Quinn is the only one whose work I have ever seen before), and scholars and critics will look in vain for evidences of the skill and erudition displayed by such masters of the horror story as Edgar Allan Poe, Ambrose Bierce and Algernon Blackwood."

When Weird Tales' editor Farnsworth Wright proposed a class-action suit against Asbury's illegal edition, which had basically reprinted stories from Christine Campbell Thomson's anthologies without permission and with no acknowledgement of their original appearances, the US publisher reportedly withdrew the book from distribution rather than pay any royalties or damages.

Meanwhile, Christine Campbell Thomson's final Jules de Grandin selection, "The Curse of the House of Phipps," appeared in her sixth volume, At Dead of Night (1931). It had originally been published the previous year in the January issue of Weird Tales.

"The House of Horror" received a further outing from Thomson in 1937 when she reprinted it again in The "Not at Night" Omnibus, which collected thirty-five stories from the earlier books and was the final volume in the series.

"This Not at Night Omnibus has been a dream of my own for some time now," wrote Thomson. "I only hope that most readers will like at least a large proportion of what I have chosen, and that no one will imagine that non-inclusion is any disparagement of quality."

Meanwhile, the influence of *Weird Tales* and its contributors began to spread beyond the shores of the US and UK, and the first translations of stories started turning up on other continents.

Edited by future novelist José Mallorqui in Barcelona for Editorial Molino of Buenos Aires, Argentina, *Narraciones Terrorfícas* (Terrifying Stories) was a Spanish-language pulp magazine which ran for seventy-six issues, from 1939 until 1952. It featured new and classic horror stories, including many that had originally appeared in the pages of *Weird Tales*.

As with the "Not at Night" series, it is not clear if the *WT* authors were even aware that their work was being translated for overseas markets.

The first Jules de Grandin story to appear in *Narraciones Terrorfícas* was "The Venomed Breath of Vengeance" (*WT*, August 1938), which was published in the second issue in 1939. That same year it was followed by "The House of Horror" in the eleventh issue, and the following year "The Poltergeist of Swan Upping" (*WT*, February 1939) and "The House Where Time Stood Still" (*WT*, March 1939) appeared in the eighteenth and twentieth issues, respectively.

"The House Where Time Stood Still" was also reprinted in the 1941 hardcover anthology *The Other Worlds*, edited by novelist Phil Strong for the Wilfred Funk, Inc. imprint. The following year it was reissued by Star Books/Garden City Publishing Co., Inc. as *The Other Worlds: 25 Modern Stories of Mystery and Imagination*.

"No anthology of current periodical horrors would be complete without a small sample of the best known supernatural detective in weird fictions," explained Strong, who was best known for his 1932 novel *State Fair*. "After all, in more conventional whodunnit [*sic*] fiction, there was the great Sherlock Holmes, quite as incredible as the small Jules de Grandin.

"'The House Where Time Stood Still' is one of Seabury Quinn's best stories and one of his worst. It is one of the ugliest and most ingenious; and on the other hand it demonstrates to an exaggerated degree his deplorable determination to have everything turn out right up to, and unhappily beyond, the point of using definitely farcical devices."

As with Herbert Asbury some years before him, you get the feeling that, as a sophisticated New Yorker, Phil Strong felt that editing a book of science fiction and horror stories selected from the pulp magazines was somehow beneath him—which might explain why *The Other Worlds* was his only venture into the genre.

Seabury Quinn held a different opinion: "It is an undisputed fact," he wrote in 1948, "that more *Weird Tales* writers are 'tapped' for inclusion in anthologies than those of any other pulp magazines, that many of its regular contributors are also 'names' in the slick-paper field, and that a high percentage of them have had one or more successful books published."

During the 1940s and early 1950s, Canadian and British publishers reprinted their own editions of *Weird Tales* with different advertisements and, in the case of the Canadians, different artwork during the years of World War II. Otherwise, these were, for the most part, straight facsimiles of the American publication and included all Quinn's later de Grandin stories that appeared in those issues. The final new story about the French occult investigator, "The Ring of Bastet," appeared in the September 1951 issue of the declining pulp magazine.

Following the demise of *Weird Tales* in 1954, the Dalrow Publishing Company stepped in to fill the gap in Britain with a weird fiction digest magazine entitled *Phantom*, which first appeared in April 1957 and ran for sixteen monthly issues. The title was basically an unofficial continuation of *Weird Tales*, and reprinted a number of stories from that publication, including the Jules de Grandin novella "The Body-Snatchers" (*WT*, November 1950) in the fourteenth issue (May 1958).

British publisher and editor Herbert van Thal recalled "The House of Horror" from its publication in Christine Campbell Thomson's "Not at Night" anthologies when he included it in the first volume of his perennial paperback anthology series, *The Pan Book of Horror Stories* (1959). "Bertie," as van Thal was known to friends, returned to the character again in 1964 when he used "Clair de Lune" (*WT*, November 1947) in *The Fifth Pan Book of Horror Stories*. He had discovered the story in Leo Margulies' anthology *The Ghoul Keepers*, which had been published by Pyramid Books three years earlier.

"'*Nom d'un nom*, friend Trowbridge!'—and one of the truly great characters of fantastic writing is on the hunt for some new horror, outrage or supernatural skulduggery [sic]," wrote Margulies. "For a quarter-century, dapper Jules de Grandin and his reserved sidekick pursued astonishingly varied forms of evil through the pages of *Weird Tales*, Trowbridge staunch and baffled, de Grandin peppery, ingenious, and ever debonair. *WT* is no more, but it is a pleasure to revive Jules de Grandin and see him once again in action against the powers of darkness."

The Austrian-born Dr. Kurt Singer, who described himself as some kind of secret agent in his jacket-flap biography, was another anthology editor who drew upon Quinn's character for his story compilations for British publisher W. H. Allen. Starting with "Lords of the Ghostlands" (*WT*, March 1945) and "Catspaws" (*WT*, July 1946) in *Kurt Singer's Ghost Omnibus* (1965), the following decade he reprinted "Vampire Kith and Kin" (*WT*, May 1949)—one of three stories by the author—in *Ghouls and Ghosts* (1972), "Clair de Lune" in *Satanic Omnibus* (1973), and "The Hand of Glory" (*WT*, July 1933) in *They Are Possessed: Masterpieces of Exorcism* (1976).

Three years before his death in 1969 at the age of 80, Seabury Quinn saw ten revised and updated versions of his Jules de Grandin stories collected in *The Phantom-Fighter* from Mycroft & Moran, the crime and mystery imprint of

August Derleth's legendary genre publisher Arkham House (which is actually the publishing house credited on the dust-jacket spine).

"The ten tales comprising this volume have been chosen with a dual purpose," explained Quinn in his brief introduction, "By Way of Explanation." "(1) to present ten typical incidents in the early career of the little phantom-fighter, and (2) to detail his methods of combating what the Catechism refers to as spiritual and ghostly enemies. He is, for example, as far as I know, the first one to electrocute a troublesome revenant, to cause a zombie to return to its grave by smuggling a bit of meat into its diet, and certainly the first to anesthetize a vampire before administering the *coup de grâce*."

In the same piece, the author also claimed that de Grandin's adventures "total almost 300," although the actual number is ninety-three.

Limited to just over 2,000 hardcover copies and subtitled "Ten Memoirs of Jules de Grandin, sometime member of *la Sûreté Général, la Faculté de Medicine Légal de Paris*, etc., etc.," *The Phantom-Fighter* included two stories that had their titles changed from their original publication—"The Horror on the Links" was amended to "Terror on the Links," while "The Curse of the House of Phipps" became "The Doom of the House of Phipps"—most probably for copyright protection.

"In any event," continued Seabury Quinn, "if the stories in this, the first collected sheaf of Jules de Grandin's adventures, serve to help the reader to forget some worrysome [*sic*] incident of the workaday world, even for an hour or two, both Jules de Grandin and I shall feel we have achieved an adequate excuse for being."

Following the end of the pulp magazines in the 1950s due to the growing market in paperback books, editor and science fiction author Robert A. (Augustine) W. (Ward) Lowndes was working for a low-rent New York publishing company called Health Knowledge, Inc. when publisher Louis C. Elson asked him to edit a new horror digest.

"Doc" Lowndes had always been a horror enthusiast—he'd even received a couple of encouraging letters from H. P. Lovecraft back in 1937 when he was still a young fan—and the result was *Magazine of Horror and Strange Stories*, launched in August 1963. Produced on a miniscule budget of $250 per issue (with payment of a penny a word), the new periodical was split between original fiction and classic reprints.

The magazine was enough of a success to allow Lowndes to follow it with a number of other titles for the company, including *Startling Mystery Stories* in the summer of 1966. From the very first edition of this new publication "stressing the eerie, bizarre, and strange type of mystery," Lowndes began reprinting Seabury Quinn's Jules de Grandin stories in the majority of issues, starting with "The Mansion of Unholy Magic" (*WT*, October 1933).

"I wanted to try some of the de Grandin stories to see if readers of the 1960s would be fascinated with them," Lowndes later recalled. "I had re-read them and found they still retained their appeal to me, after thirty years. But I could not help but notice that they did contain elements—such as ethnic dialects long out of fashion, a writing style which to contemporary young readers might seem more appropriate to the Edwardian era, and an underlying affirmation of patriotic and moral values which the younger generation were ridiculing when not angrily condemning. I determined, however, to try a few; and then continue unless a decided majority of the readers' letters indicated dissatisfaction or worse.

"Surprise! There were some complaints along the lines I've indicated above, but even these were mixed—that is, the readers noticed these elements but said that they still enjoyed the stories; please give us more."

The Fall 1967 edition of *Startling Mystery Stories* featured the de Grandin adventure "The Druid's Shadow" (*WT*, October 1930), along with pulp reprints by Arthur J. Burks and Sterling S. Cramer, and a previously unpublished poem by Robert E. Howard. However, that issue is mostly remembered today for a short story called "The Glass Floor"—the debut of a previously unknown author named . . . Stephen King!

Although most of Seabury Quinn's Jules de Grandin stories ran to novelette or novella length, his only full-length novel featuring the character, "The Devil's Bride," was serialized over consecutive issues of *Weird Tales* from February to July, 1932. Robert Lowndes reprinted it in three parts in the March, May, and July 1969 issues of *Magazine of Horror*, accompanied by Joseph Doolin's original illustrations from *Weird Tales*.

Unfortunately, the collapse of Health Knowledge, Inc. in 1971 resulted in the end of the run of both *Startling Mystery Stories* and *Magazine of Horror*, along with their companion titles *Famous Science Fiction*, *Weird Terror Tales*, and *Bizarre Fantasy Tales*.

"The Devil's Bride" was reprinted in book form for the first time in 1971, when it appeared in Germany as *Horror Expert #9 Die Braut des Teufels*, from Wolfheart Luther Verlag, and in France as *La fiancée du démon*, by Edition Christian Bourgeois.

That same year also saw the reprinting of the de Grandin stories "Body and Soul" (*WT*, September 1928) in the hardcover anthology *Horrors Unknown*, edited by Sam Moskowitz for Walker & Co., and "The Man in Crescent Terrace" (*WT*, March 1946) in editor Vic Ghidalia's paperback anthology *The Mummy Walks Among Us* from Xerox Education Publications.

In 1973, "The Devil's Bride" was reprinted in Spanish as a standalone novel entitled *La novia del diablo* by the Mexican publisher Novaro.

"During his long, successful career Jules fought every conceivable denizen of the phantom world, but it was his dramatic encounters with vampires and werewolves that were the most memorable," observed British editor Brian J. Frost in his introductory essay "The Werewolf Theme in Weird Fiction" in the 1973 Sphere Books anthology *Book of the Werewolf,* which included the de Grandin story "The Wolf of St. Bonnot" (*WT,* Dec 1930).

Belgian-born Michel Parry was another anthology editor working in the UK during the 1970s. In 1974 he kicked off a new paperback reprint series with *The 1st Mayflower Book of Black Magic Stories* (a.k.a. *Great Black Magic Stories*) for the eponymous publisher, which included Seabury Quinn's "The Hand of Glory." He followed it with two further de Grandin reprints, "Children of Ubasti" (*WT,* December 1929) and "Incense of Abomination" (*WT,* March 1938), in *The 2nd Mayflower Book of Black Magic Stories* (1974) and *The 3rd Mayflower Book of Black Magic Stories* (1975), respectively.

In France, editor Jacques Sadoul included "The Curse of the House of Phipps" in *Les meilleurs récits de Weird Tales: Tome 1 période 1925–32* (1975), published by J'ai Lu. The second retrospective volume, published the same year, covered the period 1933–37 and featured another de Grandin novella, "The Jest of Warburg Tantavul" (*WT,* September 1934). Both stories were also in the omnibus edition, which appeared in 1989.

Born in Newark, New Jersey, Robert Weinberg was a bookseller, author, publisher, editor, and art collector. But first, and foremost, he was one of the world's leading authorities on pulp magazines.

So when Weinberg put together the pulp-reprint anthology *Far Below and Other Horrors* for FAX Collector's Editions in 1974, it was not surprising that he included the de Grandin story "The Chapel of Mystic Horror" from the December 1928 issue of *Weird Tales.*

By the mid-1970s, the pulp revival was in full swing, with the works of H. P. Lovecraft, Robert E. Howard, Clark Ashton Smith and others being rediscovered and reprinted around the world. In 1976, Weinberg was hired by Popular Library to compile a series of collections of Jules de Grandin stories.

The first volume, *The Adventures of Jules de Grandin,* appeared in August 1976 and contained seven stories, as well as Seabury Quinn's brief introductory note from *The Phantom-Fighter.* "Considering his immense popularity with the readership of *Weird Tales,* it is surprising to note how little of his work has been preserved between book-covers, either hardbound or paperback," lamented Lin Carter about the author in his introduction. "With the appearance of this book," he continued, "Jules de Grandin returns in a new, vigorous reincarnation . . . With the publication of these paperbacks, Jules de Grandin joins the immortals."

"Other psychic detectives rarely ventured into rationalizing their enemies and using scientific devices to fight them," noted Robert Weinberg in his historical Afterword. "de Grandin relied on such methods."

Just a month later, *The Casebook of Jules de Grandin* appeared with an introduction by Robert A. W. Lowndes (who, of course, had reprinted many of the de Grandin stories in his magazine *Startling Mystery Stories* some years earlier). Quinn's fellow *Weird Tales* contributor Manly Wade Wellman supplied the introduction to *The Skeleton Closet of Jules de Grandin* (October 1976), which was the last of the Popular Library editions to carry one, even though it was followed by *The Devil's Bride* (November 1976), *The Hellfire Files of Jules de Grandin* (December 1976), and *The Horror Chamber of Jules de Grandin* (February 1977).

"In the last few years, Quinn has come into a good deal of criticism for the Jules de Grandin series," Robert Weinberg observed in his afterword to this final volume. "The main thrust of these attacks was that the stories were written for money and not artistic achievement alone . . . While on the surface, a fine sounding argument, the truth is anything but so simple. Seabury Quinn was a professional author. He wrote to sell and, because of this, he had to write well. For a good part of his life, a major portion of his income was derived from writing, and he was easily the most popular writer ever to work for *Weird Tales*."

Although more collections were planned, sales did not meet expectations, and Popular Library discontinued the series after the initial six volumes, which were never reprinted. Weinberg had managed to collect about one-third of the de Grandin stories along with the only full-length de Grandin novel before the paperback revival was cancelled, but he later went on to reprint further stories in his pulp fanzines.

Each of the Popular Library editions featured a cover by Vincent Di Fate; a detailed map circa 1934 of the fictional town of Harrisonville, New Jersey, which was the focal point of many of de Grandin's cases; and portraits of the excitable French detective and Dr. Trowbridge by Stephen E. Fabian. The latter were actually recreations of the illustrations artist Virgil Finlay had done for *Weird Tales*, the originals of which could not be located at the time.

Finlay's two drawings first appeared in the September 1937 issue of the magazine, accompanying the story "Satan's Palimpsest," and were reprinted at least sixteen times over an eight-year period.

"What can I say concerning the portraits of my dearest brain-children?" Seabury Quinn wrote to the artist on July 31st that year, after receiving his advance copy of the magazine. "They are just perfect . . . Thank you for taking them right out of my brain and making them live visually."

In fact, Finlay had taken them from advertisements which had appeared the previous year in a number of pulp magazines from the Munsey chain, including *Railroad Stories* and *Detective Fiction Weekly*.

Despite the failure of the Popular Library series, Quinn's de Grandin stories were still being sought out by anthology editors: in Britain, Peter Haining reprinted "Suicide Chapel" (*WT*, June 1938) in *The Fantastic Pulps* (1975) and

"Frozen Beauty" (*WT*, February 1938) in his hardcover facsimile edition of *Weird Tales* (1976).

"In hindsight," wrote Haining in the introduction to that book, "much that Quinn wrote was hack work, although readers loved him and one wrote in 1933 that he was 'the best writer since Poe.'"

Michel Parry used "The Jest of Warburg Tantavul" in *The Supernatural Solution* (1976), a collection of "chilling tales of spooks versus sleuths," while Vic Ghidalia selected "The Blood-Flower" (*WT*, March 1927) for his anthology about the plants taking over, *Nightmare Garden* (1976).

For many readers, the Popular Library paperback reprintings had been their first introduction to Jules de Grandin, and Quinn's stories were soon turning up in fan publications. Editors Gene Marshall and Carl F. Waedt used "The House Without a Mirror" (*WT*, November 1929) in *Incredible Adventures #2* (1977), while Robert Weinberg continued to champion the series with "Satan's Palimpsest" (*WT*, September 1937) and "Living Buddhess" (*WT*, November 1937) in *Lost Fantasies #9: The Sin Eaters* (1979), which featured a cover and variant frontispiece illustration of de Grandin and Dr. Trowbridge by Stephen E. Fabian.

In 1979, the French publisher Librairie des Champs-Elysées issued a paperback collection of six stories entitled *Les archives de Jules de Grandin*. Published as part of "Le Masque—Fantastique" series, it was edited with an introduction by Danny de Laet and translated by Mary Rosenthal.

Ever-popular, "The House of Horror" was selected by editor Mary Danby for her bumper 1981 anthology from Octopus Books, *65 Great Tales of Horror.*

Never one to waste a story, Peter Haining not only used "The Poltergeist" (*WT*, October 1927) in *Supernatural Sleuths: Stories of Occult Investigators* (1986) for publisher William Kimber, but recycled it the following year in *Poltergeist: Tales of Deadly Ghosts* for the Severn House imprint.

As with Haining, Italian editor Gianni Pilo liked Seabury Quinn's werewolf story "The Wolf of St. Bonnot" so much that he reprinted it in his 1988 anthology, *I signori dei lupi*, one of a series of Lovecraftian-inspired trade paperback novels and anthologies published by Fanucci Editore, as well as in *Storie di lupi mannari* for Newton Compton in 1994.

"The House of Horror" enjoyed another outing in 1990 when Karl Edward Wagner selected it for his medical horror anthology *Intensive Scare* from DAW Books.

Along with Robert Weinberg, another champion of the de Grandin stories was prolific American anthologist Martin H. Greenberg. He used "Restless Souls" (*WT*, October 1928) for his DAW Books anthology with frequent collaborator Charles G. Waugh, *Vamps: An Anthology of Female Vampire Stories* (1987), and "The Man in Crescent Terrace" in *Mummy Stories* (1990) for Ballantine Books.

Greenberg and Waugh teamed up with Frank D. McSherry Jr. in 1990 for *Eastern Ghosts*, which was part of Rutledge Hill Press's "The American Ghost Stories" series and included "The Jest of Warburg Tantavul." The following year the editors used the story again in the hardcover anthology *Great American Horror Stories* from the same publisher.

During the late 1980s and 1990s, Greenberg, Weinberg, and Stefan R. Dziemianowicz teamed up in various combinations to produce several bumper reprint anthologies for various publishers, a number of which included Jules de Grandin stories by Seabury Quinn.

They began with "Satan's Stepson" (*WT*, September 1931) in *Weird Tales: 32 Unearthed Terrors* (Bonanza Books/Crown Publishers, 1988) and followed that with "The Man Who Cast No Shadow" (*WT*, February 1927) in *Weird Vampire Tales* (Gramercy Books, 1992), "The Jest of Warburg Tantavul" in *Nursery Crimes* (Barnes & Noble Books, 1993), and "Restless Souls" in *Virtuous Vampires* (Barnes & Noble Books, 1996).

Editors Martin H. Greenberg and Charles G. Waugh reunited for *Supernatural Sleuths: 14 Mysterious Stories of Uncanny Crime* (1996) for Roc/New American Library, which included "Children of Ubasti" (*WT*, December 1929), and Robert Weinberg teamed up with John Betancourt to reprint Quinn's final de Grandin story, "The Ring of Bastet," in *Weird Tales: Seven Decades of Terror* (Barnes & Noble Books, 1997).

Over in Europe, there was another outing for "The Man Who Cast No Shadow" in Peter Haining's *The Vampire Hunters' Casebook* (1996), and that same year French publisher Editions Fleuve Noir issued the collection *Jules de Grandin, le Sherlock Holmes du surnaturel* (Jules de Grandin, The Sherlock Holmes of the Supernatural) as #28 in its "Super Pocket" series.

French editor Barbara Sadoul used the slightly re-titled "The Wolf of Saint-Bonnot" in her 1999 werewolf anthology *Le Bal des loups-garous* (The Ball of the Werewolves) for Denoël.

Finally, in January 2001, nearly fifty years after the last de Grandin story was published in *Weird Tales*, Seabury Quinn's entire canon of Jules de Grandin stories was collected together for the first time ever by George A. Vanderburgh's Canadian small press imprint The Battered Sillicon Dispatch Box as a boxed, three-volume hardcover set entitled *The Compleat Adventures of Jules de Grandin*. This not only included all ninety-three of Quinn's stories about de Grandin, but also reprinted Robert Weinberg's afterwords to the Popular Library editions, original introductions by Weinberg, Jim Rockhill, and Seabury Quinn, Jr., and the author's own introduction to *The Phantom-Fighter*.

Meanwhile, Charlotte F. Otten reprinted "The Thing in the Fog" (*WT*, March 1933) in *The Literary Werewolf: An Anthology* (2002) published by the Syracuse University Press, and the same story turned up the following year in the Ash-Tree Press collection of eleven Quinn stories, *Night Creatures*, edited by Peter Ruber and Joseph Wrzos and limited to six hundred copies.

In 2003 the Spanish publisher Avalon re-issued the novel *The Devil's Bride* (*La novia del diablo*), which led to Valdemar Gotica publishing the six-story collection *Las cámaras del horror de Jules de Grandin* (The Horror Chambers of Jules de Grandin) the following year, with an introduction by Antonio José Navarro.

This was followed in 2005 by *La dama sin límite y otras historias* (The Lady Without Boundaries and Other Stories) from Río Henares Producciones Gráficas Pulp Ediciones, which featured six de Grandin stories and a prologue by Arturo Bobadilla. The book was named after a re-titling of the 1938 story "Incense of Abomination."

In 2009, editor Peter Straub included "The Curse of Everard Maundy" (*WT*, July 1927) in *American Fantastic Tales: Terror and the Uncanny from Poe to the Pulps*, published by the prestigious Library of America imprint, and Otto Penzler featured "The Corpse-Master" (*WT*, July 1929) in his massive 2011 anthology *Zombies! Zombies! Zombies!* from Vintage Crime/Black Lizard. Seabury Quinn's de Grandin stories were finally receiving the recognition they deserved.

"Pledged to the Dead" (*WT*, October 1937) was published in 2010 as a chapbook by TGS Publishing and reissued the following year under the Ægypan imprint as a thin hardcover, while a trade paperback reprinting of *The Devil's Bride: Mysteries of Jules de Grandin* in 2012 by the UK imprint Scorpionic/Creation Oneiros also included the novella "The House of the Golden Masks" (*WT*, June 1929).

The following year, Positronic Publishing issued both "Satan's Stepson" and "Eyes in the Dark" (*WT*, November 1946) as stand-alone chapbooks.

Luigi Cozzi's Italian imprint Profondo Rosso (named after the Little Shop of Science Fiction and Horror founded by Dario Argento in Rome in 1989) published the six-story collection *Jules de Grandin: il cacciatore di fantasmi* (Jules de Grandin: The Ghost Hunter) in 2014, which also included the 1934 map of Harrisonville and Stephen Fabian's portraits of de Grandin and Dr. Trowbridge from the Popular Library paperbacks. The same publisher followed it in 2015 with *Jules de Grandin: La sposa del diavolo* (Jules de Grandin: The Devil's Bride).

That same year, La Hermandad del Enmascarado published *El horror de los páramos* (The Horror of the Moors) in Spain. Containing sixteen stories and an introduction by Javier Jiménez Barco, it was the first volume in that country's own series of "The Complete Adventures of Jules de Grandin."

"It is good to think and think again of Seabury Quinn," recalled pulp writer Manly Wade Wellman in 1976; "what he did and how he acted; this full-blooded, good-humored, hospitable, wise friend, whose taste in food and drink and reading and writing always seemed so admirable, who lived his long life to a rewarding full. He has gone to where things of evil are only diverting topics of conversation. I hope he knows that this book is being printed, that it is still happily baleful nighttime under the Harrisonville moon, that Jules de Grandin knows how to drive the hideous wickedness back to its unhallowed grave."

Now, more than ninety years after the character was first introduced in the pages of *Weird Tales*, the enduring legacy of Seabury Quinn's supernatural detective series continues to be celebrated in this new five-volume series of *The Complete Tales of Jules de Grandin*, as the exploits of "the occult Hercule Poirot" are brought back into print once again to enthrall a whole new generation of readers.

—Stephen Jones
London, April 2017

BLACK MOON

BLACK
MOON

Suicide Chapel

A LTHOUGH THE CALENDAR DECLARED it was late May the elements and the thermometer denied it. All day the rain had streamed torrentially and the wind keened like a moaning banshee through the newly budded leaves that furred the maple boughs. Now the raving tempest laid a lacquer-like veneer of driven water on the window-pane and howled a bawdy chanson down the chimney where a four-log fire was blazing on the hearth. Fresh from a steaming shower and smelling most agreeably of Roman Hyacinth, Jules de Grandin sat before the fire and gazed with unconcealed approval at the toe tip of his purple leather slipper. A mauve silk scarf was knotted Ascot fashion round his throat, his hands were drawn up in the sleeves of his deep violet brocade dressing-gown, and on his face was that look of somnolent content which well-fed tomcats wear when they are thoroughly at peace with themselves and the world. "Not for a thousand gold Napoléons would I set foot outside this house again tonight," he told me as he dipped into the pocket of his robe, fished out a pack of "Marylands" and set one of the evil-smelling things alight. "Three times, three separate, distinct times, have I been soaked to saturation in this *sacré* rain today. Now, if the Empress Josèphine came to me in the flesh and begged that I should go with her, I would refuse the assignation. Regretfully, *mais certainement*, but definitely. Me, I would not stir outside the door for—"

"Sergeant Costello, if ye plaze, sor," came the rich Irish brogue of Nora McGinnis, my household factotum, who appeared outside the study entrance like a figure materialized in a vaudeville illusion. "He says it's most important, sor."

"*Tiens*, bid him enter, *ma petite*, and bring a bottle of the Irish whisky from the cellar," de Grandin answered with a smile; then:

"*C'est véritablement toi, ami?*" he asked as the big Irishman came in and held cold-reddened fingers to the fire. "What evil wind has blown you out on such a fetid night?"

"Evil is th' word, sor," Costello answered as he drained the glass de Grandin proffered. "Have ye been radin' in th' papers of th' Cogswell gur-rl's disappearin', I dunno?"

"But yes, of course. Was she not the young woman who evaporated from her dormitory at the Shelton School three months ago? You have found her, *mon vieux*? You are to be congratulated. In my experience—"

"Would yer experience tell ye what to do when a second gur-rl pops outa sight in pracizely th' same manner, lavin' nayther hide nor hair o' clue?"

De Grandin's small blue eyes closed quickly, then opened wide, for all the world like an astonished cat's. "But surely, there is some little trace of evidence, some hint of hidden romance, some—"

"Some nothin' at all, sor. Three months ago today th' Cogswell gur-rl went to 'er room immejiately afther class. Th' elevator boy who took her up seen her walk down th' hall, two classmates said hello to her. Then she shut her door, an' shut herself outa th' wor-rld entirely, so it seems. Nobody's seen or heard o' her since then. This afthernoon, just afther four o'clock, th' Lefètre gur-rl comes from th' lab'ratory, goes straight to 'er room an'"—he paused and raised his massive shoulders in a ponderous shrug—"there's another missin'-persons case fer me to wrastle wid. I've come to ask yer help, sor."

De Grandin pursed his lips and arched his narrow brows. "I am not interested in criminal investigation, *mon sergent*."

"Not even to save an old pal in a hot spot, sor?"

"*Hein?* How is it you say?"

"'Tis this way, sor. When th' Cogswell gur-rl evaporated, as ye say, they gave th' case to me, though be rights it b'longed to th' Missin' Persons Bureau. Well, sor, when a gur-rl fades out that way there may be anny number o' good reasons fer it, but mostly it's because she wants to. An' th' more ye asks th' family questions th' less ye learn. 'Had she anny, love affairs?' sez you, an' 'No!' sez they, as if ye'd been set on insultin' her. 'Wuz she happy in her home?' ye asks, an' 'Certainly, she wuz!' they tells ye, an' they imply ye've hinted that they bate her up each night at eight o'clock an' matinees at two-fifteen. So it goes. Each time ye try to git some reason for her disappearin' act they gits huffier an' huffier till finally they sez they're bein' persecuted, an' ye git th' wor-rks, both from th' chief an' newspapers."

"Perfectly," de Grandin nodded. "As Monsieur Gilbert says, a policeman's life is not a happy one."

"Ye're tellin' me! But this time it's still worse, sor. When I couldn't break th' Cogswell case they hinted I wuz slowin' down, an' had maybe seen me best days. Now they goes an' dumps this here new case in me lap an' tells me if I fail to break it I'll be back in harness wid a nightsthick in me hand before I've checked another birthday off. So, sor, if ye could—"

"*Pas possible!* They dare say this to you, the peerless officer, the pride of the *gendarmerie*—"

"They sure did, sor. An' lots more—"

"Aside, Friend Trowbridge; aside, *mon sergent*—make passageway for me. Await while I put on my outside clothing. I shall show them, me. We shall see if they can do such things to my tried friend—*les crétins!*"

So INCREDIBLY SHORT WAS the interval elapsing before he rejoined us with his hat pulled down above his eyes, trench coat buttoned tight beneath his chin, that I could not understand until I caught a flash of violet silk pajama leg bloused out above the top of his laced boots.

"Lead on, my *sergent*," he commanded. "Take us to the place which this so foolish girl selected for her disappearance. We shall find her or otherwise!"

"Would ye be manin' 'or else,' sor, I dunno?"

"*Ah bah*, who cares? Let us be about our task!"

"Sure, we got a full description o' th' clothes she wore when she skedaddled," Costello told us as we drove out toward the fashionable suburb where the Shelton School was located. "She wuz wearin' orange-colored lounging pajamas an' pegged orange-colored slippers."

"Pegged?" de Grandin echoed. "Was she then poor—"

"Divil a bit o' it, sor. Her folks is rich as creases, but she wuz overdrawn on her allowance, and had to cut th' corners til her next check came."

"One comprehends. And then—"

"There ain't no then, sor. We've inventoried all her wardrobe, an' everything is present but th' duds she wore when she came in from class. Not even a hat's missin'. O' course, that don't mean nothin' much. If she'd set her heart or lammin', she coulda had another outfit waitin' for her somewheres else, but—"

"Quite but, my friend," de Grandin nodded. "Until the contrary appears, we must assume she went away *sans trousseau.*"

With characteristic fickleness the shrewish storm had blown itself away while we drove from the city, and a pale half-waning moon tossed like a bit of lucent jetsam in a purling surf of broken clouds as we drew up beneath the porte-cochère of the big red brick dormitory whence Emerline Lefètre had set forth for her unknown goal six hours earlier.

"Yas, suh," replied the colored elevator operator, visibly enjoying the distinction of being questioned by the police. "Ah remembers puffickly erbout hit all. Miss Lefètre come in from lab. She seemed lak she was in a powerful hurry, an' didn't say a thing, 'ceptin' to thank me for de letters."

"The letters? Do you by any happy circumstance remember whence they came?"

"Naw, suh. Ah don' look at de young ladies' mail, 'ceptin' to see who hit's for. I recolleck dese letters mos' partickler, though, 'cause one of 'em wuz smelled up so grand."

"Perfumed?"

"An' how, suh. Jus' lak de scents de conjur doctors sell, on'y more pretty-smellin'. Dat one wuz in a big vanilla envelope. All sealed up, it wuz, but de odor come right through de paper lak hit wuz nothin' a-tall."

"*Merci bien.* Now, if you will kindly take us up—"

THE LITTLE ROOM WHERE Emerline Lefètre dwelt was neat and colorless as only hospital, barrack or dormitory rooms can be. No trace of dust marred imitation mahogany furniture. Indifferent reproductions of several of the less rowdy Directoire prints were ranged with mathematical precision on the walls. The counterpane was squared with blocks of blue and white so virginally chaste as to seem positively spinsterish. "*Mon Dieu*, it is a dungeon, nothing less," de Grandin murmured as he scanned the place. "Can anybody blame a girl for seeking sanctuary from such terrible surround—*quel parfum horrible!*" His narrow nostrils quivered as he sniffed the air. "She had atrocious taste in scent, this so mysteriously absent one."

"Perhaps it's the elegant perfume the elevator operator mentioned," I ventured. "He'd have admired something redolent of musk—"

"*Dis donc!* You put your finger on the pulse, my friend! It is the musk. But yes. I did not recognize him instantly, but now I do. The letter she received was steeped in musk. Why, in Satan's name? one wonders."

Thoughtfully, he walked slowly to the window, opened it and thrust his head out, looking down upon the cement walk some fifty feet below. Neither ivy, waterspout nor protuberance of the building offered foothold for a mouse upon the flat straight wall.

"I do not think she went that way," he murmured as he turned to look up at the overhanging roof.

"Nor that way, either, sor," Costello rejoined, pointing to the overhanging of mansard roof some seven feet above the window-top.

"U'm? One wonders." Reaching out, de Grandin tapped an iron cleat set in the wall midway of the window's height. From the spike's tip branched a flange of a turnbuckle, evidently intended to secure a shutter at some former time. "A very active person might ascend or—*parbleu!*"

Breaking off his words half uttered, he took a jeweler's loop out of his rain-coat pocket, fixed it in his eye, then played the beam of his electric torch upon the window-sill, subjecting it to a methodical inspection.

"What do you make of this, my friends?" he asked as he passed the glass to us in turn, directing his light ray along the gray stone sill and indicating several tiny scratches on the slate. "They may be recent, they may have been here since the building was erected," he admitted as we handed back the glass, "but in cases such as this there are no such things as trifles."

Once more he leant across the window-sill, then mounted it and bent out till his eyes were level with the rusty iron cleat set in the wall.

"*Morbleu*, it is a repetition!" he exclaimed as he rejoined us. "Up, my *sergent*, up, Friend Trowbridge, and see what you can see upon that iron."

Gingerly, I clambered to the sill and viewed the rusty cleat through the enlarging-glass while Costello played the flashlight's beam upon it. On the iron's reddish surface, invisible, or nearly so, to naked eyes, but clearly visible through the loop's lens, there showed a row of sharp, light scratches, exactly duplicating those upon the window-sill.

"Bedad, I don't know what it's all about, sor," Costello rumbled as he concluded his inspection, "but if it's a wild-goose chase we're on I'm thinkin' that we've found a feather in th' wind to guide us."

"*Exactement*. One is permitted to indulge that hope. Now let us mount the roof.

"Have the care," he cautioned as Costello took his ankles in a firm grip and slid him gently down the slanting, still-wet slates. "I have led a somewhat sinful life, and have no wish to be projected into the beyond without sufficient time to make my peace with heaven."

"No fear, sor," grinned Costello. "Ye're a little pip squeak, savin' yer presence, an' I can swing ye be th' heels till mornin' if this rotten brickwor-rk don't give way wid me."

Wriggling eel-like on his stomach, de Grandin searched the roof slates inch by careful inch from the leaded gutter running round the roof bank's lower edge to the lower brick ridge that marked the incline's top. His small blue eyes were shining brightly as he rejoined us.

"*Mes amis*, there is the mystery here," he announced solemnly. "Across the gutter to the slates, and up the slates until the roof's flat top is reached, there is a trail of well defined, light scratches. Moreover, they are different."

"Different, sor? How d'ye mean—"

"Like this: Upon the window-sill they are perceptibly more wide and deep at their beginning than their end—like exclamation marks viewed from above. In the gutter and upon the roof they are reversed, with deeper gashes at the lower ends and lighter scratches at their upper terminals."

"O.K., sor. Spill it. I'm not much good at riddles."

A momentary frown inscribed twin upright wrinkles between de Grandin's brows. "One cannot say with surety, but one may guess," he answered slowly, speaking more to himself than to us. "If the marks were uniform one might infer someone had crawled out of the window mounted to the gutter by the ringbolt set into the wall, then climbed upon the roof. An active person might accomplish it. But the situation is quite otherwise. The scratches on the slates reverse the scorings on the window-sill."

"You've waded out beyond me depth now, sor," Costello answered.

"*Tiens*, mine also," the Frenchman grinned. "But let us hazard a conjecture: Suppose one wearing hobnailed boots—or shoes which had been pegged, as Miss Lefètre's were—had crawled out from this window: how would he use his feet?"

"To stand on, I praysume, sor."

"*Ah bah*. You vex me, you annoy me, you get upon my goat! Standing on the sill and reaching up and out to grasp that iron cleat, he would have used his feet to brace himself and pivot on. His tendency would be to turn upon his toes, thereby tracing arcs or semicircles in the stone with the nails set in his shoes. But that is not the case here. The scorings marked into the stone are deeper at beginning, showing that the hobnailed shoes were scratching in resistance, clawing, if you please, against some force which bore the wearer of those shoes across the windowsill. Digging deeply at beginning, the nail marks taper off, as the shoes slipped from the stone and their wearer's weight was lifted from the sill.

"When we view the iron cleat we are upon less certain ground. One cannot say just how a person stepping to the iron would move his feet in climbing to the roof; but when we come to read the slates we find another chapter in this so puzzling story. Those marks were left by someone who fought not to mount the roof; but who was struggling backward with the strength of desperation, yet who was steadily forced upward. Consider, if you please: The fact that such resistance, if successful, would have resulted in this person's being catapulted to the cement path and almost surely killed, shows us conclusively the maker of those marks regarded death as preferable to going up that roof. Why? one asks."

"PARDON ME, SIR, ARE you from headquarters?" Slightly nasal but not at all unmusical, the challenge drawled at us across the corridor. From the doorway of the room set opposite to Emerline's a girl regarded us with one of the most indolent, provocative "come-hither" looks I'd ever seen a woman wear. She was of medium height, not slender and not stout, but lushly built, with bright hair, blond as a well-beaten egg, worn in a page-boy bob and curled up slightly at the ends. From round throat to high white insteps she was draped in black velvet pajamas which had obviously not been purchased ready-made, but sculptured to her perfect measure, for her high, firm, ample breasts pushed up so strongly underneath the velvet that the dip of the fabric to her flat stomach was entirely without wrinkles. Her trousers were so loose about the legs they simulated a wide skirt, but at the hips they fitted with a skin-tight snugness as revealing as a rubber bathing-suit. From high-arched, carefully penciled brows to blood-red toenails she was the perfect figure of the siren, and I heard Costello gasp with almost awe-struck admiration as his eyes swept over her.

"We are, indeed, *ma belle*," de Grandin answered. "You wish to speak with us?"

Her blue eyes widened suddenly, then dropped a veil of carefully mascaraed lashes which like an odalisque's thin gossamer revealed more than it hid. They were strange eyes to see in such a young face, meaningful and knowing, a little weary, more than a little mocking. "Yes," she drawled lazily. "You're on the case of Emerline Lefètre, aren't you?"

"Yes, *Mademoiselle*."

"Well, I'm sure she disappeared at five o'clock."

"Indeed? How is it that you place the time?"

A shrug which was a slow contortion raised her black-draped shoulders and pressed the pointed breasts more tightly still against her tucked-in jacket. "I was in bed all afternoon with a neuralgic headache. The last lab period today was out at half past four, and I heard the girls come down the hall from class. There's not much time till dinner when we come in late from lab, and a warning bell rings in the dorm at three minutes before five. When it went off this afternoon it almost split my head apart. The rain had stopped; at least I didn't hear it beating on my window, but the storm had made it dark as midnight, and at first I thought it was a dream. Then I heard some of the girls go hurrying by, and knew that it was five o'clock, or not more than a minute past. I was lying there, trying to find energy to totter to the bureau for some mentholated cologne, when I heard a funny noise across the hall. I'm sure it came from Emerline's room."

"A funny noise, *Mademoiselle?* How do you mean?"

A little wrinkle furrowed down the smooth white skin between the penciled brows. "As nearly as I can describe it, it was like the opening quaver of a screech owl's cry, but it was shut off almost as it started. Then I heard a sound of stamping, as though there were a scuffle going on in there. I s'pose I should have risen and investigated, but I was too sick and miserable to do more than lie there wondering about it. Presently I fell asleep and forgot about it till I heard you in her room just now." She paused and patted back a yawn. "Mind if I go in and have a look around?" she asked, walking toward us with a swinging, aphrodisiacally undulating gait. The aura of a heavy, penetrating perfume—musk-based patchouli essence, I determined at a hasty breath—seemed hovering round her like a cumulus of tangible vapor.

As far as Jules de Grandin was concerned her blandishments might have been directed at a granite statue. "It is utterly forbidden, *Mademoiselle*. We are most grateful for your help, but until we have the opportunity to sweep the place for clues we request that no one enter it."

"WHAT D'YE MEAN, SWEEP th' place for clues, sor?" asked Costello as we drove toward home.

"Precisely what I said, *mon vieux*. There may be clues among the very dust to make this so mysterious puzzle clear."

Arrived at the house, he rummaged in the broom cupboard, finally emerging with my newest vacuum sweeper underneath his arm. It was a cleaner I had let myself be argued into buying because, as the young salesman pointed out, instead of a cloth bag it had a sack of oiled paper which when filled could be detached and thrown away. To my mind this had much merit, but Nora McGinnis begged to disagree, and so the old cloth-bellows sweeper was in daily use while the newer, sanitary engine rested in the closet.

"Behold, my friend," he grinned, "there is a virtue to be found in everything. Madame Nora has refused to use the sweeper, thereby making it impossible for you to get return on your investment, but her stubbornness assists me greatly, for here I have a pack of clean fresh paper bags in which to gather up our evidence. You comprehend?"

"Ye mean ye're goin' to vacuum-sweep that room out to th' Shelton School?" Costello asked incredulously.

"Perfectly, my friend. The floor, the walls, perhaps the ceiling. When Jules de Grandin seeks for clues he does not play. Oh, no."

The door of Emerline Lefètre's room was open on a crack as we marched down the corridor equipped with vacuum sweeper and paper refills, and as de Grandin thrust it open with his foot we caught the heavy, almost overpowering odor of patchouli mixed with musk.

"*Dame!*" de Grandin swore. "She has been here, *cette érotofurieuse*, against my express orders. And she has raised the window, too. How can we say what valuable bit of evidence has been blown out—*morbleu!*"

Positively venomous with rage, he had stamped across the room to slam the window down, but before he lowered it had leant across the sill. Now he rested hands upon the slate and gazed down at the cement pavement fifty feet below, a look of mingled pain and wonder on his face.

"Trowbridge Costello, *mes amis*, come quickly!" he commanded, beckoning us imperiously. "Look down and tell me what it is you see."

Spotlighted by a patch of moonlight on the dull-gray cement walk a huddled body lay, inert, grotesque, unnatural-looking as a marionette whose wires have been cut. The flash of yellow hair and pale white skin against the somber elegance of sable velvet gave it positive identification.

"How th' divil did she come to take that tumble?" Costello asked as we dashed down the stairs, disdaining to wait on the slowly moving elevator.

"*Le bon Dieu* and the devil only know," de Grandin answered as he knelt beside the crumpled remnant of the girl's bright personality and laid a hand beneath her generously swelling breast.

The impact of her fall must have been devastating. Beneath her crown of gold-blond hair her skull vault had been mashed as though it were an eggshell; through the skin above her left eye showed a staring splinter of white bone where the shattered temporal had pierced the skin; just above the round neck of her velvet jacket thrust a jagged chisel-edge of white, remnant of a broken cervical vertebra. Already purple bruises of extravasated blood were forming on her face; her left leg thrust out awkwardly, almost perpendicularly to her body's axis, and where the loose-legged trouser had turned back we saw the Z-twist of a compound comminutive fracture.

"Is she—" began Costello, and de Grandin nodded as he rose.

"Indubitably," he returned. "Dead like a herring."

"But why should she have jumped?" I wondered. "Some evil influence—a wild desire to emulate—"

He made a gesture of negation. "How far is it from here to the house wall?" he asked.

"Why, some eighteen feet, I judge."

"*Précisément*. That much, at least. Is it in your mind her fall's trajectory would have been so wide an arc?"

"What's that?"

"Simply this, by blue! Had she leaped or fallen from the window she should have struck the earth much nearer to the building's base. The distance separating ground and window is too small to account for her striking thus far out; besides it is unlikely that she would have dived head first. Men sometimes make such suicidal leaps, women scarcely ever. Yet all the evidence discloses that she struck upon her head; at least she fell face forward. Why?"

"You imply that she was—"

"I am not sure, but from the facts as we observe them I believe that she was thrown, and thrown by one who had uncommon strength. She was a heavy girl; no ordinary person could have lifted her and thrown her through a window, yet someone must have done just that; there is no evidence of struggle in the room."

"Shall I take charge, sor?" asked Costello.

De Grandin nodded. "It will expedite our work if you will be so kind. When she is taken to the morgue I wish you would prevent the autopsy until I have a chance to make a more minute inspection of the body. Meantime I have important duties elsewhere."

METHODICALLY, AS THOUGH HE'D been a janitor—but with far more care for detail—he moved the vacuum sweeper back and forth across the floor of the small tragic room, drew out the paper bag and sealed and labeled it. Then with a fresh bag in the bellows he swept the bed, the couch, the draperies. Satisfied that every latent trace of dust had been removed, he shut the current off, and, his precious bags beneath his arm, led the march toward my waiting car.

A sheet of clean white paper spread across the surgery table made background for the miscellany of fine refuse which he emptied from the sweeper's bags. Microscope to eye, he passed a glass rod vigorously rubbed with silk back and forth across the dust heap. Attracted by the static charge fine bits of rubbish adhered to the rod and were subjected to his scrutiny. As he completed his examination I viewed the salvage through a second microscope, but found it utterly uninteresting. It was the usual hodgepodge to be culled by vacuuming a broom-cleaned room. Tiny bits of paper, too fine to yield to straw brooms' pressure, little flecks of nondescript black dust, a wisp or two of wool fiber from the cheap rug, the trash was valueless from any viewpoint, as far as I could see.

"*Que diable?*" With eyes intently narrowed he was looking at some object clinging to his glass rod.

"What is it?" I demanded, leaning closer.

"See if you can classify it," he returned, moving aside to let me look down through the viewhole of the microscope.

It was a strand of hair three-quarters of an inch or so in length, curled slightly like a human body hair, but thicker, coarser in its texture. Reddish rusty brown at tip, it shaded to a dull gray at the center and bleached to white transparency about the base. I saw it was smooth-scaled upon its outer surface and terminated in a point, showing it had never been cut or, if clipped, had sufficient time to grow to its full length again.

"Let us proceed," I heard him whisper as he moved his polished rod again across the heap of sweepings. "Perhaps we shall discover something else."

Slowly he moved the rod across the furrowed edges of the dust heap, pausing now and then to view a fresh find. A splinter of straw, a tiny tag of paper, fine powdered dust, these comprised his salvage, till: "Ah?" he murmured, "ah-ha?" Adhering to the rod there was another wisp of hair, almost the counterpart of his first find, except it was more nearly uniform in color, dull lack-luster rust all over, like an aged tomcat's fur, or the hair of some misguided woman who has sought a simulation of her vanished youth by having her gray tresses dyed with henna.

"What—" I began, but he waved me silent with a nervous gesture as he continued fishing with his rod. At last he laid the rod aside and began to winnow the dust piles through a fine wire screen. Half an hour's patient work resulted in the salvaging of two or three small chocolate-colored flakes which looked for all the world like grains of bran and when field close to our noses on a sheet of folded paper gave off a sweetly penetrating odor.

"You recognize them?" he asked.

"Not by sight. By their smell I'd say they contained musk."

"Quite yes," he nodded. "They are musk. Crude musk, such as the makers of perfumery use."

"But what should that be doing in a young girl's room—"

"One wonders with the wonder of amazement. One also wonders what those hairs did there. I should say the musk flakes were contained in the brown envelope the elevator boy delivered to Mademoiselle Lefètre. As for the hairs—"

The tinkle of the telephone broke off his explanation. "Yes, my *sergent*, it is I," I heard him answer. "He is? Restrain him—forcefully, if necessary. I shall make the haste to join you.

"Come, let us hurry," he commanded as he set the 'phone down.

"Where, at this hour o' night, for pity's sake?"

"Why, to the morgue, of course. Parnell, the coroner's physician, insists on making an autopsy on the body of Miss Henrietta Sidlo within the hour. We must look at her first."

"Who the devil was Miss Henrietta Sidlo?" I asked as we commenced our hurried journey to the city morgue.

"The so attractive blond young woman who was killed because she could not mind her business and keep from the room we had forbidden her to enter."

"What makes you so sure she was killed? She might have fallen from the window, or—"

"Or?" he echoed.

"Oh, nothing. I just had a thought."

"I rejoice to hear it. What was it, if you please?"

"Perhaps she thought as you did, that Miss Lefètre had climbed to the roof, and tried to emulate the feat experimentally."

I had expected him to scout my theory, but he nodded thoughtfully. "It may be so," he answered. "It seems incredible that one should be so foolish, but the Sidlo girl was nothing if not unbelievable, *n'est-ce-pas?*"

Beneath the searing glare that flooded from the clustered arclights set above the concave operating-table in the morgue's autopsy room her body showed almost as pale as the white tiles that floored and walled the place. She had bled freely from the nose and ears when skull and brain were smashed at once, and the dried blood stained her chin and cheeks and throat. De Grandin took spray-nosed hose and played its thread-like stream across her face and neck sponging off the dried blood with a wad of cotton. At length: "What is it that you see?" he asked.

Where the blood and grime had washed away were five light livid patches, one some three inches in size and roughly square, and extending from it four parallel lines almost completely circling the neck. At the end of each was a deeply pitted scar, as if the talons of some predatory beast had sunk into the flesh.

"Good heavens," I exclaimed; "it's terrible!"

"But naturally. One does not look for beauty in the morgue. I asked you what you saw, not for your *impression esthetique.*"

I hesitated for a breath and felt his small blue eyes upon me in a fixed, unwinking stare, quizzical, sardonic; almost, it seemed, a little pleading. Long years ago, when we had known each other but a day, he and I had stood beside another corpse in this same morgue, the corpse of a young girl who had been choked and mauled to death by a gorilla. "Sarah Humphreys—" I began; and:

"*Bravo, bravissimo!*" he whispered, "You have right, my friend. See, here is the bruise left by the heel of his hand; these encircling marks, they are his fingers; these jagged, deep-set marks the wounds left by his broken nails. Yes, it is so. There is no thumb print, for he does not grasp like men, he does not use his thumb for fulcrum."

"Then those hairs you found when you swept up the room—"

"*Précisément.* I recognized them instantly, but could not imagine how they came there. If—one moment, if you please!"

Bending quickly he took the dead girl's pale plump hands in his and with his penknife tip skimmed underneath the rims of her elaborately lacquered nails, dropping the salvage into a fresh envelope. "I think that we shall find corroboration in a microscopic test of these," he stated, but the bustling entrance of the coroner's physician cut him short.

"What's going on here?" Doctor Parnell asked. "No one should touch this body till I've finished my examination—"

"We do but make it ready for you, *cher collègue*," de Grandin answered with fictitious mildness as he turned away. Outside he muttered as we climbed into my car: "There are fools, colossal fools, damned fools, and then there is Parnell. He is superlative among all fools, friend Trowbridge."

Three-quarters of an hour later we put the scrapings from the dead girl's nails beneath a microscope. Most of the matter was sheer waste, but broken and wedged firmly in a tiny drop of nail stain we came upon the thing we sought, a tiny fragment of gorilla hair.

"*Tiens*, she fought for life with nature's weapons, *cette pauvre*," he murmured as he rose from the examination. "It is a pity she should die so young and beautiful. We must take vengeance for her death, my friend."

AMBER BROCADE CURTAINS HAD been drawn against the unseasonably chilly weather and a bright fire crackled on the hearth of the high-manteled fireplace of the lounging-room of the Lefètre home in Nyack. Harold Lefètre greeted us restrainedly. Since dinnertime the day before he had been interviewed by a succession of policemen and reporters, and his nerves and patience were stretched almost to the snapping-point.

"There isn't anything that I can add to what you've been already told," he said like one who speaks a well-learned piece. "Emerline was just past seventeen, she had no love affairs, wasn't especially interested in boys. Her scholastic standing was quite good, though she seldom got past B grades. She was not particularly studious, so it couldn't have been a nervous breakdown forced by overstudy. She stood well enough in marks not to have been worried over passing her examinations; she was happy in her home. There is no reason, no earthly reason I can think of, for her to disappear. I've told you everything I know. Suppose you try looking for her instead of quizzing me."

Costello's face flushed brick-red. He had been against the interview, expecting a rebuke would be forthcoming.

De Grandin seemed oblivious to Lefètre's censure. His eyes were traveling round the charming room in a quick, stock-taking gaze. He noted with approval the expensive furniture, the bizarre small tables with their litter of inconsequential trifles, cinnabar and silver cigarette-containers, fashionable magazines, bridge markers, the deep bookshelves right and left of the big fireplace, the blurred blues and mulberries of the antique china in the unglassed cabinets. In a far, unlighted corner of the room his questing glance seemed resting, as though he had attained the object of his search. In apposition to the modern, western, super-civilized sophistication of the other bric-à-brac the group of curios seemed utterly incongruous; a hippopotamus leg with hoof intact, brass-lined to form a cane stand and holding in its tube a sheaf of African assagais. Above the group of relics hung a little drum no bigger than a sectioned coconut, with a slackly tensioned head of dull gray parchment. "*Monsieur*," the Frenchman suddenly demanded, "you were in Africa with Willis Cogswell in 1922?"

Lefètre eyed him sharply. "What has that to do—"

"It was Monsieur Cogswell's daughter who vanished without trace three months ago, *n'est-ce-pas?*"

"I still don't see—"

"There were three members of your African adventure, were there not: yourself, and Messieurs Cogswell and Everton?"

Anger flamed in our host's face as he turned on Costello. "What has all this got to do with Emerline's case?" he almost roared. "First you come badgering me with senseless questions about her, now you bring this 'expert' here to pry into my private life—"

"You did not part with Monsieur Everton in friendship?" de Grandin broke in imperturbably. Then, as if his question were rhetorical: "But no. Quite otherwise. You and he and Monsieur Cogswell quarreled. He left you vowing vengeance—"

"See here, I've had enough of this unwarranted—"

"And ninety days ago he struck at Willis Cogswell through the dearest thing that he possessed. Attend me very carefully, *Monsieur*. You have heard that shock caused Monsieur Cogswell to collapse, that he died of a heart seizure two days following his daughter's disappearance—"

"Of course, he did. Why shouldn't he? He'd been suffering from angina for a year, had to give up business and spend half his time in bed. His doctor'd warned him anything exciting might prove fatal—"

"*Précisément.* He fell dead in his library. His butler found him dead upon the floor—"

"That's true, but what—"

De Grandin drew a slip of folded paper from his pocket. "This was in your friend's hand when the butler found him," he answered as he held the missive toward our host. It was a piece of coarse brown paper, torn, apparently from a grocery bag, and penciled on it in black chalk was one word: *Bokoli.*

The anger faded from Lefètre's face; fear drained his color, left him gray.

"You recognize the writing?" asked de Grandin.

"No, no, it can't be," Lefètre faltered. "Everton is dead—we—I saw him—"

"And these, *Monsieur*, we found among the sweepings from your daughter's room," de Grandin interrupted. "You recognize them, *hein?*" Fixed with adhesive gum to a card of plain white paper, he extended the gorilla hairs we'd found the night before.

Utter panic replaced fear in our host's face. His eyes were glassy, bright and dilated as if drugged with belladonna. They shifted here and there, as though he sought some channel of escape. His lips began to twist convulsively.

"This—this is a trick!" he mumbled, and we saw the spittle drooling from the corners of his mouth. "This couldn't be—"

His hands shook in a nervous frenzy, clawing at his collar. Then suddenly his knees seemed softening under him, and every bit of stiffness left his body so that be fell down in a heap before the hearth, the impact of his fall rattling the brass tools by the fireplace.

Involuntarily I shivered. Something evil and soft-footed seemed to shuffle in that quiet room, but there was no seeing it, no hearing it, no way of knowing what it was; only the uncanny, hideous feel of it—clammy, cold, obscenely leering.

"Now—so!" de Grandin soothed as he lowered his flask from the reviving man's lips. "That is better, *n'est-ce-pas?*"

He helped Lefètre to a chair, and, "Would it not be well to tell us all about it?" he suggested. "You have had a seething pot inside you many years, *Monsieur*; it has boiled, then simmered down, then boiled again, and it has brought much scum up in the process. Let us skim it off, *comme ça*"—he made a gesture as if with a spoon—"and throw it out. Only so shall we arrive at mental peace."

Lefètre set his face like one who contemplates a dive in icy water. "There were four of us on safari through Bokoliland," he answered; "Cogswell, his wife Lysbeth, a Boer settler's daughter, Everton and I. We'd found the going pretty rough; no ivory, no trading fit to mention, no gold, and our supplies were running low. When we reached Shamboko's village the men were all out hunting, but the women and old men were kind to us and fed and lodged us. In normal circumstances we'd have waited there until the chief came back and tried to do some trading, but on the second evening Everton came hurrying to our hut half drunken with excitement.

"'I've just been to the Ju-Ju house,' he told us. 'D'ye know what they've got there? Gold! Great heaps and stacks o' yellow dust, enough to fill our hats and pockets, and a stack o' yellow diamonds bigger than your head. Let's go!'

"Now, the Bokoli are a fairly peaceful folk, and they'd take a lot from white men, but if you monkey with their women or their Ju-Ju you'd better have your life insurance premiums all paid. I'd seen the body of a man they'd 'chopped' for sacrilege one time, and it had put the fear o' God in me. They'd flayed the skin off him, not enough to kill him, but the torment must have been almost past standing. Then they'd smeared honey on the raw nerve ends and staked him down spread-eagled in a clearing in the jungle. The ants had found him there— millions of the little red ones—and they'd cleaned the flesh off of his bones as if they had been boiled.

"I wasn't having any of that, so I turned the proposition down, but the others were all for it. Finally I yielded and we sneaked down to the Ju-Ju house. It was just as Everton had said. The gold was piled in little pyramidal heaps before the idol in a semicircle, with the diamonds stacked up in the center. The offerings must have been accumulating over several centuries, for there's little gold in the Bokoli country, and no diamonds nearer than five hundred miles. But there the stuff was, ready for our taking.

"We stuffed our haversacks and pockets and set out for the coast within an hour, anxious to put as many miles as possible between us and the village before the medicine man paid his morning visit to the Ju-Ju and found out what we'd done.

"Everton began to act queer from the start. He'd sneak away from camp at night and be gone hours at a time without an explanation. One night I followed him. He made straight for a clearing by the river and sat down on the grass as if waiting someone. Presently I saw a shadow slipping from the bush and next moment a full-grown gorilla shambled out into the moonlight. Instead of rushing Everton the monster stopped a little distance off and looked at him, and Everton looked back, then—think I'm a liar if you wish—they *talked* to one another. Don't ask me how they did it; I don't know. I only know that Everton addressed a series of deep grunts to the great beast and it answered him in kind. Then they parted and I trailed him back to camp.

"Three days later the Bokoli caught us. We'd just completed dinner and were sitting down to smoke when all at once the jungle seemed alive with 'em, great strapping blacks with four-foot throwing spears and bullhide shields and vulture feathers in their hair. They weren't noisy about it. That was the worst of it. They appeared like shadows out of nowhere and stood there in a ring, just looking at us. Old Chief Shamboko did the honors, and he was as polite about it as the villain in a play. No reproaches for the diamonds and the gold dust we'd made off with, though they must have represented his tribe's savings for a century or more. Oh, no, he put it squarely to us on the ground of sacrilege. The Ju-Ju was insulted. He'd lost face. Only blood could wash away the memory of the insult, but he'd be satisfied with one of us. Just one. We were to make the choice. Then he walked back to the ring of warriors and stood waiting for us to announce which one of us would go back to be flayed alive and eaten up by ants. Pretty fix to be in, eh?"

"You made no offer to return the loot?" de Grandin asked.

"I'll say we did. Told him he might have our whole trade stock to boot, but he wasn't interested. The treasure we had taken from the temple had been tainted by our touch, so couldn't be put back, and only things dug from the earth were suitable as offerings to the Ju-Ju, so our trade stuff had no value. Besides, they wanted blood, and blood was what they meant to have."

"One sees. Accordingly—?"

"We tossed for it. Lysbeth, Cogswell's wife, drew out a coin and whispered something to her husband. Then he and Everton and I stood by as she flipped it. Cogswell beat us to the call and shouted 'Heads!' And heads it came. That left Everton and me to try.

"He shouted 'Tails!' almost before the silver left her hand. It came up heads again, and I was safe."

"And so—"

"Just so. The Bokoli couldn't understand our words, of course, but they knew that Everton had lost by his demeanor, and they were on him in a second, pinioning his arms against his sides with grass rope before he had a chance to draw his gun and shoot himself.

"Considering what he was headed for, you could hardly blame him, but it seemed degrading, the way he begged for life. We'd seen him in a dozen desperate fixes when his chance of coming through alive seemed absolutely nil, but he seemed like another person, now, pleading with us to shoot him, or die fighting for him, making us the most outlandish offers, promising to be our slave and work for ever without wages if we'd only save him from the savages. Even old Shamboko seemed to feel embarrassed at the sight of such abysmal cowardice in a white man, and he'd ordered his young men to drag their victim off when Everton chanced to kick the silver coin which sent him to his fate. The florin shone and twinkled in the moonlight when he turned it over. Then he and I and all of us realized. It was a trick piece Lysbeth used, an old Dutch florin with two heads. There hadn't been a chance her man could lose the toss, for she'd told him to call heads, and she'd flipped the coin herself, so none of us could see it was a cheat.

"Everton turned sober in a second. Rage calmed him where his self-respect was powerless to overcome his fear of torture, and he rose with dignity to march away between the Bokoli warriors. But just before he disappeared with them into the bush he turned on us. 'You'll never know a moment's safety, any of you,' he bellowed. 'The shadow of the jungle will be on you always, and it'll take the dearest things you have. Remember, you'll each lose the thing you love most dearly.'

"That was all. The Bokoli marched him off, and we never saw him again."

"But, *Monsieur*—"

"But two weeks later, when we were almost at the outskirts of the Boer country, I woke up in the night with the sound of screaming in my ears. Cogswell lay face downward by the campfire, and just disappearing in the bush was a great silver-backed gorilla with Lysbeth struggling in his arms."

"You pursued—"

"Not right away. I was too flabbergasted to do more than gape at what I saw for several seconds, and the big ape and the woman were gone almost before you could say 'knife.' Then there was Cogswell to look after. He'd had a dreadful beating, though I don't suppose the beast had more than merely flung him from his way. They're incredibly powerful, those great apes. Cogswell had a dislocated shoulder and two broken ribs, and for a while I thought he'd not pull through. I pulled his shoulder back in place and bandaged him as best I could, but it was several weeks before he regained strength to travel, and even then we had to take it slowly.

"I kept us alive by hunting, and one day while I was gunning I found Lysbeth. It was a week since she'd been stolen, but apparently she'd never been more than a mile or so away, for her body hung up in a tree-fork less than an hour's walk from camp, and was still warm when I found it.

"The ape had ripped her clothing off as he might have peeled a fruit, and apparently he'd been none too gentle in the process, for she was overlaid with scratches like a net. Those were just play marks, though. It wasn't till he tired of her—or till she tried to run away—he really used his strength on her. Down her arms and up her thighs were terrible, great gashes, deep enough to show the bone where skin and flesh had been shorn through in places. Her face was beaten absolutely flat, nose, lips and chin all smashed down to a bloody level. Her neck was broken. Her head hung down as if suspended by a string, and on her throat were bruise marks and the nailprints of the great beast's hands where he had squeezed her neck until her spinal column snapped. I"—Lefètre faltered and we saw the shadow of abysmal horror flit across his face—"I don't like to think what had happened to the poor girl in the week between her kidnapping and killing."

Costello looked from our host to de Grandin. "'Tis a highly interestin' tale, sor," he assured the Frenchman, "but I can't say as I sees where it fits in. This here now Everton is dead—ain't he?" he turned to Lefètre.

"I've always thought—I like to think he is."

"Ye saw 'im march off wid th' savages, didn't ye? They're willin' workers wid th' knife, if what ye say is true."

De Grandin almost closed his eyes and murmured softly, like one who speaks a poem learned in childhood and more than half forgotten: "It was December 2, 1923, that Lieutenant José Garcia of the Royal Spanish Army went with a file of native troops to inspect the little outpost of Akaar, which lies close by Boko-liland. He found the place in mourning, crazed with sorrow, fear and consternation. Some days before a flock of fierce gorillas had swept down upon the village, murdered several of the men and made away with numerous young women. From what the natives told him, Lieutenant Garcia learned such things had happened almost for a year in the Bokoli country, and that the village of the chief Sham-boko had been utterly destroyed by a herd of giant apes—"

"That's it!" Lefètre shrieked. "We've never known. We heard about the ape raids and that Shamboko's village had been wrecked by them, but whether they destroyed it before Everton was put to death or whether they came down on it in vengeance—Cogswell and I both thought he had been killed, but we couldn't know. When his daughter disappeared I didn't connect it with Africa, but that paper Cogswell clutched when he dropped dead, those hairs you found in Emer-line's room—"

"*Exactement*," de Grandin nodded as Lefètre's voice trailed off. "Perfectly, exactly, quite so, *Monsieur*. It is a very large, impressive 'but.' We do not know, we cannot surely say, but we can damn suspect."

"But for th' love o' mud, sor, how'd, this here felly git so chummy wid th' apes?" Costello asked. "I've seen some monkeys in th' zoo that seemed to have more sense than many a human, but—"

"You don't ask much about companions' former lives in Africa," Lefètre interrupted, "but from scraps of information he let drop I gathered Everton had been an animal trainer in his younger days and that he'd also been on expeditions to West Africa and Borneo to collect apes for zoos and circuses. It may be he had some affinity for them. I know he seemed to speak to and to understand that great ape in the jungle—d'ye suppose—"

"I do, indeed, *Monsieur*," de Grandin interrupted earnestly. "I am convinced of it."

"SURE, IT'S TH' NUTTIEST business I iver heard of, sor," Costello declared as we drove home. "'Tis wild enough when he stharts tellin' us about a man that talks to a gorilly, but when it's intaymated that a ape clomb up th' buildin' an' sthold th' gur-rl—"

"Such things have happened, *mon ami*," de Grandin answered. "The records of the Spanish army, as well as reports of explorers, vouch for such kidnappings—"

"O.K., sor; O.K. But why should th' gorillies choose th' very gur-rls this felly Everton desired to have sthold? Th' apes ye tell about just snatch a woman—any woman—that chances in their way, but these here now gorillies took th' very—"

"*Restez tranquil*," de Grandin ordered. "I would think, I desire to cogitate. *Nom d'un porc vert*, I would meditate, consider, speculate, if you will let me have a little silence!"

"Sure, sor, I'll be afther givin' ye all ye want. I wuz only—"

"Nature strikes her balance with nicety," de Grandin murmured as though musing aloud. "Every living creature pays for what he has. Man lacks great strength, but reinforces frailty with reason; the bloodhound cannot see great distances, but his sense of smell is very keen; nocturnal creatures like the bat and owl have eyes attuned to semi-darkness. What is the gorilla's balance? He has great strength, a marvelous agility, keen sight, but—*parbleu*, he lacks the sense of smell the lesser creatures have! You comprehend?"

"No, sor, I do not."

"But it is simple. His nose is little keener than his human cousins', but even his flat snout can recognize the pungent scent of crude musk at considerable distance. We do not know, we cannot surely say the Cogswell girl received an envelope containing musk upon the night she disappeared. We know that Mademoiselle Lefètre did." Abruptly:

"What sort of day was it Miss Cogswell disappeared?" he asked Costello.

The Irishman considered for a moment; then: "It wuz a wet, warm day in March, much like yesterday," he answered.

"It must have been," de Grandin nodded. "The great apes are susceptible to colds; to risk one in our northern winter out of doors would be to sign his death warrant, and this one was required for a second job of work."

Costello looked at him incredulously. "I s'pose ye know how old th' snatchin' monkey wuz?" he asked ironically.

"Approximately, yes. Like man, gorillas gray with age, but unlike us, their gray hairs show upon their backs and shoulders. A 'silverback' gorilla may be very aged, or he may still be in the vigor of his strength. They mature fully at the age of fourteen; at twenty they are very old. I think the ape we seek is something like fifteen years old; young enough to be in his full prime, old enough to have been caught in early youth and trained consistently to recognize the scent of musk and carry off the woman who exuded it."

"Th' tellyphone's been ringin' for a hour," Nora McGinnis told us as we drew up at my door. "'Tis a Misther Lefètre, an' he wants ye to call back—"

"*Merci bien*," de Grandin called as he raced down the hall and seized the instrument. In a moment he was back. "Quick, at once, right away, my friends," he cried. "We must go back to Nyack."

"But, glory be, we've just come down from there," Costello started to object, but the look of fierce excitement in the Frenchman's face cut his protest short.

"Monsieur Lefètre has received a note like that which killed his friend Cogswell," de Grandin announced. "It was thrust beneath his door five minutes after we had gone."

"And this," de Grandin tapped the scrap of ragged paper, "this shall be the means of trapping him who persecutes young girls."

"Arrah, sor, how ye're goin' to find 'im through that thing is more than I can see," Costello wondered. "Even if it has his fingerprints upon it, where do we go first?"

"To the office of the sheriff."

"Excuse me, sor, did ye say th' sheriff?"

"Your hearing is impeccable, my friend. Does not *Monsieur le Shérif* keep those sad-faced, thoughtful-looking dogs, the bloodhounds?"

"Be gob, sor, sure he does, but how'll ye know which way to lead 'em to take up th' scent?"

De Grandin flashed his quick, infectious grin at him. "Let us consider local geography. Our assumption is the miscreant we seek maintains an ape to do his bidding. Twice in three months a young girl has been kidnapped from the Shelton School—by this gorilla, we assume. America is a wondrous land. Things which would be marvels otherwise pass unnoticed here, but a gorilla in the country is still sufficiently a novelty to excite comment. Therefore, the one we seek desires privacy. He lives obscurely, shielded from his neighbors' prying gaze. Gorillas are equipped to walk, but not for long. The aerial pathways of the trees are nature's high roads for them. *Alors*, this one lives in wooded country. Furthermore, he must live fairly near the Shelton School, since his ape must be able to go there without exciting comment, and bring his quarry to his lair unseen. You see? It is quite simple. Somewhere within a mile or so of Shelton is a patch of densely wooded land. When we have found that place we set our hounds upon the track of him whose scent is on this *sacré* piece of paper, and—*voilà!*"

"Be gorry, sor, ye'll have no trohble findin' land to fit yer bill," Costello assured him. "Th' pine woods grow right to th' Shelton campus on three sides, an' th' bay is on th' other."

THE GENTLE BLOODHOUNDS WAGGED their tails and rubbed their velvet muzzles on de Grandin's faultlessly creased trousers. "Down, noble ones," he bade, dropping a morsel of raw liver to them. "Down, canine noblemen, peerless scenters-out of evil doers. We have a task to do tonight, thou and I."

He held the crudely lettered scrap of paper out to them and bade them sniff it, then began to lead them in an ever-widening circle through the thick-grown pine trees. Now and then they whimpered hopefully, their sadly thoughtful eyes upon him, then put their noses to the ground again. Suddenly one of them threw back his head and gave utterance to a short, sharp, joyous bark, followed by a deep-toned, belling bay.

"*Tallis au!*" de Grandin cried. "The chase is on, my friends. See to your weapons. That we seek is fiercer than a lion or a bear, and more stealthy than a panther."

Through bramble-bristling thicket, creeping under low-swung boughs and climbing over fallen trees, we trailed the dogs, deeper, deeper, ever deeper into the pine forest growing in its virgin vigor on the curving bay shore. It seemed to me we were an hour on the way, but probably we had not followed our four-footed guides for more than twenty minutes when the leprous white of weather-blasted clapboards loomed before us through the wind-bent boughs. "Good Lord," I murmured as I recognized the place. "It's Suicide Chapel!"

"Eh? How is it you say?" de Grandin shot back.

"That's what the youngsters used to call it. Years ago it was the meeting-place of an obscure cult, a sort of combination of the Holy Rollers and the Whitests. They believed the dead are in a conscious state, and to prove their tenets their pastors and several members of the flock committed suicide *en masse*, offering themselves as voluntary sacrifices. The police dispersed the congregation, and as far as I know the place has not been tenanted for forty years. It has an evil reputation, haunted, and all that, you know."

"*Tenez*, I damn think it is haunted now by something worse than any of the old ones' spooks," he whispered.

The ruined church was grim in aspect as a Doré etching. In the uncertain light of an ascending moon its clapboard sides, almost nude of paint, seemed glowing with unearthly phosphorescence. Patches of blue shadow lay like spilled ink on the weed-grown clearing round the edifice; the night wind keened a mournful threnody in the pine boughs. As we scrambled from the thicket of scrub evergreen and paused a moment in reconnaissance the ghostly hoot of an owl echoed weirdly, through the gloom.

De Grandin cradled his short-barreled rifle in the crook of his left arm and pointed to the tottering, broken-sided steeple. "He is there if he is here," he announced.

"I don't think that I follow ye," Costello whispered back. "D'ye mane he's here or there?"

"Both. The wounded snake or rodent seeks the nearest burrow. The cat things seek the shelter of the thickets. The monkey folk take to the heights when they are hunted. If he has heard the hounds bay he has undoubtlessly— *mordieu!*"

Something heavy, monstrous, smotheringly bulky, dropped on me with devastating force. Hot, noisome breath was in my face and on my neck, great, steelstrong hands were clutching at my legs, thick, club-like fingers closed around my arms, gripping them until I thought my biceps would be torn loose from my bones. My useless gun fell clattering from my hands, the monster's bristling hair thrust in my eyes, my nose, my mouth, choking and sickening me as I fought futilely against his overpowering strength. Half fainting with revulsion I struggled in the great ape's grasp and fell sprawling to the ground, trying ineffectually to brace myself against the certainty of being torn to pieces. I felt my head seized in a giant paw, raised till I thought my neck would snap, then bumped against the ground with thunderous force. A lurid burst of light blazed in my eyes, followed by a deafening roar. Twice more the thunderous detonations sounded, and as the third report reverberated I felt the heavy weight on top of me go static. Though the hairy chest still bore me down, there was no movement in the great encircling arms, and the vise-like hands and feet had ceased their torturing pressure on my arms and legs. A sudden sticky warmness flooded over me, wetting through my jacket and trickling down my face.

"Trowbridge, *mon vieux, mon brave, mon véritable ami*, are you alive, do you survive?" de Grandin called as he and Costello hauled the massive simian corpse off me. "I should have shot him still more quickly, but my trigger finger would not mind my brain's command."

"I'm quite alive," I answered as I got unsteadily upon my feet and stretched my arms and legs tentatively. "Pretty well mauled and shaken, but—"

"S-s-sh," warned de Grandin. "There is another we must deal with. *Holà l'haut!*" he called. "Will you come forth, *Monsieur*, or do we deal with you as we dealt with your pet?"

STARK DESOLATION REIGNED WITHIN the ruined church. Floors sagged uncertainly and groaned protestingly beneath our feet; the cheap pine pews were cracked and broken, fallen in upon themselves; throughout the place the musty, faintly acrid smell of rotting wood hung dank and heavy, like miasmic vapors of a marsh in autumn. Another smell was noticeable, too; the ammonia-laden scent of pent-up animals, such as hovers in the air of prisons, lazarets and primate houses at the zoo.

Guided by the odor and the searching beam shot by de Grandin's flashlight, we crossed the sagging floor with cautious steps until we reached the little eminence where in the former days the pulpit stood. There, like the obscene parody of a tabernacle, stood a great chest, some eight feet square, constructed of stout rough-sawn planks and barred across the front with iron uprights. A small dishpan half filled with water and the litter of melon rinds told us this had been the prison of the dead gorilla.

De Grandin stooped and looked inside the cage. "*Le pauvre sauvage*," he murmured. "It was in this pen he dwelt. It was inhuman—*pardieu!*" Bending quickly he retrieved a shred of orange satin. He raised it to his nose, then passed it to us. It was redolent of musk.

"So, then, Jules de Grandin is the fool, the *imbécile*, the simpleton, the ninny, the chaser-after-shadows, *hein?*" he demanded. "Come, let us follow through our quest."

Th' place seems empty, sor," Costello said as, following the wall, we worked our way toward the building's front. "If there wuz anny body here—Howly Mither!"

Across our path, like a doll cast aside by a peevish child there lay a grotesque object. The breath stopped in my throat, for the thing was gruesomely suggestive of a human body, but as de Grandin played his flashlight on it we saw it was a life-sized dummy of a woman. It was some five feet tall, the head was decorated by a blond bobbed wig, and it was clothed in well-made sports clothes—knit pull-over, a kilted skirt of rough tweed, Shetland socks, tan heelless shoes—the sort of costume worn by eight in ten high school and college girls. As we bent to look at it the cloyingly sweet scent of musk assailed our nostrils.

"Is not all plain?—does it not leap to meet the eye?" de Grandin asked. "This was the implement of training. That hairy one out yonder had been trained for years to seek and bring back this musk-scented dummy. When he was letter-perfect in discovering and bringing back this lifeless simulacrum, his master sent him to the harder task of seeking out and stealing living girls who had the scent of musk upon them. *Ha*, one can see it plainly—the great ape leaping through the shadowed trees, scaling the school roof as easily as you or I could walk the streets, sniffing, searching, playing at this game of hide-and-seek he had been taught. Then from the open window comes the perfume which shall tell him that his quest is finished; there in the lighted room he sees the animated version of the dummy he has learned to seize and carry to this *sacré* place. He enters. There is a scream of terror from his victim. His great hand closes on her throat and her cry dies out before it is half uttered; then through the treetops he comes to the chapel of the suicides, and underneath his arm there is—*morbleu*, and what in Satan's name is that?"

As he lectured us he swung his flashlight in an arc, and as it pointed toward the ladder-hole that led up to the ruined belfry its darting ray picked up another form which lay half bathed in shadows, like a drowned body at the water's edge.

It was—or had been—a man, but it lay across our path as awkwardly as the first dummy. Its arms and legs protruded at unnatural angles from its trunk, and though it lay breast down the head was turned, completely round so that the face looked up, and I went sick with disgust as I looked on what had once been human features, but were now so battered, flattened and blood-smeared that only staring, bulging eyes and broken teeth protruding through smashed lips told life had once pulsed underneath the hideous, shattered mask. Close beside one of the open, flaccid hands a heavy whip-stock lay, the sort of whip that animal trainers use to cow their savage pupils. A foot or so of plaited rawhide lash frayed from the weighted stock, for the long, cruel whip of braided leather had been ripped and pulled apart as though it had been made of thread.

"God rest 'is sinful soul!" Costello groaned. "Th' gorilly musta turned on 'im an' smashed 'im to a pulp. Looks like he'd tried to make a getaway, an' got pulled down from them stheps, sor, don't it?"

"By blue, it does; it most indubitably does," de Grandin agreed. "He was a cruel one, this, but the whip he used to beat his ape into submission was power-less at the last. One can find it in his heart to understand the monster's anger and desire for revenge. But pity for this one? *Non!* He was deserving of his fate, I damn think."

"All th' same, sor—Howly Saint Patrick, what's that?" Almost overhead, so faint and weak as to be scarcely audible, there sounded a weak, whimpering moan.

"Up, up, my friends, it may be that we are in time to save her!" the little Frenchman cried, leaping up the palsied ladder like a seaman swarming up the ratlines.

We followed him as best we could and halted at the nest of crossbeams mark-ing the old belfry. For a moment we stood silent, then simultaneously flashed our torches. The little spears of light stabbed through the shrouding darkness for a moment, and picked up a splash of brilliant orange in the opening where the bell had hung. Lashed to the bell-wheel was a girl's slim form, arms and feet drawn back and tied with cruel knots to the spokes, her body bowed back in an arc against the wheel's periphery. Her weight had drawn the wooden cycle down so that she hung dead-center at its bottom, but the fresh, strong rope spliced to the wheel-crank bore testimony to the torment she had been subjected to, the whirling-swinging torture of the mediæval bullwheel.

"Oh, please—please kill me!" she besought as the converging light beams played upon her pain-racked face. "Don't swing me any more—I can't—stand—" her plea trailed off in a thin whimpering mewl and her head fell forward.

"Courage, *Mademoiselle*," the small Frenchman comforted. "We are come to take you home."

"Β UT NO, *MON SERGENT*," Jules de Grandin shook his head in deprecation as he watched the ice cube slowly melting in his highball glass, "I have a great appreciation of myself, and am not at all averse to advertising, but in this case I must be anonymous. You it was who did it all, who figured out the African con-nection, and who found the hideaway to which the so unfortunate Miss Lefètre was conveyed. Friend Trowbridge and I did but go along to give you help; the credit must be yours. We shall show those fools down at headquarters if you are past your prime. We shall show them if you are unfit for crime detection. This case will make your reputation firm, and that you also found what happened to the Cogswell girl will add materially to your fame. Is it not so?"

"I only wish to God I did know what happened to poor Margaret Cogswell," the big detective answered.

De Grandin's smiling face went serious. "I have the fear that her fate was the same as that of Monsieur Cogswell's first wife. You recall how she was mauled to death by a gorilla? I should not be surprised if that ten-times-cursed Everton gave the poor girl to his great ape for sport when he had tired of torturing her. Tomorrow you would be advised to take a squad of diggers to that chapel of the suicides and have them search for her remains. I doubt not you will find them."

"An' would ye tell me one thing more, sor?"

"A hundred, if you wish."

"Why did th' gorilly kill th' Sidlo gur-rl instead o' carryin' her away?"

"The human mind is difficult enough to plumb; I fear I cannot look into an ape's mentality and see the thoughts he thinks, *mon vieux*. When he had stolen Mademoiselle Lefètre and borne her to the ruined chapel of the suicides the ape turned rebel. He did not go back to his cage as he was wont to do, but set out on another expedition. His small mind worked in circles. Twice he had taken women from the Shelton School, he seems to have enjoyed the pastime, so went back for more. He paused upon the roof-ledge, wondering where he should seek next for victims, and to him through the damp night air the pungent scent the Sidlo girl affected came. *Voilà*, down into the room he dropped, intent on seizing her. She was well built and strongly muscled. Also she was very frightened. She did not swoon, nor struggle in his grasp, but fought him valiantly. Perhaps she hurt him with her pointed fingernails. *En tout cas*, she angered him, and so he broke her neck in peevish anger, as a child might break its doll, and, again child-like, he flung the broken toy away.

"It was a pity, too. She was so young, so beautiful, so vital. That she should die before she knew the joys of love—*morbleu*, it saddens me. Trowbridge, my friend, can you sit there thus and see me suffer so? Refill my glass, I beg you!"

The Venomed Breath of Vengeance

I SHOOK MY HEAD reprovingly as Jules de Grandin decanted half an ounce of cream into his breakfast coffee and dropped two sugar lumps into the mucilaginous concoction.

"You're sending out an invitation to gastritis," I said warningly. "Don't you realize that mixing two such active ferments as cream and sugar in your coffee—"

He leveled an unwinking stare at me. "Am I to have no pleasure?" he demanded truculently. "May I not have the doubtful joy of getting sick without your interference? How do you amuse yourself while you preach of creamless sugar, I ask to know?"

"All right, how do I?" I responded as he paused for comment.

"By reading the obituary columns of *le journal*, to see how many of the poor misguided ones who follow your advice have gone to their long rest, where doctors prate no more of cream and sugar—"

"These don't happen to have been my patients," I cut in laughing, "but there's something queer about the way they died. Listen:

THIRD SHERVERS DIES MYSTERIOUSLY

Truman Shervers, 25, son of the late Robert Shervers, well known importer, and brother of the late Jepson Shervers, yachtsman, of Larchmont, N.Y., was found dead in bed at the family residence in Tuscarora Avenue yesterday morning by Mazie O'Brien, a maid in the household, when she went to his room to ascertain why he had not come down to breakfast with the family, as was his usual custom. Doctors MacLeod and William Lucas, hastily summoned, pronounced him dead of heart failure. The deceased had never been heard to complain of illness of that character, and seemed in perfect health when he went to bed the night before.

An air of gruesome mystery is lent to the occurrence by the fact that Mr. Shervers is the third member of his family to suffer sudden death within a month. His father, the late Robert Shervers, noted as an authority on Oriental art, was found dead in the library of the family home about a month ago, while his brother Jepson was discovered in a dying condition when a New York state trooper found his car crashed against a tree beside Pelham Park Boulevard, Mount Vernon, N.Y., two weeks later. He died without regaining consciousness. Members of the family when interviewed by *Journal* reporters declared all three deaths were ascribed to heart failure.

"What do you make of it?" I asked as I laid the paper by and helped myself to salted mackerel.

"*Tiens*, what does one ever make of death? The gentlemen appear to have been afflicted with a cardiac condition which they did not know about, and down they went, like dominoes in line, when it attacked them."

"Humph," I nodded, unconvinced. "I knew Jepson Shervers rather well, and saw him only three days before he died. He was feeling tiptop at the time and jubilant because he'd just received reports from his insurance broker that his application for fifty thousand increase in his policies had been approved. Insurance doctors don't usually overlook such things as cardiac conditions, especially where fifty thousand dollars is involved. Truman's death is even harder to explain. I saw him at the Racquet Club last Monday, and he'd just completed half an hour's work-out on the squash courts. That's pretty strenuous exercise for a cardiac."

"No autopsy was held?"

"Apparently not. The doctors all seemed satisfied."

"Then who are we to find fault with their diagnoses?" He drained a fresh cup of unsweetened coffee and rose. "Luncheon at half-past one, as usual? Good. I shall be here. Meantime, I have some matters to attend to at the library."

"THIS WAY, GENTLEMEN," THE frock-coated young man with smooth brushed hair, perfectly arranged cravat and mild, sympathetic manners met us at the door and ushered us to the back parlor of the Shervers house, where folding chairs had been set out in concentric semicircles with the casket as their focal point.

Nothing in the way of mortuary service had been omitted by the Martin Funeral Home. Behind a bank of palms a music reproducing device played the Largo from the *New World Symphony* so softly that its notes were scarcely audible:

Going home, going home,
I'm just going home ...

A linen runner spanned the scatter rugs that strewed the polished floors, making it impossible for anyone to trip or stumble as he passed from door to sitting-room. When folding chairs were broken out for late arrivals they opened with the softest clicks instead of sharp reports. We followed soundlessly in our conductor's wake, but as he paused beside the archway to permit us to precede him, I halted involuntarily. "*Comment?*" demanded Jules de Grandin in a whisper.

"That youngster," I returned, nodding toward the young mortician; "he's enough like Truman Shervers to have been his twin."

"I know that my Redeemer liveth, and that He shall stand at the latter day upon the earth . . ." Doctor Bentley began the office for the burial of the dead. A subdued flutter of fans, the soft swish-swish of unaccustomed black silk garments being adjusted by their wearers in the semi-hysteria women always show at funerals, the faint, muted murmurings of late arrivals at the front door, occasional low, distance-softened noises from the street outside accompanied the words.

". . . We brought nothing into the world and it is certain we can carry nothing out . . . the Lord gave and the Lord hath taken away . . ." the solemn words of the liturgy proceeded. De Grandin raised his hand and thrust his forefinger between his neck and collar. It was hot as only August in a rainy spell can be, and with Gallic worship of convention he had donned his cutaway and stiff--starched linen, disdainfully refusing to put on a mohair jacket and soft shirt as I did. The air was almost unsupportable in the close-packed room. The heavy, cloyingly sweet perfume of tuberoses fell upon our senses like a sickening drug. Next to us a woman swayed upon her chair and turned imploring eyes upon the tight-shut window. Why hadn't they availed themselves of Mr. Martin's chapel? I wondered. His rooms were large and air-conditioned; people need not sit and stifle in them, but . . . The lady on my left moaned softly. In a moment, I knew, she'd be sick or fainting.

Softly, treading noiselessly on feet accustomed to step without sound, the young mortician who had ushered us into the parlor tiptoed to the window, raised the lace-bordered blind and took the sash knobs in his hands. Watching idly, I saw him straighten with the effort of forcing up a sash warped in its casings by the spell of humid weather, and heard the faint squeak as the sash gave way and slid slowly upward. Something like this always happened when they had a funeral in the home, I ruminated. If only they had used the Martin chapel . . .

Like a flash de Grandin left his seat and dashed across the room, clasping arms about the young man's shoulders. In the act of opening the window the youngster had swayed back, almost as from a blow in the chest, and was sagging to the floor, sinking with a look of almost comical surprise upon his small, well modeled features.

"*Courage, mon brave,*" de Grandin whispered, closing ready arms about the fainting man. "Lean on me, it is the heat."

I rose and joined them hurriedly, for despite his reassuring words I knew that it was neither the humidity nor temperature which had stricken the young undertaker. His face was pale with a blue tinge, his lips were almost purple, as though he stood beneath the neon light in a quick-picture photographer's. "Easy, son," I comforted as we helped him down the hall; "we can't afford to have folks getting all excited at a time like this."

We reached the passage leading to the kitchen and eased our charge down to the floor while de Grandin bent to loose the black and white cravat which bound his stiffly starched wing collar.

"Ah—so. Is not that better?" he asked as he bent above the gasping youth. "You will be all well in just one little minute—"

"My God, sir, he popped up right in my face!" the boy cut in, his words mouthed difficultly, as though something soft and hot lay upon his tongue. "It was as if he waited there for me, and when I put the window up—" Thicker and thicker, softer and more soft his utterance came; finally it died away in a soft, choking gurgle. His head fell back against my arm, and I saw his jaw relax.

"Lord, let me know my end, and the number of my days; that I may be certified how long I have to live. . . ." Doctor Bentley's voice came smoothly, sonorously, from the room beyond. "O spare me a little that I may recover my strength before I go hence. . . ."

Despite the almost suffocating heat I shuddered. There was something horrifyingly appropriate in the service being read beyond that archway.

The young funeral director lay dead at our feet.

DE GRANDIN DRUMMED A tattoo on the silver head of his black walking-stick as we drove homeward from the funeral. "My friend," he announced, suddenly, "I do not like that house."

"Eh?" I responded. "You don't like—"

"By blue, I do not. It is an evil place. it has the smell of death and tragedy upon it. I noticed it the moment that I entered, and—"

"Oh, come, now," I derided. "Don't tell me you had a psychic spell and foresaw tragedy—"

"Indeed, I did. Not that poor young man's deplorable decease, but—"

"I understand," I interrupted, "but I don't believe there's anything partaking of the super-physical about it. Just one of those coincidences that make life seem so curiously unreal at times. The average person finds something faintly grotesque in an undertaker's death—just as there's something faintly comic in a doctor's being ill—and the fact that he happened to die so tragically during the funeral service, when so much emotional energy was focussed on the thought of death—"

He squeezed my elbow with a quick grip of affection. "My good friend!" he exclaimed. "I understand you. You will not scoff at me, and so you rationalize the entirely illogical death of that poor young man to let me down without hurt feelings. I wish I could agree with you, but I cannot. When I declare there is an aura of misfortune, tragedy and death about that house I speak no more than simple truth. Some things there are we see without beholding, or hear without sound. Attend me carefully: As a spider lurks in secret at the center of her web, so death waited in that place. And just as many flies pass by the spider's snare unharmed, yet some eventually are caught, just so I knew the moment that I crossed the threshold that death would strike again, and soon, inside those portals. I think that we are lucky to have come away with whole skins."

"Perhaps you're right," I murmured. "It was certainly a most uncanny—"

"You saw him die," he interrupted. "Would you certify the cause of death?"

"It looked like some sort of heart seizure, there was marked cyanosis, labored breathing, difficulty in enunciation—"

"Agreed," he broke in, "but what was it that he said as we assisted him?"

"Oh, something about someone's waiting for him; you know what strangely garbled statements dying people make. The boy was agonizing, dying. His entire system of co-ordination was deranged, the nerves connecting thought and speech were short-circuited—"

He prodded me with a stiff forefinger. "Three persons, three members of a single family, have met death within a month. In every case the cause assigned was heart failure, an almost meaningless term, medically speaking. In no instance was there any history of cardiac disturbance; in one case the deceased was certified as being in sound health within a day or so of dying. No autopsies were had, nothing but objective symptoms led the doctors to ascribe the deaths to heart conditions. Now a young and healthy man succumbs in the same way. Tell me, if you were asked to give his cause of death, would you say it was heart failure?"

"Yes," I answered. "If it were impossible to have an autopsy and I could not have his medical history, I'd say, with no other evidence than that we have at present, that his death was due to heart failure.

His noncommittal exclamation was half a swallow, half a grunt.

"Now then," he faced me at the dinner table the next evening, "we are somewhat farther in our quest."

"Are we? I didn't know we had one."

"Indubitably. The so strange deaths among the *famille* Shervers, the equally inexplicable dispatch of the young mortuarian, the insistence on heart failure as the cause of each—*ah bah*, they did not make the sense. They outraged my ideas of propriety, they intrigued me. Yes. Assuredly."

"And so—"

"And so I got permission to attend the autopsy on the young man's body at the morgue today."

"And the finding was—"

"A failure of the heart, by blue!"

"I take it you do not agree?"

"Name of a piebald porcupine, my friend, you take it right! I begged, I pleaded, I entreated them to analyze the poor one's blood, for it was of a chocolate color, and I thought I smelled a characteristic odor. But would they do it? *Non!* Parnell, the coroner's physician, he laughed at me. At Jules de Grandin! 'See,' he said while grinning like a dog, 'here are the heart. It have ceased to function. Therefore it was a failure of the heart which killed him.'

"There was nothing one could do. One was present as a guest, and entirely without official status. And so I made him a most courteous bow. '*Monsieur*,' I said, 'permit me to congratulate you on your sublime ignorance.' Thereupon I came home to my dinner."

For upward of an hour he was busy in the surgery, and I had begun to wonder if he planned to spend the evening there when he emerged in shirt sleeves, his cuffs rolled back and a look of exultation on his face.

"Behold, observe, give attention," he commanded as he waved a test-tube like a banner shaken out in triumph. "When Parnell *l'idiot de naissance* refused to test the poor young undertaker's blood I held my lips—as much as could have been expected—but though my tongue was circumspect my hands were not. Oh, no; I was a thief, a pilferer, a criminal. I filled a little so small vial with blood wrung from a sponge and hid it in my pocket. I have subjected it to an analysis, that blood, and these things I have found: The blood are chocolate brown, not red as blood should be; on distillation I found tiny yellow globules which smelled of crushed peach kernels; when ether had been added and permitted to evaporate I found an aniline apparent by its odor, and the isonitrille test confirmed its presence. What do you say to that, *hein?*"

"Why, it sounds like poisoning by nitrobenzol, but—"

"*Précisément*, that but, he puts an obstacle before us, *n'est-ce-pas?* That nitrobenzol, he kills quickly; one cannot take him in his mouth, then walk around while he awaits his action. No. He acts by making it impossible for blood to take up oxygen, therefore his victims have the blue face—cyanosis. Yes?"

"Yes, of course, but—"

"Very well, then. If this odor of the kernel of the peach has not been smelled, and we see his victim fall, we might be led to think he suffered failure of the heart, *n'est-ce-pas?*"

"That's so, but—"

"*Bien oui*. Here in this mortuarian we have a case which might be heart failure. It misleads my good Friend Trowbridge, who is nobody's fool, it misleads that *sale chameau* Parnell who is everybody's fool, but it does not mislead me. Oh, no. I am a very clever fellow, and follow where my nose directs. Now, if the young man dies of nitrobenzol poisoning, and everyone but Jules de Grandin thinks he dies of a weak heart, are it not entirely possible those members of the Shervers family succumbed to the same subtle poison? Are it not even probable?"

"Possible, of course," I nodded, "but not highly probable. In the first place, there's no earthly reason for any of them to have committed suicide, yet nitrobenzol's not the kind of drug one can administer murderously. Its characteristic odor and sharp bitterness of taste would warn intended victims. Besides, we were right beside him when that poor boy died. One moment he was well, next instant he was falling in profound narcosis, and within two minutes he was dead. No one could have given him the poison; he could not have taken it himself and walked across the room to attempt to open the window. No, I'm afraid your theory isn't tenable, de Grandin."

He regarded me a moment, round-eyed as a puzzled tom-cat. At length: "You said the young mortician bore resemblance to the Monsieur Shervers in whose funeral he participated? We may have something there. Is it not possible some evilly-intentioned person mistook him for a member of the Shervers family, and struck him down—"

"By administering $C_6H_5NO_2$ in broad daylight, without anybody's seeing him?" I asked sarcastically.

"*Précisément.* Exactly as you say."

"But that is utterly fantastic—"

"I quite agree with you. It is. But fantasy may be fact, too. If a thing exists we must accept it, whether it is capable of proof or otherwise. Meantime"— methodically he turned his cuffs down and snapped the fastenings of his smoked pearl links—"let us go and tender our condolences to survivors of the Shervers family. It would be a gracious gesture—and we may find out something which we do not know at present."

OLD EUSTACE SHERVERS COWERED in the tufted Turkish armchair set before the fireless fireplace of the stiffly formal parlor of the house where he had brought his bride some six and sixty years before when, a young lieutenant fresh from service under Farragut, he had come home from war to take his place in the importing business founded by his Anglo-Indian father. He was a pitiable figure, vulture-bald and crippled with arthritis, half blind with presbyopia, bent with the weight of eighty-seven years. Almost destitute of blood-kin, too, for all his family had preceded him except his great-grandson Elwood, Jepson's son, back from school in England to attend his father's funeral, and still at home when tragedy deprived him of his uncle. Now the old man fumbled with his black-thorn cane and stared at us with blue, almost blind eyes.

"Yes, gentlemen," he said in the cracked voice old age imposes on its victims, "it almost seems a curse is on our family. First came Robert's death, from heart failure, they said, though he seemed as vigorous as anyone could be, then Jepson, and now Truman. Jepson wanted more insurance, you know, and when the doctors said it was his father's heart that killed him he went down at once for examination. The doctors looked him over carefully, and certified his health as perfect. His application for $50,000 more insurance was approved, although the policies had not been issued when they found him dead in his car on the Pelham Road.

"Now Truman's gone the same way. He'd been designated for examination for the Marine Corps, and the naval surgeons gave him perfect ratings. Although he'd studied hard to pass his written tests, he'd kept in perfect trim, and apparently he was in the best of health. Why, on the day before the night he died he played six games of squash and won them all. Could anyone about to die of heart failure have done that?"

"It seems unlikely, *Monsieur*," de Grandin answered as he gazed with more curiosity than courtesy at the family portraits hanging on the walls. Abruptly: "Who is that one, if you please?" he asked, nodding to an oval picture done indifferently in oils and representing a young man in scarlet tunic piped with blue, a small mustache and rudimentary goatee.

His sudden change of subject shocked me hardly more than his unconcealed curiosity, and I saw old Shervers draw his bloodless lips across his false dentition at the exhibition as he answered rather stiffly, "That is my father, sir, Captain Hardon Jennings Shervers of the artillery corps of the British India Company, who fought with marked distinction through the Mutiny and helped to execute the white man's justice on the bloody dogs who massacred the women in the Cawnpore dungeons. He emigrated to America shortly afterward and engaged in Oriental trade—"

"*Pardonnez-moi, Monsieur*, is one to understand your father was commander of a battery which blew the Mutiny ringleaders from the cannon's mouth?"

"That is correct, sir. I was a lad at the time, but I well remember how the terror of those executions spread throughout all India, how the Hindoos cringed away in fear whenever a *sahib* passed"—his purblind eyes turned backward on the savage memory and his rheumatism-knotted fingers tightened on the silver knob of his thorn stick—"I tell you, gentlemen, not for a century will those heathen forget what we did to them that day!"

"*Tiens*, I damn think you have right, *mon ancien*," de Grandin murmured; then, irrelevantly: "Tell me, if you please, how did your most respected father die?"

Once more the old man's withered lips were puckered back against his false teeth as though a drawstring tightened them. "He died of heart disease."

"And had he suffered long with the complaint?"

"He had not; no, sir. Like my son and grandsons, he was in what seemed to be good health up to the time he died. He passed away while sleeping."

"One sees." For a moment he was silent, studying the bent old man as an Egyptologist might took upon some relic of a vanished time and race. At length he rose and bowed with Continental courtesy. "Thank you for your information, and again we ask you to accept our sympathy," he said.

"Nom d'un nom d'un nom d'un nom," he muttered as we drove home, "it is a puzzle with two tails we have here, good Friend Trowbridge! I have grasped one of them, but the other still eludes me."

"What the deuce?" I queried.

"Precisely, exactly, quite so. I ask the same. Consider: We have here a family descended from a British officer who officiated at the blowing from the guns of Sepoy Mutineers. We heard the old one boast about the white man's vengeance and say that never in a hundred years would Indians forget. *Tenez*, I think he spoke more truly than he knew when he said that, for the corollary of the white man's vengeance is the vengeance of the Indian. If they hold the memory of those executions for a hundred years who shall say they do not hold the thought of retribution for an equal time?"

"But holding grudges and satisfying them aren't necessarily the same thing."

"*Mais non*, but think: Old Monsieur Shervers' father died of heart disease. He was in good health, there were no warning symptoms, but he died. So did his grandsons. In every case it was the same. All were apparently in good health, all were stricken dead by heart disease. Even the young mortician who had the sad misfortune to resemble one of them was smitten by the same malady, apparently. *Mordieu*, coincidence's arm is long, but these happenings pull it out of joint. It does not make the sense. Death is not obliged to give us notice of our dispossession from our bodies, but usually he does so. Not so with these ones. First they are strong and vigorous; then *pouf!* they are not even sick. They die. What is the answer?"

"But your blood tests seem to indicate the undertaker died of nitrobenzol poisoning."

"They do, indeed, and I should like to wager that if we could perform similar tests upon the others' blood we'd find that they too died of just that sort of 'heart disease.' I am convinced these so-called natural deaths are most unnatural. That dying lad was not delirious when he declared one was waiting for him by the window."

"Who was it, have you any idea?"

"Not the slightest, or, to be more accurate, only the slightest. I think that I can guess what he was, but who? *Hélas, non*. I grope, I feel about with searching fingers like the blind man who has lost his dog and stick, but darkness shuts me in on every side. I am at fault. It is as well that it grows late. Let us go to bed and sleep upon the problem. Tomorrow I may see more clearly."

"IT IS UNFORTUNATE WE could not see young Monsieur Elwood last night," de Grandin told me at the breakfast table next morning. "He might have added something to the old one's statement which would help us understand the case. Old people have their eyes set on the past; the modern viewpoint might be helpful—"

"I'll call and ask him to drop over," I volunteered. "We'd better not go over there, it might excite the old man."

Picking up the breakfast room telephone I dialed the Shervers' number, heard the smooth purr of the dial tone give way to the rhythmic buzzing of the automatic signal; then, "Hello?" I called as a woman's muffled voice came to me on the wire. Queer, I thought, it seemed almost as if her words were choked with crying, but:

"Good Lord!" I dropped the monophone back in its cradle and stared at Jules de Grandin in incredulous dismay.

"*Comment?*" he looked up from his plate of sausages and cakes.

"Eustace Shervers died last night. They say that it was—"

"*Non!* Do not tell me; let me guess; it was the heart disease, *n'est-ce-pas?*"

"That makes the fourth death in a month—"

"And unless we act with speed a fifth will follow quickly, I damn think!"

Dashing to the telephone he called the Martin Funeral Home, found that the old man's body had not yet been taken from his house, and with a muttered farewell ran full-tilt toward the front door and out into the street as though he were pursued by all the fiends of Pandemonium.

In half an hour he was back and shut himself up in the surgery. Occasionally I could hear the clink of glass on glass mingled with the low hum of his voice as he sang his private and entirely indecent version of a French translation of *Saint James' Infirmary Blues*. When he emerged there was a look of triumph on his face as he thrust a test-tube forward for inspection. "*C'est tout de même,*" he declared. "The old one's blood test shows the same reaction as the poor young mortuarian's. He too was poisoned by administration of nitrobenzol, and died of 'heart disease'."

"How'd you get a specimen—" I began, but he waved my question airily aside.

"One does not serve for years as agent of *le sûreté* and not learn tricks, my friend. I met the body of Monsieur Eustace as it came to the embalming-room. I requested that I be allowed to look at it, and while no one was looking I filled a syringe with his blood. *Voilà.* I brought it back with me; I tested it, and here it is, with every evidence of poison in it."

"But why, how—" I began.

"Why? *C'est tout simple.* The father's sins were visited upon the son—and on the sons' sons and their sons. The white man's vengeance which old Eustace boasted of last night begot the vengeance of the Hindoos. Did he not say they never would forget? *Parbleu*, it seems that they have not!

"As to the how, the *modus operandi* of the poisonings, that is for us to find, but find it out we must, unless we wish to see the funeral of the last one of the Shervers family."

"SURELY, YOU'RE NOT SERIOUS, Doctor?" Young Elwood Shervers looked curiously at the small Frenchman. "Why, it's utterly preposterous! Who would want to wipe the Shervers family out? We've never injured anyone that I can think of, and as for a family curse, or Nemesis, as you have termed it, it's too absurd to talk about. Of course, I'm grateful for your interest, and all that sort o' thing, but—well, we're English stock, you know. If we were French or Irish we might have family *Dames Blanches* or banshees, but" —the slightest trace of patronage showed in his voice—"we're not, and we haven't. And that's definitely that."

De Grandin took a quick puff at his cigarette and narrowed his eyes against the smoke, looking hard at Elwood. "*Monsieur*, this is no laughing matter, I assure you. Inspect the record, as your so magnificent Al Smith advises: Your first American ancestor fell victim to a heart attack, yet no one suspected he was menaced by the ailment. Your father and your uncles died, all in the prime of health, two of them with fresh certificates of health from doctors trained and paid to find the slightest defect. 'Heart, disease—heart failure,' the cause of death is given as monotonously as the chanting of an auctioneer who invites bids—"

"Oh, yes, we've been all over that," young Shervers interrupted. "But it's not a bit of use, sir. There must have been a strain of cardiac weakness somewhere, although no one suspected it. When Truman died, the strain and shock were just too much for poor old Grandpa Eustace. The wonder is the poor old chap hung on so long. Now, I'm a different temperament, I'm—"

"You are most woefully mistaken, *Monsieur*. Granting sorrow joined with shock to bring death to your relatives, what of the other one, the young mortuarian who died in this house during your uncle's funeral?"

Elwood fumbled at the red and blue necktie which marked him as a public school man. "Coincidence?" he muttered.

"Coincidence, my friend, is what the fool calls fate," de Grandin shot back. "The coincidence which caused the young man's death was that he happened to resemble Truman Shervers. We saw him cross the room to raise a window; we saw him stagger back as though he had been struck; we heard him say that someone waited for him at the window; we saw him die within two minutes. And did he also die of heart disease? By blue, he did not! Listen carefully:

"Human sight is fallible. A skilled physician looking at the blue-hued face of one who dies from nitrobenzol poisoning might be misled to think that he had died of heart failure. But chemistry makes no mistakes. When this and that is mixed with that and this, reactions are invariable. There is no room for argument. So when I tell you that I made a test of the young undertaker's blood and found that be was dead of nitrobenzol poisoning I do not make a statement which can be debated." He paused, then, earnestly: "The same tests prove your *gran'père* died of nitrobenzol poisoning, *Monsieur.*"

"What?" Elwood looked to me for confirmation or denial.

I nodded. "We can't explain it, Elwood, but undoubtedly the tests were positive. It was poison and not heart disease that killed them both."

Elwood Shervers' patronizing manner vanished like a morning mist before the rising sun. "Good Lord!" he almost wailed. "If that's so, what's to hinder them from killing me?"

"Only Jules de Grandin, my young friend."

"Then what do you advise, sir? I'll do anything in reason—"

"Ha, the fear of death, like fear of God, is the beginning of wisdom, it appears. Your behavior is a matter of concern, *Monsieur*. Walk, ride, play golf, do exactly as you please, but always in the company of others. Meanwhile, at home, be careful not to stand by any opened door or window, and permit no one to interview you while you are alone. You comprehend? It is not a rigorous routine."

"Oh, I say, you must be spoofing, aren't you? If someone's out to do me in, as you seem sure he is, why should I give 'em opportunity to slip the old stiletto in my back by walking in the street, yet keep away from open doors and windows in the house? Are they like the influenza, coming in on drafts?"

"*Mais oui*, they are as subtle as *la grippe*, but infinitely more deadly, I assure you. This evening we shall call upon you. If they run true to form your periods of greatest danger will be between sunset and daybreak."

"Right-ho, I'll follow through with your prescription, Doctor, and we'll gather round the festive board for dinner about seven."

DINNER WAS NOT WHAT might be called a jovial meal. Shervers forked vaguely at the food upon his plate and I did little more than play with mine. De Grandin, as always appreciative of good food, did full justice to the soup and fish and roast and kept Ordway, Shervers' butler, occupied with the chablis bottle and the claret cruet. But time and time again I caught his keen glance straying to the long windows at the north end of the room. As for me, my eyes were hardly turned away from them, for the observation he had made as we drove over ran insistently against my inner ears: "We do not know in what guise death will come but we are certain it will try to enter through the windows."

At last we had completed the ordeal by food and moved into the little drawing-room where Ordway brought us coffee, chartreuse and cigars. The room was rather small, not more than twenty long by eighteen feet in width, and in its furnishings one read the Shervers family's traits and history. A few examples of Georgian mahogany were almost lost among an assemblage of more exotic pieces, a Dutch-Chinese highboy, a teakwood table set with tortoise-shell, Chinese panels, Japanese prints, old Russian and Greek ikons, carved Italian candlesticks, books bound in Persian covers, Bokhara rugs upon the floor. In the bow window was a tabouret of Chinese red and on it a tall vase of Peking blue held a bouquet of summer roses. Above a fireplace fashioned in Damascus tiles was crossed a pair of swords, that worn by Eustace Shervers when he fought with Farragut at Mobile Bay and the one his father wore when he served the guns that blasted back the Sepoy Mutineers at Lucknow.

Shervers filled his chartreuse glass and his hand shook so the green liqueur slopped over and dripped down on the silver tray. "Damn!" he muttered, then, half peevishly, half challengingly to de Grandin: "You're certain that my ancestor's connection with the execution of the mutineers is what's behind all this?"

"I am convinced of it, *Monsieur*."

"Well, I'm convinced you're off your rocker. Of course, I don't know much about these Hindoo Johnnies, but they can't be quite as fierce as you make out. There were some of 'em at school with me in England, and they seemed as mild as milk-and-water. Suppose my great-great-grandfather did officiate at antemortem exercises for some of 'em, that was a hundred years ago, almost, and you'd hardly think these crumpets would retain a grudge that long. Why, they always seemed a cross between white rabbits and black guinea-pigs to me. Nothing vindictive about 'em."

There was something almost pitying in the look de Grandin gave him. "Mild-mannered, did you say, *Monsieur*? *Bien oui*, so is the serpent when he lies at ease and suns himself upon a rock; so is the tiger, in repose. Have you never stood before a tiger's den at the menagerie and wondered how the lovely, sleepy-seeming creature lying there like an enlarged edition of the fireside tabby-cat could he considered fierce and dangerous?

"My friend, if you had said these so demure ones were bred from cobras crossed with tigers you would have come much nearer to the truth than when you said they seemed like cross-breeds of the rabbit and the guinea-pig. Your father's grandsire's father knew the breed much better, I assure you. He had been born and reared in India, he knew of Nana Sahib and the things he did at Cawnpore."

"Nana?" echoed Elwood. "I always thought that was a woman's name. Didn't Zola write a novel—"

"*Morbleu*—and you have been to school! Attend me, if you please, while I amend your education: Nana Sahib was the leader of the mutineers at Cawnpore. After he had put the British garrison to death with most revolting tortures, he forced two hundred Englishwomen and their children into a small cellar, then sent professional butchers in to kill them. *Parbleu*, for upward of two hours their cries and screams and prayers for mercy filled that dismal cellar while the ruthless killers slaughtered them as if they had been sheep, sparing neither infirm beldame, tender toddling babe nor young and lovely maiden. There we have a sample of the so mild manners of the crossbred guinea-pigs and rabbits which you spoke of. It was an act of useless cruelty this Nana Sahib did; he knew the British under Havelock were almost within striking distance of his trenches. He ordered these assassinations only that his innate lust for cruelty and blood might be appeased. Now hear me, if you please"—he thrust a finger rigid as a bayonet at our host—"these ones we have to deal with, I believe, are lineal descendants of the men who carried out the bloody Nana's orders, or others very like them. India sleeps, you think? *Mais certainement*, but while she sleeps she dreams a dream of vengeance. The recollection of the crushing defeat fifty thousand Englishmen administered to almost as many million Indians rankles in her racial consciousness like a splinter in a festered sore. They owe a debt of deep humiliation to the English, and every Briton killed is so much interest on the long-delayed account. You comprehend? It is more than merely probable that you and yours have been marked for assassination since the day the guns your grandsire served blew captured mutineers to bits in vengeance for the Massacre at Cawnpore. Yes, certainly. Of course."

The look upon young Shervers' face reminded me of that a half-grown child might wear while listening to an adult tell a tale of Santa Claus. He drained his pousse-café glass at a gulp. "I think you're talking rot," he growled. "Furthermore, I'd just as lief be killed by those assassins whom you talk about as smother here with all the windows down." He glared defiantly at de Grandin, then rose and crossed to the bow-window. "I'm goin' to let some air in here."

"Don't!" I cried, and:

"*Insensé, imbécile, nigaud!*" de Grandin shouted. "*Nom d'un sacré nom*, you will destroy yourself completely!"

With an impatient gesture Elwood threw the curtains back, ran up the lace-edged blind and raised the sash.

Something like a long-drawn, venomous hiss—yet strangely like a cough—came to us from the outside darkness. There was a flash of white eyes in a swarthy face, the gleam of white teeth in a smile of gloating triumph, and the window-shade cord swayed as though a light breeze blew it.

Shervers staggered backward, both hands raised to clutch his throat, then stumbled crazily as though a cord had stretched across the floor to snare his feet, and dropped full length, face-upward, on the Mosul carpet.

Crash—tinkle! The shattering of splintered glass accompanied the roar de Grandin's pistol made as he snatched the weapon from his dinner jacket pocket and fired point-blank at the momentary silhouette of the dark face and evil smile that showed outside the window. A mocking laugh responded and the tap of fleeing feet came back to us from the brick walk that circled round the house and let into the alley.

"See to him—artificial respiration!" de Grandin cried as he vaulted through the window in pursuit of the dark visitant.

I turned the fainting man face-downward, rolled my dinner coat into a wad and thrust it underneath his chest, then began applying Schaefer's method, pressing firmly down upon the costal margins, swinging back, then bearing down again, counting twenty rapidly between each alternating pressure. "Ordway!" I shouted. "Ordway, bring some brandy and water!"

"Yes, sir?" The butler tiptoed through the doorway, his disapproval of my rowdy manners written plainly on his smoothly shaven face. "Did something happen?"

"Nothing much," I answered tartly. "Only someone nearly murdered Mr. Elwood. Get some water and brandy, and be quick about it!"

It might have been five minutes, though it seemed much longer, before the boy began to breathe in shuddering sighs instead of stifled gasps. I bent my arm behind his shoulders, raised him and poured brandy mixed with water down his throat. "Easier now?" I asked.

He shuddered as though he were chilled. "He—he seemed waiting out there for me—popped right up in my face! It"—he coughed and retched—"it was like fire—like smoke—like something that exploded in my face!"

A grisly feeling of malaise came over me. "He seemed waiting out there for me"—the words the dying funeral director gasped when we helped him from the window where he had been stricken! I had the eerily uncomfortable feeling that small red ants were running up my spine and neck and through my hair. "Ordway," I called again, "see to Mr. Elwood. Give him a sip of brandy every few minutes, and fan him steadily with something. I'll be back directly."

Climbing through the window I looked around for Jules de Grandin. There was no sign of him. "Hi, de Grandin!" I called. "Where are you?"

"Ohé, mon vieux—à moi!" the hail came from the rear of the garden. "Come and see the fish that we have caught!"

The gleam of his white shirt-front guided me to where he sat upon the grass, a cigarette between his lips, a smile of utter satisfaction with himself upon his face. Thirty feet or so away something writhed upon the shadowed lawn and cursed venomously in a whining voice with thick-tongued words. "Good heavens, what is it?" I asked.

For answer he drew out his pocket flashlight and shot its beam upon his quarry. In the diffused circle of pale orange light I saw an undersized dark man, emaciated as a mummy, sparsely bearded, turbaned. There was something horribly reminiscent of a June-bug on a string about the way he clawed a little distance on the grass, then stopped abruptly with a cry or curse of pain and slipped back, as if he had been pinioned by a tether of elastic. Then I saw. Biting cruelly on his left leg were the saw-toothed jaws of a steel trap, and anchoring the trap was a strong chain made fast to a stout peg.

"Good Lord, man! What—" Involuntarily, I stepped forward to release the tortured prisoner.

"Keep back, my friend!" de Grandin warned. "*Retirez vous!*"

The warning came a thought too late. As I leant forward the trapped man roused upon an elbow, pursed his lips and blew his breath into my face. I stepped backward, choking. Overwhelmingly powerful, the fumes of some gas, hot and scalding-bitter, stung my throat and nostrils, strangling me. The world seemed whirling like a carousel gone crazy, blindness fell upon me, but it was a blindness shot with bursting lights. My head seemed swelling to the burstingpoint. Dully, I felt, yet scarcely felt, the impact of my fall. Half senseless, I realized I lay upon my back, weak, limp and sick as though anesthetized with ether, yet with slowly rising consciousness returning.

"Wha—what?" I gasped, then choked and coughed and gasped again.

"*C'est un empoisonneur vicieux!*" I felt my wrists seized in a firm grip as Jules de Grandin pumped my arms up and down vigorously. Gradually the breath refilled my lungs, the dizziness subsided, and I sat up, staring round me in bewilderment. "You said it was a vicious poisoner—"

"*Mais oui.* I did, indeed, my friend. He is just that, the naughty fellow. Everything is all clear now, but there remain some things to be attended to." Methodically he cut a long switch from a lilac bush and stripped its leaves off. "Behold how I apply the antidote," he ordered as he advanced upon the prisoner and struck him a cruel cut with the peeled withe.

I watched in a paralysis of fascination. Oddly, repulsively, the pantomime was more like the torture of a snake than the torment of a man. The wretched creature on the ground writhed and wriggled like a serpent, clawed the grass, whined and hissed. Time and time again he tried to reach de Grandin, rearing up upon his elbows, thrusting forth his head and blowing at him with a hissing sibilation.

"*Sa-ha!*" The little Frenchman leaped back nimbly, as from a physical attack, and struck and struck the prisoner again, now on his skull-thin face, now across the writhing shoulders or the twisting back, now on the legs.

The poor wretch slowly weakened in his efforts to defend himself. Between the pain of merciless beating and the torture of the steel trap clamped about his ankle, he was tiring rapidly, but de Grandin was relentless. "Blow, breathe at me, exhale, *diablotin!*" and the swish and clapping impact of his lash gave punctuation to his orders.

"Stop it, man!" I cried, almost sickened at the spectacle.

The look he turned on me made me shrink back, a hand involuntarily raised in defense. Once as a lad I'd tried to take a baby chick from my pet cat, and the recollection of the transformation of my gentle playmate to a snarling small edition of a tiger had never quite been banished from my mind. It was such a transformation that I witnessed now. His lips curled back in a snarl that bared his small, sharp teeth, his little blond mustache reared upward like the whiskers of a furious tomcat, de Grandin seemed an incarnation of the god of vengeance.

"Keep clear!" he ordered savagely. "This affair is mine, to handle as my judgment dictates."

I retreated. It would have taken one far bolder than I was to try to take his prey away from him.

Cut—lash! His whip descended on the groveling man until it seemed that he desisted more from weariness than mercy. At last he threw the switch aside and stood looking at the trembling, sobbing wretch stretched on the grass before him. "I think that is enough," he told me matter-of-factly. "His venom-sac should be exhausted now."

"Whatever are you talking about?"

"Tout à l'heure," he cut me short. "At present we have duties to perform, my friend." Twisting his handkerchief into a cord he bound the prisoner's wrists securely at his back; then: "Put your foot down here, if you will be so good," he ordered, pointing to an arm of the steel trap, and rested his foot on the other prong, heaving downward at the saw-toothed jaws and releasing the man's ankle from their grip.

"Go, march, en avant!" he commanded, digging the muzzle of his pistol in the captive's back and pushing him toward the house. To me:

"Will you be kind enough to telephone the police and inform them that we have a tenant ready for the bastille?"

All spirit seemed to have been whipped out of our prisoner. The demoniacal gleam had faded from his eyes, his shoulders sagged, once or twice he shuddered and shook as if with overmastering sobs. "Jo hoegha so hoegha—what is written must come to pass!" he muttered.

"Beard of a green goat, never have you said a truer word, my wicked one!" de Grandin agreed as he thrust his pistol deeper in the small of the man's back.

"BUT NO, MY FRIENDS," he told us as, highball glass in hand, he faced us in the Shervers' little drawing-room, "it was all most beautifully simple, or, more exactly, beautifully complex."

Resting his glass on the mantelpiece he spread his finger fanwise and ticked the first point off upon his thumb.

"To commence at the beginning: It seemed strange to me when Doctor

Trowbridge first related how the Shervers family was being stricken by heart disease in series. Such things do occur, of course, but they are of sufficient unusualness to excite our wonder. However, I was but mildly interested until that day we came here to the funeral and saw young Monsieur Oldham, the mortician, die. His death seemed due to heart disease, but there were certain things about it which rang warning bells inside my brain. His face was cyanotic—blue-hued—which is evidence of heart failure, but not the sort of evidence which excludes all other diagnoses. Also, about him, on his linen, in his breath, there was a subtle, faint perfume. Not of *l'eau de Cologne*, not *parfum social*, but of bitter almonds—crushed peach kernels. Why?

"That odor is found in a number of strong poisons, in prussic acid, in its deadly volatile derivative, hydrocyanic gas. But these kill very quickly. The young man had seemed well and strong—then he was dead. He could not have committed suicide by such means, and it seemed impossible anyone had killed him; yet he was very dead, and my experiments were later to convince me that he died from breathing fumes of nitrobenzol. However, we anticipate.

"When we called upon your venerable ancestor and saw his father's portrait on the wall, I found a basis for these deaths, but still I did not see the way the murders were committed.

"It is a matter of historic record that some of those who helped to execute the Sepoy Mutineers—and their children and their children's children—died in circumstances so unusual as to point to vengeance killings, and in some instances these were of a nature which precluded anything but magic having been involved." Elwood Shervers gave vent to a snort of incredulity; de Grandin stared him down as a master might stare down a noisy pupil in the class room, and proceeded:

"But if a ghost pursued the Shervers family, working out an ancient blood feud, he would be discriminating. He would not kill the poor young mortuarian because he was unfortunate enough to bear a close resemblance to the Shervers. Human beings make such errors in the flesh, they do not make them when they are translated into spirit form. Furthermore, a ghost would not employ the simple way of poison. They have other ways of doing violence, those ones. Accordingly, I was obliged to seek a human agency in this.

"The young Monsieur Oldham had gasped out something of a man—or thing—which waited for him at the window just before he had his fatal seizure. Well then, we were to seek for one who lurked at windows. Your uncles died in bed or sitting in the house. A murderer could enter at the window and administer the poison to them while they slept. Your father died upon the highway, presumably of a heart failure. But he was in a closed coupé. Had someone asked a ride of him and been taken in his car, conditions would have been ideal for that one to have gassed him as they rode. Your grandsire died in bed, but he was old and weak. A burglar might have entered through the window, released the deadly gas upon him, then left all quietly. The gas of nitrobenzol is highly volatile. In half an hour there would remain no telltale odor to arouse suspicion. Only an autopsy would disclose the true nature of his death, and the mistaken diagnosis of heart failure precluded the necessity of a post-mortem.

"There seemed a ritual in these killings. One of the oldest Eastern curses is: 'May you see your children and your children's children blotted out, and live to die alone in bleak despair, without the hope of progeny.' Such a course, it seemed, these killings took. Sons and grandsons perished, called to death from perfect health, while your grandsire lingered on. You alone were spared, perhaps because the killer thought he had dispatched you when he killed young Monsieur Oldham.

"This we could not have. We must act with speed if you were to be saved. The killer might go home, believing his work done, then months or years afterward find he was mistaken, and come back to complete the extirpation of your family. We had to force his hand immediately. Therefore I asked you to display yourself in public, but to have a care of open doors and windows.

"Our strategy succeeded. The miscreant who sought your life became aware of his mistake; he would come back, I knew; but how or where he'd strike I did not know. Accordingly, I made the preparation for his coming. I visited your house this afternoon and saw the way a man would take if he desired to hasten from a ground-floor window to the alley, whence he could make his get-away unseen. Then in his way I placed a steel trap, trusting he would step into it as he ran. I desired you should be seen through the window, but I did not wish to have you open it. But you disobeyed my orders, and almost forfeited your life in doing so. Into your face he blew the poison fumes; then off he ran pell-mell and —stepped in Jules de Grandin's trap.

"The fact that Doctor Trowbridge was at hand to give first aid enabled you to live where others died. Had we known the nature of his illness we could have saved the poor young Monsieur Oldham, too, but"—he raised his shoulders in a shrug—"ignorance has cost more lives than one.

"Now I had thought the poisoner was armed with some sort of a tank in which he kept his gas in concentrated form; therefore I followed him with caution until I saw him stumble in the trap and saw his hands were empty. Then I almost made the fatal error. I advanced on him; he roused upon his hands and blew his breath on me. *Parbleu*, I thought that instant was my last! But we were in the open air, and he struck too quickly, before I had come near enough. I revived, and Doctor Trowbridge came and suffered as I had.

"'Jules de Grandin, what sort of man is it who breathes out sudden death?' I asked myself.

"'Think, Jules de Grandin, you great stupid-head,' I reply to me, 'are he not an Indian, a Hindoo, and in India do they not have persons who are bred from infancy to ply the trade of poisoner?'

"'It is exactly as you say, my clever Jules de Grandin,' I reply. 'Some of these poisoners are so venomous the mere touch of their hand will kill an ordinary man; others can blow poison breath, exactly like the fabled dragons of the olden days—'"

"You mean to say that man could kill a person merely by breathing on him?" I interrupted. "I've heard about those Indian poisoners, but I'd always thought the stories old wives' tales."

"The beldame's talc is often just a garbled version of a scientific truth," he answered. "Consider, if you please:

"You know how quickly human bodies set up tolerance to medicine. The man who suffers pain and takes an opiate today will take a dose three times as large next year, a dose which would be fatal to an ordinary man, yet which will hardly register upon a system which has been habituated to the drug. The pretty ladies who take arsenic for the sake of their complexions become habituated to the poison till they can take an ounce or more a day, yet not be inconvenienced by it. It is like that with these ones, only more so. Habituated to the deadliest of poisons from their early infancy, these naughty men can ingest doses large enough to kill a dozen ordinary persons, yet feel no evil consequences.

"How did this one work? It was as simple—and as subtle—as a juggler's trick. Nitrobenzol, known commercially as oil of mirbane or artificial oil of almonds, is highly deadly. Fifteen drops compose a lethal dose, and its fumes are almost deadly as its substance. Upon inhaling them one becomes unconscious quickly—remember the young mortuarian—and death comes in a few minutes. The victim's face is cyanotic, having a blue tinge, as though heart failure were responsible. That is because the poison works by making it impossible for blood to take up oxygen. One cannot greatly blame the doctors who were misled. External symptoms all said 'heart disease,' and there was no reason why foul play should be suspected.

"Very well. Before going on a foray this one drank a quantity of nitrobenzol. It is highly volatile, and his stomach's warmth rendered it still more so. He approached a victim all unarmed. Could anyone suspect him? *Non.* Ah, but when he came within a breathing-distance, by a sudden torsion of the muscles of his thorax and abdomen, he induced an artificial eructation—the poison gas was belched forth from his mouth, his victim fell and—*voilà tout!*"

"I see," I exclaimed, "that's why you beat him so unmercifully! You wanted him to discharge all the poison gas his stomach contained.... I'm very glad, de Grandin; I'd thought that you were merely taking vengeance on him—"

He flashed his quick, infectious grin at me. "You are very good and very kind—too much so, sometimes, good Friend Trowbridge—but there are times when I have serious reason to believe you are not as well equipped with brains as you might be. Of course, I beat the miscreant. Was it his life against ours? While he still retained the power to spew the poison gases out we dared not go near him, nor could the police take him, for he needed but to breathe to free himself. I am not a cruel man, but I am logical. I do the needful when the need for doing it arises. Yes."

"But this poison—" began Shervers.

"Poison assumes many guises," interrupted Jules de Grandin. "At present, if you please, I should like some from that lovely bottle standing at your elbow." He drained his highball glass and held it out to be replenished.

Black Moon

T HE AUGUST SUN HAD reigned all day as mercilessly as a tsar whose ukase is a sword and whose sword is sudden death. Now in the evening cool we were dining in the garden, and dinner was unusually good, even for such a virtuoso of cuisine as Nora McGinnis. Tiny clams chilled almost crisp and served with champagne *brut* were followed by green turtle soup and pale dry sherry, then roast young guinea-hen and ginger ice with white Burgundy. Now the spicy sweetness of Chartreuse and the bitterness of Java coffee put a period to a meal which might have brought a flush of envy to Lucullus' face. "*Tiens*, my friend, I am in a pious mood, me," announced Jules de Grandin, his little round blue eyes bright in the candlelight. "But certainly, of course—"

"Are you repenting of past sins, or sins to be committed?" I replied.

He grinned at me. "Observe," he ordered. "In Tarragona, where the good Carthusian brethren work so hard to make this precious stuff, they say that drinking one small glass of it is equal to attending three low masses. *Parbleu*, I make amends for laxness in devotions—" He poised the cruet of green liqueur to decant a second drink, but the *wisp-wisp* of swift feet on close-cropped grass broke in upon his solemn rite.

"If yez plaze, sors, there's a gintleman to see yez," announced Nora.

Nora resents callers after office hours. More than once she has turned my patients off with sharp-tongued rebuke when they rang the door-bell around dinnertime, but now her eyes were shining with suppressed elation, and she seemed to labor with some weighty secret as she bore the message of the interruption to our after-dinner confab.

"A visitor—*grand Dieu des porcs!*—are we to be eternally annoyed by them?" de Grandin answered tartly. "Bid him depart, *ma chère*, tell him we are indisposed, that we died this afternoon and now await the coming of the undertaker—"

"And if she did he'd not believe a word of it; he's too familiar with your shameless lies, you little blighter!" a deep voice challenged as a big form vaulted from the side porch and came striding toward us through the deepening twilight.

"*Comment? Mais non!* It cannot be, and yet it is, by blue!" de Grandin cried. "Hiji, *mon brave, mon cher camarade, mon beau copain*—is it truly thou, or has some spirit put your form upon him?" In a moment he had grasped the big intruder by the shoulders, drawn him to him in a bear-hug and stood on tiptoe to impress a kiss on both his cheeks.

"Give over, you small devil, d'ye want the neighbors talkin'?" exclaimed the new arrival, thrusting back the little Frenchman, but retaining a tight hold upon his shoulders. "Trowbridge, old top, how are you?" With his free hand he grasped mine and almost paralyzed it in a vise-tight grip.

"Ingraham!" I gasped, amazed. "My boy, I'm glad to see you!"

"Glad enough to offer me a whisky-soda?" he asked as he drew a chair up to the table.

Nora had the bottle and siphon at his side almost before he could finish speaking, and as he poured about four ounces of the liquor in his glass and diluted it with rather less than that much soda I observed him carefully. Sir Hadding-way Ingraham Jamison Ingraham, known to all his intimates as Hiji, late of the Sierra Leone Frontier Police, member of the British Army Intelligence, detective extraordinary and adventurer-at-large, was taller by almost two feet than Jules de Grandin, and lean with the leanness of the practiced athlete. Although his small mustache was black, his hair was iron-gray, and his long, thin, high-cheeked face was burned almost the hue of old mahogany. With de Grandin and Costello and Inspector Renouard of the French Cambodian *gendarmerie* he had smashed a bold conspiracy to spread devil worship throughout Asia, and more than once we'd talked of him and mourned his absence when we'd found ourselves in places where a man with a strong arm and ability to shoot straight would have come in handy. Now, dropped from the summer evening sky, apparently, he sat beside us, drinking whisky-soda as composedly as though we'd seen each other at the breakfast table.

"What is it brings you here, my friend?" de Grandin asked. "Is it that you offer us a chance to go with you on some adventure? One hopes so most de-voutly. Life grows stale and tiresome in New Jersey—"

The big Englishman grinned at him. "Still on the go, eh, Frenchy? Too bad I have to let you down, but I'm a married man these days, with a wife and kids and everything that goes with it. Also, I'm no longer in the Army. I'm a member of his Majesty's Consular Service, quiet and respectable as a retired parson."

The Frenchman's eager little face went long, and Hiji grinned at him almost maliciously as he reached into his dinner coat and drew a sheaf of papers from his pocket. "Glance these over," he commanded as he spread the documents upon the tablecloth. "Just a little routine stuff about commercial matters." He raised his glass and took a long sip, gazing at de Grandin over the tall tumbler's rim.

With a grimace of distaste the Frenchman spread the papers out before him. They seemed to be newspaper clippings pasted on stiff sheets of foolscap and numbered in rotation. What possible interest Jules de Grandin could have in production and consumption, imports and exports, I could not conceive, but I saw his narrow brows draw down in concentration as he read, and when he looked up there was a lightning-glint in his small, deep-set blue eyes. "Me, I am greatly interested in this species of commercialism," he declared. "Is it that you invite us to assist in your investigations?"

"Just what I dropped in for," answered Hiji. "Can you come?"

The little Frenchman spread his hands in a wide gesture. "Can the pussycat devour liver, or the duck perform aquatic feats?" he asked. "When do we depart?"

"What's it all about?" I cut in. "I never knew you cared two pins for commerce, de Grandin, yet—"

"Observe them, if you please," he broke in as he thrust the papers toward me. "They do not make sense, I agree, but they promise something interesting, I damn think."

As far as I could see, the cuttings were without relation to each other. The first, dated a year back, bore the head:

STUDENTS' PRANK SEEN IN POLICE FIND

PARTS OF BODIES FOUND IN BAY BELIEVED

DISSECTING-ROOM RELICS—MURDER MYSTERY BLOWS UP

The item related the finding of a gunny-sack in the Chesapeake not far from Reedville, Virginia, which when opened proved to contain several human arm and leg bones from which the flesh had been almost completely cut away. Local police had at first believed them evidence of murder, but when physicians declared the grisly relics were from several bodies the theory that medical students had tossed the sack into the bay near Norfolk was accepted as the most likely explanation.

Less than an inch in length, and without relation to the first, the second cutting bore the head: "FARM AND DOMESTIC HELP SCARCE," and related that domestic and field helpers were at a premium in Westmoreland, Richmond and Northumberland Counties, though there had been no great migration to the North.

"CAMP MEETINGS LOSE APPEAL" the third clipping was headlined, and told of the almost total failure of attendance at recent camp and bush meetings among the colored population of the Norfolk section, something without precedent in the memory of the oldest inhabitants.

Entirely unrelated to the first three items, as far as I could see, was the clipping from a New York Negro daily telling of the gory murder of the proprietor of a Harlem café. The body had been found almost denuded of clothing, scored and slashed as if a savage beast had clawed it. Robbery had not been the motive, for the dead man's well-filled wallet was intact, and a diamond scarf-pin was still in his tie. He had no enemies, as far as the authorities could learn. Indeed, he had been very popular, especially with the Southern Negroes of the district.

The final story dealt with the unexplained murder of a Captain Ronald Sterling, apparently a gentleman of some importance in Westmoreland County. He had, according to the clipping, been found dead on his front lawn, his face, neck and breast so horribly mutilated that identification was possible only by his clothes. While every circumstance pointed to death being due to some ferocious beast, a careful check-up of the death scene disclosed no animal tracks, though numerous human footprints were discovered on the sandy driveway. No one had been approached, for the police had been unable to formulate a tenable theory in the case.

"H'm, perhaps there's some connection in these stories, but I can't find it if there is," I said as I passed back the papers.

Ingraham produced a small black pipe and a tin of Three Nuns and began tamping the tobacco in the briar as he looked quizzically at us. "There doesn't seem to be any common denominator, I'll admit," he answered, "but I think there is. So do my bosses. You see, there have been quite a number of Jamaican and Barbadian Negroes coming to this country lately, and some of your G-gentlemen seem to think they're mixed up in this business. His Majesty's Government thinks otherwise; I've been deputed to prove we're right."

"But what is 'this business,' as you call it?" I demanded. "I don't see any possible connection between medical students' pranks and failing attendance at camp meetings with murders in Virginia and Harlem—"

"No"—Hiji took a few quick puffs to get his pipe alight—"I don't suppose you do, but there are data not shown in the clippings. For instance, those bones washed up by the Chesapeake were charred by fire. Exposure to the water rendered positive opinion difficult, but the little flesh remaining on them appeared to have been acted on by heat. Bluntly, they'd been cooked.

"Second, there have been a number of strange Negroes seen in that section of Virginia and southeastern Maryland. They're West Indians, not from Jamaica or Barbados, but from Martinique and Haiti, men and women speaking English with a strong French patois accent. That's where we come in. Your people don't seem able to distinguish between our Negroes and those from the non-British islands.

"Now, as to connection between these murders: Jim Collins, the proprietor of that Harlem hot spot, wasn't a West Indian. He went north from Virginia something like a year ago, and he went from Captain Sterling's place. It's known that he corresponded with Sterling after coming north, and a letter was received from him two days before Sterling's death."

"D'ye know what it said?"

He nodded. "Just five words: 'Some of them are here.' I think it was 'some of them,' whoever they were or are, who killed both him and Captain Sterling. The same technique was followed in each case. Furthermore, there have been three more deaths like those of Collins and the captain, though I haven't clippings on them. One was in Maryland, almost across the bay from Sterling's place; one was in South Carolina, one in Louisiana. Add the fact that Negro churches in those localities have been steadily losing in attendance to these murders occurring hundreds of miles apart, and I think you have something. Sterling's death might have been laid to some freak of criminology, or to some wild beast escaped from a circus, but you can't advance that theory to account for the other killings. Collins writes a letter saying, 'Some of them are here,' and dies next day. Sterling receives it and dies exactly the same way two days later. A circus beast might have killed Collins or Sterling, but it couldn't have traveled from New York to Virginia in that short time. Or, say it was a criminal pervert. Those Johnnies aren't usually so choicy. Like our Jack the Ripper or your own sadistic murderers, they take their victims where they find 'em. Why should one of 'em kill the Negro Collins in New York, then hop a train to travel to Virginia just to kill the white man Sterling? And even if he did do that, would he be likely then to cross the bay to Maryland, kill a Johnny there, then travel down to Carolina and cross the country into Louisiana just to kill two more?"

"You think it was a gang?"

"I'm sure of it, and—"

"One moment, if you please!" de Grandin broke in. "Await me here; I must know something." Jumping up, he ran into the house, where a moment later we saw a glow of light shine through the study windows. In a minute he returned, announcing: "I have looked in last year's almanac. One week before that sack of bones was found in Chesapeake Bay there was a total lunar eclipse, visible from that portion of Maryland and Virginia."

"Well, what of it?" I demanded. "What's a lunar eclipse to do with—"

The little Frenchman looked at the big Englishman, and each saw confirmation of a thought in the other's glance.

"The Black Moon!" Hiji said as he let his breath out softly through his teeth.

"Precisely," nodded Jules de Grandin. "Also, according to the almanac, another eclipse will occur there in three days."

"I think we'd better do a move," replied the Englishman. "Can you put me up tonight, Trowbridge?"

A T OUR BACKS THE sun rose from the Chesapeake; underfoot the shaky little pier swayed with each rising wave; ahead of us the bay showed as clear of any sign of craft as the ocean around Juan Fernandez when Crusoe was cast on its beach. An hour earlier the steamboat which had brought us up from Norfolk had deposited us and a tall, handsome, dark young woman on the dock from which the motor ferry was supposed to operate, and since that time we had seen nothing more than sea-gulls on the water.

"Lost," Ingraham muttered as he knocked the dottle from his pipe against his heel. "We've been marooned, men, and if we can't reach Sterling's Landing by tomorrow—"

"Pardon me, sir, did I understand you all are goin' to Sterling's Landing?" the tall young woman who was our fellow castaway broke in. "May I inquire your business there? I'm Captain Sterling's daughter," she added, softening the apparent sharpness of her question. "You see, I'm his sole survivor, and—"

"Of course, one understands, *Mademoiselle*," de Grandin answered with a bow. "I am Doctor Jules de Grandin and these are Doctor Samuel Trowbridge and Sir Haddingway Ingraham of the British Consular Service. We have come to make investigation of the disaffection of your local Negro population—"

The young woman—she was no girl, but five or six and twenty—shuddered slightly, despite the rising August heat.

"I'd like to know about that, too," she answered. "Papa wrote me of it just before he died. It seems the colored people all refused to work, and some of them were insolent. A pa'cel of strange darkies came and squatted on our land, and when he warned them off they defied him—"

"Do"—the little Frenchman spoke deliberately as he eyed her narrowly—"do you connect your father's death with this, *Mademoiselle?*"

"I really couldn't say, sir. You see, I'm on the stage, and was playin' in St. Louis when word came of my father's death. I came as quickly as I could, but"—she paused and bit her lip, then: "I had to wait until I had the money to come home."

Again the little Frenchman nodded. Following his quick glance I read the sign upon her wardrobe trunk: "Coralea Sterling, Moonlight Maidens, Theatre." Some months before, the Moonlight Maidens burlesque troupe had played in Harrisonville, and from theatrical reports I'd gathered they were not very successful.

"May we count upon your help, *Mademoiselle?*" de Grandin asked.

"Of course. I'll be very glad to put you all up at the house, and if there's any way that I can help you find out—"

The hooting of the little ferry's air-whistle broke in, and in a moment we were headed down the bay for Sterling's Landing.

THE STERLING MANSION PROVED a disappointment. Far from being the Southern manor house of tradition, it was a fairly comfortable old farmhouse, badly in need of repair, set back from the sand by-road in a plot of rather unkempt lawn with an avenue of honey-locust leading from its gate. A kitchen garden mostly weeds was at its back door, and behind that was a farm of thirty-five or forty acres in a state of almost utter fallowness. Mortgages, I guessed, had been the chief crop of that land for many years. Inside, the house was fairly clean, with some pieces of good furniture of the Victorian era, some family portraits dating to the days before the Civil War, and several chambers with large, comfortable beds. No one met us at the landing, and we took turns carrying the luggage to the house, then at Miss Sterling's request went down to the village store, where we laid in a supply of canned goods, supplemented by a ham and some fresh eggs and vegetables. By noon we had fire going in the kitchen range and made a comfortable meal.

The interval that followed was a pleasant one. We all turned in to wash and put away the dishes, and as I looked at Coralea enveloped in her big apron I had a hard time visualizing her shuffling and strutting back and forth across a darkened stage while she felt for concealed fasteners in her gown and discarded piece on piece of costume till she stood revealed in pristine nudity beneath the spotlight's purple glare. With uncanny understanding de Grandin read my-thought. "One often wonders at the lure the theatre has," he whispered. "I have known mothers to desert their children and wives desert their comfortable homes to dance and sing in third-rate music halls, enduring poverty and social ostracism cheerfully. One cannot explain it, one only knows that it is so."

I nodded, but before I could reply our hostess spoke: "Can I trouble you gentlemen to make one more trip to the Landin'? There are some more things we'll be needin' from the sto'e, and while you're gone I'd like to visit 'round the neighborhood a little. I can borrow a horse next door at Hopkins'."

Half an hour later we set out for the small general store, while Coralea waved to us as she walked in the opposite direction, her slim, tall form almost boyish in khaki jodhpurs and checked riding-coat.

While I made the purchases, Hiji and de Grandin engaged some store-porch loafers in confab, and though our actual business occupied a scant half-hour it was mid-afternoon before we started on our homeward walk.

"It all fits in," said Hiji. "We see a disaffection among the local blacks who refuse work, no matter what the wages are. Negroes are naturally religious, yet there's a steady fallin' off in church attendance. Next we have four terrifyin' murders, identical in technique, but widely separated. Each victim has no known enemies, each was popular among the colored folks. Collins, the Harlem Negro, was something of a leader of his race and highly thought of by both whites and blacks. Sterling enjoyed the confidence of local colored residents, the Carolina victim was a social worker deeply loved by all the colored folks, and the fourth was a young Baptist missionary from the North who by his eloquence and kindness had won a host of friends, both white and black, and was more than holding his own against the ebb-tide in church membership. Then crack-o! someone murders him, and his congregation falls to pieces. Why should these people, so widely separated by distance, race, vocation and background, have been killed in the same manner?

"Then, here's another puzzle: The bones they found down here appear to have been relics of a cannibal feast. There's never been a case of cannibalism heard of in this country; yet—there it is.

"If these murders had been done in Africa I'd say they were the work of Leopard Men. Furthermore, the Human Leopards make a practice of eating their victims, and their big cannibal parties are held during an eclipse—at the time of the 'Black Moon.' It looks almost as if this deviltry had been imported from West Africa."

"But only indirectly," said de Grandin. "Me, I have another theory. The islands of the Caribbean reek with voodoo, the black sorcery imported with the slaves from Africa. It began in Haiti before Dessalines threw off French government; it grew upon the ruins of the church the black imperialists tore down. It is said Ulestine, daughter of President Antoine-Simone, was high priestess of the cult. Its blasphemies and obscenities run through the island's culture as tropic breezes rustle through the jungle trees. There at the time of the Black Moon the 'Goat Without Horns' has been sacrificed on voodoo altars; there the drums have bidden worshippers to the shrine of the White Queen; there a priesthood more terrible than that of Baal has ruled supreme since 1791. *Ha*, but with the coming of American marines the scene was changed. Precisely as you ran down the Leopard Men, my Hiji, the Americans hunted down the sorcerers of voodoo until their power was broken utterly. Now, I damn think, they have decided on a bold stroke. Here"—he swung his arm in a wide arc—"right here, it seems, they have decided to set up their bloody altars and force the native blacks to join with them in a worship which blends jungle bestiality with the depravity of decadent European superstition. Unless I miss my guess, my friends, we are at grips with *obeah*, voodoo—call it what you will, it makes no difference—"

The furious drumming of a horse's hoofs broke through his words, and round the turning of the sandy road a maddened beast came rushing, bearing down upon us like a miniature cavalry charge. Clinging to the pommel of the saddle, with no effort to control the frenzied steed, was Coralea Sterling, hat gone, her long black hair whipped out behind her like a fluttering signal of distress. Her eyes were round with horror, her cheeks gray with the waxen hue that comes from but one cause. One glance at her blenched, terrified, drawn face told all. Sheer, ghastly fear had seized her by the throat, strangling back the scream her grayed lips were parted to utter.

"Runaway!" cried Hiji, and poised to launch himself at the maddened horse's bridle, but the girl waved him frantically aside. Then we noticed that the unspurred heels of her tan riding-boots were beating an hysterical tattoo against the horse's sides. She was urging it to greater speed.

Like an express train flashing past a way-station, horse and rider thundered past us, while we gaped in wonder. Then:

"*Grand Dieu des chats!*" de Grandin cried, and sprang into the dusty road, dragging at the handle of his sword-stick. Something eery whipped along the highway, weaving in and out between the tracks left by the fleeing horse, something I could not see, but which left a little zig-zag trail of kicked-up dust like a puff of wind gone crazy. De Grandin brought the slim blade of his sword-cane down upon the dancing dust with a cutting, lash-like motion, and something brown and gray, with a flash of yellowish-white underside, squirmed up from the baked roadway and writhed about his blade like the serpent on Mercury's caduceus. A strumming like a chorus of a hundred summer locusts in unison sounded as he struck and whipped his sword-blade back, then struck again.

"Nice work, old son—good Lord!" Hiji thrust his hand into his jacket pocket and snatched his blue steel Browning out, firing point-blank into the road six feet or so behind de Grandin. A little spurt of dust kicked up where the steel-capped bullet struck, and with it rose a writhing thing as thick as a man's arm and half again as long.

"*Merci beaucoup, mon ami*," de Grandin grinned. "I had not noticed him, and had you not been quick I fear I should not long have noticed anything. It seems our bag is full, now; let us count the game."

Dizzy with bewilderment, I stepped out into the road. At de Grandin's feet, still quivering, but stone-dead beneath the lashing of his sword-cane, lay a diamond-headed rattlesnake, its tail adorned with ten bone buttons. Beyond the little Frenchman, where Hiji's bullet had almost shot its head away, another snake lay squirming in death agony, thrashing up the road dust into tiny, inch-high sand dunes.

I looked at both the loathsome things with a shudder of repulsion, but Hiji and de Grandin had eyes only for the second snake. "By George!" the Englishman turned the thing over with his foot.

"*Mais oui, précisément*," the Frenchman nodded. "You recognize him?"

"Quite. I've been to Martinique and Haiti."

I stared from one to the other, puzzled as a child whose elders spell out words. De Grandin pointed first to one dead reptile, then the other. "This," he told me, "is a rattlesnake, native of this section, and this," he touched the other with his sword-tip, "is a fer-de-lance, found in both Martinique and Haiti, but never in this country, except in zoos. You comprehend?"

"Can't say I do."

"*Non.* I am not sure that I do, either; but I should guess those naughty people we suspect have brought in snakes as well as most deplorably bad manners with them. What say you, *mon Hiji?*"

But the big Englishman was intent on a fresh find. "What d'ye make o' this, Frenchy?" he asked, poking a knot of gum like substance lying in the road.

De Grandin bent and looked at it intently, lowered his head until his nostrils almost touched it, and sniffed daintily. "I recognize him," he replied, "but I cannot call his name."

"Me, too," the Englishman agreed. "A cove who used to live in Haiti showed me some of it once. Those black blighters down there make a mixture by some secret formula and put it where it will be stepped in by someone they don't love so awfully much. Maybe they smear it on his motor tires or on his horse's hooves. It's all one, as far as results go. No sooner does the poor bloke go out than all the bally snakes in seven counties pick his spoor up and go after him. In a little while he gets rid of the stuff or dies by snakebite, for the stuff's attractive to the little scaly devils as valerian is to a cat."

"I think that you have right, my friend."

"You think? You know dam' well I'm right! Didn't you see how the gal was kickin' her cob to more speed when the poor brute was already giving all it had? That was no runaway; that was panic flight. And the snakes—did you ever see a snake, 'specially a lazy rotter like a rattler, pursue a human bein' for all he was worth? Watch this!" He tossed the knot of gum into the roadside grass and motioned us to stand back.

We waited silently ten, fifteen, twenty minutes; then: "Look sharp!" commanded Hiji. A rustling sounded in the short, dry grass, a little spurt of sun-baked dust showed in the center of the road. Converging on the spot where he had thrown the gum were several snakes: two full-grown rattlers, a small, slim copperhead; finally, sliding like the flickering shadow of a whiplash drawn across a horse's flank, a six-foot black snake.

"Convinced?" asked Hiji as he turned away.

"No," said Coralea, "I can't remember when I first saw them. I'd been the rounds, callin' on the neighbors and tryin' to find out something about Papa's death. The last place I stopped at was Judge Scatterhorn's, but I don't remember anything suspicious. A colored lad was out in front when I came out and led my horse up to the carriage block, but—oh!" She stopped abruptly, one hand raised to her mouth.

"Yes, *Mademoiselle?*" de Grandin prompted.

"I tossed a dime to him as I rode off, for he'd held my stirrup very nicely, but instead of takin' it he let it fall into the road and muttered something—"

"He held your stirrup, did you say?" de Grandin interrupted.

"Yes he did, and—"

"*Mademoiselle*, where are your ridin'-boots?"

"My—my ridin'-boots?"

"*Précisément.*"

"Why, in the cupboard of my room—"

Without a word the Frenchman rose and hurried up the stairs. In a moment we heard the sharp double crack of his small pocket pistol, and a minute later he came down the stairs with two dead snakes looped across the stick he'd taken from her bedroom window. "They were in your closet, Mademoiselle. When you went to get a change of clothing you would have found them waiting for you. I dislike to say so, but it would be safer if you burned those boots. One can replace burned boots, but it is not often one recovers from a fatal snakebite."

D INNER WAS A GAYER meal than I had looked for. Somewhere Coralea had found a store of wine, and with this, tinned soup, fried ham and eggs and a liberal portion of fresh melon, we did very well. But though we chatted cheerfully as we did the dinner dishes there was an air of gathering restraint which seemed to seep into the lamplit kitchen as though it were a chilling fog no door could quite shut out. Shadows flickering in the corners took on strange shapes of menace, and more than once I drew my hand back quickly, thinking I had seen the looping convolutions of a coiled snake as I reached to place a piece of china in the cupboard. By the time the last dish had been wiped and stored away our nerves were at the snapping-point. I jumped as if I had been stung when a hail came from the front door.

"Miss Sterling; oh, Miss Coralea, is your 'phone in workin' order? Judge Scatterhorn's been killed."

"You and Doctor Trowbridge go and take a look—medical chaps are better qualified for that sort o' work—I'll stay here and keep the jolly home fires burnin'," Hiji said as we gave over efforts to get service from the telephone. "Sing out when you come to the door, though; I'm liable to have a nervy finger on the trigger."

A little knot of white men grouped round something on the ground before the Scatterhorn veranda, a railroad lantern shedding its uncertain light upon their dusty boots. Two or three Negroes, eyes rolling in abysmal terror till they seemed all whites, hung on the outskirts of the crowd, studiously avoiding a glance at the blanket-covered object round which the white men gathered.

"Pardon, gentlemen, we are physicians," apologized de Grandin as we pushed our way among the crowd, knelt and turned the blanket back.

Judge Scatterhorn lay as he had died, his arms outstretched, fingers clutching at the yielding sand of the driveway. His throat and chest were horribly lacerated, as though he had been clawed and bitten by some savage beast; across his cheeks and brow ran several hideous gashes; as de Grandin turned him gently over we saw six deep cuts upon his back, running parallel from shoulder-blade to waist, and so deeply incised that the bone had been laid bare in several places.

"When did this atrocity occur?" de Grandin asked as we completed our examination.

"'Bout half an hour back," a member of the crowd replied. "We just got word of it. Mis' Semmes 'phoned us."

"Ah? And who is Madame Semmes?"

"She's th' Judge's sister. Wanna see her?"

"I regret to intrude, but it would be well if I might question her." The little Frenchman put the blanket back upon the dead man's face and rose, brushing the sand from his knees.

"*Madame*, we do not waste your time in idle curiosity," he told the trembling woman when she met us in her parlor, "but much depends upon our having first-hand information now. Will you tell us all you can?"

"We've had no servants for the last two weeks," the bereaved lady answered, "and George and I made out the best we could. He'd been out this evenin', and I heard him drive into the yard about three-quarters of an hour ago. Presently I caught his step as he walked round to the front door—we've kept the back door barred since all the servants left—then I heard a frightful scream, and the sound of someone strugglin' on the porch. George called, 'Don't come out, Sally!' then there was the sound of more thrashin' around, and—and when I finally lit a lamp and ventured out, I found him there—like that."

"Was it your brother who screamed, *Madame?*"

"No. Oh, no. It sounded more like the scream of a wildcat."

"And did you hear anything else?"

"I—I think—but I'm not quite sure—I heard somebody laughin', a terrible, high-pitched laugh; then I heard someone or something runnin' off among the laurels."

The little Frenchman looked at her intently for a moment. "You say that you have been without domestic servants for some time, *Madame*. Why is that?"

The woman shuddered. "My brother was a justice of the peace. For some time, now, there have been strange Negroes in the district. None of them has been disorderly, but they're a sullen lot, and we considered them a bad influence on the local colored people. So when one of them was picked up by the constable last month my brother sentenced him to road work as a vagrant. The fellow grinned at him before they took him off and told George, 'You'll regret this, you infernal *blanc*'—I don't know what he meant by that, but he spoke English with so strong an accent that perhaps it was an insult in some foreign language. At any rate, our servants left us the next mornin', without explanation and without even waitin' for their wages, and we've had no help of any sort since then."

De Grandin took his chin between a thoughtful thumb and forefinger. "Mademoiselle Sterling called on you this afternoon?"

"Yes, she did."

"And was it one of your servants who held her stirrup?"

A slight flush mounted to our hostess' face. "Perhaps you didn't understand," she answered. "I told you that we'd been without help for two weeks."

"Forgive my seeming rudeness, *Madame*, but Mademoiselle Coralea told us that a strange young colored lad was waiting at the front door when she left, and helped her set her foot into the stirrup."

We left the bereaved lady with her grief, and at the doorway de Grandin gave a snort of impatience. "Me, I am the stupid-head!" he confided. "I have left my pocket lens. Will you be good enough to go and fetch it from our room, Friend Trowbridge? I fear the crowd has destroyed most of the evidence, but I may be able to find something helpful to us. I shall wait you here."

I was none too pleased with the assignment, but there was no way of getting out of it; so I started up the road toward Sterling's home, grasping my heavy stick and walking faster with each step. The moon rode high and round in a clear sky, and the wind that blew up from the bay, moaned and sighed among the roadside cedars like the ghosts of lovers parted in the days when North and South contended bloodily for this Virginia land. Nearer and nearer I approached the Sterling homestead, faster and faster I walked. By the time I reached the driveway I was almost running.

The house lights shone between the trees with beckoning cheerfulness; I had not more than fifty yards to go until I reached the door, but the memory of Judge Scatterhorn's disfigured face was with me like the image of a walking nightmare. I pursed my lips to whistle a signal to Hiji, but it was no use. Walking required all my breath, and the muscles of my face were stiff as if a winter chill had gripped them.

A heavy growth of vines screened the porch from the front lawn, and the rustling of their leaves in the light breeze was like the clapping of dry, long-dead hands applauding some obscene comedy. I launched myself at the short flight of steps that led to the veranda like a winded runner entering the home stretch, then rolled floundering to the sandy driveway beneath a sudden devastating impact from above.

Something long and black, twisting, clutching, grappling, dropped upon me from the string-piece of the porch roof, hurtling through the air like a panther pouncing on its prey, clawing, grasping, tearing at my throat, gnashing teeth in berserk rage, screaming like all the fiends of hell in chorus. I felt myself borne to the earth beneath its loathsome weight, felt the cruel, cutting claws shear through the padding of my jacket shoulders, felt the gush of warm blood as they sank into my flesh.

I tried to draw the pistol which de Grandin bad insisted that I carry. My right arm was pinioned to my side between my body and the ground. I tried to strike at the thing with my fist. A talon hand, strong as a steel vise, gripped my wrist until I thought the bones would surely break. "This is how Judge Scatterhorn was killed!" I thought as I bridged my body, rising on a shoulder as I sought desperately to free myself.

A blaze of sudden light seared my eyes, a report like a field gun's sounded in my ear. There was a light impact, like a stone flung into moist sand, and the thing above me stiffened, then went limp. Something warm and sticky-feeling, something which I felt instinctively was red, began to soak the clothes above my breast.

"Bull's-eye, by Jove!" Hiji called delightedly, rushing forward from the shadow, his Browning gleaming in the lamplight filtering through the porch vinery. "Potted the beggar neat as neat. Couldn't 'a' done it better if I'd practised on him for an hour!

"Up you come, Trowbridge." He rolled the body off me and thrust forth a helping hand. "Cheerio. You're all right, old thing!"

I wasn't quite as certain of my all-rightness as he seemed to be as I sat up slowly and stared around. Close behind him, her face pale and set, but without a trace of fear, stood Coralea, a dark cloak masking her light dress.

"We were sittin' in the parlor after you all'd gone," she explained, "when suddenly Sir Haddingway said, 'S-s-sh! There's something prowling round outside.' I thought maybe it was you all coming back, but he insisted on investigatin', so I came along, too. We slipped out a side window and circled round the house, keepin' down behind the bushes till we came to the front lawn. Just as we got there we saw someone or something climb one of the porch posts and crawl along the string-piece up above the steps. Sir Haddingway couldn't shoot it from there, for the beam was between it and us, so we waited.

"Directly we heard you comin' up the drive and knew that it would jump on you, so Sir Haddingway had his pistol ready to shoot it before it could do much harm."

"H'm, I'm glad he didn't wait much longer," I replied. "His idea of harm and mine don't seem to coincide."

"Trowbridge, old fellow, you're not much hurt, are you?" cried Hiji penitently. "I'd 'a' shot him sooner, but I was afraid of hittin' you—"

"Oh, I don't think there's any damage sticking-plaster and some antiseptic can't take care of," I responded as I got unsteadily upon my feet.

"Right-o," Hiji answered with enthusiasm. "Here comes the blighted little Frenchman. Wait till we show him our bag. First blood for us, eh, what?"

"Trowbridge, *mon vieux*, is it thou?" de Grandin called as he strode up the drive. "I decided that it was too dark to make out anything tonight, so—*mon Dieu*, what have we here?"

Hiji struck an attitude. "This w'y, gents an' lydies, yer ludships an' yer 'ighnesses!" he called in whining singsong. "Come see the gryte he-normous wild man, shot in 'is nytive 'abitat by Hiji, the gryte 'unter. Come one, come hall, and see the gryte, he-normous marvel—"

"*Que diable?*" de Grandin cut in testily, glancing from my torn and blood-stained clothing to the dark bulk of the thing Hiji had shot. "Be silent, you great zany, and tell me what goes on here!"

Coralea, supplied the information, repeating substantially what she had told me, but making it appear Hiji's shot was almost supererogation, since, according to her version, I had already worsted my antagonist and Hiji shot him merely to relieve him of his suffering.

The little Frenchman viewed my tattered clothing skeptically. "Hiji, my friend, I am indebted to you," he declared. "Me, I have often thought Friend Trowbridge might be better for a slight amount of murdering, but always I have wished to do it with my own two hands. You have preserved him for my vengeance." But there was no affectation in the tears that glinted on his lashes as he threw both arms around me and kissed me on each cheek, murmuring, "*Mon vieux, mon cher, mon brave camarade!*"

He drew a hand across his eyes and turned away, playing his flashlight upon the sprawling body. It was a man, very tall, very thin, with cord-like muscles standing out on arms and legs. Save for a breech-clout of gunny-sacking he was naked, but his black skin was smeared with patches of dun-colored pigment in each of which was a rosette of five small dark-brown dots, the design bearing a striking resemblance to a leopard's spots.

Fastened to his hands by thongs were metal appliances like brass knuckles, only instead of bearing knobs, their rings were supplied with long, sharp blades which curved above the fingers, making each hand a clawed talon. About his head was bound a band of skin which proved to be the scaly hide of a full-grown fer-de-lance such a snake as we had seen pursuing Coralea that afternoon.

"By George," said Hiji as de Grandin shut his light off, "he's got the full regalia on. I've seen his kind in the Reserved Forest Area more than once—hanged a few dozen of 'em, too."

The Frenchman smiled, a thought unpleasantly. "Unless I'm more mistaken than I think, some necks will test the strength of ropes before we finish with this present business of the monkey," he declared.

T HE BIG CLOCK IN the hall ticked slowly. All of us were tired, but sleep was farthest from our thoughts. My shoulder hurt abominably, and every whisper of a breeze-blown leaf against the window-panes seemed charged with menace. Once or twice I started up, sure that I saw a grinning, painted face beyond the window, but each time search showed that imagination had been playing tricks on me. "If we could only find the blighters' lair we'd clean 'em out in jig-time," muttered Hiji. "In most ways they've run true to form, murderin' people with their 'leopard claws' and terrifyin' all the local blacks so they don't dare squeak on 'em, but there's one thing puzzles me. In Africa these human leopards gather for their pow-wows several days before the Black Moon, and send their signals to the party out by means of drums. They should be usin' something of the kind round here—"

"That's hardly likely," I objected. "So far they've managed to conduct their raids in secrecy. If they beat drums at their meetings they'd give away their gathering-place, and—"

Across the sultry summer night there came a low, slow-swelling sound. Something like the rumble of a giant kettledrum, but also like the low, sustained note of a bass viol it was, beginning on a low, deep note and slowly rising in intensity, if not in pitch: "*Ro-o-om, ro-o-om, rum-rum-rum; ro-o-om, ro-o-om, rum-rum-rum,*" its rhythm swelled and sank with a monotonous, menacing insistence.

Hiji leaped across the room, dashed the window up and thrust his head out, listening intently. "That's it!" he told us as he wheeled around. "The jungle telegraph, the night-drum of the Leopard People! What're we waitin' for? Let's go! Yoicks away, lads; the chase is on!"

We started for the door, but. "Wait a moment, wait for me!" cried Coralea. "You all aren't goin' out to hunt those savages and leave me here alone; I'm goin' with you. Give me a half a minute to put on some other clothes!"

She was somewhat longer than the stipulated thirty seconds, but it was little later when she reappeared in boyish riding-togs, twisting her long hair in a knot and stuffing it into a cap as she ran down the stairs. Bound to her slender waist by a wide leather belt was a powder-and-ball revolver of Civil War model, its eight-inch barrel knocking trim, straight knees each step she took.

"Let's go!" she cried as she rejoined us, and before we realized her intent she was through the door, across the veranda and speeding down the driveway beneath the honey-locust trees, heading for the open road.

We followed, catching up with her just as she reached the gate, and paused a moment, seeking bearings.

"*Ro-o-om, ro-o-om, rum-rum-rum; ro-o-om, ro-o-om, rum-rum-rum!*" the drums' deep monotone rolled across the darkened landscape, surging forward and receding like the sound of distant surf.

"It's over there," said Hiji, nodding toward a low, tree-crested line of hills that raised their bulk beyond the intervening fallow fields.

"It can't be there," objected Coralea. "There's an abandoned Negro cemetery in the hollow of those hills; a pair of murderers are buried there, and you couldn't get a darky within half a mile of it in daylight, much less at midnight."

Hiji's teeth flashed white beneath the black of his mustache. "You may know the superstition of your local blacks, but you don't know voodoo. Graveyards and haunted places are their favorite gathering-spots. Earth from graves of executed felons is a favorite ingredient of their charms. I vote we try the jolly old bury-ing-ground."

"I, too," de Grandin concurred. "But let us step with caution. We may be seen by members of the cult who come in answer to those devils' church bells."

Cautiously we made our way across the fields, dropping to all-fours occasionally where the visibility was high, crawling, running half bent over, gradually approaching the thick-wooded knoll behind which growled the drums' low monody. By the time we reached the hill crest we were crawling on our stomachs like a scout patrol of soldiers reconnoitering an enemy's position.

Light gleamed in the little valley shut in by the hills. A bonfire of fat pine sent its orange-yellow flames mounting ten feet, painting the whitewashed headboards and occasional stone markers of the graves with startling highlights, casting purple shadows on surrounding trees and bramble bushes.

Where light and shadow met, a circle of dark forms was huddled in a wide, loose ring, the gleam of a once-white shirt or a soiled Mother Hubbard giving clue to the spectator's sex. A low, slow-moaning chant, like that heard when the mourners are about to 'get religion' at a Negro gospel meeting, sounded from the group. Now and then there was a movement, a flash of fire-lit clothing or the gleam of bared teeth or of rolling eyeballs, which told that a fresh member of the congregation had arrived in response to the summons of the drums.

More and more they came, creeping stealthily up to the firelight's margin. From fifty to a hundred the group grew; now there were two hundred votaries about the fire, at last at least five hundred. And still the drums tolled their insistent "ro-o-om, ro-o-om; rum-rum-rum" through the night.

I heard Coralea's small smothered "Oh!" and Hiji's sigh of excitement coupled with de Grandin's almost frenzied flow of bubbling French profanity as a figure glided from behind a tombstone. It was a woman, so old and thin and wrinkled there was something almost obscene in the picture she presented, as if a mummy had come from the tomb or the corpse of one dead of senility had risen from its grave to mock and gibber at the living. Her skinny arms and legs, bare in the mounting firelight, seemed smeared with mingled filth and ashes. Her lich-like form was nude save for a length of dirty calico which hung across her back, loose ends split and tied about her waist and hips to form a sort of apron. The upper end of the cloth had been bound about her gray-wooled head to make a turban, and round and round this weird head-dress had been wound strings of gleaming beads. "Teeth!" muttered Hiji. "Human teeth! They knock 'em out and string 'em to make amulets."

"Ouranga!" came a greeting from the crone as she danced round the firelit circle. "Ouranga!" In one emaciated hand she held a black snake whip; in the other was a dried gourd-shell which she waved to and fro, making its seeds rattle furiously against the sun-dried rind. Back and forth before the fire she tripped and stumbled, leaping, sometimes, sometimes shuffling in a sort of buck-and-wing; then pirouetting on her toes like a ghastly caricature of Columbine. "Ouranga!"

From the trembling congregation sounded echoes of her hail, not deep-voiced, but high and thread-thin, frightened, more than half hysterical: "*Ouranga, ouranga; ouranga!*" Then, in a high-swelling chorus, "*Voodoo!*"

With a mincing, shuffling step the old hag circled round the fire, clattering her rattle, flourishing her whip, pausing now and then, and each time she halted the men and women groveling before her shrank back in the shadows as though she menaced them with a live snake.

"*Ouranga!*" shrieked the crone again, and half a dozen men came struggling from the shadows, pushing three cowering wretches, two men and a woman. The luckless trio were flung face-downward on the ground, where they lay quaking, too terrified to utter pleas for mercy.

"*Ouranga!*" the witch cried furiously, leaping forward to bring down her whip on the prostrate victims' backs. Repeatedly she cried the mystic word, accompanying each repetition with a cut of her cruel lash until dull scarlet stains showed through the groveling wretches' scanty clothing.

"Back-sliders from the cult," said Hiji in a whisper. "Not much inducement for 'em to leave the fold, eh what?"

The hag had ceased her flogging, more from weariness than mercy, and the chastened apostates crawled like beaten dogs to the ranks that hovered in the shadows. We saw the others draw away from them as from contagion as they found seats on the ground.

A long black shadow cut between the fire and us, and a tall, thin man came dancing out between the tombstones, pausing for a moment with uplifted hands, then falling prostrate on the sand before the voodoo priestess. In every detail he was like the man who had attacked me; painted like a leopard, hands armed with sharp, cruel iron claws, he might have been the same man raised from the dead by some unholy miracle.

The *obi* witch addressed him in a flood of cackling gibberish, and he responded in the same jargon. Finally, rising to his knees, he circled round the fire, half crawling, half dancing, waving clawed hands in the air as if he tore the life from an unseen victim. Graphically, in pantomime, we saw him re-enact the murder of Judge Scatterhorn. We saw him creep up to the quiet house, secrete himself among the shrubbery, lie in waiting for his victim. His eyes glared horribly, his teeth gleamed like the fangs of some wild thing as he arched his back and sprang. A leap, a scream like that of a demented fiend, and he swept in an arc through the air, striking with his iron-taloned hands straight at his quarry's throat, then rolling thrashing on the ground, as if locked in a death-grip with some phantom adversary. At last he lay stretched out upon the dried grass, breathing hard from his exertions, then rolled upon his face before the hag, reaching out his gaffed hands till they almost touched her feet.

"*Bon—bon!*" The *obi* witch commended, and the leopard man leaped up and joined the circle. His work had won approval from the voodoo cult's high priestess.

The bonfire had begun to burn itself to embers, and a moaning, low, almost a whimpering singsong, passed from lip to lip about the ring of squatting men and women. "*Dhan ghi—dhan ghi!*" we heard them cry. Two men staggered forward with a large pine packing-case between them. The box was reminiscent of the outside cases used to enclose caskets at cheap funerals, but was fitted with a hinged lid secured by heavy hasps and padlocks. With a sudden shock I realized that what I'd thought were painted spots were really holes bored through the planks. "De Grandin," I whispered, "there's something *live* inside there!"

"*Mais oui, mais certainement,*" he answered imperturbably. "These naughty followers of *vaudois* are worshippers of a great snake they call the 'White Queen.' Observe them, if you please."

One of the bearers set his end of the case down and ran back to the shadows, returning in an instant with a squawking cockerel. The voodoo priestess snatched the fowl from him, drew a knife from her turban and slit its throat with a quick slash.

Now her dance was like the antics of a maniac. Laughing insanely, fiendishly, muttering unintelligible charms, shrieking and crying, she whirled and turned in the fast-waning firelight, waving the stiffening body of the slaughtered cock about her head till the spurting blood from its cut neck sprayed on the worshippers, who crouched together in an ectasy of shuddering fear. Twice she leaped upon the box with the hinged top, and each time the congregation shrieked in wild, ecstatic glee. Once she clawed at its locked lid until I thought that she would open it, but apparently she reconsidered, and the lid remained closed on the dread god of the *obi* people.

"I think the convocation will be ending soon," de Grandin whispered. "Let us depart before they break their meeting up. We cannot hope to fight them single-handed, and if they should discover us—" It was not necessary for him to proceed; imagination more than supplied details missing from his statement.

Creeping flat to earth, we wriggled down the hill, reached an unplowed field and rose to run across it. "Hiji!" exclaimed de Grandin. "Where is he?"

Apparently he had dematerialized. A moment earlier he had lain beside us in our ambuscade; none of us had seen him leave, but—he was gone.

"We must go back," the Frenchman announced firmly. "We cannot leave him in their hands, they would—*mon Dieu!* Down, down for your lives, my friends!"

Coming toward us through the gloom there bulked a monstrous form. It was like some giant spider walking on its two hind legs, but larger than a cow. We dropped down to the turf, not daring to draw breath lest our respirations betray us; then: "I say, de Grandin, is that you?" Low, but distinctly cheerful, Hiji's voice came to us.

"*Bien oui*, it is I, and not another, but who in heaven's name are you?" the Frenchman answered.

"Why, Frenchy, don't you recognize your little playmate?" Hiji answered plaintively. "And I've brought our other little friend along, too. The cove who mauled Trowbridge this evenin', don't you know? While we were lyin' there and watchin' all the voodoo doin's, I thought I could find work for him, so I hustled back and got him."

I breathed more easily. What we had mistaken for a monster was the Englishman, walking upright with the dead leopard man across his shoulders.

"Just wait for me a mo'," Hiji bade. "I'll be comin' back this way, and when I come you'd best be on your toes and ready to make distance."

He trudged off in the darkness with his grisly burden. Ten minutes passed, fifteen, half an hour; then as if in response to a signal there rose such a pandemonium of shouts and screams and yells from the abandoned cemetery as might have waked the dead who slept there.

A moment later Hiji came abreast of us, running like an antelope. "Run, you blighters; cut and run for it, or you'll not see tomorrow's sunrise!" he cried pantingly. "Don't let 'em sight you!"

We ran. My heart was pounding like a battering-ram against my ribs long before we reached the Sterling house, but, amazingly, there was no pursuit.

We faced each other in the lamplit parlor. "Tell me, *mon beau sauvage*, what was it that you did to them?" de Grandin ordered.

"Oh, just gave a demonstration of my kind of magic. The beggars were waitin' a report from the feller who jumped Trowbridge, so I took care they jolly well got it. When I got back to their council fire I was put to it for a means of deliverin' him, and a young tree gave me the idea. They were raisin' such a bally row I could a sung *God Save the King* at top voice and never have been heard; so I had no trouble loppin' off the sapling's limbs, then climbin' it and draggin' my deceased friend after me. I lodged him in the tree-fork, then swung down, bringin' the tree down with me, and let go. It straightened up, of course, when I released my weight, and shot him like a stone out of a catapult, right plump into the middle of their pow-wow, neat as wax. You should have heard 'em bellow when he landed at their hospitable fireside."

"*Parbleu*, my friend, we did," de Grandin answered. "We did, indeed, and—*mordieu*, why can we not?"

"Eh?" answered Hiji.

"You have given me the idea, the hunch, the inspiration. But certainly. These devil-doings we beheld tonight were but the dress rehearsal to the ceremonies they will hold tomorrow when the moon is in eclipse. Why should we not prepare more magic for tomorrow night? Why should we not frighten them until they call upon the hills to fall upon them and hide them from the vengeance of our medicine?"

"All right, why should we not?" demanded Hiji. "If you've any ideas for a charade, spill 'em. Depend on me to rally round, old son."

"By blue, my friend, I think that you can be of service. Tell me, can you recall the chants these Leopard People sang in Africa?"

"Er—yes, I think I can. They went something like this." From half-closed lips he hummed a syncopated, wordless tune, an eery, eldritch thing resembling our swing music as the bitter scent of hydrocyanic acid gas resembles the perfume of crushed peach leaves, a wicked tune that made the listener think of pitchblack midnights and rifled graves and evil deeds done in the darkness of the moon. As he hummed he beat time with his finger on the table top, a sharp, staccato beat of broken rhythm.

De Grandin bent his gaze on Coralea as Hiji hummed. "What does the music make you think of, *Mademoiselle?*" he asked.

"Oh"—she shook her shoulders in disgust—"it stirs me all up. It makes me want to rend and tear and scratch, as if I were a savage cat. It rouses all the elemental brute in me."

"Fine, excellent, superb!" he applauded. "I had hoped you would say something of the sort. Tomorrow night we do it. Yes, by blue, and you shall help us, for you are a psychic, *Mademoiselle!*"

"TROWBRIDGE, MON VIEUX, I have a task for you," he told me as we rose next morning. "Be good enough to take a launch and go to Monsieur Townsend at Elizabeth City. Among other things he keeps a stock of fireworks, and I should greatly like to have one hundred rockets of the largest size available. You will kindly bring them back to me as soon as possible—"

"Rockets?" I echoed stupidly. "You mean skyrockets?"

"Nothing less, my wise one. Large, fine rockets, filled with balls of colored fire and powder which goes *swis-s-s-sh!* You comprehend?"

"No, can't say that I do, but I'll get 'em for you," I replied as I finished shaving. "Anything else you'd like?"

"No, unless you wish to get some Roman candles, also."

The afternoon was far spent when I returned with the fireworks, and my companions seemed on edge with excitement. We made a hurried, almost silent meal, and just before dusk Hiji and Coralea set out for some mysterious rendezvous. Looking grim as the governor of a prison on a hanging-day, the Englishman was back within an hour, and I decided that he must have taken her to some safe place while we faced the voodoo worshippers. A little later, he came into the parlor with a pair of odd contraptions. One was an ordinary rubber comb with an envelope of tissue paper pasted over it, the other a small copper kettle the flat lid of which had been clamped down and fastened with a rim of sealing-wax.

"You have tested them?" de Grandin asked.

"Absolutely. Everything's as right as rain."

"*Très bon.* Be ready when the signal comes."

We waited nervously. Neither Hiji nor de Grandin seemed inclined to talk, and both seemed listening for some signal. The daylight faded slowly, and night came on with faltering, indecisive steps. Jays and sparrows put themselves to bed with noisy good-night chirpings. Every now and then de Grandin or the Englishman went out upon the porch and looked up at the sky as though they sought some portent there. At last: "It comes, my, friends, it comes!" de Grandin cried excitedly. "Behold him, if you please!"

Following his pointing finger we looked up to the zenith. The moon, as full and round and yellow as a disk of gold alloyed with silver, swam in a cloudless sky, but nicking the smooth margin of its circle there appeared a tiny sliver of black shadow. Slowly, slower than the minute hand of a run-down old clock, the shadow moved, spreading gradually across the glowing lunar disk.

"The time has come, *mes amis*," de Grandin announced. "You know the part you are to play, my Hiji. May good fortune wait upon your work. *À bientôt.*"

"Carry on, old feller," the Englishman tucked his paper-covered comb and kettle underneath his arm and gave us each a handclasp. "Keep your heads down, and if things go wrong and I get there first, I'll tell the Devil that you're on the way, and have him burn a sulfur-candle in the window for you. Cheerio." He turned and stalked off in the darkness.

"We also have our work, my friend," de Grandin told me as he bent and took a bundle of skyrockets in his arms, motioning me to take the sheaf which he had made of the remainder.

Quietly we walked across the fields while the shadow of the eclipse grew larger with each step we took. We bent double as we reached the hill range and step by cautious step began the ascent toward the wooded knoll that overlooked the voodoo meeting-place. Half-way up I paused for breath, and as I looked around I caught a flash of fluttering drapery in the gathering shadows of the road.

"Wha—what's that?" I asked. Upon a night like this the age-old fears came crowding back, and the thing I saw was like a brooding, sheeted ghost that watched us as we mounted to our doom.

"Look farther, if you please, my friend," he answered with a laugh, "and tell me what it is you see."

I looked. Far down the road, as motionless as something carved of stone, there stood another sheeted figure, gigantic, menacing, immobile. And a little farther down the road another, and another—and another. Silent, sheeted sentinels of the night, grim specters from the olden times when dead men walked on moonless nights . . . my scalp began to prickle and my breath came faster. "What in heaven's name are they?" I gasped.

"Night riders," he replied. "A hundred of them, all in ghost-clothes, all with rifles, all ready for the signal we shall give, my friend."

"Whatever do you mean—"

He eased his burden to the turf and bent toward me. "Today we have been busy while you were away, my friend. The local colored folk are good and honest men and women, but they are firmly bound by racial fears. When these *sacré* villains from the Caribbean came here they seduced them from their simple, peaceful ways, telling them that they would bring a government like that of Haiti in the days of Henri Christophe here. Every man should be a marquis or a duke or count, every woman have a title, too, and the white oppressor should be driven from the land. Moreover, those who doubted or refused to help them were intimidated, some were even killed. Such was the fate of James Collins, whom they tracked to Harlem and murdered. You saw the sway these voodooists have on the local blacks last night. It is a kind of superstitious awe they hold them in, and only by a greater magic can that hold be broken. The authorities could harry them and hunt them, perhaps they could convict them of the murders which they have committed, but I doubt it. For where could they find a colored man or woman who would dare to testify against them? *Ha*, but if we can put on a show which seems to overmatch the voodoo magic, if we can swoop down on them with all the dreaded panoply of the sheeted riders of the night, and take their voodoo priests and priestesses before their very eyes and hang them to convenient limbs—what then?"

"But that's sheer terrorism—"

"And what is it these villains practice here? Philanthropy? I tell you, good Friend Trowbridge, only by a show of extra-legal might can we put this horror down. When we have done our part the sheeted riders will close in. They know the local blacks, and those they know will be allowed to escape. As for the voodoo men—such men as those who killed Judge Scatterhorn and Captain Sterling, and almost did the same to you—I damn think that the ropes are now all ready for their necks. Yes, certainly. Of course."

I was about to protest, but the midnight calm was shattered by the sudden rumble of a drum: "*Ro-o-om, ro-o-om; rum-rum-rum!*" As on the night before, the devilish sound seemed welling from the very center of the earth, swelling and expanding till it filled the highest heavens with its maddening discord.

"Up, up, my friend, our work is waiting for us!"

With our rockets bundled in our arms we scrambled up the grassy slope and halted in the woods which fringed the hilltop. Quickly de Grandin set his rocket-sticks into the earth, sighting each one carefully, as though he were a battery commander about to launch a charge of grapeshot at advancing cavalry.

The voodoo fire was burning in the hollow of the hills, the dusky worshippers were crouched in fascinated terror at the shadows' edge, the voodoo priestess danced and postured in the space between the tombstones. "*Ouranga, ouranga; voodoo!*" came the litany of the black rite as the priestess and her congregation worked themselves into a frenzy.

"*Dhan ghi, dhan ghi!*" the cry rose from the swaying audience. "The White Queen, show the White Queen to us. Let her testify!"

"*Ouranga, ouranga!*" shrieked the withered hag in red as she danced and leaped among the graves, twisting and writhing in an ecstasy of self-induced hypnosis. "*Dhan ghi, dhan ghi!*" She shook her claw-like hands up at the moon, which now was almost hidden in eclipse.

Now four men came shuffling forward, and between them they were bundling two more creatures, half-grown Negresses, poor, terrified, impotent things so utterly unnerved by fear that they could scarcely struggle in their captor's hands. "*Grand Dieu, les boucs; les boucs sans bois*—the human sacrifices, goats without horns!" de Grandin whispered. "Have we made a mistake, will they reverse the ceremony, and have the feast before the White Queen testifies?"

The sacrifices were flung down before the fire and the voodoo witch bent over them, touching each with her gourd rattle, then dancing off again.

"*Dhan ghi, dhan ghi!*" the chant rose louder, more insistently, and another group of men came staggering out into the firelight; between them bumped the long, hole-decorated box we'd seen the night before.

"Ah?" murmured Jules de Grandin. "It seems that I was not mistaken, after all."

The bearers dropped the box unceremoniously and scuttled off, racing back to join their fellows in the circle, for plainly their fear of the goddess in the box was greater than their faith in the high priestess' magic to protect them when the great snake issued forth.

"*Dhan ghi, dhan ghi!*" The bag was stepping in a constantly accelerated pace about the box, her knees raised level with her waist, her scrawny, splay-boned feet extended straight in a continuation of her spindling shanks. "*Dhan ghi, dhan ghi, dhan ghi!*"

Now from between her tightly compressed lips there came a whining singsong chant, a rising, quavering cry like that snake-charmers make before the serpents issue from their baskets. For a moment she paused by the box, then snatched the lid up in her claws, springing back two yards or so to avoid the great snake's head in case it started out of the case suddenly.

De Grandin's teeth were fairly chattering, and a flow of weirdly garbled French profanity came sprawling from his lips like sparks that sputter from a dampened fuse.

We waited breathless. A pall of silence fell upon the worshippers. We could hear a sudden hissing sizzle in the fire as a fresh stick fell into the flames.

"*A-a-ah!*" de Grandin let his breath out slowly. "She comes. Behold her, good Friend Trowbridge!"

No wicked, wedge-shaped, scale-mailed head arose from the voodoo tabernacle. No forked tongue darted menace at the posturing priestess and cowering congregation. Nothing at all came from the box.

Instead, high overhead, seemingly dropping from the zenith where the moon's pale countenance was masked, there came the whiffing notes of a slow, syncopated, wordless chant, an eery thing that made the listener think of pitch-black midnights and graves from which the dead were torn, and evil deeds done in the darkness of the moon. And with the rasping, scobbing music came the sound of a tom-tom which beat in sharp staccato, its broken measures reaching to the very, marrow of our spines.

The *obi* woman looked up to the sky from which the eldritch music seemed to drip like venom from a manchineel tree. Nothing met her gaze. Only the insistent, buzzing, susurrating notes swooped downward as from some discarnate unclean spirit perched among the swaying pinetrees' boughs.

The witch's hideous old face took on a look of wonder, then of worry, finally of blind, unreasoning panic. But her terror was no more than the prelude to that which followed, for something slowly rose from the long box beyond the dying fire.

A tall, lean thing it was, brown-skinned, ash-smeared, a mop of matted white hair stringing round its skull-like face. Wisps of age-rotted cloth were loosely bound around it, like grave-clothes falling from a putrefying corpse, and where the rags left chocolate-colored body bare great patches of a leprous gray showed in a ghastly contrast.

Faster and faster dripped the ghost-tune from the treetops; louder and more menacing the phantom drum-beats came. The hideous thing leaped from its box, vaulted the fire and stood face to face with the old voodoo witch. The hag drew back her arm as if to strike the specter with her lash; the visitant reached suddenly into the fire, seized a blazing pine branch from the flames and felled the priestess with a single blow.

Before the *obi* woman could retain her feet the thing turned to the fire, striking it repeatedly with a green branch, flailing out the sinking blaze until it flickered lower, lower—finally died to a dull-glowing heap of coals.

And now a thing too terrible to credit happened. The spirit of the beaten fire seemed transferred to the body of the hideous creature from the box, for its limbs and face began to glow with horrifying, smoky luminance, a glow such as dead things give off in marshes in the darkness of the night.

Higher, shriller, rising to a keening wail that sent horripilations rippling through my skin, the ghostly music lifted, while the tom-tom's tempo quickened till each plangent beat seemed driving deep into our vertebræ, and like a sulfurous silhouette against the background of the night the fiery thing danced and shuffled back and forth between the sunken-mounded graves, its glowing feet in measure with the skirl of spectral music, its smoldering body seeming hung midway between the earth and sky as it whirled and turned and leaped and bounded where the voodoo witch-fire had been burning. Now, rag by filthy, rotting rag it tore its moldering grave-clothes off, and as each fetid fragment fell upon the earth fresh horrors met our fascinated gaze. Ribs, pelvic bones and sternum seemed made of living fire which shone through the integument of chocolate-colored skin as marsh-fire might shine through the drifting brume of foul miasmal vapors.

A moaning, low but pregnant with unutterable dread, broke from the congregation as they saw their witch-priestess felled by this awful apparition which glowed with smoldering inward fire and summoned ghost-tunes from the moonless midnight sky.

"Men and women of the race," a voice sang from the specter's burning throat, "I bring you testimony. Daughter am I to *Iblis*, Chief of Devils; even of the *bori* of the jungle am I daughter.

"Voodoo is unclean; voodoo is forbidden those who would not feel the vengeance of the *bori*. Get ye to your homes, ye foolish ones; to your work go ye, for to labor is to praise the jungle people of your fathers.

"Where is your witch-woman now? Where is her magic? Could she stand before the power of the spirits of the jungle? Could her fire burn one who carries fumes of hell within her body, or can her magic save ye from my wrath?

"Back to your homes, before I call on you the curse of *Mai-Aska*, who brings scars and rashes. To your cabins, followers of false gods, or on you will I bring the wrath of *Kuri-Yandu*, who swells the joints with misery. See, ye fools who trust in voodoo, even now I call the stars down from the sky to crush you with their weight. On you I call the curse of *Mai-Ja-Chikki*, who will blind you for your sins. Behold!"

She reached her fire-gloved hands up toward the moonless sky and a swishing like the roar of flooding water when the rivers overflow their banks came from the pine trees, while curve on lambent curve of fire swept through the darkness as though a storm of meteors had been blown from hell by Satan's all-destroying breath.

"*Morbleu*, but it is perfect, it is excellent, it is *magnifique!*" de Grandin whispered in delight as he raced along the line of rockets, setting fire to them and, as they soared roaring through the air, setting fresh ones in their places.

The rockets reached their apogees and hissed down to the earth, bursting into fiery constellations. It seemed as if the heavens were alive with falling, bursting stars; the wrath of fire and brimstone that burned Sodom and Gomorrah, the promised day of awful fate when earth should be consumed by fire seemed on us as the blazing, shattering missiles crashed down from the zenith.

Screams of terror, frenzied, hopeless pleas for mercy, sounded on all sides.

"Oh, Lawd, Ah's got it! Ah's gone blind, mah eyes is out!" cried one man, clawing at his dazzled eyes. Another and another took the wail up, and in a moment rustlings in the bushes told where congregation members crawled away for sanctuary, deserting the outlanders who had held them captive in a thrall of superstition.

But now the clatter of shod hoofs came from the highway, and fresh shouts of dismay rose from the frightened fugitives as the sheeted riders of the night closed in upon the voodoo rendezvous. They were a fearsome sight—steeds and riders masked in fluttering white with fiery eyes aglare through peepholes in their draperies, torches blazing in their hands, guns or whips upraised in menace.

The ghostly riders opened ranks to let the fleeing voodoo worshippers scuttle off to safety, but with the voodoo leaders it was different. Within a moment six outlandishly dressed men and the old *obi* priestess had been corralled and bound with ropes. "I think our bag is full," de Grandin murmured; "they have them all."

"Wha—what will you do with them?" I faltered, wild stories of the condign justice meted out by night riders recurring to me.

"Do? *Parbleu*, what should they do with such ones? Have we not seen them taken as they gloated over the commission of a foul crime? Can we not testify against them from our own knowledge? *Mais certainement*, my friend. Within the hour they will lie all safe in *la bastille*. Tomorrow, at the latest, the *juge d'instruction* hears our evidence. After that—*morbleu*, one wishes one could be as sure of reaching heaven as one is that they will be convicted by the county court and suffer condemnation for their crimes! Come, let us go. This evening's work is finished, I damn think."

AN HOUR LATER WE gathered in the Sterling parlor. Lamplight shone upon the tall, mint-garlanded tumblers, ice clinked pleasantly. The juleps were delicious.

"No," Hiji laughed, "I didn't have a bit of trouble. They were all so bally intent on the doin's in the cemetery that I shinned up the tree without a single blighter spottin' me. After that"—he took another long drink—"how do you Yankees say? It was in the bag."

"Whatever—" I began, but de Grandin hastened to explain before I had a chance to frame my question.

"*Mais; c'est tout simplement, mon vieux*. One only needs to think things through, and *voilà*." He turned as footsteps echoed in the hall and Coralea came in, her face and hands and arms aglow from recent vigorous scrubbing. "*Messieurs*, permit me to present *la grande prêtresse de vomdois*, the superwitch." Coralea blushed rosily beneath her soap-and-water glow.

"The superwitch?" I echoed. "You mean—"

"*Précisément.* I had been wondering how we might turn the tables on those naughty people from the Caribbean, and when Hiji flung the body of their executed comrade into camp the idea came to me like that—*pouf!* 'These so evil fellows have laid hold upon the superstition of the local colored folk by force of fear; they have worked on their imagination, they have convinced them that they, are all-powerful,' I say to me.

"'Exactly so, you have it right, my perspicacious self,' I answer me. 'Jules de Grandin, you and I must convince them that we have the greater power. We must induce them to go back to their homes and resume their simple, peaceful mode of life.'

"'You have summed the situation up exactly, Jules de Grandin,' I tell me, 'But how are we to do these things?'

"Then I engage myself in deep conference. We have *matériel* at hand, it only waits our use. Hiji knows the demon music of the Africans, those bad, fierce Leopard Men of the West Coast beside whom these voodooists are but inept amateurs; he can reproduce it, but we must find a way to carry it to them and make them think it comes from superhuman agencies. Also, it is for us to make the magic of these voodoo people seem a weak and ineffective thing. We must put shame on them, as Moses shamed the magic-makers of the Pharaoh. How to do it? Then I recall Mademoiselle Coralea is a *danseuse*. She is clever, she is talented, she knows these people, and she has said the music of the Leopard Men arouses all her evil instincts. 'Mademoiselle Coralea,' I apostrophize her, 'you shall be our superwitch. You shall dance before the voodoo council of fire. You shall put shame on their *mamaloi*.'

"So I approach her with my proposition. At first she is afraid, but she is the *artiste*, the rôle appeals to her dramatic nature, and so at last she gives consent. Thereupon we get our properties together. Hiji makes a tom-tom of an old kettle, and a pipe out of a piece of paper wrapped around a comb. Together in the barn we make the music, very softly, and Mademoiselle Coralea perfects her dance. We make a costume for her out of cheesecloth which we drag around the barnyard till it looks as old as sin's own self. We smear her with a chocolate paste. We buy up all the matches at the village store and boil them; then with the sulfurous paste we paint a skeleton upon her so that her bones will seem to shine clear through her skin when it is dark.

"Then Hiji and I set forth to find the 'White Queen.' We find her lying in her box out in the cemetery, and—it took but two shots to dispatch her. Afterward we clean her box with disinfectant, and into it goes Mademoiselle Coralea. *Parbleu,* I think it took more courage to lie curled up in that snake's ex-den than it took to face the voodoo people in the open!

"In a tree above the graveyard we hung a telephone transmitter with an amplifier attached to it. These we connected to a wire and a telephone receiver which were hidden in a near-by tree, and into this our Hiji sang his tune and beat upon his kettle-drum. *Tiens*, the effect was most realistic, *n'est-ce-pas?* When the music seemed to come from nowhere, when the voodoo priestess was struck down by the fiery visitant which leaped out of the snake box, when the stars began to fall from heaven as our rockets took their flight—*parbleu*, it was so good a piece of stagecraft that even I who knew the plot was half afraid, myself!"

Coralea's pink cheeks were dimpled with a smile, "Doctor de Grandin, I think I owe you something for tonight," she told him.

"How is that, *Mademoiselle?*"

"That dance I did tonight; if it was good enough to make those people think I was a demon from the jungle it ought to be successful in the theatre. I'll get Sir Haddingway to play the Leopard People's music on a record for me; then as soon as Papa's estate has been settled I'll go to New York. That dance should be good for a month's engagement at the Irving Place Opera House. After that—well, other burlesque actresses have gone to Hollywood. Why shouldn't I?"

"Why not, indeed, *ma plus belle héroïne?*" replied de Grandin. "À *votre triomphe!*"

We clinked our glasses on the toast.

The Poltergeist of Swan Upping

"DEAR TROWBRIDGE," READ THE letter from Scott Thorowgood:

As you know, I bought the old house at Swan Upping on the Mullica last July and at once set out to renovate it. Restoration was completed in October and we moved in the middle of that month. Almost immediately things began to happen—unpleasant things. Servants swore they met with spectral persecutions in halls and on the stairs, bed-clothes were jerked of at night. Crockery and kitchenware fell from shelves and hooks without apparent reason, and last Wednesday morning a maid was set on as she went upstairs and thrown so violently that she sustained a broken collarbone. Neither my daughters nor I have seen anything nor been troubled in any way, and if it were not for the girl's injury I should say the whole thing is attributable to some malicious gossip; but her hurts are real enough—as I who pay her hospital bills can testify—and she persists in saying she was the victim of assault and not of accident.

Thus far it's been more annoying than frightening, but if things keep up this way we shall have to close the house for want of help, as we find it practically impossible to keep servants in the place. Do you think you can persuade Doctor de Grandin, of whose success with occult pests I've heard considerable, to come and "fumigate" Swan Upping for us? I shall, of course, be willing to pay whatever fee he asks.

"Well, can I persuade you?" I asked, passing the letter to de Grandin. "I know you're not much interested in the fee, but—"

"Who says so?" he demanded as he laid the letter down. "Why should I not be?"

"Why, I know you've turned down cases time and time again when the fees offered were almost fantastic—"

"*Précisément.* You have right, my friend. I reserve the right to take such cases as appeal to me, and to decline others. But in such cases as I take the laborer is worthy of his hire, and I think that your friend Thorowgood is one who has respect for money, whether in himself or others. This letter has a tone of command in it. One assumes *Monsieur* Thorowgood is used to having what he pays for and paying well for what he gets. *Bien.* I shall serve him well, and he shall pay accordingly. I shall be interested in both the fee and this so snobbish ghost who gives attention only to the servants and leaves the master of the house alone. When do we leave?"

"He says to take the train to Upsam's Station, then wait for him to pick us up. There's only one train down a day in wintertime. We'll have to pack immediately."

JULES DE GRANDIN THRUST his small pointed chin another inch into the collar of his fur coat, drove his hand into his pockets till his elbows all but disappeared, and eyed me with a stare as icy as the fading winter afternoon. "Me," he announced bitterly, "I am a fool of the first magnitude!"

"Indeed?" I replied. "I'm glad to hear you confess it. I've suspected something of the sort at times, but—"

"I am," he insisted, "the prize zany of the winter's crop. Five little hours ago we were warm and comfortable in Harrisonville. Now, if you please, observe us—marooned here in a trackless wilderness, retreat cut off, progress impossible. *Mon Dieu,* I perish miserably!"

"Oh, it's not that bad," I comforted. "Thorowgood will surely be here in a little while. If he can't come himself he'll send somebody—"

"*Mais oui,* and they will find our stiffening dead corpses on the station platform—"

"Maybe that's our man, now," I interrupted as an ancient car of the model which made Detroit famous in the days before the war drew up beside the waiting-platform and an aged Negro wrapped almost to the eyes in a sheep-coat descended and ambled toward the stack of freight piled at the station's farther end.

"At any rate, it is a sign of rescue," de Grandin nodded and hurried toward the dusky motorist. "*Holà, mon brave,*" he greeted. "How much will it cost us to be conveyed to Swan Upping? You know the place, of course."

"Yassuh, Ah knows hit," the other answered with a marked lack of enthusiasm.

"Very well, my priceless Jehu. What is your price for transportation thither?"

The colored man spoke with a rich Virginia accent. Obviously, he was not indigenous to southern Jersey. Just as obviously, he was much impressed by the fur coat de Grandin wore. "Cap'n, suh," he answered as he touched his battered hat, "mah bizness ain't been good dese las' two months."

"Indeed? One grieves to hear it. But we shall pay you royally, reward you with a princeling's ransom for taking us to Swan Upping. We are thoroughly disgusted with the scenery hereabouts, and would away to bright new scenes. Accordingly—"

The Negro gazed at him with something close akin to rapture. With the uneducated man's love of large words he was entranced with Jules de Grandin's eloquence, yet . . . Regretful resolution hardened in his wrinkled face. "Con'ol, suh," he interrupted, "mah bizness has been pow'ful bad dis season. Folks ain't haulin' like dey uster."

"One gathered as much; and from these preliminaries one assumes your price will be enormous. Very well, then. A dollar each? Two dollars?"

"Naw, suh."

"*Grand Dieu*, a profiteer, a usurer, a *voleur de chemin!* How much, then, my grand rascal? Three dollars each? I swear we'll pay no more!"

"Doctah, suh"—such munificence seemed to warrant a new title of respect—"Ah'd suttinly enjoy to make me six dollahs, but you all cain't hire me to take yuh to Swan Uppin'. Not dis time o' day, suh."

"Eh, how is that? Surely it cannot be so far—"

"Hit ain't so far to go, suh. Dat ain't whut's worryin' me. Hit's de gittin' back dat counts. Ah ain't aimin' to go pesticatin' round no daid folks' bizness."

"I do not understand. What have the dead to do with taking us to Swan Upping?"

"Plenty, suh. Dey's got a plenty to do wid hit. Don't yuh know dat place is *ha'nted?*"

"Bosh!" I broke in. "You know there aren't such things as ghosts?"

"Yassuh. Ah knows hit right enough in daytime, but de sun is settin' fast, an' it'll be pitch-black befo' we gits dere. Ah ain't goin' nowheres near dat place in darkness, suh."

There the matter rested. Plead, argue and cajole as we would, we could not prevail on him to take us to Swan Upping. With a regretful look at us he re-entered his decrepit chariot, set his wheezing motor going and drove off into the lengthening shadows, leaving us as hopelessly cut off at the small way-station as survivors of H.M.S. *Bounty* were on Pitcairn Island.

The prospect was not too inviting. Festoons of dripping icicles hung from the platform's open-sided shelter, patches of half-melted snow alternated with still larger patches of foot-fettering mud, and a chill wind whipped the waters of the Mullica into angry little whitecaps, then hurried on to howl a keening dirge around the corners of the boarded-up summer hotel. There was neither waiting-room nor ticket office, for the station consisted of a board platform roofed over at one end to afford temporary shelter to freight and such unfortunates as had to wait the trains that stopped on signal only. Nowhere, look as we would, could we descry a sign of anyone who might have been a messenger from Swan Upping. Meanwhile the sun was sinking steadily behind the western timberline, and long blue shadows reached out toward us like malignant fingers.

"We should have motored down," I said. "Railway service to this section of the state's not anything to brag about in winter, and—"

"*Morbleu*, we should have waited for the summer!" de Grandin interrupted. "Then, at least, we might have slept outdoors and sustained ourselves on berries. As it is, a gruesome death awaits us—*heurra*, it is a rescue!"

A station wagon pulled up alongside the platform, and Scott Thorowgood, wrapped to the heels in a chinchilla ulster, climbed from the driver's seat to wring my hand.

"Hullo, Trowbridge," he greeted heartily. "Mighty glad to meet you, Doctor de Grandin. Hope my little accident didn't inconvenience you too much. I got a flat just as I left the place and had to stop and change the wheel. Got your duffle ready? Fine, let's go."

"We were beginning to feel like orphans of the storm," I confessed as our vehicle got under way. "There was no way of telephoning you, and we thought there might have been some slip-up in train schedules. When we didn't find you here we tried to make arrangements with an old colored man to drive us over, but the deal fell through. He not only wouldn't entertain an offer, but intimated rather broadly that Swan Upping's—"

"I know, I know; don't tell me!" Thorowgood broke in. "It's all around the county, now. We just got a fresh staff from a New York employment office, but if they're here a week it'll set a record. Houseful of week-enders too."

"You say these tales of haunting are all new, *Monsieur?*" de Grandin asked. "There is no legend of an ancient ghost?"

"No, our spook is this year's model, with all the late improvements," Thorowgood responded, swinging from the main road into a long private lane. "The original Swan Upping house dates back to Colonial days, and probably there's been enough deviltry pulled off there to warrant a battalion of ghosts moving in and making it a permanent headquarters, but as far as I can ascertain no one ever heard of any ghostly visitants till we moved in. Usually old deserted houses get an unsavory reputation, but in this case the rule's reversed. Everything was quiet as a Quaker meeting till we came here. The carpenters and plumbers had hardly moved out when the ghost moved in, and began scaring my cooks and maids and laundresses out of their wits. We've had about five hundred percent labor turnover since October, and if you can't rid us of the ghost we'll either have to close the house or do our own cooking and washing.

"I thought at first it might be someone trying to scare me into selling. I've put a lot of money in the place, and it would make an ideal summer boarding-house; so, fantastic as it sounds, I thought that maybe someone might have had a notion I could be scared off and forced to sell out at a loss. That got my dander up, and I hired a crew of detectives to come and give the place a going over—"

"Indeed? And what did they discover?"

"Nothing. Not a blessed thing. The spook lay low while they were in the house, and we couldn't have asked a quieter time. Then, the very day they left, Daisy Mullins, the only one of all the servants who's been with us straight through, was set upon as she went up the stairs and thrown down the entire flight. She broke her collarbone and hurt her head, poor kid, but the harm it did her body isn't half as serious as what her mind suffered. I was over to see her in the hospital this morning, and she's almost a nervous wreck. The doctors tell me she may go into St. Vitus' dance."

"U'm? And what manifestations have you yourself observed?"

Thorowgood bit the end from a cigar and set it glowing with the dashboard lighter. "Nothing!" he exploded. "Neither my daughters nor I have seen anything out of the ordinary. No one but the servants has been troubled. That's what made me think it might have been some malicious person, or perhaps a practical joker, behind it all. I've offered a thousand dollars reward for the arrest and conviction of anyone caught playing ghost, but thus far no one's laid claim to it.

"Welcome to Spooky Hollow, gentlemen." He brought the station wagon to a halt beneath the porte-cochère and slammed the front door open. "Want to question the servants before dinner?"

"No, thank you," answered de Grandin. "I shall take the opportunity to look the terrain over before I form a plan of action, if you please."

"Certainly, certainly. You're the ghostologist on this case. It's up to you to prescribe whatever treatment you think proper."

WHEN HE DID SWAN Upping over, Thorowgood had taken thought for his guests' comfort. Our cozy room mocked at the winter darkness fingering at the window-panes. Bright curtains of glazed chintz hung at the casements, two fat armchairs had been drawn up to the blazing fire, a maple wall-case held a row of books—Heiser's *American Doctor's Odyssey*, Link's *Return to Religion* and Madame Curie's biography were three titles I saw at a glance. On the mantelpiece was a low bowl of Danish copper, jade-mellow with patina, in which a bouquet of flamboyant Cherokee roses was set. Immediately adjoining was a bathroom done in orchid tile with a deep, luxurious tub, a glassed-in shower and a row of great, fluffy towels warming themselves on a heated rack. "Name of a small green man," de Grandin murmured as his little blue eyes lighted with appreciation, "food never tastes so good as when one has been fasting, *hein*, my friend? Stand aside and let me pass, if you will be so good. I desire to defrost my frozen bones."

Half an hour later, shaved, showered, clothed and immeasurably cheered, we went out into the hall. "Now for dinner and the ghost of Monsieur Thorowgood!" announced Jules de Grandin.

It was a royal feast our host spread out that night. Besides de Grandin and me there were several people from New York and Philadelphia, a scattering of business associates from Newark and a little man whose name I understood was Bradley, but whose address I did not catch at introduction. Wild duck, shot in the Jersey marshes ten days before and gamed to perfection, stewed green celery tops, quince jelly, spoon bread golden as new-minted coin, and burgundy as mellow as midsummer moonlight, combined to make the dinner a Lucullian banquet, and ten o'clock had sounded on the tall timepiece in the hall and echoed from the banjo clock in the library before the long Madeira cloth was cleared of silver and Wedgewood.

It was with something of the gesture of a prestidigitator ordering silence for his foremost trick that Thorowgood smiled at us benevolently as he turned to Perriby the butler. "Perriby," he ordered, slipping a small key from his watch-chain, "two bottles of the cognac de Napoléon, 1810."

"Mr. Thorowgood, sir, please"—Perriby returned to the dining-room, his florid face slightly paler than its wont, his long, smooth-shaven upper lip tremulous, and with no bottles in his hands—"may I speak with you a moment, sir, in private?"

"What's the matter?—where's that brandy?"

"If you please, sir, I'd rather not go into that smoke house. I thought I saw—"

"Oh, good Lord—you, too? Take a couple of the boys. Take half a dozen, if two aren't enough, and get that brandy."

"Yes, sir." The servant bowed with frigid respect and departed.

"He's brand-new here," Thorowgood half whispered to de Grandin. "I had to get a new outfit last week when Daisy Mullins took her tumble, and I've been as careful as I could to keep this gossip from reaching 'em, but—Lord! I hope the superstitious fools don't shy at their own shadows and drop a bottle of that cognac. That stuff cost me eighteen dollars a fifth, and the only thing needed to set me staring mad would be—"

"Mr. Thorowgood, sir!" The butler was once more at his elbow, and his face was gray with fright.

"Eh? What's the matter now? Don't tell me that you saw—"

"Oh, sir," the servant interrupted, his thick, throaty voice gone high and almost squeaky, "it's Meadows, sir. Meadows, the stable boy. 'E's dead, sir!" Excitement had played havoc with his carefully acquired aspirates, and his h's fell like autumn leaves in Vallambrosa.

"Dead?" Thorowgood repeated.

"Yes, sir. Kilt. You see, I asked 'im and Smith and Little to haccompany me to the smoke 'ouse, like you said, sir, hand they went, though most reluctantly. When I hunlocked the door somethink hinside 'issed at us, as hif it were a snyke, sir. I thought hit might be someone myking gyme of us, hif you don't mind me saying so, sir, and was about to hadmonish 'im, when Meadows, who always was a most wexatious little fighter, hif I may say so, sir, rushed right into the 'ouse, and next hinstant we 'eard 'im scream hand choke, and when I played the flashlight hinto the 'ouse, there 'e lay, all sprawled hout, as you might say, and directly I looked at 'im I knew 'e was—"

"Dead?"

"Quite so, sir. The hother boys are bringin' 'im back now. I ran ahead to tell you—"

"I'll bet you did!" his master cut in grimly. "All right. That'll do." To us:

"Will you examine him, please? It's probable he's only stunned or fainted. Perriby's such a hare-brained fool. . . ."

But the butler's diagnosis was correct. Meadows, undersized and wiry as a jockey or a flyweight fighter, was quite dead, and must have died instantly. His eyes were opened widely, almost forced from their sockets. His mouth gaped slightly and his tongue thrust forth between his teeth, as though death caught him in the act of gagging.

De Grandin took the dead boy's face between his palms and raised his head a little. It was as though the head were coupled to the body by a cord rather than a column of bone and muscle, for there was no resistance as it nodded upward. "Le cou brisé," he told me. "His neck is broken, as if he had been hanged."

"But he wasn't hanged," I insisted, "and there's no mark of violence. Might he not have fallen—"

"Non," he answered positively. "Those eyes, that tongue, the whole expression of his face bear testimony of throttling. Tremendous, sudden pressure was applied, making death almost immediate, and while there was undoubtedly a subconjunctival ecchymosis, it did not have time to show lividity before he died. In an hour, maybe two, we may find bruises. Certainly the autopsy will disclose a fractured hyoid bone as well as broken vertebræ."

"By heaven, this is too much!" Thorowgood stormed when he told him of our findings. "It was bad enough when this ghost hung round the place and scared my servants into fits, but murder is no joke, and murder has been done tonight. I suppose I'll have to notify the police and hold everybody here till they have finished their investigations. Meantime, I'm offering two thousand dollars, spot cash, to anyone who puts the finger on this murderer for me.

"Might as well get it over with, I suppose," he added as he squared his shoulders and went to notify the guests that no one was to leave till given permission by the police.

I T WAS DORIS THOROWGOOD who put the company's consensus into bald words. "Well," she announced, "I'm sorry for poor Meadows and all that, but we can't bring him back by being gloomy. I'm going to dance. Who's with me?"

Apparently they all were, for the radio was soon relaying latest swing selections from New York and Newark, and the faint *wisp-wisp* of thin-soled slippers on the polished floor mingled with the strains of syncopated music.

"Not dancing, gentlemen?" Little Mr. Bradley paused beside us.

De Grandin eyed him coldly. "I think the dead deserve some courtesy, even if he was no more than a mere stable boy," he answered.

"I agree with you, sir. It is an evil thing to dance in a house where death lurks. Indeed, I have a feeling we shall witness more misfortune."

"Specifically?" de Grandin raised his eyebrows quizzically.

"No, not specifically, but generally. The moment I came in this house I felt an atmosphere of menace."

"You are psychic, *Monsieur!*"

"Naturally." From his waistcoat pocket Bradley drew a card which he presented to the Frenchman. Leaning forward I read:

THADDEUS BRADLEY
Clairvoyant

He was a little man, not exactly dwarfish, but so well below the average stature that he scarcely reached de Grandin's chin. He was curiously stooped, too, whether as the result of a crippled shoulder or deliberate pose I could not quite determine. By contrast, he had a large head with a shock of curling black hair, a wide forehead with delicately curved brows, a hooked, assertive nose and dark-brown eyes, set a -thought too close together.

The little Frenchman looked at him with increased interest. "Tell me," he asked, "do you know anything about this house, *Monsieur?* Did Monsieur Thorowgood tell you—"

"Yes, sir, he did. He told me he'd been troubled by some spirit entities which were frightening his servants and had injured one of them. He asked me to come up from Philadelphia and see what I could do to find the ghost, if—"

"Did he say it was a ghost?"

"Well, not exactly. He said the servants said it was a ghost, but he thought it was something human. However, I'm known to possess psychic powers, and if I think the house is haunted-which I do, most certainly—"

Anger kindled in de Grandin's small blue eyes. "When did he summon you?" he interrupted.

"This morning, Doctor. I arrived shortly before noon—"

"*Le cochon, porc!* Does he think he can do this to me?"

"Eh, what's that?"

"Did he not tell you I was coming, that he had engaged my services—"

"Well, now you mention it, he did. Yes, sir. He said you had a reputation as a ghost-breaker, but he wanted to have my opinion, too—"

"*Parbleu*, this is intolerable, this is monstrous, this is not to be endured! He has made me insulted. That I should be spied upon—"

"Oh, now, don't take it that way, sir. I'm sure Mr. Thorowgood meant nothing by it. Just wanted to be sure, you know. It's just as if he called another doctor in for consultation in a case of illness. Anyway, what do we care? He's got to pay us each a fee. He doesn't think there are such thing as ghosts. Let's convince him of his error. Maybe we could hold a séance for him, find the ghost and drive it out then each collect his fee. That way everybody's satisfied—"

Before the rising fury in the Frenchman's eyes he quailed to silence "Charlatan, impostor," de Grandin almost hissed, "you would involve me in a fraud? You would manufacture a ghost to put fear into Monsieur Thorowgood that you may collect a fee—*parbleu*, yes! Why not?"

"Wha—what is it?" stammered Bradley.

"You would hold a séance, *hein*? You would produce a rapping-of-the-table, perhaps go in a trance and relay messages from some defunct Indian sachem? *Très bon*. You shall conduct a séance, my fine friend, but it shall be genuine. Let us see if we can make this evil entity produce himself. Perhaps he will materialize—"

"No, no! Not that, sir. Not me; I can't do that! I'm not a spirit medium; I can contact controls and get through messages—I really can!—but when it comes to trying to materialize—I'm scared to monkey with it. I've seen some things—"

"*Corbleu*, my friend, as yet you have seen nothing. You have your choice. Either you will hold a séance here and now, or I denounce you publicly, tell everyone that you are an impostor who declared he would find a ghost here, whether it—"

"No, no, don't do that, sir; it would ruin me!"

"You are an apt pupil, *mon ami*; you apprehend my meaning perfectly. Which is it to be, a séance or denunciation?"

T HE GUESTS WERE ALL enthusiastic. Dancing might be fun, but a séance, with a dead man practically in the next room . . . "My dear," I heard Letitia Thorowgood exclaim, "it's priceless—definitely! Maybe we can make poor Meadows tell who killed him, and why."

Every stage trick of the charlatan was evident as Bradley prepared for the séance. Lights were turned off in the drawing-room and the adjoining hall, the guests were seated round the wall in a wide circle, with hands joined, and Doris Thorowgood took her place at the piano, softly playing *Abide With Me*. Bradley seated himself at a small table with a nickel-plated paper-knife held upright in his hand. At his request de Grandin played a flashlight's ray upon the knife so that it stood out in the darkness like a lighted tower at night.

"No one is to speak or move until I give permission," cautioned Bradley, gazing fixedly at the knife-point gleaming in the dark.

Silence settled on the room. From the hall outside we heard the pompous, slow tick of the tall clock; softly, softer than the clock-tick, barely audible to us, came the piano's notes:

I fear no harm with Thee at hand to bless,
Ills have no weight and tears no bitterness;
Where is death's sting, where, grave, thy victory? . . .

The paper-cutter wavered, swayed from right to left, and dropped to the floor with a light tinkle. Bradley's eyes closed and his head, leaned back against the chair, fell a little sideways as the neck muscles relaxed.

And in that instant pandemonium broke loose. The music from the hallway banged *fortissimo* in the syncopated strains of *Satan Takes a Holiday*, and from Doris Thorowgood there came a laugh as eery as the blindfold-gropings of a lost mind; a wild, high-mounting burst of mirth that seemed to froth and churn and boil, then change from merriment to torture and geyser up into a stream that rose, flickered like a flame of torment, went up and up until it seemed no human throat could stand its strain, then dropped again until it was a chuckle of indecent glee.

Bradley was on his feet, hugging himself in sudden agony, his tortured face turned up to the groined ceiling, and with a crash as deafening as a thunder-clap every piece of fragile porcelain in a wall-cabinet was dashed down to the floor as though a giant broom had swept it from the shelves.

Then from the hall, foul as a suspiration from a charnel house, a gust of wind came sweeping, incredible, filthy, furious as a cyclone. I retched at it, I heard the man next to me give a gasp and then a gagging choke. This was no mere fetor, it was the very noisome breath of Death, charged with the rottenness of putrefaction stored up since the first beginnings of mortality.

"Lights, lights, *pour l'amour d'un bouc!*" I heard de Grandin shout.

But there were no lights. When Thorowgood shook off his lethargy of disgust and pressed the wall-switch, a sharp *click* sounded, but the room remained as black as Erebus, and meanwhile filthiness unnamable, illimitable terror and disgust, filled the house to stifling overflowing. Coughing, strangling, almost fainting I stumbled to a window and wrenched at it. The sash was firmly set as if built in the masonry.

"*In nomine Domini conjuro te, sceleratissime, abire ad tuum locum!*" de Grandin's conjuration sounded, not loud, but with a force of earnestness more compelling than a shout. Then *crash!* he hurled a flower-bowl through the window. The shattered glass sprayed outward not more from his missile than from the pressure of the nameless, obscene filthiness that filled the house to inundation, and I gasped great lungfuls of revivifying air as a drowning man might fight for precious breath.

From the hallway the piano sounded, beating out its rhythm with the heavy, unaccented tone of an electric mechanism, and in accompaniment to the cacophony of beaten keys and tortured strings the wild, demoniac peals of laughter gushed from Doris' lips.

"Mademoiselle Doris, stop it, I command you!" de Grandin ordered sharply, but still the music sounded stridently, still she laughed like a witch-thing delighted at the success of some hell-brew she had concocted.

"Ha, so? Then this must be the way of it!" He gave her a resounding slap on the right cheek, then turned his hand and struck the other cheek a stinging blow.

The treatment was effective, for she raised her hands from the piano and held them to her smarting face, hysteria gone before the stimulus of sudden pain.

"One regrets heroic measures," he apologized as she looked at him in hurt wonder, "but there are times when they are necessary. This was one of them."

Bradley had fallen on his back and lay quaking spasmodically, hands pressed against his midriff, little buzzing noises sounding from his throat, as though he breathed through some obstruction.

"Up, man, up!" de Grandin cried, seizing him beneath the arms and dragging him up to his feet. "So! Bend over!" He bent the choking fellow forward almost as if he were a swimmer overcome by water, signaled me to hold his head between my hands, and struck him sharply on the back between the shoulders with the heel of his left hand. With the first two fingers of his right hand he traced a cross against the man's bent back, and murmured something in swift Latin of which I caught but a few words: ". . . *Deus, in nomine tuo . . . exorcizo uos . . . uade retro, Satanas . . .*"

Bradley gave a tortured choke, like one about to strangle, and from his lips there came what seemed to be a puff of smoke. But it was no light ethereal vapor, for it plummeted to the floor and hit the polished oak with a soft slap, almost like the smacking of an open hand. For a moment it lay there like a little cone of swirling vapor, or, perhaps a pile of fine-ground powder, but suddenly it appeared to take on semblance of a shape not well defined, but vague and semi-formed, like a mass of colloid substance, or a jelly-fish which had been brought up from the bay. It was hard to define it, for it seemed to shift its outline, flowing, quivering, ever changing, now resembling a splash of albumen, now drawing in upon itself until it was almost a perfect circle, then lengthening until it seemed to be an ovoid.

The thing disgusted me. It seemed like some great spider tentatively stretching out its claws in search of prey. De Grandin seemed to realize its potency for evil, too, for while he kept the beam of the flashlight upon it and muttered Latin conjurations at it through clenched teeth, I noticed that he stood well back from it, as though he feared that it might spring at him. But it did not spring. Rather, it seemed at somewhat of a loss which way to go or what to do until, as if it formed quick resolution, it rolled as swiftly as a drop of mercury released from a thermometer to the shattered window, mounted to the sill so quickly that we had difficulty following its movement, and disappeared into the night.

"What was it?" I asked rather shakily. "I never saw a thing like that before—"

"*Parbleu*, you have not missed much amusement!" the Frenchman answered. "I cannot tell you what it was, my friend, but I know that it was very evil. It was that which killed the poor young Meadows—I would not give a centime for the life of anyone whom it attacked."

"It seemed to come from Bradley's throat—"

"Perfectly. Had we not acted quickly—and been lucky—it would have possessed him completely."

"Possessed? You mean in the Biblical sense?"

"*Précisément*, nothing less; our institutions for the insane are filled with people similarly afflicted."

"Something's choking me," moaned Bradley. "It's in my throat—"

"*Non*, it is no longer there," de Grandin soothed. "You feel the secondary pains, my friend. You fainted but you are all better, now. I should prescribe a glass of brandy. Indeed, I think that I shall join you in the medicine."

"THEN YOU'VE NO IDEA what it could be?" I asked as we prepared for bed.

"On the contrary, I have several. When I first heard Monsieur Thorowgood's account of these strange happenings I was inclined to think he might be right in attributing the so-called phenomena to the servants' superstition or to human agencies. Even the murder of the stable boy might fit in with such a theory. Then this Thaddeus Bradley one accosted us, and I had the idea. 'This person doubtless is a charlatan,' I tell me, 'but he has played at spiritism for a long time. The claims of spiritualism are debatable, to say the least. I have had a wide experience with the occult, but I would not say that it is possible for so-called mediums to get in contact with the spirits of the dead at will. On the other hand, I am convinced that there are many entities, both formed and unformed, who wish to break the barriers between the human and the super-human, or sub-human. For such as these the average medium is a gateway to desire. When he or she is entranced and off guard they enter through the breach left by his absent consciousness, usually with dire results to mankind. Also, although the usual medium is an arrant fraud, the very atmosphere in which he lives is favorable for such spirit-raids. I had no idea this Bradley could evoke the spirit which has worked his mischiefs in this place, but if I could make him go into the mummery of a séance we could get, perhaps, a glimpse of what we are opposed to. Conditions were ideal. Bradley focused all attention on himself, and every mind was intent on some manifestation of the otherworldly. The bars were down, the frontier was unguarded—if some malignant spirit hovered round the house and sought to force an entrance, this was his ideal opportunity. *Eh bien*, he recognized it!

"By his force he made Mademoiselle Doris pliant to his will. By the psychoplasm generated by the concentrated thought of all the company he assumed a sort of form and solidarity, and forced himself right into Bradley's throat. Had we not expelled him he would have found asylum there, fed and fattened on the poor man's physiopsychic substance, gained strength, and, like the fever germ which generates in one body, kills its host, then fares forth for more killing, would in time have issued from poor Bradley's corpse to wreak more havoc in the world."

"You think we've overcome it—whatever it is?"

"That would be a foolish boast at this time. I fear we have but started our campaign. We have balked, but not defeated it. Tomorrow, or the next day, or perhaps the next, we shall come to grips with it."

"You think it may be a malignant ghost, a murderer's, perhaps?"

"It may be, but I do not think so. I have met with such as that upon occasion, and usually they have a sort of pseudo-substance of their own. This one had not, but had to build himself a form of psychoplasm. As yet he is not very strong. He has not the staying power. His strength, by which his capacity for evil is bounded, flows and ebbs, like the tides. Whether he will grow too swiftly for us—"

"Then you think that it's an—"

"An elemental? *Bien oui*. I think that this is what for want of better nomenclature we call a 'spirit,' but it has never lived in human form. Evil, spiteful and dangerous it unquestionably is, but as yet it is evil discarnate. Should it become completely carnate our work will be that much more difficult."

"You've referred to psychoplasm several times. Just what is it?" I asked.

"*Tiens*, what is electricity? We know how to produce it, we can harness it to our needs, we recognize its results when we see them, but we have no definition for it. So with psychoplasm. It is something like the animal magnetism to which Mesmer attributed his success at hypnotism. It seems to be of nervous origin and physiologically connected with the internal secretory organs. As nearly as we can define it, it is an all-penetrating, imponderable emanation which normally is dissipated quickly, but under certain conditions can be stabilized and energized by the intelligence of the living, or by discarnate intelligence. Often, but not always, it is luminous, the spirit-light we see at séances. Less often—*grâce à*

Dieu!—it can in favorable conditions be made the vehicle to transmit force. It was through concrescence of this emanation that they which attacked Bradley became visible. But one wonders—"

He broke off, staring straight before him.

"What is it?"

"Where, by what means, did it get the necessary force to kill the Meadows boy?"

"Why—"

He waved my suggestion aside, and continued, speaking slowly, as though he thought aloud. "*Tenez*, we have more cause for worry. The psychoplasm which is loosed at every séance is the product of the minds of everybody present. It is put forth as a force.

"It leaves the body and the mind. Then what becomes of it? Is it reabsorbed? Perhaps. But does one reabsorb the very psychoplasm he put out? There is the question. We cannot surely say. Once it leaves its power house, or reservoir, it is beyond control of him from whom it emanated. It is quite likely to be seized and directed by"—he checked the possibilities off on his fingers—"stronger wills in the circle at the séance, lower, baser forms of discarnate intelligence, or by true ghosts, the spirits of ex-humans. Mademoiselle Doris was intent upon her music; she was also in a neutral state of mind, half doubting, half expecting something, though she knew not what. Certainly she was not intent on guarding from outside assaults. Thus she was an ideal prey for some mischievous thought-form."

"Great heavens, you think she was possessed, then?"

"No-o, neither possessed nor obsessed."

"What's the difference? I always thought the terms synonymous."

"By no means, not at all. In possession the demon steals the possessed's mind and personality. It is like vampirism, except the vampire animates a corpse; the possessing demon takes a living body from which he has forced its rightful occupant, and uses it for his own ends. In obsession the malignant spirit uses both mind and body of his victim, crippling or misdirecting the mentality, but not entirely ousting it.

"Mademoiselle Doris is nervous and high-strung, selfish, emotional, shallow, inclined to be erratic. When the spirit form attempted to invade her consciousness she gave way physically at once, and played a strain of wild and mocking music, as it bade. Mentally, she closed the bulkheads of her consciousness by going off into hysteria. Obsession has this much in common with hypnotism, it must have a mind on which to operate. No one can hypnotize an idiot or lunatic, neither can an idiot be obsessed. A person in the grip of hysteria is practically insane; therefore she was safe for the time being. But if he comes back to attack her while her mind is off its guard in sleep, or when she is controlled by evil thoughts, as in a fit of anger—*eh bien*, we may find our task a more complex one."

"But do we know it was hysteria and not possession?" I persisted. "That awful, ghoulish laugh and the expression on her face seemed scarcely human—"

He nodded thoughtfully. "Your question is well put, my friend. But did not you notice how she came back to her senses when I slapped her in the face?"

"Yes, but—"

"No buts, if you will be so kind. In the possessed state the victim is unconscious of deeds done and words said. Thus far your case is good, but it is also true that one possessed is markedly insensitive to pain. The demon sitting at the wheel can feel no pain inflicted on the body he possesses; *alors*, we find a state of anesthesia in the possessed or obsessed. Hot objects may be handled with impunity, electric shocks are not felt.

"But was it so with Mademoiselle Doris? *Non*. I did not strike her hard, although I struck her sharply. Had she been truly possessed I might have beat her till her face was bloody, yet she would not have ceased her playing or her diabolic laughter. You see?"

"Yes, I suppose so. What's our next move?"

He patted back a yawn. "At present, *mon vieux*, I have a rendezvous with Morpheus. Á *bientôt*."

Beachwood Hospital where Daisy Mullins' broken clavicle was mending was a private institution with no wards and only about a hundred beds. As we strode along the corridor amid the faint but all-pervading atmosphere of antiseptics, drugs and shut-in humanity, I reflected Thorowgood had not been niggardly in providing treatment for his injured maid.

"Queer thing about that girl," said Doctor Broemel as he piloted us down the hallway, "she's not in much pain—it's just a simple fracture and it's healing beautifully—but her nerves are shot to pieces. She hardly speaks except to keep imploring us for a night nurse. That's absurd, of course. She doesn't need a night nurse any more than I need feather dusters on my heels. Of course, a tumble down a flight of stairs is quite a shock, but she should be well out of it by now. She's been here five days, and besides the broken clavicle and some slight contusions on the head she's as sound as a nut."

"Does she give reasons for desiring a night nurse?" de Grandin asked.

"No, she doesn't. Just keeps saying she's afraid to be left alone—with four nurses within twenty feet of her! Queer things, women patients."

"You are imparting information to us?" de Grandin answered as we stopped before the door to Daisy's room.

The place was all white tile and white enamel, with a narrow bed of spotless white. Daisy Mullins was half propped to a sitting posture, one hand strapped across her chest, a band of white gauze wound around her injured head, another bandage drawn beneath her chin to hold the first one firm. Somehow, with the

wimple-like white cloths about her head and face, she had the look of a young
nun, a nun carved out of tallow. Her cheeks seemed absolutely bloodless, so did
her lips; her eyes seemed far too large for her countenance, and though they
were light blue they seemed dark and cavernous against the pallor of her face.
She glanced at us without interest. Indeed, I could not say she looked at us at
all. Rather, it seemed, she was trying to see something just beyond her range of
vision, and feared with desperate fear that she might sight it. It would be hard to
make her tell us anything, I thought.

De Grandin laid the flowers and the huge box of bonbons he had brought
upon the bedside table, and stood gazing at her for a moment. Then, with his
quick, infectious smile, "*Mademoiselle*, we have come to ask your help in fighting
it," he announced.

The fear in her was suddenly a live thing, writhing like a wounded snake
behind her eyes. "It?" she echoed in a whisper.

"Precisely. It. We cannot call it him or her; it is a thing—a very naughty
thing, but we shall beat it, with your help."

"You can't fight it, it's no use. How can you fight a thing that you can't even
see?"

"Ah, that is what you think, but you do not know me. I am a very clever
person. I have neither fear of it nor doubt that I can conquer it, but I need your
help. Will you not give it to me?"

"What d'ye want me to do?"

"Only tell us all about your accident—*non*, I mean your injury. Precisely how
did it happen? We must know about this thing we are to fight, how it looked—"

"I tell you it didn't look at all. I couldn't see it. Only feel—and smell—it!"

"But if you could not see it, *Mademoiselle*, is it not possible that you fell down
the stairs—"

"I didn't trip, I didn't fall; it threw me." The dammed-back memories of her
ordeal flooded to her lips and she spoke rapidly, as if she had to finish in a given
time. "It was last Wednesday morning, when I was takin' Miss Doris' breakfast
tray up. I was goin' up the back stairs, and had reached the landin' on the second
floor when it set on me. I didn't see nothin', there wasn't anything to see; but all
at once I felt a pair o' hands about my throat, shakin' me till I dropped the tray,
and then it threw me down the stairs so hard I tumbled half a dozen somersets as
I went down, and then I must 'a' fainted, for the next thing I knew—"

"Quite yes, we know what happened next, but what of your assailant? Is it
dark at the hall landing?"

"No, sir. It's quite light, for there's a window at the stair turn, and the sun was
shinin'. If anything had been there I'd 'a' seen it, but there wasn't nothin' there,
just an awful smell and then the hands around my throat—"

"Hands, *Mademoiselle*?"

"Well, no, sir, not exactly hands. It was more like someone wrapped a loop o' Turkish towel around me, and drew it tight an' sudden. A wet, cold towel, sir."

"And what kind of smell was it?"

"Dreadful, sir. It like to smothered me—like sumpin' dead."

"Which did you notice first, the smell or the choking sensation?"

She wrinkled her smooth bandaged brow a moment, then: "I think it was the smell. I remember thinkin' that a rat must 'a' crawled into the walls and died, and just then it grabbed me."

De Grandin tweaked the waxed ends of his mustache. "A frightful smell, a choking grasp upon your throat, a blow that knocked you down the stairs," he recapitulated. "It was a most unpleasant experience—"

"An' that's not all, sir."

"No? What then?"

"It was here last night!"

"Name of a small blue man! Here, you say?"

"Yes, sir, that it was. I woke up last night about half-past nine, and smelt it in the room. Then, just as I was fixin' to cry out it snatched the bed-clothes off'n me an' piled 'em on my face. I know I wasn't dreamin', sir. How could I pull my covers off and put 'em on my face? They're tucked in at the foot and sides, and I'm that helpless with my arm strapped up against me—"

"It is because of this you want a night nurse?" he broke in.

"Yes, sir. I'm scared. I'm terrible scared o' it."

"Very well, then you shall have one. I shall speak about it as we leave, and see you have a nurse with you all night."

"Oh, gee, thanks, sir!" The tired blood washed back in her wan cheeks. "I'll feel lots safer, now."

"THIS IS THE CRAZIEST business I ever heard of," I declared as we drove from the hospital. "There's no sense to any of it. Swan Upping's never had the reputation of being haunted, and certainly there's nothing about the Thorow-goods to attract ghostly visitants. Scott's as pragmatic as the iron pipe he man-ufactures, and from what I've seen of them I'd say that neither of his daughters is interested in anything appertaining to spirits, except the kind cocktails are made of. Why should a ghost move in on them?"

He nodded. "Why, indeed?"

"And it's such a silly, clownish sort of ghost. Scaring servants, snatching blankets off the beds, smashing crockery—"

"And killing people," he put in.

"Exactly. And killing people. If it confined itself to buffoonery or to malig-nancy I could understand it, but it seems like a peevish child turned loose in a toy shop. First it plays stupid, prankish tricks; then it kills as ruthlessly as a spoiled child might smash a toy; then goes back to silly, beetle-headed capers. Sometimes it's good-natured, sometimes vicious—"

"*Non.* There you make the mistake, *mon vieux.* It is never good-natured; always it is malignant."

"Why, but—"

"Consider, if you please: everything it does brings some measure of discomfort to someone, whether it be but the annoyance of knocking pots and pans and plates off of the kitchen shelves, tweaking bed-clothes off of sleepers, throwing a poor, frightened girl downstairs, or breaking the neck of a stable boy. You have compared it to a naughty child. A *juste titre.* Have you ever seen a small, dull-witted, rather vicious child play with a fly? Have you observed how he pulls off its wings, then watches it intently as it crawls in agony, thereafter pulling off its legs, one at a time, and pausing between torments to observe its helpless antics? Finally, you will recall, he kills it; not to put a period to its sufferings—oh, no—merely because he has grown tired of the cruel sport and can think of nothing else to do. There is playfulness of a sort in such actions, but there is a viciousness and cruelty, too. Does not all this remind you of the harmless pranks, as you have called them, of this poltergeist?"

Little chills of apprehension had begun to chase each other up my spine as he talked. To be confined in a house with an unseen but powerful malignancy, to be the subject of oafish experiments of a thing with the mentality of a four-year-old moron and the strength of a gorilla . . . "Is there any way for us to overcome this thing?" I asked.

For several seconds he did not reply, gazing straight before him, thoughtful-eyed, tapping out a devil's tattoo on the silver handle of his cane. At last: "The thing confronting us is technically a poltergeist, though it displays some aspects I have not seen in such phenomena before. The distinguishing characteristics of poltergeist hauntings are aimless violence unaccompanied by materialization of the manifesting entity. Generally these mischievous phenomena are associated directly or indirectly with children, adolescents, old, fragile people or those whose strength has been reduced by long illness. The skeptic's explanation is to attribute mischief or a desire to mystify or to be revenged on someone by the child, the invalid or the old one. However, it has been demonstrated that if the child or invalid suspected be removed and an accredited medium substituted, the disturbing manifestations will be continued as effectively as ever." He paused a moment, as if reaching out for loose thought-threads, and:

"Let's see if I understand you," I broke in. "A child, or someone in poor health, is generally associated with the antics of a poltergeist. Is there any explanation?"

"We cannot say, exactly. On a few occasions people in poor health, especially sufferers from enervating fevers or chronic disorders, have been seen to glow with, or exude, faint luminosity. This is scientifically attested. The haloes traditionally associated with the saints were not due to artists' whims, nor, as has sometimes been suggested, to poetic reference to the Pentecostal flames which shone on the Apostles. The records of the early and mediaeval church testify that people noted for their piety and asceticism were often seen to radiate luminous auras. What the connection between bodily frailty and the emanation of this light may be we do not know; we only know there seems to be some. But may we not assume this luminosity is akin to astral light, psycho-physical in origin, and identical with psychoplasm? I think so. *Très bon.* The weakling child, the frail old man or woman, the invalid, can supply this force, then—"

"What about the adolescents? They are not often very frail—"

"*Précisément.* But they are peculiar people. We might almost say they are a third sex. As a physician you know of the derangement of the mind and body which accompanies adolescence; no one knows better that 'the long, long thoughts of youth' are often thoughts of suicide. The powerful derangements of our complex human organism accompanying adolescence make the boy or girl at that stage an ideal source of psychoplasm."

"But why the spiritualistic medium? They're mostly grown men and women; childish-minded, often, and sometimes rather frail, but—"

"Quite yes. But the medium who does not exude psychoplasm is no medium at all. Whether one is mediumistic because he is supplied with superabundant psychoplasm, or whether he is thus well stocked with it because he is a medium is as profitless to discuss as the question of priority between the chicken and the egg. *En tout cas*, mind cannot affect matter without the intervention of a human intermediary, whether it be a child, an invalid, an adolescent or a medium. One of these is always present. He supplies the needed psychoplasm to make the manifestation possible, serves as dynamo to generate the necessary energy—"

"But you just said that poltergeists do not materialize."

"*Bien oui.* Ordinarily they do not; also ordinarily they are harmless, though annoying. This one is very far from harmless, this one has partially materialized, and may succeed in doing so entirely. *Alors*, we can but reason by analogy. We cannot treat this as an ordinary poltergeist, nor can we look on it as a malignant strangler merely.

"We must adapt our strategy to meet unusual conditions, and proceed most carefully."

A note lay on de Grandin's dressing-table:

Dear Doctor: After what occurred in this house last night I do not dare stay here another minute. I am convinced the whole place reeks with evil and probably is haunted by a savage elemental which has but one desire, to work harm to humanity. Only fire can cleanse a place so fearfully attainted, and

I have advised Mr. Thorowgood to burn the whole place, house, furniture and furnishings, without delay. Only by so doing can he hope to rid the neighborhood of a deadly peril, and it is my opinion that if he remains here with his family or permits this house to be inhabited, dreadful tragedy will result. For Mr. Thorowgood's sake, as well as your own, I hope you will add your advice to mine, and urge on him the need for acting quickly.

Yr. obt. svt.
Thaddeus Bradley.

"Well, what about it?" I demanded as I passed the letter back to him. "I've always heard that fire's a cure for hauntings."

His thrifty Gallic soul was horrified at the suggestion. "Burn this fine house, this so exquisite furniture? But no, I will not hear of it. We do not know just how this thing came in, nor why, but if it entered it can leave. Our problem is to provide an exit."

"Do you think it's an elemental?"

"*Je ne sais pas.* It may be so. The aimlessness of its violence indicates a very low mentality, and yet—" He broke off, staring into space.

"Yes?" I prompted.

"Have you not noticed an increasing method in its acts? At first it seemed experimenting, trying out its power; then when it had thrown the Mullins girl downstairs it murdered Meadows, then sought to give itself a ponderable form, to force an entrance into Monsieur Bradley's body. What will its next move be, more killing or a fresh effort to materialize? Which would you do, were you a poltergeist?"

"If I were a polt— don't be absurd!"

"I was never more serious, my friend. Conceive yourself as evil, infinitely evil, loving wickedness for its own sake and desiring above everything to gain strength that you might work more harm. What would you do?"

"Why, I suppose I'd try to draw vitality from some fresh victim. There's no strength to be had from the dead—"

"*Par la barbe d'un bouc vert!* Why had I not considered that? Come, my friend, let us hasten, let us rush, let us fly!"

"Where, in heaven's name—"

"To the hospital. At once. And we do go in heaven's name, too."

"You are invaluable, incomparable, my old one," he assured me as the big car gathered speed. "Had you not given me the suggestion—"

"Whatever are you talking of?"

"Of you, my priceless old one, and the hint that you let fall unwittingly. Did not you say, 'There's no strength to be had from the dead'?"

"Of course. Is there?"

"How do we know it? Who can say? In common with all discarnate intelligences, this thing we are opposed to gains strength from body emanations. Someone in that house had furnished these until it found itself sufficiently supplied with force to throw the poor young Mullins person down the stairs, to kill the so unfortunate young Meadows, finally to brave us all at the séance and make a bold attempt to take the Bradley person's body by assault. Is that not so?"

"Why, I suppose so, but—"

"No buts, I do entreat you. Where else had it been yesternight? At half-past nine, to be specific?"

"Why, you can't mean the—"

"By blue, I do. I do, indeed! At half-past nine the Mullins girl was wakened by its noisome stink and felt it snatch the covers from her. She was its point of contact. It had handled her before, had overcome her. Is it not probable it had its motivating psychoplasm from her at the first?

"*Bien.* Let that question pass. We can return to it anon. What interests us immediately is that in a place devoted to the sick, the dying and the dead it would have found a feast of strength-imparting emanations, and that within half an hour of its visit there it returned to Swan Upping to do the poor young Meadows man to death.

"Now, attend me: Granted that such things thrive on vital force exuded from the human body, can we say with certainty—can we say at all, indeed—the flow of such force stops with death? Certainly, it continues during sleep. Is it not possible that the very process of disintegration of the body strengthens it? We know there are two kinds of death, somatic and molecular. A man 'dies' legally and perhaps medically when his respiration ceases and his heart stops beating. But though the man is dead his individual cells live on for varying periods. The brain, for instance, lives in this way for a possible ten minutes, while the muscle of the heart may survive twice that long. As for the hair-roots and the nails, they are the same a week succeeding death as they were when it occurred. Why should these emanations stop at death? The graves of saints become the shrines where miracles are wrought; many of the most revolting vampire phenomena are associated with unhallowed tombs. Why could not this thing have stored up energy from the sick, the dying and the dead in that hospital, then, after killing Meadows, used the vital force set free by him as rigor mortis crept upon him—"

"That's too fantastic—"

"*Parbleu,* the whole thing is fantastic! The fantastic seems to be the commonplace. Should things keep on as they are going, only the commonplace will be fantastic, I damn think!"

"IS THERE GOOD REASON for retaining the young Mullins woman here, *Monsieur?*" he questioned Doctor Broemel.

"Actually, there isn't, Doctor," Broemel answered. "Naturally, she's more comfortable here with our facilities than she would be at home, but she's certainly sufficiently advanced to go, if you desire it."

"*Merci beaucoup*," de Grandin smiled.

Five minutes later, as we entered Daisy's room:

"*Mademoiselle*, we have the pleasant tidings for you. It has been decided that you leave the hospital—"

"But I can't do that, sir. I have no home. I'd been livin' in a furnished room in New York before I came down here in October, and I don't think Mr. Thorowgood will want me round the place, unable to dress myself, and everything—"

"*Ah bah*, you make the mistake. It is not to Swan Upping that you go, nor to a furnished room, but to an hotel at Asbury Park. A nurse will go with you to see that you are taken care of; arrangements will be made with a physician at the shore to inspect the progress of your healing fracture, and you shall stay there as the guest of Monsieur Thorowgood until you are all well. Are not those joyous tidings?"

The girl burst into tears. "Y-you mean he's doing all this just for me and my salary goes on, too, just like he said it would?"

"Indubitably, *Mademoiselle*."

"When do I leave?"

"At once. As soon as you can get your clothes on. A motor is waiting to convey you to the shore."

"Oh, sir," she sobbed happily, "I'll never be able to tell him how delighted and surprised I am—"

"*Corbleu*," de Grandin chuckled as we left the hospital, "I damn think he will be the surprised one, although, perhaps, he will not be delighted, when he learns what I have done in his name."

"What's our next move?" I asked as we drove back to Swan Upping.

"To ask some questions of Monsieur Thorowgood. One part of my surmise has proved correct. Undoubtlessly it was the Mullins girl from whom this haunting thing drew strength. You heard her say she came here in October. That must have been soon after Monsieur Thorowgood moved in. She is the perfect type, thin, inclined to anemia, undernourished. It was from her he drew his first vitality. Yes, certainly."

"Then why did he turn on her—"

"*Tiens.* He had no further use for her. He had gained sufficient strength from her to go about his own nefarious business; accordingly, he cast her away, literally."

"Yes," Thorowgood told us, "the house was practically rebuilt, but we used old material as much as possible. The addition to the north wing where the servants' quarters are, and the smoke house which we use for wine cellar, were entirely built of old red brick and old timber. They've pre-served the weathered colors beautifully, haven't they? No one would guess they weren't a part of the original house—"

"By blue, my friend, you would be surprised at things which people guess!" de Grandin interrupted. "Can you tell us where these bricks and timbers came from?"

"Why, yes. I picked 'em up at Blakeley's lumber yard at Toms River."

"Ah-ha, we make the progress. Excuse us, if you please. We go to interview this Monsieur Blakely."

His little round blue eyes were dancing with excitement; every now and then he gave a chuckle as we drove pell-mell toward Toms River.

"What are you so pleased about?" I asked. "You look like the cat that's just dined on the canary."

"Not quite, my friend," he answered with an impish grin. "Say rather that I look like one about to dine upon roast poltergeist." He raised his hands before him and brought them slowly toward each other. "We have him in a vise. Why did he trouble no one but the servants? Why was it that he failed to annoy guests or family Until last night? Because he was a snob? *Mais non.* Because the servants' quarters and the smoke house where the so unfortunate young Meadows met his death were built of olden brick and timber—"

"What has that to do with it? The bricks and timbers of the main house are old as those they built the north wing and the smoke house with—"

"*Mais certainement,* but of a different origin undoubtlessly. Regard me, if you please:

"Thoughts are things. We cannot see or touch or weigh them, but they are things. They have the power to impress themselves upon inanimate objects, on sticks and stones and bricks, and like wheat buried with the mummy they may lie dormant for an age, then sprout to life when given new and favorable environment. The sorcerer who treasures earth from an unhallowed grave or the rope which hanged some master criminal is practising more than mere symbolism, I assure you.

"Again: In every case of poltergeist activities we find that two things are essential, physical limits, as of walls, and some mediumistic person to transform the stored-up evil force from static to dynamic. Here we have the ideal combination, bricks and boards and timbers which undoubtlessly have been in contact with some evil-living, evil-thinking persons, and a source of psychoplasm—Daisy Mullins—to energize the accumulated force, to focus it and make it possible for it to have a physical and fulminant effect."

"Aren't you taking a lot for granted?"

He fairly glowered at me. "When you see a patient with high temperature,

nose-bleed, abdominal tenderness and distension and an inclination toward profound lethargy, do you have to take a blood test, must you see the typhosus bacil-
lus in your microscope before you decide he is suffering from enteric fever and
begin appropriate treatment? Of course not. So in this case. So many diagnostic
factors are apparent that I have no hesitancy in predicting what we shall learn
when we speak with the peerless lumberman at Toms River."

"SURE, I REMEMBER THAT junk," the Blakeley foreman said. "It lay around
our yard ten years. I thought that we were stuck with it for keeps till Mr.
Thorowgood saw it."

"Ah, yes, and could you tell us where it came from?"

"Sure. Centermead, Doc Bouton's sanitarium. The old man ran a private
bughouse there for close on thirty years, and went crazy as a basketful o' eels
before he finally killed hisself. Say, how'd you 'a' liked to be shut up in a nut college with the doctor loony as a chinch-bug, beatin' up an' torturin' the patients,
an' even killin' 'em, sometimes?"

Jules de Grandin drew a deep breath. "By damn, I can inform the cross-eyed
world such treatment would have driven off my goat," he answered solemnly.

The foreman was still gaping when we drove away.

"You see, it matches perfectly," he said triumphantly. "Every necessary element is present. The long association with the mad—the living dead—the lust-
ful cruelty of a doctor who had yielded up his sanity through contact with the
sick in mind, the suffering, the torture, the despair. . . . But yes, could these
bricks and timbers speak they would relate a tale to give us nightmare of the soul
for many years to come. It is small wonder that the haunting influence acts with
low intelligence; it is the tincture, the very distillate of compressed madness with
which these bricks are saturated to the overflowing point. All that was needed
was the energizing force supplied by Daisy Mullins."

"And what do we do next?"

"*Mais cela parle tout seul*—the thing speaks for itself. We have but to demolish that north wing and smoke house, remove the source of the infection, and
the hauntings will be cured. My friend, this Jules de Grandin is one devilish
clever fellow. Is he not?"

"I've heard you say so," I returned.

A wrecking-crew was already at work when we caught the solitary eastbound
train for Harrisonville next morning.

"DOCTOR DE GRANDIN?" A Western Union messenger accosted us as we
drew up before my house. "I have an urgent message for you."

The missive was brief with telegraph terseness, but imperative: "Men unable
to continue work because of accidents stop need your advice immediately."

"Take the extension and listen as we talk, if you please," he asked me as he rang up Thorowgood. "I should like to have you hear the conversation.

"*Allo?*" as the connection was made. "It is I, de Grandin. What seems to be the matter, if you please?"

"Plenty," Thorowgood answered tersely. "You'd hardly left when things began to happen. A workman fell off the roof and broke his leg. He swore somebody pushed him, but I smelled liquor on his breath, so I can't be sure o' that. Then another man got a broken arm when half a dozen bricks fell on him; one of 'em hit his foot with a pick-ax and nearly cut it off. The place looked like a battlefield, and the men quit cold. Told me to go jump in the lake when I offered double time if they'd stay on the job. What're we going to do?"

"*Eh bien*, he is of the obduracy, this one. He does not take his ouster calmly."

"See here, this is no time to wisecrack. This thing has hurt a girl, killed a man and injured half a dozen others. Now it takes possession of my house. How're we going to get rid of it?"

"I would suggest you leave him in possession overnight. Move your entourage to an hotel, and come back tomorrow morning with a fresh crew of workingmen prepared to dynamite the walls. Also, bring back the young Mullins girl. I have need of her. Doctor Trowbridge and I will motor down and meet you I at Swan Upping in the morning. *Au 'voir*, my friend.

"You will excuse me?" he asked as he put the monophone back in its cradle. "I have work to do. There are authorities to be consulted and *matériel* to be collected. I shall be back for dinner."

It was not until dessert that he spoke concerning his work of the afternoon. Then, irrelevantly: "You know the works of Judge Pursuivant?" he asked.

"Who?"

"The very learned, very able, very well-informed Keith Hilary Pursuivant. What a scholar, what a man! His book *The Unknown that Terrifies* is worth the ransom of an emperor to any occultist. I read him this afternoon, and in him I found comfort. Silver, says the learned Judge, is specific protection against every form of evil. You apprehend?"

"Was that bundle you brought home some magic formula of his?"

"Not precisely," he grinned. "*Monsieur le Juge* supplied the thought, I follow his suggestion. I secured a supply of silver wire and netting."

"Silver wire—for goodness sake!"

"*Précisément, mon vieux.* For goodness' sake, no less."

"But why silver? Wouldn't any other metal do as well?"

"By no means. Silver, as the learned judge has pointed out, with a number of citations, is a potent force against all evil. Iron, most earthly of all metals, is abhorrent to the ghostly tribe, so much so that when Solomon King of Israel reared his temple to the Most High God with the help of Hiram King of

Tyre and that great architect Hiram the Widow's Son, no tool of iron was heard to ring throughout the building operation, since they were helped by friendly *djinn* who could not have abided in the neighborhood of sharpened iron. But for discarnate evil, evil vague and without definition, silver is the better metal. Ghostly foes incapable of being killed to death with leaden bullets, witches, werewolves and vampires, all are vulnerable to silver shot. Does not your own Monsieur Whittier, who was a very learned man as well as a great poet, mention it? But certainly. In his narrative of the garrison beleaguered by a phantom foe he relates:

> "Ghosts or witches," said the captain, "thus I foil the Evil One!"
> And he rammed a silver button from his doublet down his gun.

"And you expect to overcome this powerful thing with silver netting and some wire?" I asked incredulously.

"I expect to overcome him in that manner," he replied in a flat, toneless voice, fixing an unwinking stare of challenge on me.

THE SCENE WHICH GREETED us at Swan Upping was reminiscent of a circus about to strike camp. Two trucks stood idling on the rear driveway; a crew of wreckers waited to commence work; back and to one side was a small red wagon with the word EXPLOSIVES lettered ominously on its sides and front.

"*Très bon.* All is prepared, I see," de Grandin smiled. "Where is the Mullins girl, if you please?"

"Waiting there with the nurse," Thorowgood waved toward a limousine.

"Ah, yes. Will you excuse me while I persuade her?" For some five minutes he engaged her in a whispered conversation, then came hurrying back to us. "She has consented, it is well," he told us as he cut the wrappings of his parcel.

His preparations were made quickly. A bed of blankets was laid in the partially demolished smoke house and Daisy Mullins lay on it. Working deftly he enveloped her in length on length of silver-wire gauze, laminating each fold on the next until she was encased in the light netting like a mummy in its wrappings. Only at her mouth did he permit an opening, and over this he hinged a little door of netting and tied a length of thread to it.

"*Bien,*" he patted her encouragingly. "I shall be but little longer, *Mademoiselle.*"

With heavier silver wire he wove a basket-like covering for her, leaving something like six inches between her body and the cage.

"You are quite comfortable?" he asked. She nodded, looking at him with wide eyes in which her confidence in him was struggling with abysmal fear. From the pocket of his jacket he drew a little mirror to which a string had been attached. This he twisted round his left forefinger, permitting the glass to hang pendulumwise. "Eyes upon the mirror, if you please," he ordered, as he began to swing it slowly back and forth.

"Tick—tock; tick—tock!" he recited in a monotone, keeping time to the slow oscillation of the glass. "The clock is ticking, Mademoiselle, slowly, slowly, ver-ry slowly. Tick—tock; tick—tock; you are ver-ry tired. You are so very weary you must sleep; sleep is the thing you most desire. Sleep and rest, rest and sleep. Tick—tock; tick—tock!"

The girl's eyes wavered back and forth, following the gleaming arc the mirror marked, but as he droned his monody they became heavy-lidded, finally closed. "Sleep—sleep," he whispered. "Tick—tock; sleep—sleep!"

"Now what—" I began, but he silenced me with a fierce gesture and stood looking at the sleeping girl intently.

For perhaps two minutes he stood statue-still regarding her; then carefully, like one who tiptoes through a room where a restless sleeper lies, he bent down, took a length of silver wire in his right hand, and grabbed the thread attached to the hinged door above her mouth. "Regardez, s'il vous plaît!" he whispered almost soundlessly.

I started, but kept silent. From between her lightly parted lips a little thread of vapor issued. "Breath," I told myself. "It's cold today . . ."

But it was not breath. Scarcely thick enough for liquid, it was yet too ponderable to be called vapor, and seemed to have a semi-solid, gelatinous consistency. Too, it flowed in quasi-liquid fashion across her lower lip, but with a quivering instability, like quicksilver. Then it seemed to lighten and assume a gaseous buoyancy and hover in midair above her. It was taking form, too, of a sort, not definite, but shifting, changing, seeming to flow and melt upon itself and, ameba-like, to put forth gastropodal extensions of its substance. Like an animalculum in tainted water it floated driftingly above the girl's lips, joined to her lightly opened mouth by a ligament of smoky-seeming semi-fluid; waxing larger every second. In the quarter light of the smoke house it gleamed and glistened with a putrid phosphorescent glow. Gradually, insensibly at first, but growing stronger every instant, the foul effluvium of its overpowering stench spread through the place, fulsome, nauseous, sickening.

"I think that is enough, me," de Grandin said, and gave the string he held a sharp pull. The hinged deadfall above the girl's face-covering dropped, shearing through the foggy wisp that issued from her lips. The inchoate, amorphous thing that floated over her suddenly contracted, bent its finger-like extensions in upon itself, like a spider curling up when sprayed with an insecticide. Then it bounced toward de Grandin as surely and purposefully as though it saw him and intended to attack him.

He raised his two-foot length of silver wire like a sword, but its protection was unneeded. The almost shapeless mass of foulness that rushed at him struck full against the silver cage that he had woven over Daisy, and, as if it struck a spring, bounced back again.

There was something fascinating, and revolting, in its antics. It was like one of those toys of the physical laboratory called Cartesian devils which, as the membranes of their bottles are pressed down or released, rise, sink or float according to the pressure. Up it surged until it struck the wire cage; then down again it recoiled till it touched the silver netting which he had wrapped round the girl. Then up it rushed again, only to be driven back by contact with the silver cage.

"*Dans les mâchoires de l'étau!* I have you in the vise, my most unpleasant one!" de Grandin cried triumphantly. "Take her up, Friend Trowbridge; help me with her, if you will."

Carefully we lifted the unconscious girl and bore her to the waiting car. As we came out into the light I noticed that the foul thing hovering over her became transparent, almost invisible. But its overpowering stench remained to tell us it was there.

ELECTRIC DRILLS WORKED FURIOUSLY, dynamite was placed at proper intervals, and at a signal battery plungers were thrust down. There was a detonation and a rumbling roar, and walls and roofs of servants' quarters and smoke house came toppling down in ruins.

The wreckers worked with methodical speed. Load after load of shattered brick and timber was piled upon the trucks and hustled to the river, Humped into the turbid, frosty water, and replaced by other loads. By noon the wreckage had been cleared away, and only empty gaping cellars and a brash of broken bricks and mortar told where the structures had been.

"Stand back, my friends!" de Grandin ordered. "I am about to liberate him!"

Holding a lash of wire defensively, he bent and wrenched an opening in the cage above the sleeping girl.

"Begone, avaunt, aroint thee, naughty thing!" he commanded, switching vigorously at the almost invisible globular shape that hovered in midair above her body.

There was a flicker, as of unseen lightning, and a soughing *whish!* as if a sudden strong wind blew past us. In a moment the foul odor faded, growing fainter every instant. Before five minutes had elapsed it had disappeared.

"And that, my friends," he told us, "is indubitably that."

THE DINNER HAD BEEN perfect as only the inspired chef of the Reading Club could make it. Oysters and champagne, turtle soup with dry sherry, sole with chablis, partridge with Château Lafite . . . de Grandin passed a lotus-bud shaped brandy snifter back and forth beneath his nose and turned his eyes up to the ceiling with a look of ecstasy. *"What is it that the vintners buy one-half so precious as the stuff they sell?"* he misquoted Omar Khayyám.

"Never mind the poetry," Thorowgood commanded. "How'd you do it? I know you put it over, but—"

"But it was so simple, *Monsieur*," supplied Jules de Grandin. "Simple like the binomial theorem or the hypothesis of the Herr Professor Einstein. Yes." He warmed the glass between his cupped palms, inhaled again, then drank as if it were a solemn rite he practised.

"My friend Judge Pursuivant gave me the necessary hint," he added. "Granted silver would repulse this thing, we were enabled to confine it while we wrecked the buildings from which it emanated. So we put the Mullins girl in his way, enabled him to half-materialize, and then—*eh bien*, he was excessively annoyed when he found what we had done to him, *n'est-ce-pas?*

"It required but a brief investigation to find that these bricks and timbers came from an old house where evil had run riot. Evil thoughts, evil sentiments, evil instincts, despair and violent death had washed those bricks like ocean waves. They were saturated with it. They were very reservoirs of wicked power, waiting only for some mediumistic help to bring them into focus, just as sunlight needs a burning-glass to enable it to start a fire. This focussing medium was supplied—all unconsciously—by the poor Mullins girl. The static power of evil became dynamic force by use of psychoplasm which it stole from her. You thwarted it when you removed her to the hospital, but it pursued her thither, renewed its strength killed the stable boy and almost took possession of the Bradley person's body. When we removed her from the hospital its source of energy was weakened, but it still had strength enough to fight the wreckers off.

"Then I took counsel with myself. We would bring the Mullins girl to it. We would place her in a deep, hypnotic sleep. There was its chance. It could not resist the opportunity of strengthening itself from her. Ha, but it did not take me into its calculations! I had made arrangements, me. Her I enclosed in silver netting, so it could not do her injury. Only her mouth did I leave unprotected, and as soon as it had partially materialized so we could see it, I dropped the trap across its source of energy, and left it high and dry, unable to retreat, unable to go forward, hemmed in on every side by silver. Then while we held him incommunicado we pulled down his nest about his ears. We robbed him of his power house, his source of potency.

"Experience has taught us that a poltergeist cannot operate without material limits, such as walls, and neither can he operate without an energizing medium. We may compare him to gunpowder. Drop it loose upon the earth and nothing happens. Touch fire to it and it goes up in harmless flame and smoke. But confine it in a twist of paper, and touch fire to it, and *pouf!* we have the grand

Fourth of July explosion. So with the poltergeist. The walls are to him as the paper covering is to the squib, *le pétard*, the—how do you call him?—the crack-er-of-fire? Very well. It needs then but the medium to set him off, and there he is. Unconfined, he is harmless. Remember how those bricks lay for ten years in Monsieur Blakeley's lumber yard and nothing untoward happened? That was because they lay in the open. But when you built them into solid walls—"

"D'ye think it'll be safe to have that Mullins girl around the house? She's been a faithful little thing, standing by me when the other servants ran out, but—"

"You need not distress yourself, *Monsieur*. The evil-saturated bricks have been dumped in the river. They are no longer a potential source of harm. Just as the poltergeist could not function without her, she cannot energize a power which is not present."

"Where do you suppose that poltergeist force went?" I put in.

"*Tenez*, who can say? Where does the flame go when one blows the candle out? He is obliterated, dispersed, swallowed up—*comme ça!*"

He raised the brandy snifter to his lips and drained it at a gulp.

The House Where Time Stood Still

T HE FEBRUARY WIND WAS holding carnival outside, wrenching at the window fastenings, whooping round the corners of the house, roaring bawdy chansons down the chimney flues. But we were comfortable enough, with the study curtains drawn, the lamps aglow and two fresh oak logs upon the andirons taking up the blazing torch their dying predecessors flung them. Pleased with himself until his smugness irritated me, Jules de Grandin smiled down at the toe of his slim patent-leather pump, took a fresh sip of whisky-soda, and returned to the argument.

"But no, my friend," he told me, "medicine the art is necessarily at odds with medicine the science. As followers of Æsculapius and practitioners of the healing art we are concerned with individual cases, in alleviating suffering in the patient we attend. We regard him as a person, a complete and all-important entity. Our chief concern for the time being is to bring about his full recovery, or if that is not possible, to spare him pain as far as in our power lies, *n'est-ce-pas?*"

"Of course," I rejoined. "That's the function of the doctor—"

"*Mais non.* Your term is poorly chosen. That is the function of the physician, the healer, the practitioner of medicine as an art. The doctor, the learned savant, the experimenting scientist, has a larger field. He is unconcerned with man the individual, the *subspecies aeternitatis.* Him he cannot see for bones and cells and tissues where micro-organisms breed and multiply to be a menace to the species as a whole. He deals with large, great bodies like—"

"Sir Haddingway Ingraham an' Sergeant Costello, if ye plaze, sors," interrupted Nora McGinnis from the study entrance.

"Yes, *parbleu,* exactly like them!" de Grandin burst out laughing as the two six-footers hesitated at the doorway, unable to come through together, undecided which should take precedence.

"Regard, observe them, if you please, Friend Trowbridge!" he ordered as he looked at the big visitors. "*Quel type, mais quel type; morbleu, c'est incroyable!*"

To say that the big Briton and the even bigger Celt were of a common type seemed little less than fantastic. Ingraham—Sir Haddingway Ingraham Jamison Ingraham, known to all his friends familiarly as Hiji, was as typically an Englishman of the Empire Builder sort as could be found in literature or on the stage. So big that he was almost gigantic, his face was long and narrow, high-cheeked, almost saddle-leather tanned, with little splayed-out lines of sun-wrinkles about the outer corners of his eyes. His hair was iron-gray, center-parted, smooth as only brilliantine and careful brushing could make it, and by contrast his small military mustache was as black as the straight brows that framed his deep-set penetrating hazel eyes. His dinner clothes were cut and draped with such perfection that they might as well have borne the label Saville Row in letters half a foot in height; and in his martial bearing, his age and his complexion, you could read the record of his service to his king and country as if campaign ribbons had adorned his jacket: the Aisne, Neuve Chapelle, the second Marne, and after that the jungle or the veldt of British Africa, or maybe India. He was English as roast beef or Yorkshire pudding, but not the kind of Briton who could be at home in London or the Isles, or anywhere within a thousand miles of Nelson's monument, save for fleeting visits.

Costello was a perfect contrast. Fair as the other was dark, he still retained his ruddy countenance and smooth, fresh Irish skin, although his once-red hair was almost white. If Hiji was six feet in height the sergeant topped him by a full two inches; if the Englishman weighed fourteen stone the Celt outweighed him by a good ten pounds; if Ingraham's lean, brown, well-manicured hand could strike a blow to floor an ox, Costello's big, smooth-knuckled fist could stun a charging buffalo. His clothes were good material, but lacked elegance of cut and were plainly worn more for protective than for decorative purposes. Smooth-shaved, round-cheeked, he might have been an actor or a politician or, if his collar were reversed, a very worldly, very knowing, very Godly bishop, or a parish priest with long experience of the fallibility of human nature and the infinite compassion of the Lord.

Thus their dissidence. Amazingly, there was a subtle similarity. Each moved with positively tigerish grace that spoke of controlled power and almost limitless reserves of strength, and in the eyes of each there was that quality of seeing and appraising and recording everything they looked at, and of looking at everything within their range of vision without appearing to take note of anything. As usual, de Grandin was correct.

Each bore resemblance to the other, each was the perfect type of the born man-hunter, brave, shrewd, resourceful and implacable.

"But it is good to see you, *mes amis!*" de Grandin told them as he gave a hand to each and waved them to a seat beside the fire. "On such a night your company is like a breath of spring too long delayed. Me, I am delighted!"

"Revoltin' little hypocrite, ain't he?" Hiji turned to Costello, who nodded gloomy acquiescence.

"*Comment?* A hypocrite—I?" Amazement and quick-gathering wrath puckered the small Frenchman's face as if he tasted something unendurably sour. "How do you say—"

"Quite," Hiji cut in heavily. "Hypocrite's the word, and nothin' less. Pretendin' to be glad to see us, and not offerin' us a drink! On such a night, too. Disgustin' is the word for it."

"*Mea culpa, mea maxima culpa!*" wailed de Grandin. "Oh, I am humiliated, I am desolated, I am—"

"Never mind expressions of embarrassment, you little devil. Pour that whisky; don't be sparin' o' your elbow!"

In a moment Scotch and soda bubbled in the glasses. Ice tinkled in Costello's. "None in mine, you blighted little thimblerigger; d'ye want to take up space reserved for whisky?" Hiji forbade when de Grandin would have dropped an ice-cube in his glass.

Refreshed, we faced each other in that silence of comradery which only men who have shared common perils know.

"And now, what brings you out on such a night?" de Grandin asked. "Smile and grin and play the innocent as you will, I am not to be imposed upon. I know you for the sybarites you are. Neither of you would thrust his great nose out of doors tonight unless compulsion forced him. Speak, thou great ungainly ones, thou hulking oafs, thou species of a pair of elephants. I wait your babbling confidences, but I do not wait with patience. Not I. My patience is as small as my thirst is great—and may I never see tomorrow's sunrise if I see it sober!"

Hiji drained his glass and held it out to be refilled. "It's about young Southerby," he answered gloomily. "The poisonous little scorpion's managed to get himself lost. He's disappeared; vanished."

"Ah? One is desolated at the news." De Grandin leant back in his chair and grinned at Ingraham and Costello. "I am completely ravaged at intelligence of this one's disappearance, for since I have abandoned criminal investigation in all its phases, I can look upon the case objectively, and see how seriously it affects you. May I prescribe an anodyne?" he motioned toward the syphon and decanter.

"Drop it, you little imp o' Satan!" Ingraham replied gruffly. "This is serious business. Yesterday we had a matter of the greatest importance—and secrecy— to be transmitted to the embassy in Washington. There wasn't a king's messenger available, and we did not dare trust the papers to the post; so when young Southerby—dratted little idiot!—stepped in and told the Chief he'd do his Boy Scout's good deed by runnin' the dispatches down to Washington, they took him on. He's been knocking round the consulate a year and more, gettin' into everybody's hair, and the Chief thought it would be a holiday for the staff to get him out from under foot awhile. The little blighter does know how to drive a car, I'll say that for him; and he's made the trip to Washington so often that he knows the road as well as he knows Broadway. Twelve hours ought to do the trip and leave him time for meals to spare, but the little hellion seems to have rolled right off the earth. There ain't a trace o' hide or hair of him—"

"But surely, you need not concern yourself with it," de Grandin interrupted. "This is a matter for the police; the good Costello or the state constabulary, or the Federal agents."

"And the newspapers and the wireless, not to mention the cinema," broke in Hiji with a frown. "Costello's not here officially. As my friend he's volunteered to help me out. As a policeman he knows nothin' of the case. You'll appreciate my position when I tell you that these papers were so confidential that they're not supposed to exist at all, and we simply can't report Southerby's disappearance to the police, nor let it leak out that he's missin' or was carryin' anything to Washington. All the same, we've got to find those precious papers. The Chief made a bad blunder entrustin' 'em to such a scatterbrain, and if we don't get 'em back his head is goin' to fall. Maybe his won't be the only one—"

"You are involved, my friend?" De Grandin's small eyes widened with concern.

"In a way, yes. I should have knocked the little blighter silly the minute that he volunteered, or at least have told the Chief he wasn't to be trusted. As it was, I rather urged him to accept the offer."

"Then what do we wait for? Let us don our outdoor clothes and go to seek this missing young man. You he may elude, but I am Jules de Grandin; though he hide in the lowest workings of a mine, or scale the sky in a balloon—"

"Easy on, son," Hiji thrust a hand out to the little Frenchman. "There's nothin' much that we can do tonight."

"I've already done some gum-shoe wor-rk, sor," Costello volunteered. "We've traced 'im through th' Holland Tunnels an' through Newark an' th' Amboys and New Brunswick. Th' trail runs out just th' other side o' Cranberry. It wuz four o'clock when he left New York, an' a storm blew up about five, so he musta slowed down, for it wuz close to eight when he passed Cranberry, headed for Phillydelphia, an'"—he spread his hands—"there th' trail ends, sor, like as if he's vanished into thin air, as th' felly says."

De Grandin lit a cigarette and leant back in his chair, drumming soundlessly on the table where his glass stood, narrowing his eyes against the smoke as he stared fixedly at the farther wall.

"There was mingled rain and snow—sleet—on all the roads last night," he murmured. "The traffic is not heavy in the early evening, for pleasure cars have reached their destinations and the nightly motorcade of freight trucks does not start till sometime near eleven. He would have had a lonely, slippery, dangerous road to travel, this one. Has inquiry been made for wrecks?"

"That it has, sor. He couldn't 'a' had a blowout widout our knowin' of it. His car wuz a Renault sports model, about as inconspicuous as a ellyphunt on a Jersey road, an' that should make it a cinch to locate 'im. That's what's drivin' me nuts, too. If a young felly in a big red car can evaporate—howly Mither, I wonder now, could that have any bearin'—" He broke off suddenly, his blue eyes opened wide, a look almost of shocked amazement on his face.

"A very pleasant pastime that, my friend," de Grandin put in acidly as the big detective remained silent. "Will you not confide your cause for wonder to us? We might wish to wonder, also."

"Eh? O' course, sor." Costello shook his shoulders with a motion reminiscent of a dog emerging from the water. "I wuz just wonderin'—"

"We gathered as much—"

"If sumpin' else that's happened, recently, could have a bearin' on this case. Th' Missin' Persons Bureau has had lookouts posted several times widin th' past three months fer persons last seen just th' other side o' Cranberry—on th' Phillydelphia side, that is. O' course, you know how so many o' these disappearances is. Mostly they disappear because they wants to. But these wuz not th' sort o' cases ye'd think that of. A truck driver wuz th' first, a fine young felly wid a wife an' two kids: then a coupla college boys, an' a young gur-rl from New York named Perinchief. Th' divil a one of 'em had a reason for vamoosin', but they all did. Just got in their cars an' drove along th' road till they almost reached Cranberry, then—bingo! no one ever heard o' one of 'em again. It don't seem natural-like. Th' state police an' th' Middlesex authorities has searched for 'em, but th' devil a trace has been turned up. Nayther they nor their cars have been seen or heard from. D'ye think that mebbe there is sumpin' more than coincidence here?"

"It may not be probable, but it is highly possible," de Grandin nodded. "As you say, when people disappear, it is often by their own volition, and that several persons should be missed in a short period may quite easily be coincidental. But when several people disappear in a particular locality, that is something else again. "Is there not something we can do tonight?" he turned to Ingraham.

"No," the Englishman replied, "I don't believe there is. It's blacker than the inside of a cow out there, and we can't afford to attract attention lookin' for the little blighter with flashlights. Suppose we do a move tomorrow before dawn and see what we can pick up in the neighborhood where Southerby was last reported."

DAWN, A RAW, COLD February dawn well nigh as colorless and uninviting as a spoiled oyster, was seeping through the lowering storm clouds as we drove across the bridge at Perth Amboy and headed south toward Cranberry. Hiji and

Costello occupied the rear seat; de Grandin rode beside me, chin buried in his greatcoat collar, hands thrust deep in his pockets.

"See here," I asked him as an idea struck me, "d'ye suppose this lad has skipped? You heard Hiji say how valuable the papers he was carrying are, and apparently he begged to be allowed to carry them. These youngsters in the consular and diplomatic service usually live beyond their means, and sometimes they do queer things if they're tempted by a large amount of cash."

"I wish I could believe that," he returned, cowering lower in his seat. "It would have saved me the discomfort of emerging from a warm bed into a chill morning. But I know *les anglais*, my friend. They are often stupid, generally dull; socially they are insufferable in many cases, but when it comes to loyalty Gibraltar is less firm. Your English gentleman would as soon consider eating breakfast without marmalade as selling out his honor or running from an enemy or doing anything original. Yes."

A little light, but no sunshine, had strengthened in the sky when we drew up beside the roadway a half-mile beyond Cranberry. "All right," Hiji called as he dismounted; "we might as well start here and comb the terrain. We have a fairly good line on our bird up to this point, and—hullo, there's a prospect!"

He nodded toward a corduroyed Italian, obviously a laborer, who was trudging slowly up the road walking to the left and facing traffic, as pedestrians who hope to survive have to do on country highways.

"*Com' esta?*" de Grandin called. "You live near here?"

The young man drew his chin up from his tightly buttoned reefer and flashed a smile at him. "*Si, signor,*" he returned courteously, and raised a finger to his cap. "I live just there, me."

With a mittened hand he waved vaguely toward a patch of bottom land whence rose a cumulus of early-morning smoke.

"And you work long hours, one surmises?"

Again the young man smiled. "*Si,* all day I worka; mornin', night, all time—"

"So you walk home in darkness?"

A smile and nod confirmed his surmise.

"Sometimes the motors cause you trouble, make you jump back from the road, *hein?*"

"Not moch," the young Italian grinned. "In mornin' when I come to work they not yet come. At night when I come back they all 'ave gone away. But sometimes I 'ave to jomp queek. Las' night I 'ave to jomp away from a beega rad car—"

"I think we are upon the scent, my friends!" de Grandin whispered. Aloud: "How was that? Could he not see you?"

The young man shrugged his shoulders. "I theenk 'e craz'," he answered. "Always I walka dees side a road, so I can see car come, but dees a one 'e come from other side, an' almost bang me down. Come ver' fast, too, not look where he go. Down there"—again he waved a vague hand down the road—"'e run into da woods. I theenk 'e get hurt, maybe, bot I not go see. I ver' tired, me, and want for to get 'ome."

De Grandin pursed his lips and rummaged in his pocket for a coin. "You say the young man left the road and ran into the woods? Did you see his car?"

"*Si, signor.* Heef I don' see heem I not be 'ere now. Eet was a beega rad car, lika dose we see in old contry, not small like dose we see 'ere."

"And where did this one leave the road?"

"You see dose talla tree down by de 'ill op dere?"

"Perfectly."

"'E go off road about a honnerd meters farther on."

"Thank you, my peerless one," the Frenchman smiled, as he handed the young man a half-dollar. "You have been most helpful." To us: "I think that we are on the trail at last."

"But I can't think that Southerby would have stopped to take a drink, much less get drunk," objected Ingraham, as we hastened toward the point the young Italian indicated. "He knew how devilishly important those things were—"

"Perhaps he was not drunk," the Frenchman cut in cryptically as we walked toward the little copse of evergreens which lay back from the road.

An earth cart-track, deeply rutted with the winter rains, ran through the unkempt field which fringed the road and wound into the heart of the small wood lot, stopping at the edge of a creek which ran clattering between abrupt banks of yellow clay.

"Be gob," Costello looked down at the swirling ochre water, "if yer little friend ran inter this, he shure got one good duckin', Hiji."

"*Eh bien,* someone has run into it, and not so long ago," de Grandin answered, pointing to a double row of tire tracks. "Observe them, if you will. They run right down the bank, and there is nothing showing that the car was stopped or that its occupant alighted."

"By Jove, you're right, Frenchy," Ingraham admitted. "See here"—he indicated a pair of notches in the bank—"here's where he went down. Last night's storm has almost washed 'em away, but there the tracks are. The blighted little fool! Wonder how deep, it is?"

"That is easily determined," de Grandin drew his knife and began hacking down a sapling growing at the water's edge. "Now"—he probed experimentally—"one may surmise that—*morbleu!*"

"What is it?" we exclaimed in chorus.

"The depth, my friends. See, I have thrust this stick six feet beneath the surface, but I have not yet felt bottom. Let us see how it is here." He poked his staff into the stream some ten feet beyond his original soundings and began to switch it tentatively back and forth. "Ah, here the bottom is, I think—*non*, it is a log or—*mon Dieu*, attend me, *mes amis!*"

We clustered around him as he probed the turbulent yellow water. Slowly he angled with his pole, swishing it back and forth, now with, now against the rushing current, then twirled it between his hands as if to entangle something in the protruding stubs of the roughly hacked-off boughs.

"Ha!" he heaved quickly upward, and as the stick came clear we saw some dark, sodden object clinging to its tip, rising sluggishly to the surface for a moment, then breaking free and sinking slowly back again.

"You saw it?" he demanded.

"Yes," I answered, and despite myself I felt my breath come quicker. "It looked like a coat or something."

"Indubitably it was something," he agreed. "But what?"

"An old overcoat?" I hazarded, leaning over his shoulder to watch.

"Or undercoat," he replied, panting with exertion as he fished and fished again for the elusive object. "Me, I think it was an—ah, here it is!" With a quick tug he brought up a large oblong length of checkered cloth and dragged it out upon the bank.

"Look at him, my Hiji," he commanded. "Do you recognize him?"

"I think I do," the Englishman responded gravely. "It's the tartan of the clan MacFergis. Southerby had some Scottish blood and claimed alliance with the clan. He used that tartan for a motor rug—"

"Exactement. Nor is that all, my friend. The minute I began exploring with this stick I knew it was not bottom that I touched. I could feel the outlines of some object, and feel something roll and give beneath my pressure every now and then. I am certain that a motor car lies hidden in this stream. What else is there we cannot surely say, but—"

"Why not make sure, sor?" Costello broke in. "We've found th' car, an' if young Misther Southerby is drownded there's nothin' to be hid. Why not git a tow-line an' drag whativer's in there out?"

"Your advice is excellent," de Grandin nodded. "Do you stay here and watch the spot, my sergeant. Hiji and I will go out to the road and see if we can hail a passing truck to drag whatever lies beneath that water out. Trowbridge, my friend, will you be kind enough to go to yonder house"—he pointed to a big building set among a knot of pines that crowned a hill which swept up from the road—"and ask them if they have a car and tow-line we may borrow?"

THE STORM WHICH HAD been threatening for hours burst with berserk fury as I plodded up the unkempt, winding road that scaled the hill on which the old house stood enshrouded in a knot of black-boughed pine trees writhing in the wind. The nearer I drew to the place the less inviting it appeared. At the turning of the driveway from which almost all the gravel had been washed long since, a giant evergreen bent wrestling with the gale, its great arms creaking, groaning, shaken but invincible against the storm. Rain lashed against the walls of weathered brick; heavy shutters swung and banged and crashed, wrenched loose from their turn-buckles by the fury of the wind; the blast tore at the vines that masked the house-front till they writhed and shuddered as in torment; even the shadowy glimmer of dim light glowing through the transom set above the door seemed less an invitation than a portent, as if warning me that something dark and stealthy moved behind the panels. I pulled my hat down farther on my brow and pushed the collar of my greatcoat higher up around my ears.

"Someone's up and stirring," I told myself aloud as I glanced up at the feeble glow above the door. "They can't very well refuse to help us." Thus for the bolstering of my morale. Actually, I was almost shaking with a sort of evil prescience, and wanted more than anything to turn and run until I reached the roadway where my friends were waiting.

"Come, man, don't be a blithering fool!" I bade myself, and seized the rusty iron knocker stapled to the weather-blasted door.

There was something reassuring in the shock of iron upon iron. Here was reality; just a commonplace old farmhouse, run down and ruinous, but natural and earthy. I struck the knocker twice more, making it sound sharply through the moaning wind and hissing rain, waited for a moment, then struck again.

What sort of response I'd expected I had no accurate idea. From the ruinous appearance of the place I had surmised it had been used as a multiple dwelling, housing several families of day-laborers, perhaps a little colony of squatters washed up by the rising tide of unemployment which engulfed our centers of industry. Perhaps a family of discouraged farmer folk used a portion of it and closed off the rest. Had a Negro or Italian answered my impatient knock I should not have been startled, but when the door swung open and a tall man in semi-military uniform looked at me with polite inquiry I was fairly breathless with surprise. A liveried chauffeur opening the door of the old ruin seemed somehow as utterly incongruous as a Zulu chieftain donning dinner-clothes for tribal ceremonies.

His expression of inquiry deepened as I told my errand. It was not until I had exhausted five minutes in futile repetitions that I realized he understood no word I spoke.

"See here," I finally exclaimed, "if you don't understand English, is there anybody here who does? I'm in a hurry, and—"

"In-gliss?" he repeated, shaking his head doubtfully. "No In-gliss 'ere."

"No," I responded tartly, "and I don't suppose you've any Eskimos or Sioux here, either. I don't want an Englishman. I have one already, and a Frenchman and an Irishman, to boot. What I want is someone who can help me haul a motor car out of the brook. Understand? Motor car—sunk—brook—pull out!" I went through an elaborate pantomime of raising a submerged vehicle from the muddy little stream.

"You'll be sorry for this!" I threatened, leaping from the cot. "I don't know who you are, but you'll know who *I* am before you're done with me—"

"Oh, yes, I know perfectly who you are," he corrected in a gentle, soothing voice. "You are Abraham Stravinsky, sixty-five years old, once in business as a cotton converter but adjudged a lunatic by the orphans' court three weeks ago and placed in my care by your relatives. Poor fellow"—he turned sorrowfully to his companion—"he still thinks he's a physician, Mishkin. Sad case, isn't it?"

He regarded me again, and I thought I saw a glimmer of amusement in his solicitous expression as he asked: "Wouldn't you like some breakfast? You've been sleeping here since we had to use harsh measures day before yesterday. You must be hungry, now. A little toast, some eggs, a cup of coffee—"

"I'm not hungry," I cut in, "and you know I'm not Stravinsky. Let me out of here at once, or—"

"Now, isn't that too bad?" he asked, again addressing his companion. "He doesn't want his breakfast. Never mind, he will, in time." To me:

"The treatment we pursue in cases such as yours is an unique one, Stravinsky. It inhibits the administration of food, or even water, for considerable periods of time. Indeed, I often find it necessary to withhold nourishment indefinitely. Sometimes the patient succumbs under treatment, to be sure; but then his insanity is cured, and we can't have everything, can we? After all, Stravinsky, the mission of the sanitarium is to cure the disease from which the patient suffers, isn't it, Stravinsky?

"Make yourself comfortable, Stravinsky. Your trouble will be over in a little while. If it were only food you are required to forgo your period of waiting might be longer, but prohibition of water shortens it materially—Stravinsky."

The constant repetition of the name he'd forced upon me was like caustic rubbed in a raw wound. "Damn you," I screamed, as I dashed myself against the door, "my name's not Stravinsky, and you know it! You know it—you *know it!*"

"Dear, dear, Stravinsky," he reproved, smiling gently at my futile rage. "You mustn't overtax yourself. You can't last long if you permit yourself to fly into such frenzies. Of course, your name's Stravinsky. Isn't it, Mishkin?" He turned for confirmation to the other.

"Of course," his partner echoed. "Shall we look in on the others?"

They turned away, chuckling delightedly, and I heard their footsteps clatter down the bare floor toward the other end of the corridor on which my room faced.

In a few minutes I heard voices raised in heated argument, seemingly from a room almost directly underneath my cell. Then a door slammed and there came the sound of dully, rhythmically repeated blows, as if a strap were being struck across a bed's footboard. Finally, a wail, hopeless and agonized as if wrung from tortured flesh against the protest of an undefeated spirit: "Yes, yes, anything— *anything!*"

The commotion ceased abruptly, and in a little while I heard the clack of boot heels as they went upon their rounds.

THE HOURS PASSED LIKE eons clipped from Hell's eternity. There was absolutely no way to amuse myself, for the room—cell would be a better term for it—contained no furniture except the bed. The window, unglazed, small and high-set, faced an L of the house; so there was neither sky nor scenery to be looked at, and the February wind drove gusts of gelid rain into the place until I cowered in the corner to escape its chilling wetness as though it were a live, malignant thing. I had been stripped to shirt and trousers, even shoes and stockings taken from me, and in a little while my teeth were chattering with cold. The anesthetic they had used to render me unconscious still stung the mucous membranes of my mouth and nose, and my tongue was roughened by a searing thirst. I wrenched a metal button from my trousers, thrust it in my mouth and sucked at it, gaining some slight measure of relief, and so, huddled in the sleazy blanket, shivering with cold and almost mad with thirst, I huddled on the bed for hour after endless hour till I finally fell into a doze.

How long I crouched there trembling I have no idea, nor could I guess how long I'd slept when a hand fell on my shoulder and a light flashed blindingly into my face.

"Get up!" I recognized the voice as coming from the man called Mishkin, and as I struggled to a sitting posture, still blinking from the powerful flashlight's glare, I felt a broad web strap, similar to the one with which I had at first been pinioned, dropped deftly on my arms and drawn taut with a jerk.

"Come," my jailer seized the loose end of my bond and half dragged, half led me from my cell, down the stairs and through a lower hall until we paused before a door which had been lacquered brilliant red. He thrust the panels back with one hand, seized me by the shoulder with the other, and shoved me through the opening so violently that, bound as I was, I almost sprawled upon my face.

The apartment into which I stumbled was in strong contrast to the cell in which I'd lain. It was a large room, dimly lighted and luxurious. The walls were gumwood, unvarnished but rubbed down with oil until their surface gleamed like satin. The floor of polished yellow pine was scattered with bright Cossack rugs, barbarian with primary colors. A sofa and deep easy-chairs were done in brick-red crushed leather. A log fire blazed and hissed beneath the gumwood over-mantel and the blood-orange of its light washed out across the varnished floor and ebbed and flowed like rising and receding wavelets on the dark-red walls. A parchment-shaded lamp was on the table at the center of the room, making it a sort of island in the shadows, and by its light I looked into the face of the presiding genius of this house of mystery.

He had taken off his dark-lensed glasses, and I saw his eyes full on me. As I met their level, changeless stare I felt as if the last attachments of my viscera had broken. Everything inside me had come loose, and I was weak to sickness with swift-flooding, nameless terror.

In a lifetime's practice as physician one sees many kinds of eyes, eyes of health and eyes diseased, the heaven-lighted eyes of the young mother with her first-born at her breast, the vacant eye of fever, the stricken eye of one with sure foreknowledge of impending death upon him, the criminal's eye, the idiot's lack-luster eye, the blazing eye of madness. But never had I seen a pair of eyes like these in a human face. Beast's eyes they were, unwinking, topaz, gleaming, the kind of eye you see in a house cat's round, smug face, or staring at you speculatively through the bars that barricade the carnivores' dens at the zoo. As I looked, fascinated, in these bestial eyes set so incongruously in a human countenance, I felt—I knew—that there was nothing this man would not do if he were minded to it. There was nothing in those yellow, ebony-pupiled eyes to which one could appeal; no plea addressed to pity, decency or morals would affect the owner of these eyes; he was as callous to such things as is the cat that plays so cunningly and gently with a ball one moment, and pounces on a hapless bird or mouse so savagely the next. Feline ferocity, and feline fickleness, looked at me from those round, bright, yellow eyes.

"Forgive the lack of light, please, Doctor Trowbridge," he begged in his soft, almost purring voice. "The fact is I am sensitive to it, highly photophobic. That has its compensations, though," he added with a smile. "I am also noctiloptic and have a supernormal acuity of vision in darkness, like a cat—or a tiger."

As he spoke he snapped the switch of the desk lamp, plunging the apartment into shadow relieved only by the variable fire-glow. Abruptly as a pair of miniature motor lights switched on, the twin disks of his eyes glowed at me through the dimness with a shining phosphorescent gleam of green.

"That is why I wear the Crookes'-lensed glasses in the daytime," he added with an almost soundless laugh. "You won't mind if we continue in the darkness for a little while." The vivid glow of his eyes seemed to brighten as he spoke, and I felt fresh chills of horror ripple up my spine.

Silence fell, and lengthened. Somewhere in the darkness at my back a clock ticked slowly, measuring off the seconds, minutes. . . . I caught myself remembering a passage from Marlowe's *Doctor Faustus*:

O lente, lente currite, noctis equi!
The stars move still, time runs, the clock will strike,
. . . and Faustus must be damn'd!

The shadowed room seemed full to overflowing with manifested, personalized evil as the magician's cell had been that night so long ago in Wurtemberg when Mephistopheles appeared to drag his screaming soul to everlasting torment. Had the floor opened at my feet and the red reflection of the infernal pit shone on us, I do not think I should have been surprised.

I almost screamed when he spoke. "Do you remember—have you heard of—Friedrich Friedrichsohn, Doctor Trowbridge?"

The name evoked no memories. "No," I answered.

"You lie. Everyone—even you half-trained American physicians—knows of the great Friedrichsohn!"

His taunt stung a mnemonic chord. Dimly, but with increasing clarity, recollection came. Friedrich Friedrichsohn, brilliant anatomist, authority on organic evolution . . . colonel-surgeon in the army which Franz Josef sent to meet its doom on the Piave . . . shellshocked . . . invalided home to take charge of a hospital at Innsbruck—now memory came in a swift gush. The doctors in Vienna didn't talk about it, only whispered rumors went the rounds of schools and clinics, but the fragmentary stories told about the work they'd found him at, matching bits of shattered bodies, grafting amputated limbs from some to others' blood-fresh amputation-wounds, making monsters hideous as Hindoo idols or the dreadful thing that Frankenstein concocted out of sweepings from dissecting-rooms. . . . "He died in an insane asylum at Korneusburg," I replied.

"Wrong! Wrong as your diagnoses are in most instances, *mein lieber Doktor.* I am Friedrich Friedrichsohn, and I am very far from dead. They had many things to think of when the empire fell to pieces, and they forgot me. I did not find it difficult to leave the prison where they'd penned me like a beast, nor have I found it difficult to impose on your credulous authorities. I am duly licensed by your state board as a doctor. A few forged documents were all I needed to secure my permit. I am also the proprietor of a duly licensed sanitarium for the treatment of the insane. I have even taken a few patients. Abraham Stravinsky, suffering from dementia præcox is—was—one of them. He died shortly after you arrived, but his family have not yet been notified. They will be in due course, and you—but let us save that for a later time.

"The work in which I was engaged when I was interrupted was most fascinating, Doctor. Until you try it you cannot imagine how many utterly delightful and surprising combinations can be made from the comparatively few parts offered by the human body. I have continued my researches here, and while some of my experiments have unfortunately failed, I have succeeded almost past my expectations in some others. I should like to show you them before—I'm sure you'll find them interesting, Doctor."

"You're mad!" I gasped, struggling at the strap that bound my arms.

I could feel him smiling at me through the dark. "So I have been told. I'm not mad, really, but the general belief in my insanity has its compensations. For example, if through some deplorable occurrence now unforeseen I should be interrupted at my work here, your ignorant police might not feel I was justified in all I've done. The fact that certain subjects have unfortunately expired in the process of being remodeled by me might be considered grounds for prosecuting me for murder. That is where the entirely erroneous belief that I am mad would have advantages. Restrained I might be, but in a hospital, not a tomb. I have never found it difficult to escape from hospitals. After a few months' rest I should escape again if I were ever apprehended. Is not that an advantage? How many so-called sane men have *carte blanche* to do exactly as they please, to kill as many people as they choose, and in such manner as seems most amusing, knowing all the while they are immune to the electric chair or the gallows? I am literally above the law, *mein lieber Kollege.*

"Mishkin," he ordered the attendant who stood at my elbow, "go tell Pedro we should like some music while we make our tour of inspection.

"Mishkin was confined with me at Korneusburg," he explained, as the clatter of the other's boot heels died away beyond the door. "When I left there I brought him with me. They said he was a homicidal maniac, but I have cured his mania—as much as I desired. He is a faithful servant and quite an efficient helper, Doctor Trowbridge. In other circumstances I might find it difficult to handle him, but his work with me provides sufficient outlets for his—shall we call it eccentricity? Between experiments he is as tractable as a well-trained beast. Of course, he has to be reminded that the whip is always handy—but that is the technique of good beast-training, *nicht wahr?*

"Ah, our accompaniment has commenced. Shall we go?"

Seizing the end of my tether, he assisted me to rise, held the door for me, and led me out into the hall.

Somewhere upstairs a violin was playing softly, *Di Provenza il Mar*, from *Traviata*. Its plaintive notes were fairly liquid with nostalgic longing:

From land and wave of dear Provence
What hath caused thy heart to roam?
From the love that met thee there,
From thy father and thy home? ...

"He plays well, *nicht wahr?*" Friedrichsohn's soft voice whispered. "Music must have been instinctive with him, otherwise he would not remember—but I forget, you do not know about him, do you?" In the darkness of the corridor his glowing eyes burned into mine.

"Do you remember Viki Boehm, *Herr Doktor?*"

"The Viennese coloratura? Yes. She and her husband Pedro Attavanta were lost when the *Oro Castle* burned—"

His almost silent laughter stopped me. "Lost, *lieber Kollege*, but not as you suppose. They are both here beneath this roof, guests of their loving *Landsmann*.

Oh, they are both well, I assure you; you need have no fears on that score. All my skill and science are completely at their service, night and day. I would not have one of them die for anything!"

We had halted at a narrow lacquered door with a small design like a coronet stenciled on it. In the dim light of a small lamp set high against the wall I saw his face, studious, arrogant, unsmiling. Then a frigid grimace, the mere parody of a smile, congealed upon his lips.

"When I was at the university before the war"—his voice had the hard brittleness of an icicle—"I did Viki Boehm the honor to fall in love with her. I, the foremost scientist of my time, greater in my day than Darwin and Galileo in theirs, offered her my hand and name; she might have shared some measure of my fame. But she refused. Can you imagine it? She rebuffed my condescension. When I told her of the things I had accomplished, using animals for subjects, and, of what I knew I could do later when the war put human subjects in my hands, she shrank from me in horror. She had no scientific vision. She was so naïve she thought the only office of the doctor was to treat the sick and heal the injured. She could not vision the long vistas of pure science, learning and experimenting for their own sakes. For all her winsomeness and beauty she was nothing but a woman. *Pfui!*" He spat the exclamation of contempt at me. Then:

"Ah, but she was beautiful! As lovely as the sunrise after rain, sweet as springtime in the Tyrol, fragile as a—"

"I have seen her," I cut in. "I heard her sing."

"So? You shall see her once again, *Herr Doktor.* You shall look at her and hear her voice. You recall her fragile loveliness, the contours of her arms, her slender waist, her perfect bosom—see!"

He snatched the handle of the door and wrenched it open. Behind the first door was a second, formed of upright bars like those of a jail cell, and behind that was a little cubicle not more than six feet square. A light flashed on as he shoved back the door, and by its glow I saw the place was lined with mirrors, looking-glasses on the walls and ceiling, bright-lacquered composition on the floor; so that from every angle shone reflections, multiplied in endless vistas, of the monstrous thing that squatted in the center of the cell.

In general outline it was like one of those child's toys called a humpty-dumpty, a weighted pear-shaped figure which no matter how it may be laid springs upright automatically. It was some three feet high and more than that in girth, wrinkled, edematous, knobbed and bloated like a toad, with a hide like that of a rhinoceros. If it had feet or legs they were invisible; near its upper end two arm-like stubs extended, but they bore no resemblance to human pectoral limbs. Of human contours it had no trace; rather, it was like a toad enlarged five hundred times, denuded of its rear limbs and—fitted with a human face!

Above the pachydermous mass of shapelessness there poised a visage, a human countenance, a woman's features, finely chiseled, delicate, exquisite in every line and contour with a loveliness so ethereal and unearthly that she seemed more like a fairy being than a woman made of flesh and blood and bone. The cheeks were delicately petal-like, the lips were full and sensitive, the eyes deep blue, the long, fair hair which swept down in a cloven tide of brightness rippled with a charming natural wave. Matched by a body of ethereal charm the face would have been lovely as a poet's dream; attached to that huge tumorous mass of bloated horror it was a thousand times more shocking than if it too had been deformed past resemblance to humanity.

The creature seemed incapable of voluntary locomotion, but it was faced toward us, and as we looked at it, it threw its lovely head back with a sort of slow contortion such as might be made by a half-frozen snake. There was neither horror nor hatred, not even reproach, in the deep-blue eyes that looked at Friedrichsohn. There was instead, it seemed to me, a look of awful resignation, of sorrow which had burned itself to ashes and now could burn no more, of patience which endures past all endurance and now waits calmly for whatever is to be, knowing that the worst is past and nothing which can come can match that which is already accomplished.

"Her case was relatively simple," I heard Friedrichsohn whisper. "Mishkin and I were cruising in a motorboat off shore when the *Oro Castle* burned. We picked her and her husband up, gave them a little drink which rendered them unconscious and brought them here. She gave us very little trouble. First we immobilized her by amputating both legs at the hip; then, in order to make sure that she would not destroy herself or mar her beauty, I took off both arms midway between shoulder and elbow. That left a lovely torso and an even lovelier face to work with.

"You're wondering about her beautifully swollen trunk? Nothing could be simpler, *herr Kollege*. Artificially induced elephantiasis resulted in enormous hypertrophy of the derma and subcutaneous tissue, and we infected and reinfected her until we had succeeded in producing the highly interesting result you observe. It was a little difficult to prevent the hypertrophy spreading to her neck and face, but I am not the greatest doctor in the world for nothing. She suffers nothing now, for the progress of her condition has brought a permanent insensitiveness, but there were several times during the progress of our work when we had to keep her drugged. Elephantiasis begins as an erysipelatous inflammation, you know, and the accompanying lymphangitis and fever are uncomfortable.

"Internally she's quite healthy, and Mishkin makes her face up every day with loving care—too loving, sometimes. I caught him kissing her one day and beat him for an hour with the knout.

"That put a chill upon her ardor. I do not let him feed her. That is my own delightful duty. She bit me once—the lovely little vixen!—but that was long ago. Now she's as tame and gentle as a kitten.

"Ingenious, having her room lined with mirrors, isn't it? No matter which way she may look—up, down or sidewise—she cannot fail to contemplate herself, and compare her present state of loveliness with what she once possessed."

"Viki!" he rattled the bars of her cage. "Sing for our guest, Viki!"

She regarded him a moment with incurious, thoughtful eyes, but there was no recognition in her glance, no sign that she had heard his command.

"Viki!" Again he spoke sharply. "Will you sing, or must we get the branding-iron out?"

I saw a spasm of quick pain and apprehension flash across her face, and: "That is always effective," he told me, with another soft laugh. "You see, we altered Pedro Attavanti, too. Not very much. We only blinded him and moved his scalp down to his face—a very simple little grafting operation—but he went mad while we were working on him. Unfortunately, we were short of anesthetics, and non-Aryans lack the fortitude of the superior races. Once a day we let him have his violin, and he seems quite happy while he plays. When Viki is intractable we have an excellent use for him. She can't bear to see him suffer; so when we bring him to her door and let her watch us burn him with hot irons she does whatever we ask her.

"Shall we get the irons, Viki," he turned to the monstrous woman-headed thing in the cell, "or will you sing?"

The hideous creature threw its lovely head back, breathing deeply. I could see the wattled skin beneath the throat swell like a puffing toad as it filled its lungs with breath; then, clear and sweet and true as ever Viki Boehm had sung upon the concert stage, I heard her voice raised in the final aria of *Faust:*

Holy angels, in heaven blest,
My spirit longs with thee to rest . . .

Surely, the ecstatic melody of that prison scene was never more appropriately sung than by that toad-thing with a lovely woman's head.

The song still mounted poignantly with an almost piercing clarity as Friedrichsohn slammed the door and with a jerk that almost pulled me off my feet dragged me down the hall.

"You'll be interested in my heart experiment, *Herr Doktor*," he assured me. "This is a more ambitious scheme, a far more complicated—"

I jerked against the harness that confined me. "Stop it!" I demanded. "I don't want to see your fiend's work, you sadistic devil. Why don't you kill me and have done with—"

"Kill you?" The mild, surprised reproach in his voice was almost pathetic.

"Why, Doctor Trowbridge, I would not kill anyone, intentionally. Sometimes my patients die, unfortunately, but, believe me, I feel worse about it than they do. It's terribly annoying, really, to carry an experiment almost to completion, then have your work entirely nullified by the patient's inconsiderate death. I assure you it upsets me dreadfully. A little while ago I had almost finished grafting arms and legs and half the pelt from a gorilla to an almost perfect human specimen, a truck driver whose capture caused me no end of trouble, and would you believe it, the inconsiderate fellow died and robbed me of a major triumph. That sort of thing is very disconcerting. Shall we proceed?"

"No, damn you!" I blazed back. "I'll see myself in Hell before—"

"Surely, you're not serious, Doctor?" He dropped his hand upon my shoulder, feeling with quick-kneading fingers for the middle cervical ganglion. "You really mean you will not come with me?" With a finger hard and pitiless as a steel bolt he thrust downward on my spine, and everything went red before me in a sudden blaze of torment. It was as if my head and neck and throat were an enormous exposed nerve on which he bore with fiendish pressure. I felt myself reel drunkenly, heard myself groan piteously.

"You will come with me now, won't you, *lieber Kollege?*" he asked as he released the pressure momentarily, then bore down on my spine again until it seemed to me my heart had quite stopped beating, then started up again with a cold, nauseating lurch. I could see his eyes blaze at me through the dark, feel his fingers fumbling at my skull-base.

"Don't—don't!" I panted, sick with pain. "I'll—"

"*Ist gut.* Of course you will. I knew that you would not be stubborn. As I was saying, this next experiment I propose making is more ambitious than any I have tried before. It involves the psyche quite as much as the body. Tell me, Doctor, is it your opinion that the physical attraction we call love springs more from contemplation of the loved one's face or figure?"

He tapped me on the shoulder with a rigid forefinger, and I shrank from the contact as from a heated iron. Sick revulsion flooded through me. What atrocity was hatching in the diseased mind of this completely irresponsible mad genius?

"Why—I—what do you mean?" I stammered stupidly. My head and neck still pained me so that I could hardly think.

"Precisely what I say, *mein lieber Kollege,*" he snapped back acidly. "Every day we see cases which make us wonder. Men love and marry women with faces which might put Medusa to shame, but with bodies which might make a Venus jealous. Or, by contrast, they fall in love with pretty faces set on bodies which lack every element of beauty, or which may even be deformed. Women marry men with similar attributes. Can you explain these vagaries?"

"Of course not," I returned. "Human beings aren't mere animals. Physical attraction plays its part, naturally, but intellectual affinity, the soul—"

"The psyche, if you please, *mein Kollege*. Let us not be mediæval in our terminology."

"All right, the psyche, then. We see beneath the surface, find spiritual qualities that attract us, and base our love on them. A love with nothing but the outward-seeming of the body for foundation is unworthy of the name. It couldn't last—"

"Fool!" he half laughed and half snarled. "You believe in idealistic love—in the love that casteth out fear and endureth all things?"

"Absolutely"

"So do those two down there—"

He had halted at a turning of the hallway; as he spoke he pressed a lever, sliding back a silent panel in the floor. Immediately beneath us was a small room, comfortably furnished and well lighted. On a couch before the open fire a boy and girl were seated, hand in hand, fear written on their faces.

He was a lad of twenty-two or so, slightly made, with sleek, fair hair and a ruddy, fresh complexion. I did not need to hear him speak to know that he was English, or that I had the answer to the disappearance of the British consul's messenger.

The girl was younger by a year or so, and dark as her companion was blond.

Their costumes and positions were reminiscent of domestic bliss as portrayed in the more elaborate motion pictures; he wore a suit of violet pajamas beneath a lounging-robe of purple silk brocade, and a pair of purple kid house-boots. She was clothed in an elaborate hostess coat of Persian pattern, all-enveloping from throat to insteps, but so tight from neck to hips that it hid her lissome form no more than the apple's skin conceals the fruit's contours. From hips to hem it flared out like a ballerina's skirt. Laced to her feet with narrow strips of braided scarlet leather were brightly gilded sandals with cork soles at least four inches thick, and the nails of her exquisitely formed hands and feet were lacquered brilliant red to match the sandal straps.

"No," she was saying as Friedrichsohn slid back the panel, "it isn't hopeless, dear. They're sure to find us sometime—why, you were a king's messenger; the consulate will turn the country inside out—"

His bitter laugh broke in. "No chance! I've stultified myself, blasted my name past all redemption. They'll let me rot, and never turn a hand—"

"Neville! What do you mean?"

He put his elbows on his knees and hid his face in his cupped hands. "I should have let 'em kill me first," he sobbed, "but—oh, my dear, you can't imagine how they hurt me! First they beat me with a strap, and when that didn't break my spirit the little man with the black glasses did something to my neck—I don't know what—that made me feel as if I had a dentist's drill in every tooth at once. I couldn't stand the dreadful pain, and—and so I signed it, Lord, forgive me!"

"Signed what, dearest?"

"A letter to the consul tellin' him I'd sold the papers that he'd trusted with me to the Germans, and that I'd hooked it with the money. I shouldn't have found it hard to die, dear, but the pain—the awful pain—"

"Of course, my dear, my poor, sweet dear"—she took his head against her bosom and rocked it back and forth as if he were a fretful child and she his mother—"I understand. Rita understands, dear, and so will they when we get out of here. No one's responsible for things he's done when he's been tortured. Think of the people who denied their faith when they were on the rack—"

"And of the ones who had the stuff to stick it!" he sobbed miserably.

"Honey, listen. I don't love you 'cause you're strong and masterful and heroic; I love you 'cause you're you." She stopped his wild self-accusation with a kiss. Then back again to her first theme:

"They're sure to find us, dear. This is Twentieth Century America. Two people can't just disappear and stay that way. The police, the G-men—"

"How long have we been here?" he interrupted.

"I—I don't quite know. Not being able to look out and see the sun, I can't form estimates of time. We don't know even when it's night and when it's day, do we? All I remember is that I was late in leaving Philadelphia and I was hurrying to avoid the evening traffic from New York when, just outside of Cranberry, something flew against my face and stung me. I thought at first that it was a mosquito, but that was silly. Even Jersey skeeters don't come around in February. The next thing I knew I was awfully dizzy and the car was rocking crazily from one side of the road to the other; then—here I was. I found myself in a soft bed, and my clothes were gone, but these sandals and this house-coat were laid out for me. There was a bathroom letting off my chamber, and when I'd finished showering I found breakfast—or maybe it was luncheon or dinner—waiting for me on a tray beside the bed. They don't intend to starve us, sugar, that's a sure thing. Haven't you been well fed, too?"

"Yes, I have. My experience was about the same as yours, except that I've seen them, the tall, thin man who looks like a walkin' corpse, and the little pipsqueak with black glasses. But I didn't see 'em till today—or was it yesterday? I can't seem to remember."

The girl knit her smooth brows. "Neither can I. I've tried to keep count of the meals they've served, allowing three meals to a day, so I could form some estimate of the time I've been here, and I've tried so hard to lie in wait and catch the one who serves 'em; but somehow I always seem to fall asleep, no matter how I strive to keep awake, and—it's funny about sleeping, isn't it? When you wake up you can't say if you've just dozed for five minutes or slept around the clock—"

The boy sat forward suddenly, gripping both her hands in his. "That's it! I'm sure of it! No wonder time seems to stand still in this place! They drug us—dope us some way, so that we go to sleep whenever they desire it. We don't know how long these drugged sleeps last. We may have been here weeks, months—"

"No, dear," she shook her head. "It isn't summer, yet. We haven't been here months."

"We may have been." Wild panic had him in its grip, his voice was rising, growing thin, hysterical. "How can you tell?"

"Silly!" She bent and kissed him. "Call it woman's intuition if you like, but I am sure we haven't been cooped up here for a month."

They sat in silence a few minutes, hand interlaced in hand; then:

"Rita?"

"Yes, dear?"

"When we get out—if we get out, and if I square myself with the Chief—will you marry me?"

"Try to keep me from it, Mister Southerby, and you'll find yourself right in the middle of the tidiest breach-of-promise suit you ever saw! D'ye think that you can compromise me like this, sit here with me, dressed as we are, and without a chaperon, then ride off gayly? You'll make an honest woman of me, young feller me lad, or—" Her mask of badinage fell away, leaving her young face as ravaged as a garden after a hail storm. "Oh, Neville, you do think they'll find us, don't you?"

It was his turn to comfort her. "Of course, of course, my darling!" he whispered. "They'll find us. They can't help but find us. Then—"

"Yes, honey, then"—She snuggled sleepily into his arms—"then we'll always be together, dear, close—so close that your dear face will be the first thing that I see when I awake, the last I see before I go to sleep. Oh, it will be heaven . . . heaven."

"I shall be interested to find out if it will. Time will tell, and I think time will side with me." Friedrichsohn pressed the spring that slipped the silent panel back in place, and rose, helping me up from my knees. "It will be an interesting experiment to observe, *nicht wahr, mein Kollege?*"

"Wha—what d'ye mean?" I stammered, my voice almost beyond control. What dreadful plan had taken form behind that high, white brow? Would he subject this boy and girl to dreadful transformation? I had seen the remnant of the lovely Viki Boehm. Did he dare . . .

His soft, suave voice broke through my terrified imaginings. "Why, simply this, *mein lieber Kollege:* They are ideal subjects for my test; better, even, than I had dared hope. I caught the girl by the simple device of waiting by the roadside with an airgun loaded with impregnated darts. The slightest puncture of the epidermis with one of my medicated missiles paralyzes the sensory-motor nerves instantly, and as she told the young man, when she woke up she was in bed in one of my guest rooms.

"But my experiment requires Jill to have a Jack, Joan a Darby, Gretel a

Hänsel, and so I set about to find a mate for her. Eventually this young man came along, and was similarly caught. I had arranged for everything. Their sleeping-quarters open on a common sitting-room, his to one side, hers upon the other. Each morning—or each night, they can't tell the difference—I permit them to awaken, open the automatic doors to their rooms, and let them visit with each other. When I think that they have made love long enough I—ah—turn the current off and put them back to sleep."

"How do you mean—"

"Have not you noticed a peculiar odor here?"

"Yes, I smelled the incense when I first came in—"

"*Jawohl.* That is it. I have perfected an anesthetic gas which, according to the strength of its concentration, can put one in a state of perfect anesthesia in a minute, a second, or immediately. It is almost odorless, and such slight odor as it has is completely masked by the incense. Periodically I put them to sleep, then let them re-awaken. That is why they cannot guess the intervals of time between their meetings, and—what is more important—when they begin to reason out too much, I see that they become unconscious quickly. I turned the anesthetic on when he began to guess too accurately concerning my technique a moment ago. By this time both of them are sleeping soundly, and Mishkin has taken them to bed. When I see fit, I shall allow them to awake and eat and take their conversation up where they left off, but I do not think they will. They are too preoccupied with each other to give much thought to me—just now, at least."

"How long have they been here?" I asked. "I heard her say that she came first—"

"What is time?" he laughed. "She does not know how long she's been my guest; neither does he, nor you, *Herr Doktor*. It may have been a night I let you sleep, in Stravinsky's cell, or it may have been a week, or two—"

"That's nonsense," I cut in. "I should have been half starved if that were so. As it is, I'm not even feeling hungry—"

"How do you know we did not feed you with a nasal tube while you were sleeping?"

I had not thought of that. It upset my calculations utterly. Certainly in normal circumstances I should have been ravenous if I'd been there but four and twenty hours. A longer period without nourishment and I should have felt weak, yet I felt no hunger. . . .

"To return to our young lovers," Friedrichsohn reminded me. "They are better suited to my purpose; better, even, than I'd thought. When I captured him I could not know that they had known each other for some time, and were more than merely mildly interested in each other. Since they have been my guests, propinquity has made that interest blossom into full-blown love. Tomorrow, or the next day—or the next day after that—I think I shall begin to work on them."

"To—work—on—them?"

"*Jawohl, mein lieber Kollege.* You saw the fascinating beauty treatment I gave Viki Boehm? *Ist gut.* I shall put them quietly to sleep and subject them to precisely similar ministrations. When they awake they'll find themselves in the dove-cote I have prepared for them. It is a charming, cozy little place where they can contemplate each other as the little lady said, where the face of each shall be the first thing that the other sees when he awakes, the last thing he beholds before he goes to sleep. It is larger than the chamber I assigned to Viki—more than twice as large—and one of them shall rest at one end of it while the other occupies the other, facing him. It has been lined with mirrors, too, so that they can see themselves and each other from both front and back. That is necessary, *Herr Doktor,* since they will not be able to turn around. Lacking legs, a person finds himself severely handicapped in moving, *lieber Freund.*"

"But why should you do this to them?" I faltered, knowing even as I asked the question that reason had no part in his wild plans.

"Can you ask that after our discussion of the merits of the face and form as stimulants of love? I am surprised and disappointed in you, *mein Kollege.* It is to see if love—the love they pledge so tenderly to each other—can stand the sight of hideous deformity in the loved one. Their faces will be as they are now, only their forms will be altered. If they continue to express affection for each other I shall know the face is that which energizes love, but if—as I am sure they will—they turn from each other in loathing and abhorrence, I shall have proven that the form is more important. It will be a most diverting comedy to watch, *nicht wahr, Herr Doktor?*"

Horror drove my pulses to a hurrying rhythm. Something sharp, something penetrating as a cold and whetted knife-blade, seemed probing at my insides. I wanted to cry out against this outrage, to pray; but I could not. Heaven seemed unreal and infinitely far away with this phosphorescent-eyed monstrosity at my elbow, his pitiless, purring voice outlining plans which outdid Hell in hellish ingenuity.

"You can't—you can't do this!" I gasped. "You wouldn't dare! You'll be found out!"

"That's what Viki Boehm said when I told her of the future I had planned for her," he broke in with a susurrating laugh. "But they didn't find me out. They never will, *Herr Doktor.* This is a madhouse—pardon me, a sanitarium—duly licensed by the state and impervious to private inquiry. People expect to hear cries and shrieks and insane laughter from such places. Passersby and neighbors are not even curious. My grounds are posted against trespassers; your law insures my privacy, and no one, not even the police, may enter here without a warrant. I have a crematory fully equipped and ready to be used instantly. If attempts are made to search the house I can destroy incriminating evidence—inanimate and animate—in a moment and without trouble. I shall prosecute my work uninterrupted, *lieber Kollege*—and that reminds me, I have a proposal to make you."

He had reached the red-walled room again, and he pushed me suddenly, forcing me into a chair.

"There are times when I feel Mishkin is inadequate," he said, taking out a cigarette and setting it alight. "I have taught him much, but his lack of early training often makes him bungle things. I need a skilled assistant, one with surgical experience, capable of helping me in operations. I think you are admirably fitted for this work. Will you enlist with me—"

"*I?*" I gasped. "I'll see you damned first."

"Or will you fill Stravinsky's coffin?"

"Stravinsky's—coffin?"

"Exactly. You remember that I told you Abraham Stravinsky was a patient here and that he died the day you came? *Jawohl.* His family have not yet been notified of his death. His body is preserved and waiting shipment. Should you accept my offer I shall notify his relatives and send his corpse to them without delay. If you decline"—the green eyes seemed to brighten in the gloom as they peered at me—"I shall put him in the crematory, and you shall take his place in the coffin. He was a Hebrew of the orthodox persuasion, and as such will have a plain pine coffin, rather than a casket. I have several boxes like that ready, one of them for you, unless you choose to join me. You are also doubtless aware that the rules of his religion require burial of the dead within twenty-four hours of death. For that reason there is small fear that the coffin will be opened. But if it should be, his family will not know that it is you and not their kinsman whom they see. I shall say he died in an insane seizure, as a consequence of which he was quite battered in the face.

"You need not fear, *mein lieber Kollege*: the body will be admirably battered—past all recognition. Mishkin will attend to all the details. He has a very dexterous talent with the ax, but—"

"But he will not exercise it, I damn think!" From behind me Jules de Grandin spoke in ordinary conversational tone, but I recognized the flatness of his voice. Cyclopean fury boiled in him, I knew. Friedrichsohn might be insane, fierce and savage as a tiger; de Grandin was his match in fierceness, and his clear French brain was burdened with no trace of madness.

"*Kreuzsakrament!*" As de Grandin stepped before me Friedrichsohn launched himself across the table, leaping like a maddened leopard. "You—"

"It is I, indeed, thou very naughty fellow," de Grandin answered, and as the other clawed at him rose suddenly into the air, as if he were a bouncing ball, brought both feet up at once, and kicked his adversary underneath the chin, hurling him unconscious to the floor. "*Tiens*, a knowledge of *la savate* is very useful now and then," he murmured, as he turned and loosed the strap that bound my arms and transferred it to his fallen foeman. "So, my most unpleasant friend, you will do quite nicely thus," he said, then turned to me.

"*Embrasse moi!*" he commanded. "Oh, Trowbridge, *cher ami, brave camarade*, I had feared this stinking villain had done you an injury. *Alors*, I find you safe and sound, but"—he grinned as he inspected me—"you would look more better if you had more clothing on!"

"There's a chest behind you," I suggested. "Perhaps—"

He was already rummaging in the wardrobe, flinging out a miscellany of garments. "These would be those of Monsieur Southerby"—he tossed a well-cut tweed suit on the floor—"and these a little lady's"—a woolen traveling-suit with furred collar came to join the man's clothes. "And this—ah, here they are!" My own clothes came down from the hooks and he thrust them at me.

"Attire yourself, my friend," he ordered. "I have work elsewhere. If he shows signs of consciousness, knock him on the silly head. I shall return for him anon."

Hurrying footsteps clattered on the floor outside as I dragged on my clothes. A shout, the echo of a shot. . . .

I flung the door back just in time to see de Grandin lower his pistol as Mishkin staggered toward the front door, raised both arms above his head and crashed sprawling to the floor.

"My excellent de Grandin!" Jules de Grandin told himself. "You never miss, you are incomparable. *Parbleu*, but I admire you—"

"Look, look!" I shouted. "The lamp—"

Clawing blindly in the agony of death, Mishkin's hand had knocked one of the red-globed oil lamps from its place before a statuary niche. The lacquer-coated, oil-soaked walls were tinder to the flame, and already fire was running up them like a curtain.

"In there," I cried. "Southerby and a young girl are locked up there somewhere, and—"

"Hi, Frenchy, where the devil are you?" Hiji's hail came from the transverse corridor. "Find Trowbridge yet? We've got Southerby and a—" He staggered out into the central hall with the still unconscious Southerby held in his arms as if he were a sleeping babe. Behind him came Costello with the girl, who was also sunk deep in anesthesia.

"Whew, it's gettin' hotter than Dutch love in here!" the Englishman exclaimed. "We'd best be hookin' it, eh, what?"

"Indubitably what, my friend," de Grandin answered. "One moment, if you please." He dashed into the red room, reappearing in a moment with arms filled with clothes. "These are their proper raiment," he called, draping the garments over Hiji's shoulder. "Take them to the garage and bid them dress themselves becomingly for public appearance. Me, I have another task to do. Assist me, if you will, Friend Trowbridge."

Back in the red-walled room he raised the fallen madman, signing me to help him. "The place will be a furnace in a moment," he panted, "and me, I am not even one of the so estimable young Hebrews who made mock of Nebuchadnezzar's fiery wrath. We must hasten if we do not wish to cook!"

He had not exaggerated. The oil-soaked walls and floors were all ablaze; lashing, crackling flames swept up the stairway as if it were a chimney flue.

"Good heavens!" I cried, suddenly remembering. "Up there—he's got two others locked in cells—"

Down from the upper story, clear and sweet and growing stronger, came a voice, the voice of Viki Boehm:

So stürben wir, um ungetrennt,
Ewig einig ohne end . . .

So should we die, no more to part,
Ever in one endless joy . . .

The mounting notes of a violin accompanied the words of Tristan and Isolde's plea for death which should unite them in the mystic world beyond life.

"*Mon Dieu! Concede misericors, Deus . . .*" De Grandin looked up at the fire-choked stairway. "There is no chance of reaching them—"

The crash of breaking timbers drowned his words, and a gust of flame and sparks burst from the stairwell as the draft was forced down by the falling floors. The song had died; only the roar of blazing, oil-soaked wood sounded as we bent our heads against the smoke and staggered toward the door. "It is their funeral pyre—*fidelium animae per misericordiam Dei, requiescat in pace!*" de Grandin panted. "A-a-ah!"

"What's the matter?" I asked. "Are you—"

"Bid Hiji or Costello come at once!" he groaned. "I—am—unable—"

"You're hurt?" I cried solicitously.

"*Vite, vite*—get one of them!" he choked.

I rushed through the front door and circled around the house toward the garage. "Hiji—Costello!" I shouted. "Come quickly, de Grandin's hurt—"

"*Pardonnez-moi, mon ami*, on the contrary I am in the best of health, and as pleased as I can be in all the circumstances." At my very heels de Grandin stood and grinned at me.

"You got clear? Good!" I exclaimed. Then: "Where's Friedrichsohn?"

There was no more expression in his small blue eyes than if they had been china eyes in a doll's face. "He was detained," he answered in a level voice. "He could not come."

Suddenly I felt an overmastering weakness. It seemed to me I had not eaten for a year; the cold bit at my bones as if it were a rabid wolf. "What day is it?" I asked.

"You are unpatriotic, my friend. It is the anniversary of the Great Emancipator's birth. Did not you know?"

"February twelfth? Why, that's today!"

"*Mon Dieu*, what did you think it was, tomorrow or yesterday?"

"But—I mean—we left Harrisonville on the morning of the twelfth, and I've been in that place at least—"

He glanced down at his wrist watch. "A little over two hours. If we hasten we shall be in time to lunch at Keyport. They have delicious lobster there."

"But—but—"

"Doctor Trowbridge, Doctor de Grandin, these are Miss Perinchief and Mr. Southerby," Hiji broke in as he and Costello came from the garage shepherding a most ecstatic-looking pair of youngsters.

"I've seen—" I began; then: "I'm very glad to meet you both." I acknowledged the introduction.

He made me tell him my adventures from the moment I had left him by the brook where Southerby's car was foundered, listening with tear-filled eyes as I described the loathsome things Friedrichsohn had made of Viki Boehm and her husband, weeping unashamedly when I recounted what I'd overheard while I looked through the trap-door into the room in which young Southerby and Rita Perinchief confessed their love. "And now, in heaven's name, what were you doing all that time?" I asked.

"When you failed to return we were puzzled. Costello wished to go to the farmhouse and inquire for you, but I would not permit it. One took at that place and I knew it had the smell of fish upon it. So I posted them out by the great tree at the turning of the driveway, where they could be in plain sight while I crept around the house and sought an opening. At the last I had to cut the lock away from the back door, and that took time. I do not doubt the Mishkin rascal watched them from some point of vantage. *Bien*. While he was thus engaged Jules de Grandin was at work at the back door.

"At last I forced an entrance, tiptoed to the front door and unfastened it, signaling to them that all was well. I was waiting for them when I saw that *sale chameau* Friedrichsohn come down the stairs with you.

"'Can this be endured?' I ask me. 'Can anyone be permitted to lead my good Friend Trowbridge as if he were a dog upon a leash? *Mais non*, Jules de Grandin, you must see to this.' So I crept up to the room where he had taken you and listened at the keyhole. *Voilà tout*. The rest you know."

"No, I don't," I denied. "How did Hiji and Costello know where to look for Southerby and Rita?"

"*Tiens*, they did not know at all, my friend. They came in and looked about, and they espied the Mishkin rogue on guard before their prison door. He ran, and they broke down the door and brought the prisoners out. They should have shot him first. They have no judgment in such matters. *Eh bien*, I was there. It is perhaps as well. I have had no target practice for a long, long time—"

"Did they find the papers Southerby was carrying?"

"But yes. Friedrichsohn set no value on them. They were in the desk of the room where you first saw him. Hiji has them safely in his pocket."

"It seems incredible I was in there such a little while," I mused. "I could have sworn that I was there at least a week—"

"Ah, my friend, time passes slowly in a prison. What you thought was hours' space as you lay shivering in that cell was really only half an hour or so. Time does not pass at all, it stands entirely still while you are sleeping. They rendered you unconscious with their gas, and woke you in perhaps five minutes. Suggestion did the rest. You thought that you had slept around the clock-dial, and since you could not see the sun, you had no clue to what the hour really was. Sleep and our own imaginings play strange tricks upon us, *n'est-ce-pas?*"

The BROILED LIVE LOBSTER was, as he had promised, delicious. Luncheon done, de Grandin, Hiji and Costello marched toward the bar, with me bringing up the rear. Neville Southerby and Rita Perinchief cuddled close together on a settle set before the fireplace in the lounge. As I passed the inglenook in which they snuggled side by side, I heard her: "Honey lamb, I think I know how Robinson Crusoe felt about his island when they'd rescued him. He kept remembering it all his life, and even though he'd undergone a lot of hardships there, he loved it. Somehow, I'll always feel that way about the place that madman shut us up in. Just suppose they'd never found us . . . suppose we'd stayed there always, just the two of us, being with each other always, looking at each other . . . we might have been changed some by being cooped up, but—"

"*Morbleu*, my friend, you look as if you'd seen a most unpleasant ghost!" de Grandin told me as I joined them at the bar and reached unsteadily for a drink.

"I have," I answered with a shudder. "A most unpleasant one."

Mansions in the Sky

"**V**RAIMENT**,**" JULES DE GRANDIN looked up from his reading, parentheses of concentration between his brows. "It is precisely as he says, that Monsieur Kipling."

"Eh?" I answered, stifling an incipient yawn. It was raining, steadily and coldly, and had been since mid-afternoon. An icy wind soughed through the bare gray trees, and flocks of sparrows huddled shivering in the shelter of the dripping eaves. The study fire was dying, and I was almost waterlogged with sleepiness. "What's true?" I murmured with scant interest.

"Why, this epigram he makes, my friend:

The sins ye do by two and two
Must be paid for one by one.

"I dare say," I returned, "but if you don't mind, I think that I'll turn in."

The phone bell rang a short, sharp stuttering warning, first querulously, then insistently, finally with a frantic, drilling clamor. I half decided to ignore it; the night was foul, and I was dog-tired after a long, trying day. But habit overcame my inclination. "Hullo?" I challenged gruffly as I took the instrument from its cradle.

"Doctor Trowbridge, will you come right away, please? It is my niece. She has hurt herself; perhaps she may be dead already—"

"Hold on," I cut in, "who is this?"

"Kimon Sainpolis, Doctor. It is my niece Stephanola. She is badly hurt."

"What's the nature of the injury?" I began, but the sharp click of the phone thrust back into its hooks broke my query off half uttered, and I turned toward the surgery for my first-aid kit with a sigh of exasperation.

De Grandin joined me at the front door, his trench coat belted and his felt hat already turned down in anticipation of the outside rain.

"Where to, *mon vieux?*" he asked. "May not I go, also? It is dull work, staying by oneself when others are about their business."

"Of course, glad to have you," I responded as I climbed into my car and shot the starter. "Kimon Sainpolis, the Greek importer, just called. It seems his niece has met some sort of accident—pretty serious, too, I gathered, for he said she might be dead."

We turned into the boulevard and headed toward the heights where Sainpolis, grown rich with vending wine in Prohibition days, and richer still since his activities were legalized, had built his big stone mansion.

THE WIND WAS BITTER as a witch's curse as we began to mount the hill, and by the time we reached our destination there was a glaze of ice across my windshield reminiscent of the frosting on old-fashioned barroom mirrors. It was almost midnight, but every window in the house was bright as we drew up at the curb and hastened up the path of marble tiles that led to the wide porch.

Inside there was the sound of voices speaking in the stage-whisper of ill-suppressed excitement as the butler met us at the door and ushered us across the hill. Somewhere upstairs a woman laughed and wept by turns in the shrill timbre of hysteria.

"Doctor Trowbridge, this is kind of you, indeed," Sainpolis exclaimed as he rushed down the wide stairs to greet us. "I am almost frantic—Doctor de Grandin!" he acknowledged my introduction with a deep bow, "I am honored that you, the great occultist, have consented to come out with Doctor Trowbridge! My niece—"

"Where is she?" I broke in sharply. Out patient might be dying while we stood there talking.

"Upstairs, sir. She is—oh, but it is terrible! How shall I ever face my brother, her poor father? He sent her to me from the old country when she was only three years old. Now—" He wrung his slender white hands in an agony of despair. "You will help me keep it secret, Doctor?"

"Where is she?" I repeated. "And what's wrong with her?"

"Ah, yes, of course, Doctor. You must know all—all—if you are to help me. Come."

Up the thickly carpeted steps we followed him, down a hallway wide enough to have served a hotel, till we paused before a partly-opened door.

"In there!" he whispered as he stood aside and waved dramatically. "You will find her in there, gentlemen."

De Grandin was before me by the fraction of a step, and as he crossed the threshold he came to a sharp halt, letting his breath out in a low *"Ha?"*

Before an ormolu-framed cheval glass, like a *couturière's* dummy overturned, a girl lay on the slate-gray carpet. The sheer rose chiffon of her evening dress was crumpled round her like the petals of a wilting flower, pale yellow hair like wind-blown floss swirled round her face, a silver brocade evening sandal had slipped off one silk-sheathed foot and lay gaping emptily upon its side.

All this I saw at first glance. My second look showed what de Grandin had seen at first.

Below the golden head, where it rested on the velvet carpet, was a sickening dark-red stain, slowly spreading as the gilt clock on the dressing-table ticked the seconds away nervously.

"Good heavens!" I exclaimed. "Suicide!"

"Quite yes," de Grandin nodded. "It was not us, but the funeral director and the coroner Monsieur Sainpolis should have called."

"But we mustn't have the coroner!" our host wailed from the doorway. "I appeal to you as doctors to prevent a scandal. I have called you to attend my niece. If she is dead, you can certify—"

"Be quiet, if you please," de Grandin ordered sharply. "Not one word from you! Answer me: When did this happen?"

"Not fifteen minutes ago," Sainpolis answered. "We had been to the theatre, Madame Sainpolis, my niece and I. Stephanola had been nervous and upset all afternoon; during the final intermission she complained of feeling faint and begged us to allow her to come home. We let her go, but before she had been gone five minutes we decided to follow her. Our car drove up just as she dismissed her taxi, and we entered the house not two minutes behind her. We heard her slam her door; before we could get halfway up the stairs we heard a shot. See"—he pointed to the tiny pistol lying by her outstretched hand—"it was with that she did it."

De Grandin eyed him levelly. "You can assign no reason for this so unfortunate occurrence?"

Sainpolis raised his shoulders in a shrug of eloquent negation. "You know as much as I do, sir. My niece was only twenty-two and was affianced to an estimable young man. As far as I know they had no quarrel."

"U'm?" de Grandin tweaked his small mustache. "She had shown no signs of melancholy—what of this afternoon?"

Sainpolis looked thoughtful. "I could not call it melancholy," he replied at length, "but she has certainly been nervous at times. Six months or so ago she lost a pair of gloves. They were practically new, and quite expensive, but it seemed to me she brooded over their loss far more than she should. It was certainly not natural."

Abruptly he returned to his original theme: "You will help me, gentlemen? You can say it was not suicide—I will say she hurt herself while playing with the toy pistol, and that I summoned you in all haste; you can bear me out in your statements. The disgrace of a suicide in the family will practically ruin me—my brother will declare a feud on me—she will be denied the last rites of the church—"

De Grandin motioned him to silence. "If you are troubled only on those scores, *Monsieur*, we can certainly assist you," he answered. "*Mademoiselle* your niece was rendered melancholy by the loss of her so pretty gloves; she brooded on their loss; *alors*, she shot herself. *Voilà*. Sane people do not do such things, and the church will not refuse its comfort to a person who has killed herself while mad. We can give you our opinion that she must have been of unsound mind when she destroyed herself. Do not make yourself uneasy on that account, *Monsieur*."

"But the police," Sainpolis almost wailed. "They will spread the news broadcast—"

"Excuse me, sir," the butler paused discreetly at the entrance, eyes carefully averted from what lay on the floor, "there's a gentleman from the police here asking for Miss Stephanola. I've told him she is indisposed—"

I had not thought Sainpolis' face could have been paler than it was already, but at the serving-man's announcement the blood seemed visibly to drain out of his countenance, leaving it as livid as the features of a long-dead corpse. "The—police?" he choked. "Tell them to go away, tell them anything. They must not know; we cannot see them now—"

"*Pardonnez-moi, Monsieur*, there you do make the great mistake," de Grandin interrupted. "A crime has been committed here, the crime of suicide. The police must be notified. Await me, and touch nothing in this room!" Tiptoeing down the corridor he leaned across the marble balustrade and looked down to the lower hall.

Below us stood a big red-headed man, looking interestedly, but not at all with awe, at the articles of almost priceless vertu with which Sainpolis had adorned his house. As he turned we saw his face, smooth-shaven, florid, curiously calm.

"*Gloire!*" de Grandin exclaimed delightedly. "We are in luck, it is the good Costello. *Holà, mon vieux!*"

The big detective started at the little Frenchman's hail, and, "Glory be, Doctor de Grandin, sor, who'd 'a' thought to find you here?" he answered with an eye-crinkling smile. "It's on th' level, then, about th' lady's bein' laid up?"

"*Hélas, mon brave*, it is more serious than that," de Grandin replied. "We were called in haste to tend her, but a greater one than we arrived before us."

"Arra, sor, ye mane she's dead?"

"Completely."

"What wuz it, sor?"

"It seems to have been suicide by gunshot."

The utterly expressionless expression which policemen, undertakers and lawyers can assume at will spread across Costello's face.

"Does it, now, indade?" he answered. "That's that, then. We'd best be lookin' round a bit before th' coroner's men mess everything up wid their chicken-tracks."

"You will leave us, if you please, *Monsieur*," de Grandin ordered Sainpolis as we re-entered the death chamber. "There are certain observations to be made which might distress you."

As the worried little man crept out he bent above the body. The pistol lying on the floor was little larger than a toy, and as nearly as I could determine was of .22 caliber. When de Grandin held it to me after a quick inspection I followed his example and put the muzzle to my nose. Faint, but quite perceptible, the sulfurous reek of burnt gunpowder came to me.

That the weapon had been held against the girl's head there was no doubt, for the wound disfiguring the scalp had been torn into a cross-shaped scar by escaping gases plowing up the tissue, and the skin each side of the aperture was tattooed in converging lines like wheel-spokes by dark powder-stains. An area of slightly burned flesh ringed the hole, and a disk of powder-blackening half an inch or so in diameter marred the skin. From the irregularity of the wound it was evident that the bullet had crashed through the temporal bone at the junction of the coronal and squamous sutures, and had been directed upward to the brain.

"*Bien*," de Grandin nodded. "All indicia of self-destruction are apparent. Now, if the fingerprints upon the pistol are the poor young person's—"

"Yis, sor," Costello broke in with what seemed to me unnecessary emphasis, "I'm particu'ly anxious to git a sample o' her fingerprints. "

"*Mais, c'est très simple*," answered de Grandin as he lit a wax match, let its oily flame discolor the smooth surface of a hand mirror and, one after another, proceeded to rub lampblack on the dead girl's well-manicured finger-tips, then transfer impressions to a sheet of paper from a memorandum pad which lay upon the rosewood writing-desk.

"You are satisfied it was a suicide, *mon sergent?*" he asked as he completed his task.

"It seems so, sor," Costello answered, "but—"

"Yes—but?" de Grandin prompted.

"Oh, nothin', sor. I wuz just wonderin' how she got hep."

"She which?" the Frenchman asked. "This 'hep', what is he, if you please?" but before the sergeant could reply, "*Ohé, la pauvre!*"

"What's that, sor?"

"Observe." He motioned toward the far side of the room where a *prie-dieu* stood against the wall, a shelf containing two extinguished candles, a covered crucifix and a rosary fastened to the wall above it. "*Cette pauvre*," he repeated. "See, she veiled the cross before she shot herself all dead!" Stepping across the room he bowed formally to the cross and lifted off the tulle scarf which obscured it. "*Parbleu*, this is a most unusual-looking prayer book," he added as he bent and picked a slender volume bound in gold-stamped vellum from the velvet cushions of the prayer-bench.

"Regard him, if you please," he ordered, holding out the little book for our inspection.

We saw its covers were secured by a gold clasp held by a tiny padlock.

"Hey, sor, ye can't do that widout a search warrant!" Costello warned sharply.

"No? You amaze me, my friend." From his hip, where he wore it lashed to his back brace-straps—"*pour les circonstances imprévues*"—de Grandin drew his double-edged apache knife and calmly forced the book's lock. It gave way with a snap, revealing not a volume of devotions, but a blank book whose pages were thickly covered with a fine, irregular script.

"French!" exclaimed Costello in disgust as he glanced at the small writing. "A lotta good that'll do me."

"It may," de Grandin replied with a grin. "There have been times when I believed I understood that language. Perhaps I can translate it for you." He thrust the volume in his pocket, and:

"Ye can't do that, sor," protested the detective. "It's agin th' law."

"So in an unhappier day was bootlegging but I have the recollection no one ever stopped to think about it," answered the small Frenchman. "Luckily I am under no compulsion to observe the niceties of police etiquette, and undoubtlessly this small book will prove of help to us. Permit me to suggest you look out of the window for a moment, my friend. The view tonight is very fine."

Astonishingly, as the big detective turned his back upon him, he dropped upon his knees beside the crumpled little body, joined his hands and bowed his head in silent prayer a moment.

"*Eh bien,*" he rose and brushed his trouser knees, "let us be upon our way, my friends. It seems we have accomplished all we can here. We are agreed it was a suicide? *Très bon.* Let us notify the coroner to that effect."

"AND NOW, MY OLD one, tell me what this 'hep' is," he demanded of Costello as we gathered round the study fire. "You have the idea how the poor young *demoiselle* contracted it?"

Costello grinned. "Sure, sor, it ain't a thing, it's sumpin' that ye feel. Like"— his eyes roved round the room in search of inspiration—"well, sor, ye're hep when ye're jerry-like as if a felly tried to snatch yer overcoat in a restaurant, an' ye realized what it wuz that he wuz up to as he started to do it."

The frown of fierce fixed concentration faded from de Grandin's face. "One comprehends entirely, *mon vieux*. When one is hep he has become wise, *n'est-ce-pas?*"

"Sure, now, sor, ye wouldn't 'a' been kiddin' me?" Costello asked reproachfully.

"By no means, my incomparable one. But what was it that the so unfortunate young woman had become hep to?"

Once more Costello looked serious. "I ain't sayin' she destroyed herself on this account, but it's worth considerin'," he replied, reaching in his pocket and drawing forth a slip of folded paper. "This come by special delivery to Headquarters about ten o'clock, an' I'd come out to ask th' pore young gur-rl about it when I finds she's up an' shot herself."

The paper was a noncommittal sheet of cheap white bond such as can be had at any ten cent store, and the message which it bore was composed of words and letters cut from a newspaper, capitals and lowercase characters oddly assorted:

if you waNt to DIshcover who made the burglaries in THIS city YOu should looK at stePhanolA SainpOlis fingERprintS

That was all.

Costello cleared his throat. "We ain't exactly advertisin' it, sor, but these burglaries that's been committed here th' past six months has been done mighty slick, an' we haven't got to first base wid 'em. It a'most seems as if th' felly that's pulled 'em has gone out of his way to leave his fingerprints around. A'most like he signs his jobs, ye might say. Three-four times we've made a pinch, an' it looked as if we had dead wood on 'em, but when we come to matchin' up th' fingerprints th' whole case melted."

"You could not identify the culprits' prints left at the scene of crime?"

"No, sor, that we couldn't. There ain't no record of 'em here or in th' criminal or non-criminal files in New York an' Washin'ton."

"You have a copy of the miscreant's prints with you?"

"Right here, sor." The sergeant drew a second slip of paper from his wallet and laid it on the table.

Glass in hand, he and de Grandin compared the copy with the set of prints made of the dead girl's digits. Even I, who am no expert, could read the damning likeness as I compared them through the lens. The wanted criminal's fingerprints and those of Stephanola Sainpolis were identical.

"Bates hell, sors, don't it?" asked Costello. "Here's a young gur-rl, rich and well brought up an' wid no nade to want fer annything longer thin it takes to ask fer it; yet off she goes an' takes to burglary. One o' them fool thrill-hunters, she wuz, I'd say, an' just to make th' game more dang'rous she went an' left her fingerprints all over every job she pulled."

He returned the papers to his pocket, and: "Wonder who it wuz that tipped us off, an' why?" he added thoughtfully. "Belike she had a partner in th' wur-rk, some uneddycated crook who got mad at her when she wouldn't come across wid more swag, an' double-crossed her for revenge."

"I think you're wrong there, Sergeant," I told him. Ever since I'd seen the treacherous message I'd been wrestling with memory, and recollection came to me just as he finished speaking. "When I was a youngster serving my internship at old Bascomb Hospital I used to see notes sent the clinic by our foreign out-patients. Part of my work was translating them into English for the records and I remember how our English sibilants confused them. You'll note the sender of this note says 'dishcover' for 'discover.' Our English 'sh' and 'ch' and the combinations of our sibilants 'c,' 'z' and 's' are things few foreigners except the Scandinavians and Dutch ever seem able to grasp unless they've had more than ordinary training in English orthography. They'll use 'sh' for the combination of 'c' and 's,' or 's' and 'c'—as in 'discover'—eight times out of twelve. I believe whoever pasted up this note was foreign born and quite unused to writing English. He may speak it fairly well, but when it comes to writing it he's virtually illiterate."

"*Parbleu*, my friend, you put the finger squarely on it!" de Grandin exclaimed. "Me, I made those very mistakes which you point out when I was studying English. The girl has slipped from Friend Costello's net by suicide, but he may be able to arrest the one who betrayed her, thus meting out poetical and criminal justice at the same time. Tomorrow I will translate her diary," he added to Costello. "It may be we shall find some clue in it."

H E WAS IN THE library most of the next day, and when he joined me at dinner there was an oddly sad expression on his face.

"Find anything in the diary?" I asked.

"Much; a great deal," he replied with something like a sigh, "but I must ask your indulgence. Wait until the good Costello joins us, so we need have only one narration of the story."

Police routine delayed Costello until after nine o'clock, and several times I thought de Grandin would explode with impatience. Within two minutes after we had gathered in the study he stood before us like a teacher about to address his class, the dead girl's diary in one hand, a sheaf of notes clutched in the other.

"My friends," he began impressively, "we three owe a humble apology to the dead. All of us condemned her as a criminal who chose suicide as an escape from justice last night. It was not so. She was the victim of a villain blacker than the devil's lowest coal-vault. Attend me. Here is the story which her journal tells:

"Two years ago, when she was only twenty, she was attending school near Morristown. A fashionable school it was, one where the pupils were continually chaperoned, except when they were most in need of supervision. It seems the girls had found a way of getting out unseen at night and going to the near-by city, almost at will. *Eh bien*, I think the managers of that school took more trouble to investigate their pupils' families' bank accounts than they did to look up their background, for assuredly they had some queer fish there. One of them was a girl whom the diary designates as Amy, and it was she whom the poor young Mademoiselle Sainpolis shared rooms with. *Tiens*, she shared other things as well, for anon this Amy took her to a roadhouse near the school, and there they met a man called Niccolo—last name unknown.

"He had a way with women, this one. A handsome dog he must be, and a vain and vicious one.

"This poor one thought that she was seeing life when she met him; even when she learned he was a criminal she was more thrilled than shocked, and when he dared her to take cocaine she was still more fascinated. *Tenez*, the path down to Avernus is a smooth one. Within two months she had joined him in a criminal foray, acting as his lookout while he burglarized a house.

"In her journal she recounts how she suffered with remorse next day, and vowed to have no more to do with him. Within a week she kept another rendez-vous, and this time they held up a dining-car.

"Then fear came to the aid of conscience. The papers told of the blond girl who helped the highwayman, and she was sure she would be recognized if she remained near Morristown. She wrote her uncle, begged to be allowed to come home, and left the school next day.

"Earnestly she strove to make amends for her misdeeds. Every day she went to church, each night she prayed for hours for forgiveness. It seemed her prayers were answered, for in a short time she met a young man named Strapoli, and their love was almost instantaneous. They were affianced, preparations for their wedding were in progress, then"—he paused and waved his hand as if announcing an arrival—"Niccolo re-entered. She, as she thought, was done with him, but he had not by any means concluded his relationship with her. Oh, no.

"She was beautiful, she was wealthy, she was much to be desired. He meant to have her. *Ha*, but he was subtle, that one!

"He called her on the telephone, and she, poor innocent, went in mortal fear to the appointed place. She offered him whatever he desired if only he would leave her, and he reproached her for her lack of faith, told her he knew they lived in different worlds, and all he wanted was to say goodbye and beg some little keepsake from her. What do you think he asked for a souvenir, *hein?*"

Pausing, he looked expectantly from me to Costello; then, as we made no answer: "Her gloves, by damn, he asked her gloves of her! You comprehend?"

"I recall Sainpolis said she'd lost a pair of gloves six months or so ago, but I don't see the connection," I answered. "She knew where they were—"

"*Précisément.* That is exactly why she was driven first to desperation, then to madness, finally to self-destruction. The gloves were glacé kid, and almost new, she says so in her diary. She gave them to him gladly, and came home with a great fear gone from her; but in a few days all her dreams of happiness were dissolved. Why did he ask her gloves? I ask you."

Vaguely recollection knocked upon the door of my memory. "Didn't Portia and Nerissa beg Bassanio's and Gratiano's gloves after the trial in *The Merchant of Venice* in order to plague them later on?" I asked.

"*Tu parles, mon vieux.* But what they did in sport this one did in deadly earnest. From the gloves he had matrices of her fingerprints made, and these he had cemented to the fingertips of rubber gloves—"

"Be gorry, sor, I git it!" Costello almost roared. "That's why th' burglar wuz so careless wid his fingerprints—that's why we couldn't match 'em up, no matter how we tried—"

"*Exactement.* And this Niccolo, this reptile, this snake in human guise, wrote to his victim, telling her each time he projected a burglary and informing her that her fingerprints would be found at the scene of crime.

"Imagine yourselves that! She scanned the papers every day to learn if any clue had been discovered. Nothing; nowhere; never! All the papers told her that the burglar left his fingerprints, but his identity—"

"Well, for goodness' sake, why didn't she denounce him?" I interjected. "She could have told the police that her fingerprints were forged—"

He threw me a God-give-me-patience look. "Quite yes, but if he were apprehended her adventures into crime would have come to light, also. Remember that, my friend. Only in his safety lay her own. Also, she was much in love with Monsieur Strapoli, and stood in mortal fear of scandal. She dared not speak, yet if she remained quiet she was still in danger. *Misère de Dieu,* how she must have suffered!

"For six months this went on, six months she lived and moved beneath the shadow of this Damocletian sword; for half a year she roasted in a Hell of fear, grilled on the iron of her conscience. Then came the last blow to her shattered morale.

"Not content with having made a criminal of her, not satisfied with having introduced her to the habit of cocaine, this species of a camel must make a final demand. She must, he told her, dismiss the young Strapoli and accept him as her fiancé. He would have her beauty and her wealth at once and live in idleness upon the fortune which she brought him.

"She might have given him the money, but herself she denied him, and he took revenge. Only yesterday he notified her that unless she married him forthwith he would denounce her to the police.

"Last night she and her aunt and uncle went to the theatre, to a play called *Evil Communications.* It is a melodrama dealing with a blackmail plot. In it the heroine who has forsaken her criminal associates and married happily is about to be denounced by one with whom she has been involved in crime. She sees her happiness about to be destroyed, her children branded with her hidden infamy. She kills herself. The suggestion took hold on Mademoiselle Sainpolis. She left the theatre, left her aunt and uncle, hurried home and—*tiens*, the rest we know. We came, the good Costello came; but she had gone."

"Bedad," commented Costello, "I'd like to have 'bout fifteen minutes private conversation wid this Niccolo. Me an' a two foot length o' rubber hose."

S HE WAS VERY LOVELY in her casket. The scars of autopsy had been obliterated by the skill of the embalmers, a gown of white lace—fashioned for her wedding day—enfolded her slim form, a white lace mantilla draped her shining hair; in the slender, oleander-white hands crossed piously upon her virgin bosom a rosary was twined. Our testimony had convinced the priest, and her funeral was held in church with the lovely, long-drawn ceremony of high mass as celebrated by the Greek communion, a choir of forty voices singing *a cappella* and incense rising in an almost choking cloud of sweetness. Six young girls robed in white and veiled like brides were pallbearers; floral offerings filled two open touring-cars which headed the procession from St. Helena's to the tiny Greek Orthodox cemetery.

"M ISTER STRAPOLI, IF YE plaze, sors," announced Nora McGinnis shortly after dinner the evening following the funeral. "He says as how he ain't a patient," she added rather grimly, for the rule against admitting patients after office was of her own devising, and one she imposed on both my clientele and me with rigorous inflexibility.

The young man who came in a moment later was typical of the city's café life. His dinner suit was of exaggerated cut, trousers fitted snugly at the waist and hips but bellowing into flowing bottoms at the foot; a purple grosgrain cummerbund was bound so tightly round his waist as to suggest a corset, his double-breasted jacket sloped sharply from the shoulders to the waist, then flared above the hips. Black hair, rather long, was brushed straight back without a part and trained down on his cheeks in long sideburns. The bandoline with which it was dressed gave it a finish flat and shiny as a skullcap of black patent leather. He was the perfect "sheik" type, reminiscent of the days when Valentino and Novarro were the *beaux idéals* of motion picture lovers. He was lithe and graceful as a panther in his movements, but somehow the impression which he gave was of a panther which has been hunted till the fear of hounds and guns is in its sleek pelt like a barb.

"Doctor de Grandin?" he asked tentatively in a light but musical voice.

"I am he," de Grandin answered, eyeing him with none too much approval. "What is it that you wish?"

"I am Anthony Strapoli. Stephanola Sainpolis was—we were to have been married."

The little Frenchman shot me a quick glance as if to warn me, "Silence, my friend, tell him nothing. Let me handle this." To the young man:

"You have our deepest sympathy, *Monsieur*. I, who have had the experience, know how the heart bleeds at the thought that we shall not see those we love again—"

"But I have seen her, sir. I saw her last night. That's why I've come to you. They tell me you know all about such things."

De Grandin's narrow brows rose slightly. "You imply you saw her in the spirit?"

"No, sir. In the flesh. I swear it!"

For an instant the small Frenchman eyed him narrowly; then: "Say on, *Monsieur*, I listen."

The young man dropped into a chair and fixed his large dark eyes upon de Grandin's small blue ones. "It wasn't any ghost or spirit I saw, sir," he announced earnestly. "It was Stephanola, in the very body I have known and loved.

"I lead the band at Casa Ayer, and last night was a special occasion, our first broadcast on a national hook-up, so I couldn't be away, though it almost broke my heart to go through with it. I played at both the dinner and the supper shows, and it was two o'clock before we were through, almost three when I reached home. I was so tired that I could hardly stand, but when I went to bed I couldn't sleep; so, sometime between three and four I got up and went to the bathroom for a dose of veronal. I took a stiff shot and was going back to bed when I happened to look into the living-room. Something white was shining there."

"Shining, *Monsieur?*" de Grandin repeated in a flat voice.

"Yes, sir. At first I thought it was the moonlight on the polished floor, but when I looked again I saw it was the lower part of a white dress, a woman's long white gown. I stepped into the room, and there was Stephanola. Don't look at me like that, sir. I tell you she was there!"

"But certainly," de Grandin soothed. "Conditions were ideal for the vision. The broken heart, the tired, frayed nerves, the sedative—"

"It wasn't any vision, as you call it. It was my girl, there in the living, breathing flesh. She stood there in her bridal gown, the one they used to bury her, with the white lace veil across her golden hair, just as I'd hoped to see her at the altar.

"At first I was afraid. Everyone's afraid of ghosts, even if they're of the ones they've loved; so I began to cross myself, and said, 'In the name of the Father, and of the Son—'

"But before I finished she put her hand out to me. 'Don't say it, Tony,' she begged. 'If you do I'll have to go away, and I don't want to leave you so soon.'

"So there I stopped with my hand in the air, right where I'd touched myself upon the forehead when I began to form the cross, and the invocation half pronounced.

"She stepped toward me, and I saw the motion of her train against the floor, and when the moonlight shone on her she cast a shadow. Ghosts don't make shadows, so I began to lose my dread of her, and when she put her hand on mine it was cool and soft, just as it always was, not cold and ghostly.

"'Tony dear,' she whispered, and I could feet her breath against my cheek, 'you've got to help me. I need your help most dreadfully, my dear. I'm a sinner, Tony, for I took the life that wasn't mine to take, but there is a way open for me to forgiveness if you'll help me. Won't you help me, please, Tony?'

"She looked so beautiful and sorrowful and appealing that before I realized what I did I'd put my arms around her and was drawing her to me. I could feel her in my arms, feel the pressure of her body against mine. It was no ghost I held, but a sweet living girl, the same one I'd embraced a thousand times before.

"She didn't shrink from me nor hold back when I bent to kiss her, but—I don't quite know how to say it—something—something I could feel, but couldn't see, seemed to come into the room just then. I can't describe it, really. It wasn't palpable, and yet it was. I couldn't see nor hear nor feel it, but I knew it was there. A thing invisible and soundless had displaced some of the room's air—you know how it is when you're standing in a phone booth and someone else crowds in, but doesn't touch you? And I had a sense of being watched."

"Watched? Inimically?" de Grandin prompted as the boy stopped with a puzzled frown.

"No, sir. It was as if someone very sad, but not at all hostile, stared at me with a long, calm look." His shapely slim hands made a gesture of futility. "It's just impossible to describe, sir. There was no chill, no fear, no sensation I can name at all, but I suddenly felt she and I were not alone, and kissing her right then would be —well, sort of indecent.

"She stepped back from my arms and put her hands upon my shoulders. 'Listen, Tony dear,' she told me, 'listen carefully; this is terribly important. See.' From her dress she drew a big red rose and put it in my hand. 'This is from me, dear, the only gift that I can give you now. Do you recognize it?'

"I looked, and thought I did. Among the flowers I'd sent for her funeral was a spray of Gloire de Dijon roses, twenty-two of them, one for each year of her life. 'Keep it, Tony,' she added, 'it will help you realize this is not a dream you're having. Kneel dearest.'

"The veronal had started working by this time and I was getting dizzy. I don't know whether I knelt purposely or whether I stumbled and fell, but next moment I was on my knees before her and she held her hands against my lips. Somehow that—that presence—which came into the room with her didn't seem forbidding any more, and I kissed her fingers, starting with the little finger of her right hand, counting off ten kisses, and ending with her left little finger. Then, very gently, she drew her hands from mine and laid them on my eyes."

The look of simulated interest with which de Grandin had regarded Strapoli gave way to an amiable frown of concentration. "And when she did this you saw something?" he demanded almost sharply.

The young man's shoulders came up in a puzzled shrug. "Yes, sir, I did, but it didn't seem to make much sense."

"Suppose you tell us what you saw, and let us be the judges of its sense or senselessness, *Monsieur.*"

"At first I saw nothing but indistinguishable blackness, just as you always do when you first close your eyes; then, as the pressure of her fingers on my lids seemed to grow, the black appeared to fade to a dark blue, and soon this was all shot with stars, like the sky on a clear night before the moon has risen. Then slowly, like the fade-in in a motion picture, the image of a house appeared against the sky, not quite shutting out the star-specked heavens, but seemingly imposed on them. It was a big house, something like this, but with more grounds around it, and with evergreens growing by the porch. I saw it plainly, but in miniature, as if it were very far away, or as if I looked at it through the wrong end of an opera glass. There were no lights in any of the windows, but a sort of soft illumination, like moonlight, made it plain as day to me."

"And what occurred then, if you please? "

"Nothing, sir. I knelt there, looking at that house through my closed eyelids for what seemed several minutes; then I felt the pressure on my lids lighten, and when I opened my eyes I was alone, kneeling in the center of the room with a big red rose in my hand.

"I started to get up, but the veronal had taken hold, and I fell forward in a heap and lay there in a drugged sleep till almost noon today. When I recovered consciousness I'd have thought it all a dream, if it were not for this." From the breast pocket of his dinner coat he drew a tissue paper parcel, handling it as reverently as if it were a sacred relic.

The soft white wrappings came away, revealing a great red Gloire de Dijon rose, slightly wilted and with several petals coming loose, but still retaining its deep color and breathing forth a rich scent from its golden heart.

"This was still clutched in my hand when I waked," he told us. "Something, I don't know what, told me that it was from the spray I'd sent to Stephanola, and as quickly as I could I dressed and hurried to the cemetery. All the floral tributes were in place around her grave or on it, and almost at the mound's head, where her breast would be, they'd put my spray of roses. I counted every blossom on it. There were twenty-one left."

Slowly de Grandin poured three drinks, tendering one to our guest, one to me.

"No, thanks," the young man refused. "Sometimes I drink a little wine. I never touch hard liquor."

"*Mon Dieu*, and you have such an amiable face, too!" de Grandin exclaimed in a shocked voice. Then: "*Eh bien*, whatever else you were last night, you were not drunk when you beheld this vision, *mon vieux.*"

A reproachful look came into the young man's dark eyes. "You don't believe me, sir!" he almost wept.

"*Par la barbe d'un bouc vert*, I do, my friend," the little Frenchman answered earnestly, "but there are some features of your vision which daunt me. Precisely, what is it that you would have me do?"

Strapoli smiled sadly. "I think I've come to you for moral support more than anything else," he replied. "Mr. Sainpolis told me you were an expert in the occult, and I'd like to have your opinion—" He paused, swallowed once or twice; then, hurriedly: "Did I do wrong to let the vision stay, or should I have sent it—her—away with an invocation of the Trinity? I went to Father Anastapoul this morning and told him everything, and he tells me I was wrong. He says the living have no right to contacts with the dead except through prayer, and that demons often take the forms of those we loved in life to lure us to damnation."

"The reverend father has some factual basis for his statement," de Grandin answered with a thoughtful nod. "It is unfortunately all too true that what we thought the spiritual manifestation of one we loved turns out to be a foul succubus, but I should say the evidence in this particular case seems to point otherwhere. Tell me, *Monsieur*, what does your own heart say?"

"Why, that I did no wrong, sir. I believe it was Stephanola, not her ghost or spirit, but herself, and that she came to me for help because she loves me, just as I love her. There's nothing I would not have done for her when she was living; why should I deny her aid, now that she's dead?"

Tears were streaming down his face, and other tears were glinting on de Grandin's lashes as he answered, "Why, indeed, my friend? Do not attempt to evoke her as you value your salvation do not seek communication with her through a spiritualistic medium—but if she comes again unbidden, receive her as a lover should. You would not have hurt her living; can you find it in your heart to hurt the helpless dead?"

"WHAT D'YE MAKE OF it?" I asked as the door closed on our visitor. "Did he actually see her, or was it just a tired brain in a tired body, plus a dose of veronal, that gave him an hallucination?"

He shrugged his shoulders. "*Le bon Dieu* knows, not I. There is much truth in that old saying that the wish is father to the thought. Who of us has not heard the voice of one whom he has loved and lost—perhaps beheld him? Such experiences come oftenest when we are in that no man's land between full consciousness and sleep. It is entirely possible he wished so hard for her that his tired senses heard the pleadings of his heart and vouchsafed him a vision. On the other hand, we have the rose for evidence."

"Yes, but the rose might have been there all the time," I argued. "Gloire de Dijons were her favorite flowers; he might possibly have bought one, put it in a vase, and then forgotten it. And as for one blossom being missing from the spray out in the cemetery, the wonder is that there were any left. I noticed how the young men hurried with the flowers following the funeral. If Mr. Martin had caught them he'd have given them a lecture. I've often heard him say the floral tributes deserve almost as great care as the body, because they're tokens of love."

"An estimable man, that Monsieur Martin," he returned. "He is a funeral director in a thousand. Come, let us go and drink to him."

"Bedad, sor, he's at it again, th' impident spalpeen!" Sergeant Costello stalked into our breakfast room, his usually florid face gone almost apoplectic with fury.

"*Morbleu*, do you say so? And who in Satan's foul name is he, and what has he been at?" de Grandin answered with a grin.

"Why, this here now felly, th' one that ye were afther readin' about in Miss Sainpolis' diary. Bad cess to 'im, wid th' pore young gur-rl hardly cold in her grave he's goin' round burglarizin' houses an' lavin', fingerprints all over th' place. Ouch, it's' th' brazen one he is! Belike he thinks we didn't check her fingerprints when we found that she wuz dead, an' o' course, he don't know nothin' about th' diary, so he thinks he's safe as long as—"

"One moment, if you please!" de Grandin shut him off. "Me, I feel the birth-pains of an idea stirring in my brain. I have what you call the hunch!" He raised a hand to enjoin silence; then: "Where did he commit this latest outrage?"

"'Twas Misther Westmorsham's house, out on th' Bordentown Road, sor. Th' family wuz to Atlantic City, an' th' servants had been given time off. This mornin' they come back to find th' house picked clean as a wishbone, wid furs an' silverware and jools and Lord knows what all carted off.

"An' how d'ye s'pose he got in? Why, through th' front door, if ye plaze. Jimmied it and walked right in, as bold as brass. We know he done it sometime between midnight an' this mornin', for th' harness bull on th' beat tried th' door at twelve an' one, an' agin at half-past three. At half-past six this mornin' a prowl car passin' by seen it wide open, an' when they went in to investigate they found th' whole place gutted clean as any carcass in a butcher-shop."

"*Parbleu*, it strikes a chord, my friends!" de Grandin cried. "Me, I have the idea. *Oui-da, ma petite pauvre*, I get the message which you sent!"

"Howly Moses, Doctor Trowbridge, sor, d'ye let him sthart his drinkin' so early in th' mornin'?" Costello asked me in well-simulated reproach.

"Never mind the ill-timed witticisms, thou great stupid one," de Grandin shot back. "Come with me, at once, immediately, right away. Take me to this house of Monsieur Westmorsham, let me look at it, and I will show you how to lay this miscreant by the heels. Come, hurry, we waste time!"

T HE SUPPER SHOW WAS more than half done when the captain showed us to our table at the Casa Ayer. The slow, deliberately erotic notes of "Mood

Indigo" trickled like a spate of hot spiced wine from the battery of saxophones set in the front rank of the orchestra while several young and shapely women cavorted on the dance floor in a flood of purple light.

De Grandin waved the menu card aside. "I have not the hunger," he announced. "Bring me a dozen lobster sandwiches and a pint of champagne *brut*, no more."

I ordered a Welsh rarebit and a mug of ale, and looked around the darkened room. Here and there a man's shirtfront or a woman's shoulders gleamed in dim highlight, but for the most part the whole place was steeped in shadow. On the stand before the orchestra I descried our visitor of the night before leading the musicians with the deftness of long practice, his task mechanical as drawing breath.

At the table next to us a party of two women with their escorts talked in strident tones, decrying music, food and entertainment. As a match flared I caught sight of them. The women were the sort one might expect to see at night clubs, powdered, painted, curled and bleached until all semblance of their natural selves had vanished. Curiously, although they wore the irreducible minimum of clothes, they seemed overdressed. One of the men faced from me; the other I saw full face in the orange flare of the match, and instinctively I hated him. Somehow, for all his obviously freshly-shaven face and spotless linen, he seemed unclean. Dark-skinned he was, swarthy as a mulatto, with curling black hair, full, red lips and dancing black eyes. But though he smiled it seemed to me he did so more in contempt than merriment, and the gleam in his eyes was decidedly more malicious than jocund. Handsome he was, certainly, but in the way that Mephistopheles is pictured; cruel, arrogant and vicious.

"My Gawd," I heard him sneer, "d'je ever see a cornier show?"

The match winked out, and as the darkness hid him from me I heard the clinking chime of metal on the tiled floor. He had offered the ultimate in insults to the club's talent, flung a fistful of coppers to them.

The lights flashed on and de Grandin beckoned to a waiter, handing him a note. In a moment young Strapoli joined us.

"You have something to tell me, sir?" he asked as we shook hands.

"Not now, a little later, perhaps," returned de Grandin. "First, I would have you tell me something. You recognize this picture, *hein?*" From his pocket he produced a small photograph and showed it to Strapoli.

The young man studied it a moment, and I saw his face go pale. "Yes, sir!" he replied emphatically. "That's the house I saw last night when Stephanola put her hands against my eyes. I'd recognize it anywhere. It's a real place, then?"

"*Assurément*, very real," de Grandin answered somewhat grimly, "and your recognition of it makes clear something which has puzzled me. I think I know now what it is that *Mademoiselle la Morte Amoureuse* attempts to tell us, and why. Attend me, if you please, my friend: It is more than merely probable that she will come to you again, and when she comes it is a certainty that she will show another of these mansions in the sky to you."

"Yes, sir?" expectantly.

"*Précisément.* When this occurs you are to notify me instantly. You comprehend?"

"But suppose she comes at night, as she most likely will—"

"Whether morning, noon or night, my friend, you are to let me know immediately. It is of the greatest importance."

Mystified, but willing to co-operate, Strapoli turned to rejoin his band, but as he passed the table next to ours he tripped, stumbled, and fell full length upon the floor.

"You"—he rose, eyes blazing as he faced the dark-skinned man who had flung coppers to the dancers—"you tripped me!"

"Yeah, I tripped yuh. So what?" the other countered, rising from his chair and lurching forward menacingly.

Strapoli's hand drew back, but before he had a chance to strike, the other was upon him, bringing up his knee and striking him violently in the stomach. It was as foul a blow as I had ever seen, and Strapoli crumpled to the floor, the breath completely knocked from him.

"Get fresh wid me, punk, will ya?" snarled the swarthy one. "For two cents I'd send yuh where I sent—" he broke off, laughing, and turned to his companions.

"C'mon, let's blow this lousy joint," he ordered.

Astoundingly, none of the waiters or attendants made a move to stop him as he swaggered from the place, and as we lifted Tony to his feet I whispered, "Don't you want to prosecute him? He attacked you without provocation, and both Doctor de Grandin and I will testify we saw him start the fight—"

"Oh, no, sir, thank you," he mumbled as he rearranged his clothes. "We wouldn't dare do that."

"No, and why, not?" asked de Grandin.

"That's Niccolo Frezzi—Nick the Brute—sir; he's the toughest mug in town. They'd lie for me and beat me up if I had him arrested. No one ever dares to cross him.

"He's suspected of all kinds of crimes, but the police can't pin anything on him, and if anybody dares appear against him, even in a traffic case, he's sure to get a dreadful beating in a day or two. Everybody knows that Nick the Brute does it, but there's never any legal proof of it, so—"

He brushed a fleck of dust from his sleeve and walked unsteadily to his place on the bandstand.

IT WAS HARDLY DAYLIGHT when the call came. Strapoli's voice was half hysterical.

"She's been here, sir," I heard him tell de Grandin as I picked up the extension telephone which stood beside my bed. "What? Yes, sir; she showed me another house—"

"*Très bon*, my friend, arise and dress. I shall join you instantly—"

In five minutes we were rushing through the dawn-gray streets toward Strapoli's apartment, pausing only to pick up Costello.

"Sure, an' this hunch o' yours had better be a good one," the sergeant growled as he climbed in beside us. "Gittin' a man up at th' crack o' dawn—"

"Be quiet," broke in de Grandin. "Unless I am much more mistaken than I think we shall crack other things beside the dawn before we finish this day's work. You have a two-foot length of hose in readiness?"

"Hose?—Fer th' love o' Mike, sor—"

"*Exactement.* Did not you say you would enjoy a conversation with this so vile Niccolo—you and a length of rubber hose?"

"O' course, sor, but—"

"No buts, my friend. I have the idea who this Niccolo is. If all goes as I think that it will go, I shall deliver him into your hands before so very long."

STRAPOLI WAITED FOR US on his doorstep.

"Sorry I couldn't call you sooner," he apologized, "but I fell asleep again when Stephanola left, and just woke up a little while ago."

"Never mind," de Grandin answered. "You are sure that you can recognize the house she showed you."

"Certain, sir."

"*Très bien.*" Slowly, looking carefully from right to left we cruised the residential sections of the city, beginning at the eastern suburbs, weaving slowly across town, finally threading through the wider avenues of the west end.

Abruptly, "There it is; I recognize it!" Tony called as we idled past a big house in Tunlaw Street. "I'd know it anywhere."

Costello consulted a typed list. "Yep, this is one of 'em," he announced. "Th' Fanshaws live here, but they're all in Florida. We have instructions to kape a special watch on it."

"U'm? Let us see how well instructions have been carried out," de Grandin replied as we walked across the lawn.

Step by careful step we circled the place, testing door and window fastenings. Everything was in order.

"All right, sor, an' where do we go from here?" the sergeant asked.

De Grandin took his chin between his thumb and forefinger. At length: "Who has the keys?" he asked.

Costello referred to his list again. "They're at th' family lawyer's, but—"

"No buts, if you will be so kind. Secure them all soon, and bring at least two officers to mount guard in the house. The robber has not yet appeared, but I am confident he will."

All day we waited for a summons to the Fanshaw house, but none came. By dinner time de Grandin was as nervous as a cat; when nine o'clock had sounded he was almost frantic.

"She cannot do this," he declared. "But no, she cannot make the fool of Jules de Grandin."

"What the deuce are you maundering about?" I asked.

"No matter, let us go and see for ourselves. I will phone Monsieur Strapoli to accompany us; he is not due at Casa Ayer till eleven."

The big old house was quiet as a tomb as Strapoli, de Grandin, Costello and I let ourselves in at the kitchen door.

"Seen anything?" the sergeant asked the patrolman waiting in the kitchen.

"Everything quiet as the stock exchange on Sunday, sir."

"Umph? What's next, sor?" the sergeant asked de Grandin.

"First we reconnoiter the terrain, then we sit and wait his coming. Be assured, he will come, my friends. The dead do not make jokes."

From room to room we walked, led by the beam of his flashlight. The place was still with that dead silence peculiar to deserted houses, and I had an eery feeling we were not alone, that unseen eyes were on us, watching with sardonic amusement.

"*Halte la!*" de Grandin ordered as we paused upon the threshold of the drawing-room. "A *silence*, he is coming, I think!"

Softly, so softly that it might have been mistaken for the scraping of a wind-blown branch against the window-pane, a sound came to us from the high French window overlooking the side garden. It came again, louder this time; then a sharp click sounded as the sash swung inward.

Against the back-drop of the cloudy starless night the window showed oblong and dark; dark and empty, like a hole. Then, barely darker than the outer darkness, we saw it: a man's form cased in skin-smooth tights, head covered by a tight hood—no chance for fallen hairs to give police a clue—hands encased in what seemed rubber gloves.

For a moment he paused on the sill like a cat about to leap down from a fence; then soundlessly he dropped into the room and seemed to fade into the shadows.

We were four to one, and two of us were armed, but for an instant terror gripped me by the throat. There was something so inhuman in the tight-clothed burglar, such a suggestion of uncanny cruelty and power. . . .

De Grandin broke the spell. "*Eh bien, Monsieur le Voleur,* you are very welcome!" he announced. "We have waited long, but not with patience—"

Flashlights cleft the blackness, and like miniature lightnings came the flamings of two pistols, then a third. Boots pounded on the hardwood floors as the two patrolmen rushed to join us. I saw a shadow loom against the window for an instant, then saw it topple inward as a whirring missile struck it.

"Tur-rn on th' lights, ye omadhauns!" Costello bellowed, and after a brief fumble a switch clicked, almost blinding us with the sudden brilliance from the chandelier Before the window lay a figure cased in clinging black silk jersey like an acrobat's costume, save that a hood-like helmet covered neck and chin and head, leaving only a small oblong of face visible, and this was barred by the wisp of a black silk mask. Beside the supine body lay de Grandin's little automatic; a larger weapon was half clutched in one of the man's flaccid, rubber-gloved hands.

Costello leaned and snatched the mask off of the fellow's face. I recognized him instantly: the man who threw the coppers at the Casa Ayer, then tripped and beat Tony Strapoli.

"Well, well," the sergeant chuckled. "Nick th' Brute in person, an' not a movin' pitcher. We got dead wood on 'im at last—"

"He is also the Niccolo mentioned in the poor Sainpolis girl's diary," de Grandin added.

"Th' divil!"

"Not quite, but almost, *mon sergent.* See, I saved him for you. I might have shot him, but I chose to throw my pistol at his head and stun him."

"Whatever for, sor? Why should ye be so tender—"

The little Frenchman grinned, "Did not I hear you once remark that you would like a quarter-hour's conversation with this one —you and a piece of rubber hose? Very well, then. You would not enjoy such a conversation with a wounded man."

"Be gob, ye're right, sor. It'll be a pleasure—"

"Doctor!" one of the patrolmen called. "This feller's hit bad—"

In our excitement we had failed to notice that Strapoli was not with us. Now we turned to see him lying by the farther wall, a spreading stain across his shirtfront. From the corners of his mouth there welled twin rivulets of blood. De Grandin gave a softly deprecating exclamation. "C'est *trop fort*—he is shot through the lung, my friend. See, it is a pulmonary hemorrhage!"

Strapoli's pulse was weakening rapidly, almost all semblance of expression had faded from his eyes, yet as we knelt beside him he achieved the vestige of a smile.

"Mon *pauvre garçon*," whispered de Grandin, "we have him in a vise, he cannot wriggle from the clutches of the law this time, and we shall make him pay through the nose—"

Strapoli paid no heed. His almost-vacant eyes were fixed on something which we could not see, something which appeared to be a foot or so above and before him. He raised his hands, palms facing, then drew them downward toward him.

The pantomime was perfect. He held a face between his palms, drew it closer, closer to his own . . . "Stephanola!" he murmured, and we saw his lips form in a kiss, then fall apart as a bright cataract of blood poured through them, and he fell back, supine, on the floor.

The two policemen arranged him, folded hands across his breast, dropped a coat over his face. De Grandin knelt in prayer a moment, then bounded up to join Costello.

"An' it'll be th' hot squat for yours, bozo," the sergeant was saying almost jocularly to the man in tights who was now regaining consciousness. "Ye've made a monkey o' th' law a long, long time, but this time we've put th' finger on ye. Ye'll not be batin' th' rap this time. Them rubber gloves ye're wearin', wid th' pore gur-rl's prints stuck on 'em, will pin a dozen burglaries on ye, but ye'll niver do a day o' time for 'em. Oh, no, my bucko! Ye've kilt a man in th' commission o' th' felony o' housebreakin', an' it's th' electric chair that ye'll be warmin' before firecrackers pop, so help me."

The two patrolmen were arguing. "Of course I didn't put it there," denied one hotly. "Where the devil would I get it in this empty house; besides do I look like an undertaker or sumpin'?"

"Well, where'd it come from, then?"

"Whist, ye divils, have ye no shame? Where's ye're rayspict for th' dead?" Costello, reproved in a bull-bellow. "What's all th' fussin' for?"

"Aw, Sarge, Milligan says I put this flower on 'im, an' I told him he was fulla prunes. Where'd I get a flower in this place?"

"What flower?" broke in Costello.

"This one, right here, sir," the young patrolman pointed to Strapoli's body.

Clasped in the pale hands folded on his breast Strapoli held a lovely Gloire de Dijon rose, fresh, dew-jeweled, breathing out a cloud of perfume from its golden heart.

"Do not dispute, *mes enfants*," de Grandin ordered. "We know the donor of that flower." He laid a hand upon his breast and made a sweeping bow to the great empty room. "*Félicilations, mes amis*," he said, as if congratulating an affianced couple.

"QUITE YES, BUT HOW can one explain it otherwise?" he said as we forgathered in my study shortly after midnight. "Did not she give the explanation when she first appeared to young Strapoli? But certainly. 'I have sinned, but there is a way open to forgiveness,' she told him. Of course, if she could bring this so vile Niccolo to justice she would acquire merit, perhaps attain to pardon for her self-destruction.

"She and the young Strapoli were in love, hence *en rapport*. She could, it seems, appear to him at will, while others could not sense her presence.

"When first he told us of his experience, how she laid her hands upon his eyes and made him see that mansion in the sky, I thought the whole occurrence too fantastic to be other than a dream.

"*Ha*, but next morning when you came with tidings of the burglary, I had at once the thought:

"'He saw a house, a big, fine, empty house last night . . . such a mansion has been burglarized . . . Jules de Grandin, get a picture of that house and show it to the young Strapoli. If he recognizes it as the one his vision showed him, that is what she meant.'

"*Parbleu*, I did; he did, and the case was proved. *Assurément*.

"'She has foreknowledge of the naughty Niccolo's intentions,' I tell me. 'When next she gives her lover the impression of a house, we have only to go there and wait his coming.'

"*Tenez*, she came again. She showed him another house; he told us; we searched until we found the house of his vision. We waited there—*voilà*."

The House of the Three Corpses

W E WERE WALKING HOME from Mrs. Douglas Lemworth's garden party.
Once a year the Old Dragon of Harrisonville Society holds a "fair" for
blind and crippled children, and if you are engaged in the professions
you attend, buy several wholly useless knickknacks at outrageous prices, drink a
glass of punch or cup of tea and eat a cake or two, then leave as unobtrusively as
possible. Even in most favorable conditions her parties are horrendous; tonight it
had been a foretaste of Purgatory.

Though dark had long since fallen, the city sweltered in the mid-June heat.
Sidewalks and roadways were hot to the touch; even the moon, just past the
full and shaped like a bent pie-plate, seemed panting in a febrile sky. Absolutely
stirless, the air seemed pressing down like a black blanket dipped in steaming
water, and as Jules de Grandin simmered outwardly he boiled with fury within.

"*Grand Dieu des chats*," he fumed, what an abominable *soirée*! It was not bad
enough that they should stifle us with vapid talk and senseless laughter, that
they should force us to be polite when we wished to shed our coats and shoes and
act the rowdy; *non*, *cordieu*, they must pile insult upon injury and give us *sacré*
lemon punch to drink! I am outraged and affronted. I am maimed for life; never
shall I get my face straight from that dreadful taste!"

Despite my own discomfort I could not forbear a grin. The look of wrathful
incredulity upon his face when he discovered that the lemonade was only lemonade was funnier than anything I'd seen in months.

"Well, cheer up," I consoled as we turned from the side street into the avenue, "we'll be home soon and then we'll have a Tom Collins."

"Ah, lovely thought!" he breathed ecstatically. "To shed these so uncomfortable clothes, to feel the cool gin trickle down our throats—*morbleu*, my friend,
is not that strange?"

"Eh?" I answered, startled by his sudden change of subject. "What?"

"Regard her, if you please. *La porte de la maison*, she is open."

Following the direction of his nod I saw the door of a big house across the street swing idly on its hinges, displaying a vista of dimly lighted hall.

In almost any other section of the city opened front doors on a night like this would have been natural as hatless men or girls without their stockings; but not in Tuscarora Avenue. That street is the last outpost of the pre-Depression era. House-girls in black bombazine and stiff white lawn may still be seen at work with mop and pail upon its low white-marble stoops at daybreak, lace curtains hang in primly white defiance of a changing world at its immaculately polished windows, house-men in uniform come silent-footed as trained cats to take the visitor's hat and gloves and walking-stick; no matter what the temperature may be, Tuscarora Avenue's street doors are never left open. "Perhaps"—I began; then—"good heavens!"

Sharp and poignant as an acid-burn, wordless, but hair-raising in intensity, the hail came to us from the open door.

"*Allons!*" de Grandin cried. "*Au secours!*"

We dashed across the street, but at the mansion's small square porch we paused involuntarily. The place seemed so substantially complacent, so smugly assured. . . . "We shall feel like two *poissons d'avril* if what we heard was someone crying out in a bad dream," he murmured as he tapped his stick on the sidewalk. "No matter, better to be laughed at for our pains than emulate the priests and Levites when someone stands in need of help."

He tiptoed up the steps and pushed the pearl button by the open door.

Somewhere inside the house a bell shrilled stridently, called again as he pressed on the button, and repeated its demand once more as he gave a last impatient jab. But no footsteps on the polished floor told us that our summons had been heard.

"Humph, looks as if we were mistaken, after all," I murmured. "Maybe the cry came from another house—"

"*Sang du diable!* Look well, my friend, and tell me if you see what I see!" Low and imperative, his whispered command came. Through the open door he pointed toward the end of the wide hall where an elaborately carved balustrade marked the ascent of a flight of winding stairs.

Just below the stair-bend stood a Florentine gilt chair and in it, hunched forward as though the victim of a sudden case of cramps, sat a man in house-servant's livery, green trousers and swallowtail coat corded with red braid, yellow-and-black waistcoat striped horizontally, and stiff-bosomed shirt.

I took the major details of the costume in subconsciously, for though his shirtfront was one of the least conspicuous items of his regalia, it seized and held my gaze. Across its left side, widening slowly to the waistcoat's V, was a dull reddish stain which profaned the linen's whiteness as a sudden shriek might violate a quiet night. And like a shriek the stain screamed out one single scarlet word—Murder!

De Grandin let his breath out in a suppressed "*ha!*" as he stepped across the threshold and advanced upon the seated man.

"Is he—he's—" I began, knowing all the time the answer which his nod confirmed.

"*Mais oui*, like a herring," he replied as he felt the fellow's pulse a moment, then let the lifeless hand fall back. "Unless I err more greatly than I think, he died *comme ça*"—he snapped his fingers softly; then:

"Come, let us see what else there is to see, but have the caution, *mon vieux*, it may be we are not alone."

I reached the door which let off from the rear of the hall first and laid my hand upon the knob, but before I had a chance to turn it he had jerked me back. "*Mais non*," he cautioned "not that way, my friend; do this."

Touching the handle lightly he sprang the latch, then drew back his foot and drove a vicious kick against the polished panels, sending the door crashing back against the wall.

Poised on his toes he waited for an instant, then grasped the handle of his cane as if it were a sword-hilt and the lower part as though it were a scabbard and pressed soundlessly through the doorway. "*Bien*," he whispered as he looked back with a nod, "the way seems clear." As I joined him at the threshold:

"Never open doors that way, my friend, when you are in a house whose shadows may conceal a murderer. Not long ago, to judge by the condition of that poor one yonder, someone did a bloody killing; for all we know he is still here and not at all averse to sending us to join his other victim. Had he lurked behind this door he could have shot you like a dog, or slit your gizzard with a knife as you came through, for you were coming from a lighted room into the dark, and would have made the perfect mark. *Hé*, but the naughty one who would assassinate de Grandin needs to rise before the sun. I am not to be caught napping. By no means. Had a wicked one been standing in concealment by that door, his head would surely have been soundly knocked against the wall when I kicked it, much of the fight would have been banged from him, and the advantage would be mine. You apprehend?"

I nodded appreciation of his wisdom as we stepped from the dim light of the hall into the faint gloom of the room beyond.

It was a dining-room, a long, high-ceilinged dining-room appointed with the equipment of gracious living. A long oval mahogany table of pure Sheraton design occupied the center of the floor, its polished surface giving back dim mirrorings of the pieces with which it had been set. In the center a silver girandole held a flat bouquet of early summer roses, a silver bowl of fruit—grapes, pomegranates and apricots—stood near the farther end, while a Sheffield coffee service graced the end near us. A demi-tasse of eggshell lusterware stood near the table edge; another lay upon its side, its spilled contents disfiguring the polished wood. A pair of diminutive liqueur glasses, not entirely drained, stood near the coffee cups, their facets reflecting the flickering light of two tall candles burning in high silver standards at each end of the table. A chair had been pushed back as though its occupant had risen hastily; another lay upon its side on the floor. To me it seemed as if the well-bred silence of the room was holding its breath in shocked surprise at some scene of violence lately witnessed.

"Nobody's here," I whispered, unconsciously and instinctively lowering my voice as one does in church or at a funeral. "Maybe they ran out when—"

"You say so?" he broke in. "*Regardez, s'il vous plaît.*"

He had seized one of the candles from the table and lifted it above his head, driving the shadows farther back into the corners of the room. As the light strengthened he pointed toward a high three-paneled Japanese screen which marked the entrance to the service-pantry.

Something hot and hard seemed forming in my throat as my eyes came to rest at the point toward which his pointing stick was aimed. Protruding from behind the screen an inch or so into the beam of candlelight was something which picked up the rays and threw them back in dichromatic reflections, a woman's silver-kid evening sandal and the ox-blood lacquer of her carefully kept toenails.

He strode across the room and folded back the screen.

She lay upon her side, a rather small, plump woman with a mass of tawny hair. One delicately tinted cheek was cradled in the curve of her bent elbow, and her mane of bronze-brown hair was swirling unconfined about her face like a cascade of molten copper. Her white-crêpe evening gown, cut in the severe lines which proclaimed the art of a master dressmaker, displayed a rent where the high heel of her sandal had caught in its hem, her corded girdle had come unfastened and trailed beside her on the floor, and on the low-cut bodice of her frock was a hand-wide soil of red—such a stain as marked the shirtfront of the dead servant in the hall.

One glance at her face, the startled, suffering expression, the half-closed eyes, the partly opened lips, told us it was needless to inquire further. She too was dead.

"*Eh bien,*" de Grandin tweaked the needle-points of his mustache, "he was no retailer, this one. When he went in for murder he did it in the grand manner, *n'est-ce-pas?* Put the screen back, if you please, exactly as we found it. We must leave things intact for the police and the coroner."

He led the way into the wide, bay-windowed drawing-room at the front of the house, raised his candle a moment; then: "*Nom d'un nom d'un nom d'un nom,* another!" he exclaimed.

He had not exaggerated. Lying on the low ottoman beside the door communicating with the hill was a man in dinner clothes, dark-skinned, sleek, well groomed, hands folded peacefully upon his breast, silk-stockinged ankles crossed, and on the white surface of his dress shirt was the same ghastly stain which we had found upon the servant in the hall and the murdered woman in the dining-room.

De Grandin eyed the oddly composed corpse in baffled speculation, as if he added up a column of figures and was puzzled at the unexpected answer. "*Que extraordinaire!*" he murmured, then, amazingly, gave vent to a low chuckle. "*Comme le temps de la prohibition, n'est-ce-pas?*"

His Gallic humor failed to register with me. "I don't see anything so droll about it," I scowled, "and what had Prohibition to do with—"

"*Tenez*, ever literal as a sausage, are you not, my old one? Cannot you see the connection? Observe him closely, if you please. No one ever died like that, not even in his bed. No, certainly. He was carried here and arranged thus, much in the way the gangsters of the Prohibition era laid their victims out when they had placed them on the spot.

"But yes, this business is clear as water from a spring. It fairly leaps to meet the eye. This was no robbery, no casual crime. It was carefully premeditated, planned and executed in accordance with a previously-agreed-upon program, as pitilessly as the heartlessness of Hell. The servant might have been, and doubtless was, killed to stop his mouth, the woman looks as if she might have died in flight, but this one? *Non.* He was killed, then dragged or carried here, then carefully arranged as if to fit into his casket."

Something evil and soft-footed seemed to stalk into that quiet room. There was no seeing it or hearing it, only the feeling, sudden and oppressive, as if the mid-June heat evaporated and in its place had come a leering, clammy coldness. Small red ants seemed crawling on my scalp; there was an oddly eery prickling in the hollows of my legs behind the knees. "Let's get out of here," I pleaded. "The police—"

He seemed to waken from a revery. "But yes, of course," he assented, "the police must be notified. Will not you call them, *mon vieux?* Ask for the good Costello; we need his wisdom and experience in such a case."

I scurried back into the entranceway, picked up the receiver, and dialed police headquarters. No buzzing answered as I spun the dial. The rubber instrument might have been a spool of wood for all the life it showed. Again and again I snapped the hook down, but without result.

"You have them—he is coming, the good sergeant?" de Grandin asked, emerging from the dining-room with the candle in one hand, his sword-stick in the other.

"No, I can't seem to get any response," I answered.

"U'm?" He pressed the instrument against his ear a moment. "One is not surprised. The wires have been cut."

He put the phone back on its tabouret and his small, keen face, flushed with heat and excitement, was more like that of an eager tomcat than ever.

"My friend," he told me earnestly, "I damn think we have put our feet into a case which will bear scrutinizing."

"But I thought you'd given up criminal investigation—"

"*En vérité*, I have so; but this is something more. Tell me, what does ritualistic murder suggest to your mind?"

"One of two things, a malevolent secret society or a cult of some sort."

He nodded. "You have right, my friend. Murder as such is criminal, though sometimes I think it fully justified; but the killing of a man with ritual and deliberation is an affront not only to the law, but to the Lord. It is the devil's business, and as such it interests me. Come, let us go."

We hurried to the cross street, walked a block down Myrtle Avenue and found an all-night pharmacy.

"*Holà, mon vieux*," I heard him call as his connection with headquarters was established, "I have a case for you. *Non*, great stupid one, not a case of beer, a case of murder. Three of them, *par la barbe d'un corbeau rouge!*"

Then he closed the phone booth door to shut the traffic noises out, and his animated conversation came to me only as an unintelligible hum.

"The sergeant tells me that the owners of the house have been living on the Riviera since last year," he told me as we started toward the murder mansion. "They rented it furnished to a family of Spaniards some eight months ago. That is all he knows at present, but he is having an investigation made. As soon as he has viewed the scene he'll take us to headquarters, where we may find—"

"Look out!" I warned, seizing his elbow and dragging him back to the curb as he stepped down into the street. A long, black, shiny, low-slung car had swung around the corner, driven at a furious pace and missing him by inches.

"*Bête, misérable!*" he glared at the retreating vehicle. "Must you rush him to his grave so quickly?"

I stared at him, astonished. "What—"

"It was a hearse," he explained. "One of those new vehicles designed to simulate a limousine. *Eh bien*, one wonders if it fools the dead man as he rides in it and makes him think he is alive and going for a pleasure trip?" He set a cigarette alight, then muttered angrily: "I saw his number. I shall report him to the good Costello."

The big police car, driven like the wind and turning out for no one, drew alongside the curb just as we reached the house, and Costello ran across the sidewalk to shake hands.

"There musta been some doin's here, from what you tell me, sor," he greeted.

"There were, indeed, my friend. Three of them there were, one in the entranceway, one in the dining-room, one in the—*mon Dieu*, Friend Trowbridge, look!"

I glanced past him into the hall, steeling my nerves against the sight of the dead houseman keeping silent vigil over his dead employers, then gasped in sheer astonishment. Everything was as we'd left it; the hall lamp still glowed warmly in its shade of bronze fretwork, the big gilt chair still stood below the curve of the stairway, but—the murdered man had disappeared.

Costello mopped his streaming forehead with a sopping handkerchief. "Where's this here now dead guy, sor?" he asked.

De Grandin muttered something unintelligible as he led us through the hall, across the darkened dining-room, and pushed back the carved screen. Nothing but the smudge of shadow where our bodies blocked the candlelight was there.

"*Parbleu!*" de Grandin muttered, tugged the tip of his mustache, and turned upon his heel to lead us to the drawing-room. The low ottoman, upholstered in brocaded satin, stood in the same position against the damask-draped wall, but on it was no sign or trace of the dead man we'd seen ten minutes earlier.

Costello drew a stogie from his pocket and bit its end off carefully, blowing wisps of tobacco from his mouth as he struck a match against his trousers. "There doesn't seem to be much doin' in th' line o' murder here right now, sor," he announced, keeping eyes resolutely fixed upon the match-flame as he drew a few quick puffs on his cigar. "Ye're sure ye seen them dead folk here—in this house? These buildin's look enough alike to be all five o' th' Dionne quints. Besides, it's a hot night. We're apt to see things that ain't there. Maybe—"

"'Maybe' be double-broiled upon the grates of blazing hell!" de Grandin almost shrieked. "Am I a fool, a simpleton, a zany? Have I been a physician for thirty years, yet not be able to know when I see a dead corpse? *Ah bah*, I tell you—"

Upstairs, apparently from the room immediately above us, there came a sudden wail, deep, long-drawn, rising with swift-tightening tension till it vanished in the thinness of an overstrained crescendo.

"Howly Mither!" cried Costello.

"Good heavens!" I ejaculated. "What the—"

"*Avec moi, mes enfants!*" de Grandin shouted. "Come with me. Corpses come and corpses go, but there is one who needs our help!"

With cat-like swiftness he rushed up the steps, paused a moment at the stairhead, then turned sharply to the left.

I was close behind him as he scuttled down the hall and kicked against the door that led into the chamber just above the drawing-room. Panting with the labor of the hurried climb, Costello stood at my elbow as the door flew back with a bang and we almost fell into the room.

Sitting in the middle of the floor, stockinged feet straight out before her, like a little girl at play, was a young woman—twenty-one or -two, I judged— dressed in a charming dinner frock of pastel blue georgette, a satin sandal in each hand. As we entered she shook back the strands of her almost iridescent black hair from before her face and beat against the floor with her slippers, like the trap-drummer of a band striking his instruments, then fell to laughing—a high-pitched, eery laugh; the laugh of utter, irresponsible idiocy.

"*Sí, sí, sí, sí!*" she cried, then fell into a sort of lilting, rhythmic song. "*Escolopendra! La escolopendra! La escolopendra muy inhumana.*" She drummed a sort of syncopated accompaniment to the words against the floor with her sandals, then raised the tempo of her blows until the spool-heels beat a sustained *rat-tat* on the boards as though she were attempting to crush some vile crawling thing that crept invisible around her on the floor.

"*Escolopendra, escolopendra!*" The words rose to a shriek that thinned out to a squeaking wail as she leaped unsteadily to her silk-cased feet and her wisp of frock swirled round her slender graceful legs when she bounded to the center of the bed and gathered her skirts round her, for all the world like a woman in deadly terror of a mouse.

"*Esto que es?*—what is this?" Costello asked as he stepped forward. "What talk is this of *una escolopendra*—a centipede—*chiquita?*"

"*Ohé, caballero,*" the girl cried tremulously, "have pity on poor Constancia and save her from the centipedes. They are all about, scores of them, hundreds, thousands! Help, oh, help me, I implore you!" She held her little hands beseechingly to him, and her voice rose to a thin and rasping scream as she repeated the dread word, "*escolopendra—escolopendra!*"

"Whist, mavourneen, if' 'tis centipedes as scares ye, ye can set yerself aisy. Sure, it's Jerry Costello as won't let one of 'em come near ye."

Reaching up, he gathered her into his arms as if she were a child. "Come on, sors," he suggested, "let's git goin'. This pore gur-rl's real enough, 'spite of all th' gallopin' corpses that ye've seen around here."

De Grandin in the lead, we hastened down the hall, and were almost at the stairs when he halted us with upraised hand. "A *silence;*" he commanded, "*écoutez!*"

Very faintly it came to us, more a whimper than a moan; low, frightened, weak. "*Morbleu,*" de Grandin exclaimed as he turned the handle, kicked the door, and disappeared into the bedroom like a diving duck.

I followed, and Costello, with the girl still in his arms, came after me. In a wicker chair beside the chamber's window sat a young man, the mad girl's brother, judging by their strong resemblance to each other, gently rocking to and fro and moaning softly to himself. He was dressed in dinner clothes, but they were woefully disheveled.

His collar had been torn half from his shirt; his tie, unknotted, hung limply round his neck; the bosom of his shirt had been wrenched from its studs and bellied out from his chest like the sail of a full-rigged ship standing before the wind.

"Howly Moses!" Costello tilted his straw hat down on his nose, then pushed it back upon his head. "Another of 'em?"

"Gregorio, *hermano mio!*" the girl Costello carried cried. "Gregorio—*las escolo pendras—*"

But the young man paid no heed. He bent forward in his chair, eyes riveted upon his shoe-tips, and hummed a sort of tuneless song to himself, pausing now and then to utter a low moan, then smile foolishly like a man fuddled with liquor.

"Hey, Clancy," Costello hurried to the stairhead and called down, "come up here on th' run; we got a couple o' nuts!"

The burly uniformed patrolman came up the stairs three at a time, joined us in the bedroom and drew the drooling youth up from his chair. "Up ye come, young felly me lad," he ordered. "Come on out o' this, an' mind ye don't make anny fuss."

The boy was docile enough. Tottering and staggering as though three-quarters drunk, but otherwise quite tractable, he went with Clancy down the stairs and made no effort at resistance as they thrust him into the police car.

Costello placed the girl in the back seat beside her brother and turned uncertainly to de Grandin. "Well, sor, now we got 'em, what're we goin' to do wid 'em, I dunno?" he asked.

"Do with them?" the little Frenchman echoed acidly. "How should I know that? What does one usually do with lunatics? Take them riding in the park, take them to dinner and the theatre, buy them lollipops and ice cream—if all else fails, you might convey them to the City Hospital. Me, I go to research that never-quite-sufficiently-to-be-anathematized house. I tell you that I saw three corpses there, as dead as mutton and as real as taxes. I shall not rest till I have found them. Can they play hide-and-seek with me? Shall three cadavers make the monkey out of me? I tell you no!"

"O.K., sor, I'll go wid ye," agreed Costello, but to me he whispered, "Stay wid 'im, Doctor Trowbridge, sor. I'm feared th' heat has touched 'im in th' head."

With the little Frenchman in the lead we marched into the hall again and, following the line of our first search, paused before the screen that masked the entrance to the service-pantry.

"See, look, observe," he ordered as he found the light switch and snapped the current on. "I tell you that a woman's body lay right here, and—*a-ah?*" He dropped upon his knees and pointed to a globular black button on the polished hardwood floor.

"U'm?" Costello grunted noncommittally, bending forward to inspect the globule. "What is it, sor, a bit o' jet?"

"Jet?" de Grandin echoed in disgust. "*Grand Dieu des porcs*, where are your eyes? Touch it!"

The sergeant put a tentative forefinger on the gleaming orb, then drew back suddenly, his heat-flushed face a thought paler. Where his finger had pressed it the button had gone flat, lost its rotundity and become a tiny pool of viscous liquid. What he had mistaken for a solid substance was a great drop of partly congealed blood.

"Bedad!" he wiped his finger on his trousers, then scrubbed it with his handkerchief. "What wuz it, sor? It looks like—"

"*Précisément.* It is," the Frenchman told him in a level, toneless voice. "That is exactly what it is, my friend. The heart's blood from the poor dead woman whom neither I nor good Friend Trowbridge saw here before we called you."

"Well, I'll be—" Costello began, and:

"One can almost find it in his heart to hope you will," cut in de Grandin. "You have made me the insult, you have intimated that I did not know a corpse when I beheld one, that I had hallucinations in the head—*ah bah*, at times you do annoy me past endurance!"

Grinning half maliciously, half derisively, he straightened from his knees and nodded toward the stairs.

"Let us go up and see what else it was Friend Trowbridge and I imagined when we first came to this house of the three corpses," he ordered.

We climbed the winding stairs, every sense alert for token of the unseen murderers or their victims, and walked down to the room where we had found the mad girl raving of the centipedes.

"Now," de Grandin cast a quick, stock-taking glance around the chamber, "one wonders why she babbled of '*las escolopendras.*' Even the insane do not harp upon one string without some provocation. It might have been that—stand back, my friends; beware!"

We stared at him in open-mouthed amazement, wondering if the room's influence had affected him, but he paid us no more heed than if we had been bits of lifeless furniture. Slowly, stepping softly on his toes, silent-footed as a cat that stalks a mouse, he was creeping toward the chintz-draped bedstead in the center of the room. And as he advanced noiselessly I heard a faint, queer, clattering sound, as though some mechanical toy, almost run down, were scratching on the bare, bright polished floor beyond the shadow of the bed.

Chin thrust forward, lips drawn back in a half snarl, mustache aquiver, the little Frenchman advanced some three feet or so, then quickly slipped the rapier blade from his sword-stick and stood poised, one foot forward, one drawn back, knees slightly bent, his bright blade slanting down in the beam of the electric light.

"*Sa-ha!*" He stabbed swiftly at the shadows and whipped his blade back. As he held the steel aloft for our inspection we saw a thing that writhed and twisted on its point, an unclean thing—six inches or so long; a many-jointed, horn-armored bit of obscenity which doubled convulsively into a sharp horseshoe-curve, then bent itself into a U, and waved a score or more of crooked, claw-armed legs in pain and fury as it writhed.

"Observe her very carefully," he ordered. "Medusa on a hundred legs, 'la escolopendra.' I have seen her kind in Africa and Asia and South America, but never of this size. One does not wonder that the poor young *mademoiselle* was frightened into idiocy by the knowledge that this lurked among the shadows of the room. It is a lucky thing I heard her clawing on the floor a moment since and recognized her footsteps; had she gotten up a trouser-leg and sunk her venomed mandibles in one of us—*tiens*, that one would soon have found himself immersed in flowers, but unable to enjoy their scent. Yes, certainly."

"Ye said a mouthful there, sor," Costello agreed. "I've seen 'em in th' Fillypines—'twas there I learnt th' Spanish lingo so's I understood th' pore gur-rl's ravin's—an' no one needs to tell me about 'em. Shtep careful, sors; perhaps there's more of 'em about. They hate th' light like Satan hates th' Mass, an' our pants would make a fine place for their hidin'. It's glad I am ye seen th' poison little divil first, Doctor de Grandin, sor."

"CALLING ALL CARS; ATTENTION all cars," a voice was droning through the police car's radio as we left the house. "Be on the lookout for a funeral car—a limousine hearse—license number F373-471. Reported stolen from in front of 723 Westmorland Street. License number F373-471. That is all."

"Ah-ha," de Grandin exclaimed. "Ah-ha-ha?"

"What is it, sor?" Costello asked.

"The joke has been on me, but now I think that we shall turn the laugh on them. One sees it all. But of course!"

"What—" I began, but he motioned me to silence.

"The hearse which almost ran me down, whence did it come, Friend Trowbridge?"

"Down this street; it almost clipped you as we started to cross at—"

"*Précisément, exactement*; quite so. You have very right, my friend. And the address whence the stolen car was pilfered, where is it, *mon sergent?*"

"Right round th' corner, sor. 'Bout halfway between this street an' Myrtle Avenoo—"

"Perfectly. It fits together like a picture-puzzle. Consider, if you please: Three bodies lie here, a hearse is stolen just around the comer; the bodies disappear, so does the hearse. Find one and you shall find the others, I damn think."

"THANK YOU KINDLY, GENTLEMEN; all contributions to our stock of assorted nuts are gratefully received." Doctor Donovan, in charge of H-3, the psychopathic ward at City Hospital, grinned amiably at us. "You say you found 'em babbling in a house in Tuscarora Avenue? Pair o' howlin' swells, eh? Well, we'll try to make 'em comfortable, though they can't have caviar for breakfast, and we're just fresh out o' *pâté de foie gras*. Still—"

"Doctor Donovan"—an interne pushed the superintendent's office door four inches open and nodded to our host.

"Yes, Ridgway?" asked Donovan.

"It's about the man and woman just brought in. It looks to me as if they had been drugged."

"Eh? The devil! What makes you think so?"

"Doctor Amlie took the girl and I examined the man. He seemed half drunk to me, and as I was preparing the test for alcoholism an urgent message came from Doctor Amlie.

"I left my patient with a male nurse and hurried over to the women's section. Amlie was all hot and bothered. 'What d'ye think o' this?' she asked me as she pointed to a spot of ecchymosis bigger than a silver dollar on her patient's arm. It was just above the common tendon of the triceps, and surrounded the pit of a big needle wound. Looked to me as if she'd had a hypo awkwardly administered. She couldn't 'a' given it to herself.

"Amlie wanted to test for morphine or cocaine, but I talked her out of it. Cocaine's hardly ever injected except for surgery, and morphine makes 'em lethargic. This girl was almost hysterical, jabbering Spanish or Italian, I don't know which, and stopping every other moment to giggle. Then she'd seem about to fall asleep, and suddenly wake up and go through the whole turn again.

"I'd just finished reading Smith's *Forensic Medicine in the East*, and had a hunch."

"Uh-huh?" Donovan encouraged.

"Well, sir, I withdrew one-point-fifty-four cc's of blood from her arm, directly in the ecchymosed area, and gave it the Beam test, using ethyl chloride instead of alcoholic potash—"

"Talk English, son; I'm rusty on my toxicology," Donovan broke in. "What'd you find?"

"Galenical cannabis indica, sir."

"U'm? Any objective symptoms?"

"Yes, sir. Her reflexes were practically nil, the heart action was markedly accelerated and the pupils dilated. Just now she seems about to drop off to sleep, but there are periods of hysteria recurring at gradually increasing intervals."

"Uh-huh. How about your patient?"

"Doctor Amlie came over to the male section with me and we put my man through the same tests. Everything checked, but his symptoms are more marked. I'd say he had a heavier dose, but both of 'em have been doped with cannabis indica injected intravenously."

"How long d'ye think this condition'll last?"

"According to the text books not much longer than an ordinary drunk. They should sleep it off in eight to ten hours, at most."

"*Pardon*," de Grandin interrupted, "but is there not some way that we can hold these persons *incommanicado*? In France it would be easy, but here—"

"Sure, there is," Costello broke in. "You an' Doctor Trowbridge say you seen three corpses in that house, an' ye believe that they wuz murthered. These kids wuz found there, an' might know sumpin' 'bout it. We can hold 'em as material witnesses any reasonable time."

"Very good, take the necessary steps to keep them in restraint, and when they are recovered from their drugged sleep let me see them."

"SAY, TROWBRIDGE," DOCTOR DONOVAN's voice came to me on the telephone next morning, "who wants to break in to see a nut?"

"Who wants to what?" I answered, mystified.

"You heard me right, feller. There was some monkey business down here last night, and one of those kids you and de Grandin and Costello brought here is mixed up in it. Can you and de Grandin come down here?"

Dawkins, the night chief orderly of the psychopathic ward, was waiting for us in the superintendent's office when we reached the City Hospital, and launched upon his story without preface.

"I was sittin' just inside the safety door—the grating, you know—and it was just ten minutes after one when the funny business started," he told us.

"How do you place the time with such exactitude?" de Grandin asked.

Dawkins grinned. "I went on duty at eleven, and wouldn't be relieved till seven in the morning. About one o'clock I began to get pretty sleepy, so I sent Hosmer to the kitchen for a pot o' coffee and some sandwiches. It seemed to me he took a little longer than he should, and I'd just looked up at the electric clock on the wall just opposite my chair when I heard a funny-sounding noise.

"It wasn't quite like anything I'd ever heard before, for while it was a sort of whistling, like a sudden wind, it was also something like the humming of a monster bee, perhaps an airplane."

De Grandin tweaked his mustache ends. "You say it combined a hum and whistle?"

"That's just about the way to describe it, sir."

"Very good, and then?"

"Then I saw the shadow, sir. You know, there's a ceiling light in the main corridor—the one connecting the ambulance entrance with the emergency ward—just around the corner from the hallway leading to H-3. Anybody standing around the corner of the junction of the two corridors, but between that light and the angle made by our hallway branching off, casts a shadow down our hall. Many a time I've spotted nurses and orderlies standing to talk there when they should have been about their duties. Well, when I heard this funny noise I got up, and as I did I saw this shadow. It wasn't any of the hospital employees. It was someone with a derby hat on, and it looked to me as if he had a club or something in his hand. I didn't like his looks too much."

"You were suspicious? Why?"

"Well, we haven't had anything of the kind happen for some years, but in the old days when the gangs were running liquor, two-three times gunmen broke into the hospital and shot up fellers we had in here. Once they rubbed out an orderly because he tried to stop 'em.

"So I started down to the other end of the ward. Dennis was on duty there, and he's a pretty good one to have with you in a scrap. O' course, we aren't allowed to carry weapons—not even billies—in H-3. Too much chance of some lunatic's getting hold of 'em and going on a rampage. But I wanted Dennis to take a gander at this guy's shadow, and if he thought what I did, we could call up the main office and have someone with a gun come round and grab him from behind while we went out to tackle him in front. So I started down to get Dennis."

"Yes, and then?"

"Well, sir, just as I got abreast of 34, the room they'd put Doctor Ridgway's patient in, I heard a sound that seemed to cut through the queer noise I've been telling you about, like someone filing a piece of metal.

"The patient was asleep and I thought he might be snoring—some of 'em make mighty funny noises-but when I looked through the peep-hole in the door I saw a feller on the outside, cutting through the window grating.

"You know how our windows are. There's a strong steel netting on the outside, then the glass, then another grating on the inside. This feller was working on the outside grating with a saw of some sort, and had already cut a hole two inches long.

"D'ye know what I think?"

"Nothing would delight us more than hearing it, my friend."

"Well, sir, I think that funny noise I heard was made to cover up the noise the saw made as it cut that grating."

"Your theory does great credit to your perspicacity. Did you see the one who sought to cut the grating?"

"Not very good, sir. He seen me about the same time that I spotted him, and ducked down out o' sight. Funny thing about him, though. I'd say he was a for-eigner. Anyhow, he was mighty dark and had black hair and a large nose."

Donovan took up the story: "Dawkins turned in the alarm, and we rushed around to see about it. Of course, we found no one in the main corridor, but that's not strange. There's no guard at the ambulance entrance, and anyone can come or go that way at will. If we hadn't found the cut screen we'd have thought he dreamed it.

"Now, what I want to know is this: Who'd want to help those kids escape? As I understand it, they're being held as witnesses to a murder—"

"*Excusez-moi!*" de Grandin cut in; then, to Dawkins: "Will you take me to the window this one tried to cut through, if you please?"

They were back in less than three minutes, and a grim look set upon the little Frenchman's face as he opened his folded handkerchief and spread it out on Donovan's desk. "*Regardez!*" he directed.

Upon the linen lay some particles of glass, evidently portions of a smashed test-tube, and the crushed but clearly recognizable body of a four-inch centipede.

"THERE IS A BLACK dog running through my brain," he complained as we sat waiting in the study after dinner the next evening. "This case puzzles me. Why should it not be one thing or the other? Why should it be a hybrid? Somewhere"—he spread his hands as if to reach for something—"just beyond my fingertips the answer lies, but I cannot touch it."

"What puzzles you particularly?" I asked. "What they've done with the missing bodies?"

"Ah, *non*. That is comparatively simple. When the police find the stolen hearse, as they are sure to do in time, they will find the bodies in it. It is the half-caste nature of the case which causes me confusion. Consider him, if you please." He spread his fingers out fanwise and checked the items on them:

"We come on three dead corpses. There is nothing strange in death. It has been a scientific fact since Eve and Adam first sinned. All indications are that they were murdered. Murder, in and of itself, is no novelty. It has been going on since Cain slew Abel; but surrounding circumstances are unusual. Oh, yes, very. The servant and the woman had been left as they had died, one in his chair, the other on the floor; but the man is carried to the drawing-room and laid out carefully. Is it that the killers first arranged him, and were about to do the same for their two other victims when we were attracted by the young girl's scream, and interrupted them? There is a thought there.

"Then about the young man and his sister. Both had been drugged with hashish and left in their respective rooms to be killed by poison centipedes. Why? one wonders. Why were they not killed out of hand, like the three others; why were they drugged instead of being bound and gagged when they were left as prey for the vile myriapods?

"And why should they be Spaniards, as they obviously are?"

Despite myself I grinned. "Why, for the same reason that you're French and I'm American," I answered. "There's nothing strange about a Spaniard being Spanish, is there?"

"In this case, yes," he countered. "If they had been Orientals I could under-stand some phases of the puzzle—the hashish and the so vile piping heard about the hospital when the attempt to drop the centipede into the young man's room was made. But their being Spanish upsets all my theories.

"Hashish is a drug peculiar to the East. They eat it, smoke it; sometimes, though not often, they inject it. *Alors*, we may assume that he who used it on these children was an Eastern, *n'est-ce-pas?*

"As for the so peculiar music—the 'funny sound'—which the good Dawkins heard, I know her. She is a very high, shrill sound produced by blowing on a specially prepared reed, and has a tendency to shock the sensory-motor nerves to a paralysis; something like the shrieking of the Chinese screaming boys, whose high, thin, piercing wail so disorganizes the hearer's nervous system that his marksmanship is impaired and often he is rendered all but helpless in a fight. Our agents in the Lebanon mountains report this music his been used by—*mon Dieu*, I am the monumental stupid-head! Why did I not consider it before?"

"What in the world—" I began, but before I had a chance to frame my question Nora McGinnis announced from the study entrance:

"Sergeant Costello an' a young lady an' man, sors, if yez plaze."

"Good evenin', gentlemen," the big detective greeted. "I brought 'em, as ye asked. These are Señorita and Señor Gutierrez y del Gado de Jerez."

Though the youngsters had been confined in the hospital it was evident that access to their wardrobe had not been denied them, and their appearance was far different from that of the babbling imbeciles we'd found in Tuscarora Avenue. The lad was positively seal-sleek; if anything, a thought too perfect in his grooming. He wore more jewelry than good taste required and smelled unnecessarily of lilac perfume.

As for Constancia, only the knowledge that she'd been in custody continuously, and so could not have sent a substitute, enabled me to recognize the wild-haired, panic-ridden girl of the previous night in the self-contained and assured young woman who occupied the chair opposite me. I'd forgotten how intensely black her hair was when we'd rescued her. Now it seemed even blacker. Drawn severely back in a French roll and parted low on the left side, it glinted like a grackle's throat in the lamplight. Dressed with pomade, two curls like inverted question marks were plastered close against her cheeks where a man's sideburns would be, and were rendered more noticeable by the long pendants of green jade that hung nearly to her creamy shoulders from her ear-lobes. Her backless, strapless evening gown of shimmering black satin fitted almost as tightly as a stocking, covering to some extent but by no means concealing any of her narrow, lissome figure. Her ear-pendants and the emerald clasps of her stilt-heeled sandals were her only jewelry and the only spots of color in her costume. The vivid carmine of her painted lips glowed like a red rose fallen in the snow, for her face, throat, shoulders and tapering arms and hands were dead-white in their pallor as the petals of a gardenia. Despite her immaturity of figure and youthfulness of face—she seemed much younger than on the night we'd first seen her—there was a strange allure about her, and I caught myself comparing her to Carmen in a Paris frock or Francesca da Rimini with Rue de la Paix accessories.

Ankles crossed demurely, hands folded in her lap, she cast a glance from burnished-onyx eyes on Jules de Grandin. "Señor," she murmured in a throaty rich contralto, very different from her reedy ravings of the other night, "they tell me that our parents are—have been killed. Is it truly so?" Her English was without accent, save for a shortening of the *i*'s and a slight rolling of the *r*'s.

"Alas, I fear that it is true, *señorita*," de Grandin answered. "Can you tell me any reason anyone should wish them harm?"

Her sultry eyes came up to his beneath their curling fringe of long black lashes, and if it had been possible, I'd have said their darkness deepened. "I cannot tell you who wished evil to them," she replied, "but I know they lived in fear of someone or some thing. I am seventeen years old, and never in my life have I lived long enough in any place to know it well or call it home or make a lasting friendship. Always we have been upon the move, like gipsies or an army. London, Paris, the Riviera, Zurich, Rome, California, New York—we have flown from one to another like birds pursued by hawks that will not let them rest in any tree. Never have we owned a home—no, not so much as the beds we slept on. I grew up in villas rented ready furnished, in *pensions* and hotels. We were like the orchid that draws sustenance from the air and never sinks its roots into the soil beneath it. The nearest to a home I ever had was the three years that I was at convent school near Cologne. I think if they had let me stay there I should have found that I had the vocation, but"—her narrow naked shoulders came up in a shrug—"it was like the rest. No sooner had I learned to love it— found peace and contentment there—than they took me away."

"One sympathizes with you, *señorita*. You have no idea who or what it was your parents fled?"

"No, *caballero*. I only know they feared it greatly. We would come to rest in some new place, perhaps a little *pension* in Paris or Berlin, perhaps a furnished cottage in some English village, or a hotel in Switzerland, when one day *Mama* or the *Padre* would come in with fear upon his face, looking backward as he walked, as though an *asesino* dogged his steps, and, 'They are here,' or 'I have seen them,' one would tell the other. Then in hot haste we packed our clothing and effects—always we lived with porte-manteux in readiness—and off we rushed in secrecy, like criminals fleeing from the law.

"But I do not think the *Padre* ever was a criminal, for everywhere we went he was most friendly with the police. Always when we came to live in some new place the *cuartel general de policia*—the police headquarters—was one of the first places which he visited. Is that the way a fugitive from justice acts?"

"That's right, sor," Costello confirmed. "Colonel Gutierrez came to head-quarters when he first moved here nine months ago, an' asked 'em to give orders to th' man on his bate to give special attention to his house. Told 'em he'd been burglarized three times in his last residence, an' his wife wuz on th' verge of a breakdown."

De Grandin nodded as he turned back to the girl. "The sergeant called your father Colonel Gutierrez, *señorita*. Do you know what army he served in?"

"No, *señor*, he had quit the military service before I was born. I never heard him mention it, nor did I ever see a picture of him in his uniform."

The Frenchman nodded understandingly. Apparently this conversation, so meaningless to me, confirmed some theory he had formed. "What of the night we found you?" he asked. "Precisely what occurred, *señorita?*"

Young Gutierrez leaped up and advanced a step toward Jules de Grandin. "*Señor,*" he exclaimed, as he clasped his slender, ring-laden hands in a perfect ecstasy of entreaty, "we—my sister and I—are in the dreadful trouble. These scoundrels have put the slight upon us. They have slain our parents. Blood calls for blood. It is the *rifa*, the *contienda*—the blood-feud—we have with them. We call on you to help us get revenge!"

"Gregorio! *Hermanito mio!*" the girl called softly as she rose and laid a hand upon her brother's arm. "*Silencio, corazonito pequeño!*" To us she added rapidly in English:

"Forgive him, *señores*. He lives in a small world of his own. He is, alas, *un necio dulce*—one of God's little ones."

There seemed magic in her touch, for the young man quieted immediately, and sat silently with her hand clasped in his as she responded to de Grandin's query.

"We had finished dinner, and Gregorio and I had been excused while *Mama* and the *Padre* had their coffee and liqueur. He—my brother—and I were going to the cinema and were changing from our dinner clothes when I heard a sudden cry downstairs. It was my mother's voice, pitched high and thin, as if she suffered or were very frightened."

"*A-a-ah?*" de Grandin cut in on a rising note. "And then, if you please?"

"I heard no more, but as I ran to see if I could be of help a hand was laid upon my doorknob and two men rushed into my room. One held a cane or stick of some sort in his hand and as I shrank back from him he thrust it at me. There must have been a pin or steel point on it, for it pierced my arm and hurt me dreadfully, but only for a moment."

"A moment, *señorita?* How do you mean?"

She looked at him and managed a wan smile. "There was the oddest feel-ing spreading through me—like a sudden deathly fatigue, or, perhaps, a sort of numbness. I still stood upon my feet, but I had no idea how I kept on them. I seemed to have grown to a giant's height, the floor seemed far away and unreal, as the earth does when you look at it from the top of a high tower; and I knew that in a moment I should fall upon my face, but even as I realized it I knew that I'd not feel it. I felt as if I never should feet anything again.

"Then I was on the floor, with the cool boards pressing on my cheek. I had fallen, I knew, but I had not felt the impact. One moment I was standing; the next I lay upon the floor, with no recollection how I got there.

"One of the men had a small cage of woven willow, something like the little straw cages that the Japanese keep crickets in, and suddenly he upset it and shook it. Something—several things—came tumbling, squirming, out of it, and I recognized them as great centipedes—the deadly poisonous *escolopendras* whose bite is terrible as that of a tarantula. Then they laughed at me and left.

"The centipedes were writhing toward the corners of the room as I tried to rise and run, but I could not. The numb, half-paralyzed sensation was gone, but in its stead I seemed to suffer from a sudden overpowering dizziness. And my eyes were playing tricks on me. The lamplight seemed to glow and glitter with prismatic colors, and the edges of the room began to curl in on me, like the petals of a folding flower. I was in deadly terror of the centipedes, but somehow it seemed I was too tired to move.

"Then one of them came running at me from the shadow of the bed. Its eyes looked bigger than the headlights of a motor car and seemed to glow with fire-red flashes. Somehow I managed to sit up and tear the sandals off my feet and beat the floor with them. I couldn't reach to strike the centipede, for if I leaned this way or that I knew that I would topple over, and then my face would be down on the floor where it was! But when I pounded on the floor with my shoes it seemed to be afraid and ran back to the shadows.

"I have no idea how long I sat there and drummed upon the floor, but presently I heard a woman scream and scream, as though she'd never stop. After a little while I realized it was I who screamed, but I was powerless to stop it. It might have been five minutes or an hour that I sat and screamed and drummed on the floor with my shoes; I could not say. But presently my door was opened and you gentlemen came in. To God and you I owe my life, *señores*." The smile with which she swept us was positively ravishing;

"*Eh bien, señorita*, we are indebted to you for a very lucid exposition of that so trying night's occurrences," de Grandin said. "We need not trouble to interrogate your brother. From all that we have seen we may assume that his experiences were substantially the same as yours.

"You have heard about the attempt on his life at the hospital?"

"But yes," she answered tremulously. "Is there no safety for us anywhere? What have we done to anyone? Why should anybody wish to harm poor us."

"Please understand me, *señorita*," he returned. "It is for your own safety, not because we think of you as criminals, that we have arranged to lodge you in the city prison. Even in the hospital you are not safe, but in the prison with its fast-locked doors and many guards your safety is assured. As for who it was that orphaned you and then administered a drug and tried to kill you with the poison centipedes, I do not know, but I shall find out, never fear. I am Jules de Grandin, and Jules de Grandin is a very clever fellow."

"B E TH' WAY, SOR," Costello whispered as he prepared to escort the young people to the safety of the prison, "they've found th' missin' hearse. It wuz in th' bay, where it'd been run off Whitman's Dock. The plates wuz missin', but Joe Valenti, th' Eyetalian undertaker, identified it."

"Ah, that is good. The bodies were in it, of course?"

"No, sor, they weren't. Th' Harbor Squad's draggin' th' bay on th' off chance they mighta dropped out, but I don't think they'll find 'em. Th' hearse doors wuz all shut when it wuz fished up, an' hardly any water had seeped in. 'Tain't likely th' bodies fell out of it."

T HE SERGEANT CAME TO dinner three nights later, and did full justice to the *ragout irlandais* which Nora had prepared for his especial benefit. Not until the meal was over and we had adjourned to the study would de Grandin speak about the case; then, as he took his stance before the empty fireplace: "My friends," he announced as he drew a sheaf of papers from his pocket, "I damn think I have the answer to our puzzle. You will remember *Señorita* Gutierrez knew her father had resigned his commission before her birth, and had never spoken of his military service in her hearing. Perhaps you wondered at it. We old soldiers are not wont to minimize the tales of our adventures. Yet there was good reason for his reticence.

"I have his record here. I have cabled to the *Sûrêté* and the *Ministère de la Guerre*, and they replied at length by air mail via South America.

"Constantino Cristóbal José Gutierrez y del Gado de Jerez was, we knew, a Spaniard; we did not know he quit his country in extraordinary haste with the *guardia civil* upon his heels. When the Barcelona riots broke out in 1909 he was a young subaltern fresh from military school at Toledo, where he had been educated in the traditions of Pizarro and Cortez. You recall what happened after that uprising? How Francisco Ferrer the great educator was tried by a court-martial? *Tiens*, when a military court tries a soldier it metes out substantial justice. When it tries a civilian one may wager safely that it was convoked to find him guilty of all charges.

"Our young *sous-lieutenant* was among the prosecution's witnesses and when the trial was completed the sentence sent the defendants to the firing-party.

"The whole world shuddered at the outrage, and the pressure of mankind's opinion was so great that three years later another military court revoked the first one's findings, and branded testimony given against Ferrer and his co-defendants as perjury.

"Gutierrez, now a captain, took offense at this supposed reflection on his veracity, challenged one of the court to a duel and killed him at the first pass. His opponent was a major, partly crippled by a wound he had received in Cuba, very wealthy and of an influential family. Captain Gutierrez killed his own career in the Spanish army when he killed his adversary, and had to flee in greatest haste to avoid arrest.

"*Eh bien*, he landed where so many disappointed soldiers land, in the Foreign Legion. He had the blood of the *Conquistadores* in him, that one. Embittered, bold and reckless, he was the *légionnaire par excellence*. By the end of the Great War he was a colonel.

"Then, as now and always, the Riffs and Druses were in revolt, actual or prospective, and Colonel Gutierrez when assigned to the Intelligence proved successful in obtaining military information from the captured rebels. The Spaniard has a flair for torture, my friends. Cruelty is as native to him as delicacy is to a Frenchman. Some few of Colonel Gutierrez' prisoners escaped, some he released when they had served their turn. All went back home crippled and deformed, and his popularity with the hillmen waned in inverse ratio to the number of their tribesmen he disfigured.

"*Tenez*, at length an elderly Druse gentleman named Abn-el-Kader fell into our brave colonel's none too gentle hands, and with him was captured his daughter Jahanara, called *lalla aziza*, the beautiful lady. She was indeed a lovely creature, just turned thirteen, which in the East meant budding into womanhood, with copper-red hair rolling low upon her snowy forehead and passionate, dreamy, wistful eyes into which a man looked once, then never cared to look away again.

"*Eh bien*, he was stubborn, that one. He was not at all talkative. Rather than disclose his tribesmen's plans he chose to die, which he did in circumstances of elaborate discomfort, and Jahanara was not only a prisoner, but an orphan as well.

"*Corbleu*, my friends, romance is much like history in that the more it changes the more it is the same wherever it is found. Race, religion and the custom of blood-feud as old as the Lebanon Hills stood between them, but the captor had become the captive, and *Monsieur le Colonel* was eyebrow-deep in love with Lalla Aziza Jahanara. One wonders if she loved or hated him the more when they first kissed, whether she would not rather have drunk his heart's blood than his eager, panting breath as he took her in his arms. *Tiens*, love conquers all, as Ovid says. In a little while she wed the man at whose command her father died in torment.

"But though the prince had wed his Cinderella it was not to be his lot to live in peaceful happiness with her. Oh, no! The Druses are a prideful, stiff-necked people. Their ancient tribal law forbids their women marrying outside their race. They have a proverb, 'No Druse girl mates with any but a Druse, and if she does, her father and her brothers track her down and slit her heart, though she be lying in the Sultan's arms.' The Druse maids understand this perfectly. Before they come of marriageable age they swear an oath to keep the ancient tribal law on pain of death—death by the knife of vengeance for themselves, and if, they have borne hybrid children—'may they be the prey of centipedes.'

"You apprehend, my friends? Cannot you understand why Colonel Gutierrez quit the Legion and with his Druse bride, and later with his half-blood children, lived a hunted, fugitive existence, seeing a threat in each strange face, starting frightfully at every vagrant shadow, never feeling safe in any one place very long? Yes, certainly.

"Ordinarily only the unfaithful Druse woman and her children are the objects of the tribal Nemesis, but the hillmen had a long score to settle with the colonel. The memory of the missing hands and feet, the burnt-out eyes, the slit and speechless-babbling tongues of their blood brethren festered like a canker-sore in their minds. They owed him a long-standing debt of vengeance. *Tiens*, it seems they paid it."

"REGARD HIM, IF YOU please," he ordered me at breakfast two days later, handing me a copy of the morning *Journal*.

GUTIERREZ CHILDREN RETURN HOME

the headline read, and under it a short item:

Senorita Constancia Gutierrez and her brother Gregorio, who have been undergoing treatment at City Hospital for the past few days, are now fully recovered and have returned to their residence, 1502 Tuscarora Avenue, where they will hereafter be at home to their many friends.

"Is it not magnificent?" he asked.

"I don't see anything magnificent about it," I returned. "It doesn't even seem like good make-up to me. How did they ever come to stick an unimportant little item like that on the first page instead of burying it in the Society column? Who cares whether Constancia and Gregorio have gone home or not?"

"You and I do, by example," he answered with a grin. "The good Costello does, but, most important of us all, several gentlemen from the Djebel Druse are greatly interested in their movements. As long as they were lodged in City Prison they were safe. Now that they are home again—"

"Good heavens, d'ye mean that you're deliberately exposing them to—"

"*Mais oui*, my friend. We set the trap, we wait, we spring, *parbleu!* One might recast the old jingle to read:

"Will you walk into my parlor?"
Said de Grandin to the Druses.

The cry came quivering down the hall, shrill, sharp, fright-freighted.

For half an hour we had waited in the darkened room adjoining that in which Constancia and her brother were, ears strained to catch the slightest sound which might betray arrival of the Druses. Downstairs, patrolmen waited in the drawing-room and kitchen, two others lurked in ambush, in the back yard. Our baited trap seemed escape-proof, yet . . .

The scream came once again, then stopped abruptly, like a radio-transmission when the dial is curtly turned.

"*Morbleu*, they have won through!" de Grandin cried as he blew his police whistle and we tumbled through the door and dashed into Constancia's room.

From downstairs came the police guard, clattering and pounding on the steps. The bedroom fairly boiled with armed men, but nowhere was there any sign of the youngsters.

"No one came through th' front way," a policeman told Costello, and:

"Same wid th' kitchen," supplemented another. "A mouse couldn't 'a' got past us—"

"The screen is out," de Grandin interrupted, "and a drain pipe runs within a foot of the window. A moderately agile climber might have—"

"Hey, youse down there!" Costello bawled to the patrolmen in the back yard, "seen anybody?"

There was no answer. "*Ah bah*, we waste the time," de Grandin snapped. "It is probable they knifed the guards as they did the servant when they killed the colonel and his lady. After them!"

"They can't 'a' took 'em very far," Costello panted as we rushed downstairs. "Th' alley's too narrow for a car; they'll have to carry 'em."

The two patrolmen lay inert as corpses on the lawn, but a hurried glance assured us they were merely stunned, and we left them and rushed out into the alley.

Where the luminance of a street lamp gleamed dully from the alley-head at the cross street we saw a group of hurrying figures, and de Grandin raised his pistol. "*Canaille!*" he rasped, and fired. One of the fugitives fell staggering, but the others hurried on, and as they neared the light we saw they struggled with two shrouded figures.

They had perhaps two hundred feet start of us, and de Grandin did not dare to fire again for fear of injuring the captives. Though we raced at top speed they reached the cross street before we could close the gap sufficiently to fire with safety, and as we emerged from the alley we saw them scrambling into a car waiting at the curb with engine running. Next instant they roared past us and we caught a glimpse of Constancia's blanched face as she peered through the tonneau window.

Half a dozen blasts on Costello's whistle brought two squad cars rushing round the corner, and the chase was on.

Perhaps a quarter-mile away, but losing distance with each revolution of the wheels, our quarry sped. De Grandin hung upon our running-board, his pistol raised, waiting opportunity to send a telling shot into the fleeing car.

Eight, ten, a dozen blocks we raced at breakneck speed, our sirens cleaving through the sultry darkness like lightning lances. We were less than half a block behind them when they swerved sharply to the right and darted down a cross street. When we reached the corner they had disappeared.

Like hounds at fault we looked about us. To the left a creek cut through the town, and most streets ended at it, only one in each five being bridged. The two cross streets to the right were torn up for repaving; they could not have fled that way, and no glimmering tail light showed in the street in which we stood.

Most of the houses in the block were deserted, and any of them might afford a refuge for the Druses and their prisoners, but nowhere, look sharply as we would, could we espy a sign of their old motor. From house to darkened house we went, looking in the back yards for some trace of the car. At last:

"My friends, come quickly!" called de Grandin. He was standing at the creek bank, pointing to the shallow muddy water. Nose-foremost in the stream was a decrepit motor, its tail light still aglow. "*Tiens*, it seems to be a habit with them, throwing their equipage into the water," he remarked; then: "*En avant, mes enfants. A la maison!*

"No, be of the quietness," he warned as Costello put his shoulder to the door. "Let me do it." From his pocket he produced a thin strip of metal, worked at the lock for a moment; then, "*Entrez!*" he invited as the lock snapped back with a soft click.

Down the narrow, dust-strewn hall we crept, tried several doors without result, then began to mount the stairway, treading on the extreme outer edges of the boards to avoid betraying creaks.

An oblong of slate-gray against the darkness told us where a window opened from the upper hall, and toward it we stole silently, halting as de Grandin gave a low hiss. Thin as a honed razor-blade, but not to be mistaken in the gloom, a narrow line of faint light trickled from beneath a tight-closed door.

"You are ready, *mon sergent?*"

"Aye, sor."

Like twin battering-rams they launched themselves against the door. Its flimsy panels splintered as if they were matchwood, and in the subdued light of a single electric bulb pendant from the ceiling we saw three men facing two figures lashed to chairs.

Constancia Gutierrez sat facing us, and beside her was her brother. Both were gagged with wide strips of adhesive tape across their lips; both had their shoes and stockings stripped away; more wide bands of adhesive tape bound their feet and ankles to the chair legs in such manner that they could not lift them from the floor.

One of the men was emptying a small cage of woven wicker work as we crashed in, and as its little door flapped open we saw three writhing centipedes come tumbling out and strike the dusty floor beside the girl's bare feet.

A moan of terror—a scream of anguished horror muted by the gag across her lips—came from Constancia as the poisonous insects struck the floor; then her head fell forward as her senses failed.

At the crashing of the door the three men wheeled upon us, and there was something almost military in the singleness of their gesture as they reached beneath their unkempt jackets, ripped out eighteen-inch knives and rushed at us. "*Ya Rabaoiu!*—O foreigners!" one cried, but his words were drowned out by the thunderous roar of pistols.

De Grandin's little automatic seemed to blaze a single stream of fire, Costello's big revolver bellowed like a field gun. It was as if the three men walked into a wall. Like troops obeying a command they halted, wavered, stumbled. One hiccupped, gasped and slumped down slowly, bending at the knees. Another spun half around and fell full length upon his face. The third stood goggling at us, empty-eyed and open-mouthed, then stepped back shufflingly, seemed to trip on nothing and fell flat on his back.

"Excellent, superb, magnificent!" de Grandin commented. "We be marksmen, thou and I, *mon sergent.*" With a leap he cleared the foremost body, bounded up into the air and came down heavily, flat-footed. His small feet banged on the bare floor like the metaled shoes of a tap-dancer as he ground the centipedes to unclean pulp beneath his heels.

"Here's sumpin' I can't figure, sor," admitted Costello as we proceeded with our search of the house.

A surprising miscellany had turned up in the half-hour we'd been working since we sent Constancia and Gregorio under escort to the hospital. In the room adjoining we had found the Druses' living-quarters, an evil-smelling, unkempt room with four bed-rolls, some cook-pots and valises filled with none too clean clothing. In the basement was a table like a carpenter's work bench, two pressure tanks, an airpump, several airbrushes of varying sizes, and, plugged into an electric outlet, a large fan. The table and the floor were mottled with dried spots of what looked like shellac, some white stuff resembling plaster of Paris, and here and there dull-glowing patches like metallic paint.

Now Costello handed us a filled-in printed form. It was a deed entitling José Gutierrez to full rights of burial in a six-grave plot in St. Rose's Cemetery—"Lot No. 3, Range 37, Section M."

"St. Rose's is a Cath'lic cemetery," Costello reminded us; "what th' divil were these haythens doin' wid a deed from it?"

De Grandin scarcely seemed to hear. His little eyes seemed all pupil, like those of a startled cat; his small blond mustache was fairly twitching with excitement. "The fan, the plaster, the blow-guns," he murmured. "One blows the paint and plaster with the airbrush, one dries it quickly with the fan, one then—*mais oui*, it is entirely possible. Come, my friends, let us hasten with all speed to the cemetery of the sainted Rose. I think our trail ends there!"

By no stretch of the imagination could the cemetery super-intendent's greeting have been called cordial when, in response to Costello's thunderous banging on his door, he finally let us into his small, cluttered office.

"Sure, I sold a plot to Josie Gooteez," he admitted. "He an' his three brothers come to get it last Thursday. They wuz Mexicans or sumpin', I think. Anyhow, they didn't speak good English."

"And they made immediate interments?" asked de Grandin.

"Naw, they ain't buried nobody yet. But they stuck up a couple o' monuments. Damndest-lookin' things yuh ever seen, too. They come here yesterday wid two statoos in a truck, an' set 'em up theirselves—'fore th' cement bases wuz quite finished dryin'."

"Indeed? And of what were these so weird statues, if you please?"

"Huh, your guess is good as mine about that. They looked as if they had been meant to represent a man an' woman, but they ain't so hot. Seemed to me as if they'd molded 'em in cement, then painted 'em with bronze paint, like a radiator. We hadn't ought to let such things be put up here, but that plot's in th' cheapest section, an' almost anything goes there. That's where th' haythens and such-like bury."

THE SUPERINTENDENT'S CRITICISM OF the effigies was entirely justified by all artistic canons. Standing on twin concrete bases, some eight feet apart, two statues faced each other. One was of a woman, one a man, and both were execrably executed.

The woman's costume seemed to be some sort of evening gown, but its folds were obscured by the clumsiness with which they had been reproduced. Of her features little could be discerned; the face had been so crudely shaped as to resemble a half-chiseled stone portrait. Only humps and hollows in appropriate places told where eyes and nose and mouth were.

The male figure was as uncouth as the other. Only after looking at it for some time were we able to determine that its clothes were meant to represent a dinner suit. Like the woman's, his face was little more suggestive of a human countenance than a poorly executed plaster mask.

"*Mordieu—quel imparfait!*" muttered Jules de Grandin. "They must have been in hot haste, those ones. Me, I could do a better piece of work myself."

For a moment he stood staring at the concrete atrocities, then walked across the gravelly lawn to a partly opened grave. The diggers had left tools beside the trench when they knocked off working for the day, and he took up a pick-ax, weighed it in his hand a moment, then approached the woman's statue.

"My friends," he announced, "here we end our search. *Regardez!*"

The statue swayed upon its base as he struck it with the flat side of the pick, waited for a moment, then struck a second time.

"Hey, what th' devil do you think you're doin'?" stormed the superintendent. "I'll have th' law on you—"

"Take it aisy, feller," soothed Costello. "I'm the law, an' if he wants to bust that thing to pieces you're not goin' to sthop 'im. Git me?"

The Frenchman drew his pick back once more and launched a battering smash against the statue's knees. This time it shattered like a piece of broken crockery, and where a three-foot flake of cement dropped away there showed a stretch of something pale and almost colorless. No need to tell a doctor what it was. Every first-semester student of anatomy knows dead human flesh at sight.

"Good Lord, sor, is it her?" Costello gasped.

"Indubitably it is she, my friend," de Grandin answered. "It is none other than Señora Gutierrez. And that monstrosity"—he pointed toward the other statue with his pick-ax—"conceals her husband. Call your men, *mon sergent*. Have them take these dreadful things away and break them up, then put the bodies in the city morgue."

"H'm, wonder what they did wid th' other one?" the sergeant asked.

"The servant?" The Frenchman pointed to the disturbed earth between the statues' bases. "I cannot say with certainty, but it is my guess that if you dig there you will find him."

"**O**NE RECONSTRUCTS THE CRIME," he told us sometime later at my house. "I was as much at sea as you when first we went into that house where they had taken Señorita Gutierrez and her brother. Coupled with the disappearance of the bodies from the stolen hearse, the spots of paint and plaster on the cellar floor, the airbrushes and the drying-fan should have told me how the corpses had been hidden, but it was not till you found the burying-deed that I had the idea. Even then I thought that they had bought the burial plot and put the bodies in it after casing them in cement so the earth would not cave in upon them too soon and thus disclose their hiding-place.

"But when the superintendent told us of the statues and we looked upon their dreadful crudity, the whole thing became clear to me.

"*Toutefois*, the credit goes to you, *mon sergent*. It was you who put the riddle's key into my hands when you showed me that burial-deed. Yes, it is unquestionably so.

"Do not forget to tell them when you make your report to headquarters."

He helped himself to an enormous drink, and:

"*Quelle facétie monumentale!*" he murmured with a wry face.

"What's a 'monumental joke'?" I demanded.

"*Pardieu*, the one those so abominable ones played on Colonel Gutierrez and his lady—to make them stand as monuments above their own graves!"

Stoneman's Memorial

The Adventures of the Famous Little
Ghost Breaker since his last
Escapade in *Weird Tales*

In answer to numerous inquiries concerning the whereabouts and activities of Dr. Jules de Grandin and Capt. Sir Haddingway Ingraham Jameson Ingraham (less formally known as Hiji) during the past three years I am happy to be able to supply the following data:

De Grandin went to France immediately upon the outbreak of hostilities in 1939 and was serving in Syria when the truce was made with Germany and the French Republic abolished. The fiery little patriot at once repudiated Vichy and all its works, made his way to Africa and joined the Free French forces of Gen. Charles de Gaulle and became a captain in the *corps de santé*. A severe case of enteritis, contracted during the unsuccessful attack on Dakar, and the tardy realization of his superiors that he was far more valuable as an intelligence and liaison officer than as a military surgeon caused him to be sent to England and later to this country, where he at once went to see Dr. Samuel Trowbridge at Harrisonville, N.J.

Hiji, who was a captain of Houssa policemen in British West Central Africa (and enjoying it hugely) when Poland was invaded, resigned his commission and became a major of infantry in the B.E.F. In the retreat from Dunkerque his right femur was shattered by a shell fragment, and he was invalided out of service and sent as an attaché to the British Consulate General at New York. He can be seen limping down Fifth Avenue or lower Broadway almost any day, and usually has Sunday dinner with Dr. Trowbridge. Lady Ingraham, his wife, is serving at home in the Women's Territorial Auxiliary, and both he and she declare, "When this shindy's over we're goin' to Surrey or America or some nice, quiet place and settle down to raisin' flowers and kids and bulldogs.—S.Q.

T HE REUNION HAD BEEN a huge success. Norah McGinnis, delighted at de
Grandin's return, had fairly outdone herself with dinner, and if she had not
quite killed the fatted calf for him her oysters with champagne, turtle soup
with dry sherry, filet of sole with graves and roast pheasant with burgundy was a
more than merely satisfactory substitute. Now with the firelight beating back the
shadows with its rosy lashes and casting changing highlights on the drawn curtains, I looked about the study much as a proud father might regard his family at a
Thanksgiving homecoming. The room was redolent with a mixture of cigar smoke,
the scent of burning apple wood and the bouquet of old whiskey and older brandy.

Across the hearth from me sat Jules de Grandin, small-boned and delicately
built, sensitive and neurotic as a woman, with a few more lines in his forehead, a
few more tiny wrinkles round the corners of his eyes, a slightly tensed look in his
gaze, but obviously happy as a schoolboy on a holiday. His little, round blue eyes
were agleam with pleasure, his small wheat-blond mustache was fairly quivering
with ecstatic joy as he passed the fragile, bubble-thin inhaler back and forth
beneath his nose before he took a reverent sip of the pale cognac that was old
when Andrew Jackson held New Orleans from the British. Hiji, a little thinner
than I'd known him in the old days, and with several white hairs showing in the
little black mustache that was in such sharp contrast to his pewter-colored hair,
seemed to fill the sofa with his broad ruggedness. He had absorbed prodigious
quantities of Scotch and water since we came from the table, and with each
succeeding drink the tense lines in his face seemed softening. Detective Sergeant Costello, smooth-shaven, ruddy-faced, white-haired and even bigger than
Hiji, filled his easy chair completely, and like Hiji took enormous quantities of
Scotch, but took it without water. His smooth, pink face and blue, ingenuous
Irish eyes were curiously misleading. He had the look, and often the precise
manner of a suffragan bishop, plus an emergency vocabulary that would have
been the envy of an army mule-skinner.

Ten minutes out of Newark Airport the night plane for the West roared
overhead, its motors droning like a swarm of angry hornets. Hiji poured the last
four ounces of his drink down in a single gulp and looked up quizzically. "Not
long since we'd been duckin' for the cellar when we heard one o' those blokes,
eh, Frenchy?" he asked de Grandin.

"*Tu parles, mon vieux*," the little Frenchman agreed with a smile. "Me, I
am—how do you say him? muscle-tied?—from running into rabbit-holes when
they appeared. *Parbleu*, but it was execrable, no less. When one has finished
dinner, one desires to relax, to feel the pleasant combination of the process of
digestion and slow poisoning by alcohol and nicotine. But did *les Boches* think
of that? Damn no! They spoiled my after-dinner rest at least a thousand times.
Cochons! If one were to come to me now and tell me, 'Jules de Grandin, here
is fifty thousand francs. It is all yours if you will rise and move from where you

sit'—*morbleu*, but I would tweak him by the nose and hurl the proffered bribe back in his face. I would let nothing interfere with the luxury of this hour—"

"Beg pardon, sor," Norah came to the study door apologetically, "but there's a young man askin' fer th' Sergeant, Dr. Trowbridge. He says as how—"

"Arrah, Norah darlin', hold yer whist!" broke in Costello reprovingly. "Did ye not hear Dr. de Grandin say we couldn't be disturbed th' now? Tell th' young felly to come round to Headquarters in th' mornin'. 'Tis meself's off duty now, an'—"

"But, Sergeant acushla, 'tis one of yer own lads as wants ter see ye," she persisted. "He says as how his name is Dennie Flannigan, an'—"

"Does he, now, bad cess to th' young omadhaun? Well—" he looked at us apologetically, then, to de Grandin:

"Would ye be afther listinin' to th' lad, Dr. de Grandin, sor? He's in bad trouble, so he is, and likely to be in worse before all's said an' done. Ye see, his father, Dennie Flannigan—God rest 'is soul!—wuz me buddy when I wuz first appointed to th' force, an' many a night we walked th' same beat together. Killed in th' line o' duty, he wuz, too, an' I'm responsible for young Dennie's appointment.

"There's been some trouble round about th' town these last few weeks, sor. A killer's on th' loose, and devil a hand can we lay on 'im, so th' newspapers is givin' us a goin' over. Well, sor, 'twas Dennie's hard luck to be walkin' down th' street th' other night when th' killer wuz out. He heard a woman scream an' ran to help her, an' caught th' murderer almost red-handed."

"Eh?" Jules de Grandin raised slim black brows. "Since when has it been a misfortune to catch a criminal at his crimes, *mon brave?*"

"That's just it, sor. I said he almost caught 'im. But not quite. Th' killer's on th' lam, ye see, an' Dennie orders 'im, to halt, an' when he doesn't he lets fly wid everything he has. Pumps five shots into him, an' still he keeps on runnin'.

"Well, anyone can miss a shot or two sor, I've done it meself, but five shots in succession at almost point-blank range, that ain't so good. An' th' alibi he turned in didn't help his case much, either."

"*Qu'est-ce donc?* What was his excuse?"

Costello's eyes were wide and serious, not mocking or ironical, as he looked in de Grandin's face. "He said it wuz a stone man, sor."

"*Que diable?* My ears have played me false. I thought I heard you say he said it was a man of stone, my Sergeant."

"That's right, sor. He said it was a stone man—a statue that ran like it wuz livin'. He says his bullets had no more effect on it than they'd have had on a stone wall. He knows he didn't miss, an' I believe him, for he's a good shot, but—"

"Drunk, that's what he was," commented Hiji, helping himself to a fresh drink. "Drunk as a goat, seein' livin' statues and pink elephants. That's what's the matter."

Costello nodded gloomily. "That's what th' assistant commissioner says, too, but I've got me doubts about it. Dennie's a member o' th' Cath'lic Total Abstinence Society, an' if he'd had a drink 'twa sumpin' new for 'im."

"Always has to be a first time, you know, old son."

"*Taisez-vous!* Be silent, species of camel!" de Grandin ordered sharply. "Who art thou to point the finger of derision at a drunkard?" Then, to Costello:

"And you believe this, *mon sergent?*"

"Well, sor," Costello was embarrassed but deadly serious, "I wouldn't go that far but I don't think th' lad wuz lyin'. Not knowingly, anyhow."

"A Frenchman and an Irishman," commented Hiji sadly to his almost-empty glass, "tell either of 'em that the moon's made o' green cheese, and they'll believe you—"

"Attend me, if you please, my friend," de Grandin interrupted as he leaned toward Hiji, two little wrinkles deepening suddenly between his brows, "shake off your drunkenness a moment, if you will be so kind. To refuse to deny is not to affirm. Me, I have the open mind, so has the good sergeant. So have you up to a certain point, but no further. If I tell you that a listener to the radio can hear a speaker's words a thousand miles away before those in the same room hear it you say, 'Very likely, that is scientific.' But when you hear an honest policeman encountered what he thought was a stone statue running down the street you scoff and say that he was drunk. Yet fifty years ago one statement would have seemed as absurd as the other, *n'est-ce-pas?*"

Hiji grinned at him and smothered back a hiccough. "You've definitely got something there, Frenchy. I apologize. Have Costello bring his stone-man-seein' copper in and let's hear what he's got to say. I'll suspend judgment till his story's told, but it had better be good. I can't afford to take time from my drinkin' to listen to old wives' tales."

Patrolman Dennis Flannigan was a fine, honest-looking youngster. "Black Irish"—smooth, clear skin, black curly hair and eyes so dark a brown that they seemed black.

"Have a seat, Dennie lad," commanded Costello when introductions were completed, and:

"Have a drink?" asked Hiji as the young policeman settled in a chair.

"No, thank you, sir, I never use it," he refused, and Costello shot a glance of triumph at the Englishman.

De Grandin nodded affably. "Quite right, *mon enfant*. You have as much right not to drink as I have to do so." Then with one of his quick, elfin smiles, "The Sergeant tells us you had an unique experience the other night; that you met a miscreant in armor that defied your bullets as a tin roof turns the rain aside. It must have been a great surprise to you, *n'est-ce-pas?*"

A stubborn look came in the youngster's face. "It wasn't armor, sir," he contradicted. "The man—the thing—was solid stone, and turned my bullets as if they'd been made o' putty."

"Eh, how is it that you say? A man of stone? You seriously expect us to believe that?"

"No, sir, I don't. I don't expect anyone to believe me. If someone told me the same thing I'd say he was drunk or crazy or both, but it's the truth, sir, just the same.

"It was last Sat'day night, or Sunday morning, about ten minutes after twelve. I can fix the time pretty well, for the clock in St. Dominic's tower had just finished striking midnight when I turned in my call from the box at Bay and Tunnell Streets. My next call was from Fox and Pettibone, and I'd covered almost half the distance to it when I heard a woman screaming bloody murder somewhere down the block where Blake Street crosses Tunnell.

"There's all sorts o' cries, sir, and pretty soon a cop gets so he knows 'em. At first I thought this woman had a case o' jim-jams—it's a rough neighbor-hood, with lots o' drinkin' and the like o' that goin' on all night—but when she screamed the second time I knew the fear o' death was on her, so I took out down the block as fast as I could leg it.

"Blake Street ain't so well lighted, and some of the tough kids in the neighborhood are almost always breaking the few lights they have, but there was a street light burnin' almost in the middle of the block, and I could see almost as well as if it had been daytime. Something white was bending down above what seemed to be a woman, shaking her like a bulldog would a cat, and I knew there was a murder being done, so I let out a yell and drew me gun.

"Just as I came up with 'em the white thing dropped the woman—no sir, that ain't quite right—it didn't drop her, it threw her half across the street, like a man could throw a bundle of old clothes, sir, and then, without even turning round went down Blake Street toward the waterfront. That's when I saw it plain, sir, for it passed right under the street light. It was a marble statue, sir; a marble statue, bone-white and just about a man's size, maybe a little smaller, but heavier. Lots heavier. I could hear its stone feet clumpin' on the sidewalk as it walked away, and when it broke into a run it sounded like a steam-hammer that's been stepped up to about a hundred an' eighty strokes a minute."

"U'm?" de Grandin tweaked the ends of his mustache. "One sees. And what transpired then, if you please?"

"Well, sir, I'd seen these here now livin' statues in the theatre—you know, the kind they have when actors put on white tights and smear white powder on their hands and hair and faces, then pose against a black background? I thought at first this guy was in some sort o' costume like that, with maybe metal bottoms on his shoes, so I shouted to him to halt, and when he kept on goin' I fired at him. My first shot must have missed, so I let him have four others, and while he had a good head-start o' me I don't think that I missed him all four times. In fact, I know I didn't."

"*Comment?* What makes you so positive?"

A flush washed up the young man's cheeks and brow as he thrust a hand inside his blouse and drew a twist of paper from an inner pocket. "This, sir," he answered as he tore the paper open and dropped its contents into Jules de Grandin's hand. "I saw that fly from it as it ran down the street. I know my bullet knocked it off when it struck and ricocheted."

De Grandin outlined his chin with the thumb and forefinger of one hand while he balanced the white marble splinter in the hollow of the other. "U'm?" he commented, and again, "U'm?" Then, abruptly, "How was he dressed, this naughty stone person?"

"He wasn't, sir."

"Eh, how is it you say?"

"He was necked, sir. Stripped bare as your hand, and I could see the light shone on his back and shoulders as he ran, but—it's funny how you notice little things without even realizin' you're looking at 'em—there was no play of muscles underneath his skin as he ran. He was all smooth and white and shiny, just like any other statue, and when I saw the chip fly off of him I reached down and picked it up whilst I was runnin' after him. He lost me, though, sir. Turned the corner of James and Blake about a dozen—maybe twenty—yards ahead of me, and when I got there he was gone. I hunted for him for awhile, then went back to the woman."

"She was dead, sir, and all broken up. It was as if she'd been a rag doll that some spoiled brat had torn up. Her face was all crushed in, her neck was limp as rope and it seemed to me like both her shoulders had been broken."

"Yes? And then?"

"There wasn't anything to do but call the precinct, sir, so I put in a call and waited by her till the wagon came from the morgue. Then I filed my report, sayin' just what I've told you, and when the assistant commissioner read it he went wild. Told me I was crazy, or had been drinkin' while on duty, and gave me half an hour to draw a new report or stand charges. I wouldn't do it, sir. It was a stone thing, not a man, that killed that woman, whether anybody believes it or not. So now I'm relieved of duty and if I can't prove it was a livin' statue that committed that murder I guess I'll have to turn me badge in."

"Ah-ha. You showed this bit of stone to *Monsieur le Commissaire?*"

"Yes, sir," grimly, "I showed it to him."

"And what did he say to it?"

"Applesauce."

"*Comment?* He said sauce of the apple, no more? He made no move to investigate—"

"He was drunk, I'm tellin' you," asserted Hiji gravely. "Drunk as an owl. Too beastly intoxicated to take the proper steps. Blasted inefficiency, that's what it is. If one of my Houssas told me he'd seen a ju-ju runnin' through the forest and showed me where he'd chipped a piece of it away with his rifle, d'ye think I'd talk about applesauce, or marmalade or jam? You know ol' Hiji better'n that! No, sir, drunk or sober, I'd investigate. That's what I'd do."

The shadow of a smile lurked underneath the tightly waxed ends of de Grandin's small blond mustache. "I am like Balaam's ass, all ears, my friend," he declared. "How, by example, would you investigate this case?"

Hiji looked at him with the long, earnest stare of one far gone in liquor. "Oh, so you think I wouldn't know what to do, eh? Think I'm too drunk to know my business? Listen, my small French friend, once a policeman always a policeman. The constable says the bloke was naked, doesn't he? That ain't particularly shockin', but it's interestin'. There's lots o' statuary around this town, but not much of it's nude, 'specially the male figures. Who the devil wants to look at a nude man? Think customers would go to burlesque houses to see some cove march up an down the stage an' strip his shorts and singlet off? You know they wouldn't. All right, then, the hunt's considerably narrowed down. So I'd check up every statuary group containin' nude male figures, and look at 'em all closely to see if they showed bullet marks or had a piece chipped off 'em. Then, when I found one answerin' the prescription I'd know I had the murderer, and I'd hang him. Yes, sir, hang him higher than I hanged old Mebili the witch-doctor when he started monkey-shines up in the Luabala Country—"

"*Nom d'un porc d'un nom d'un porc!*" de Grandin interrupted in delight. "It may be that it is the whiskey and not you who speaks, my old, my priceless one, but whether it be you or alcohol that speaks, you talk the good, hard sense. But yes!

"Go home and have no further fear of discharge, *mon enfant*," he told Dennis Flannigan. "I, Jules de Grandin, will assist you, and though we have a case of utmost difficulty, we shall win, for Jules de Grandin is one devilish clever fellow. Assuredly."

When Flannigan had gone he turned once more to Hiji with the pleased expression of a cat that contemplates a bowl of cream. "Come, *brave compagnon*," he invited as he poured a fresh supply of liquor into their glasses, "it has been long since we were satisfactorily drunk together. For why are we waiting?"

DESPITE THE OFTEN-QUOTED COPYBOOK axiom to the effect that wine is a mocker and strong drink an abomination they were both as fresh as the proverbial daisy when they came down to the dining room next morning and did more than ample justice to a breakfast of orange juice, cereal, pancakes and sausage and broiled mackerel. Hiji, who must report at the consulate at ten, limped off to catch the nine-fifteen train for New York and, his seventh cup of well-creamed coffee disposed of, de Grandin grinned at me across the empty table.

"What time are office hours today, *mon vieux?*" he asked, lighting a vile-smelling French cigarette.

"No office hours this morning," I answered. "I've a patient to look in on at Mercy Hospital and two more at the Consolidated. After that I'm free till five this afternoon."

"*Bien,*" he nodded, "and you will kindly chauffeur me around the town, as in the good old days?"

"Be glad to. Where shall we go first?"

"U'm," he considered a moment. "To the police headquarters, if you will be so kind. I would have a word with *Monsieur l'Inférieur Commissaire. Ah bah,* a fool he must be, that one!"

WENDELL WINTERBOTHAM, FIRST ASSISTANT police commissioner, sat behind his glass-topped wide desk decorated with twin fountain pens, a telephone, brass-bound desk blotter and an amber glass bud-vase in which stood a single crimson rose and smirked at Jules de Grandin with the deprecating, irritating smile of a man who was not born yesterday. "And you seriously expect me to put credence in this absurd story, Dr. de Grandin?" he asked.

"I seriously do, *Monsieur le Commissaire.* I do not say, or even think, it was a stone man who committed this murder, but I do believe the young policeman thinks it was, and the marble splinter which he shot from it—and which I hear he showed to you in support of his story—gives some weight to his belief. It may well be the miscreant wore some fantastic sort of disguise—"

"Bosh! Who'd go around in such a get-up to commit a murder? It just doesn't make sense—"

"Assuredly, *M'sieur.* Nor does it make sense that he beat his victim almost to a pulp when one blow would have killed her. When Sergeant Bertram disinterred the bodies of the dead from Paris cemeteries and bashed them with a grave-digger's spade, that made no sense, either; when Jack the Ripper killed his victims in the London slums and mutilated their corpses, that made no sense to normal men, but—" he gestured the ending with a wave of his hand—"there are strange things buried in the secret mausoleums of the mind, *Monsieur le Commissaire.* Lust for power, lust for cruelty, lust for murder—savage urges to deface and rend and tear and slay our fellow being, they are all there. And while we keep them under lock and key they are still there, lying like the vampires to arise and walk from their coffins when the opportunity arises. But certainly. This murderer, this killer, he may be eminently respectable by day, an honored lawyer or doctor, perhaps a businessman or even clergyman. That is when he plays the rôle of Dr. Jekyll. But when the ghost of Mr. Hyde comes forth to prowl, what power of deepest hell may not be loosed?"

"H'm." The commissioner grew thoughtful. He was not a stupid man, only opinionated and "practical." Before becoming assistant commissioner he had been director of a mail order house, and prided himself on having brought hard-headed business efficiency to public service. "You think we may be dealing with a homicidal maniac?"

De Grandin raised his narrow shoulders in the sort of shrug that no one but a Frenchman can achieve. "*Comme qui dirait?* The ear-marks of the killing point to it. If, as we may assume, this is a second Sergeant Bertram we deal with—he was a mellow-mannered, lovable young man when not gripped by his mania—it may well be that he puts on the disguise of a statue when he goes upon his killing quests. It may be that he has devised a sort of armor that will defy bullets—"

"A crazy man?" scoffed Winterbotham.

"As you say, *M'sieur*, a crazy man. But a crazy man who is brilliant and talented in normal times and uses his great talents to assist him in the crimes he commits when his second, evil personality is uppermost. It could be so, *n'est-ce-pas?*"

"Why, yes, I suppose so. Wait a minute—" Winterbotham pressed a button underneath his desk, and, to the clerk who answered the summons, "Bring me the files in the Jukes, Mahoney and Ebbert cases, please."

He ruffled through the papers, then: "I hadn't thought of it, Doctor," he confessed, "but what you say puts a new light on this case. Here's Sally Jukes, a woman of no lawful occupation, arrested several times for vagrancy and half a dozen times for soliciting. She was killed in Deal Street shortly after midnight three weeks ago. Her—"

"One moment, if you please, *Monsieur le Commissaire*," de Grandin interrupted. "The other two, the Mahoney and Ebbert women, what were their occupations, if you know?"

The commissioner gave a slight start. "No known—or, rather, too well known means of support—"

De Grandin nodded. "There was no question, then, I take it, concerning their morals, which, *hélas*, were all on the wrong side of the question mark?"

"That's right, Doctor. All three were—"

"*Exactement.* And how, if you please, did *la* Jukes meet her end?"

"The coroner's report shows death was due to dislocation of the spinal column between the second and third cervical vertebrae. There was also a fracture of the right occiput, and the frontal bone, both shoulders—"

"*Précisément, M'sieur.* And were not the two other women similarly broken?"

"Ye-es," the commissioner thumbed through the records of the other cases. "You're right, Doctor. The coroner's physician's findings in all three cases are almost identical. We don't know that all three were killed by the same person, of course, but the technique of the murders—"

"Was the calling card of the assassin, by blue! Did not I say it?"

Winterbotham's somber eyes showed traces of amusement. "What do you want me to do, Doctor? Accept young Flannigan's report? Give out to the newspapers that an animated statue's running amok, that the police can't catch it, that their bullets can't hurt it, and that no man's life is safe?"

"By no means, M'sieur. Tell the press you have a clue, a dozen of them, if you wish, and that you're satisfied the killings have no connection with each other and were perpetrated by different persons. That will pique the murderer's vanity, and will also lull him into feeling safe. Make no mistake, he reads the papers, this one. He gloats in secret at the thought that he has foiled the police, that he can murder with impunity. Yes, certainly. Bien. Let him gloat. Soon comes our turn. Meantime, I pray you, do not be too hard on the young Flannigan. He is an honest boy, else he would not stick to his story so stubbornly."

"All right, Doctor. I think your advice is sound, and I'll not press charges against Flannigan. May we count on your cooperation?"

"A hundred and forty-five percent, M'sieur!"

We shook hands all around at parting, and for a moment I was fearful that de Grandin would implant a kiss on Winterbotham's cheeks for promising to restore Dennis Flannigan to duty.

"Non, merci," he denied when I suggested that I drive him on his other errands. "I shall do very nicely afoot, my friend. I have important missions to perform, and you are due at the hospitals. Go call upon your patients, but bid Madame Nora to wait dinner for me. Unless I am more mistaken than I think, I shall have the appetite of the ostrich when I return."

H E WAS HOME IN time to mix the cocktails, and as I sipped the pale gold fluid from the beaded glass I realized with a pang that not since he had left for France when war broke out had I tasted a perfect Martini. These were pluperfect, with the vermouth cutting the flavor of the gin just enough to leave the dryness intact, the Angostura blending faultlessly with both. "Was it a successful day" I asked as I helped myself to a second portion from the frost-encrusted shaker.

"Eminently, my friend," he assured me. "I have found that which I sought; now I desire to hear that—"

"Dinner is served, if ye plaze, sor," announced Nora from the doorway, and de Grandin who would no more think of keeping dinner waiting than of whistling in church was silent till the soup was served. Then, as Nora put the plate of steaming mulligatawny before him, "Tell me, Friend Trowbridge, do you know the Spring of Temperance?"

"The Spring—" I countered, wondering if he were being facetious, then as recollection dawned, "you mean the fountain in Dunellan Park? Why, yes, I've seen it, but I don't believe I ever really noticed it. Why do you ask?"

He spread a dab of butter on his hot roll and give me a quick, level glance. "Me, I saw her today. I examined her most carefully, and—"

"You mean—" the look in his eyes gave me the clue, but it seemed so utterly fantastic—"there were bullet marks on it"

"Four," he replied sententiously. "The young Flannigan did not lie to us, or to the *commissaire de police*. But no. Also, I matched the little marble splinter which he left with me into a little, so small notch knocked from the arm of the standing male figure."

Nora set the joint before me, a rolled beef-roast, brown and crisp on the outside with glaced potatoes turned in its juice, and for a moment there was silence as I carved, then, when she'd left us to ourselves once more: "You will recall the group of statuary, perhaps? A child and young woman bend above the basin of the fountain, back of them, and leaning toward the spring, is a male figure, nude as are the other two, and slightly less than full life-size."

"Yes, I remember now. It caused considerable scandal when it was unveiled. Some of our ladies' organizations thought its undraped figures might corrupt youth. That's why they put it in Dunellan Park instead of—"

"One comprehends," he cut in. "The female mind, especially in America, is something which no one can understand—or perhaps which one understands entirely too well if he is versed in psychology. But it is of the statues that I speak, not of their aesthetic qualities. I searched the city with the comb of the fine teeth, and was all but despairing when at last I came upon that group. 'Jules de Grandin,' I then said to me, 'it is here your quest ends, either in success or failure.' 'You are entirely correct, as usual, Jules de Grandin,' I reply to me, and forthwith I examined every square inch of those *sacré* statues' marble hide.

"And what did I discover? *Morbleu*, upon the back of the male standing figure I found three small, shallow, flattened pits with gray discolorations which indubitably were the marks of soft-nosed leaden bullets. But certainly. And on the triceps of the figure's left arm was a little nitch, also discolored as from a lead missile, and into it I set the marble splinter left with me by the young Flannigan. *Parbleu*, it fitted perfectly, like the slipper on the little, dainty foot of *Cendrillon*. Yes. Certainly. Of course."

"You're certain they were bullet marks? Children, especially boys, are everlastingly committing acts of vandalism—"

"*Ah bah!* You ask me if I know the tell-tale mark of the bullet on stone? Me, Jules de Grandin, the soldier? My friend, I know him as I know the lines of my own hand. Have I not seen him on the walls where military executions have been carried out? Of course. I tell you, good Friend Trowbridge, there is no doubt about it. Fantastic and incredible as it may seem, it was that statue which repelled the bullets of young Flannigan, that very marble image that killed Lucy Ebbert, and by almost inescapable inference Sally Jukes and Mae Mahoney also."

"Well," I forced a smile that did not go much below the surface, for despite the absurdity of his statement his deadly earnest manner made me feel uncomfortable, "if that's the case we're in a bad fix. As Winterbotham said this morning, a marble statue is running amok and the police are powerless against it. If a marble image can come to life and go on a rampage, what is to prevent those bronze colossi in Military Park from taking the warpath?"

"Jules de Grandin," he returned smiling. He did not make the statement boastfully, but simply, as an existing fact. "I shall take measures to insure their tranquility, my friend."

"What measures?"

He drew his shoulders upward in a shrug of complete eloquence. "How should I know? The time is not yet ripe, my friend. When it has come, *pardieu*, Jules de Grandin will be there also!"

"You certainly think highly of yourself," I admitted, "but it seems to me you've taken on a job that's worthy of your best this time. If bullets won't stop this stone murderer, the only thing left to do is smash it with a sledge hammer, and you'd find yourself involved with the police if you tried that. I doubt if even your persuasiveness could convince the Park Department that one of their prize groups of statuary has developed homicidal tendencies. Besides, if one statue has come alive to commit murder, what's to stop the rest? You can't tear down or break up every piece of sculpture in the city. Why, counting the monuments in the cemeteries, there must be at least—"

"You are informing me?" he broke in with a slightly worried frown. "No, my friend, as you say, we cannot embark on a course of wholesale image-smashing. Besides, this business of the monkey, if I interpret it correctly, is more a symptom than a disease. One does not treat a case of ache, by example, by local applications, one treats the gastro-intestinal disturbance which is the etiological factor. So it must be in this case. We must reach the underlying cause of all this nonsense, and remove it—or him."

I nodded and, irrelevantly, it seemed to me, he asked abruptly: "This Monsieur Joseph Stoneman, who was he, if you please? A plaque set in the fountain's base informs the beholder that he bestowed it on the city as a memorial to his son who was, one takes it, killed in the war."

"No, he wasn't killed in battle," I rejoined. "He met his death in a speakeasy brawl. Joe Stoneman was a manufacturer of carbonated beverages and made a fortune out of them. His Jingerade and Kolatonik were famous at one time, but since repeal of prohibition they've lost popularity."

"Ah? The public ceased insulting its collective stomach with his nostrums when once more it had a chance to drink light wines and beer?"

"Not quite. Stoneman was almost fanatically opposed to alcohol in every and any form. He was one of our foremost dry crusaders, and almost succeeded in getting a bill through the legislature prohibiting the use of alcohol as a solvent in medicines. It took the combined efforts of the Medical Society and Pharmacists' Association to defeat it. He was credited with donating almost fantastic sums to finance the dry cause, too."

"One sees completely. It was an excellent advertisement for his own non-intoxicating beverages."

"No one believed that. He seemed so utterly sincere, but when repeal became operative one of the first things he did was to set up a huge brewery and advertise his beer almost as extensively as he had his soft drinks. His advertising campaign announced that as long as people were to be allowed to drink intoxicants anyway he felt it his duty to make a good beer which they would drink in preference to hard liquor. Nobody believed him. His former associates in the dry cause turned against him as a traitor and saloon proprietors and tavern keepers, remembering how he'd led the prosecutions for infraction of the prohibition laws refused to handle his beer, so both his soft drink and beer businesses fell flat and he sold his brewery and factories and retired."

He frowned thoughtfully. "One sees. And what of his son's death? You said it occurred in a speakeasy? Strange the son of such a father should die so."

I nodded. "It was something of a scandal. The youngster was a harum-scarum sort of lad, and while his father sought to dry up liquor at the source, he worked industriously to cut down the supply from the consumer's angle. One evening there was a brawl in a speakeasy, and when the police came they found young Stoneman lying in the street outside the place with his head staved in and his neck broken—"

"*Morbleu*, can such things be?" he almost shouted.

"Eh?" I jerked back. "What d'ye mean?"

"His injuries, my friend. He had his head staved in; he had his neck broken—so did the three women killed by the statue. Do not you see some connection?"

"I don't quite see what you're driving at," I confessed.

The smile he flashed at me was infectious as a yawn. "I am not sure that I do, either," he admitted. "It is a puzzle picture that we work on, my friend. As yet we have but a few pieces, and the pattern is obscure, but presently we shall have more, and then we shall see order emerging from this apparent chaos. Meantime, why distress ourselves unduly? Shall not we go to the study for coffee?"

H E CAME BUSTLING IN next afternoon and thrust a copy of the journal into my hand. "We must surely go to this, my friend," he informed me, indicating an item on the third page with the tip of a well manicured finger. "It will be of the interest."

The paragraph announced that Dr. Bradley-Stoker of the Universities of

Edinburgh and Dublin would lecture on the secret writings of Cornelius Agrippa that night at Sawyer Hall.

"I don't think I'd be interested," I told him. "Why don't you go alone? I've had a rather trying day and—what's the matter with you?" He was grinning like a small boy who observes a portly gentleman in a high hat coming toward him on a snowy day.

"Me, I promise you will not be bored," he assured me. "It may be possible the learned doctor will not show up for his lecture, but I am certain that another will."

"Who?"

"Wait and see, my friend. If all goes as I think that all will go I shall explain to you completely. I have been busy as a hive of bees today. I have made investigation of the death of young Monsieur Stoneman, and some of the things I found out give me furiously to think. The speakeasy where he was done to death was in Tunnell Street, that most unsavory thoroughfare where Sally Jukes came to her end, and near which both the Ebbert and Mahoney women were murdered. Moreover, all three of them had been among those present when he was killed. There was another there also, one Nellie Cook, and this afternoon I saw and talked with her."

"Yes?" I asked, puzzled. "And what is the connection—"

"She is, according to the popular phrase, down on her luck at present, having been but recently released from jail. Once she was a singer, a night club entertainer, and specifically a *chanteuse* in the Hard-Boiled Owl, the speakeasy where the young Stoneman met his finish. *Tiens*, he was the devil of a fellow, that young man. He thought that he could best professional gamblers at their own craft, and on the night that he was killed had been engaged in a crap game with three young gangsters, boy friends of the girls, who had, in every probability, inveigled him into playing. *Tenez*, a blind man could foresee the outcome. He lost and lost again, then finally decided he had been cheated and made demand for his money, threatening to expose the dive and have his father prosecute it and all its inmates.

"Thereupon the three young gentlemen who rejoiced in the names of Handsome Harry, Gentleman Jim and Lefty Louis set upon him with brass knuckles and blackjacks. When they were finished with him he was entirely wrecked."

"Did the girl tell you this? I never heard anyone was prosecuted for his murder."

"But no. The gentlemen involved made themselves scarce, and either through loyalty or fear of reprisal the girls refused to implicate them. Their story was that they and the young Stoneman had been innocently drinking when three strange hoodlums rushed in and assaulted him, apparently for no reason."

"I should think she'd be afraid to tell you this, even now," I objected. "Gangland has a way of dealing with informers."

"Quite yes, but in this instance there is little fear. Gentleman Jim and Handsome Harry met their several deaths some years ago in a gang battle; Lefty Louis recently went to his reward in the tuberculosis ward of a state prison. So of all those witnessing or taking part in *l'affaire* Stoneman only this Cook woman remains. You will see her tonight at the lecture."

I laughed outright. "A discourse on the secret charms and spells of Cornelius Agrippa seems the least likely place to meet a superannuated trull."

Nevertheless, she will be there. I have made sure of it. Today I took her to the shops and bought her everything that she needed, including several drinks, a manicure and a fresh hair-bleach. She was pathetically grateful, and will be more grateful still for the fee I have promised her if she acts and speaks exactly as I have instructed her."

A NEAT PLACARD ANNOUNCED THE lecture when we arrived at Sawyer Hall, but it appeared that Dr. Bradley-Stoker would not have a large house. The ticket seller yawned in his booth and the doorman had no duties to perform. When we went in we found we had the little auditorium to ourselves except for a fat man and a woman muffled to the ears in a fur-collared coat. For half an hour we sat there, then an usher stepped out on the stage and announced Dr. Bradley-Stoker had been called out of town on urgent business. Accordingly there would be no lecture, and our money would be refunded to us at the box office.

The fat man was before us at the window, and what little of him I could see I disliked instinctively. When he turned his face it seemed to me his puffy red cheeks threatened to engulf his little eyes completely. It was a face like that of some sleek, sleepy cat, more animal than human.

The woman crowded on our heels, and indignation fairly exuded from her. "It's an imposition," she told no one in particular in a sharp, strident voice, "bringing us out on a night like this for nothing!"

As she voiced her protest Jules de Grandin gave a start of surprise and then turned toward her. "Why, Mademoiselle Nellie!" he exclaimed. "This is indeed a pleasure. May I present my friend Dr. Trowbridge? Friend Trowbridge, this is Mademoiselle Nellie Cook."

With the quick suspicion of a wink at me he continued, keeping his voice up, "I did not know that you were interested in Cornelius Agrippa, *Mademoiselle*." The quick flick of his eyes bade me take notice of the fat man at the ticket seller's window.

I turned my head a little and was aware of a sharp feeling of revulsion. The man was regarding us with a cold, steady look, the sort of look a cat might have before a mouse-hole, and at the woman's reply I could see a sudden gleam in his dull eyes, as if their lead had been scratched to malicious brightness.

"I surely am interested," she was assuring de Grandin, and she, too, spoke much louder than seemed necessary. "Why, they say he had some sort of charm by which he could make stone images come to life and do whatever he commanded them. That's what I wanted to hear about particularly tonight. You know—" there was a sharp catch in her voice, as though her breath had halted momentarily—"I can't get it out of my head that poor Sally and Mae and Lucy were not killed by some fiend as the papers seem to think, but—" her voice sank to a sharp whisper that could have been heard in a boiler shop—"but by *an animated statue*, Doctor!"

W E DROVE A BLOCK or two in silence, then: "Well, did I put it over all right, sir?" she asked de Grandin. "I gave the act all I had."

"You did it excellently, *Mademoiselle*," he replied. "Here is your promised reward." A bill changed hands, and, "Where can we put you down?" he asked.

"Any place where I can get a drink. Ugh! When I think of how that little fat guy looked at me I feel cold right down to my toes and need a good, stiff snifter."

The little Frenchman nodded sympathetically. "I quite agree, *Mademoiselle*. And I suggest that you stay indoors till the new moon appears, also."

"I'll think about it," she returned with a laugh as she climbed down from the car, "but after a girl's just finished a college course she wants to get out under the bright lights, you know. G'night, sir, and thanks."

"Now what the deuce is all this nonsense?" I demanded as we turned toward home. "I don't believe there was a lecture scheduled for tonight at all, and—"

"My perspicacious, good Friend Trowbridge," he broke in with a chuckle. "Of course there was not! The learned Dr. Bradley-Stoker exists in my mind and nowhere else. I hired the hall, I put the notice in *le Journal*, I hired the usher to make the announcement—"

"Of all the silly, childish charades!" I exclaimed. "Whatever were you thinking of to play a prank like that?"

"It was no prank, my friend," be answered soberly. "It was a stratagem of war, and it was most successful. We know now who our foeman is, and we can make plans for his defeat."

"I'm hanged if I understand."

"Very well. Consider: The things which Mademoiselle Nellie told me today gave me the clue. Perhaps it was not likely, but it was entirely possible that these women's deaths had some connection with the killing of the young Stoneman. The fountain was unveiled a year ago, I understand. At that time the Jukes girl and her three companions were 'in college' as they call it. That is to say, they were in jail for vagrancy, shoplifting and similar petty crimes. Very well. A month ago the Jukes woman was released. True to the customs of her kind, she went at once to her old neighborhood and—*voilà*, she was killed. By all accounts she did not die pleasantly."

"Then the Mahoney baggage comes from the jail. She, too, went back to her old haunts and—you have read the coroner's report in her case."

"The Ebbert girl was discharged from prison two weeks ago. Like the other two she goes back to her old associates, like the other two she dies, but this time someone sees the killer at his work. You comprehend?"

"I certainly do not."

He breathed a sigh of exasperation, then, patiently: "Four women are suspected of complicity in the killing of a young man. The young man's father has a statuary group erected as a memorial—in a low, unfashionable part of town, by the way—and as the women, then incarcerated, are released they meet a death much like that of the young man.

"Our young Policeman Flannigan swears he saw a marble statue kill the Ebbert girl.

"Now, arranging for the lecture by the mythical Dr. Bradley-Stoker was not all I did this afternoon. By no means. I read and reread certain of Cornelius Agrippa's charms and spells. By the use of certain magic formulae the magus claimed to be able to vivify marble statues, and make them do his will for good or ill, but only at the dark or in the waning of the moon, and only at the midnight hour between Saturday—the old Sabbath—and Sunday, the new day of worship.

"So I arrange this wholly false lecture, and arrange to have the Cook woman come to it, and to say certain things in the hearing of one I am convinced will also be there. It all transpired as I planned, my friend."

"See here," I demanded as we turned in my driveway, "was that evil-looking little fat man just ahead of us at the box office—"

"Of course," he anticipated my question. "Who else could it be but Monsieur Joseph Stoneman, father of the killed young man and donor of that statuary group to this fair city?"

THE NIGHT WAS COLD with a cruel, penetrating chill that gnawed at our bones like a starved wolf. A gray rain slashed against the flat fronts of the grimy tenements in Tunnell Street, as halfway down the slattern row of shabby houses a door opened for a moment on the storm, showed a fuzzy square of faint light, then closed with a bang.

Muffled to the ears in a raincoat, Nellie Cook slipped from the house, paused a moment on the worn doorstep, then stepped out into the flooding street. For a moment she pressed close against the house front, seeming to hold her breath and listen. She cast a quick glance up and down the street and, keeping to the shadows, crept down the sidewalk. Frightened though she obviously was, I noticed that she walked with shortened, gliding steps and provocatively swaying hips.

For several days de Grandin had been coaching her, schooling her in her entrance, directing where she was to walk, regulating the speed of her movements. Now she was letter-perfect in the rôle, and, the dress rehearsals having been concluded, we were ready for the performance. Since we had met her in the lobby of the lecture hall the new moon had gone through its phases, and we had reached another dark period. The storm had kept the usual crowd of Saturday night revelers indoors, and as the girl emerged from the house the gong in the clock tower of St. Dominic's Church, six blocks away, boomed the first deep, resounding stroke of midnight.

Beside me in the doorway huddled Jules de Grandin. His face seemed pinched with cold, but the twitching of his little blond mustache and the intermittent quiver of his lips was purely the result of nervous tension, I knew.

He and Hiji had been deep in consultation all afternoon, and shortly before dinner the Englishman had made a hurried trip to New York, returning somewhere about nine with a small paper parcel which he handled with extreme tenderness. Now he and Costello were ensconced in a doorway at the far end of the block, and all of us watched Nellie as she walked slowly through the pelting rain.

A street light's haze revealed the pale blur of her face as she passed under it. I knew that it was sharp and unintelligent, with hard, malicious eyes and only feeble traces of the common prettiness it once had, but in the distance, softened by the rain-filtered lamp rays, it looked fragile and appealing, and clearly terror-ridden.

She paused a moment underneath the light, looked backward fearfully, then went on toward the farther corner.

"This is so utterly inane!" I grumbled as a drop of water from the doorway's lintel fell like an icicle down the upturned collar of my raincoat. "We'll get nothing but pneumonia for our pains, and—"

"*Zut!* Quiet, my friend," warned de Grandin in a sharp whisper. "We are not here for pleasure, I assure you, and—*ah, barbe d'un bouc vert*, behold him!"

Something sounded on the flagstone walk almost beside us, dully, heavily, like stone striking stone. *Clump—thump, thump—clump!* and walking like a robot, yet with speed almost equal to a run, a white shape passed us.

A cold as hard and dull as death itself seemed added to the chill of the rain-drenched night air, and I felt the breath catch in my throat like a hard, solid ball.

Agleam with rain, and moving with a stride as purposeful as Fate, yet with no play of flexing muscles showing under its white surface, a graven image—a white marble statue—passed us in the wake of the retreating girl.

"*Hola!*" shouted de Grandin, leaping out into the rain and struggling with some object in his trench coat pocket. "*Hola, M'sieur le Statuaire! Halte la!*"

The moving marble horror gave no sign of hearing, but heavily, yet swiftly, with the surety of inexorable Nemesis, made toward the woman.

Now we saw it fully revealed in the fuzzy glow of the street lamp. There was no expression in its carven features. Calm and composed and utterly oblivious of everything around them, its marble eyes stared straight ahead.

The woman heard the pounding of the marble feet and turned for a swift glance across her shoulder. Her scream was something horrible to hear. A bubbling, frothing, mounting geyser of sheer terror, winding upward, growing shrill and shriller till it seemed to pierce our eardrums like a probing needle.

She reeled blindly in midstep, clutching at the rain-flogged empty air with fingers gone as stiff as rigor mortis, then, seeming to realize that if she fainted she was lost, she gathered skirts and raincoat up above her knees and darted like an arrow from a bow toward the cross street.

The stone pursuer broke into a run. Not the heavy, clumsy jog-trot that might have been expected from an automaton, but the lithe, swift racing of a trained athlete, every step instinct with grace and only the hard thudding of its stone feet on the stone sidewalk to make us know it was an animated rock, not flesh and blood, that rushed through the downpouring tempest.

There was no doubt of the result. Before she'd traversed fifty steps the terror-stricken woman stumbled and fell to her knees, and for a moment as she turned toward her pursuer we saw her face like one of those old Grecian horror masks, mouth squared in agony of terror, eyes almost forcing from their sockets, cheeks gone a sort of dreadful, deathly gray despite the daubs of paint on them.

Costello's burly form came cannoning from the doorway where he hid. "Stand back, ye murderin' haythin!" he roared, raised his service pistol and let fly a stream of bullets at the charging marble horror.

The thing paid no more heed to them than it did to the pelting rain drops. We heard the spat of lead on stone, the screaming whine of a bullet as it ricocheted, but on the statue ran, its carved feet drumming on the flagstones of the walk.

"Duck, Sergeant!" we heard Hiji shout as he leaped past Costello, shoved him aside and faced the onrushing stone monster.

We saw him balance on his sound foot, raise his maimed leg almost waist-high, press something hard against his thigh, then bend forward as he hurled a missile, putting every ounce of weight and strength behind it.

The roar was utterly deafening, and the burst of sudden fire that came with it was blinding as the dazzling blaze of a flashbulb. I could feel the force of detonation beating on me like a dozen fists as it was echoed back from the house fronts.

For a long moment everything was dark, then as my eyes regained their vision, I saw a heap of marble debris on the sidewalk forty feet or so away, smashed white stone that seemed strangely like a corpse dismembered by some hideous force, here a marble hand, and there a bit of what had been an arm or leg or torso. Almost at my feet a calm, serene white marble face stared up into the pelting rain, and I had a quick qualm of wonder that it did not close its lids against the battering drops.

"Bingo!" I heard Hiji call. "Got him square amidships with the first throw, Frenchy. Jolly lucky that I did, too, or you and Trowbridge would be in the happy huntin' grounds by now."

"*Mon brave, mon superb,* my infinitely splendid Hiji!" de Grandin cried delightedly. "You are, as you have said, a marvel!"

"Who said that? Not I. You do all the boastin' around here, you little devil!"

"No matter, there is glory enough for all," the little Frenchman returned. "What though it was the agile brain of Jules de Grandin that conceived the plan of shattering him to pieces with a hand grenade because he could not be stopped with bullets? It was the fine, strong arm and fine, true, accurate aim of Hiji that gave him the *coup de grâce.* But certainly!

"Now," practically, he added, "let us see to these ones."

Costello had been knocked unconscious by the detonation of the bomb, but his loss of consciousness was short-lived, for even as we bent above him he shook himself like a dog emerging from the water. "Howly Mither!" he exclaimed. "What wuz it? Wuz I kilt entirely?"

"*Mais non, mon sergent,* you are very much alive," denied de Grandin with a laugh. "You were struck senseless for a little so short time, but now you are all right. Of course. Give him to drink from your flask, Hiji," he added as he ran to help me with the swooning woman.

As far as I could find she had no injury of any kind. No broken bones, no cuts, no wounds. Apparently unconsciousness had been induced by fright alone.

I took her head in the bend of my elbow and held my flask beneath her nose, letting the fumes of the brandy act as a restorative. In the weak light from the street lamp, with the rain upon her face, she looked almost pretty. The long, dark, heavily mascaraed lashes lay in half moons on her cheeks, the wilful, child-ish mouth was relaxed and robbed of its petulance and cynicism. The tendrils of bright hair that slipped beneath the brim of her storm hat seemed really golden, not the result of a skillful bleaching.

"Gimme!" she roused as the scent of the brandy reached through her unconsciousness, grasped the flask in both hands and drank greedily. "Gosh!" she let her breath out with a gulping sigh and drank again, then drew her hand across her mouth, leaving a bright stain of carmine lipstick on it. "That was sumpin', wasn't it?"

"It was, indeed, *ma belle,*" de Grandin agreed as he rose from his knees beside her. "It was indubitably something."

He looked at her a long minute, then: "What is it you would want, my little one? If you will say the word I shall be glad to find employment for you, or defray expenses of your schooling while you prepare yourself for a position. You have courage and resourcefulness, and could go far—"

"Yeah, far as the nearest gin-mill," she interrupted. "It's no dice, Doc. You can comb an' brush her all you want, an' tie a ribbon round her neck an' call her all the pet names that you know, but an alley cat is still an alley cat, an' sooner or later she'll go back to her alley. I'm no good an' never was. I know it an' you know it. Me take a job? That's a big laugh! You know I couldn't hold one twenty minutes."

The look he gave her was direct and level, but not at all censorious. "*Tu parles, ma petite*," he agreed with a quick smile. "Here is something for your services to Jules de Grandin," he pressed a roll of bills into her hand, "and here is something for yourself alone." Taking her cheeks between his palms he bent her face back and kissed her upon the mouth.

"Gosh, Doc," she gave him a look in which surprise and pleasure were mingled, "you ain't such a cold number yourself. Why don't—" she slurred her voice in imitation of Mae West—"why don't you come up an' see me some time?"

"Should I require the service of a brave and loyal woman again you may be sure that I shall call on you, *Mademoiselle*," he answered with a friendly smile.

"Okay, Doc, be seein' you in the pictures." She gave him a nod of farewell and turned toward her house.

"Too bad," I murmured as I watched her walk off slowly through the rain. "She has the makings of something fine—"

"*Ah bah*, my friend, you sentimentalize!" he chuckled. "Did not you hear her? She understands herself perfectly, and was most just in her estimate. None but a fool would try to make a silk purse of a sow's ear, or force a different way of life on women such as that. It is her destiny to be a waster, so she will go through life a petty criminal, harried by the police, picked up on trifling charges, serving short terms in jail, then, as she put it so concisely, 'returning to her alley.' The pity is not that she is what she is, but that she was born in our time. In ancient Greece, or the Alexandria of the Ptolemies, or even in medieval Europe, there was a niche and place for such as she, a sort of honorable dishonor. *Eh bien*, they had more religion and less morals in those days, I damn think."

He shrugged as only a Frenchman can when he wishes to disclaim responsibility. The fault was Fate's, not his. And: "Hiji, thou species of an elephant," he added, "have you forgotten we have other duties to perform? Come, let us be upon our errand. *Allez vous promener!*"

"Right you are, my diminutive frog-eatin' friend," agreed the Englishman. "Carry on."

T HE BIG OLD HOUSE in Albemarle Road looked gaunt and lonely. Built of gray stone with a wide porch across the front and sides, it had the jigsaw ornaments of the Victorian period set in the angles of its gables, and iron urns on high stone pedestals on its front lawn. Now, huddled in the fringe of evergreens planted almost at its foundations, it had the look of an old man who wraps his cloak about him and withdraws from life. Rain lashed against its windows, flattening on the pines, rain sluiced down its gutters, wind-driven rain washed across its porch floor like waves that sweep across the decks of a ship in a storm.

De Grandin seized the heavy iron knocker hanging on the solid Flemish oak front door and beat a devil's tattoo with its ring. No answer came to his first summons, but at the third insistent drumming a glow showed in the fanlight above the door, and the heavy panel swung back a few inches. "Who is it?" came the challenge in a rather high-pitched voice.

The little Frenchman put his foot in the crack of the door before he replied: "Those who wish to talk with you about the memorial you erected to your son in the park, M'sieur."

The exclamation answering him was almost like a squeak. The door swung nearly shut, then, wedged against his foot, came to a halt, and: "Hiji, my friend, I think I need your shoulder's weight," he told the big Englishman.

The door crashed back before the mighty push that Hiji gave it, and we were in the hallway of the old house. I looked around me with amazement. The place was a litter of bad taste. Heavy furniture of the kind fashionable in the "awful eighties" stood about the walls, bronze statuary worthy of the worst the cemeteries have to offer loomed on onyx pedestals, the pictures in their heavy gilt frames showed impossible landscapes. The only light in the room came from an old gas chandelier which, dripping colored prisms, hung from the center of the ceiling. There was a musty smell about the house, a taint of dried leather, of dust and mildewed fabrics. "Tudieu, my friends," de Grandin remarked, "I damn think we have come into the Castle of Despair."

He looked at the short, fat man in the flowered silk dressing gown, and: "You wish to tell us of that memorial, M'sieur?" he asked. "Or shall we tell you?"

"I—I don't know what you mean!" the other stammered, and the little, thin, high-piping voice that came from that great mass of fat struck me as being nothing less than shocking.

Joseph Stoneman was not an impressive figure, but he was sinister. Despite his moon face and pot belly there was none of the traditional jollity of the fat man about him, and the little eyes that looked out from the folds of fat that framed them were absolutely terrible.

"Monsieur," de Grandin's voice was flat and leveL and he kept his sharp gaze on the fat face of the other, "since you will not tell us, let me tell you of that memorial. Six weeks ago it left its pedestal and walked by night through Tunnell Street. There it encountered Sally Jukes, and what it did to her was most unpleasant.

"A week later it waylaid Mae Mahoney, and when its work was done there was another case for the coroner. Then Lucy Ebbert met him as she walked the street, and—"

A quick and dreadful change came over Stoneman's face. Gone was the childish, sullen, stupid look, gone the dullness from his eyes. His fat jaws quivered like the dewlaps of a hound that works its teeth, his little, puffy mouth began to twist convulsively. "Yes, yes!" he squeaked. "I know it; I sent him—I tracked them down like rats, the sluts that lured my poor boy to his ruin. One by one I tracked them down, and had them killed the way their gangster lovers killed him. All, all are gone, now—Jukes, Mahoney, Ebbert, Cook!"

"There you make the mistake, M'sieur. Mademoiselle Cook is very much alive, as we can testify, and your statue he is—pouf!—eliminated."

"You lie," the other told him. "You can't hurt him. He's proof against your bullets—"

"But not against my dynamite, M'sieur."

"Dynamite?" the other echoed unbelievingly. "You dared to dynamite my lovely statue—my executioner?"

"Quite yes, M'sieur. Your statue is a heap of rubble, nothing more, and we are here to make you answer for your crimes."

A sly, triumphant look came into Stoneman's little eyes. "You can't" he jeered. "Who'd believe the truth when you told it? What sober-minded jury would convict me on your testimony—or fail to send you to a madhouse?

"They'll put you safely away, and I shall be free to impose my will on the world. I'll recite the magic spell not once, but fifty or a hundred times. Think of it, I'll have a company—a regiment—of marble executioners to do my bidding, and all who offend me shall meet death. I'll wipe out alcohol and vice and sin, and I shall be the sole judge of what's right and what is wrong. I shall be like God. I shall—"

"You shall be nothing at all, M'sieur," de Grandin interrupted in a low, hard voice. "You are the only man alive who knows the secret spell of the magus to bring the dead, cold stone to life, and knowing that, you know too much for the good of mankind.

"Trowbridge, Costello," he turned to us, "will you accommodate me by retiring to the porch for a moment? I shall not keep you waiting longer than our work requires."

The Sergeant cast a meaning look at me, and, "Yis, sor," he agreed. "It'll be a pleasure, so it will."

We closed the door behind us and turned up our collars to the storm. Costello drew me to an angle of the wall, "We don't know nothin', do we, Dr. Trowbridge, sor?" he asked softly.

It was not long before they joined us, locking the door carefully after them. "Hélas, I bring you the sad news, as the papers in the morning will report. Monsieur Joseph Stoneman, the eminent philanthropist, committed suicide tonight. It appears that he hanged himself with the belt of his dressing gown."

Death's Bookkeeper

J ULES DE GRANDIN, LOOKING even more diminutive and dapper in his uniform of major in the *Service des Rensiegments* than in civilian attire, regarded the highly polished tip of his tan boot with every sign of approval as he exhaled two columns of smoke through narrow nostrils. Dinner had been something of a function that evening, for at a little place in East Fifty-Third Street he had found that afternoon a half-case of Nuits St. Georges which he had borne home triumphantly just in time to grace the capon which Nora McGinnis had been simmering in claret for our evening meal. Now, fed to repletion, with coffee on the stand at his elbow and something like a thimbleful of green Chartreuse left in the *pousse café* beside his cup, he seemed utterly at peace with all the world. "The day has been a trying one at the *Bureau des Rensiegments*, my friend," he confided as he took a half-swallow of Chartreuse and followed it with a sip of black coffee. "I am tired like twenty dogs and half as many so small puppies. I would not budge from this chair if—"

The shrilling of the telephone sawed through his statement and with a nod of apology I picked up the instrument. "Yes?" I inquired.

"This is Michaelson, Doctor," the woman's voice came to me from the other end of the wire.

"Yes!" I repeated. Miss Michaelson was night supervisor of the maternity floor at Mercy Hospital, and when she called I knew what impended.

"Mrs. Morrissey in Fifty-Eight—"

"How long?" I interrupted.

"Not more than half an hour, sir. Maybe less. If I were in your place—"

"If you were in my place, I should be in yours, and not have to drive thirty blocks through zero weather," I broke in somewhat rudely. "Have them make the delivery room ready, if you please, and give her half a grain of morphine if the pain becomes too great. I'm starting right away."

To de Grandin I explained: "Just one of those things that keep life from becoming too dull for the doctor. The population of New Jersey is due for an addition in the next half hour, and I have to be there as part of the welcoming committee—"

"Will you permit that I go with you to assist?" he asked. "Me, I have so long been busily engaged in reducing the sum total of humanity that it will be a novelty to take part in its increase. Besides, my hand grows awkward for the lack of practice."

"I'll be delighted," I assured him as I hunted up my case of instruments and got into my greatcoat. "But I thought you were too tired—"

"*Ah bah!*" The little laughter-wrinkles deepened at the outer corners of his eyes "That Jules de Grandin, he is what you call?—the cramper-in-the-stomach? He is always complaining, that one. You must not put too much credence in his lamentations."

I T WAS AN ORDINARY case. Miranda Morrissey was young and strong, and de Grandin's obstetrical skill was amazing. "So—now—my small sinner," he spanked the small, red infant's small, red posterior with a wet towel, "weep and wail, and breathe the breath of life in the process. What?" as the baby refused to respond to his command. "You will not? By blue, I say you shall! You are too young to defy your elders. Take that, *petit diablotin!*" He struck a second, sharper blow, and a piping, outraged wail answered the assault. "Ah, that is better—much better!" He wrapped the now-wriggling small, wrinkled bundle of humanity in a warmed turkish towel and bore it toward the bed where Miranda rested with all the pride of a cook carrying a *chef-d'oeuvre*. "Behold your man-child, mother," he announced as he laid the baby on her bosom. "He is not happy now, but in your arms he will find happiness. *Le bon Dieu* grant the world in which he has been borh may be a better one than that into which we came!"

As we walked down the corridor he drew his hand across his eyes wearily. "There is something more solemn in a birth than a death," he confided. "For the dead one all is over, his troubles are behind him, he is quits with life and fate. But for the one who is beginning life—*hèlas*, who can say what he has stepped into? A quarter-century ago when little boys came into the world we thought they were inheritors of peace and safety and security; that we had won the war to end all war. Today?" He spread his hands and raised his shoulders in the sort of shrug no one but a Frenchman can attain, "Who can prophesy, who can predict what—*barbe d'un bouc vert*, who in Satan's name is that?" he broke off sharply.

I looked at him in amazement. His small, pointed chin was thrust forward and in his little round blue eyes there was the flash of sudden anger, while his delicate, slim nostrils twitched like those of a hound scenting danger or quarry. "Who? Where?" I asked.

"Yonder by the elevator, my friend. Do not you see him? *Parbleu*, if the Iscariot had descendants, I make no doubt that he is one of them!"

I looked where his glance indicated and gave a shrug of disgust. "That's Coiquitt," I answered. "Dr. Henri Coiquitt."

"*Hein?*"

"I don't know much about him, and the little that I do know is not good. He came here since you went away. You never heard of him."

"Thank God for that," he answered piously. "But something tells me I shall hear more of him in the future, and that he shall hear of Jules de Grandin."

The object of our colloquy turned toward us as the elevator stopped in answer to his ring, and in the light that flowed from the car we saw him outlined clearly as an actor in a spotlight on a darkened stage. He was a big man, six feet tall, at least, and his height seemed greater because of his extreme slenderness. He was in black throughout, a long loose cape like a naval officer's boat-cloak hung from his shoulders, his broad-brimmed hat was black velour; his clothes, too, seemed to be of a peculiar shade of black that caught and pocketed the light. The only highlight in his costume was the band of white that marked his collar above his wide, flowing black cravat, and in complement to the somberness of his attire his skin was pale olive and his lips intensely red. As we stepped into the car beside him we caught the scent of perfumed soap and bath powder, but underneath the more agreeable odor, it seemed to me, there was a faint, repulsive smell of decay and corruption.

Coiquitt bowed gracefully as we joined him, and de Grandin, not to be outdone in courtesy, returned the bow punctiliously, but for a moment, as their glances crossed, both men seemed poised and alert, like duelists who seek an opening in each others' guards. I felt a shiver of something like awe run through me. It seemed to me as if I sat in a box seat and watched a drama staged by Fate unfold. These men had never heard of each other, never before set eyes on each other, yet in the glance of each there shone a sudden hatred, cold and deadly as a bared knife. They were like two chemicals that waited only for a catalyst to explode them.

Traveling so smoothly we were scarcely aware of its motion, the elevator drew to a stop at the ground floor, and Coiquitt stepped soundlessly across the corridor to the reception room. At the door Camilla Castevens rushed to meet him. "How is he, Doctor?" we heard her ask in a trembling whisper. "Is he—is there any improvement?"

He bowed to her with a superb gentility, yet the gesture had a hint of mockery in it, I thought. "Of course, Miss Castevens. Did I not promise you—" He turned and cast a glance half quizzical, half mocking, at de Grandin and me, and with a guilty start I realized we had halted almost at his elbow, drinking in each word he and Camilla said to each other.

"Good evening, Dr. Trowbridge," Camilla nodded coldly as she recognized me, and with an answering bow I took de Grandin's elbow and guided him toward the door, feeling like a naughty little boy who had been caught eavesdropping on his elders' conversation.

"Now, what in Satan's name is it all about?" the little Frenchman demanded as we stepped into the stinging cold of the February night.

I laughed without humor. "I wish I knew. Dr. Coiquitt is a newcomer to Harrisonville, as I told you. Where he came from goodness only knows. We know only that he had credentials from half a dozen European universities, and had no difficulty in obtaining a license to practice. Since he set up shop in Dahlonega Road he's raised the very devil with the medical profession."

"Ah? How is that, is he a quack?"

"I only wish I knew. He's certainly not orthodox. The first case I have real knowledge of is one he took from Perry. I think you know Perry. First-rate heart man. He'd been treating Mrs. Delarue for angina pectoris, and having no more luck with her than was to be expected in the circumstances. Then somehow Delarue met Coiquitt and took the case from Perry. Within two months his wife was as completely cured as if she'd never had a moment's illness. That started it. Case after case the rest of us had given up as hopeless was taken to Coiquitt, and in every instance he effected a complete cure, even with Bernice Stevens, who was so far gone with carcinoma hysteria that none of us would operate, because there wouldn't have been enough left of her to bury when we'd cut the morbid growth away."

"U'm?" be pursed his lips. "I take it there is something more here than mere professional jealousy, my friend?"

I shook my head hopelessly. "Of course, there is. We'd have been chagrined to have a stranger take our cases and effect cures when we'd abandoned all hope, but that could have happened. Only—" I paused, at loss for words to continue, and he prompted softly. "Yes, only—"

"Well—oh, this sounds utterly absurd, I know—I'd never think of mentioning it to anybody else, but—hang it all, man, it seems to me there's something like black magic in his cures."

"Ah-ha? How do you say?"

"In every instance where a cure has been effected someone in the patient's family has taken ill and died within a year. Sometimes sooner, but never later."

He was silent for a moment, then, "Perhaps," he admitted thoughtfully. "The Greeks knew of such things—"

"How's that?"

"I cannot say, at least not now, *mon vieux*. I did but think aloud, and not to any great effect, I fear."

IT MIGHT HAVE BEEN a week later, perhaps ten days, when Camilla Castevens called on me. She was a tall young woman with copper hair and steady blue eyes, past the first flush of her youth—some thirty-two or -three—but with the added attractiveness that early maturity gives to a woman. In the light of the consulting-room lamp her face looked sad, her cheeks seemed hollow, and her red lips dipped in a pathetic downward curve. "I'm frightened, Dr. Trowbridge," she confessed.

I found it hard not to be sarcastic. It was on the tip of my tongue to ask her why she did not take her fears to Dr. Coiquitt, but better sense prevailed, and instead I looked at her inquiringly. Like the priest, the doctor has to be long-suffering and patient.

"I—I'm terribly afraid," she went on as I said nothing to help her. "I don't want to die."

"Few of us do, my dear."

"But I shall have to if"—she paused a long, agonized moment, then with a burst of something like hysteria—"if Richard is to get well. He says I must!"

"He? Who?"

"Dr. Coiquitt, sir. Don't you know, haven't you noticed? He was treating Mrs. Delarue for an incurable ailment. She got well—yes, well, when all the other doctors said she hadn't a chance!—but her son Donald who was her idol died just as he was about to receive his commission in the Air Corps when his plane crashed in his final practice flight. Oh, I know you'll say it was coincidence; that his plane would have cracked up just the same if his mother had died instead of getting well. But it didn't. She got well and he died. Then there was Bernice Stevens. Nobody thought she had an earthly chance, and she herself prayed daily for death to release her from her dreadful suffering; but he took her case and cured her—and Bert Stevens died within ten months. Of cancer, too. Perhaps that was coincidence, also. How many coincidences do we have to have to make a certainty, Doctor?

"I'll tell you—" She leaned forward, and in the light of my desk lamp her eyes seemed hard and expressionless as blue gems inlaid in an ivory face. "I have proof! The man's a wizard; just as much a wizard as those dreadful men they hanged and burned in mediæval days. He is—he *is!*" Her voice rose almost to a shriek, and as I smiled incredulously, "Listen:

"You know that Richard Bream and I have been in love for years. We went in grade school together, and to high school, and afterwards to college. We'd planned to be married just after commencement, but the depression came along just then, and Richard couldn't get a start in his law practice. They took his furniture for debt, and evicted him from his office, and he couldn't get even a clerk-ship anywhere; finally he was forced to take a place as a soda dispenser in a drug store—Richard Bream, Esquire, bachelor and master of laws, Phi Beta Kappa and Sigmu Nu Tau, a soda-jerker at ten dollars a week, and glad to get that much! I had twelve dollars weekly from my work as a stenographer, but two people can't live on twenty-two dollars a week, and besides, I had mother to look after. Then finally Rick secured a place as law clerk with Addleman and Sinclair, and just as we were planning to get married his father died, and he had his mother to support. It was just one thing after another, Doctor. Every time we thought our period of waiting was over something came up to destroy our hopes. I've heard the Indians sometimes tormenting their prisoners by tying them to stakes and lighting fires around them, then, when the torture had become unbearable, offering the poor wretches bowls of cool water, only to dash them from their lips as they were about to drink. That's the way it's been with Rick and me for nearly twelve years, Doctor. We've starved and thirsted for each other, and time and again it seemed our period of waiting had come to a close when"—she raised her hands in a gesture of futility—"something else happened to postpone our marriage. At last the war came, and Rick got his commission. There seemed nothing that could halt us now, and then—this unsuspected heart ailment appeared; Rick was discharged from the Army on a medical certificate and went to Dr. Dahlgren and half a dozen other specialists. All told him the same thing. He might live one year, maybe two—he might drop dead any minute.

"I wanted to get married right away. I'm making fifty dollars a week now, and that would keep us. I could love and cherish him for whatever time remained to us, and—oh, Doctor, I love him so!" She broke down utterly and bowed her head upon her clasped hands, crying almost silently with body-shaking sobs. At last: "I was desperate, Dr. Trowbridge. I'd heard about the wonderful cures Dr. Coiquitt had made, and went to see him." A shudder, more of horror than of fear, it seemed to me, ran through her. "I tell you, the man is a wizard, sir.

"His office is more like a necromancer's den than a physician's place. No daylight penetrates it; everything about the place is black—black floors, black walls, black ceiling; black furniture upholstered in black silk brocade. The only light in the place is from a black-shaded lamp on the desk where he sits and waits like a—like a great spider, sir! He wasn't kind and sympathetic as a doctor ought to be; he wasn't glad to see me; he didn't even seem surprised that I had come. It was as if he knew I'd have to come to him, and had been waiting with the patience of a great cat sitting at a rat-hole.

"When I told him about Rick's case he seemed scarcely interested; but when I'd finished talking he said in that heavy foreign accent of his: 'These matters have to be adjusted, Miss Castevens. I can cure your lover, but the risk to you is great. Do you love him more than you love life?'

"Of course I vowed I did, that I would gladly die if Rick could live, and he smiled at me—I think that Satan must smile like that when a new damned soul is brought to him.

"'For every one who leaves the world another comes into it,' he told me. 'For every one who cheats Death, Death must have another victim. I have pondered long upon this matter; I have learned the wisdom of the ancients and of people you Americans in your ignorance call savage. I know whereof I speak. I do not prescribe for the ailing. I give my medicine—and thought—to the well, and they, by sympathy, affect the suffering. If you will agree to do just as I say I can cure your lover, but it may be that your life will be the forfeit demanded for his. You must understand this clearly; I would not have you embark on the case unknowingly.'

"Well, it sounded utterly absurd, but I was desperate, so I agreed. He went into a back room and I heard him clinking glass on glass, then presently he came out with a syringe which he thrust into my arm and drew blood from it. Then he disappeared again for a short time, and finally came back with a tall glass in which some black liquor steamed and boiled. 'Drink this,' he ordered, and as you drink it pronounce after me, "Of my own free will and accord I agree to give myself in his stead, whatever may betide." I took the glass into both hands and drained it at a gulp as I pronounced the words he told me, and instead of being boiling hot the liquid seemed as cold as ice—so cold it seemed to send a chill through every vein and artery in my body, to make my toes and fingers almost ache with sudden chill, and freeze my heart and lungs until I breathed with difficulty.

"Before I left he gave me another bottle filled with black liquor and told me, 'Take this three times a day, once before each meal and once before you say your prayers at night. You do pray, don't you?

"'Yes, sir,' I answered. 'Every night and morning.'

"'So much the better. Take an extra dose of this before your morning prayer, then, and I shall call on Mr. Bream in the morning, make a careful note of his condition and report to you. In three days he should begin to improve. In two months he should be completely recovered.' That was all, and I left that queer, black-walled den of his feeling foolish as if I'd been to consult a fortune-teller.

"But the next day when I called the hospital to inquire after Richard they told me he was showing marked improvement and his improvement has been constant ever since."

"That's wonderful," I commented, and she caught me up abruptly, sarcastically:

"Yes, isn't it? It's wonderful, too, that as Richard gained in strength I've lost weight steadily, and for the past two weeks have suffered agonizing pain in my right breast and arm, and have these dreadful smothering fits when it seems that a pillow has been clamped across my nose and mouth. I tell you, Doctor Trowbridge, I am dying; dying surely as if I had been sentenced to death by a court. Rick's getting well, and, of course, I want that; but I'm afraid, sir, terribly afraid. Besides, if I die, what shall we have gained? Rick will have life, but not me, and I—I shall have nothing at all!" Her voice rose to a wail of pure despair.

"Camilla!" I admonished sharply. "Such things don't happen. They can't—"

"By blue, my friend, I think they do and can," de Grandin's sharp denial came as he stepped into the consulting room. "You must excuse me, *Mademoiselle*," he bowed to Camilla, "but I could not help hearing something of the things you said to Doctor Trowbridge as I came in. You need have no fear your confidence will be violated. I too, am a physician, and whatever I have heard is under the protection of my oath of confidence. However," he lifted brows and shoulders in the faint suggestion of a shrug, "if you will consent that I try, I think perhaps that I can help you, for I am Jules de Grandin, and a very clever person, I assure you."

Reminded by his announcement that the amenities had not been observed. I introduced them formally, and he dropped into a seat facing her. "Now, if you please," he ordered, "tell me all that you have told Friend Trowbridge, and leave out nothing. In cases such as this there are no little things; all is of the importance, and I would know all that I may be of assistance to you. Begin at the beginning, *Mademoiselle*, if you please."

She rehearsed the story she had told me, and he nodded emphatic agreement as she finished. "I do not know how he does it, *Mademoiselle*," he admitted as she brought her recital to a close, "but I am as convinced as you that there is something unholy about this business. What it is remains for us to find out. Meantime, if you will oblige us by submitting to a physical examination"—he rose and nodded toward the examination room—"we should like to assure ourselves of your condition; perhaps to prescribe treatment."

There was no doubt in either of our minds when we had finished our inspection. There was a widespread area of dullness round her heart, the pulmonary second sound was sharply accented, and a murmur was discernible in the second interspace to the left of the sternum at the level of the third rib, so harsh as to be audible over the entire pericardium. Camilla Castevens was undoubtedly a victim of myocarditis, and in an advanced, almost hopeless stage.

"I shall not hold the truth from you, *Mademoiselle*," de Grandin told her gravely when she returned to the consultation room. "You are a very ill person, and in utmost danger. These"—he scribbled a prescription for some three-grain amyl nitrite capsules—"will ease the pain when it comes on. Crush one in your handkerchief and inhale the fumes freely. For the rest," his slender fingers tapped a fuguelike rhythm on the edge of the desk, "we shall have to seek the cause of your illness, and it is not in you, I assure you. Do not hesitate to call on us if you feel the need of our assistance."

"And I should dismiss Dr. Coiquitt?"

"Not at all; by no means. Desist from taking his nostrums, if you have not already done so, but permit him to attend your fiancé by all means——"

"But look here," I protested, "if your theory is correct he's already done Camilla immeasurable harm. If we permit him to stay in the case——"

"We shall know where he is and what he's up to, *parbleu*," de Grandin returned.

"He will be within the orbit of our observation. When the hunter stalks the tiger, he tethers a goat to a stake in a clearing, and waits in concealment till the striped one makes his appearance. Then, when the moment is propitious, he fires, and there is one more handsome rug to decorate a floor. So it is in this case. *Mademoiselle* and *Monsieur* her fiancé are the bait which we leave for this debased species of a charlatan. Do keep up your courage, *Mademoiselle*," he cast a smile of reassurance at Camilla, "and we shall do the rest. Be brave; we shall not fail you."

"The pair of you are crazy as a brace of loons," I fumed when she had taken her departure. "I can understand Camilla. It's the power of suggestion working on her. There's a book about that sort of thing in the library, written by a man named Manly Wade Wellman. He's made a study of the matter and decided that if belief in illness is induced in someone who firmly believes what is told him, he will become ill—even die—of the disease he has been told he has. It may be that Camilla had a tendency toward a weak heart. Now, if Coiquitt induced her to believe she would develop myocarditis, and administered some evil-tasting drug to be taken regularly and so keep her attention fixed on the suggestion, it might easily be that her constant worry and the fear of impending sickness and death have combined to make that latent heart-weakness active. But as for your believing such rubbish—"

"Ah, *bah*, my friend," he patted back a yawn, "you bore me. Always you must rationalize a thing you do not understand, taking the long route around the barn of Monsieur Robin Hood in order to arrive at a false conclusion.

"It was the power of suggestion, you say? Let us for the sake of argument admit that suggestion could induce such an organic condition as that we found in Mademoiselle Camille. *Très bien*. So much for her. But was it also suggestion that caused Madame Stevens to recover from advanced carcinoma—and her husband to develop it and die almost as she regained health? Was it the power of suggestion that pulled the young man's plane out of the sky and dashed him to his death against the earth? Coincidence, you say. Perhaps in one case, and possibly in two, but in the three of which we know, and in the many which we damn suspect coincidence has ceased to take a great part. *Parbleu*, to say otherwise would be to pull the long arm of coincidence clear out of joint! *Non*, my friend. There is something more sinister in this business-of-the-monkey we are dealing with. Just what it is I do not know, but I shall make it my affair to secure the necessary information, you may be assured."

"How'll you go about it?" I demanded, nettled by his air of assurance.

He spread his hands and raised his shoulders. "How should I know? The case requires thought, and thought requires food. There is an excellent dinner awaiting us. Let us give it our attention and dismiss this never-quite-sufficiently-to-be-anathematized Coiquitt person from our thoughts a little while."

H E WAS RATHER LATE to dinner the next evening, and Nora McGinnis was calling on high heaven to witness that the *coq au vin blanc* she had prepared especially for him would be entirely ruined when he bustled in with that peculiar smile that told he was much pleased with himself on his face.

"Me, I have done research at the city hall this afternoon," he told me. "At the bureau of *statistiques vitales* I delved into the records. This Coiquitt person is the very devil of a fellow. A hundred cases he has had since he began the malpractice of medicine in the city, and I find he has prolonged a hundred lives for a greater or less time, but at the cost of an equal number. He is not righteous, my friend. He has no business to do such things. He annoys me excessively, *par les cornes d'un crapaud!*"

Despite myself I could not forbear a grin. "What are you going to do about it?" I asked.

He tweaked the waxed ends of his small mustache alternately, teasing them to needle-sharpness. "I do not quite know," he confessed. "At times I think perhaps it would be best if I went—*mon Dieu*, is it that we are attacked?"

The front doorbell had given a quick, anguished peal, almost as if it wailed in pain, and as the shrilling of the gong ceased someone beat upon the panels with a frenzied knock.

I hurried to answer the summons, and Camilla Castevens almost fell into my arms. "Oh, Dr. Trowbridge," she gasped as I steadied her, "he's found out that I came to you! I don't know how he did it, but he called me on the 'phone a little while ago and told me that my time is up. Rick will get well—he seemed positively gloating when he told me that—but I must die tonight—" Her voice trailed off in a gasp and if I had not held her she would have slumped to the floor in a swoon.

I carried her into the study and stretched her on the sofa while de Grandin bathed her temples with cologne and held a glass of brandy to her lips when she revived a little.

She was pitiable in her terror. Her lower lip began to quiver and she caught it savagely between her teeth to steady it. Her fingers twisted and untwisted themselves, and at the base of her throat we could see the pulsing of an artery as her tortured heart jumped like a frightened rabbit with each beat. "Be calm, *ma pauvre*," de Grandin ordered gently. "You will do yourself an injury if you give way. Now, tell us just what happened. You say he threatened you?"

"No, sir. I wouldn't call it a threat so much as a statement—like a judge pronouncing sentence. He told me I should never see another sunrise—"

"*Nom d'un bouc vert!* Did he, indeed? And who in Satan's stinking name is he to pass judgment of life and death upon his fellow creatures, and especially on the patients of Jules de Grandin and Samuel Trowbridge, both reputable physicians? Do you rest quietly beside the fire, *Mademoiselle*. If you should have a fit of oppression use the amyl nitrite capsules we gave you. If you desire it, a little brandy cannot do you harm. Meanwhile—come, Friend Trowbridge," he turned to me imperatively, "we have important duties to perform."

"Duties? Where?"

"At Dr. Coiquitt's, in the street of the funny name, *pardieu!* We shall talk with that one, and in no uncertain words—"

"We can't go barging in on a man like that—"

"Can we not, indeed? Observe Jules de Grandin, if you please, my friend, and you shall see the finest instance of barging ever barged, or I am one infernal, not-to-be-believed liar. Come, *alons; allez-vous-en!*"

Dr. Coiquitt's house in Dahlonega Road loomed dark as Dolorous Garde against the smalt blue of the winter sky. In keeping with his bizarre personality its owner had had the place painted black, with no relieving spot of color, save for the silver nameplate on the door that bore the single word Coiquitt. No chink showed in the tightly drawn shutters, no ray or spot of light came from the house, but not to be deterred by the tomblike air of the place de Grandin beat a tattoo on the panels with the handle of his military swagger stick. "*Nom d'un nom d'un nom d'un artichaut*," he promised savagely, "I shall stand here hammering until I bring the filthy place down on his ears, or till he answers me!"

At last his persistence was rewarded. A shuffling step sounded beyond the portal and the door drew back on a crack, not swinging on hinges, but sliding in a groove on oiled bearings. It would have taken a battering-ram to force the place, I thought, as I noted the strong steel of the track in which the heavy oak door traveled.

A Negro, heavy-set and obviously powerful, but dreadfully hunchbacked, peered at us through the aperture. "The doctaire is not seeing patients now," he announced in an accent I could not quite place, but which sounded vaguely French.

"Nevertheless, he will see us, *mon vieux*," de Grandin promised, and launched into a torrent of words, speaking in a patois I could not make out, but which the other understood instantly.

"One moment, if you please, M'sieu," he begged as he drew back the door and stood aside for us to enter. "I shall be pleased to tell the doctaire—"

"*Non*, by no means," de Grandin denied. "Do not disturb him at his lucubrations. We shall go to him all quietly. I know that he will see us gladly."

"*Bien*, M'sieu. You will find him at the head of the stairway," the servant answered as we stepped across a long hall carpeted in black, with black, lack-luster walls and ceilings.

"He is a Haitian, that one," de Grandin confided as we crept up the black-carpeted stairway. "He thinks that I am an initiate of voodoo, a *papaloi*. I did not tell him that I was—in just so many words—but neither did I deny it. And now"—he halted, braced himself as for a physical encounter, and struck the black-enameled door before us with his knuckles.

"*Entrez*," a deep voice answered, and we stepped across the threshold.

The room was positively bewildering. It ran across the full width of the house, some thirty feet or more, and the floor above had been removed so that the vaulted ceiling was at least eight yards above us. The floor was of some black and shining composition, strewn with rugs of leopard skin with the heads and claws left on, and the glass eyes set in the beasts' stuffed heads blazed at us with a threatening fury. The walls were dull black and emblazoned with a great gold dragon that seemed marching round and round the room, while across the farther end was built a divan upholstered in black silk and strewn with red and cloth-of-gold pillows. Here and there against the walls were cabinets of ebony or buhl containing large and strangely-bound books, scientific paraphernalia and bits of curiosa such as skeletons of small animals, stuffed gila monsters and serpents coiled as if forever in the act of striking, and baby crocodiles. A human skeleton, fully articulated, swung from a frame of ebony like a gallows, and in a tiled fireplace there stood a retort hissing over a great bunsen burner. Incongruously, on a book-strewn table in the center of the room, there was a massive silver vase containing a great bouquet of orchids.

The man who sat at the table raised his eyes as we entered, and as I met his gaze I felt a sudden tingling in my spine—the sort of feeling one has when in the reptile house at the zoo he looks down into a pit filled with lizards and nameless crawling things.

Coiquitt's eyes were black as polished obsidian and strangely shiny, yet unchanging in their stare as those of one newly dead, and almost idly, as one takes minute note of such trifles at such times, I noticed that the lids above the odd, unchanging eyes had a faint greenish tinge and a luster like that of old silk. For a moment he raked us with a glance of cold, ophidian malignancy, then abruptly lowered his lids, as if he drew a curtain between us and his thoughts.

"Good evening, gentlemen—dare I say colleagues?" There was suave mockery that threatened to become stark savagery at any moment in his voice. "To what am I indebted for the honor of this wholly unexpected and I'm sure quite undeserved visit?"

The anger that had shown in Jules de Grandin's face had given way to a puzzled frown, and beneath his sharply waxed, diminutive mustache his lips were pursed as if he were about to whistle. For a long moment he made no reply, and his silence seemed to goad the other into sudden fury. "*Quoi?*" he demanded almost shrilly. "Is it that you come to see a marvel, and are stricken speechless at the sight? I am not on display, my simple ones. Speak up and state your business and be off!"

"*Morbleu!*" Surprise seemed to have forced the word from de Grandin.

"What is it that you—" began the other, but de Grandin ignored him completely.

"Not Coiquitt!" he almost shouted at me. "Not Coiquitt, Trowbridge, *pour l'amour d'un porc louche!* It is Dessiles, Pierre Dessiles, the apostate, false alike to his country and his Aesculapian oath as a physician! Dessiles the necromancer, the *sale espion*, dismissed from the *faculté de médicine*, convicted of conniving with the filthy *Boche* to sell his country's secrets, and condemned to penal servitude for life on Devil's Island!" He leveled his small swagger stick at the other as if it were a weapon and continued his denunciation: "I had heard he had escaped from confinement and made his way to Haiti and become a member of the voodooists, and when I first saw him at the hospital I was almost sure I recognized him, though when he turned to face me I was just as certain that I was mistaken, for in the olden days his eyes were gray, now they are black. I do not know how he has done it, but I know beyond a doubt now that he is Dessiles, despite the changed color of his eyes. I cannot be mistaken in that voice, that monstrous egotism of the ass who struts about in a lion's skin. However much the leopard has succeeded in effacing his spots or Dessiles in changing his eye-color, the leopard still is but an overgrown, great pussy-cat and Dessiles remains a stinking charlatan and traitor!"

"*Touché!*" the man behind the table laughed with a low hard raucousness like the crackling of crushed paper. "You are right on every count, my little droll one, and since your knowledge goes no farther than yourself, and you shall go no farther than this room, you might as well know all." With an almost incredibly quick motion he flung open a drawer in the table and snatched a heavy automatic pistol from it, swinging it in a quick arc between de Grandin and me, steady as a pendulum and deadly as a serpent poised to strike. "Be seated, gentlemen," he ordered rather than invited. "When the time has come to say *au 'voir* you may stand, if you wish, but until then I must insist that you sit—and keep your hands in plain sight."

I collapsed into the nearest chair, but de Grandin looked about him deliberately, chose a comfortable divan, and dropped on it, resting his short swagger stick across his knees and beating a tattoo on it with lean, nervous fingers. "And now," he prompted, heedless alike of the menacing, blank stare in Coiquitt's glassy eyes and the threat of the pointed pistol, "you were about to regale us with the story of your adventures, were you not, *Monsieur?*"

"I was about to say that I survived the green hell of the *Île du Diable*. They penned me in like a brute beast, stabled me on stinking straw in a sty no pig with *amour propre* would consent to live in, made me drag a ball and chain behind me, starved me, beat me—but I survived. And I escaped. Through swamps that swarmed with crocodiles and poison snakes and reeked with pestilence and fever, I escaped. Through shark-infested waters and shores that swarmed with gendarmes on the watch for me, I escaped, and found safe sanctuary in the *houmforts* of the *voudois*.

"They welcomed me for my learning, but, *pardieu*, they had much to teach me, too! I learned, by example, how to make a *zombi*, how to draw the soul from the body and leave only an automaton that moves and breathes, but has no mind or reason. I learned from them how it is possible to cast the illness out of one and into another—even how to swerve the clutching hand of death from one to another. Poor little fool, do you know that in the mountain fastnesses of Haiti there are men and women still young and strong and virile who were old when Toussaint l'Ouverture and Henri Christophe raised the banner of revolt against the French? How? Because, *parbleu*, they know the secret I alone of all white men have learned from them—how to turn the hand of death from one man to another. But there must be a willing victim for the sacrifice.

"There must be one who says that he will die in place of the other. Granted this, and granted the such power as I possess, the rest is easy. Life begins at forty, some Yankee has said fatuously. *Pardieu*, it can begin again at seventy or eighty or a hundred, or flow back strong and vibrant into one who lies on death's doorsill, provided always there is one who will become the substitute of him whose time is almost sped.

"That is the secret of the cures I've made, my silly little foolish one. I have not changed the score. Death still collects his forfeit, but he takes a different victim; that is all. Yet I grow rich upon the hope and the credulity of those who see only the credit columns of the ledger Death keeps. They do not realize, the fools! that every credit has its corresponding debit, and when Death finally strikes his balance, 'Too bad,' they say, 'he had so much to live for, yet he died just as she regained health.' Ha-ha, it is to laugh at human gullibility, *mes enfants*. You, by example, would never stoop of practicing such chicanery, I am certain. Oh, no! If you could not effect a cure you would permit the patient to die peacefully, and raise your hands and eyes to heaven in pious resignation. Me, I am different. As long as there are fools there will be those to prey on them, and I shall keep Death's books, collect my stipend for my work, and be known as the great doctor who has never lost a case—"

"I fear you have lost this one, *cher savant*," the ghost of an ironic grin appeared beneath the waxed ends of de Grandin's small mustache. "We have heard all we desired, and—"

"And now the time has come to say, '*Adieu pour l'éternité!*'" the other broke in savagely as he leveled the pistol, steadying his elbow on the table. "You think—"

"*Non*, by blue, it is that I damn know!" de Grandin's voice was hard and sharp as a razor as he raised one knee slightly, pressed his hand against the leather knob of his swagger stick and gave it a sharp half-turn.

The report was no louder than the bursting of an electric light bulb, and there was no smoke from the detonation of the cartridge in the gun-barrel hidden in the cane, but the missile sped to its mark with the accuracy of an iron-filing flying to a magnet, and Coiquitt swayed a little in his chair, as if he had been struck by an unseen fist. Then, between the widow's peak of the black hair that grew well down on his forehead and the sharply accented black brows above the glassy, unchanging black eyes, there came a spot of red no larger than a dime, but which spread till it reached the size of a quarter, a half-dollar, and finally splayed out in an irregular red splash that covered almost the entire forehead. There was a look of shocked surprise, almost of reproof, in the cold visage, and the black, lack-luster eyes kept staring fixedly at de Grandin.

Then suddenly, appallingly, the man seemed to melt. The pistol dropped from his unnerved hand with a clatter and his head crashed down upon the table, jarring the great silver bowl of orchids till it nearly overturned, and dislodging a pile of books so they crashed to the floor.

"And that, unless I am much more mistaken than I think, is that, my friend," de Grandin rose and walked across the room to stand above the dead man slumped across the table. "The English, a most estimable people, have a proverb to the effect that the one who would take supper with the devil would be advised to bring with him a long spoon. *Eh bien*, I took that saying to heart before coming to this place, *mon vieux*. This little harmless-seeming cane, she is a very valuable companion in the tight fix, I do assure you. One never knows when he may find himself in a case where he cannot make use of his pistol, when to make a move to draw a weapon would be to sign one's own death warrant; but he who would shoot quickly if he saw you reach for a weapon would never give a second thought or glance to this so little, harmless seeming stick of mine. No, certainly. Accordingly, when he had bidden us be seated and threatened us with his pistol, I took great care to seat myself where I could aim my cane at him as I held it across my knees, with nothing intervening to spoil the shot I knew I must take at him sooner or later. *Tiens*, am I not the clever one, *mon vieux*? But certainly, I should say yes."

"You certainly got us out of a tight fix," I admitted. "Five minutes ago I shouldn't have cared to offer a nickel for our chance of getting out of here alive."

He looked at me reproachfully. "While I was with you, Friend Trowbridge?"

For a moment he bent over the man sprawled across the table, then, "Ah-ha!" he cried jubilantly. "Ah-ha-ha! Behold his stratagem, my friend!"

I went a little sick as I looked, for it seemed to me he gouged the dead man's eyes out of their sockets, but as I took a second glance I understood. Over his eyeballs, fitted neatly underneath the lids, Coiquitt had worn a pair of contact lenses that simulated natural eyes so well that only a fixed stare betrayed them, and they were made with black irides, entirely concealing the natural gray of his eyes.

"He had the cunning, that one," de Grandin grudgingly admitted as he dropped the little hemispheres of glass upon the table. "He made but one great mistake. He underestimated Jules de Grandin. It is not wise to do that, Friend Trowbridge."

"How will you explain his death," I asked. "Of course, you shot in self-defense, but—"

"But be stewed in sulphur and served hot with brimstone for Satan's breakfast," he broke in. "The man was an escaped convict, a traitor to France and a former agent of the *Boche*. I am an officer of the Republic, and had the right to apprehend him for the American authorities. He resisted arrest, and"—his shrug was a masterpiece, even for him—"he is no longer present. *C'est tout simple, n'est-ce-pas?*"

The telephone began to ring with a shrill insistence and instinctively I reached for it, but he put out his hand to arrest me. "Let it ring, my friend. He is past all interest in such things, and as for us, we have more important business elsewhere. I would inspect Mademoiselle Camille—"

"You think she may have—"

"I do not know just what to think. I have the hope, but I cannot be sure. Come, hasten, rush, fly; I entreat you!"

CAMILLA LAY UPON THE study sofa much as we had left her, and smiled wanly at us as he hurried into the room. "You did see him, didn't you?" she asked with something akin to animation in her voice.

"We did, indeed, *Mademoiselle*," de Grandin assured her, "and what was much more to the point, he saw us."

"I knew you must have talked to him and made him relent, for just a little while ago—it couldn't have been more than ten or fifteen minutes—I had another dreadful attack, and just when I had given up all hope and knew that I was dying it stopped, and I found I could breathe freely again. Now I feel almost well once more. Perhaps"—hope struggled with fear in her eyes—"perhaps I shall recover?"

"Perhaps you shall, indeed, *Mademoiselle*," he nodded reassuringly. "Come into the examination room if you will be so kind. It is that we should like to see what we can see."

It was amazing, but it was true. The most minute examination failed to show a symptom of angina pectoris. There was no area of dullness, no faint suggestion of a heart murmur, and her pulse, though rather light and rapid, was quite steady.

"Accept our most sincere congratulations, *Mademoiselle*," de Grandin murmured as he helped her from the table. "It seems you are on the highway to complete recovery."

"Oh!" her exclamation was a small, sad sound, and there was an enmeshed, desperate look in her eyes. "Rick! If I get well, he'll—"

De Grandin made a little deprecating sound with his tongue against his teeth. "It may be even as you say, *ma chère*. I would not give you the false hope. Again, it may be quite otherwise. Have you courage to go with us to the hospital and see?"

T HE SUPERVISOR OF THE third floor where young Bream's room was met us at the elevator. "It's really amazing," she confided as we walked down the corridor. "Mr. Bream has been improving steadily these past six weeks, but shortly after ten o'clock tonight he had a dreadful paroxysm, and we thought it was the end. We had to get Dr. Carver the house physician, for all our efforts to get Dr. Coiquitt on the 'phone were useless. Dr. Carver gave us no hope, but suddenly—almost miraculously, it seemed to me—the spasm passed and Mr. Bream began to breathe freely. In a little while he fell asleep and has been resting ever since. I never knew a patient sick as he was with myocarditis to recover fully, but—"

"Strange things are happening every day, *Madame*," de Grandin reminded her. "Perhaps this is one of them."

I had not treated Bream, and so had no basis of comparison between his condition as I found him and his former state, but careful examination revealed nothing alarming.

His pulse was weak and inclined to be thready, and his respiration not quite satisfactory, but there was no evidence of organic affection. With bed-rest and good nursing he should make an excellent prospect for some life insurance salesman in a year or less, I thought. De Grandin agreed with me, and turned to Camilla, eyes agleam with delight. "You may congratulate him on his impending recovery, *Mademoiselle*," he whispered, "but do it softly—gently. The aching sweetness of a lover's kiss—*morbleu*, but it can play the very devil with a normal heart, when one is not so strong—have the discretion, *Mademoiselle*."

"I'm hanged if I can understand it," I confessed as we left the hospital. "First Bream is dying, then Coiquitt, or Dessiles, seems to cure him, but makes Camilla wilt and wither like a flower on the stem as he improves. Then, when you shoot him, she makes an amazing recovery and Bream seems practically well. If he had retrogressed as she recovered—"

He chuckled delightedly. "He called himself Death's Bookkeeper. *Très bon*. He was balancing the books of Death when I shot him, and as you say so drolly in America, caught him off his balance. The scales were even. She he had sent the psychic message to, but not in quite enough force. Had he endured five little minutes longer, he might have forced her to her death. As it was I damn think I did not delay one little minute too long in eliminating him. At the same time he endeavored to cause her to die he attempted to undo the work he had done for young Monsieur Bream, but his death cut short that bit of double-dealing, also, and the young man lapsed again into the state of almost-wellness he had attained when the *sale trompeur* tried to kill him to death. Yes, undoubtedly it is so. I can no more explain it than I can say why a red cow who eats green grass gives white milk. I know only that it is so.

"And in the meantime, if we walk a block in this direction, then turn twenty paces to the left, we shall arrive at a place where they purvey a species of nectar called an old-fashioned—a lovely drink with quantities of lovely whiskey in it. Why do we delay here, my friend?"

The Green God's Ring

S T. DUNSTAN'S WAS PACKED to overflowing. Expectantly smiling ladies in cool crêpe and frilly chiffon crowded against perspiring gentlemen in formal afternoon dress while they craned necks and strained ears. Aisles, chancel, sanctuary, were embowered in July roses and long trailing garlands of southern smilax, the air was heavy with the humid warmth of summer noon, the scent of flowers and the perfume from the women's hair and clothes.

The dean of the Cathedral Chapter, the red of his Cambridge hood in pleasing contrast to the spotless white of linen surplice and sleek black cassock, pronounced the fateful words, his calm clear voice a steady mentor for the bridegroom's faltering echo:

"I, Wade, take thee Melanie to be my wedded wife, to have and to hold from this day forward—"

"From this day forward," Dean Quincy repeated, smiling with gentle tolerance. In forty years of priesthood he had seen more than one bridegroom go suddenly dumb. "From this day forward, for better, for worse—"

His smile lost something of its amusement, his florid, smooth-shaven face assumed an expression of mingled surprise and consternation which in other circumstances would have seemed comic. Swaying back and forth from toes to heels, from heels to toes, the bridegroom balanced uncertainly a moment, then with a single short, hard, retching cough fell forward like an overturned image, the gilded hilt of his dress sword jangling harshly on the pavement of the chancel.

For what seemed half a minute the bride looked down at the fallen groom with wide, horrified eyes, then, flowing lace veil billowing about her like wind-driven foam, she dropped to her knees, thrust a lace-sheathed arm beneath his neck and raised his head to pillow it against the satin and seed pearls of her bodice. "Wade," she whispered in a passionless, cold little voice that carried to the farthest corner of the death-still church. "Oh, Wade, my belovèd!"

Quickly, with the quiet efficiency bred of their training, the young Naval officers attending the fallen bridegroom wheeled in their places and strode down the aisle to shepherd panic-stricken guests from their pews.

"Nothin' serious; nothin' at all," a lad who would not see his twenty-fifth birthday for another two years whispered soothingly through trembling lips as he motioned Jules de Grandin and me from our places. "Lieutenant Hardison is subject to these spells. Quite all right, I assure you. Ceremony will be finished in private—in the vestry room when he's come out of it. See you at the reception in a little while. Everything's all right. Quite—"

The pupils of de Grandin's little round blue eyes seemed to have expanded like those of an alert tomcat, and his delicate, slim nostrils twitched as though they sought to capture an elusive scent. "*Mais oui, mon brave*," he nodded approval of the young one-striper's tact. "We understand. *Certainement*. But me, I am a physician, and this is my good friend, Dr. Trowbridge—"

"Oh, are you, sir?" the lad broke in almost beseechingly. "Then for God's sake go take a look at him; we can't imagine—"

"But of course not, *mon enfant*. Diagnosis is not your trade," the small Frenchman whispered. "Do you prevail upon the congregation to depart while we—*attendez-moi*, Friend Trowbridge," he ordered in a low voice as he tiptoed toward the chancel where the stricken bride still knelt and nursed the stricken bridegroom's head against her bosom.

"*Sacré nom!*" he almost barked the exclamation as he came to a halt by the tragic tableau formed by the kneeling bride and supine man. "*C'est cela même.*"

There was no doubting his terse comment. In the glassy-eyed, hang-jawed expression of the bridegroom's face we read the trade mark of the King of Terrors. Doctors, soldiers and morticians recognize death at a glance.

"Come, Melanie," Mrs. Thurmond put a trembling hand upon her daughter's shoulder. "We must get Wade to a doctor, and—"

"A doctor?" the girl's voice was small and still as a night breeze among the branches. "What can a doctor do for my poor murdered darling? Oh, Wade, my dear, my dear," she bent until her lips were at his ear, "I loved you so, and I'm your murderess."

"*Non, Mademoiselle*," de Grandin denied softly. "You must not say so. It may be we can help you—"

"Help? *Ha!*" she almost spit the exclamation at him. "What help can there be for him—or me? Go away—get out—all of you!" she swept the ring of pitying faces with hard bright eyes almost void of all expression. "Get out, I tell you, and leave me with my dead!"

De Grandin drew the slim black brows that were in such sharp contrast to his wheat blond hair down in a sudden frown. "*Mademoiselle*," his voice was cold as icy spray against her face, "You ask if any one can help you, and I reply they can. I, Jules de Grandin can help you, despite the evil plans of pisacha, bhirta and preta, shahini and rakshasha, I can help—"

The girl cringed from his words as from a whip. "Pisacha, bhirta and preta," she repeated in a trembling, terrified whisper. "You know—"

"Not altogether, *Mademoiselle*," he answered, "but I shall find out, you may be assured."

"What is it you would have me do?"

"Go hence and leave us to do that which must needs be done. Anon I shall call on you, and if what I have the intuition to suspect is true, *tenez*, who knows?"

She drew a kneeling cushion from the step before the altar rail and eased the dead boy's head down to it. "Be kind, be gentle with him, won't you?" she begged. "Good-by, my darling, for a little while," she laid a light kiss on the pale face pillowed on the crimson cushion. "Good-by—" Tears came at last to her relief and, weeping piteously, she stumbled to her mother's waiting arms and tottered to the vestry room.

"HEART?" I HAZARDED AS the bridal party left us alone with the dead man. "I should think not," he denied with a shake of his head. "He was on the Navy's active list, that one, and those with cardiac affections do not rate that."

"Perhaps it was the heat—"

"Not if Jules de Grandin knows his heat prostration symptoms, and he has spent much time near the Equator. The fires of hell would have been cold beside the temperature in here when all those curious ones were assembled to see this poor one and his belovèd plight their troth, but did he not seem well enough when he came forth to meet her at the chancel steps? Men who will fall prone on their faces in heat collapse show symptoms of distress beforehand. Yes, of course. Did you see his color? Excellent, was it not? But certainly. Bronzed from the sea and sun, *au teint vermeil de bon santé*. We were not thirty feet away, and could see perfectly. He had none of that pallor that betokens heat stroke. No."

"Well, then"—I was a little nettled at the cavalier way he dismissed my diagnoses—"what d'ye think it was?"

He lifted narrow shoulders in a shrug that was a masterpiece of disavowal of responsibility. "*Le bon Dieu* knows, and He keeps His own counsel. Perhaps we shall be wiser when the autopsy is done."

We left the relatively cool shadow of the church and stepped out to the sun-baked noonday street. "If you will be so kind, I think that I should like to call on the good Sergeant Costello," he told me as we reached my parked car.

"Why Costello?" I asked. "It's a case of sudden unexplained death, and as such one for the coroner, but as for any criminal element—"

"Perhaps," he agreed, seeming only half aware of what we talked of. "Perhaps not. At any rate, I think there are some things about this case in which the Sergeant will be interested."

We drove a few blocks in silence, then: "What was that gibberish you talked to Melanie?" I asked, my curiosity bettering my pique. "That stuff about your being able to help her despite the evil plans of the thingabobs and whatchamay-callems? It sounded like pure double talk to me, but she seemed to understand it."

He chuckled softly. "The pisacha, bhirta and preta? The shahini and rak-shasha?"

"That sounds like it."

"That, my friend, was what you call the random shot, the drawing of the bow at venture. I had what you would call the hunch."

"How d'ye mean?"

"Did you observe the ring upon the index finger of her right hand?"

"You mean the big red gold band set with a green cartouche?"

"*Précisément.*"

"Not particularly. It struck me as an odd sort of ornament to wear to her wedding, more like a piece of costume jewelry than an appropriate bridal deco-ration, still these modern youngsters—"

"That modern youngster, my friend, did not wear that ring because she wanted to."

"No? Why, then?"

"Because she had to."

"Oh, come, now. You can't mean—"

"I can and do, my friend. Did not you notice the device cut into its setting?"

"Why, no. What was it?"

"It represented a four-faced, eight-armed monstrosity holding a straining woman in unbreakable embrace. The great God Siva—"

"Siva? You mean the Hindu deity?"

"Perfectly. He is a veritable chameleon, that one, and can change his form and color at a whim. Sometimes he is as mild and gentle as a lamb, but mostly he is fierce and passionate as a tiger. Indeed, his lamb-like attributes are generally a disguise, for underneath the softness is the cruelty of his base nature. *Tiens,* I think that he is best described as Bhirta, the Terrible."

"And those others with outlandish names?"

"The pisacha and preta are a race of most unlovely demons, and like them are the rakshasha and shahini. They attend Siva in his attribute of Bhirta the Terrible as imps attend on Satan, doing his foul bidding and, if such a thing be possible, bettering his instructions."

"Well?"

"By no means, my friend, not at all. It is not well, but very bad indeed. A

Christian maiden has no business wearing such a talisman, and when I saw it on her finger I assumed that she might know something of its significance. Accordingly I spoke to her of the Four-Faced One, Bhirta and his attendant implings, the shahini, raksash and pischa. *Parbleu*, she understood me well enough. Altogether too well, I damn think."

"She seemed to, but—"

"There are no buts, my friend. She understood me. Anon I shall understand her. Now let us interview the good Costello."

DETECTIVE-SERGEANT JEREMIAH COSTELLO WAS in the act of putting down the telephone as we walked into his office. "Good afternoon, sors," he greeted as he fastened a wilted collar and began knotting a moist necktie. "'Tis glad I'd be to welcome ye at any other time, but jist now I'm in a terin' hurry. Some swell has bumped himself off at a fashionable wedding, or if he didn't exactly do it, he died in most suspicious circumstances, an'—"

"It would not be Lieutenant Wade Hardison you have reference to?"

"Bedad, sor, it ain't Mickey Mouse!"

"Perhaps, then, we can be of some assistance. We were present when it happened."

"Were ye, indeed, sor? What kilt 'im?"

"I should like to know that very much indeed, my friend. That is why I am here. It does not make the sense. One moment he is hale and hearty, the next he falls down dead before our eyes. I have seen men shot through the brain fall in the same way. Death must have been instantaneous—"

"An' ye've no hunch wot caused it?"

"I have, indeed, *mon vieux*, but it is no more than the *avis indirect*—what you would call the hunch."

"Okay, sor, let's git goin'. Where to first?"

"Will you accompany me to the bride's house? I should like to interview her, but without official sanction it might be difficult."

"Howly Mackerel! Ye're not tellin' me she done it—"

"We have not yet arrived at the telling point, *mon ami*. Just now we ask the questions and collect the answers; later we shall assemble them like the pieces of a jigsaw puzzle. Perhaps when we have completed the mosaic we shall know some things that we do not suspect now."

"I getcha," Costello nodded. "Let's be on our way, sors."

THE THURMOND PLACE IN Chattahoochee Avenue seemed cloaked in brooding grief as we drove up the wide driveway to the low, pillared front porch. A cemetery quiet filled the air, the hushed, tiptoe silence of the sickroom or the funeral chapel. The festive decorations of the house and grounds were as incongruous in that atmosphere of tragedy as rouge and paint upon the cheeks and lips of a corpse.

"Miss Melanie is too ill to be seen," the butler informed us in answer to Costello's inquiry. "The doctor has just left, and—"

"Present our compliments to her, if you please," de Grandin interrupted suavely. "She will see us, I make no doubt. Tell her it is the gentleman with whom she talked at the church—the one who promised her protection from Bhirta. Do you understand?"

"Bhirta?" the servant repeated wonderingly.

"Your accent leaves something to be desired, but it will serve. Do not delay, if you please, for I am not a patient person. By no means."

Draped in a sheer convent-made nightrobe that had been part of her trousseau, Melanie Thurmond lay rigid as death upon the big colonial sleigh bed of her chamber, a madeira sheet covering her to the bosom, her long auburn hair spread about her corpse-pale face like a rose gold nimbus framing an ivory ikon. Straight before her, with set, unseeing eyes she gazed, only the faint dilation of her delicate nostrils and the rhythmic rise and fall of her bosom testifying she had not already joined her stricken lover in the place he had gone a short hour before.

The little Frenchman approached the bed silently, bent and took her flaccid hand in his and raised it to his lips. "*Ma pauvre,*" he murmured. "It is truly I. I have come to help you, as I promised."

The ghost of a tired little smile touched her pale lips as she turned her head slowly on the pillow and looked at him with wide-set, tearless sepia eyes. "I knew that it would come," she told him in a hopeless little voice. Her words were slow and mechanical, her voice almost expressionless, as though she were rehearsing a half-learned lesson: "It had to be. I should have known it. I'm really Wade's murderess."

"Howly Mither!" Costello ejaculated softly, and de Grandin turned a sudden fierce frown on him.

"*Comment?*" he asked softly. "How do you mean that, *ma petite roitelette?*"

She shook her head wearily from side to side and a small frown gathered between her brows. "Somehow, I can't seem to think clearly. My brain seems seething—boiling like a cauldron—"

"*Précisément, exactement, au juste,*" de Grandin agreed with a vigorous nod. "You have right, my little poor one. The brain, she is astew with all this trouble, and when she stews the recrement comes to the surface. Come, let us skim it off together, thou and I"—he made a gesture as if spooning something up and tossing it away. "Thus we shall rid our minds of dross and come at last to the sweet, unadulterated truth. How did it all start, if you please? What made you know it had to happen, and why do you accuse yourself all falsely of the murder of your *amoureux?*"

A little shudder shook the girl's slim frame, but a hint of color in her pallid cheeks told of a returning interest in life. "It all began with The Light of Asia."

"*Quoi?*" de Grandin's slim brows rose in Saracenic arches. "You have reference to the poem by Sir Edward Arnold?"

"Oh, no. This Light of Asia was an Oriental bazaar in East Fifty-Sixth Street. The girls from Briarly were in the habit of dropping in there for little curios—quaint little gifts for people who already seemed to have everything, you know.

"It was a lovely place. No daylight ever penetrated there. Two great vases stood on ebony stands in the shop windows, and behind them heavy curtains of brocaded cloth of gold shut off the light from outside as effectively as solid doors. The shop—if you could call it that—was illuminated by lamps that burned scented oil and were encased in frames of carved and pierced teakwood. These, and two great green candles as tall as a man, gave all the light there was. The floors were covered with thick, shining Indian rugs, and lustrous embroideries hung against the walls. The stock was not on shelves, but displayed in cabinets of buhl and teak and Indian cedar—all sorts of lovely things: carved ivories and moulded silver, hand-worked gold and tortoise-shell, amethyst and topaz, jade and brass and lovely blue and green enamel, and over everything there hung the scent of incense, curiously and pungently sweet; it lacked the usual cloying, heavy fragrance of the ordinary incense, yet it was wonderfully penetrating, almost hypnotic."

De Grandin nodded. "An interesting place, one gathers. And then—"

"I'd been to The Light of Asia half a dozen times before I saw The Green One."

"The Green One? *Qui diable?*"

"At the back of the shop there was a pair of double doors of bright vermilion lacquer framed by exquisitely embroidered panels. I'd often wondered what lay behind them. Then one day I found out! It was a rainy afternoon and I'd dropped into The Light as much to escape getting wet as to shop. There was no other customer in the place, and no one seemed in attendance, so I just wandered about, admiring the little bits of *virtu* in the cabinets and noting new additions to the stock, and suddenly I found myself at the rear of the shop, before the doors that had intrigued me so. There was no one around, as I told you, and after a hasty glance to make sure I was not observed, I put my hand out to the nearer door. It opened to my touch, as if it needed only a slight pressure to release its catch, and there in a gilded niche sat the ugliest idol I had ever seen.

"It seemed to be carved of some green stone, not like anything I'd ever seen before—almost waxen in its texture—and it had four faces and eight arms."

"*Qu'est-ce-donc?*"

"I said four faces. One looking each way from its head. Two of the faces seemed as calm as death masks, but the one behind the head had a dreadful sneering laugh, and that which faced the front had the most horrible expression—not angry, not menacing, exactly, but—would you understand me if I said it looked inexorable?"

"I should and do, *ma chère*. And the eight arms?"

"Every hand held something different. Swords, and sprays of leafy branches, and daggers—all but two. They were empty and outstretched, not so much seeming to beg as to demand an offering.

"There was something terrible—and terrifying—about that image. It seemed to be demanding something, and suddenly I realized what it was. It wanted me! I seemed to feel a sort of secret, dark thrill emanating from it, like the electric tingle in the air before a thunderstorm. There was some power in this thing, immense and terrifying power that gave the impression of dammed-up forces waiting for release. Not physical power I could understand and combat—or run from, but something far more subtle; something uncanny and indescribable, and it was all the more frightening because I was aware of it, but could not explain nor understand it.

"It seemed as if I were hypnotized. I could feel the room begin to whirl about me slowly, like a carousel when it's just starting, and my legs began to tremble and weaken. In another instant I should have been on my knees before the green idol when the spell was broken by a pleasant voice: 'You are admiring our latest acquisition?'

"It was a very handsome young man who stood beside me, not more than twenty-two or -three. I judged, with a pale olive complexion, long brown eyes under slightly drooping lids with haughty brows, and hair so sleek and black and glossy it seemed to fit his head like a skullcap of patent leather. He wore a well-cut morning coat and striped trousers, and there was a good pearl in his black poplin ascot tie.

"He must have seen the relief in my face, for he laughed before he spoke again, a friendly, soft laugh that reassured me. 'I am Kabanta Sikra Roy,' he told me. 'My dad owns this place and I help him out occasionally. When I'm not working here I study medicine at N.Y.U.'

"'Is this image—or idol, or whatever you call it—for sale?' I asked him, more to steady my nerves by conversation than anything else.

"The look he gave me was an odd one. I couldn't make out if he were angry or amused, but in a moment he laughed again, And when he smiled his whole face lighted up. 'Of course, everything in the shop's for sale, including the proprietors—at a price,' he answered, 'but I don't think you'd be interested in buying it.'

"'I should say not. But I just wondered. Isn't it some sort of god, or something?'

"'Quite so. It is the Great Mahadeva, third, but by far the most important member of the Hindu Triad, sometimes known as Siva the Destroyer.'

"I looked at the thing again and it seemed even more repulsive than before. 'I shouldn't think you'd find a quick sale for it,' I suggested.

"'We don't expect to. Perhaps we'll not sell it at all. In case we never find a buyer for it, we can put in our spare time worshiping at its shrine.'

"The utter cynicism of his reply grated on me, then I remembered having heard that many high caste Hindus have no more real faith in their gods than the educated Greeks and Romans had in theirs. But before I could be rude enough to ask if he really believed such nonsense, he had gently shepherded me away from the niche and was showing me some exquisitely carved amethysts. Before I left we found we had a dozen friends in common and he'd extended and I'd accepted an invitation to see Life With Father and go dancing at the Cotillion Room afterward.

"That began the acquaintance that ripened almost overnight into intimacy. Kabanta was a delightful playfellow. His father must have been enormously rich, for everything that had come to him by inheritance had been given every chance to develop. The final result was this tall, slender olive complexioned man with the sleek hair, handsome features and confident though slightly deferential manner. Before we knew it we were desperately in love.

"No"—her listless manner gathered animation with the recital—"it wasn't what you could call love; it was more like bewitchment. When we met I felt the thrill of it; it seemed almost to lift the hair on my head and make me dizzy, and when we were together it seemed as if we were the only two people in the world, as if we were cut off from everyone and everything. He had the softest, most musical voice I had ever heard, and the things he said were like poetry by Laurence Hope. Besides that, every normal woman has a masochistic streak buried somewhere deep in her nature, and the thought of the mysterious, glamorous East and the guarded, prisoned life of the zenana has an almost irresistible appeal to us when we're in certain moods. So, one night when we were driving home from New York in his sports roadster and he asked me if I cared for him I told him that I loved him with my heart and soul and spirit. I did, too—then. There was a full moon that night, and I was fairly breathless with the sweet delirium of love when he took me in his arms and kissed me. It was like being hypnotized and conscious at the same time. Then, just before we said good night, he asked me to come to The Light of Asia next evening after closing time and plight our troth in Eastern fashion.

"I had no idea what was coming, but I was fairly palpitant with anticipation when I knocked softly on the door of the closed shop shortly after sunset the next evening.

"Kabanta himself let me in, and I almost swooned at sight of him. Every shred of his Americanism seemed to have fallen away, for he was in full Oriental dress, a long, tight-waisted frock coat of purple satin with a high neck and long, tight sleeves, tight trousers of white satin and bright red leather shoes turned up at the toes and heavily embroidered with gold, and on his head was the most gorgeous piece of silk brocade I'd ever seen wrapped into a turban and decorated with a diamond aigret. About his neck were looped not one nor two but three long strands of pearls—pink-white, green-white and pure-white—and I gasped with amazement at sight of them. There couldn't have been one in the three strands that was worth less than a hundred dollars, and each of the three strands had at least a hundred gems in it. The man wore twenty or thirty thousand dollars worth of pearls as nonchalantly as a shop girl might have worn a string of dime store beads.

"'Come in, White Moghra Blossom,' he told me. 'All is Prepared.'

"The shop was in total darkness except for the glow of two silver lamps that burned perfumed oil before the niche in which the Green God crouched. 'You'll find the garments of betrothal in there,' Kabanta whispered as he led me to a door at the rear, 'and there's a picture of a Hindu woman wearing clothes like those laid out for you to serve as a model. Do not be long, O Star of My Delight, O Sweetly Scented Bower of Jasmine. I swoon for the sight of you arrayed to vow love undying.'

"In the little anteroom was a long, three-paneled mirror in which I could see myself from all sides, a dressing-table set with toilet articles and cosmetics, and my costume draped across a chair. On the dressing-table was an exquisite small picture of a Hindu girl in full regalia, and I slipped my Western clothes off and dressed myself in the Eastern garments, copying the pictured bride as closely as I could. There were only three garments—a little sleeveless bodice like a zouave jacket of green silk dotted with bright yellow discs and fastened at the front with a gold clasp, a pair of long, tight plum-colored silk trousers embroidered with pink rosebuds, and a shawl of thin almost transparent purple silk tissue fringed with gold tassels and worked with intricate designs of lotus buds and flowers in pink and green sequins. When I'd slipped the bodice and trousers on I draped the veil around me, letting it hang down behind like an apron and tying it in front in a bow knot with the ends tucked inside the tight waistband of the trousers. It was astonishing how modest such a scanty costume could be. There was less of me exposed than if I'd been wearing a halter and shorts, and not much more than if I'd worn one of the bare-midriff evening dresses just then becoming fashionable. For my feet there was a pair of bell toe rings, little clusters of silver bells set close together like grapes in a bunch that tinkled with a whirring chime almost like a whistle each time I took a step after I'd slipped them on my little toes, and a pair of heavy silver anklets with a fringe of silver tassels that flowed down from the ankle to the floor and almost hid my feet and jingled every time I moved. On my right wrist I hung a gold slave bracelet with silver chains, each ending in a ball of somber-gleaming garnet, and over my left hand I slipped a heavy sand-moulded bracelet of silver that must have weighed a full half pound. I combed my hair straight back from my forehead, drawing it so tightly that there was not a trace of wave left in it, and then I braided it into a queue, lacing strands of imitation emeralds and garlands of white jasmine in the plait. When this was done I darkened my eyebrows with a cosmetic pencil, raising them and accenting their arch to the 'flying gull' curve so much admired in the East, and rubbed green eye-shadow upon my lids. Over my head I draped a long blue veil sewn thickly with silver sequins and crowned it with a chaplet of yellow rosebuds. Last of all there was a heavy gold circlet like a clip-earring to go into my left nostril, and a single opal screw-earring to fasten in the right, giving the impression that my nose had been pierced for the jewels, and a tiny, star-shaped patch of red court plaster to fix between my brows like a caste mark.

"There is a saying clothes don't make the man, but it's just the opposite with a woman. When I'd put those Oriental garments on I *felt* myself an Eastern woman who had never known and never wished for any other life except that behind the purdah, and all I wished to do was cast myself prostrate before Kabanta, tell him he was my lord, my master and my god, and press my lips against the gold-embroidered tips of his red slippers till he gave me leave to rise. I was shaking as if with chill when I stepped from the little anteroom accompanied by the silvery chiming of my anklets and toe rings.

"Kabanta had set a fire glowing in a silver bowl before the Green God, and when I joined him he put seven sticks of sandalwood into my hands, telling me to walk around the brazier seven times, dropping a stick of the scented wood on the fire each time I made a circuit and repeating Hindu invocations after him. When this was done he poured a little scented water from a silver pitcher into my cupped hands, and this I sprinkled on the flames, then knelt across the fire from him with outstretched hands palm-upward over the blaze while I swore to love him, and him only, throughout this life and the seven cycles to come. I remember part of the oath I took: 'To be one in body and soul with him as gold and the bracelet or water and the wave are one.'

"When I had sworn this oath he slipped a heavy gold ring—this!—on my finger, and told me I was pledged to him for all time and eternity, that Siva the Destroyer was witness to my pledge and would avenge my falseness if I broke my vow. It was then for the first time I heard of the pisacha, bhirta and preta, shahini and rakshasha. It all seemed horrible and fantastic as he told it, but I believed it implicitly—then." A little rueful smile touched her pale lips. "I'm afraid that I believe it now, too, sir; but for a little while I didn't, and so—so my poor lover is dead."

"*Pauvre enfant*," de Grandin murmured. "*Ma pauvre belle créature.* And then?"

"Then came the war. You know how little pretense of neutrality there was. Americans were crossing into Canada by droves to join up, and everywhere the question was not 'Will we get into it?' but 'When?' I could fairly see my lover in the gorgeous uniform of a risaldar lieutenant or captain in the Indian Army, leading his troop of wild Patans into battle, but Kabanta made no move. When our own boys were drafted he was deferred as a medical student. At last I couldn't stand it any longer. One evening at the shore I found courage to speak. 'Master and Lord,' I asked him—we used such language to each other in private—'is it not time that you were belting on your sword to fight for freedom?'

"'Freedom, White Blossom of the Moghra Tree?' he answered with a laugh. 'Who is free? Art thou?'

"'Thou art my lord and I thy slave,' I answered as he had taught me.

"'And are the people of my father's country free? You know that they are not. For generations they have groaned beneath the Western tyrant's lash. Now these European dogs are at each other's throats. Should I take sides in their curs' fight? What difference does it make to me which of them destroys the others?'

"'But you're American,' I protested. 'The Japanese have attacked us. The Germans and Italians have declared war on us—'

"'Be silent!' he commanded, and his voice was no longer the soft voice that I loved. 'Women were made to serve, not to advise their masters of their duty.'

"'But, Kabanta—'

"'I told you to be still!' he nearly shouted. 'Does the slave dare disobey her master's command? Down, creature, down upon your knees and beg my pardon for your insolence—'

"'You can't be serious!' I gasped as he grasped me by the hair and began forcing my head down. We'd been playing at this game of slave and master—dancing girl and maharajah—and I'd found it amusing, even thrilling after a fashion. But it had only been pretense—like a 'dress-up party' or the ritual of a sorority where you addressed someone you'd known since childhood as Queen or Empress, or by some other high-sounding title, knowing all the while that she was just your next door neighbor or a girl with whom you'd gone to grammar school. Now, suddenly, it dawned on me that it had not been play with him. As thoroughly Americanized as he appeared, he was still an Oriental underneath, with all the Oriental's cynicism about women and all an Eastern man's exalted opinion of his own importance. Besides, he was hurting me terribly as he wound his fingers in my hair. 'Let me go!' I demanded angrily. 'How dare you?'

"'How dare I? Gracious Mahadeva, hear the brazen Western hussy speak!' he almost choked. He drew my face close to his and asked in a fierce whisper, 'Do you know what you vowed that night at The Light of Asia?'

"'I vowed I'd always love you, but—'

"'You'd always love me!' he mocked. 'You vowed far more than that, my Scented Bower of Delight. You vowed that from that minute you would be my thing and chattel—vowed yourself to Siva as a voluntary offering, and accepted me—as the God's representative. As Gods are to humanity, so am I to you, O creature lower than the dust. You're mine to do with as I please, and right now it pleases me to chastise you for your insolence.' Deliberately, while he held my head back with one band in my hair, he drew one of his moccasins off and struck me across the mouth with its heel. I could feel a thin trickle of blood between my lips and the scream I was about to utter died in my throat.

"'Down!' he commanded. 'Down on your face and beg for mercy. If you are truly penitent perhaps I shall forgive your insolence.'

"I might have yielded finally, for flesh and blood can stand only so much, and suddenly I was terribly afraid of him, but when I was almost beyond resistance we heard voices in the distance, and saw a light coming toward us on the beach. 'Don't think that I've forgiven you,' he told me as he pushed me from him. 'Before I take you back you'll have to walk barefoot across hot coals and abase yourself lower than the dust—'

"Despite the pain of my bruised lips I laughed. 'If you think I'll ever see you again, or let you come within speaking distance—' I began, but his laugh was louder than mine.

"'If you think you can get away, or ever be free from your servitude to me, you'll find that you're mistaken,' he jeered. 'You are Siva's, and mine, for all eternity. My shadow is upon you and my ring is on your finger. Try to escape the one or take the other off.'

"I wrenched at the ring he'd put on my hand. It wouldn't budge. Again and again I tried to get it off. No use. It seemed to have grown fast to the flesh; the more I tried to force it off the tighter it seemed to cling, and all the time Kabanta stood there smiling at me with a look of devilish, goading derision on his dark handsome features. At last I gave up trying and almost fainting with humiliation and the pain from my bruised mouth I turned and ran away. I found my car in the parking lot and drove home at breakneck speed. I suppose Kabanta managed to get a taxi. I don't know. I never saw him again."

"*Très bon,*" de Grandin nodded approval as she completed her story. "That is good. That is very good, indeed, *ma oisillone.*"

"Is it?" the irony of her reply was razor-thin.

"Is it not?"

"It is not."

"*Pourquoi? Nom d'un chameau enfumé!* For why?"

"Because he kept his word, sir. His shadow *is* upon me and his ring immovably upon my finger. Last year I met Wade Hardison, and it was love at first sight. Not fascination nor physical attraction, but love, real love; the good, clean, wholesome love a man and woman ought to have for each other if they expect to spend their lives together. Our engagement was announced at Christmas, and—"

"*Et puis?*" he prompted as her voice broke on a soundless sob.

"Then I heard from Kabanta. It was a post card—just a common penny post card, unsigned and undated, and it carried just eleven words of message: 'When you remove the ring you are absolved from your oath.' He hadn't signed it, as I said, but I knew instantly it was from him.

"I tried desperately to get the ring off, wound my fingers with silk, used soap and olive oil, held my hand in ice cold water—no use. It wouldn't budge. I couldn't even turn it on my finger. It is as if the metal had grown to my flesh and become part of me. I didn't dare tell anyone about it, they wouldn't have believed me, and somehow I didn't have the courage to go to a jeweler's and have it filed off, so ..."

The silence that ensued lasted so long one might have thought the girl had fainted, but the short, irregular, spasmodic swelling of her throat told us she was fighting hard to master her emotion. At last:

"Two days ago," she whispered so low we had to bend to catch her words, "I had another note. 'He shall never call you his,' was all it said. There was no signature, but I knew only too well who the sender was.

"Then I told Wade about it, but he just laughed. Oh, if only I had had the courage to postpone our wedding Wade might be alive now. There's no use fighting against Fate," her voice rose to a thin thread of hysteria. "I might as well confess myself defeated, go back to Kabanta and take whatever punishment he cares to inflict. I'm hopelessly enmeshed, entrapped—ensnared! I am Siva's toy and plaything, and Kabanta is the Green God's representative!" She roused to a sitting posture, then fell back, burying her face in the pillow and shaking with heart-breaking sobs.

"Kabanta is a species of a cockroach, and Siva but an ape-faced piece of green stone," de Grandin answered in a hard, sharp voice. "I, Jules de Grandin tell you so, *Mademoiselle*; anon I shall say the same thing to them, but much more forcefully. Yes, certainly, of course."

"THAT DAME'S AS NUTTY as a fruit cake," Costello confided as we left the Thurmond house. "She goes an' gits herself involved with one o' these here fancy Hindu fellies, an' he goes an' tells her a pack o' nonsense, an' she falls fer it like a ton o' brick. As if they wuz anny such things as Shivas an' shahinnies an' raytors an' th' rest o' it! Begob, I'd sooner belave in—"

"You and I do not believe, my friend," de Grandin interrupted seriously, "but there are millions who do, and the power of their believing makes a great force—"

"Oh, come!" I scoffed. "You never mean to tell us that mere cumulative power of belief can create hobgoblins and bugaboos?"

"*Vraiment*," he nodded soberly. "It is indeed unfortunately so, my friend. Thoughts are things, and sometimes most unpleasant things. Yes, certainly."

"Nonsense!" I rejoined sharply. "I'm willing to agree that Melanie could have been imposed on. The world is full of otherwise quite sane people who are willing to believe the moon is made of green cheese if they're told so impressively enough. I'll even go so far as to concede she thinks she can't get the ring off. We've all seen the cases of strange inhibitions, people who were convinced they couldn't go past a certain spot—can't go off the block in which they live, for instance. She's probably unconsciously crooked her finger when she tried to pull it off. The very fact she found excuses to put off going to a jeweler's to have it filed off shows she's laboring under a delusion. Besides, we all know those Hindu are adepts at hypnotism—"

"*Ah, bah!*" he broke in. "You are even more mistaken than usual, Friend Trowbridge. "Have you by any chance read *Darkness Out of the East* by our good friend John Thunstone?"

"No," I confessed, "but—"

"But be damned and stewed in boiling oil for Satan's supper. In his book Friend Thunstone points out that the rite of walking barefoot seven times around a living fire and throwing fuel and water on it while sacred *mantras* are recited is the most solemn manner of pronouncing an irrevocable oath. It is thus the neophyte is oath-bound to the service of the temple where she is to wait upon the gods, it is so when the wife binds herself forever to the service and subjection of her lord and husband. When that poor one performed that ceremony she undertook an oath-bound obligation which every Hindu firmly believes the gods themselves cannot break. She is pledged by fire and water for all time and eternity to the man who put the ring of Siva on her finger. While I talked to her I observed the amulet. It bears the device of a woman held in unbreakable embrace by Four-Faced Siva, and under it is written in Hindustani, 'As the gods are to mankind so is the one to whom I vow myself to me. I have said it.'

"As for her having the ring filed off—she was wiser than she knew when she refrained from that."

"How d'ye mean?" Costello and I chorused.

"I saw an instance of it once in Goa, Portuguese India. A wealthy Portuguese planter's *femme de la main gauche* had an *affaire* with a Hindu while her protector was away on business. She was inveigled into taking such a vow as Mademoiselle Thurmond took, and into having such a ring slipped on her finger. When she would have broken with her Hindu lover and returned to her *purveyor* she too found the ring immovable, and hastened to a jeweler's to have it filed off. *Tiens,* the life went out of her as the gold band was sawn asunder."

"You mean she dropped dead of a stroke?" I asked.

"I mean she died, my friend. I was present at the autopsy, and every symptom pointed to snake bite—except the stubborn fact that there had been no snake. We had the testimony of the jeweler and his two assistants; we had the testimony of a woman friend who went with her to the shop. All were agreed there had been no snake near her. She was not bitten; she merely fell down dead as the gold band came off."

"O.K., sor; if ye say it, I'll belave it, even if I know 't'aint so," Costello agreed. "What's next?"

"I think we should go to the morgue. The autopsy should be complete by this time, and I am interested in the outcome."

D R. JASON PARNELL, THE coroner's physician, fanned himself with a sheaf of death certificates, and mopped his streaming brow with a silk handkerchief. "I'm damned if I can make it out," he confessed irritably. "I've checked and rechecked everything, and the answer's the same each time. Only it doesn't make sense."

"*Qu'est-ce donc?*" de Grandin demanded. "How do you say?"

"That youngster has no more business being dead than you or I. There wasn't a God's earthly thing the matter with him from a pathological standpoint. He was perfect. Healthiest specimen I ever worked on. If he'd been shot, stabbed or run down by a motor car I could have understood it; but here he is, as physiologically perfect as an athlete, with positively no signs of trauma of any sort—except that he's as dead as a herring."

"You mean you couldn't find a symptom—" I began, and he caught me up before I had a chance to finish.

"Just that, Trowbridge. You said it. Not a single, solitary one. There is no sign of syncope, asphyxia or coma, no trace of any functional or organic weakness. Dammit man, the fellow didn't die, he just stopped living—and for no apparent reason. What'n hell am I goin' to tell the jury at the inquest?"

"*Tiens, mon ami*, that is your problem, I damn think," de Grandin answered. "We have one of our own to struggle with. There is that to do which needs immediate doing, and how we are to do it only *le bon Dieu* knows. Name of a little blue man, but it is the enigma, I tell you."

Sergeant Costello looked unhappily from Parnell to de Grandin. "Sure, sors, 'tis th' screwiest business I've ever seen entirely," he declared. "First th' pore young felley topples over dead as mutton, then his pore forsaken bride tells us a story as would make th' hair creep on yer neck, an' now you tell us that th' pore lad died o' nothin' a-tall. Mother o' Moses, 'tis Jerry Costello as don't know if he's comin' or goin' or where from an' where to. Can I use yer 'phone, Doc?" he asked Parnell. "Belike th' bhoys at Headquarters would like to know what I'm about."

We waited while he dialed Headquarters, heard him bark a question, and saw a look of utter unbelief spread on his broad perspiring face as some one at the other end answered. "'T'ain't so!" he denied. "It couldn't be.

"We wuz just up to see her, an' she's as limp as a wet wash—"

"What is it, *mon sergent?*" de Grandin asked. "Is it that—"

"Ye can bet yer bottom dollar it is, sor," the Sergeant cut in almost savagely. "It sure is, or I'm a monkey's uncle. Miss Thurmond, her we just seen layin' in th' bed so weak she couldn't hold up her head, has taken it on th' lam."

"*Diable!*" de Grandin shot back. "It cannot be."

"That's what I told 'em at Headquarters, sor, but they insist they know what they're a-talkin' about; an' so does her old man. 'Twas him as put the call in to be on th' lookout fer her. It seems she lay in a half stupor when we left her, an' they'd left her alone, thinkin' she might git a bit o' rest, when zingo! up she bounces, runs to th' garage where her car wuz parked, an' rushes down th' street like th' divil wuz on her trail."

"*Ha!*" de Grandin's hard, dry, barking laugh had nothing whatever to do with amusement. "*Ah-ha-ha!* I am the greatest stupid-head outside of a *maison de fous, mes amis.* I might have damn anticipated it! You say she ran as if the devil were behind her? *Mais non,* it is not so. He was before her. He called her and she answered his summons!"

"Whatever—" I began, but Costello caught the little Frenchman's meaning.

"Then what th' divil are we waitin' fer, sor?" he demanded. "We know where he hangs out. Let's go an' peel th' livin' hide off 'im—"

"*Ma moi, cher sergent,* you take the words out of my mouth," the small Frenchman shot back. "Come, Friend Trowbridge, let us be upon our way."

"Where to?" I asked.

"Where to? Where in the foul name of Satan but to that so vile shop called The Light of Asia, where unless I am more greatly mistaken than I think the dove goes to a rendezvous with the serpent. Quickly. Let us hasten, let us rush; let us fly, *mes amis!*"

The rain that had been threatening since early afternoon came down in bucketsful as we crept slowly through East Fifty-Sixth Street. It poured in miniature Niagaras from cornices and rolled-up awnings, the gutters were awash, the sidewalks almost ankle-deep with water.

"*Halte la!*" ordered de Grandin, and I edged the car close to the curb. "My friends, we are arrived. Be quiet, if you please, make no move unless I request it, and—" he broke off with a muttered "*nom d'un coq!*" as a wind-whipped awning sluiced a sudden flood of icy water over him, shook himself like a spaniel emerging from a pond, and laid his hand upon the brass knob of the highly varnished door.

Amazingly the door swung open at his touch and we stepped into the dim interior of The Light of Asia.

The place was like a church whose worshipers had gone. The air was redolent of incense, the darkness was relieved by only a dim, ruddy light, and all was silent—no, not quite! At the far end of the long room a voice was singing softly, a woman's voice raised in a trembling, tear-heavy contralto:

Since I, O Lord, am nothing unto thee,
See here thy sword, I make it keen and bright . . .

"*Alons, mes enfants,* follow!" whispered Jules de Grandin as he tiptoed toward the rear of the shop.

Now the tableau came in view, clear-cut as a scene upon a stage. In an elevated niche like an altar place crouched a green stone image slightly larger than man's-size, the sightless eyes of its four faces staring out in cold, malevolent obliviousness. Below it, cross-legged on a scarlet cushion, his hands folded palm-upward in his lap, was a remarkably handsome young man dressed in an ornate Oriental costume, but these we passed by at a glance, for in the foreground, kneeling with her forehead pressed against the floor, was Melanie Thurmond dressed as she had been when she took her fateful vow and had the ring of Siva put upon her hand. Her hands were raised above her bowed head, and in them rested a long, curved scimitar, the ruddy lamplight gleaming on its jeweled hilt and bright blade with ominous redness.

"Forgive, forgive!" we heard her sob, and saw her beat her forehead on the floor in utter self-abasement. "Have pity on the worm that creeps upon the dust before thy feet—"

"Forgiveness shall be thine," the man responded slowly, "when dead kine crop the grass, when the naked rend their clothes and when a shining radiance becomes a void of blackness."

"Have mercy on the insect crawling at thy feet," the prostrate woman sobbed. "Have pity on the lowly thing—"

"Have done!" he ordered sharply. "Give me the sword."

She roused until she crouched upon her knees before him, raised the scimitar and pressed its blade against her lips and brow in turn, then, head bent low, held it out to him. He took it, balancing it between his hands for a moment, then drew a silk handkerchief from his sleeve and slowly began polishing the blade with it. The woman bent forward again to lay her brow against the floor between her outstretched hands, then straightened till she sat upon her crossed feet and bent her head back till her slender flower-like throat was exposed. "I wait the stroke of mercy, Master and Lord," she whispered as she closed her eyes. "'Twere better far to die at thy hands than to live cut off from the sunshine of thy favor. . . ."

There was something wrong with the Green God. I could not tell quite what it was; it might have been a trick of light and shadow, or the whorls of incense spiraling around it, but I could have sworn its arms were moving and its fixed, immobile features changing expression.

There was something wrong with me, too. A feeling of complete inadequacy seemed to spread through me. My self-esteem seemed oozing out of every pore, my legs felt weak, I had an almost irresistible desire to drop upon my knees before the great green idol.

"Oom, mani padme hong!" de Grandin cried, his voice a little high and thin with excitement. "Oom, mani padme hong!"

Why I did it I had no idea, but suddenly I echoed his invocation, at the top of my voice, "Oom, mani padme hong!"

Costello's rumbling bass took up the chant, and crying the unfamiliar sylla-bles in chorus we advanced toward the seated man and kneeling woman and the great, green gloating idol. "*Oom, mani padme hong!*"

The man half turned and raised his hands in supplication to the image, but even as he did so something seemed to happen in the niche. The great green statue trembled on its base, swayed backward, forward—rocked as if it had been shaken by a sudden blast of wind, then without warning toppled from its embra-sure, crushing the man seated at its feet as a dropped tile might crush a beetle.

For a long moment we stood staring at the havoc, the fallen idol lying athwart the crushed, broken body of the man, the blood that spread in a wide, ever-broadening pool about them, and the girl who wept through lowered lids and beat her little fists against her breast, unmindful of the tragedy.

"Quickly, my friends," bade de Grandin. "Go to the dressing room and find her clothes, then join me here.

"*Oom, mani padme hong!* The gods are dead, there is no power or potency in them, my little flower," he told the girl. "*Oom, mani padme hong!*" he bent and took her right hand in his, seizing the great ring that glowed upon her forefinger and drawing it away. "*Oom, mani padme hong!* The olden gods are powerless—they have gone back to that far hell from whence they hailed—" The ring came off as if it had been several sizes too large and he lifted her in his arms gently.

"Make haste, my friends," he urged. "None saw us enter; none shall see us leave. Tomorrow's papers will record a mystery, but there will be no mention of this poor one's name in it. Oh, be quick, I do beseech you!"

"NOW," I DEMANDED AS I refilled the glasses, "are you going to explain, or must the Sergeant and I choke it out of you?"

The little laughter wrinkles at the outer corners of his eyes deepened momen-tarily. "*Non, mes amis,*" he replied, "violence will not be required, I assure you. First of all, I assume you would be interested to know how it was we overcame that green monstrosity and his attendant by your chant?"

"Nothin' less, sor," Costello answered. "Bedad, I hadn't anny idea what it meant, or why we sang it, but I'm here to say it sounded good to me—I got a kick out o' repeating it wid ye, but why it wuz, I dunno."

"You know the history of Gautama Buddha, one assumes?"

"I niver heard o' him before, sor."

"*Quel dommage!* However"—he paused to take a long sip from his glass, then—"here are the facts: Siddhartha Gautama Buddha was born in India some five hundred years before the opening of our era. He grew up in a land priest-rid-den and god-ridden. There was no hope—no pride of ancestry nor anticipation of immortality—for the great mass of the people, who were forever fixed in mis-erable existence by the rule of caste and the divine commands of gods whom we

should call devils. Buddha saw the wickedness of this, and after years of medita-
tion preached a new and hopeful gospel. He first denied the power of the gods
by whose authority the priests held sway, and later denied their very existence.
His followers increased by thousands and by tens of thousands; they washed the
cursed caste marks from their foreheads, proclaimed themselves emancipated,
denied the priests' authority and the existence of the gods by whom they had
been terrorized and downtrodden for generations. Guatama Buddha, their leader,
they hailed and honored with this chant: 'Oom, mani padme hong!—Hail, thou
Gem of the Lotus!' From the Gulf of Bengal to the Himalayas the thunder of
their greeting to their master rolled like a mighty river of emancipation, and the
power of it emptied the rock temples of the olden deities, left the priests without
offerings on which to fatten. Sometimes it even overthrew the very evil gods
themselves. I mean that literally. There are recorded instances where bands of
Buddhists entering into heathen temples have by the very repetition of 'Oom,
Mani padme hong!' caused rock-hewn effigies of those evil forces men called
Vishnu and Siva to topple from their altars. Yes, it is so.

"En conséquence tonight when I saw the poor misguided mademoiselle about
to make a sacrifice of herself to that four-faced caricature of Satan I called to
mind the greeting to the Lord Gautama which in olden days had rocked him and
his kind from their high thrones, and raised the ancient battle cry of freedom
once more. Tiens, he knew his master, that one. The Lord Gautama Buddha had
driven him back to whatever hell-pool he and his kind came from in the olden
days; his strength and power to drive him back was still potent. Did not you see
it with your own four eyes, my friends?"

"U'm," I admitted somewhat grudgingly. "You think it was the power of the
Green God that called Melanie back to The Light of Asia tonight?"

"Partly, beyond question. She wore his ring, and material things have great
power on things spiritual, just as spiritual things have much influence on the
material. Also it might well have been a case of utter frustration. She might
have said in effect, 'What is the use?' Her lover had been killed, her hopes of
happiness blasted, her whole world knocked to pieces. She might well have rea-
soned: 'I am powerless to fight against my fate. The strength of the Green God is
too great. I am doomed; why not admit it; why struggle hopelessly and helplessly?
Why not go to Kabanta and admit my utter defeat, the extinction of my personality, and take whatever punishment awaits me, even though it be death? Sooner
or later I must yield. Why not sooner than later? To struggle futilely is only to
prolong the agony and make his final triumph all the greater.' These things she
may have said to herself. Indeed, did she not intimate as much to us when we
interviewed her?

"Yes," he nodded like a china mandarin on a mantelpiece, "it is unquestionably so, my friends, and but for Jules de Grandin—and the Lord Gautama

Buddha assisted by my good friends Trowbridge and Costello—it might have been that way. *Eh bien,* I and the Buddha, with your kind assistance, put an end to their fine schemes, did we not?"

"You seriously think it was the force of the Green God that killed Wade Hardison?" I asked.

"I seriously do, my friend. That and naught else. The Green One was a burning glass that focused rays of hatred as a lens does sunlight, and through his power the never-to-be-sufficiently-anathematized Kabanta was enabled to destroy the poor young Hardison completely."

He stabbed a small, impressive forefinger at me. "Consider, if you please: What was the situation tonight? Siva had triumphed. He had received a blood-sacrifice in the person of the poor young Hardison; he was about to have another in the so unfortunate Mademoiselle Melanie, then *pouf* comes Jules de Grandin and Friend Trowbridge and Friend Costello to repeat the chant which in the olden days had driven him from power. Before the potency of our chant to the Buddha the Green One felt his power ebbing slowly from him as he retreated to that far place where he had been driven aforetime by the Lord Gautama. And what did he do as he fell back? *Tenez,* he took revenge for his defeat on Kabanta. He cast the statue of himself—a very flattering likeness, no doubt—down from its altar place and utterly crushed the man who had almost but not quite enabled him to triumph. He was like a naughty child that kicks or bites the person who has promised it a sweet, then failed to make good the promise—"

"But that idol was a senseless piece of carved stone," I protested. "How could it—"

"*Ah bah,* you irritate me, my friend. Of course the idol was a senseless piece of stone, but *that for which it stood was neither stone nor senseless.* The idol was but the representation of the evil power lurking in the outer darkness as the tiger lurks in ambush. Let us put it this way: The idol is the material and visible door through which the spiritual and invisible force of evil we call Siva is enabled to penetrate into our human world.

"Through that doorway he came into the world, through it he was forced to retreat before the power of our denial of his potency. So to speak, he slammed the door as he retreated—and caught Kabanta between door and jamb. *En tout cas,* he is dead, that miserable Kabanta. We are well rid of him, and the door is fast closed on the evil entity which he and the unwitting and unfortunate Mademoiselle Melanie let back into the world for a short time.

"Yes," be nodded solemnly again. "It is so. I say it. I also say that I should like my glass refilled, if you will be so gracious, Friend Trowbridge."

Lords of the Ghostlands

J ULES DE GRANDIN PASSED the brandy snifter back and forth beneath his nose, savoring the bouquet of the fine champagne with the keen appreciation of a connoisseur. He took a light, preliminary sip, and his expression of delight became positively ecstatic. "*Parbleu*," he murmured, "as my good friend François Rabelais was wont to say, 'Good wine is the living soul of the grape, but good brandy is the living spirit of the wine,' and—"

"The devil!" Dr. Taylor broke in as a nervous movement of his elbow dislodged the bubble-thin inhaler from the tabourette beside his elbow and sent it crashing to the floor.

"*Quel dommage*—what a pity!" consoled de Grandin. "To lose the lovely crystal is a misfortune, *Monsieur*, but the *vieux cognac*, he are priceless, to lose her are a calamity, no less!"

"You're not just saying that!" Dr. Taylor answered grimly. "That's the last bottle of Jérôme Napoleon in my cellar, and heaven only knows when I'll get a replacement. These things always seem to run in threes. This morning at breakfast I upset my coffee cup, this afternoon I nearly dropped a bit of absolutely priceless papyrus in the fire, now"—he broke off with a grimace of self-disgust —"I hope I've completed the cycle."

"One understands, *Monsieur*," de Grandin nodded commiseratingly. "It is the times—the strain of war, the—"

"We can't blame this on the war," Taylor denied. "I hate to confess it, but I've been jumpy as a bit of popcorn in a popper for the past few days. My goat's gone."

"*Comment?*" de Grandin's brows went up the barest fraction of an inch. "He was a valuable animal, this goat of yours, *Monsieur?*"

Despite himself our host gave vent to a short laugh. "Very, Dr. de Grandin. Unless I get him back again I shall—oh, I'll not pull your leg. To lose one's goat is an American idiom meaning to become utterly demoralized. It's that dam' mummy that is driving me almost to distraction."

This time de Grandin was not to be caught napping. "Translate, if you will be so kind, Friend Trowbridge," he begged. "Is it another of his idioms—is the mummy to which he refers a genuine *cadavre*, or perhaps a papa's wife, or a mother—"

"No!" Dr. Taylor held explosive laughter in by main force. "This is no idiom, Dr. de Grandin. I wish it were. The fact is that though I'm not superstitious I've had a bad case of the jitters since last week when they brought out a new mummy at the Museum. It had been greatly delayed in transit due to the war, and when it came it took us all by surprise. Several of our younger men have joined the services, so I took it in charge. I wish I hadn't now, for unless I'm much mistaken it's what's called 'unlucky,' and—well, as I've said, I'm not superstitious, but . . ."

"I should think that any mummy might be called unlucky," I put in rather fatuously. "To be jerked out of the quiet restfulness of your grave and shipped across four thousand miles of water, then exhibited for people whom you'd call barbarians to gawk at—"

My faint attempt at humor was completely lost on Dr. Taylor. "When an Egyptologist refers to a mummy as unlucky he has reference to its effect on the living, not to its peculiar luck or lack of it," he cut in almost sharply. "Call it nonsense if you will—and probably you will—but the fact is there seems some substance to the belief that the ancient gods of Egypt have the power to punish those disturbing the mummies of people dying in apostasy. Such mummies are referred to in the trade as 'unlucky'—unlucky for the people who find them or have anything to do with them. Tutankhamen is the classic example of this. He was a noted heretic in his day, you know, and had given great offense to the 'Old Ones' or their priests, which in the long run amounted to the same thing. So when he died, although they gave him an elaborate funeral, they set no image of Amen-Ra at the prow of the boat that ferried him across the Lake of the Dead, and the plaques of Seb, Tem, Nepthys, Osiris and Isis were not prepared to go with him into the tomb. Notwithstanding his belated efforts to be reconciled with the priesthood, Tutankhamen was little better than an atheist according to contemporary Egyptian theology, and the wrath of gods followed him beyond the grave. It was not their wish that his name be preserved to posterity or that any of his relics be brought to light.

"Now, just consider contemporary happenings: In 1922 Lord Carnavon located the tomb. He had four associates. Carnavon and three of these associates died within a year or so of the opening of the tomb. Colonel Herbert and Dr. Evelyn-White were among the first to enter the tomb. Both died within twelve months. Sir Archibald Douglass was engaged to make X-rays of the mummy. He died almost before the plates could be developed. Six of the seven French journalists who went into the tomb shortly after it was opened died in less than a year, and almost every workman engaged in the excavations died before he had a chance to spend his pay. Some of these people died one way, some another. The fact is: *They all died.*

"Not only that: Even minor articles taken from Tut's tomb seem to exercise malign influence. There is proof absolute that attendants at the Cairo Museum whose duties keep them in or even near the room where Tutankhamen's relics are displayed sicken or die—for no apparent reason. D'ye wonder that they call him an 'unlucky' mummy?"

"*Bien, Monsieur. Et puis?*" de Grandin prompted as our host lapsed into moody silence.

"Just this," responded Dr. Taylor. "This mummy I've had wished on me is dam' peculiar. It's Eighteenth Dynasty work, that much is plain, but unlike anything I ever saw before. There is no face mask nor funerary statue, either on the mummy or in the coffin, and the case itself is bare of writing. The old Egyptians always wrote the titles and biographies of the dead upon their coffins, you know, but this case is just bare, virgin wood; a beautiful shell of thin hard cedar to which not even varnish has been applied. Most mummy case lids are held in place by four little flanges, two to a side, which sink into mortises cut in the lower section and are held in place by hardwood dowels. This case has eight, three to each side and one at each end. They must have wanted to make sure that whoever was fastened in that coffin wouldn't break out. Furthermore—and this is more than merely unusual, it's absolutely unique—the bottom of the coffin is strewn four inches deep with spices."

"Spices?" echoed Jules de Grandin.

"Spices. Yes. We haven't analyzed all yet, but so far we've identified clove, spikenard, cinnamon, aloes, thyme and ginger, mustard, capsicum and common sodium chloride."

De Grandin pursed his lips in a soundless whistle. "This are unusual, *vraiment*," he conceded. "And have you unwrapped him or perhaps X-rayed her?"

"Well, yes and no."

"*Comment? Oui et non?* Is this perhaps some of the famous double talk of which one hears so much?"

"Not exactly," our host grinned. "I meant to say that I've unwrapped the first layer of bandages, the crust or shell that's plastered with bitumen, you know, and subjected the mummy wrapped in its inner bandages, to the fluoroscope—"

"Yes? And then, *Monsieur?*" de Grandin prompted as Dr. Taylor paused so long it seemed he had no more to say.

"That's just it, Dr. de Grandin. It isn't well at all. What I've found confirms my first suspicions that I've an 'unlucky' mummy on my hands.

"Woeltjin, Dr. Oris Woeltjin, found this mummy in a cleverly hidden tomb between Nagada and Dêr El-Bahri, on the very eastern border of the Lybian Desert, territory given up as thoroughly worked over years ago. While they were excavating two of his fallaheen were bitten by tomb spiders and died in terrible convulsions. That in itself was unusual, for while the Egyptian tomb spider's an ugly-looking brute, he's not particularly venomous; I've been bitten by 'em half a dozen times and not suffered half as much as when stung by a scorpion. This must have impressed the rest of his workmen, too, for they deserted in a body, but Woeltjin stuck it out, and with the help of such neighborhood men as he could hire for double wages he finally reached the funerary chamber.

"That was only the beginning. He had the devil's own time getting down the Nile with it. Half the crew of his dahabeeyah came down with some sort of mysterious fever, several of 'em died and all the rest went overside, so it was almost two weeks before he'd finished a trip which in ordinary circumstances would have taken five days at most. The Egyptian government doesn't let you take a mummy out these days, but Woeltjin was an old hand at the game. He wheedled where he could and bribed where he had to, and finally smuggled the thing out disguised as a crate of Smyrna sponges; got it as far as Liverpool, and died.

"The mummy knocked around the wharves and warehouses at Liverpool for almost two years, the war kept it there still longer, but finally it arrived, and—believe it or not!—our shipping department actually took it for a lot of sponges and let it lie around our storeroom almost two more years. The curator discovered it purely by accident last week. Well, with that background, what I found yesterday just about confirmed my suspicions that the thing's unlucky."

Jules de Grandin leaned forward in his chair. "*Nom d'un million moustiques pestiferes, Monsieur*, what was it you discovered?" he demanded. "Me, I am consumed with curiosity."

Taylor smiled a trifle grimly. "The fluoroscope revealed the bony structure of the chest had been broken. Either she had died from an injury in what corresponded to the modern traffic accident, or"—he paused and took a sip of brandy—"she suffered death by a ritual roughly corresponding to the *peine forte et dure* of the medieval English criminal courts—crushed to death beneath a great pile of rocks, you know."

"But it might have been an accident," I objected. "Those two-wheeled chariots of ancient days weren't very stable vehicles, and it would have been quite possible—"

"Possible, but not probable, in view of what the papyrus says," Dr. Taylor cut in. "I found the sheet of writing tucked between two layers of bandages—surreptitiously, I'd say—just after I'd completed my fluoroscopic inspection."

De Grandin tweaked the needle-points of his small wheat-blond mustache. "*Tiens, Monsieur*, why do you torment us thus, making a long story still longer? What did it say, this twenty-times-accursed papyrus of yours?"

"Plenty," Dr. Taylor answered. "I haven't finished translating it, but even its beginning has an air of eerie mystery. She describes herself as Nefra-Kemmah, servant of the Most High Mother, the Horned One, the Lady of the Moon—in fine, a priestess of the Goddess Isis. You get the implication?"

I shook my head; de Grandin leveled one of his unwinking cat-stares at our host, but made no answer.

"The priestess of Isis, unlike the servants of all other Mother-Goddesses of ancient days—Aphrodite and Tanith, for instance—were vowed to chastity and were as completely celibate as Vestal Virgins or Christian nuns. If one of them forgot her sacred obligations even to the small extent of looking at or speaking to a man outside the priesthood the consequences were decidedly unpleasant. If she, as the saying goes, 'loved not wisely but too well,' death by torture was the penalty. This might take several forms. Burial alive, wrapped and bandaged like a mummy, but with the face exposed to permit breathing, was one form of inflicting the punishment. Another was to crush her erring heart to pulp beneath a great pile of stones. . . ."

"*Parbleu*," de Grandin murmured. "This poor one, then, was one of those unfortunates—"

"All signs point to it. She was a priestess, vowed to chastity on pain of death; her ribs have been crushed in; her coffin bears no inscription, not even so much as a brush mark. It seems not only death, but oblivion had been her portion. Now, perhaps, you understand why I'm inclined to be jumpy. It's all right to say 'stuff and nonsense' when you hear unlucky mummies talked of, but any Egyptologist can cite instance after instance of 'accidents' occurring to those who come in contact with the mummies of those who died under interdict."

"What else did the papyrus say—or have you gotten any farther?" I asked.

"Humph. The farther I get into it the more I'm puzzled. You know something of Egyptian medical ideas?"

"A little," Jules de Grandin admitted, "but I would not presume to discuss them with you, *Monsieur*."

Taylor smiled appreciation of the compliment.

"They had some odd notions. They thought, for instance, that the arteries contained air, that the seat of the emotions was the heart, and that anger generated in the spleen."

"Perfectly," de Grandin nodded.

"But they were far in advance of their contemporaries, and even of the Greeks and Romans, for they had partly grasped the truth that reason resided in the brain. Remember that, for what comes next ties in with it.

"The Egyptians were probably the first great people of antiquity to formulate a definite idea of immortality. That was their reason for mummification of their dead. They believed that when three thousand years had passed the soul returned to claim its body, and without a fleshy tenement to welcome it, it would have to wander bodiless and homeless in Amenti, the realm of the damned. As the Priestess Nefra-Kemmah lived during the XVIIIth Dynasty—roughly somewhere between 1575 and 1359 B.C., she should now be about ready—"

"Ah?" murmured Jules de Grandin. "Ah-ha? You think—"

"I don't think anything. I'm only puzzled. Instead of praying to the gods to guide her wandering *ka* or vital principle back to her waiting body, Nefra-Kemmah asserts—states positively—she will rise again with the help of one who lives, and by the power of the brain. That is absolutely unique. Never before, to my knowledge, has such a thing been heard of. Even those who died apostate sought the pity of the gods and begged forgiveness for their sin of unbelief, beseeching divine assistance in attaining resurrection. This little priestess declares categorically she will rise again with the help of a living human being and by the power of the brain." He drew an envelope from his pocket and scribbled a notation on it.

"Repeatedly I found these ideographs," he told us as he held the paper out for our inspection.

"The first one signifies '*arise*,' or, by extension, '*I shall arise*,' and the second means almost, though not quite, the same thing. '*Awake*,' or '*I shall awake to life*.' And always, she repeats that she will do it by the power of the brain, which complicates the message still farther."

"How's that?" I asked.

"Why, if she's a mummy she can have no brain. One of the first steps of Egyptian embalming was to withdraw the brain by means of a metallic hook inserted through the nose."

"She surely must have known that," I began, but before our host could answer we heard laughter on the porch, a key clicked in the front door, and Vella Taylor swept into the drawing room with an unusually good-looking young soldier in her wake. "Hullo, Daddy-Man," she greeted as she planted a quick kiss on Taylor's bald spot. "Good evening, Dr. Trowbridge—Dr. de Grandin. This is Harrock Hall, my most 'special-particular boy friend. Sorry, I couldn't be here for dinner tonight, but Harrock's ordered away to camp early tomorrow, so I ran around to his house. It wouldn't have seemed fair to have taken him from his mother and father on his last night home, and I knew I wanted to be with him just as much as possible, so—what're you folks drinking? Cognac?" She made a face suggestive of vinegar mixed with castor oil. "Vile stuff! Come on, treasure," she linked her hand in the young soldier's. "Let's us see if we can promote some Benedictine and Spanish brandy. That's got a scratch and tastes good, too."

"You will inform us of developments?" de Grandin asked as we prepared to go. "This so remarkable young lady who had courage to defy the priests who had condemned her and declared that in spite of their sentence to oblivion she would rise again, she interests me."

I T MUST HAVE BEEN toward three o'clock when the persistent ringing of the telephone awakened me. The voice that came across the wire was agonized, almost hysterical, but doctors get used to that. "This is Granville Taylor, Trowbridge. Can you come right over? It's Vella—she's had some sort of seizure. . . ."

"What sort?" I interrupted. "Does she complain of pain?"

"I don't know if she's in pain or not. She's unconscious—perfectly rigid, and—"

"I'll be there just as fast as gasoline can bring me," I assured him as I hung up and fished for the clothes which years of practice had taught me to keep folded on a bedside chair.

"What makes, *mon vieux?*" de Grandin asked as he heard me stirring. "Is it that Monsieur Taylor has met with the accident he feared—"

"No, it's his daughter. She's had some sort of seizure, he says—she's rigid and unconscious."

"*Pardieu,* that pretty, happy creature? Let me go with you, my friend, if you please. Perhaps I can be of assistance."

Her father had not overstated her condition when he said that Vella was rigid. From head to foot she was as stiff as something frozen; taut, hard as a hypnotist's assistant in a trance. We could not chafe her hands for they were set so stiffly that the flesh was absolutely unyielding. It might have been a lovely waxen tailor's dummy over which we bent rather than the happy, vibrant, vital girl to whom we'd said goodnight a few hours before. Treatment was futile. She lay as hard and rigid as if petrified. As if she had been dead, her temperature was exactly that of the surrounding atmosphere, the uncanny hardness of the flesh persisted, and she was unresponsive to all stimuli, save that the pupils of her set and staring eyes showed slight contraction when we flashed a light in them. There was practically no pulse perceptible, and when we drove a hypodermic needle in her arm to administer a dose of strychnine, there was no reflex flinching of the skin, and the impression we had was more like thrusting a needle through some tough waxy substance than into living flesh. As far as we could see vital functions were suspended. Yet she was not paralyzed in the ordinary sense of the term. Of that much we were certain.

"Is—is it epilepsy?" Dr. Taylor asked fearfully. "Her mother had a brother who—"

"*Non,* calm yourself, my friend," soothed de Grandin. "It is not the epilepsy, of that I can assure you." To me he added in a whisper: "But what it is *le bon Dieu* only knows!"

The dawn was brightening in the east when she began to show signs of recovery. The dreadful stiffness, so like rigor-mortis, gave way gradually, and the set and horrified expression of her eyes was replaced by a look of recognition. The rigid, hard lines faded from her cheeks and jaw, and her slender bosom fluttered with a gasp of respiration as a little sigh escaped her. The words she spoke

I could not understand, for they were uttered in a mumbling undertone, strung together closely, like an invocation hurriedly pronounced, but it seemed to me they had a harsh and guttural sound, as though containing many consonants, utterly unlike any language I had ever heard before.

Now the whisper gave way to a chant, sung softly in an eerie rising cadence with a sharply accented note at the end of every measure. Over and over, the same meaningless jargon, a weird and wavering tune vaguely like a Gregorian chant. One single word I recognized, or thought I did, though whether it really were a word or whether my mind broke its syllables apart and fitted them to the sound of a more or less familiar name I could not be sure; but it seemed to me that constantly recurring in the rapid flow of mumbled invocation was a sibilant disyllable, much like the letter s said twice in quick succession.

"Is she trying to say 'Isis'?" I asked, raising my eyes from her fluttering lips.

De Grandin was regarding her intently with that fixed, unwinking stare which I had seen him hold for minutes when we were in the amphitheater of a hospital and a piece of unique surgery was in progress. He waved an irritated hand at me, but neither spoke nor shifted the intentness of his gaze.

The flow of senseless words grew slower, thinner, as though the force behind the twitching red lips were lessening, but the weird soft chant continued its four soft minor notes slurred endlessly. Now her enunciation seemed more perfect, and almost without effort we could recognize a phrase that kept recurring: O Nefra-Kemmah nehes—Nehes, O Nefra-Kemmah!"

"Good God!" exclaimed Dr. Taylor. "D'ye get it, gentlemen? She's chanting, 'Nefra-Kemmah, awake—Arise, O Nefra-Kemmah!' Nefra-Kemmah was the name of that priestess of Isis I told you of last night, remember? In her delirium she's identifying herself with the mummy!"

"She probably heard you talking of it—"

"I'm hanged if she did. You were the only two to whom I've mentioned it outside the Museum. I knew de Grandin has a taste for the occult, and you were to be relied on, Trowbridge, but as for mentioning that mummy to anybody else—no! D'ye think I'd want my daughter to think me a superstitious old fool, or would I court the pitying smiles of other outsiders? I tell you she never heard that cursed mummy's name, yet—"

"S-h-sh, she awakes," de Grandin warned.

Vella Taylor looked from Jules de Grandin to me, then past us to her father. "Daddy!" she exclaimed. "O, Daddy, dear, I've been so frightened!"

"Frightened, dear? Of what?" Taylor dropped to his knees, beside the bed and took her hands in his. "Who's been trying to scare my little girl?"

She smiled a little ruefully. "I—I don't quite know," she confessed, "but whoever set out to do it surely got away with it. "I think it must have been those horrible old men."

"Old men, *Mademoiselle?*" de Grandin echoed. "Who and where were they, one asks to know? Tell me and I shall have great pleasure in kicking their false teeth out—"

"Oh, they weren't really men at all, just dream-images, I suppose. But they seemed terribly real, and oh, how dreadfully afraid of them I was!"

"Tell us of it, if you please, *ma belle*. You have suffered a severe shock. Perhaps it was the result of nightmare, perhaps not; at any rate, if you can bring yourself to discuss the painful subject—"

"Of course, sir. Talking of it may help sweep my memory clear. Harrock left a little after you did, for he had to catch an early train this morning, and I came right upstairs and cried myself to sleep. Sometime this morning—I don't quite know when, but it must have been a little before three, for the moon had risen late and it was very bright when I awakened—I woke up with a dreadful sense of thirst. It must have been that crying made me feel so, I can't account for it otherwise; at any rate I was utterly dehydrated, and went to get a glass of water from the bathroom tap. When I came back to my room the first thing that I noticed was that a single shaft of moonlight was slanting through the window and striking full upon the mirror," she gestured toward the full-length glass that stood against the farther wall. "Something, I don't know what, seemed urging me to go and look into the glass. When I stopped before it, it seemed the moonlight had robbed it of its power of reflection. I couldn't see myself in it at all."

"Ah?" de Grandin nodded. "You cast no shadow?"

"None at all, sir. Instead, the mirror seemed to be glossed over with a layer of opaque silver—not quite opaque, either, but rather iridescent. I could see small points of light reflected in it, and somehow they seemed moving, whirling round and round each other like a swarm of luminous midges, and burning with an intense blue, cold flame. Gradually the glowing pinpoints of light changed from their spinning to a slow, weaving pattern. The luminous sheet they spread across the mirror seemed breaking up, forming a definite design of highlights and shadows. It was as if the mirror were a window and through it I looked out upon another world.

"The place I looked into was bright with moonlight, almost as bright as day. It was a long, wide, lofty colonnaded building. I thought at first from what I'd heard Daddy say that it must be a temple of some sort, and in a moment I was sure of it, for I could hear the tinkling of sistra shaken in unison, and the low, sweet chanting of the priestesses. They knelt in a long double row, those sweet, slim girls, all gowned in robes of white linen, with bands of silver set with lapis lazuli bound about their brows. Their heads were bowed and their hands raised and held at stiff right angles to their wrists as they sang softly. Presently a young man came into the temple and walked slowly toward the altar-place. Despite the fact his head was shaven smooth, I thought him utterly beautiful, with full red lips, a firm, strong chin and great, soft, thoughtful eyes. He kept his gaze fixed on the tiles as he walked toward the altar, but just before he put aside the silver veil that hung before the face of Isis he glanced back and his eyes fell with a sort of sad reproachfulness upon the kneeling girl nearest him. I saw a flush mount up her throat and cheeks and brow, and she bent her head still lower as she sang, but somehow, though she gave no sign, I knew a thought-message had passed between them. Then slowly he passed beyond the veil and was gone.

"Suddenly to the chanting of the priestesses was joined the heavier chant of men singing in a sort of harsh harmony. Instinctively I knew what was transpiring. The young man I had seen had gone into the sanctuary of Great Isis to become one of her priests. He was being initiated into her mysteries. She would flood him with her spirit, and he would be hers for eternity. He would put away the love of woman and the hope of children, and devote himself whole-heartedly to the service of the Great All-Mother. The priestess I had seen blush knew it, too, for I could see the tears fall from beneath her lowered lids, and her slender body shook with sobs which she could not control.

"Then slowly, as if steam were forming on the mirror, everything became cloudy and in a moment the scene in the temple was completely hidden, but gradually the vapor cleared away and I was looking out into bright daylight. The sun shone almost dazzlingly on a temple's painted pylon. In the forecourt the sacred birds were feeding, and jets of water glinted jewel-bright from a fountain. A woman walked across the courtyard toward the splashing fountain, the priestess I had seen before. She was robed in a white linen shift that left her bosom and her ankles bare. Sandals of papyrus shod her slender henna-reddened feet, and jewels were on her arms. A band of silver set with lapis lazuli crowned the hair which she wore cut in a shoulder-length bob. In one hand she held a lotus bud and with the other she balanced a painted water pot on her bare shoulder.

"Suddenly, from the deep shadow cast by the high temple gate, an old man tottered. He was very feeble, but his rage and hatred seemed to impart power to his limbs as wires moved a marionette. By his red robe and blue turban and his flowing milk-white beard, no less than by his features, I knew him to be a Hebrew. He planted himself in the girl's path and let forth a perfect spate of invective. Of their actual words I could hear nothing, but subjectively I seemed to know what passed between them. He was reviling her for proselyting his son from the worship of the Lord Jehovah, for the Jewish youth, it seemed, had seen her and gone mad with love of her, because her vows made it impossible for them to wed he had abjured his race and kin and God to take the vows of Isis, so that he might be near her in the temple and commune with her in common worship of the goddess.

"The little priestess heard the old man through, then turned away contemptuously with a curt, 'Jewish dog, thou snarlest fiercely, but wherewith hast thou teeth to bite?' and the old man raised his hands to heaven and called a curse on her, declaring she should find no peace in life or death until atonement had been made; until she turned against the heathen gods she worshipped and bore testimony to their downfall through another's lips.

"'How sayest thou, old dotard?' asked the girl. 'Our gods are powerful and everlasting. We rule the world by their favor. Is it likely that I should turn from them? And if I did, how could it be that I should speak through the lips of another? Shall I become as one of those magicians the Greeks call polyphonists, who make a stick or stone of brute beast seem to talk because they have the power of voice-throwing?'

"Once more the scene shifted, and I looked out upon a moonlit night. The stars seemed almost within reach overhead, and there blew such a soft perfume on the moon-drenched air that you could almost see it take shape like dancing butterflies. In the deep blue shadow of the temple pylon crouched the priest and priestess, clinging to each other with the desperation of denied love. I saw her rest her curling shoulder-length-cut hair upon his shoulder, saw her turn her face up to his with eyes closed and lips a little parted, saw him kiss her brow, her closed eyes, her yearning, eager mouth, her pulsing throat, the gentle swell of her bare bosom . . . then like a pack of hounds that rush in for the kill, I saw the Hebrews pounce upon him. Knives flashed in the moonlight, curses hard and sharp as knife-blades spewed from their lips. 'Apostate swine, turncoat, back-slider, renegade!' they called him, and with every bitter curse there was another biting stab. He fell and lay upon the sands, his life-blood spurting from a dozen mortal wounds, and as his murderers turned away I seemed to hear the patter of bare feet upon the tiles, and half a dozen shaven-headed priests of Isis came running. 'What passes here?' their leader, an old man, panted angrily. 'Thou Jewish dogs, if thou hast—'

"The leader of the assassins interrupted with a scornful laugh: 'Naught passes here, old bare-poll, all is passed. We took one of your priests and priest-esses red-handed in infidelity. The man we dealt with, for aforetime he had been one of us; the woman we leave to thy vengeance, 'tis said thou hast a way of treating such.'

"I saw the priests seize the poor, stricken, trembling girl and lead her unre-sistingly away.

"Then once again the mirror clouded, and when it cleared I was looking full into the little priestess' face. She seemed to stand directly behind the glass, as close as my own reflection should have been, and she held out her hands beseechingly to me, begging me to help her. But my power of understanding was gone. Though I saw her lips move in appeal I could make nothing of the words she strove so desperately to pronounce, although she seemed repeating some-thing with a deadly, terrible insistence.

"Then suddenly I felt a dreadful cold come in the air, not the chill of the wind from the opened window, but one of those subjective chills we sometimes have that make us say, 'Someone is walking over my grave.' Instinctively I felt the presence of another person in my bedroom. Someone—no, some*thing* had come in while I watched the changing pictures in the mirror.

"I turned to look across my shoulder—and there they were. I think that there were five of them, though possibly there were seven—old men in long white robes with dreadful masks upon their faces. One wore a bull's head, another a mask like a jackal, another had a false-face like a giant hawk's head, and still another wore a headdress like a lion's face—"

"If they were masked how did you know they were old men?" I asked.

"I *knew* it. Their eyes were bright with a fierce, supernatural light, the kind of gleam that only those who are both old and wicked have in their eyes, and the flesh of their forearms had shrunk away from the muscles, leaving them to stand out like thick cords. Their hands and feet were knotty and misshapen with the ugliness of age, and the bones and tendons showed like painted lines against the skin.

"They grouped behind me in a semi-circle staring at me menacingly, and though they made no sound I knew that they were threatening me with something dreadful if I acceded to the little priestess' entreaty.

"'Vella Taylor, you are dreaming,' I told myself, and closed my eyes and shook my head. When I opened them again the horrible old masked men still stood there, but it seemed to me they had come a step nearer.

"The priestess in the mirror seemed to see them, too, for suddenly she threw her hands up as if to ward off a blow, made a frenzied gesture to me as if to warn me to escape, and turned away. Then she disappeared in vapor, and I was left alone with those terrific, silent shapes.

"'I won't be bluffed by anything so utterly absurd,' I declared, and started toward the door. The masked men drew together, barring my way. I turned toward the bed and they shrank back toward the corners of the room. Then I lay down and closed my eyes. 'I'll count up to a thousand,' I said. 'When I'm done counting I'll open my eyes, and they'll be gone.'

"But they weren't. In every corner of the room they hunched and crouched and panted, waiting the moment to pounce.

"I felt stark panic hammering at me; terror yarnmered at my will, abysmal fear ripped at my nerves, and when I tried to call to Daddy I could make no sound. A dreadful weight seemed pressing on me, so heavy I could not endure it; I felt it crushing out my breath, cracking my ribs, breaking every bone in my body. My eyes seemed starting from my face, I could feel my tongue protruding from my mouth, and . . ."

"Yes, *Mademoiselle*, and then?" de Grandin prompted as she ceased talking with a shudder.

"Then I saw you and Dr. Trowbridge and my own dear Daddy standing by me, and the terrible old men had gone away. You won't let them come back, will you?"

"Be assured, *Mademoiselle*, if they come back while I am here they shall indubitably wish they had not. Now it is time for you to get some rest and gather back your strength.

"Will you prepare the hypo, good Friend Trowbridge?" he asked me.

"D'YE REALIZE WHAT VELLA saw was the Infernal Assizes of Old Egypt?" Dr. Taylor whispered as we tiptoed from the bed chamber.

"The Infernal Assizes?" I repeated.

"Precisely. When a man died the Egyptians believed his soul was led by Thoth and Anubis to Amenti, where it stood trial before the judges of the Dead. These included hawk-headed Kebhsnauf, ape-headed Taumatet, dog-visaged Hapi, cat-headed Bes, and, of course, ox-headed Osiris. Similarly, when a living person was accused of heresey, a court of priests made up to represent the infernal deities tried him or her. The Priestess Nefra-Kemmah must have stood trial before just such a tribunal."

"Ah?" de Grandin murmured. "*Ah-ha? Ah-ha-ha?*"

"What is it?"

"I am persuaded, Friend Taylor, that what your daughter saw was more than 'such stuff as dreams are made on'—or, to be more explicit, just such stuff as that of which a dream is compounded, namely, thought-force. Just what it is I do not know, but somewhere there is an influence running from the mummy of the Priestess Nefra-Kemmah to *Mademoiselle* your daughter. The poor, misfortunate priestess seeks her aid, the ghostly old ones would prevent it. The daylight quickens in the east, my friend. Soon it will be full day. We shall arrange to have a nurse attend Mademoiselle Vella, and if you will be so kind we shall repair to the Museum and inspect this precious mummy of yours."

"H'm, that's a bit irregular," Taylor demurred.

"Irregular, *ha*? And by damn-it, was it not irregular for *Mademoiselle* your daughter to be vouchsafed a glimpse of the old times, to watch the unfolding of the romance of those so sadly unfortunate lovers, and to see the olden ones from the parapets of hell come trooping into her bed chamber? *Parbleu*, I damn think yes!"

WITH A PRECISION RIVALING that of a jeweler, Dr. Taylor cut away the crisscrossed bandages of yellowed linen that swathed the mummy of the Priestess Nefra-Kemmah. Yard after endless yard he reeled off, finally coming to a strong, seamless shroud drawn sackwise over the body and tied at the foot with a stout cord. The cloth of which the bag was made seemed stouter and heavier than the bandages, and was heavily coated with beeswax or some ceraceous substance, the whole being, apparently, both air- and water-tight.

"Why, bless my soul, I never saw a thing like this before!" exclaimed Dr. Taylor.

"*Monsieur*, unless I am more greatly mistaken than I have any right to suppose, I make no doubt there are at least a dozen things in this case which will be novelties to you," de Grandin answered rather grimly. "Come, cut away that seventeen-times-damned sack. I would see what lies within it.

"*Ah-ha?*" he exclaimed as with a gentle twitching motion Dr. Taylor worked the waxed bag upward from the mummy's shoulders. "*Que diable?*"

The body that came gradually in view beneath the blue-white glare of the electric lights was not technically a mummy, though the aromatic spices in the coffin and the sterile, arid atmosphere of Egypt had combined to keep it in a state of almost perfect preservation. The feet, first parts to be exposed, were small and beautifully formed, with long straight toes and narrow heels and high-arched insteps, the digits as well as the whole plantar region stained brilliant red with henna. There was astonishingly little desiccation, and though the terminal tendons of the *brevis digitorum* showed prominently through the skin the effect was by no means revolting; I had seen equal prominence of flexor muscles in living feet where the patient had suffered considerable emaciation.

The ankles were sharp and shapely, the legs straight and well turned, with the leanness of youth rather than the wasted look of death; the hips were narrow, almost boyish, the waist slender, and the gently swelling bosom high and sharp.

"*Morbleu*, Friend Taylor, you had right when you said she had suffered grievous hurt before she died," de Grandin murmured as the waxed sack slid over the body's shoulders.

I looked across his shoulder and gulped back an exclamation of horrified amazement. The slimly tapering arms had been folded demurely on the breast in accordance with Egyptian custom, but the humerus of the left arm had been cruelly crushed, resulting in a compound comminuted fracture, so that an inch or more of splintered bone had thrust through the skin above the deltoid attachment. The same cruel blow that crushed the arm had smashed the bony structure of the chest, the third and fourth ribs had snapped in two, and through the smooth skin underneath the breast a prong of bone protruded. "*La pauvre!*" de Grandin murmured. "*Fi donc!* By damn-it, if I could but come to grips with those who did this thing I should—" He paused in mid-word, pursed his lips as if about to whistle, then whispered half-thoughtfully, half-gleefully, "*Nom d'un porc vert, c'est possible!*"

"What's possible?" I demanded, but his only answer was a shrug as he diverted his gaze to the face exposed as Dr. Taylor drew the sack away. The features were those of a woman in her early youth. Semitic in their cast, they had a delicacy of line and contour which bespoke patrician breeding. The nose was small, high-bridged, a little aquiline, with slim, aristocratic nostrils. The lips were thin and sensitive, and where they had retracted in the process of partial desiccation showed small, sharp teeth of startling whiteness. The hair was black and lustrous, cut in a shoulder-length bob that seemed amazingly modern, and bound about the brows was a circlet of hammered silver set with small studs of lapis lazuli. For the rest, a triple-stranded necklace of gold and blue enamel, armlets of the same design, and a narrow golden girdle fashioned like a snake composed her costume. Originally a full, plaited skirt of sheer white linen had been appended to the girdle that circled her slim torso just beneath the bosom, but the fragile fabric had not been able to withstand the years of waiting in the tomb, and only one or two thin wisps remained.

"*La pauvre belle créature!*" de Grandin repeated. "If it were only possible—"

"I think we'd better wrap the body up again," Dr. Taylor broke in. "To tell the truth, I'm just a little nervous—"

"You fear," de Grandin did not ask a question, he made an assertion. "You fear the ancient gods of olden Egypt may take offense at our remaining here to speculate upon the manner of this poor one's death—or murder, one should say."

"Well, you must admit there've been some unexpected things happening in connection with this mummy, if you can call it that, for technically it's never been embalmed at all, just preserved by the aromatics sprinkled in the coffin, and—"

"One understands and agrees," de Grandin nodded. "There have been unexpected happenings, as you say, Friend Taylor, and unless I'm more mistaken than I think, there will be more before we finish. I should say—*gran Dieu des pommes de terre*, observe her, if you please!"

As Dr. Taylor had reminded us, the body had not been embalmed but merely preserved by the spices strewn around it and the almost hermetic sealing of the coffin and waxed shroud. It had been dehydrated in the years since burial so that blood, tissue and bones while retaining their contours had been reduced to something less stable than talcum powder. Now, beneath the impact of the fresh damp air and Dr. Taylor's gentle handling the triturated body-substance began crumbling. There was nothing horrifying in the process. Rather, it was as if we witnessed the slow disintegration of a lovely image moulded in sand or chalk-dust.

"*Sic transit bellitas mundi*," murmured Jules de Grandin as the shape before us lost its human semblance. "At least we've seen her in the flesh, which is a thing those wicked old ones never thought would happen, and you, *Monsieur* still have the coffin and her priceless ornaments for souvenirs. They are decidedly worthwhile, and—"

"Damn her coffin and her ornaments!" Dr. Taylor cut in sharply. "What frightens me is what this devilish business may do to my girl. She's already partially identified herself with Nefra-Kemmah and saw a vision of the priestly court that condemned her to be crushed to death beneath great stones. If that vision keeps recurring—isn't there some way we can break up this obsession—"

"By blue, there is, *Monsieur*," de Grandin assured him. "Precisely as a phobia may be overcome by showing him who suffers from it that it has no basis, so we can clear the vision of those wicked old ones from your daughter's mind. Of that I am persuaded. But the treatment will not be orthodox—"

"I don't care what it is. D'ye realize her sanity may be at stake?"

"Perfectly, *Monsieur*. Have we your consent to proceed?"

"Of course—"

"*Très bon*. Tonight, at your convenience, we shall call at your house, and unless I am far more mistaken than I think, we shall give battle to and wrest a victory from those shapes that haunt the darkness. Yes. Certainly. Of course."

ALL DAY HE WAS as busy and as bustling as a bluebottle fly. Calling on the telephone repeatedly, swearing poisonously improbable French oaths when he found our friend John Thunstone had been called away from New York on a case, rushing to the Library to consult some books the librarian had never heard of, but managed to dig up from dust-hidden obscurity at his insistence; finally dashing to the wholesale poultry market to secure something which he brought home in a thermos bottle and placed with loving care in the sterilizing cabinet of the surgery. At dinner he was almost silent, absent-mindedly forgetting to request a third helping of the lobster cardinal, a dish of which he was inordinately fond, and almost failing to refill his glass with Poully-Fuisse a fourth time.

"You've figured everything out?" I asked as we began dessert.

"*Corbleu*, I only wish I had," he answered as he raised a forkful of apple tart to his lips. "I used brave words to Monsieur Taylor, Friend Trowbridge, but just between the two of us I do not know if I am right or wrong. I grope, I feel my way, I stumble in the dark like a blind man in an unfamiliar street. I have an hypothesis, but it cannot yet be called a theory, and there is not time to test it. I warn you, what we do tonight may be dangerous. You can ill be spared to suffering humanity, my friend. The sick and ailing need your help. If you prefer to stay home while I give battle to these olden forces of evil I shall not feel offended. It is not only your privilege, it is almost your duty to remain away—"

"Have I ever let you down?" I broke in reproachfully. "Have I ever stayed behind because of danger—"

"*Non, par la barbe d'un bouc vert*; that you have not, *brave comrade*," he denied. "You may not be a trained occultist, but what you lack in training you make up in courage and loyalty, dear friend. You are one in twenty million, and I love you, *vieux comrade*, may the devil serve me hot with *sauce bordelaise* for his dinner if I do not!"

Shortly after nine o'clock that evening we gathered in the recreation room of Dr. Taylor's house. Vella, looking little worse for her attack of the night before, was wearing a black velvet dinner dress, quiet and unadorned, save for a great intricate gold pin which emphasized by contrast the ivory of her complexion and the dark mistiness of her black hair.

De Grandin set his stage precisely. Dribbling red liquid from his thermos bottle, he traced a double interlaced triangle across the tiled floor and placed four chairs inside it. "Now, *Mademoiselle*, if you will be so kind," he invited with a bow to Vella.

She dropped into an armchair, hands folded demurely in her lap, head lolling back against the cushions.

The little Frenchman took his stand before her, drew out a small gold pencil and held it vertically in front of her face. "*Mademoiselle*," he ordered, "you will please be kind enough to look at this—at its very tip, if you will. So. Good. Excellent. Observe him closely."

Deliberately, as one who beats time to a slow andante tune, he wove the little gleaming pencil back and forth, describing arabesques and intricate interlacing figures in the air. Vella watched him languidly from under long black lashes, but gradually her attention became fixed. We saw her eyes follow every motion of the pencil, finally converge toward each other until it seemed she made some sort of grotesque grimace; then the lids came down across her great dark eyes and her head moved slightly sidewise as her neck muscles relaxed. Her folded hands fell loosely open on her velvet clad knees, and she was, to all appearances, sleeping peacefully. Presently the regular, light heaving of her bosom and her softly sibilated, regular light breathing told us she had indeed fallen asleep.

De Grandin returned the pencil to his pocket, put his fists upon his hips and held his arms akimbo as he regarded her steadily. "You can hear me, cannot you, *Mademoiselle?*" he demanded.

"I can hear you," she repeated drowsily.

"*Bien.* You will rest a moment, then, as the inclination moves you, say whatever comes into your mind. You understand?"

"I understand."

For something like five breathless minutes we waited in silence. I could hear the great clock in the hall above: "*Tick*-tock—*tick*-tock!" and the soft hiss of a green log burning in the fireplace, then, gradually, but certainly, for no reason I could think of, the room began to grow colder. A hard, dull bitterness of cold that seemed to affect the spirit as well as the body pervaded the atmosphere; a biting, searing cold suggestive of the limitless freezing eternities of interstellar space.

"*Ah-ha!*" I heard de Grandin's small strong teeth click sharply, like a pair of castanets. "*Ah-ha-ha!* It seems you did not wait a second invitation, *Messieurs las Singeries.*" How they came there I had no idea, but there they were—a semi-circle of old men in flowing robes of white linen, masked with headgear simulating hawks, jackals, lions, apes and oxen. They stood in a grim, silent crescent, looking at us with dull, lack-luster eyes, the very embodiment of inhibitory hatred.

"*Mademoiselle*," de Grandin whispered, "the time has come for you to speak, if you can find the words."

The sleeping girl moaned softly, tried to articulate, then seemed to choke upon a word.

The semi-circle of grim silent watchers moved a step nearer, and the cold that theretofore had been a mere discomfort became a positive torture. The nearest of the shadowy masked figures reached the point of one of the interlaced triangles, paused irresolutely a moment, then shrank back.

"*Sa-ha, Monsieur Tête de Singe*, you do not like him, *hein?*" de Grandin asked with a short spiteful laugh. "Have patience, *Monsieur* Monkey-Face; there is to come that which you will like still less." He glanced across his shoulder at the girl. "Speak, *Mademoiselle*. Speak up and fear no evil!"

"Lords of the Ghostland," came a voice from Vella Taylor's lips, but it was not her voice. There was an indefinable and eerie undercurrent to the tone that sent a shiver tingling up our spines. Her words were slurred and languorous, yet strangely mechanical, as though an unseen hand were playing a gramophone:

"Revered and dreadful judges of the worlds of flesh and spirit, ye awful ones who sit on the parapets of hell, I answer guilty to the charge ye bring against me. Aye, Nefra-Kemmah who stands now before ye on the brink of deathless death, whose body waits the crushing stones of doom, whose spirit, robbed forever of the hope of fleshly tenement, must wander till time blends into eternity, confesses that the fault was hers, and hers alone.

"Behold me, awesome judges of the living and the dead, am I not a woman, and a woman shaped for love? Are not my members beautiful to see, my lips like apricots and pomegranates, my eyes like milk and beryl, my breasts like ivory set with coral? Yes, mighty ones, I am a woman, and a woman formed for joy.

"Was it my fault or my volition that I was pledged to serve the Great All-Mother or ever I had looked upon the daylight? Did I abjure the blissful agony of love and seek a life of sterile chastity, or was the promise spoken for me by another's lips?

"I gave all that a woman has to give, and gave it gladly, knowing that the pains of death, and after death the torment of the gods awaited me, nor do I deem the price too high a one to pay.

"Ye frown. Ye shake your dreadful heads upon which rest the crowns of Amun and of Kneph, of Seb and Tem, of Suti and Osiris' mighty self. Ye whisper one to other that I speak sacrilege. Then hear me yet awhile: She who stands in chains before you, shorn of all reverence as a priestess, stripped of all honor as a woman, tells ye this to your teeth; knowing that ye cannot do her greater hurt than she stands prejudged to endure. Your reign and that of those ye serve draws to a close. A little while ye still may strut and preen yourselves and mouth the judgments of your gods, but in the days to come your very names shall be forgot save when some stranger from another time and place drags forth your withered mummies from the tomb and sets them up to make a show of. Aye, and the gods ye serve shall be forgotten. They shall be sunk so low that none shall be found in the world to do them reverence; none to call on their names, not even as a curse, and in their ruined temples there shall not be found a living thing except the fearful, whimpering jackal and the white-bellied lizard.

"And who shall do this thing to them and ye? An offspring of the Hebrews. Yea, from the race of him I loved and for whose sake I trod my vows of cold sterility into the desert sand, from that race that ye despise and hate shall come a child and unto Him shall be all glory. He shall put down your gods beneath His feet and spoil them of all respect; they shall become but shadow-gods of a forgotten past.

"My name ye've stricken from the roll of priestesses of the All-Mother; no writing shall be graven on my tomb or coffin, and I shall be forgotten for all time by men and gods. So reads your dreadful judgment.

"Ye hoary-headed fools, I hurl the lie into your teeth! Upon a day in the far future men from a strange land shall delve into the tomb where ye have laid me and take forth my body from it, nor shall your spite and hatred stop them till they've looked upon my face and seen my broken bones and heard the story of my love for the Hebrew who for my sake abjured his God and became a shaven-headed servant of the great All-Mother. I swear that I shall tell the story of my love and death, and in another age and land strange men shall hear my name and weep for me—but *your names they shall never know.*

"Ye think to cast me to oblivion? I tell ye I shall triumph in the end, and it is ye who shall be utterly forgotten, nameless as the sands the wind pursues across the desert.

"Pile now your stones of doom upon my heart and still its fevered beating. To death I go, but not from out the memory of men as ye shall. I have spoken."

The girl's voice ended on a weary little sob, and de Grandin's shout of spiteful laughter slashed the silence as a sword might slash through flesh.

"And hast thou heard, thou animal-faced fools?" he asked. "Who prophesied the truth, and who was caught in the web of his own conceit, old monkey-faces? Take now your pale and breathless shades back to that shadow-land from whence they came. Ye tried your evil best to keep her from revealing her story, and ye have failed. Go—go quickly to oblivion. *In nomine Dei*, I bid ye begone now and henceforth!"

He took a step toward the half-circle of masked forms, and they gave ground before him. Another step, and they fell back another pace. They were wavering now, becoming less substantial, more shadowy; as he raised his hands and took a third step toward them they seemed merely nebulous gray vapor swirling and eddying in the light draft from the open fireplace where the logs blazed, and—suddenly they were gone.

"*Fini—triomphe—achevé—parfait!*" de Grandin drew a silk handkerchief from his cuff and wiped his brow. "Ye were strong and hateful, *Messieurs les Revenants*, but Jules de Grandin he is strong, too, and when it comes to hating—*morbleu*, who knows his power better than you?"

"WHAT WAS THAT STUFF you sprinkled on the floor of Taylor's recreation room before we began tonight, and why did it hold back those dreadful shadowy forms while Vella spoke?" I asked him as we drove homeward.

He broke off the tune he hummed with a laugh. "It was pigeons' blood, my friend. I got it from the *marchand de volaille* this afternoon. As to why it held them back, *morbleu*, I am as much at sea as you. It is one of those things we know without understanding.

"You know, by example, that in all ancient religions the priest was wont to purify the altars with the blood of the sacrifices—of the goats, lambs, doves or bullocks offered to the god?"

"Yes, I've heard that."

"And for why? Not that the blood is cleansing. *Mais non*. Blood is simply liquid tissue, and very messy stuff indeed. Why, then? Because, my friend"—he tapped me solemnly upon the knee—"the blood contained some secret, potent power to *hold the god in check*. He could not pass beyond a circle traced in it. That kept him in his place and kept him in control as one might say. He could not swoop down on the congregation past that barrier of sacrificial blood, as long as that stood between him and them they were safe from his wrath or spite or his capricious wish to do them hurt and injury. Yes. Of course. Very good. The priests of Isis wet her altars with the blood of doves. I secured a similar substance and with it traced a pentacle about us; the votaries of Isis, like their mistress, could not pass by that barrier; within it we were safe. And then, *pardieu*, when Mademoiselle Vella had delivered Nefra-Kemmah's message to us—shown those olden ones their cruel and wicked judgment had been set at naught—then, *morbleu*, they were completely undone. They had not strength nor spirit to oppose me when I ordered them to begone. *Parbleu*, I literally laughed them out of existence!" He drummed gloved fingers on the silver knob of his short military cane:

Sacré de nom,
Ron, ron, ron.
La vie est brève,
La nuit est longue—

he hummed. "Make haste, Friend Trowbridge."

"Why, what's the hurry?"

"It is dry work, this battling with those olden dusty ones, and just before we left for Monsieur Taylor's I saw a man put a bottle of champagne in the frigidaire."

"A man put champagne in our frigidaire?" I echoed. "Who—"

"*C'est moi*—I am the man, my friend, and *mort d'un rat mort*, how I do thirst!"

Kurban

THE CLOCK ON MY desk registered 6:45, the patient had been dismissed, from the house came appetizing odors and the rattle of a cocktail shaker briskly agitated. Dinner would be ready in a few minutes and—the chiming of the office bell came like a warning of impending disappointment as the late caller obeyed the "Ring and Enter" engraved on the brass plate decorating the door. Devoutly I hoped that the *pièce de resistance* would not be steak. A roast is little the worse for an extra half hour in a low oven, but a steak. . . .

"Trowbridge!" Dunscomb Doniphan strode into the consulting room. "Thank goodness I caught you in. I'm almost frantic, old man."

"Sit down," I invited, noting the deep grooves etched by worry wrinkles in his brow, the long lines like parentheses that scored his cheeks, and the tired look in his eyes. Here was fatigue as plainly to be read as sky-writing on a still day, another case of the "nervous prosperity" that had swept the country like a plague as war orders piled up and price became a matter of decreasing importance. "What seems to be the trouble?"

"Austine!" he flung the name at me as if it were a missile.

"Austine?" I echoed. "What—"

"Trowbridge, *mon vieux*, the ducklings roasting for our dinner are utterly *incinérée*, and the Martinis I have made with loving care—ah!" as he noticed Doniphan the little Frenchman paused abashed, "a thousand pardons, *Monsieur*, I did not know that Dr. Trowbridge entertained a patient—"

"This is Dr. de Grandin, Doniphan," I introduced. "Dr. de Grandin, Dunscomb Doniphan. We were in college together." The small Frenchman shook hands cordially and turned to leave, but:

"I've heard of you, Dr. de Grandin," Doniphan interposed. "I understand you're an expert in psychiatry."

"There are no experts in psychiatry," de Grandin denied with a smile. "Some of us may have penetrated a little deeper into the fog than others, but all of us are groping in that no-man's land where theory plays a game of blind man's buff with fact. However," he dropped into a chair, all thoughts of desiccated ducklings, and lukewarm Martinis gone from his mind, "if there is anything that I can do I shall be very happy. What is the problem vexing you?"

"Problem is right," responded Doniphan grimly. "It's my daughter Austine. If she were ten years younger I'd turn her over my knee and reason with her with a slipper; if she were five years younger I'd cut her spending money off and lock her in her room. But she's free, white and twenty-five, with what some people might consider a fortune inherited from her grandmother, so there's not a damn thing I can do with her."

"*Tiens, Monsieur*, this is no problem for a psychiatrist. I damn think most fathers of daughters suffer from the same complaint. Jules de Grandin is not equal to this task, neither is the good Trowbridge. What you need is a Solomon, and even he, if I recall my Scripture correctly, confessed the ways of a maid—"

"You know a crazy person when you see one, don't you?"

"U'm?" de Grandin took his narrow chin between a thoughtful thumb and forefinger. "I cannot say with certainty, *Monsieur*. We are all a little what you call crazy; some of we are just a little more so than the rest. What is the particular aberration from which your daughter suffers?"

The half-worried, half-puzzled look on Doniphan's face gave way to an expression of anger. "New Thought," he shot back. "Or Theosophy, or Yoga or Hinduism; maybe Bahaism? I don't know what they call it. All I know is that it's a lot of damn nonsense and has made an imbecile of what was once a fairly intelligent young woman." The smoldering anger in his eyes gave way to blazing rage. "Listen, you two:

"Ten months ago this Swami Ramapali came to brighten our ignorance with the light of his countenance. Where he came from, only God knows. He might have come from India or Indiana, but wherever he hails from, he's got what the women, young and old, eat up. Started out by giving little talks at afternoon gatherings, driveling about being In Tune With the Infinite and the Nothingness of Matter, and all that sort of rot. First thing we knew he'd progressed to holding regular meetings, then to forming a congregation with a temple of its own; three months ago he bought the Judson farm out by Passaic and founded a colony. Good Lord!" he snorted in disgust.

"And this colony of which you speak, *Monsieur*. It is—"

"I don't know what it is. Nobody does. Austine had been going to this faker's meetings regularly, and contributing plenty to them, judging by the entries we found in her check books since she left home. When he set up housekeeping at the Judson place she was one of the first to join him. I haven't laid eyes on her since. Neither has her mother. We've been out there half a dozen times, but she won't see us. Sends out word she's in her Silence, or some such damnfool message."

De Grandin's slender brows went up the fraction of an inch. "You suspect it to be a place where—how do you say *hein?*—untrammeled love is practiced?"

"I don't know what to think or suspect. I don't know anything about it, neither does anyone else. As nearly as we can find out, there are some thirty or forty people living here, mostly young women, though there's a sprinkling of old spinsters and a few widows. All of 'em are wealthy and all of them have cut themselves off from their families as completely as Austine has broken with us. I've been to the police. They can't, or won't, do anything. Say there's no crime charged, and all that sort of legalistic rot. Now, what I want you to do is"—he leveled a stiff forefinger at de Grandin and me in turn—"find some way of getting into that booby-hatch, sizing up the situation, and then, if you can find a shred of evidence appear before a lunacy commission and have Austine committed. I really think she's clear off her rocker over this business, but if we can get her out and away from the Swami's influence she'll come out of it. Then—it ought to be as easy to have her declared sane as it was to have her adjudged incompetent, oughtn't it?"

"It is deplorable," de Grandin murmured.

"Ain't it," Doniphan agreed inelegantly. "To think that a well-brought-up young woman—"

"Should have such a bigoted, narrow-minded parent, *parbleu!*" interrupted the small Frenchman fiercely. "This cult to which *Mademoiselle* your daughter has attached herself may be all that you suspect, and more, but at any rate it satisfies her. She finds it to her liking. And you, *Monsieur*, because it does not meet with your approval, would perpetrate this dreadful thing, have your own daughter branded *alienée*—a mad women—to he forever suspected of insanity, to have her children suspect of a strain of madness in their blood. *Pardieu*, it is entirely too much, this! Me, I will have none of it. Good day, *Monsieur!*" He rose, bowed coldly, and left the room.

"Well, Trowbridge, that's that," Doniphan murmured. "What do you say?"

"I say go slow," I temporized. "Austine may have gone off the deep end, but she'll come round in time. Just wait and see what happens."

"That your last word?"

"I'm afraid so. I couldn't lend myself to any such scheme as you propose—"

"All right. You're not the only doctor in town. I'll find one who'll be willing to listen to reason for a thousand-dollar fee."

"By the way, de Grandin," I remarked casually at dinner some nights later, "that Swami that Doniphan was so burned up about is making a talk at Mrs. Tenbroeck's this evening. Would you care to have a look at him? I must confess I'm somewhat curious after all I've heard."

He looked up from his apple tart with one of his direct cat-stares. "I think

I should, my friend. He may be a *jongleur,* quite possibly a criminal, but I should like to see this fellow who has, as Monsieur Doniphan expressed it, what the ladies devour. Yes, by all means, let us go."

THE SWAMI RAMAPALI WAS just finishing his discourse as de Grandin and I found seats in the Tenbroeck drawing room. He was a young man slightly under middle height, dark complected, but obviously not a member of the colored races. Dark hair, lustrous and inclined to curl, was smoothly parted in the middle and hung in long ringlets each side of his face, brushing the velvet collar of his dinner coat. His shirt of fine white linen was decorated with a double row of box pleats edged with fine lace, and against its immaculate whiteness there showed studs of onyx set with small star sapphires. Knotted negligently beneath his wide collar was a flowing black silk tie of the sort affected by art students of the '90's. His eyes were very large, prune-black, and held a drowsy, sensuous expression.

"All, all is only seeming," he concluded in a voice that was almost a purr. "All seeming is a fantasy, a nothingness, a part of Brahm's dream. We are but shadow-shapes in the Dream of the Infinite; what we call matter is delusion. Thought only is eternal, and that which we call thought is but the echo of an echo in the Dream of the Creator."

"*Grand dieu des porcs,* he talks the double-talk, this one!" de Grandin whispered. "What is this maundering of the nothingness of something and echoes of echoes—"

"*S-s-st!*" I hissed him into silence, for the Swami had stepped forward from his place beside the grand piano and the lights which had been lowered while he spoke were turned on. The vaguely unfavorable impression the Swami had made on me when I first saw him was heightened by the full light of the chandelier. As our hostess presented us and his somber, brooding eyes fell on me with a look of almost calculating appraisal, I had a momentary feeling of revulsion as unreasonable and inexplicable, but as tangible, as a warm-blooded creature's instinctive reaction to a snake.

He spoke no word of recognition as de Grandin and I bowed. Serene, statue-still, he received our murmured expressions of pleasure at the meeting with an air of aloofness that was almost contemptuous. Only for a fleeting instant did his expression change. Something, perhaps the gleam of mockery in the little Frenchman's gaze, hardened his large eyes for an instant, and I had a feeling that it would behoove my friend not to turn his back on the Swami if a dagger were handy.

In the dining room the long sideboard was laden with silver dishes of nuts, dried figs, dates and raisins. De Grandin sampled the contents of the first compote and turned away with a wry face. "Name of a name," he swore softly, "such vileness should be prohibited by law!"

"Isn't it simply wonderful?" a lady with more than ample bosom and a succession of assistant chins gushed in my ear. "It's in honor of the Swami, you know. His religion forbids eating anything that has been cooked or killed. Only the kind fruits of the kind earth are spread for a repast when he is present. I'm thinking seriously of taking up the diet. Poor dear Estrella Santho took it up, you know, and it did wonders—simply wonders—for her."

De Grandin fixed his set, unwinking cat-stare on her. "And this poor dear lady, where is she now, if you please?"

Our *vis-à-vis* seemed slightly taken aback, but rallied in a moment with a sad sweet smile. "She has passed on—her faith was stronger than ours. Where we linger hesitating on the brink, afraid to take the plunge she made the great decision and became a neophyte in the Swami's colony, the Gateway to Peace. She had completed the initial steps and was almost ready to become one of the *hieroi* when she was absorbed into the Infinite, she has passed her final incarnation and dwells forever in the ineffable light emanated by the Divine All—"

"In fine, *Madame*, one gathers she is defunct, deceased; dead?"

"In the language of the untaught—yes," the lady admitted. "It was so tragic, too. You see, the dwellers on the Threshold of Peace wear Eastern costume—no hampering Western clothes to take their minds from contemplation—and she was bitten by a snake—"

"A snake, *Madame?* You interest me. What sort of snake was it, if you know?"

"Really, sir," the lady had apparently become tired of his catechism, "I haven't the faintest idea. What sort of snakes usually bite people in this latitude?"

"That is precisely what one asks to know," he answered, but he spoke to the departing dowager's broad back.

"Ah-h'm?" he murmured as he drew a gold pencil from his pocket and scribbled a memorandum in his notebook. "This we shall look into, I damn think."

"What?" I demanded, but our hostess' announcement from the farther room prevented further conversation:

"The Swami has consented to perform a miracle for us. He will demonstrate the power of mind over seeming matter."

"*Qu'est-ce-qui?*" de Grandin's tightly waxed wheat-blond mustache was all a-quiver, like the whiskers of an alert tom-cat. "Come, Friend Trowbridge, this is something we must not forbear to witness, not by any means."

The drawing-room lights had been lowered again and the Swami was seated before a small table on which lay an ordinary lead pencil. He put his elbows on his knees and stared intently before him a long moment, then raised slender, ring-decked hands and moved them back and forth above the pencil. Faster and faster moved the undulating hands. It seemed, almost, they wove a pattern of invisible threads in the air. Then slowly, unbelievably, it happened. With a movement almost serpentine the pencil writhed a little, rose a full half-inch, then dropped back, the metallic band that held its rubber tip making a faint clicking sound against the polished table top. The Swami's hands wove fresh patterns above it, came together with a soft clap, then separated slowly. And as they drew apart the pencil rose unsteadily, wavered drunkenly a moment at an acute angle and, almost against its will, it seemed, balanced on its sharpened point. The half-lit room seemed vibrant with something unseen and unholy. I had a sudden feeling of uncanny dread, as if I'd witnessed the raising of a dead and stiffened body. For a moment the insensate bit of rubber, wood and graphite stood upright as a toe-dancer executing a pirouette, then, falling drunkenly side-wise, rolled off the polished table to the floor.

"How wonderful! Marvelous! Miraculous!" the whispered comments ran around the shadowed room.

The Swami leant back in his chair, a look of physical exhaustion on his face. "Thought," he murmured tiredly, "only thought is strong. What you have seen, my friends, is but a manifestation of the power of the will. That we call matter is of no consequence, no potency. The vaunted science of the West cannot explain such things; the stupid, cold religions of the West have nothing concrete to offer. Their storybooks are full of tales of miracles and wonders, all worked in the long-ago. But if you ask them for a miracle today—even such a little thing as that which I have done just now—they turn to vague excuses, saying that the age of miracles is past—"

De Grandin had tiptoed to the hall now, as the Swami paused a moment, he came back into the drawing room, his silver-headed stick beneath his elbow. "*Pardonnez-moi*, Monsieur Swami," he interrupted, "but here is one who does not subscribe to your thesis. In one of those story-books which you deride it is recorded how Pharaoh's necromancers cast their rods upon the earth and they became live, hissing serpents. And when Aaron, Moses' brother, cast his staff upon the ground, it likewise became a serpent and devoured those rod-serpents of Pharaoh's sorcerers. *Regardez-moi, s'il vous plaît*—" He dropped into a chair opposite the Swami, braced his stick between his knees and began to make passes over it. "You vitalized a little, insignificant lead pencil, Monsieur Swami. *Très bon*. Me, I shall call a walking stick to life. *Attendez!*"

He waved slim hands above the silver knob of the cane a moment, and the upright stick fell from between his knees, almost struck the floor, then, rallying with a wavering, uncertain movement, slowly rose until it stood upright upon its ferrule. For a moment it swayed gently, then rose clear of the floor and fell clattering to the polished boards at his feet.

He rose and bowed to the assemblage as if he were an actor on a stage, but no applause greeted his exhibition. "What, is there none to show appreciation of my *jonglerie?*" he demanded. "For shame, *messieurs et 'dames*. Is it that you seek an explanation? *Bien*. I show you. Lights, if you will be so kind," and as the lights snapped on, he took the cane up and showed them a three-foot length of black suture silk attached to it. "You see, I fasten this small thread to the stick, then I take the ends between my hands—so." He drew the string taut, and the cane rose till it stood upon its ferrule. "*Très bien.* Then I loosen the thread, and the cane she leans from side to side. When I once more tighten the thread she comes back to the vertical. *C'est très simple, n'est-ce-pas?* It is an old, old juggler's trick, one that I learned in boyhood. Yes, certainly.

"'Ah, but,' you say, 'the Monsieur Swami had no thread to make his pencil dance upon its tip. He are a really-truly supernatural someone.' Ah, bah!" So quickly none of us divined his purpose, he lashed a hand out, thrust his fingers into the Swami's waistcoat pocket and dragged out the pencil with which the miracle had been worked. From its upper end, close to the metal cap that held the rubber to the wood, there dangled eighteen inches of hair-fine black silk thread.

A flush stained the Swami's cheeks and brow, his great dark eyes suffused with tears of embarrassment. "It is a trick," he almost shrieked. "A trick—"

"But certainly, *mon ami,*" the Frenchman laughed delightedly. "A trick it is, and a most good one, too. Come now, confess that you did make the innocent joke tonight. They asked you for to perform some wonder, and you did do it for them. Very well you did it, too. I could not have done it better myself, and I am very clever. Let us make no hard feelings"—he clapped the Swami jovially upon the shoulder—"let us all be jolly friends together."

The amiability he sought to rouse was something less than hilarious, but at least the tension had been broken, and half an hour later we took our leave with a rather wintry good-bye from our hostess.

"NAME OF A SMALL green man!" he chuckled delightedly as we drove to my house. "Did I not make a monkey out of him, Friend Trowbridge? I think that he will not try to make the dancing pencil very soon again; not before that audience, at any rate."

"H'm," I rejoined. "You surely showed him up, but all the same I have a feeling everything was not as innocent as it seemed. There was an atmosphere of something evil—"

"*Parbleu,* you felt it, too? I am delighted!"

"Delighted!"

"But certainly. I had a feeling of *malaise,* of something sinister and ugly, directly I went into that room where he drooled his senseless dribble, but I am the suspicious one. I have traveled much among the fakirs and seen the so-called holy men at their unholy monkey-business. I do not like or trust those ones. To me they have the odor of dead fish.

"It was no parlor trick that he performed tonight, my friend. He was in deadly earnest, and would have let the imposition stand, had I not unmasked it. It was as false as his philosophy and his alleged religion, but—did you take note of that gathering?" he changed the subject abruptly.

"How do you mean?"

"Its composition. Did you notice the preponderance of women? And what sort of women? Not young, not old, but middle-aged.

"A very dangerous age indeed, my friend. Too old for romance, yet too young for resignation, and obviously well supplied with cash. Such people make the ideal victims for the charlatan. I damn think I shall follow the investigation of this Monsieur Swami further in the morning. Yes, certainly."

H E WAS LATE FOR dinner the next evening, and when he came in there was that expression in his little round blue eyes that told me he had made an important discovery. "Well?" I demanded as we took our seats.

"*Non*, my dear, good friend, I do not think that it is well," he denied as he sipped his Martini. "Upon the contrary, I fear that it is very not-so-well. I have apologized to Monsieur Doniphan and agreed to take his case."

"You mean you'll be a party to having Austine declared insane—"

"Better temporarily insane than dead, *mon vieux*. Perhaps she will be both before this business has come to its end. Attend me, if you please," he leveled his soup spoon at me. "This morning I went to the court house and asked to see the wills that have been probated in the last three months."

"Yes?"

"*Oui-da*. Among them I did find the one I sought, that of the poor dear Mademoiselle Santho, of whom the lady of the several chins told us last night. Dear she may have been, but certainly she was not poor. She had a comfortable fortune, oh, a very comfortable one or two hundred thousand dollars. And what did she do with it, I ask you? *Parbleu*, she willed it to her dear friend the Swami Ramapali! What do you make from that?"

"Undue influence?"

"Indubitably. Damn yes. But there is something more, a something sinister that does not leap immediately to the eye. She died, if you recall, of snake-bite."

"Yes, I remember hearing that."

"Very well, or, more precisely, very bad. She made her will upon a Wednesday. Upon the following day, Thursday, she was bitten fatally by a snake. Was it not a most accommodating serpent who dispatched her so conveniently and quickly?"

"Good heavens, d'ye think—"

"Not yet, my friend. I do not think. I am like a blind man in an unfamiliar place. I feel about me, grope for something which will show me where I am and how I should proceed, and what is it my searching fingers find? Nothing, *pardieu!*

Nothing at all. It may be that I raise the shadow of a bugaboo unnecessarily, but—can you spare tomorrow morning to go out to Monsieur Swami's colony where Mademoiselle Austine has taken residence? I should greatly like to see that place."

I T WAS EVIDENT THAT Swami Ramapali did not welcome visitors to the colony, for a cement wall some ten feet high surrounded the grounds, and the morning sunlight glinted on the raw edges of a triple row of broken bottles set in mortar on its top. The only entrance was a narrow door of heavy planking reinforced with iron straps and fitted at man's height with a little wicket through which callers might be inspected.

De Grandin struck a sharp, authoritative knock on the door, then, as no answer came to his hail, repeated the summons more loudly. The wicket in the door flew open abruptly and a dark face topped by a soiled white cotton turban scowled at us. "Go away," the porter ordered. "Your noise annoys the silence of this holy place."

"*Tiens*, Monsieur Dirty-Hat, you will experience even more annoyance if you do not make your door open all soon. I am Dr. Jules de Grandin and this is Dr. Samuel Trowbridge, and we would talk with Mademoiselle Austine Doniphan. Conduct us to her quickly, if you please."

The panel snapped shut suddenly as it had opened, and we were left to view the door again in silence.

"*Queue d'un rat mort*, they shall not shut their twenty-times-accursed door in our faces!" de Grandin swore. "They shall not—"

The heavy door swung open slowly and the porter greeted us with a salaam. "Be pleased to enter through the Gateway to Peace," he announced sonorously.

"Ah, now, my friend, you use the gas for culinary purposes," de Grandin complimented as we stepped across the threshold.

We followed our guide down a long alley lined with little cement hutches no larger than good-sized dog houses and, like dog houses, having only one opening shaped like an inverted U and so low that whoever entered would have to crawl on hands and knees. Crossing the alleyway were other even narrower passages, apparently forming a series of concentric circles radiating from a low one-story structure of stucco with a pagoda-like roof and low porch surrounded by a series of interlaced trefoil arches. There was no sign of life in the street through which we passed, but in the transverse alleys we caught glimpses of white-robed figures kneeling before the kennel-like houses, heads bent, hands clasped in what seemed silent contemplation. Curiously enough, several of them seemed to combine cigarettes with their devotions, for we saw them raise the little paper tubes to their mouths, draw deeply at them, and blow smoke slowly from their nostrils.

We reached the central structure, mounted the low single step that led to its veranda and paused before a curtained doorway. "Proceed into the presence of the Sublimity," our guide bade, holding back the hanging of striped cotton goods that draped the doorway, and we stepped into the almost total darkness of a bare, unfurnished room. As my eyes became accustomed to the gloom I descried a seated figure at the far side of the apartment. He was squatting on a large pillow, legs crossed, feet folded sole-upward upon his calves, hands resting palm-up in his lap, with fingertips barely touching. As far as I could see his costume consisted of a sheet of saffron-yellow cotton loosely belted at the waist, leaving arms, chest, legs and feet uncovered. His head was bowed, nor did he look up as we entered, but:

"You would speak with her who in the world was known as Austine Doniphan?" he asked in a low voice, and instantly I recognized the Swami Ramapali.

But how changed! Where there had been luxuriant dark hair the night we saw him at the Tenbroeck house we now saw only naked scalp, for his head was shaven smooth as an egg, giving him at once a curiously infantile and aged appearance.

De Grandin bent a sharp look on him "It seems that I was right, Monsieur Swami," he announced. "I could have sworn that you were crowned with a wig. Your hair, apparently, is no more genuine than your magic—"

"You would speak with her who in the world was known as Austine Doniphan?" the Swami interrupted in the same low, level voice.

"By blue, we would, and quickly, if you please, Monsieur. My patience is no longer than my nose, and nature has not gifted me with a long proboscis."

The Swami struck his hands together with a sharp clap. "Bid Savatri to the presence," he ordered as our late guide paused upon the threshold with a deep salaam.

We waited for perhaps five minutes while de Grandin and the Swami seemed to be engaged in seeing who could stare the other down, then a shaft of sunlight stabbed the shadows as the doorway curtain was pulled back and a girl stepped soundlessly into the room.

I had not seen Austine Doniphan for some time, and probably should not have recognized her if I'd passed her in the street. Certainly the odd figure which crept into our presence bore no resemblance to the girl I'd known. Her costume seemed to consist of some yards of soiled white cotton cloth wrapped round and round her body from bosom to ankles almost as tightly as mummy-bandages. Her arms and shoulders were uncovered, as were her feet and ankles, and so tightly was the cotton bound about her knees that she walked like a hobbled animal, setting one foot precisely before the other, and turning her hips with an exaggerated motion. A loose end of her winding sheet had been brought up to drape her head with a sort of veil, secured by a long wooden pin passed through cloth and hair. Her arms were held stiffly at her sides, hands at right angles to wrists, palms parallel to the floor. On her brow above the bridge of her nose a small daub of bright vermilion showed like a fresh wound against the skin.

Her eyes were large and fine, with long, silky lashes, and though her face was thin with sunken-cheeked thinness, there was no evidence of ill-health. I recognized the symptom. Primary emaciation resulting from sudden diminution of diet.

Looking neither right nor left, without so much as indicating by the lifting of an eyebrow that she saw us, she slipped forward with her oddly creeping walk and came to a halt before the Swami.

A moment she paused thus, head bent demurely, hands clasped together palm to palm, the fingers pointing downward, then like a hinged dummy she sank to her knees, raised both hands above her head, bent forward, laying them upon the floor palm-upward, and dropped her forehead between them.

"Name of a name!" de Grandin swore. "This is indecent, this! Arise, thou foolish one, stand on thy feet—"

"Rise, follower of the Eternal Truth," the Swami bade, and at the command the girl struggled to her knees, awkwardly, for the tightness of her winding-sheet was like a fetter, raised her hands above her head and joined them palm to palm, but kept her eyes downcast. "Look on these men," he ordered. "Dost thou know them?"

She cast a quick, almost frightened glance in our direction, then bent her head again. "I know one of them, Sublimity. He is a friend of my father—"

The Swami struck his palms together sharply. "Remember thy oath, Savatri! Thou has no father nor mother, nor any friends or kin. Thy every thought is centered on the Infinite Eternal—"

The girl lurched forward till she lay full-length before him and beat her forehead on the floor. "Forgive, forgive, Sublimity! Be patient with the dullest of thy pupils!" Her self-abasement was so complete that I felt almost sick with embarrassment for her.

"Proceed, then, but be mindful of your vow," he ordered.

"One of them, Sublimity, was known to me in the house wherein I dwelt in the world of ignorance," she replied in a low, frightened voice as she once more struggled to her knees. "He was a doctor—a physician who in his ignorance pretended to have power to cure the ills of the flesh—"

"Instruct him, Savatri," the Swami nodded to her.

"Dr. Trowbridge," she turned her great eyes, large and gentle as a gazelle's, full on me, "I pity you. You struggle in the dark, even as I did before the light of Truth Eternal fell on me. Do you not know, you foolish old man, that what we call the flesh, the body, all that we think material, are but the faintest shadows of shadows, and nothing real exists in the universe but thought? By treating what we call our bodies with contempt, by starving them, tormenting them, bringing them to utter and complete subjection, we weaken them but strengthen our souls. Anon we shall succeed in sloughing them away, flinging off the useless and undying—"

"*Cordieu, Mademoiselle*, you interest me," de Grandin broke in. "And the end of it is—"

"Nothing," she replied. "From the Infinite we came, and slowly toward the Infinite we struggle through countless incarnations. At last we shall attain perfection and be absorbed into the Infinite, all trace of self—of what you call the personality—forever lost and blotted out."

"Well said, my pupil," the Swami commended softly. "But is not the Way of Truth too hard for you? I have thought sometimes you were not able to endure the task of bodily subjection—"

"Sublimity!" Austine fell forward on her face and clasped her hands across her bowed neck. "Have gracious pity! Do not send me hence, I beg! If I have faltered in my duty it was not because I lacked the will; I had not strength to beat the flesh into complete subjection—"

There was something subtle and beguiling in the soft tone of his voice as he broke in: "For those who have the courage there is a short way to *Kailas*. There is a long and toilsome way, and a short, easy path.

"Omkar holds the door of *Kailas* open for those who would be reabsorbed into the Infinite without necessity for countless reincarnations—"

A tremor like a spasm shook the girl's bowed body. "Sublimity," she panted, "say that I may take that way! Give me leave to go to *Kailas* through *Kurban!* Grant permission for my entry into the Ineffable Nothingness that brings rest and oblivion. I would be *Kurban*, Sublimity!"

"*Grand Dieu!*" de Grandin breathed.

"Ah," the Swami let the syllable out slowly. "Thou hast made the choice thyself, Savatri. Remember, only thou canst make the choice—"

"I know, I know!" the girl broke in, breath coming in quick, sobbing gasps. "None but I can make the choice, none in heaven or in earth can revoke it. Record the vow, Sublimity! Freely, fully, voluntarily, I have made the choice. I will be *Kurban!*"

At a sign from the Swami she rose and turned to us. "I'm sorry, Dr. Trowbridge," she said gently, every trace of the frenzy that had possessed her completely gone. "You can never understand, neither can the others. I have come here of my own free will, and here I shall remain. In this place I have found such peace as I had never hoped to find on earth. Thank you for coming, and goodbye. I go to greater joys than ever woman knew before." She stretched a slender hand out, took mine in a firm clasp, and turned away with a murmured, "Peace be with you."

"See here," I told the Swami as Austine slipped from the room, "I don't know what all this nonsense is about, but it's obvious to me Miss Doniphan is not sound mentally. I came here to observe her, and in my opinion she's not responsible—"

"You think so?" Ramapali interrupted sarcastically. "However unusual her actions may have seemed at first, you can hardly say she seemed irrational when she left, Dr. Trowbridge. Do you honestly believe any jury would commit her to an institution if she appeared as normal as she did a moment since? Perhaps you'll see things in a different light when you have thought them over."

"*Eh bien*, Monsieur Swami, we have not yet begun our thinking, I assure you," answered Jules de Grandin. "It may be we shall meet again—"

"I greatly doubt it, Dr. de Grandin," the Swami broke in. "Now, if you will excuse me—I would resume my contemplation."

"*Au 'voir, Monsieur*, but by no means *adieu*," de Grandin answered as he turned on his heel.

I T WAS SHORTLY AFTER three o'clock that afternoon when he called up to ask permission to bring a friend to dinner. "A most delightful person, Friend Trowbridge. An Indian gentleman named Ram Chitra Das who has been most kind and helpful, and will be more so. Yes."

Mr. Das proved a pleasant surprise. I had had visions of a sloe-eyed Oriental with a pink or green turban and an air of insufferable condescension. Had I not known his origin I should have mistaken the man de Grandin brought to dinner for a Spaniard or Italian. His dark eyes were alert and keen with more than a suggestion of humor in them, his features small and regular, his tailoring faultless and his accent reminiscent of Oxford. He was, it appeared, the son of the tenth son of a Nepalese princeling who had so far forgotten the conventions as to fall in love with and actually marry a *nautchni*—a solecism comparable to an American parson's son marrying a burlesque strip-teaser. But because the old prince loved his son, and because the son was so far removed from the throne that the possibility of his succession was practically nil, the only punishment inflicted was banishment on a pension which equaled the income he would have enjoyed had he remained in the palace.

Ram Chitra Das was born in British India and for his first ten years was educated by a queer mixture of Mission School and native *gurus'* teaching. It was his father who insisted on his English education and his mother who saw that he received the training of a high-caste Hindu. "The dear old girl was frightfully keen on the princely blood, you know, even though the strain had begun to run pretty thin by the time it reached me."

When he was ten his father sent him to a good public school in England. He had been only fifteen when the World War broke out, but was given a commission as subaltern in an Indian regiment, fought in France, took his degree at Oxford after the war, and returned to India as a member of the Intelligence Section of the British Indian Police.

"Lord, no, I'm no Brahmin," he laughed when I commented on the ample justice he had done the roast beef at dinner. "The pater's caste was broken when he married the mater, you know, and whatever caste I had was smashed to bits when I crossed the ocean to England. I hadn't any desire to go through the disagreeable ceremony of having it restored. Sometimes I wonder what I really am. I was nurtured in the belief of the old gods of Hindi, and several English parsons, not to mention kind old ladies, labored manfully to make a Christian of me. The net result is that I try to follow St. Paul's advice to prove all things, and hold fast to that which is good. I've found a lot of good—and some things not entirely to my liking—in all religions."

"But you recall your early training" de Grandin asked.

"Oh, yes, just as a worldly Christian adult recalls the catechisms he learned as a child. Like this, you mean?" He looked about him, finally crossed the drawing room and took a tiny ivory figure from a curio cabinet. It was perhaps an inch high and represented a peacock with spread tail.

Placing it on the coffee table, he stared fixedly at it, elbows on knees, hands interlaced beneath his chin. A moment—two—went by, and I experienced a slight chill along my spine as I saw the carved ivory rise half an inch from the table, circle round as if in flight, then settle down at least a foot from the spot where he had placed it.

"Why, that's the trick the Swami did!" I exclaimed, but Mr. Das shook his head.

"No, Dr. Trowbridge, that's the trick this fellow you call Ramapali pretended to do, and which Dr. de Grandin exposed so neatly. I assure you I had no strings tied to your peacock, and you saw that my hands were motionless and never nearer than my chin to the ivory."

"But—that's magic. True magic."

Again he shook his head. "I wouldn't call it that, sir, although there are many who would. I don't pretend to understand it, any more than the dear old ladies who practice table tipping can explain why lifeless wood will vibrate and dance all round the parlor beneath their fingers. But just as I'm perfectly sure that spooks have nothing to do with the movements of the ladies' tables, I'm certain that neither gods nor demons had anything to do with making that bit of ivory seem to defy gravity. It's just one of those things for which we have no ready explanation—yet."

"Now," his laughing eyes became suddenly serious, "I'm interested in this Swami Ramapali, as he calls himself. From what Dr. de Grandin tells me, I think I know him. Some twenty years ago a young man named Michael Quinault was sent to jail in Bombay for practicing Christian wiles on the heathen in his blindness. He had been some sort of confidence man in the States, I understand. He certainly lacked confidence that day in Bombay when the judge sahib sentenced him to five years penal servitude for fleecing a Parsee widow out of her insurance money.

"He really should have thanked the judge, however, for jail proved just the thing he needed. No"—as I prepared a question—"it didn't reform him. It opened up new vistas. In jail he made the acquaintance of our slickest native criminals, and they can be very slick, believe me. He got a smattering of Hindustani, and a fair working knowledge of Hindu philosophy and religion. Learned something about Yoga, too. In fine, when he came out he was equipped to palm himself off as a genuine *guru*—that means holy man, or teacher, sometimes miracle-worker—on anybody not too well acquainted with the genuine article. He also had another souvenir of imprisonment. A severe case of fever had made him totally and permanently bald as an egg. That might have proved a handicap to most; it was a valuable asset to him in his new role of religious teacher and revealer of the Truth. We hear of him occasionally—he's swindled his way clear across the continent of Europe and the British Isles with his merry little masquerade, and done a handsome business in the States. His victims are nearly always women. There is a certain type of Western woman to whom anything oriental is simply resistless, just as there's a type of oriental female who can't resist a Western man. He's an adept at picking his—what is it you chaps call 'em?—suckers?

"If it were just a matter of separating credulous ladies from their cash I shouldn't be so much concerned. That sort of thing's been going on since time began, and will probably continue till eternity replaces time. But from what Dr. de Grandin tells me there's something far more serious involved here."

"Indeed?" I answered. "What?"

"Murder."

"Murder?" I echoed, horrified.

"Murder, *parbleu!*" de Grandin seconded. "Consider, if you please: This Mademoiselle Santho who willed her whole estate to the Swami Ramapali-Quinault, then so conveniently shuffled off the mortal coil by snake-bite. I was greatly interested in her. So to the Bureau of Vital Statistics I went and looked at her death certificate. It was signed by Dr. William Macwhyte of Tunlaw Mills. You know him?"

"No."

"So did I. But I made his acquaintance. According to his report he was roused from bed early in the morning to minister to a lady at the Swami's colony who had been bitten by a serpent. 'What sort of serpent?' I ask him.

"'A rattlesnake,' he tells me.

"'Indeed?' I asked to know. 'And did you satisfy yourself concerning this, *cher collège?*'

"'But certainly,' he tells me. 'She was bitten in the ankle. The venom was injected directly into the posterior tibial artery about four inches above the astragalus. Death must have supervened within a very short time. There were the characteristic punctures where the fangs had pierced the epidermis and the derma to the subcutaneous tissue; slight lividities around the wounds, and considerable coagulation of the blood.'

"Does it not leap to the eye?"

"Perhaps it leaps to yours. Not to mine."

"Forgive me, Friend Trowbridge. I do forget you are a general practitioner, and though a very skillful one, not familiar with reptile bites. The venom of the rattlesnake destroys the protoplasm of the blood, rendering it uncoagulable. It is about ninety-eight percent blood-destroying in its action. The venom of the cobra, *tout le contraire*, permits the blood to thicken, since its action is a swift paralysis, the poison attacking the nerve centers at once, and being only two to five percent blood-destroying. You see?"

"Can't say I do."

"*Mordieu*, I did forget. Perhaps you did not read him: Just two weeks prior to Estrella Santho's death two cobras—king cobras, *ophiophagus elaps*—were secretly abstracted from the reptile house at the zoological garden. I remembered reading of it in *le Journal* and wondering who would be such a great fool as to steal two six-foot tubes of sudden death. Then, when I put the pieces of the so unfortunate lady's death-puzzle together, 'Jules de Grandin,' I say to me, 'we have something here, Jules de Grandin,' and 'It are indubitably as you say, Jules de Grandin,' I reply to me, 'just what it are we have I do not rightly know, but beyond the question of a doubt, we have something.'"

He turned to Ram Chitra Das. "Tell him what *Kurban* means, if you will be so kind," he ordered.

"*Kurban*," the Indian replied, "means self-immolation, the offering of one-self voluntarily as a human sacrifice. A Hindu woman may find quick access to *Kailas*—heavenly oblivion—by voluntarily offering herself as a sacrifice on the altar of Okmar, which is one of Siva's less admirable attributes. Or a widow, who is doomed to countless incarnations for the sin of having permitted her husband to predecease her, may avert the curse by *Kurban*. Perfectly ridiculous, of course, yet it differs more in degree than kind from the Christian woman's entering a convent or enlisting in the Salvation Army or going as a nurse in a lepersorium."

"Good heavens!" I exclaimed. "We heard her say she wanted to become *Kurban*—"

"*Précisément*," de Grandin agreed. "I, too, heard it. Therefore, my friends, in half an hour Captain Chenevert of the State *gendarmerie* will meet us on the

Andover Road, and to that sixty-three-times damned colony we go to see what happens. Are you with us, *mon vieux?*" he turned to Mr. Das.

"Oh, absolutely, old thing. This Quinault bloke led our police a merry chase. I'd like to be in at the death."

A HIGHWAY PATROL CAR waited for us a mile or so out on the Andover Road, and as we drew abreast, Captain Chenevert thrust his head from a window. "Good evening, Dr. de Grandin; evening, Dr. Trowbridge," he greeted. "Pleased to meet you, Mr. Das," as de Grandin introduced our guest. "What's all this hush-hush stuff about? If I hadn't worked with you before, and didn't know you've always got something on the ball I'd have said, 'The hell with it,' tonight. I've got a big day tomorrow—"

"*Parbleu,* my worthy one, and you shall have a fine large night of it tonight, or Jules de Grandin is more greatly mistaken than he thinks! But yes."

Briefly he outlined the situation, and Chenevert's lips pursed in a soundless whistle. "Baldy Quinault?" he murmured. "Masqueradin' as a Hindu faker an' bumpin' women off with trick snakes. Well, what d'ye know? Let's get going."

"Softly, my friends, be silent, I implore you!" de Grandin bade as we drew up before the entrance-way of the colony. "We must make no noise—"

At his gestured command we flattened ourselves to the wall and he struck three peremptory knocks on the door. There was no answer, but after the third repetition of the summons the wicket shot back, and though we could not see from our positions, we knew the porter looked through the spy-hole.

De Grandin crouched out of the warder's line of vision, silent as a shadow, till the wicket slammed shut, then beat three thunderous blows upon the planking of the gate. This time the response was instantaneous. The wicket shot back violently, the porter took a second look, then, seeing nothing, slipped the heavy bar from its braces and swung the door back a few inches, thrusting his head out.

"*Merci bien; merci bien une mille fois*—a thousand thanks, my friend!" de Grandin chuckled. His blackjack swung in a short arc, not downward where its impact would have been cushioned by the fellow's turban, but sidewise, so that it took him squarely on the frontal bone and dropped him to his knees like a steer bludgeoned on the killing floor of a slaughter house.

Chenevert took over momentarily. "Two of you stay here," he ordered the four troopers who accompanied him. "If this bird comes out of it, see that he doesn't raise a holler. McCarty, you and Hansen come with me. Have your riot guns ready; we're apt to need 'em in a hurry. Okay, Dr. de Grandin. It's your ball from here on."

Not a light showed anywhere, nor was there any sign of life among the little buildings of the colony, but from the central structure came a muted wailing of reed pipes played in tuneless unison and the muttering rhythm of a tom-tom.

"*Ah-ha?*" the Frenchman whispered. "They have lost no time, these ones. Forward, *mes enfants!*"

Stepping high to avoid unseen obstacles, breathing through our mouths lest our respiration betray us, we hastened toward the central building, mounted its low single step and paused a breathless moment at its curtained doorway. "*Entrez, mais en silence!*" ordered Jules de Grandin.

Twin bronze braziers burned at the far side of the room, shedding a ruddy glow that stained rather than lightened the darkness of the place, and from them curled long spirals of heady incense as kneeling women fed handsful of aromatic powder on their glowing charcoal. The air was sickening with the mingled scents of aloes, sandalwood and cedar, and—even mixed with the perfumes of the aromatics its odor could not be disguised—cannabis indica, the *bhang*, or hashish of the East, the drugs of madness compared to which the marijuana of the West is as beer to brandy.

About the darkened room, their robes of cotton shining ghostly, leprous white against the gloom, some thirty figures, mostly women, crouched in attitudes of abject prostration, humming a low, wailing chant and emphasizing its crescendos by rising to their knees, hands held aloft, and clapping them together softly.

The mournful canticle came to a close, and from a farther doorway stepped the Swami Ramapali. His yellow robe had been replaced by a white gown of rhinestone-studded satin, a turban of white silk was bound about his head, and from its knot a brooch of brilliants caught the red reflection of the braziers' glow. Jeweled sandals shod his feet, and in his hand he held a rod of polished wood tipped with a knob shaped like an acorn. At sight of him the congregation groveled on the floor, then as a brazen gong clanged ominously rose to their knees and raised their hands in salute.

Two more deep, clanging strokes came from the unseen gong, and through the curtains of the door behind the Swami came Austine Doniphan. She, too, had changed her costume. Gone was her wrapped robe of soiled cotton, and in its place she wore a short bodice of purple satin and a full skirt of gold tissue bound about the waist and hips with a scarf of crimson silk. Silver anklets clinked and chimed with each step that she took, and band on band of silver circled wrists and arms. Her dark hair had been smoothly parted in the middle, and down the part there ran a streak of vivid red. As I glanced at her bare feet I saw their soles were painted red to match the part in her hair, and when she raised her hands in salute to the Swami I saw their palms were stained a brilliant yellow. Memory rang a horrifying bell in my mind: Years ago I had been told by a missionary that the colors daubed on Austine's head, hands and feet were thus applied to the bodies of Hindu women whose husbands had not survived them, and were never smeared on till the time and place of cremation had been fixed.

The girl bent in a deep salaam to the Swami, then as the gong boomed three full, brazen strokes, elevated hands above her head, pressed their yellow-painted palms together, and, rising on tiptoe, began gyrating rapidly. Faster and faster she whirled; the weighted hem of her gold-tissue dress rose slowly with centrifugal force until the garment stood out from her like a wheel and she was like a golden-petaled flower of which her white legs were the stem, the stiffly outstanding skirt the blades, and her body from the waist upward, the pistil.

"Look, for God's sake!" rasped Chenevert in my ear, and I choked on a horror-stricken breath as something like a narrow streak of shadow rippled from the doorway just behind the madly whirling girl. It was about the thickness of a steamship's hawser, and about its color, too, and bent and twisted sinuously in a series of conjoined W's, then coiled upon itself until the circle of its body and upreared head were like a giant, obscene Q. Then it uncoiled once more, lay upon the floor in a long, twisted line, and reared its wedge-shaped head to thrust forth a forked tongue. Slowly the steely whip of elongated body crept across the floor, nearer the girl's white, whirling feet, nearer—nearer.

The breath stopped in my throat. What was it Dr. Macwhyte had told de Grandin? Estrella Santho had died of snake-venom injected directly into her posterior tibial artery, the great blood vessel that supplies the back of the foot— about four inches above the astragalus or ankle bone.

A ripple of movement showed in the wavering light cast by the braziers and a second cobra joined the first, its sphenoid head raised inquiringly, its molasses-colored tongue flickering forward like a jet of flame.

"Don't shoot!" I heard Chenevert caution the troopers. "They're too close. We'd be sure to hit her—"

Beside me, coming unexpectedly as a clap of thunder on a clear day, there rose a sudden spiral of sound. Not strident, but soft, melodious, lilting, liquid as an ocarina played in middle register. With hands pressed tight against his lips, Ram Chitra Das was imitating the notes of an Indian flute. The music fluctuated from a slender spider-web of sound to a soft and throaty murmur like that of pigeons busy with their courtship. It was in a minor key, the mourning, sad lament that stamps all Oriental music, yet underneath its liquid, muted tones there was the faint suggestion of shrill, spiteful laughter.

The cobras heard it, and halted their zigzagging course toward the madly whirling girl. One of them raised its head questioningly, then the other. Suspiciously they paused a moment, swaying slowly, uncertainly, then turned away from Austine and faced Ram Chitra Das. The foremost snake raised half a yard of mottled body from the floor, and as it reared itself the hood behind its head expanded slowly till it looked like a gigantic toadstool fastened to the sinuous barrel of its body just behind the head. The second cobra seemed to struggle for a moment, then, like the first, began to rise. Slowly, apparently unwillingly, they rose and rose; now they were balancing upon what seemed no more than half a foot of coiled tail, and their heads swayed slowly with a circular motion in time to the flute's rhythm.

"Get her to hell away from there!" Ram Chitra Das brought his cupped hands down from his lips an instant. "I'll hold the snakes—be quick!"

"Take her, Trowbridge, *mon vieux*," de Grandin cried as he kicked his way through the groveling congregation toward the Swami. "Take her in your arms and bear her hence. This one is mine!"

Avoiding the charmed snakes as widely as I could, I put my arms about Austine and drew her to me. She made no struggle as I lifted her, but lay as limp and helpless as a woman in a swoon.

The little Frenchman's fist shot out and cracked against the Swami's chin with a sharp impact. "*Hola, mon ami*," he cried, "here is company you did not expect at your party!" A second uppercut sent the Swami reeling back against the wall, and before he could regain his balance handcuffs snapped upon his wrists. "I make you arrested for the murder of Estrella Santho and the attempted murder of Austine Doniphan, Michael Quinault alias Ramapali," de Grandin announced. "This time, *par la barbe d'un babouin rouge*, I think you will not beat the rap. No, not at all, by damn it!"

Ram Chitra Das had followed us, and stood above the swaying cobras. "*Hayah-hou!*" he cried as he ceased humming the flute-tune. "The dance is ended, favored ones of Brahm. The time for rest has come!"

Slowly, as if they had been lowered on invisible threads, the almost erect snakes sank to the floor and lay there inertly, quivering slightly, but giving no further sign of life. Unceremoniously as if he gathered up two lengths of rope Ram Chitra Das picked them up, seizing them carefully behind the head, and bore them, tails trailing flaccidly on the floor, through the doorway whence they had emerged.

"Nobody move!" Chenevert's voice rang like metal striking metal. "You're all under arrest as material witnesses. Take 'em in charge, McCarty."

"MOST OF IT'S PLAIN," I told de Grandin as he, Ram Chitra Das and I disposed of a bottle of champagne in my study some hours later. "I'm frank to admit, though, that what was plain as a pikestaff to you meant nothing to me until you'd pointed it out. But how d'ye account for Austine's apparent desire to offer herself as a sacrifice? Self-preservation is one of the strongest instinctive urges—"

"In normal people, yes," he agreed. "But this young woman, like all too many of her generation, is definitely neurotic. We all have a queer streak in us somewhere, and if the streak becomes too wide we are thrown off our mental balance. Man's innate impulse, as we know all too well, is to take, and woman's is to give.

It is this 'give complex'—a series of emotionally accented impulses in a suppressed state—that fills our hospitals with nurses, that makes daughters devote their lives to selfish parents, keeps women true to undeserving husbands. But when this natural trend in woman gets out of hand it becomes pathological. We call it masochism, sometime algolagnia. Very well. Consider:

"She is neurotically unbalanced, this Mademoiselle Austine. Guided in the proper channels her over-developed 'give impulse' might have made her a second Florence Nightingale. Alas, it had no guidance. It was left to run riot, and her inhibitions were naturally less strong than those of normal young women. When first we met her in the colony of the Swami I thought that I detected the scent of cannabis indica—hashish—on her hair and garments. This drug, as you know, has a powerful tendency to increase dormant, suppressed desires, to render them unnaturally—sometimes overwhelmingly—strong. When Captain Chenevert and I went through the Swami's private rooms we found hundreds of drugged cigarettes—tobacco mixed with hashish—what you call reefers. These he had systematically led his followers to smoke until they had become addicts, living in an unreal world of drug-created fantasy, wholly free from the inhibitions which ordinary sane people possess as brakes upon their impulses, especially their unnatural or 'queer' impulses. Yes. Certainly. Of course.

"Now, when one takes a sensitive, neurotic young woman and keeps her in a virtually continuous state of drug-intoxication for upward of three months she makes a fertile soil in which suggestion—either good or bad—may be implanted. Constantly, without remission, this so vile Quinault had dinned into her ears the suggestion that she give herself as a sacrifice—that she become *Kurban*. She had completely lost whatever inhibitions she once had. Her instinct for self-preservation was entirely blotted out, and her natural womanly instincts cried incessantly 'give—give—*give!*' with thousand-tongued insistence, until she felt the only way to happiness lay in offering herself as a sacrifice.

"You remember when she told the Swami she would become *Kurban?* She hesitated for a long moment before she made the declaration, then, all at once she burst out with the offer of herself so frenziedly that she could scarcely make her words coherent. That was entirely symptomatic. So was the calm that followed when she had made the hard choice. They had so constantly suggested the act to her that her poor drugged brain had come to regard it as inevitable. Natural love of life had fought against the act, but when she'd finally given way and made the decision to become *Kurban* she felt a positive relief. The long, hard, losing struggle had come to an end.

"The poor Mademoiselle Santho was less fortunate. Her they inveigled into making a will leaving her fortune to the unspeakable Quinault, then killed her ruthlessly. Mademoiselle Austine was next in line, and when we finish our investigation I am convinced that we shall find that every person in that colony is wealthy in his own right, and able to dispose of a neat fortune by will. Yes, I am certain.

"Some they would have killed as they killed la Santho and attempted to kill Mademoiselle Austine. The others they would have blackmailed mercilessly, for all of them were parties to the murders in a way, and would have paid and paid to keep their part in them from being known. But of course—"

"Why did you take those cobras up?" I asked Ram Chitra Das. "You could have killed them easily enough."

The Indian grinned amiably at me. "I didn't serve with the police for nothing, sir. Those snakes alive will make good evidence against Quinault when they try him for the murder of Miss Santho and the attempted murder of Miss Doniphan. They'd have been no use to us if I had killed them."

"*Mon brave*," the little Frenchman complimented. "My old wise one! *Morbleu*, but you do think of everything! Come, let us have another little so small drink"—he refilled our glasses and raised his toward the Indian—"to your cleverness, which is second only to de Grandin's, my friend!"

The Man in Crescent Terrace

"**B**UT THIS IS MOST pleasant, *vraiment*," Jules told me as we reached the corner where the black-and-orange sign announced a bus stop. "The *moteur*, he is a convenience. Yes, *Whiz-pouf!* he takes you where you wish to go all quickly, and *sifflement!* he brings you back all soon. But where there is no need for haste—*non*. It is that we grow soft and lazy substituting gasoline for walking-muscle, Friend Trowbridge. Is it not better that we walk on such a lovely evening?"

The brief October dusk had deepened into dark as if a curtain had been drawn across the sky, and in the east a star sprang out and a cluster of little stars blinked after it. A little breeze came up and rustled faintly in the almost-leafless maples, but it seemed to me a faint sound of uneasiness came from them, not the comfortable cradle-song of evening, but a sort of restrained moaning.

And with the sibilation of the wind there came the sound of running footsteps, high heels pounding in a sharp staccato on the sidewalk with a drumming-like panic made audible. The diffused glow of a street showed her to us as she ran, hurrying with the awkward, knock-kneed gait of a woman unused to sprinting, casting fearful looks across her shoulder each few steps, but never slackening her terror-goaded pace.

It was not until she was almost within touching distance that she saw us, and gave vent to a gasp of relief mingled with fright.

"Help!" she panted, then, almost fiercely, "run—run! He—it's coming. . . ."

"*Tenez*, who is it comes, *Mademoiselle?*" de Grandin asked. "Tell us who it is annoys you. I shall take pleasure in tweaking his nose—"

"*Run*—run, you fool!" the girl broke in hysterically, clutching at my lapel as a drowning person might clutch at a floating plank. "If it catches me—" Her breathless words blurred out and the stiffness seemed to go from her knees as she slumped against me, flaccid as a rag-doll.

I braced her slight weight in my arms, half turning as I did so, and felt the warm stickiness of fresh blood soak through my glove. "De Grandin," I exclaimed, "she's been hurt—bleeding—"

"*Hein?*" he deflected the sharp gaze which he had leveled down the darkened street. "What is it that you say—*mordieu*, but you have right, Friend Trowbridge! We must see to her—*hola, taxi, à moi, tout vite!*" he waved imperatively at the rattletrap cab that providentially emerged from the tree-arched tunnel of the street.

"Sorry, gents," the driver slowed but did not halt his vehicle, "I'm off duty an' got just enough gas to git back to the garage—"

"*Pardieu*, then you must reassume the duty right away, at once, immediately!" de Grandin broke in. "We are physicians and this lady has been injured. We must convey her to the surgery for treatment, and I have five—*non*, three—dollars to offer as an incentive—"

"I heard you the first time, chief," the cabby interrupted. "For five dollars it's a deal. Hop in. Where to?"

OUR IMPROMPTU PATIENT HAD not regained consciousness when we reached my house, and while de Grandin concluded fiscal arrangements with the chauffeur I carried her up the front steps and into the surgery. She could not have weighed a hundred pounds, for she was slightly, almost boyishly built, and the impression of boyishness was heightened by the way in which her flaxen blond hair was cropped closely at back and sides and combed straight back from her forehead in short soft waves. Her costume added little to her weight. It was a dress of black watered silk consisting of a sleeveless blouse cut at the neckline in the Madame Chiang manner and a pleated skirt that barely reached her knees. She wore no hat, but semi-elbow length gloves of black suede fabric were on her hands and her slim, small, unstockinged feet were shod with black suede sandals criss-crossed with straps of gold. If she had had a handbag it had been lost or thrown away in her panic-stricken flight.

"Ah—so, let us see what is to be done," de Grandin ordered as I laid my pretty burden on the examination table. Deftly he undid the row of tiny jet buttons that fastened the girl's blouse at the shoulder, and with a series of quick, gentle tweaks and twitches drew the garment over her head. She wore neither slip nor bandeau, only the briefest of sheer black-crêpe step-ins; we had only to turn her on her side to inspect her injury.

This was not very extensive, being an incised wound some four inches long beginning just beneath the right scapula and slanting toward the vertebral aponeurosis at an angle of about sixty degrees. At its commencement it was quite deep, striking through the derma to subcutaneous tissue, but at termination it trailed off to a mere superficial skin wound. It was bleeding freely, and its clean-cut edges gaped widely owing to the elasticity of the skin and the retraction of the fibrous tissue. "H'm," de Grandin murmured as he bent above the wound. "From the cleanness of its lips this cut was evidently inflicted by a razor or a knife that had been honed to razor-sharpness. Do not you agree, Friend Trowbridge?"

I looked across his shoulder and nodded.

"*Précisément.* And from the way it slants and from the fact that it is so much deeper at commencement than at termination, one may assume the miscreant who inflicted it stole up behind her, hoping to take her by surprise, but struck a split-second too late. The blow was probably directed with a slicing motion at her neck, but she was already in flight when her assailant struck. *Tiens*, as things are, she had luck with her, this little pretty poor one. A little deeper and the weapon might have struck into the rhomboideus, a little to the right, it might have sliced an artery. As it is—" He wiped the welling blood away, sponged the wound and surrounding epidermis with alcohol and pinched the gaping lips of the incision together in perfect apposition, then laid a pad of gauze on the closed wound and secured it with a length of adhesive plaster. "*Voilà*," he looked up with an elfin grin. "She are almost good like new now I damn think, Friend Trowbridge. Her gown is still too wet with blood for wearing, but—" he paused a moment, eyes narrowed in thought, then: "Excuse me one small, little second, if you please," he begged and rushed from the surgery.

I could hear him rummaging about upstairs, and wondered what amazing notion might have taken possession of his active, unpredictable French brain, but before I had a chance to call to him he came back with a pleased smile on his lips and a Turkish towel from the linen closet draped across his arm. "Regard me, Friend Trowbridge," he ordered. "See what a fellow of infinite resource I am." He wrapped the soft, tufted fabric about the girl's slim torso, covering her from armpits to knees, and fastened the loose end of the towel with a pair of safety pins. "*Morbleu*, I think perhaps a brilliant *couturier* was lost when I decided to become a physician," he announced as he surveyed his handiwork. "Does she not look *très chic* in my creation? By damn it, I shall say she does!"

"Humph," I admitted, "she's adequately covered, if that's any satisfaction to you."

"I had expected more enthusiastic praise," he told me as he drew the corners of his mouth down, "but—*que voulez-vous?*—the dress-designer like the prophet must expect to be unhonored in his own country. Yes." He nodded gloomily and lifted the girl from the table to an easy chair, taking care to turn her so her weight would not impinge upon her injured shoulder.

He passed a bottle of ammonium carbonate beneath her nostrils, and as the pungent fumes made her nose wrinkle in the beginnings of a sneeze and her pale lids fluttered faintly: "So, *Mademoiselle*, you are all better now? But certainly. Drink this, if you will be so kind." He held a glass of brandy to her lips. "Ah, that is good, *n'est-ce-pas*? *Morbleu*, I think it is so good that I shall have a small dose of the same!"

"And now," with small fists on his hips and arms akimbo he took his stand before her, "will you have the kindness to tell us all about it?"

She cowered back in the chair and we could see a pulse flutter in her throat. Her eyes were almost blank, but fear stared from them like a death's head leering from a window. "Who are—where am I?" she begged piteously. "Where is it? Did you see it?" As her fingers twisted and untwisted themselves in near-hysteria, then came in contact with the towel swathed round her. They seemed to feel it unbelievingly, as if they had an intelligence separate from the rest of her. Then she looked down, gave a startled, gasping cry and leaped from the chair. "Where am I?" she demanded. "What has happened to me? Why am I dressed in—in this?"

De Grandin pressed her gently back in the chair. "One question and one answer at a time, if you please, *Mademoiselle*. You are in the house of Dr. Samuel Trowbridge. This is he," he bowed in my direction, "and I am Dr. Jules de Grandin. You have been injured, though not seriously, and that is why you were brought here when you swooned in the street. The garment you are wearing is fashioned from a bath towel. I am responsible for it, and thought it quite *chic*, though neither you nor Dr. Trowbridge seem to fancy it, which is a great pity and leaves your taste in dress open to question. You have it on because your gown was disfigured when you were hurt; also it is a little soiled at present. That can and will be remedied shortly.

"Now," his little round blue eyes twinkled and he laughed reassuringly, "I have answered your questions. Will not you be so kind as to answer ours?"

Some of the fear went out of her eyes and she managed to contrive a little smile. People usually smiled back at de Grandin. "I guess I've been seeing too many horror films," she confessed. "I saw the operating table and the bandages and instruments, and smelled the medicines, then when I realized I was dressed in this my first thought was that I'd been kidnaped and—"

De Grandin's shout of laughter drowned her half-ashamed confession. "Mordieu, you thought that you were in the house of Monsieur Dracula J. Frankenstein, and that the evil, mad surgeons were about to make a guinea-pig or white rabbit of you, *n'est-ce-pas, Mademoiselle?* I assure you that fear is quite groundless. Dr. Trowbridge is an eminently respectable practitioner, and while I have been accused of many things, human vivisection is not one of them.

"Some three-quarters of an hour ago Dr. Trowbridge and I stood at Colfax and Dorondo Streets, waiting for an omnibus. We observed you coming toward us, running like Atalanta racing from the suitors, and obviously very much afraid. When you reached us you cried out for us to run also, then swooned in Dr. Trowbridge's arms. It was then we saw that you had been injured. *Alors,* we did the proper thing. We bundled you into a taxi and brought you here for treatment. You know why we removed your dress, and why you wear my own so smart creation.

"That puts you in possession of the facts, *Mademoiselle*. It is for you to tell us what transpired before we met. You may speak freely, for we are physicians, and anything you say will be held in strict confidence. Also, if we can, we shall be glad to help you."

She gave him a small grateful smile. "I think you've done a lot to help me already, sir. I am Edina Laurace and I live with my aunt, Mrs. Dorothy Van Artsdalen at 1840 Pennington Parkway. This afternoon I called on some friends living in Clinton Avenue, and walked through Crescent Terrace to Dorondo Street to take a number four bus. I was almost through the Terrace when—" she stopped, and we could see the flutter of a little blue vein at the base of her throat as her heart action quickened—"when I heard someone running."

"*Parbleu*, another runner?" murmured Jules de Grandin. Aloud he ordered: "Proceed, if you please, *Mademoiselle*."

"Naturally, I looked around. It was getting dark, and I was all alone—"

"One understands. And then what was it that you saw?"

"A man was running toward me. Not exactly toward me, but in the same direction I was going. He was a poor-looking man; that is, his clothes were out of press and seemed too loose for him, and his shoes scuffed on the pavement as he ran—you know how a bum's shoes sound—as if they were about two sizes too large? He seemed almost out of breath and scared of something, for every few steps he'd glance back across his shoulder. Then I saw what he was running from, and started to run, too. It was—" her hands went up to her eyes, as if to shut some frightful vision out, and she trembled as if a sudden draft of cold air had blown on her—"it was a mummy!"

"A *what?*" I demanded.

"*Comment?*" Jules de Grandin almost barked.

"All right," she answered as a faint flush stained her pale cheeks, "tell me I'm crazy. I still say it was a mummy; one of those things you see in museums, you know. It was tall, almost six feet, and bone-thin. As far as I could make out it was about the color of a tan shoe and seemed to be entirely unclothed. It ran in a peculiar sort of way, not like a man, but sort o' jerkily, like a marionette moved by unseen wires; but it ran fast. The man behind me ran with all his might, but it kept gaining on him without seeming to exert itself at all."

Her recitation seemed to recall her terror, for her breathing quickened as she spoke and she paused to swallow every few words. "At first I thought the mummy had a cane in its hand, but as it came neater I saw it was a stick about two—maybe three—feet long, tipped with a long, flat spearhead made of gold, or perhaps copper.

"You know how it is when you're frightened that way. You run for all you're worth, yet somehow you have to keep looking back. That's the way I was. I'd run a little way, then feel I *had* to look back. Maybe I couldn't quite convince myself it was a mummy. It was, all right, and it was gaining steadily on the man behind me.

"Just as I reached Dorondo Street I heard an awful cry. Not exactly a scream, and not quite a shout, but a sort of combination of the two, like '*ow-o-o-oh!*' and I looked back just in time to see the mummy slash the man with its spear. It didn't stab him. It chopped him with the edge of its weapon. That's when he yelled." She paused a moment and let her breath out in a long, quivering sigh. "He didn't fall; not right away. He sort o' staggered, stumbling over his own feet, or tripping over something that wasn't there, then reeled forward a few steps, with his arms spread out as if he reached for something to break his fall. Then he went down upon his face and lay there on the sidewalk perfectly still, with his arms and legs spread out like an X."

"And then?" de Grandin prompted softly as she paused again.

"Then the thing stood over him and began sticking him with its spear. It didn't move fast nor seem in any hurry; it just stood over him and stuck the spear into him again and again, like—like a woman testing a cake with a broomstraw, if that means anything to you."

De Grandin nodded grimly. "It does, indeed, *Mademoiselle*. And then?"

"Then I *did* start to run, and presently I saw it coming after me. I kept looking back, like I told you, and for a while I didn't see it; then all at once there it was, moving jerkily, and sort o' weaving back and forth across the sidewalk, almost as if it weren't quite sure which way I'd gone. That gave me an idea. I ran until I came to a dark spot in the road, the point between two street lamps where the light was faintest, and rushed across the street, running on tiptoes. Then I ran quietly as I could down the far side of the road, keeping to the shadows as much as possible. For a time I thought I'd shaken it, for when it came to where I'd crossed the street it seemed to pause and look about. Then it seemed to realize what I'd done and came across to my side. Three times I crossed the street, and each time I gained a few yards on it; but I was getting out of breath and knew I couldn't keep the race up much longer.

"Then I had another idea. From the way the creature ran it seemed to me it must be blind, or almost so, and followed me by sound more than sight. So next time I crossed the street instead of running I hid behind a big tree. Sure enough, when the thing came over it seemed at fault, and stood there, less than ten feet from me, turning round and round, pointing its spear first one way, then another, like a blind man feeling with his cane for some familiar object.

"It might have missed me altogether if I could have stayed stock-still, but when I got a close-up look at it—it was so terrible I couldn't keep a gasp of terror back. That did it. In an instant it was after me again, and I was dodging, round and round the tree.

"You can't imagine how horrible it was. The thing was blind, all right. Once

I got a good look at its face—its lips were like tanned leather and I could see the jagged line of its teeth where the dried-up mouth had come a little open, and both its eyes were tightly shut. But blind or not it could hear me, and it was like a dreadful game of blind man's buff, I dodging back to keep the tree between us, then crouching for a sprint to the next tree and doubling and turning around that, and all the time that dreadful thing following, sometimes thrusting at me with its spear, sometimes chopping at me with it, but never hurrying. If it had rushed or sprung or jumped at me it wouldn't have seemed half so terrifying. But it didn't. It just kept after me, seeming to know that sooner or later it would find me.

"I'd managed to get back my breath while we were dodging back and forth around the trees, and finally I made another break for freedom. That gave me a short respite, for when I started running this time I kept on the parking, and my feet made no noise on the short grass, but before I'd run a hundred feet I trod on a dried, curled-up leaf. It didn't make much noise, just the faintest crackling, but that was enough to betray me, and in another second the mummy was after me. D'ye remember that awful story in Grimms' *Fairy Tales* where the prince is captured by a giant, and manages to blind him, but finds that the charmed ring upon his finger forces him to keep calling, 'Here am I,' each time he eludes his pursuer? That's the way it was with me. The thing that followed me was blind, but any slightest sound was all it needed for direction, and no matter how still I tried to be, I couldn't help making some small noise to betray my position.

"Twice more I halted to play blind man's buff with it around the streetside trees, and the last time it slashed me with its spear. I felt the cut like a switch on my shoulder, it didn't hurt so much as smart, but in a moment I could feel the blood run down my back and knew that I'd been wounded. Then I lost my head completely and rushed straight down the sidewalk, running for my life. That would have been the end of me had it not been for the cat."

"The cat, *Mademoiselle?*" de Grandin asked.

"Yes, sir. It—the mummy—was about a hundred and fifty feet behind me, and gaining every step, when a big black cat came across the sidewalk. I don't know where it came from, but I hope that it has cream for dinner and two nice, fat mice for dessert every day for the rest of its life. You know how cats act sometimes when they see something coming at them—how they sort o' crouch down and stay still, as if they hope whatever it is that threatens 'em won't see 'em if they don't move? That's the way this cat did—at first. But when the mummy was almost on it, it jumped up and arched its back, puffed out its tail and made every hair along its spine stand straight up. Then it let out a miaul almost loud enough to wake the dead.

"That stopped the mummy in its tracks. You know how deceptive a caterwaul can be—how it rises and falls like a banshee's howl, and seems to come from half a dozen places at once? I think that's what must have happened. The mummy was attuned to catch the slightest sound vibration, like a delicate radio instrument, but it couldn't seem to locate the exact place whence the cat's miaul came.

"I glanced back once, and if it hadn't been so horrible it would have seemed ludicrously funny, that murderous blind mummy standing there, swaying back and forth as if the unseen strings that moved it had suddenly come loose, turning its leathery, unseeing face this way and that, and that big black tomcat standing stiff-legged in its path, its back arched up, its tail fluffed out, and its eyes blazing like two little spots of green fire. They might have stayed that way for two minutes, maybe more. I didn't stop to watch, but kept on running for dear life. The last I saw of them the puss was circling round the mummy, walking slowly and stiff-kneed, the way cats do before they close for a fight, never taking its eyes off the thing, and growling those deep belly-growls that angry cats give. I think the mummy slashed at it with its spear, but I can't be sure of that. I know the cat did not give a scream as it almost certainly would have if it had been struck. Then I saw you and Dr. Trowbridge standing by the bus stop, and"—she spread her slim hands in a gesture of finality—"here we are."

"We are, indeed," de Grandin conceded with a smile, "but we cannot remain so. It grows late and *Tante* Dorothée will worry. Come, we will take you to her and tomorrow you may come to have your wound dressed, or if you prefer you may go to your own family physician." He took his chin between his thumb and forefinger and looked thoughtfully at her. I fear your dress is not yet quite dry, *Mademoiselle*, and from my own experience I know blood-wet garments are most uncomfortable. We shall ride in Dr. Trowbridge's *moteur*—do you greatly mind retaining the garment I devised for you, wearing one of my topcoats above it? No one would notice—"

"Why, of course, sir," the girl smiled up into his eyes. "This is really quite a scrumptious dress; I'm sorry I said horrid things about it."

"*Tiens*, the compliment is much appreciated, *Mademoiselle*, even though it is a bit late," he returned with a bow. "Now, if we are all ready. . . ." He stood aside to let her precede us to the hall.

"Perhaps it would be best if you did not tell *Tante* Dorothée all your adventure," he advised as I drew up before the modest but attractive little house where she lived with her aunt. "She might not understand—"

"You mean she'd never believe me!" the girl broke in with what was more than the suggestion of a giggle. "I don't think I'd believe a person who told me such a story." Her air of gaiety dropped from her and her laughing eyes became serious. "I know it really couldn't have happened," she admitted. "Mummies just don't run around the streets killing people like that—but all the same, it's so!"

"*Tu, parles, ma petite*," de Grandin chuckled. "When you have grown as old as I, which will not be for many years, you'll know as I do that most of the impossible things are quite true. Yes, I say it."

"**Y**OU MEAN YOU ACTUALLY believe that cock and bull yarn she told us," I demanded as we drove home.

"But certainly."

"But it's so utterly fantastic. Mummies, as she herself admitted, don't run about the streets and kill people—"

"Mummies ordinarily do not run about the streets at all," he corrected. "Nevertheless, I believe her."

"Humph. Next thing, I suppose, you'll be calling Costello in on the case."

"If I am not much more mistaken than I think the good Costello will not need my summons," he returned as we reached my driveway. "Is not that he at our front door?"

"*Hola, mon lieutenant*," he called as he leaped from the car. "What fortunate breeze has wafted you hither?"

"Good evenin' gentlemen," Detective-Lieutenant Jeremiah Costello answered as he stepped back from the door. "'Tis luck I'm in, fer Mrs. McGinnis wuz just afther tellin' me as how ye'd driv away, wid yer dinner practic'ly on th' table, an' hadn't said a word about when ye'd come back."

"But now that we are so well met, you will have dinner with us?" asked the Frenchman.

"Thank ye kindly, sor. I've had me supper, an' I'm on duty—"

"*Ah bah*," de Grandin interrupted, "I fear you are deteriorating. Since when have you not been competent to eat two dinners, then smack your lips and look about for more? But even if you have no appetite, you will at least lend us your company and share a cup of coffee, a liqueur and a cigar?"

"Why, yes, sor, I'll be glad o' that," Costello returned. "An' would ye be afther listenin' to me tale o' woe th' while?"

"Assuredly, *mon vieux*. Your shop-talk is invariably interesting."

"Well, sors," Costello told us as he drained his demi-tasse and took a sip from the glass of old whiskey de Grandin had poured for him, "it's like this way: I wuz about to lave the office an' call it a day, fer this bein' a lootenant ain't as easy as it wuz when I wuz sergent, d'ye understand, an' I'd been hard at it since eight o'clock this mornin', when all to onct me tellyphone starts ringin' like a buzz-saw cuttin' through a nail, an' Dogherty o' th' hommyside squad's on th' other end. He an' Schmelz, as fine a lad as never ate a bite o' bacon wid his breakfast eggs an' fasted all day on Yom Kippur, had been called to take a look into th' killin' o' Louis Westbrook, also known as Looie th' Louse. He wuz a harmless sort o' bum, th' Louse, never doin' much agin th' law except occasionally gettin' drunk an' maybe just a mite disorderly, an' actin' as a stooly fer th' boys sometimes—"

"A stooly?" echoed de Grandin. "And what is that, if you please?"

"Sure, sor, ye know. A stool pigeon."

"Ah, yes, one comprehends. A *dénonciateur*, we use them in the *Sûreté*, also."

"Yes, sor. Just so. Well, as I wuz sayin', Looie'd been found dead as a mackerel in Crescent Terrace, an'—"

"*Morbleu*, do you say it? In Crescent Terrace?"

"That same, sor. An', like I says—"

"One moment, if you please. He was dead by a wound inflicted from the rear, possibly in the head, but more likely in the neck, and on his body were numerous deep punctured wounds—"

"Howly Mither! He wuz all o' that, sor. How'd ye guess it?"

"I did not guess, my friend. I knew. Proceed with your description of the homicide."

"Well, sor, like ye said, Looie had been cut down from th' rear, swiped acrost th' neck wid a sword or sumpin' like that. His spinal column wuz hacked through just about here—" he turned his head and held his finger to his neck above the second cervical vertebra. "I've seen men kilt just so when I was in th' Fillypines. They're willin' workers wid th' bolo, those Fillypino johnnies, as many a bloody Jap can certify. An' also like ye said, sor, he wuz punctured full o' deep, wide wounds all up his back an' down his legs. Like a big, wide-bladed knife or sumpin' had been pushed into him.

"Ever see th' victim o' one o' them Comorra torture-killin's—th' *Sfregio* or Death o' th' Seventy Cuts, as they calls it? Well, th' way this pore Joe had been mangled reminded me o' them, on'y—"

"A moment, if you please," de Grandin interrupted. "This Joseph of whom you speak? We were discussing the unhappy demise of Monsieur Louis the Louse; now you introduce a new victim—"

"Arrah, Dr. de Grandin, sor, be aisy," Costello cut in, halfway between annoyance and laughter, "when I say Joe I mean Looie—"

"*Ha?* It is that they are identical?"

"Yes, sor. Ye might say so."

De Grandin glanced at me with quizzically raised brows then lifted narrow shoulders in the sort of shrug a Frenchman gives when he wants to indicate complete dissociation with the matter. "Say on, my friend," he ordered in a weary voice. "Tell us more of this Monsieur Joseph-Louis and his so tragic dissolution."

"Well, sor, like I wuz tellin' ye, Looie'd done a bit o' stoolin' now an' then, but it wuz mostly small-fry, unimportant stuff puttin' th' finger on dips an' dope-peddlers, or tippin' th' department off when a pawnbroker acted as a fence; sometimes slippin' us th' office when a loft burglary wuz cookin', an' th' like o' that. We hadn't heard that he'd been mixed up with any of these now black-handers, so when he turns up dead an' all butchered like I said, we're kind o' wondering who kilt him, an' why."

"I have the answer to one part of your question, *mon lieutenant*," de Grandin informed him with a grave nod.

"An' have ye, now, sor? That's just grand. Would ye be afther tellin' me who done it, just for old times' sake? That is, if it's not a military secret."

"*Mais non. Point du tout.* He was killed by a mummy."

"A—glory be to God!" Costello drained his glass of whiskey at a gulp. "Th' man says he wuz kilt be a mummy! Sure, Dr. de Grandin, sor, ye wuz always a great one for kiddin', but this is business."

De Grandin's little round blue eyes were hard and cold as ice as they looked into Costello's. "I am entirely serious, my friend. I who speak to you say he was slain by a mummy."

"O.K., sor. If ye say so, I s'pose it's so. I've never known ye to give me a bum steer, but sayin' a gink's been kilt be a mummy is pretty close to tryin' to tell me that pigs fly an' tomcats sing grand op'ry. Now, th' question is, 'How're we gonna find this murderin' mummy?' Do they kape him in a museum, or does he run loose in th' streets?"

"*Le bon Dieu* only knows," the little Frenchman answered with a shrug, "but perhaps we can narrow down our search. Tomorrow I shall go to the morgue and inspect the corpse of Monsieur Joseph-Louis. Meantime there is something you can do to aid the search. This Crescent Terrace, as I recall it, is a little street. Secure the names of every householder and compile as complete a *dossier* on each as is possible: what his habits are, whence he comes, how long he has lived there—everything. The smallest little detail is important. There are no unimportant things in such a case as this. You comprehend?"

"I do, sor."

"*Très bon.*" He cast a speculative look at the decanter of whiskey. "There is at least three-quarters of a quart left in the bottle, my friends. Let us do a little serious drinking."

THE STREET LIGHTS WERE coming on and the afterglow was faint in the west under the first cold stars when we gathered in my study for a council of war next evening. De Grandin tapped a sheaf of neatly piled pages lying on the table before him. This Monsieur Grafton Loftus is our most likely suspect," he announced. "This is the *dossier* compiled on him by your department, Friend Costello:

> No. 18 Crescent Terrace—Loftus, Grafton. Unmarried, about fifty. Born in England. Came to this country from London four years ago. No occupation, maintains fair account in the Clifton Trust Co., periodically replenished by foreign bank drafts. Pays all bills promptly. Goes out very little, has no intercourse with neighbors. Few visitors. Nothing known of personal habits, hobbies, etc. No pets. Neighbors on each side speak of having heard

low, peculiar whistle, no tune, coming from his home at night, sometimes continuing for half hour at a time, have also noted strong smell like that of Chinese incense coming from his house at times.

"Perhaps I am a trifle dull," I said sarcastically, "but I fail to see where anything in that *dossier* gives ground for suspicion. We haven't any personal description of Mr. Loftus. Does he look like a mummy?"

"I would not say so," de Grandin replied. "I took occasion to call on him this afternoon, pretending to ask direction to the house of an entirely mythical Monsieur John Garfield. Monsieur Loftus came to the door—after I had rung his doorbell unremittingly for half an hour—and seemed considerably annoyed. He is a big man, most decidedly stout, bald-headed, with a red face and fat cheeks threatening to engulf his small eyes. His lips are very red, his mouth is small, and pouts like that of a petulant child. Also, he was distressingly uncivil when I asked most courteously for the non-existent Monsieur Garfield's address. I did not like his looks. I do not like him. No. Not at all."

"All the same, there's nothing in what you've told us to indicate he goes around disguised as a mummy and murdering inoffensive bums," I persisted.

"*Ah bah!*" he answered. "You vex me, Friend Trowbridge. Attend me, if you please. When I had seen this Monsieur Loftus I called New Scotland Yard on Transatlantic telephone, and talked with my friend Inspector Grayson, formerly of the British Intelligence. He told me much I wished to know. By example: Monsieur Loftus served with the British troops in Egypt and Mesopotamia during the first World War. While there he forgathered with decidedly unsavory characters, and was three times court-martialed for being absent without leave when native pow-wows were in progress. Of no importance, you say? Very, well, to continue: When he returned to England he became identified with several malodorous secret societies. The first of these was the Gorgons, ostensibly a nature-worship cult, but actually concerned with diabolism. He appears to have grown tired of these and joined the cult of Lokapala, which comprised as sinister a company of blackguards as could be found anywhere. They were known to have sacrificed animals with revolting cruelties, and were suspected of having indulged in human sacrifice at least on one occasion. The police broke this gang up and Loftus, with several others, was sentenced to a short term in the workhouse.

"We next hear of him as a member of the gang known as *Los Leopardos*, the Human Leopards, whose headquarters in the Shooter's Hill locality of Blackheath was raided by the police in 1938. Again the estimable Monsieur Loftus served a short term in jail. He was also implicated in the deviltries of Rowely Thorne, whose nemesis our mutual friend John Thunstone is. Now," he swept us with a cold, challenging stare, "you will admit the company he kept was something less than desirable."

"That may be so," I conceded, "but all the same——"

"But all the same he was a member of the Esoteric Society of the Resurrection. You comprehend?"

"I can't say that I do. Was that society one of those half-baked religious organizations?"

"Neither half-baked nor religious, in the true sense of the term, my friend. They were drawn from every stratum of society, from every country, every race. Scientists some of them were, men and women who had perverted their knowledge to base ends. Others were true mystics, Indian, Egyptian, Syrian, Druse, Chinese, English, French, Italian, even some Americans. They brought together the wisdom—all the secret, buried knowledge—of the East, and mated—not married—it to the science of the West. The offspring was a dreadful, illegitimate monster. Here, let me read you a transcription of an eyewitness' account of a convocation of the society:

The members of the cult, all robed in flowing white draperies, gathered in the courtyard of the society's headquarters around the replica of an Egyptian tomb with heavy doors like those of an ice box held fast with triple locks and bolts of solid silver. After a brief ceremony of worship four members of the society wearing black and purple draperies came out of the house, led by the Grand Hierophant robed in red vestments. They halted before the tomb and at a sign from the High Priest all members of the congregation stopped their ears with their fingers while the Hierophant and his acolytes mumbled the secret formula while the silver locks and bolts were being unfastened. Then the High Priest cried the Secret Word of Power while his assistants threw incense on the brazier burning before the tomb.

In a moment they emerged bearing a black-painted bier or stretcher on which lay the unwrapped body of an Egyptian mummy. Three times they bore the embalmed corpse around the courtyard that every member of the congregation might look on it and know that it was dead. Then they went back into the tomb.

More incense was burned while everybody knelt on the bare earth and stared fixedly at the entrance of the tomb. Minutes passed, then at the gaping doorway of the tomb appeared the mummy, standing upright and moving slowly and mechanically, like a marionette moved by invisible wires. In its right hand it held a short spear tipped with the tempered copper that only the ancient Egyptians knew how to make.

The Chief Hierophant walked before the mummy, blowing softly on a silver whistle each few steps, and the revivified lich seemed to bear and follow the sound of the whistle. Three times the mummy followed the High Priest in a circuit of the courtyard, then priest and living corpse went back into the tomb. The priest came out in a few moments and quickly fastened the silver locks of the tomb door. He was perspiring profusely, although the night was cold.

The strictest silence was enjoined during the entire ceremony, and instant dismissal from the society was the penalty decreed for any member making even the slightest sound while the mummy was out of the tomb. Once, it was said, a woman member became hysterical when the mummy emerged from the tumulus, and burst into a fit of weeping. The lich leaped on her in an instant and struck her down with its spear, then hacked her body to ribbons as she lay writhing on the earth. It was only by the shrilling of the High Hierophant's whistle that the thing was finally persuaded to give over its bloody work and lured back to the tomb.

"What do you think from that, *hein?*" he demanded as he finished reading.

"It sounds like the ravings of a hashish-eater, or the recollection of a most unpleasant dream," I volunteered.

There was no hint of impatience in the smile he turned on me. "I agree, Friend Trowbridge. It are assuredly *extra ordinem*—outside things' usual and accepted order—as the lawyers say; but most of us make the mistake of drawing the line of the possible too close. When I read this transcription over the 'phone to our friend Monsieur Manly Wade Wellman this afternoon he agreed it was entirely possible for such things to be.

"Now," once more he swept us with his fixed, unwinking cat-stare, "me, I have evolved an hypothesis: This so odious Loftus, who had been a member of this altogether detestable society, has made use of opportunity to cheat. While others stopped their ears as the Hierophant pronounced the secret invocation—the Word of Power as the witness to the ceremony calls it—he listened and became familiar with it. He anticipated making similar experiments, I have no doubt, but the onset of the war and the bombings of London interfered most seriously with his plans. *Alors*, he came to this country, took up residence in the quietly respectable Crescent Terrace, and proceeded with his so unholy trials. That would account for the incense his neighbors smelled at night, also for the whistlings they heard. Do not you agree?"

"I don't agree," I answered, "but if we grant your premises I see the logic of your conclusions."

"*Triomphe!*" he exclaimed with a grin. "At last good skeptical Friend Trowbridge agrees with me, even though he qualifies his agreement. We make the progress.

"And now, my friends," he turned from me to Costello, Dogherty and Schmelz, "if we are ready, let us go. The darkness comes and with it—*eh bien*, who shall say what will eventuate?"

CRESCENT TERRACE WAS A short semilunar by way connecting Clinton Avenue and Dorondo Street built up on the west side with neat houses. There were only twenty of them in the block, and their numbers ran consecutively, since a small park faced the east curb of the street.

We drew up at the far side of the park and walked across its neatly clipped lawns between beds of coleus and scarlet sage. At the sidewalk we halted and scanned the blank-faced houses opposite. "The second building from the end is Number 18," Jules de Grandin whispered. "Do you take station behind yonder clump of shrubs, Friend Costello, and Sergeants Dogherty and Schmelz will form an ambuscade just behind that hedge of hemlock. Friend Trowbridge, it is best that you remain with the Lieutenant, so that we shall have two parties of two each for reserves."

"An' where will you be, sor?" Costello asked.

"Me, I shall be the lure, the bait, the stalking-horse. I shall parade as innocently as an unborn lamb before his lair."

"But we can't let ye take th' risk all by yerself, sor," Costello objected, only to be cut short by de Grandin's sharp:

"*Zut!* You will do exactly as I say, *mon ami*. Me, I have worked this strategy out mathematically and know what I am doing. Also, I was not born yesterday, or even day before. *A bientôt, mes amis*." He slipped into the shadows silently as a bather letting himself down into dark water. In a moment we saw him emerge from the far side of the park into Clinton Avenue, turn left and enter Crescent Terrace. Somehow, as he strode along the footway with an air of elaborate unconcern, his silver-headed ebony stick tucked beneath his left elbow, he reminded me of a major strutting before a band, and heard him humming to himself as if he had not a care in the world.

He had almost traversed the three hundred yards of the short half-moon of the Terrace, walking slower and more slowly as he approached Dorondo Street. "Nothin' doin' yet," breathed Dogherty. "I been lookin' like a tomcat at a mouse-hole, an' don't see nothin'—"

"Zat so?" whispered Costello sharply. "If ye'd kape yer eyes on th' street an' not on Dr. de Grandin, maybe ye'd see more than ye have. What's that yonder in th' doorway o' Number 18, I dunno?"

Dogherty, Schmelz and I turned at his sharp question. We had, as he said, been watching Jules de Grandin, not the street behind him. Now, as we shifted our glances, we saw something stirring in the shadow that obscured the doorway of Number 18. At first it seemed to be no more than a chance ray of light beamed into the vestibule by the shifting of a tree-bough between house and street lamp, but as we kept our eyes glued to it we saw that it was a form—a tall, attenuated, skeletally-thin form moving stealthily in the shadow.

Slowly the thing emerged from the gloom of the doorway, and despite the warning I had had, I felt a prickling sensation at the back of my neck just above my collar, and a feeling as of sudden chill ran through my forearms. It was tall, as we had been told, fully six feet from its bare-boned feet to hairless, parchment-covered skull, and the articulation of its skeleton could be seen plainly through the leathery skin that clung to the gaunt, staring bones. The nose was large, high-bridged and haughty, like the beak of a falcon or eagle, and the chin was prominent beneath the sheath of skin that stretched across it. The eyes were closed and showed only as twin depressions in the skull-like countenance, but the mummified lips had retracted to show a double line of teeth in a mirthless grin. Its movements were irregular and stiff, like the movements of some monstrous mechanical doll or, as Edina Laurace had expressed it, like a marionette worked by unseen wires. But once it had emerged from the doorway it moved with shocking quickness. Jerkily, and with exaggeratedly high knee-action, it crossed the lawn, came to the sidewalk, turned on its parchment-soled feet as if on a pivot, and started after de Grandin.

The luckless bum it had pursued the night before had run from it. De Grandin waited till the scraping of its fleshless feet against the flagstones was almost at his elbow, then wheeled to face it, little round blue eyes ablaze, small teeth showing in a grin as mirthless and menacing as the mummy's own. "Sa-ha, Monsieur le Cadavre," he spoke almost pleasantly, "it seems we meet to try conclusions, hein? Monsieur Joe-Louis the Louse you killed, but me you shall not kill. Oh, no!"

Glinting like a flash of silver lightning in the street lamp's glow the blade of his sword cane ripped from its sheath, and he fell into guard position.

The mummy paid no more attention to his sword than if it had been a straw. It never faltered in its advance, but pressed upon him, broad-bladed spear raised like an axe. Down came the chopping spearhead, up went de Grandin's rapier, and for a moment steel and spear-shaft locked in an impasse. Then nimbly as an eel escaping from a gloved hand the Frenchman's weapon disengaged and he leaped back beyond the reach of the spear.

But the mummy came on relentlessly or, more exactly, insensately, with the utter lack of caution of an automaton. The rapier played lightning-like, weaving glittering patterns in the pale light of the street lamps; de Grandin danced as agilely as the shadow of a wind-blown leaf, avoiding heavy slash and devastating lunge, then closed in quickly as a winking eye, thrusting, stabbing, driving with a blade that seemed more quicksilver than steel. Once, twice, three times we saw his rapier pass clear through the lich, its point emerging four full inches from the leather-skinned back, but for all the effect his thrusts had, he might have been driving a pin into a pincushion.

The mummy could not have weighed much more than fifty pounds, and the little Frenchman's devastating thrusts drove it back on its heels like blows from a fist, rocking it from perpendicular until it leant at an angle of forty degrees to the earth, but it seemed endowed with devilish equilibrium and righted itself like a gyroscope each time he all but forced it off its balance.

"*Mais c'est l'enfantillage*—this is childishness!" we heard de Grandin pant as we closed in and sought a chance to seize his skeleton-like antagonist. "He who fights an imp of Satan as if he were human is a fool!

"Stand back, my friends," he called to us as we approached, "this is my task, and I will finish it, by blue!" He dodged back from the chopping of the mummy's spear, fumbling in his pocket with his left hand, then once more drove in savagely, his rapier slipping past the weapon of his adversary to pierce clear through the bony body.

And as the sword hilt struck against the mummy's ribs and swayed it backward, he thrust forward with his left hand. There was a click, a spurt of sparks, and the blue point of a little cone of flame as the wick of his cigarette lighter kindled.

The tiny blue flame touched the mummy's wrinkled skin, a flickering tongue of yellow fire bloomed like a golden blossom from the point of contact, and in an instant the whole bony, bitumen-smeared body of the lich was ablaze. If it had been composed of oil-soaked cotton waste it could not have caught fire more quickly or blazed more fiercely. The flame licked up its wasted torso, seized greedily upon emaciated limbs, burned scrawny neck and scraggy, parchment-covered head as if they had been tinder. The stiffness went from thigh- and shin-bones as they crumbled into ashes, and the blazing torso fell with a horrifying thud to the flagstones, flame crackling through its dryness.

"*Ha*, that was a trick you had not thought of, *Monsieur le Cadavre!*" De Grandin thrust the tip of his sword into the fast-crumbling remnants of the lich, stirring them as he might have stirred a coal-fire with a poker. "You were invulnerable to my steel, for you had no life in you to be let out with a sword, but fire you could not stand against. Oh, no, my old and very naughty one, you could kill poor Monsieur Joe-Louis the Louse, you could frighten poor Mademoiselle Edina, and wound her most sorely in the shoulder, but me you could not overcome, for Jules de Grandin is one devilish clever fellow and more than a match for all the mummies ever made in Egypt. Yes, certainly; of course!

"And now, my friends," he turned to us, "there is unfinished business on the agendum. Let us have some pointed conversation with this so offensive Monsieur Loftus."

A BRASS KNOCKER HUNG on the door of Number 18 Crescent Terrace, and de Grandin seized its ring and beat a thunderous tattoo. For some time there was no response, but finally a shuffling step came in the hall, and the door opened a few inches. The man who stared at us was big in every way, tall, broad and thick. His fat checks hung down like the dewlaps of a hound, his little mouth was red and full-lipped, like that of a spoiled child or wilful woman, and he stared at us through the thick lenses of rimless spectacles with that expression of vague but vast kindliness which extreme short-sightedness often confers. "Yes?" he asked in a soft oleaginous voice.

"Monsieur Loftus, one assumes?" de Grandin countered.

The man looked at him searchingly. "Oh, so it's you?" he replied. "You're the man who came here today—"

"*Assurément, Monsieur*, and I have returned with these gentlemen of the police. We would speak with you if you can spare us a few minutes. If you find it inconvenient—*eh bien*, we shall speak with you nevertheless."

"With me? About what?"

"Oh, various matters. The matter of the so abominable mummy you endowed with pseudo-life by means of certain charms you learned as a member of *la Société de la Résurrection Esotérique*, by example. Also about the death of Monsieur Joe-Louis the Louse which was occasioned yesternight by that same mummy, and of the attack on Mademoiselle Edina Laurace by your utterly detestable mummy-creature—"

The fat face looking at us underwent sudden transformation. The childish, peevish mouth began to twist convulsively and little streams of saliva dribbled from its corners. "You can't do anything to me!" Loftus exclaimed. "I deny everything. I never had a mummy; never raised it from the dead; never sent it out to kill—who would believe you if you tried to bring me into court on such a charge? No judge would listen to you; no jury would convict me—"

"Silence, *cochon!*" cried de Grandin sharply. "Go up the stairs and pack a valise. We take you to the *Bureau de Police* all soon."

The fat man stepped back, looking at him with an almost pitying smile. "If you wish to make a fool of yourself—"

"*Allez vous-en!*" the Frenchman pointed to the stairs. "Go pack your things, or we shall take you as you stand. Your execrable mummy we have burned to ashes. For you the fire of the electric chair awaits. Yes."

As Loftus turned to mount the stairs the little Frenchman whispered to Costello: "He has right, by damn it! He could not be convicted in a modern court of law, especially in this country. We might as well charge him with riding on a broomstick or turning himself into a wolf."

"Be dad, sor, ye've got sumpin' there," Costello admitted gloomily. "We seen th' whole thing wid our own ten eyes; we seen ye fight wid it an' finally make a bonfire out o' it, but if we tried to tell it to a judge he'd have all five o' us in th' bughouse quicker'n ye could say 'Scat!' so he would."

"*Précisément.* For that reason I ask that you will go out on the porch and await me. I have a plan."

"I don't see how ye're goin' to work it, sor—"

"It is not necessary that you see, my friend. Indeed, it is far better that you do not. Be swift and do as I say. In a moment he will be among us; then it will be too late."

We filed out the door and waited on the little roofless porch before the house. "If this ain't screwy," Dogherty began but got no further, for a sharp cry, half of protest, half of terror, sounded from the house, and we rushed back into the vestibule. The door had swung to behind us and the lock had snapped, so while Costello and Dogherty beat on it Schmelz and I raced to a window.

"We're coming!" I called as Sergeant Schmelz broke the glass, thrust his hand through the opening and undid the lock. "We're coming, de Grandin!"

Costello and Dogherty forced the front door as Schmelz and I broke through the window, and the four of us charged into the hall together. "Howly Mither!" exclaimed Costello. Loftus lay at the foot of the stairs as oddly and grotesquely lifeless as an over-stuffed scarecrow. His head was bent at an utterly impossible angle, and his arms and legs splayed out from his gross body, unhinged and nas-tily limp at knees and elbows.

De Grandin stood above him, and from the expression on his face I could not determine whether laughter fought with weeping or weeping with laughter. "*Je suis desolée*—I am completely desolated, my friends!" he told us. "Just as Mon-sieur Loftus was about to descend the stairs his foot slipped and he fell heavily. *Hélas*, I fear his neck is broken. Indeed, I am quite sure of it. He are completely dead. Is it not deplorable?"

Costello looked at Jules de Grandin, Jules de Grandin looked at Costello, and nothing moved in either of their faces. "Ye wouldn't 'a' helped him be any chanct, would ye, sor?" the Irishman asked at length.

"Helped him, *mon lieutenant*? Alas, no. He was below me when he fell. I could not possibly have caught him. It is unfortunate, disastrous, most regretta-ble—but that is how things are. Yes."

"Yes, sor," Costello answered in a toneless, noncommittal voice. "I had a hunch that's how things would turn out.

"Schmelz, Dogherty, why th' divil are ye standin' there gapin' like ye'd never seen a dead corpse before, an' ye both members o' th' hommyside squad? Git busy ye omadhauns. Tellyphone th' coroner an' tell him we've a customer for him.

"An' now, sor, what's next?" he asked de Grandin.

"*Eh bien*, my old and rare, what should men do when they have finished a good day's work?"

"Sure, Dr. de Grandin, sor, ye'd never be advisin' that we take a wee dhrap o' th' potheen, would ye?"

They exchanged a long, solemn wink.

Three in Chains

T HE MURMUR OF VOICES sounded from the drawing room as I let myself in wearily after a hard afternoon at the hospital. An interne might appreciate two appendectomies and an accouchement within the space of four hours, but an interne would need the practice and be thirty years my junior. I was dog-tired and in no mood to entertain visitors. As silently as I could I crept down the hall, but:

"Trowbridge, *mon vieux*," de Grandin hailed as I passed the partly opened door on tiptoe, "*à moi, s'il vous plaît*. This is of interest, this." Putting the best face I could upon the matter I joined him.

"May I present Monsieur and Madame Jaquay?" he asked, then with a bow to the callers, "*Monsieur, Madame*, Dr. Trowbridge."

The young man who stepped forward with extended head had fine, regular features crowned by a mass of dark hair, a broad, low forehead and deep greenish-hazel eyes set well apart beneath straight brows. The woman seated on the sofa was in every way his feminine counterpart. Close as a skullcap her short-cropped black hair, combed straight back from her forehead and waved in little ripples, lay against her small well-shaped head; her features were so small and regular as to seem almost insignificant by reason of their very symmetry. The dead-white pallor of her skin was enhanced by her lack of rouge and the brilliant lipstick on her mouth, while the greenness of her hazel eyes was rendered more noticeable by skillfully applied eye shadow which gave her lids a faintly violet-green tinge and a luster like that of worn silk.

I shook hands with the young man and bowed to the girl—she was little more—then looked at them again in wonder. "Mr. and Mrs. Jaquay?" I asked. "You look more like—"

"Of course, we do," the girl cut in. "We're twins."

"Twins—"

"Practically, sir. Our mothers were first cousins, and our fathers were first cousins, too, though not related to our mothers, except by marriage. We were born in the same hospital within less than half an hour of each other, and grew up in adjoining houses. We went to school, high school and college together, and were married the day after graduation."

"Is it not entirely charming?" Jules de Grandin demanded.

I was becoming somewhat nettled. Tired as I was I had no wish to interview two-headed calves, Siamese twins, cousins married to each other and like as grains of sand on the seashore or other natural phenomena. "Why, yes, of course," I agreed, "but—"

"But there is more—*parbleu*, much more!—my old and rare," the little Frenchman assured me. To the young man he ordered: "Tell him what you have told me, *mon jeune. Mordieu*, but you shall see his eyes pop like those of an astonished toad-frog!"

I dropped into a chair and tried my best to assume a look of polite interest as young Jaquay ran his hand over his sleek hair, cast a look of appeal at de Grandin and began hesitantly. "Georgine and I came here three months ago. Our Uncle, Yancy Molloy, made us sole beneficiaries of his will and Tofte House—perhaps you know the place?—was part of our inheritance. There were a few repairs to be made, though the place was in extraordinarily good condition for so old a structure, and we've been living there a little over two months. We've become very much attached to it; we'd hate to have to leave."

"Then why not stay?" I answered somewhat ungraciously. "If the house is yours and you like it—"

"Because it's haunted, sir."

"What!"

He colored slightly, but went on: "It's haunted. We didn't notice anything out of the ordinary for the first few days we lived there, then gradually both Georgine and I began to—well, sir, to feel alien presences there. We'd be reading in the library or sitting at table, or just going about our affairs in the house when suddenly we'd have that strange, uncanny feeling you have when someone stares fixedly at the back of your neck.

"When, we'd turn suddenly as we always did at first, there'd be no one there of course, but that odd, eerie sensation of being constantly and covertly watched persisted. Instead of wearing off it grew stronger and stronger till we could hardly bear it."

"U'm?" I commented, taking quick stock of our callers, noting their small stature, their delicacy of form and feature . . . their double cousinship amounted almost to inbreeding, fertile ground for neuroses to sprout in. "I know that feeling of malaise you refer to, and the fact that you both experienced it seems diagnostic. You young folks of today burn the candle at both ends. There's no need to hurry so; save a few sensations to be probed when you're past forty. These visual, sensory and circulatory symptoms aren't at all unusual. You'll have to take it easier, get much more rest and a lot more sleep. If you can't sleep I'll give you some trional—"

"But certainly," de Grandin cut in. "And the trional will surely stop the sound of clanking chains and dismal, hollow groans."

"What?" I turned on him. "Are you trying to tell me—"

"Not at all, by no means, my old one. But Monsieur Jaquay was endeavoring to do so when you interrupted with your prattle of the so odious trional. Say on, *Monsieur,*" he ordered our guest.

"We were getting pretty much on edge from this feeling of being watched so constantly," young Jaquay continued, "but it wasn't till last week we heard anything. We've made some pleasant friends in Harrisonville, sir, and been going out quite a bit. Last Saturday we'd been to New York on a party with Steve and Mollie Tenbroeck and Tom and Jennie Chaplin—dinner at the Wedgewood Room, to Broadway to see 'Up in Central Park,' then to Copacabana for supper and dancing. It must have been a little after three when we got home.

"Georgine had gone to bed, and I was in the bathroom washing my teeth when I heard her scream. I ran into the bedroom with the dentrifice suds still on my lips, and there she was, huddled in bed with the covers drawn up to her chin, pushing against the headboard as if she were trying to force herself through it. 'Something touched me!' she chattered. 'It was like an ice-cold hand!'

"Well—" he smiled apologetically—"you know how it is, sir. 'What?' I asked.

"'I don't know. I was almost asleep when it put its clammy fingers on me!'

"We'd had several rounds of cocktails both dinner and supper, and Burgundy with dinner and champagne at supper, but both of us were cold sober—well, not more than pleasantly exhilarated—when we got home. 'You're nuts,' I told her.

"And just as I spoke something went wrong with the lights. They didn't go out all at once. That could have been explained by a blown-out fuse or a short circuit in the feed line. This was different. The lamp began to grow dim slowly, as if a rheostat were being turned off. It was possibly a half-minute before the room was dark, but when the darkness came it was terrific. It pressed down on us like a great blanket, then it seemed to smother us completely—more completely than a thousand black cloths. You know that wild, unreasoning feeling of panic you have when you choke at table? This was like it. I was not only blinded, but bound and gagged as well. I tried to call to Georgine. The best that I could do was utter a choked, strangling gasp. I tried to go to her; it was like trying to wade waist-deep through a strong tide. The blackness in that room seemed liquefied, almost solidified.

"Then we heard it. At first it was no more than a whisper, like the sighing of a storm heard miles away, but getting louder, stronger, every second, like a storm that rushes toward you. Then the sigh changed to a moan and the moan became a howl, and the howl rose to a screech, and then rose to a piercing shriek that stabbed our eardrums like a needle. It rose and rose, spiraling upward till it seemed no human throat could stand the strain of it. Then it stopped suddenly with a deep, guttural gurgle, as if all that dreadful geyser of sound were being sucked down into a drainpipe. The silence that followed was almost worse than the noise. It was as if we had suddenly been stricken stone-deaf.

"I could feel the perspiration trickling down my forehead and into my eyes, but the sweat seemed turned to ice as the silence was smashed by the clanking of a chain. At first it was no more than a light clinking sound, as if some teth-ered beast stirred in the darkness. But like the shriek it increased in volume till it seemed some chained monster were straining at his iron leash, striving with a strength past anything that man or beast knows to break loose from its fetters."

Jaquay halted in his narrative to draw a handkerchief from his breast pocket and pass it over his brow. His wife was sobbing on the sofa, not violently, but with soft, sad little sounds, like those a frightened child might make.

"And then, *Monsieur?*" de Grandin prompted.

"Then the lights flashed on, not slowly, as they had gone off, but with a sudden blaze of blinding brightness, and there we were in our bedroom and everything was just the same. Georgine was cowering against the headboard of the bedstead, and I was standing at the bathroom door blinking like a fool in the sharp, dazzling light, with the dentifrice suds still on my lips and running down my chin to dribble on the floor."

"And there have been more—manifestations?"

Georgine Jaquay answered in her charmingly modulated contralto. "Not so—so violent, sir. George and I were pretty badly shaken by what happened Saturday night, or more precisely Sunday morning, but we were both very tired and dropped off to sleep before we realized it. Next day was bright and sunny and we'd almost succeeded in convincing ourselves the experience of the night before was nothing but a sort of double nightmare when that sensation of being watched became stronger than ever. Only now it seemed somehow different."

"*Hein?*"

"Yes, sir. As if whoever—or whatever—watched us were gloating. Our uneasiness increased as the afternoon wore on; by bedtime we were in a pretty sorry state, but—"

"Ah, but you had the hardihood, the courage, *n'est-ce-pas, Madame?* You did not let it drive you from your home?"

"We did not," Georgine Jaquay's small mouth snapped shut like a miniature steel trap on the denial. "We hadn't any idea what it was that wanted to get rid of us, but we determined to face up to it."

"*Bravissimo!* And then?"

"I don't know how long we'd been sleeping. Perhaps an hour; perhaps only a few minutes, but suddenly I wakened and sat bolt-upright, completely conscious. I had a feeling of sharp apprehension, as if an invisible alarm-bell were sounding a warning in my brain. There was no moon, but a little light came through the bedroom windows, enough for me to distinguish the furniture. Everything seemed as usual, then all at once I noticed the door. It showed against the further wall in a dark oblong. Dark. Dark like a hole. Somehow the comparison made me breathe faster. I could feel the pulses racing in my wrists and throat. The door had been shut—and locked—when we went to bed. Now it swung open, and I had a feeling unseen eyes were staring at me from the hallway while mine sought helplessly to pierce the darkness. Then I heard it. Not loud this time, but a sort of whimpering little moan, such as a sick child might give, and then the feeble clanking of a chain, as if whatever were bound by it moved a little, but not much.

"I sat there staring helplessly into the dark while every nerve in my body seemed tauntened to the breaking point, and listened to that hopeless moaning and the gentle clanking of that chain for what seemed like an hour. Then, very softly, came a woman's voice."

"A woman's, *Madame?*"

"Yes, sir. I could not possibly have been mistaken. It was low, not a whisper, but very weak and—hopeless."

"Yes, *Madame?* And what did this so small voice say, if you please?"

"'My poor darling!'"

"*Sang du diable!* It said that?"

"Yes, sir. Just that. No more."

"And were there further voices?"

"No, sir. There were a few weak, feeble moans, repeated at longer and longer intervals, and every once in a while the chain would rattle, but there were no more words."

De Grandin turned to young Jaquay. "And did you hear this so strange voice also, *Monsieur?*"

"No, sir. I slept through it all, but later in the night, perhaps just before morning, I wakened with a feeling someone stood beside the bed and watched me, and then I heard the scraping of a chain—not across our floor, but over something hard and gritty, like stone or perhaps concrete, and three people moaning softly."

"Three? *Grand Dieu des cochons,* the man says three! How could you tell, *Monsieur?*"

"Their voices were distinct and different. One was a man's, a light baritone, well-pitched, but very weak. The other two were women's, one soft and husky, like stroked velvet, a Negro woman's, I'm sure, and the other was lighter in tone, musical, but very feeble, like that of a person sinking in a swoon."

"They did not speak?"

"Not in words, sir, but from their tones I knew all three were very weak and exhausted, so far gone that it seemed nothing mattered to them."

"U'm?" de Grandin took his little pointed chin between a thoughtful thumb and forefinger. "And what did you do next, *Monsieur?*"

Jaquay looked embarrassed. "We sent for Dr. Van Artsdalen, sir."

"Ah? And who is he, if one may inquire?"

"He's pastor of the Union Church at Harbordale, sir. We told him everything that had happened, and he agreed to exorcise the house."

"*Mordieu*, did you, indeed?" de Grandin twisted the waxed ends of his small blond mustache until they were as sharp as twin needles. "And did he succeed in his mission?"

"I'm afraid he didn't, sir. He read a portion of the Scriptures from St. Luke, where it says that power was given the Disciples to cast out devils, and offered up a prayer, but—we haven't had a moment's peace since, sir."

The little Frenchman nodded. "One understands all too well, *Monsieur*. The occultism, he is neither good nor safe for amateurs to dabble in. This Doctor—the gentleman with the so funny name—may be an excellent preacher, but I fear he was out of his element when he undertook to rid your premises of unwelcome tenants. Who, by example, told him they were devils he came out to drive away?"

"Why—er—" Jaquay's face reddened—"I don't think anybody did, sir. We told him only what we had experienced, and he assured us that evil is always subject to good, and could not stand against the power of—"

"One understands completely," de Grandin cut in sharply. "The reverend gentleman is also doubtless one of those who believe savage animals cannot stand the gaze of the human eye, that sharks must turn upon their back to bite, and that you are immune from lightning-stroke if you have rubber heels upon your shoes. In fine, one gathers he is one of those who is not ignorant because of what he does not know, but because of the things he knows which are not true. What has occurred since his visit?"

"All day we feel those unseen eyes fairly boring into us; at night the sighs and groans and chain-clankings begin almost as soon as darkness comes and keeps up till sunrise. Frankly, sir, we're afraid to stay in the place after sunset."

The Frenchman nodded approval. "I think that you are wise to absent yourselves, *Monsieur*. For you to stay in that house after dark would not be courageous, it would be the valor of ignorance, and that, *parbleu*, is not so good. No, not at all.

"Attend me, if you please: I have made a study of such matters. To 'cast out devils,' may be an act of Christian faith which anyone possessing virtue may perform. Me, I do not know. But I do know from long experience that what will be effective in one case will wholly fail in another. Do you know surely what it is that haunts this house from which you have so wisely fled? Did the good *pasteur* know? Do I know? *Non, pardieu*, we grope in ignorance, all of us! We know not what it is we have to contend with. Attend me, *Monsieur*, if you please, with great carefulness. As that very learned writer, Manly Wade Wellman, has observed, there are many sorts of disembodied beings.

> In earth and sky and sea
> Strange things there be.

"There are, by example, certain things called elementals. These never were in human form; they have existed from the beginning, and, I assure you, they are very naughty. They are definitely unfriendly to humankind; they are mischievous, they are wicked. They should be given as wide a berth as possible. It is safer to walk unarmed through a jungle infested with blood-hungry tigers than to frequent spots where they are known to be, unless you are well-armed with occult weapons, and even then your chances are no better than those of the hunter who goes out to trail the strong and savage beast.

"Then there are those things we call ghosts. They cannot be defined with nicety, but as a class they are the immortal, or at least the surviving spiritual part of that which was once man or woman. These may be either good, indifferent or bad. The bad, of course, far outnumber the good, for the great bulk of humanity that has died has not been good. *Alors*, it behooves us to step carefully when we have dealings with them. You comprehend?

"*Bien*. It may well be the good *pasteur* used the wrong technique when he assumed to rid you of your so unwelcome co-tenants. He did not surely know his adversary; it is entirely possible that he succeeded only in annoying him as one might irritate but not cripple a lion by shooting him with a light rifle. *Mais oui*, it may be so. Let us now proceed with system. Let us make a reconnaissance, spy out the land, acquaint ourselves with that with which we must match forces.

"When this is done we shall proceed to business, not before. No, certainly; by no means.

"TELL ME, FRIEND TROWBRIDGE," he asked at breakfast next morning, "what do you know of this house from which Monsieur and Madame Jaquay have been driven?"

"Not much, I'm afraid," I answered. "I know it's more than a hundred years old and was built by Jacob Tofte whose family settled in New Jersey shortly after the Dutch wrested it from the Swedes in 1655."

"U'm? It is the original structure?"

"As far as I know. They built for permanence, those old Dutchmen. I've never been inside it, but I'm told its stone walls are two feet think."

"You do not know the year in which it was erected?"

"About 1800, I believe. It must have been before 1804, for there were originally slave quarters on the back lot, and slavery was abolished in New Jersey in that year."

"*Morbleu, pas possible!*"

"What?"

"Oh, nothing of the consequence, my friend. I did but entertain an idle thought. Those ghostly sighs and groans, those ghostly clankings of the chains, might not they have some connection with slavery?"

"None that I can see."

"And none, *hèlas*, that leaps to my eye, either," he admitted with a smile as he rose. "I did but toy with the suggestion." He lit a cigarette and turned toward the wall. "Expect me when I return, *mon vieux*. I have much ground to cover, and may be late for dinner—may *le bon Dieu* grant otherwise."

THE EVENING MEAL WAS long since over when he returned, but that his day's work had not been fruitless I knew by the twinkle in his little round blue eyes, and his first words confirmed my diagnosis. "My friend, I would not go so far as to say I have found the key to this mystery, but I damnation think that I can say under which doormat the key hides."

I motioned toward the decanter and cigars, a work of supererogation, for he was already pouring himself a generous drink of brandy. "*Bien oui,*" he nodded solemnly as he shot the soda hissing into his glass. "All morning I did search, and nowhere could I find a person who knew much about that execrable Tofte House until I reached the County Historical Society's archives. There I found more than ample reward for my labors. There were old deeds, old, yellowed newspapers; even the diaries of old inhabitants. Yes.

"This Jacob Tofte, he who built that house, must have been the devil of a fellow. In youth he followed the sea—*eh bien*, who shall say how far he followed it, or into what dark paths it led him? Those were the days of sailing ships, my old and rare, a man set forth upon a voyage new-married and easily might find himself the father of a five-year-old when he returned. But not our friend old Jacob. Not he! He traveled many times to Europe, more than once to China and the Indies, and finally to Africa. There he found his true vocation. Yes."

He paused, eyes gleaming, and it would have been cruel to have withheld the question he so obviously expected. "Did he become a 'blackbirder,' a slaver?" I asked.

"*Parbleu*, my friend, you have put your finger on the pulse," he nodded. "A slave trader he became, *vraiment*, and probably a very good one, which means he must have been a very bad man, cruel and ruthless, utterly heartless. *Tiens*, the wicked old one prospered, as the wicked have a way of doing in this far from perfect world. When he was somewhere between forty-five and fifty years of age

he returned to New Jersey very well supplied with money, retired from his gruesome trade and became a solid citizen of the community. Anon he built himself
a house as solid as himself and married.

"Now here—" he leveled a slim forefinger at me like a pointed weapon—
"occurs that which affords me the small inkling of a clue. The girl he married
was his cousin, Marise Tenbrocken. She was but half his age and had been affianced to her cousin Merthou Van Brundt, a young man of her own age and the
cousin, rather more distantly, of Monsieur Jacob. One cannot say with certainty
if she broke her engagement willingly or at parental insistence. One knows only
that Monsieur Jacob was wealthy while young Monsieur Merthou was very poor
and had his way to make in the world. Such things happened in the old days as
in the present, my friend."

He paused a moment, took a sip of brandy and soda, and lighted a cigar. "Of
these things I am sure," he recommenced at length. "From there on one finds
only scattered bones and it is hard to reconstruct the skeleton, much more so to
hang flesh upon the frame. Divorce was not as common in those days as now,
nor did people wash domestic soiled linen in public. We cannot surely know if
this marriage of May and October was a happy union. At any rate the old *Monsieur* seems to have found domestic life a trifle dull after so many years of adventure, so in 1803 we find him fitting out a small schooner to go to New Orleans.
Madame his wife remained at home. So did her *ci-devant fiancé*, who had found
employment, if not consolation, in the offices of Peter Tandy, a ship chandler.

"Again I have but surmise to guide me. Did the almost-whitened embers of
old love spring into ardent flame once more when Monsieur Van Brundt and
Madame Tofte found themselves free from the surveillance of the lady's husband, or had they carried on a liaison beneath old Monsieur Jacob's nose? One
wonders.

"*En tout cas*, Monsieur Jacob returned all unexpectedly from his projected
voyage to New Orleans, dropping anchor in the Bay but three weeks after he
had left. With Monsieur Tofte's arrival we find Madame Marise and her cousin,
formerly her *fiancé*, and doubtless now her lover, vanishing completely. *Pouf!*
Like that."

"And what became of them?" I asked as he remained silent.

"*Qui drait?* The devil knows, not I. They disappeared, they vanished, they
evaporated; they were lost to view. With them, perhaps went one Celeste, a
Martinique mulatress Monsieur Jacob had bought—or perhaps stolen—to be
Madame Marise's waiting maid.

"Her disappearance seemed to cause him more concern than that of *Madame*
his wife and his young cousin Merthou, for he advertised for her by handbill
offering a reward of fifty dollars for her return. She was, it seems, a valuable
property, speaking French, Spanish and English, understanding needlework and

cooking and the niceties of the toilette. One would think he would have offered more for her, but probably he was a very thrifty man. At any rate, it does not appear she was ever apprehended."

"And what became of Jacob Tofte?"

He shrugged his shoulders. "He sleeps, one hopes peacefully, in the church-yard of St. Chrysostom's. There was a family mausoleum on his land, but when he died in 1835 he left directions for his burial in St. Chrysostom's, and devised five thousand dollars to the parish. *Tiens*, he was a puzzle, that one. His very tombstone presents an enigma."

"How's that?"

"I viewed it in the churchyard today. Besides his name and vital data it bears this bit of doggerel:

Beneath this stone lies J. Tofte,
The last of five fine brothers.
He died more happy by his lone
And sleeps more sound than others.

"What do you make from that, *hein?*"

"Humph. Except that it's more generous in its substitution of adjectives for adverbs than most epitaphs, I'd say it compares favorably with the general level of graveyard poetry."

"Perhaps," he agreed doubtfully, "but me, I am puzzled. 'He died more happy,' says the epitaph. More happy than whom? And than whom does he sleep more soundly? Who are these mysterious others he refers to?"

"I can't imagine. Can you?"

"I—think—" he answered, speaking slowly, eyes narrowed, "I—think—I—can, my friend.

"I have searched the title to that property, beginning with Monsieur Jacob's tenancy. It has changed hands a surprising number of times. Monsieur Molloy, from whom Monsieur and Madame Jaquay inherited, was the fiftieth owner of the house. He acquired it in 1930 at an absurdly small price, and went to much expense to modernize it, yet lived in it less than a year. There followed a succession of lessees, none of whom remained long in possession. For the past ten years the place was vacant. Does light begin to percolate?"

I shook my head and he smiled rather bleakly. "I feared as much. No matter. Tomorrow is another day, and perhaps we shall be all wiser then."

"YOU HAVE NO OFFICE hours today, *n'est-ce-pas?*" he asked me shortly after breakfast the next morning.

"No, this is my Sabbatical," I answered. "One or two routine calls, and then—"

"Then you can come to Tofte House with us," he interrupted with a smile. "I damn think we shall see some things there today."

George and Georgine Jaquay were waiting for us at the Berkeley-York where they had taken temporary residence, and once more I was struck by their amazing likeness to each other. George wore gray flannels and a black Homburg, a shirt of white broadcloth and a pearl-gray cravat; Georgine wore a small black hat, a gray flannel mannishly-cut suit with a white blouse and a little mauve tie at her throat. They were almost exactly of a size, and their faces similar as two coins stamped from the same die. The wonder of it was, I thought, that they required words to communicate with each other.

The gentleman with them I took to be their lawyer. He was about fifty, carefully if somberly dressed in a formally-cut dark suit with white edging marking the V of his waistcoat. His tortoise-shell glasses were attached to a black ribbon and in one gray-gloved hand he held a black derby and a black malacca cane.

"This is Monsieur Peteros, Friend Trowbridge," de Grandin introduced when we had exchanged greetings with the Jaquays. "He is a very eminent medium who has kindly agreed to assist us."

Despite myself I raised my brows. The man might have been an attorney, a banker or mill-owner. Certainly he was the last one I should have picked as a practitioner of the rather malodorous profession of spiritualistic medium. Perhaps my face showed more than I realized, for Mr. Peteros' thin lips compressed more tightly and he acknowledged the introduction with a frigid "How d'ye do?"

But if the atmosphere were chilly de Grandin seemed entirely unaware of it. "Come, *mes amis*," he bade, "we are assembled and the time for action has arrived. Let us go all soon and not delay one little minute. No, certainly not."

F RAMED BY BIRCH AND oak, elm and maple, the big old house in Andover Road looked out upon a stretch of well-kept lawn. It was built of native bluestone without porches, and stood foursquare to the highway. Its walls were at least two feet thick, its windows high and narrow, its great front door a slab of massive oak. The sort of house a man who had been in the slave trade might have put up, a veritable fortress, capable of withstanding attacks with anything less than artillery.

Jaquay produced his key and fitted it into the incongruously modern lock of the old door, swung back the white-enameled panels and stood aside for us to enter. Mr. Peteros went first with me close at his elbow, and as I stepped across the sill I all but collided with him. He had come to an abrupt halt, his head thrown back, nostrils quivering like those of an apprehensive animal. There was a nervous tic in his left cheek, the corners of his mouth were twitching. "Don't you sense it?" he asked in a voice that grated grittily in his throat.

Involuntarily I inhaled deeply. "No," I replied shortly. "The only thing I "sensed" was the Charbert perfume Georgine Jaquay used so lavishly. I had no very high opinion of mediums. If Peteros thought he could set the stage to put us in a mood for any "revelations" he might later make, he'd have to try something more subtle.

We stood in a wide, long hall, evidently stretching to the rear of the house, stone-floored and walled with rough-cast plaster. The ceiling was of beamed oak and its great timbers seemed to have been hand-squared. The furniture was rather sparse, being for the most part heavy maple, oak or hickory—benches, tables and a few rush-bottomed square-framed chairs, and though it had small beauty it had value, for the newest piece there must have been at least a hundred years old. A fireplace stretched a full eight feet across the wall to the right, and on the bluestone slab that served for mantel were ranged pewter plates and tankards and a piece or two of old Dutch delft any one of which would have fetched its weight in gold from a knowing antique dealer. To our left a narrow stairway with a handrail of wrought brass and iron curved upward.

I was about to remark on the patent antiquity of the place when de Grandin's sharp command forestalled me: "It was in the bedroom you had your so strange experiences, my friends. Let us go there to see if Monsieur Peteros can pick up any influences."

Young Jaquay led the way, and we trooped up the narrow stairway single file, but halfway up I paused and grasped the balustrade. I had gone suddenly dizzy and felt chilled to the bone, yet it was not an ordinary chill. Rather, it seemed a sudden coldness started at my fingertips and shivered up into my shoulders, then, as with a cramp induced by a galvanic battery, every nerve in my body began to tingle and contract.

Just behind me, Peteros grasped my elbow, steadying me. "Swallow," he commanded in a sharp whisper. "Swallow hard and take a deep breath." As I obeyed the tingling feeling of paralysis left me and I heard him chuckle softly. "I see you felt it, too," he murmured. "Probably you felt it worse than I did; you weren't prepared for it." I nodded, feeling rather foolish.

Apparently the Jaquays had refurnished the bedroom, for it had none of the gloomy eighteenth century air of the rest of the house. The bedstead was a canopied four-poster, either Adam or a good reproduction, a tall chest of mahogany stood against one wall, between the narrow, high-set windows was a draped dressing table in the long mirror of which were reflected silver toilet articles and crystal bottles. Curtains of fluted organdie, dainty and crisp, hung at the windows. The floor was covered with an Abusson carpet.

"*Bien.*" De Grandin took command as we entered the chamber. "Will you sit there, *Madame?*" he indicated a chintz-covered chair for Georgine. "And you, Monsieur Jaquay, I would suggest you sit beside her. You may be under nervous strain. To have a loving hand to hold may prove of helpfulness. *Mais oui*, do not

I know? I shall say yes. You, Friend Trowbridge, will sit here, if you please, and Monsieur Peteros will occupy this chair—" he indicated a large armchair with high, tufted back. "Me, I prefer to stand. Is all in readiness?"

"I think we'd better close the curtains," Peteros replied. "I seem to get the emanations better in the dusk."

"*Bien. Mais certainement.*" The little Frenchman drew the brocade over-draperies of the windows, leaving us in semi-darkness.

Mr. Peteros leant back and took a silver pencil from his waistcoat pocket. Holding it upright before his face, he fixed his eyes upon its tip. A minute passed, two minutes; three. From the hall below came the ponderous, pompous ticking of the great clock, small noises from the highway—the rumble of great cargo trucks, the yelp of motor horns came to us through the closed and curtained windows. Peteros continued staring fixedly at the pencil point, and in the semi-darkness his face was indistinct as a blurred photograph. Then the upright pencil wavered from the perpendicular. Slowly, like a reversed pendulum, or the arm of a metronome, it swung in a short arc from right to left and back again. His eyes followed it, converging on each other until it seemed he made a silly grimace. The silver rod paused in its course, wavered like a tree caught in a sudden wind, and dropped with a soft thud to the carpet. The medium's head fell back against the cushions of his chair, his eyelids drooped and in a moment came the sound of measured breathing, only slightly stertorous, scarcely more noticeable than the ticking of the clock downstairs. I knit my brows and shook my head in annoyance. I could have simulated a more convincing trance. If he thought we could be imposed upon by such a palpable bit of trickery. . . .

"O-o-o-oh!" Georgine Jaquay exclaimed softly. She had raised one hand to her throat and the painted nails of her outspread fingers were like a collar of garnets on the white flesh.

I felt a sudden tenseness. Issuing from Peteros' lips was a thin column of smoke, as if he had inhaled deeply from a cigar. Yet it was not ordinary smoke. It had an oddly luminous quality, as if its particles were microscopic opals that glowed with their own inward fire, and instead of coming in a series of short puffs, as cigar smoke would have come from his mouth, it flowed in steady, even stream, like steam escaping from a simmering kettle. "*Regardez, s'il vous plaît,* Friend Trowbridge," de Grandin whispered half belligerently. "I tell you it is psychoplasm—soul stuff!"

The cloud of luminescent vapor drifted slowly toward the ceiling, then as if wafted by an unfelt zephyr coiled and circled toward the wall pierced by the curtained windows, and slowly, more like dripping water than a cloud of steam or smoke, began to trickle down the wall until it covered it completely.

It is difficult to describe what happened next. Slowly in the opalescent vapor that obscured the wall there seemed to generate small sparks of bluish light, mere tiny points of phosphorescence, and gradually, but with a gathering speed, they multiplied until they floated like a swarm of dancing midges circling round each other till they joined to form small nebulae of brightness large as gleaming cigarette ends. The nebulae became more numerous, touched each other, coalesced as readily as rain drops brought together, till they formed a barrier of eerie, intense bluish light.

There was eeriness, uncanniness about it, but it was not terrifying. Instead of fear I felt a sort of gentle melancholy. Vague, long-forgotten memories wafted through my mind . . . a girl's soft laugh, the touch of a warm hand, the echo of the muted whisper of a once-loved voice, the subtle fragrance of old hopes and aspirations.

Half dazzled, wholly mystified by the phenomenon, I watched the luminous curtain.

A sort of cloudiness appeared in its bright depths, at first no more than a dim, unformed network of small dots and dashes, but gradually they built up a pattern. As when an image appears on the copper of a halftone plate in its acid bath, a picture took form on the surface of the glowing curtain. As if through the proscenium of a theatre—or on a motion picture screen—we looked into another room.

I recognized it instantly, so did Georgine Jaquay, for I heard her gasp, "Why, it's the hall of this house!"

"*Taisez-vous!*" de Grandin snapped. "*Laissez-moi tranquille, s'il vous plaît, Madame!* Be silent!"

It was the hall we had come through less than ten minutes before, yet somehow it was not the same. A great fire blazed on the wrought-metal andirons and in a pair of brass candlesticks tallow dips were burning. The lights and shadows shifted constantly, but such illumination as there was seemed to do little more than stain the darkness. The door through which we had come opened and a middle-aged Negro dressed in a suit of coarse tow came into the apartment, bending almost double under the weight of a brass-bound trunk of sole leather. He paused uncertainly a moment, seemed to turn as if to hear some command shouted at him from outside, then shambled toward the stairway.

The door, which had swung partly shut, was kicked back violently, and across the sill a man stepped with a woman in his arms. He was a big man, tall and heavy-set, with enormous shoulders and great depth of chest, dressed in the fashion of a hundred years and more ago. His suit of heavy woolen stuff was snuff-colored, made with a long coat and breeches reaching to his knees, and his brown stockings were of knitted wool but little better than those of the Negro. I guessed his age as somewhere near fifty, for there were streaks of gray in the long hair that he wore plaited in a queue and in the short dark reddish beard and mustache that masked his lower face. He had a big nose, dark hawk-eyes, broad low forehead and high-jutting cheek-bones. His skin was darkly tanned, and though he had few wrinkles they were deep ones. He was, I thought, a well-to-do farmer, perhaps a merchant sea captain. Certainly he was no gentleman, and just as certainly he was a hard customer, tricky and, unscrupulous in bargaining and fierce and ruthless in a fight.

Of the woman we could see little, for a long hooded cloak of dark blue linsey-woolsey covered her from head to heels. What was at once apparent, however, was that she did not snuggle in his arms. She neither held his shoulders nor put her arms about his neck, merely lay quiescent in his grasp as if she rested after an exhausting ordeal, or realized the futility of struggling.

But when he set her on her feet we saw that she was very delicately made, not tall but seeming taller than her actual height because of extreme slenderness. She was pretty, almost beautiful, with a soft cream-and-carnation skin, bronze hair that positively flamed in the firelight, and eyes of luminous greenish violet with the wondering expression of a hurt child.

The man said something to her and with a start I realized we witnessed a pantomime, a scene of vibrant life and action soundless as an old-time moving picture, but legible in meaning as sky-writing on a windless day. We saw her shake her small head in negation, then as he echoed his peremptory demand, hold out her hands in a gesture of entreaty. Her face was bloodless and her eyes suffused with tears, but if she had been a bird and he a cat her appeal could not have been more futile. Abruptly he seized her left hand and raised it to a level with her eyes, and on its third finger we saw the great, heavy plain gold band that marked her as a matron. For a moment he stood thus, then flung the little hand from him as if it were a bit of dross and grasped the trembling girl in his arms, crushed her to him and bruised her shrinking lips with kisses that betrayed no trace of love but were afire with blazing passion.

When he released her she shrank back, cheeks aflame with outraged blood and eyes almost filmy with nausea, but as he repeated his command she crept rather than walked to the stairway and mounted it slowly, holding fast to the wrought-brass handrail for support.

The man turned toward the kitchen, bellowing an order and into the hall stole another girl about the age of her whom he had just mauled so lustfully. She was a mulatress, scarce larger than a child, with delicately formed features, short wavy brown hair clustering round her ears and neck in tiny ringlets, and large dark eyes as gentle—and as frightened—as a gazelle's. Despite the almost shapeless gown of woolen stuff that hung on her we saw her figure was exquisite, with high breasts, narrow hips and lean, small waist. She bore a straw-wrapped stone demijohn stopped with a broken corncob, and at his order, took a pewter tankard from the mantel and poured some of the colorless contents of her jar into it. "More!" We could not hear the word, but it required no skill in lip-reading to know what he ordered, and with a shrug that was no more than a flutter of her shapely shoulders she splashed an added half-pint of liquor into the beaker.

It was obvious; she was afraid of him, for she stayed as far away as she could, and her large eyes watched him furtively. When she had filled the mug she stood back quickly, pretending to be busy with recorking the bottle, but obviously eager to stay out of reach.

Her stratagem was futile, for when he downed the draft he wiped his mouth upon his cuff and held out his hand. "Kiss it!" we saw, rather than heard him order. She took his rough paw in her delicate gold hands and bent her sleek head over it, but he would not let her kiss its back. "Not that way!" he bade roughly, and obediently she turned it over and pressed her lips to its palm.

Why he demanded this peculiar form of homage I had no idea, but evidently de Grandin understood its implication, for I heard him mutter, "*Sale bête*—dirty beast!"

The bearded man threw back his head and laughed a laugh that must have filled the house with its bellow, then half playfully but wholly viciously he struck the girl across the face with a back-handed blow that sent her reeling to a fall beside the tiled hearth of the fireplace. The demijohn slipped from her hand, and in a moment a dark stain of moisture spread across the stones.

We saw him beckon her imperiously, saw her rise trembling to her feet and slink toward him, her wide eyes fearful, her lips trembling. Nearer she crept, shaking her head from side to side, begging mutely for mercy, and when she was within arm's length he seized her as a pouncing beast might grasp its prey. As a terrier might shake a rat he shook her, swaying her slim shoulders till her head bobbed giddily and her short curls waved like wind-whipped bunting round her ears. Protesting helplessly she opened her mouth and the force with which he shook her drove her teeth together on her tongue so that a little stream of blood came from the corners of her mouth. Then, not content with this punishment, he struck her with his fist, knocking her to the floor, then raising her again that he might strike her down once more. Three times he hit her with his knotted fist, and every blow drew blood. When he was done he left her in a little crumpled heap beside the hearthstone, her slim gold hands held to her face and bright blood dripping from her nose, her lips and her bruised cheeks.

"*Cochon, pourceau, sale chameau!*" de Grandin whispered venomously. "*Pardieu*, he was a species of a stinking swine, that one!"

The big man wiped his mouth upon his sleeve once more and, swaying slightly from the effect of the potent apple-jack, made for the stairway up which the girl he had borne into the house had crept.

The picture before us began to fade, not growing dimmer but apparently dissolving like a cloud of steam before a current of air, and in a moment little dots and lines of color danced and moved across the luminous screen, forming figures like the prisms of a kaleidoscope, then gradually merging to depict another scene.

Not very different from its present aspect, save that its lawn was not so well kept, the front yard of the house spread before us. It was early evening, and from the marshes—long since filled in and built over—rose a soft, light mist, silvery, unearthly, utterly still. The trees that rimmed the highway were almost denuded of their foliage and stood out in sharp silhouette, pointing to the pale sky from which most of the stars had been wiped by a half-moon's light. An earlier wind had blown the fallen leaves across the bricked walk with its low box borders, and the man and woman walking away from us kicked them from their path, rustling them against their feet as children love to do in autumn. At the lower end of the footway they paused and as the girl turned her face up to her escort we recognized the young woman we had seen borne into the house. The moonlight brought them into clear-cut definition. The man was young, about the girl's age, and bore a strong resemblance to her, obviously a family likeness. His clothes and linen were threadbare but scrupulously clean, and his lean drawn face showed the effect of high ambition and slender resources. What they said we had no way of knowing, but we saw her arms creep up around his neck, not passionately, but tenderly, like the tendrils of a vine, as she raised her lips for his kiss. A moment they stood thus in silent embrace, then she unclasped her arms from his neck and he turned away, walking down the moonlit high road with no backward glance and with squared shoulders, like a man who has made final, immutable decision.

Once more the scene was obscured, then took on new form, and we saw the white girl and the mulatress working feverishly packing a small nail-studded trunk. They folded linen underwear and sprinkled it with crumbled dry lavender, pressed a woolen dress down on the antique lingerie, added several pairs of cotton stockings and a pair of square-toed little buckled shoes. The box was packed and strapped, the girl ran to the door, but paused upon the threshold, the joy wiped from her face as sunlight disappears before a sudden cloud.

In the entrance stood the bearded man, and over one shoulder, as a butcher might have held a new-slaughtered calf, he bore the body of the young man we had seen before. Blood trickling from a scalp-wound told us how the boy had been bludgeoned, and on the barrel of the antique horse-pistol in the big man's right hand there was a smear of blood to which a few brown hairs adhered.

There was something utterly appalling in the big man's quietness. Methodically as if he followed a rehearsed plan he dropped the unconscious man on the bed, retraced his steps to the door and returned with three short lengths of iron chain which he proceeded to fasten round the necks of the two women and the swooning man.

Amazingly the women made no effort to resist but stood as dumbly and quiescently as well-trained horses waiting to be harnessed as he latched the fetters on their throats. Perhaps the memory of past beatings told them that submissiveness was wiser, perhaps they realized the hopelessness of entreaty or effort. It was very quickly accomplished, and in a moment the big man had shouldered the unconscious youth again, tucked the little trunk beneath his free arm, and nodded toward the door. Without a word of protest or entreaty the women went before him, holding the free ends of their neck chains in their hands as if to still their clinking.

We looked into a little room, perhaps some twelve feet square, stone-floored, stone-walled, stone-ceilinged. It was darker than a moonless midnight, but somehow we could distinguish objects. About the walls were small partitioned spaces rising four deep, tier on tier, like oversized pigeonholes, and, each was closed with a stone slab in which a heavy ringbolt had been set. Something like a swarm of small red ants seemed crawling up the backs of my knees and my spine. One did not need to be an antiquarian to recognize the crypts of an old family tomb.

Something stirred in the darkness, and as I strained my eyes toward it I saw the huddled form of a woman. I knew it for a woman by the long red hair that hung upon its head, but otherwise, although it had been stripped of clothing, it was almost unclassifiable. Emaciation was so far advanced that she was little more than a mummy. Knee- and elbow-joints stood out against the staring skin like apples on broomsticks, the hip-bones showed like ploughshares each side the pelvis, the ribs were like the bars of a grating, and every tooth was outlined through the shrunken lips.

The creature bent its skull-face to the stone pavement and licked a little moisture from the trickle of a tiny spring-fed rivulet that crossed the flags, then tried to rouse itself to a sitting posture, tried vainly again, and sank back limply. Slowly, painfully, as if it fought paralysis, it edged across the cold damp stones of the floor, stretched out a bony, tendon-scored hand toward another thing that crouched against the farther wall.

This was—or had been—a man, but now it was no better than a skeleton held in articulation by the skin stretched drum-tight over it. It seemed to rouse to semi-consciousness by the other's movement, and tried desperately to reach the withered hand stretched toward it. In vain. The chains that tethered the whimpering woman-lich and her companion were barely long enough to stretch from their ring-bolts to the floor, leaving the captives just length of leash enough to lie on the floor, but not permitting them sufficient movement to reach each other, even when their arms were stretched to fullest extent.

And as we watched the prisoners struggle futilely to bring their dying hands together we saw something flutter feebly in the darkness at the rear of the tomb. Chained like the other two the golden-skinned mulatress lay against the wall, and constantly her head turned from side to side and her emaciated body shook with unremitting spasms.

"*Cordieu*, but it was monstrous, that!" de Grandin whispered grittily. "Not content with making them die horribly by slow starvation; not content with making it impossible for them so much as to join hands in their extremity, he chained that other poor one with them that they should be denied all privacy, even in the hour of death!"

He struck his hands together sharply. "*Monsieur!*" he called. "Monsieur Peteros!"

The gruesome scene before us faded as if it had been frescoed on wax melting in quick heat, and through the semi-darkness of the room there swirled a wraith-like cloud of gleaming vapor that hovered like a nimbus above the medium a moment, then, as if he had inhaled it, was absorbed by him. "Eh?" Peteros murmured sleepily. "Did I go into a trance? What did I say?"

"Not a word, *Monsieur*," de Grandin told him. "You were as dumb as an infant oyster, but through your help we are much wiser. Yes. Certainly. Stay here and rest, for you must be exhausted. The rest of us have duties to perform. Come, *mes amis*," he looked at me and the Jaquays in turn, "let us go to that abominable tomb, that never-to-be-quite-sufficiently-anathematized sepulchre. We are a century and more too late—we cannot rescue them, *hèlas*, but we can give them what they most desire. Of a surety."

WITH A CROWBAR WE forced back the rust-bound iron door of the Tofte mausoleum and after standing back a moment for the outer air to enter de Grandin led the way into the tomb, playing the beam of his flashlight before him.

"*Voyez! Voilà que!*" he ordered as the shifting shaft of light stabbed through the murky darkness. Death lay at our feet. Arranged in orderly array as if they waited articulation by an osteologist were the bones of three skeletons. Dangling from the ring bolts of three stone-sealed crypts to the floor beside the skulls were lengths of rust-bitten iron chain. The disintegration of the prisoners' upper spinal columns had loosed the loops of iron latched about their throats. We had no difficulty determining their sex. Even if the widely-opened sciatic notches of the pelvic bones and the smoothly curved angular fronto-nasal articulation of the skulls had not denoted the female skeletons to de Grandin's practiced eye and mine the pitiful relics lying by two of the skulls would have told their story — the amethyst-set gold earrings of the white girl and the patina-encrusted copper loops that once had hung in the mulatress little ears.

The Frenchman stepped back, bowing as if he addressed three living people. "*Mes pauvres*," he announced softly, "we are come to give you release from your earth-bound state. Your pleas have been heard; you shall be together in what remains of the flesh. The evil man who boasted of his better, sounder sleep— *parbleu*, but Jules de Grandin makes a monkey out of him!"

"It is a case for the coroner," he told us as we walked back to the house. "We need not tell the things that we saw in the bedroom. The circumstances of the disappearance of Madame Tofte and Monsieur Van Brundt as they appear in the historical records, together with the advertisement crafty old Monsieur Jacob broadcast for the return of the poor Celeste, will be sufficient to establish their identity. As to the manner of their death—*eh bien*, does it not proclaim itself? But certainly."

He smiled grimly. "And that old hypocrite who lies so snugly in St. Chrysostom's churchyard—though it is late in overtaking him his sin has found him out at last. The jury of the coroner cannot help but name him as the murderer of those poor ones."

THE DINNER AT THE Berkeley-York had a huge success. *Consommé de tortue vert* with sherry, *buîtres François* with Chablis, *truite Margery* with Meursault, *coq au vin* with Nuits St. Georges and finally *crêpes Sussettes* with cointreau. As the waiter poured the coffee and Chartreuse I fully expected to hear de Grandin purr. "I suppose it's your theory that the stone and timbers of Tofte House held a certain psychic quality derived from association with the tragedy of Marise Tofte and Merthou Van Brundt, or that these unhappy lovers in the stress of their emotion passed on lasting thought-emanations to their inanimate surroundings?" I asked him. "I've heard you say that dreams or visions can be evoked in psychically sensitive persons when they're permitted to sleep in a room with a chip from a house where some atrocious crime has been committed, or—"

"I would not quite say that," he interrupted with a smile as he took a morsel of pink peppermint between his teeth and sipped a little black coffee. "This, I think, is what we might call a genuine ghost story, one where the earthbound spirits of the dead, denied the rites of Christian burial, sought constantly for help from the living.

"Consider, if you please: That Madame Marise and Monsieur Merthou were about to elope, accompanied by the slave girl Celeste, we have no doubt at all. Also, after seeing what a *bête bas* she had for husband one cannot greatly blame her, especially as she was still in love with her cousin who seems to have been a quiet, amiable young man. Yes.

"Next, we know the naughty old Monsieur Jacob laid a trap for them. He pretended to go on a long voyage, gave them barely time to renew love and make plans for eloping then *pouf!* swooped down on them like a cat on two luckless mice. The sad rest we know also.

"When he had chained them like brute beasts they died all miserably in the tomb, and their poor, starved bodies lay unburied. What then? Year after painful year they sought to tell their plight to those who came to live in that old house, but always they did fail. Those whom they begged for help were frightened and ran off.

"But finally these unhappy cousins who were thwarted in their love were visited by cousins fate had given to each other. And so it came about that we, with Monsieur Peteros' assistance, found their pitiful remains, had their killer branded as a murderer, and after proper rites laid them in consecrated ground. Yes certainly."

A grim expression settled on his lips. "That poor Celeste, the slave girl, she gave me some trouble," he confided.

"How's that?" asked Georgine Jaquay.

"The sexton of St. Chrysostom's told me the ground was reserved for the burial of white people exclusively. '*Monsieur*,' I say to him, 'this are no woman, but a skeleton I seek to have interred here, and the skeleton of a young girl of color as white as that of a Caucasian. Besides, if you persist in your pig-odious refusal I shall have to tweak your far from handsome nose.' *Tiens*, he let us bury her beside those whose death she had shared."

Georgine Jaquay gave a short neighing laugh, the sort of laugh a person gives to keep from weeping, but in a moment tears glinted on her lashes. "Do you suppose it was because they were cousins, and George and I are cousins, that they finally found peace through us?" she asked.

He raised his narrow shoulders in the sort of shrug no one but a Frenchman can achieve. "Who knows, *Madame?* It are entirely possible," he answered. Then with one of his quick elfin grins, "Or possibly it were because you and *Monsieur* your husband had the good sense to consult Jules de Grandin. He is a very clever fellow, that one."

Catspaws

W E HAD BEEN LATE leaving the Medical Society meeting and the cold rain of the early evening had changed to a wet, sleet-spurred snow, hag-ridden by a bitter wind, when we came out into the street. At the southern entrance of the Park my car gave a sharp lurch as a report like a bursting electric bulb was followed by an angry hiss and the sound of vicious slapping on the roadway. "*Grand Dieu des porc*," asked Jules de Grandin, "what in Satan's name was that?"

I swerved the car to the curb and shut off my engine. "If you don't know I haven't the heart to tell you," I answered.

He nodded sadly. "One might have guessed as much. And we have no spare tire, *naturellement?*"

"*Naturellement*," I echoed." Those things are pretty strictly rationed. We just came through a war, or hadn't you heard?"

"It is the fortune of the dog we have. What should we do?" Then before I could make a sarcastic rejoinder, "One comprehends. It is that we walk?"

"It is," I assured him as we dived into the Park's darkness, heads bent against the weather.

The gale clutched at our hats, whipped our sleeves, lashed at our coats; snow gathered on our soles in hard inverted pyramids that made the going doubly hard, now and then a laden tree bough shook its frigid burden down on us.

"*Feu noir du diable*," de Grandin cursed as a particularly vicious barrage of wet snow fell on him, "*quelle nuit sauvage!* If only —morbleu, another luckless pilgrim of the night! Observe her, Friend Trowbridge."

I followed the direction of his pointing stick and saw a woman—a girl, really—fur-swathed from neck to knees, bareheaded and shod with high-heeled sandals, judging by her awkward gait, struggling with frantic haste over the rough hummocks of frozen slush. As she drew almost abreast of us I realized she was half moaning, half sobbing to herself as she ran.

"*Pardonnez-moi, Mademoiselle*," de Grandin touched the brim of his black felt hat, "may we be of service? You seem in trouble—"

"Oh—" she gave a little scream of surprise at his voice. "Oh, yes; yes. You can help me. *You can!*" Her voice rose to a pitch half an octave below hysteria. "Please help me, I'm—"

"*Tiens*, you have the nervousness unnecessarily, *Mademoiselle*. We shall take great pleasure in assisting you. What is it?"

"I—" she gulped sobbingly for breath—"I want to get to a trolley, a taxi, any way to get home in a hurry, please. I—"

"And so do we, *ma petite*." he broke in, "but alas, there is no street car, bus or taxi to be had. If you will come with us to the other side of the Park—"

"Oh, no!" she declined fiercely. "Not that way. I'm afraid. Please don't take me back that way. He's there!"

"Eh?" he shot back sharply. "And who is 'he,' if one may ask?"

"That—that man!" she panted hoarsely, turning to resume her flight. "Oh, sir, please don't take me back. I'm terribly afraid!" Her teeth began to chatter with mingled chill and fright.

"Be quiet, *Mademoiselle!*" he ordered. "This will not do. No, not at all. What is your trouble, why do you fear to retrace your steps? Is there anybody there two able-bodied, healthy men cannot protect you from?"

"I—" the girl began again, then seemed to take a grip upon her nerves. "No, of course I'm not afraid while I'm with you. I'll go." She swung round, catching step between us.

"I was going home from a party at a friend's house," she began, speaking hurriedly. "My—my young man had to catch a midnight train for Philadelphia and couldn't take me, so I was waiting on the corner for a bus when a man drove by and asked me if I'd like a lift, and—like a fool!—I told him yes. I told him I was going to MacKenzie Boulevard, but he turned into the Park, and when we got down to the bottom of the hill he—oh, I was so terrified! I jumped out and began to run, and—and I'm afraid, sir; I'm terribly afraid of him!"

The light from one of the infrequent roadside lamps fell on de Grandin's face and showed a look of mingled wonder and amusement. "One understands, but only partly, *Mademoiselle*. You were a very foolish little person to accept a ride from a stranger. Had you never heard that she who rides must all too often pay her passage? That the young man—one assumes be was young—should have proved a wolf was not astonishing, but you evaded him. He did not harm you. Why, then, are you so distrait, so terrified? Is it that—"

Her frightened exclamation cut through his question as her hands clenched on our arms with fear-strengthened fingers. "See! There are the lights of his car. He's waiting for me—oh, I'm afraid!"

The Frenchman loosed her clutching fingers gently. "Look to her, Friend

Trowbridge. Me, I shall attend to this smasher." Striding to the car parked at the roadside he addressed its unseen occupant. "*Monsieur*, this young woman tells us you have affronted her. Me, I do not like that kind of business. Have the goodness to descend *Monsieur*, and I shall take great pleasure in tweaking your so odious nose."

No answer was forthcoming and he put a foot upon the running board. "I see you, miscreant. Silence will not give you protection. Descend and defend yourself—" He raised his head level with the face of the man at the car's steering wheel. There was a rustle of snow-covered sleeve against the casing of the car window, and: "*Mordieu*, Friend Trowbridge, come and see," he ordered as he fished into his pocket for his flashlight. "Look at him, if you please—and keep tight hold of the woman!"

I grasped the girl's wrist and leant forward as the beam of his light pierced the darkness and fell back a step, my fingers tightening on her arm involuntarily.

Bolt-upright at the wheel of the roadster was a heavy-set blond young man, bare-headed, and with the collar of his ulster open at the throat. His left hand wore a heavy glove, I noticed, while his right which rested on the wheel, was bare. His light-blue eyes, probably always prominent were widely opened in an idiotic, fixed stare and fairly popping from his face. His mouth was gaping with a hang-jawed, imbecile expression, the tongue protruding slightly, and the chin resting on the fabric of his turned-back collar.

"Oh," the girl beside me let out a shrill, squealing scream, "he's dead!"

"*Comme un maquereau*," de Grandin agreed laconically. "Nor did he die from overeating. Regard him, if you please, Friend Trowbridge." Placing his hand on the young man's sleek fair hair he moved it with a gentle rotary motion. The head beneath his hand followed its pressure as if it had been fastened to the shoulders by a loose-tensioned spring. "You agree with my diagnosis?" he asked.

"There certainly appears to be a fracture, probably at the third cervical vertebra," I agreed, "but whether he died as a result of—"

"Perfectly," he agreed. "The autopsy will disclose that." Then, to the girl: "Was this why you were so afraid to retrace your steps, *Mademoiselle*?"

"I didn't do it—truly I didn't!" she answered in a thick-tongued voice. "He was alive—alive and laughing, when I ran away. The last thing I heard as I ran was his voice calling, 'You won't get far in this storm, sister. Come back when it gets too cold for you.' Please, you must believe me!"

"H'm," he snapped his flashlight off and climbed down from the running board. "I do believe you did not do it, *Mademoiselle*. You have not strength enough. But this is a case for the coroner and the police. We must ask you to accompany us."

"The police?" her voice was little more than a whisper, but freighted with as much fear as a scream. "Oh—no! You mustn't have me arrested. I don't know anything about it—" She choked on her denial and slumped against me, then slid to the snow unconscious.

"The typically feminine escape," he murmured cynically. "Come, let us take her up, my friend. Here—so." He grasped my wrists in his hands, forming a chair for the unconscious girl. "We shall bear her easier this way. She is no great weight."

"That's why I think she told the truth when she said she didn't do it," I replied as we trudged toward the exit of the Park. "She's a frail little thing who could no more break a man's neck than I could kick a hippopotamus's ribs in."

"True," he agreed as he eased her dark head on his shoulder. "I think she tells the truth when she denies the actual killing, but someone killed him very thoroughly less than half an hour ago. It may well be that she knows more than she has told, and I propose to find out what she knows before we summon the police. If she is guilty she should suffer; if she is innocent it is our duty to protect her. *En tout cas* I propose to know the truth."

F RAIL OR NOT, THE girl's weight seemed to increase in geometrical progression as we trudged through the sticky snow. By the time we reached the Park gate I was thoroughly exhausted and the blinking lights of the taxi de Grandin hailed were like a lighthouse to a shipwrecked mariner to me.

We carried her into the house and laid her on the office couch, and while de Grandin poured a dose of aromatic ammonia in one glass and two ounces of sherry in another I unfastened her fur coat and laid it back. "I don't believe we have a right to do this," I began. "We've no official status, and no legal right to question her—good heavens!"

"*Comment?*" queried Jules de Grandin.

"Look here," I ordered. "Her chest—" Beginning just below the inner extremity of her left clavicle and extending downward almost to the upper rondure of her left breast were three paralleling vertical incisions, superficial, little more than scratches, and deeper at beginning than at termination. They were about a half-inch from each other and their lips were roughened, the skin turned back like soil at the lips of a plough-furrow. Blood had run down them and dripped upon the bodice of her low-cut party frock, and the bodice itself had been torn and ripped so that the black lace of the bandeau that confined her rather slender bosom was exposed.

"*Morbleu*," de Grandin bent across my shoulder to inspect the scratches, "*Chose étrange!* If you did not know otherwise what would you say caused those wounds, Friend Trowbridge?"

I shook my head bewilderedly. "It's past me. If they were smaller I'd say they'd been made by a cat—"

"*Tu parles, mon vieux*—you have said it. A cat and nothing else it was that made those scores in her so tender flesh, but what a cat! *Nom d'un pipe*, he must have been an ocelot at least, and yet—

"Ah, *Mademoiselle*, you waken?" he broke off as the girl's lids fluttered. "That is good. Drink this." He held the ammonia to her lips, and as she gulped it down regarded her with an unwinking stare. "You have not told us all, by any means," he added as he handed her the sherry. "The young man lifts you—*non*, how do you say him—picks you up? Yes. When he has driven you into the *parc* he becomes forward. Yes. You leap from the *moteur* in outraged modesty and flee into the storm. Yes; certainly. So much you tell us; that much we know. But—" his eyes hardened and his voice grew cold—"you have not told us how your *toilette* became torn, nor how you suffered those wounds on your thorax. No, not at all. Our eyes and our experience say those wounds were inflicted by a cat—a very large, great cat, perhaps a panther or a wildcat. Our reason rejects the hypothesis. Yet," he raised his narrow shoulders in a shrug, "*les voilà*—there we are!"

The girl shrank back as from a blow. "You wouldn't believe me!"

"*Tenez, Mademoiselle*, you would be astonished at my credulity. Tell us just what happened, if you please, and omit nothing."

She sipped the sherry gratefully, seeming to be marshalling her thoughts. "All I told you was the truth, the absolutely honest truth," she answered slowly, "only, I didn't tell you everything. I was afraid you'd say that I was lying, drunk or crazy; maybe all three. As I said, I was standing on the corner waiting for a bus when the young man drove past and asked if I'd like a lift. He seemed so nice and pleasant, and I was so cold and wretched, that I accepted his offer. Even when he turned into the Park I wasn't too much worried. I've been around and know how to take care of myself. But when he stopped the car and leaned toward me I became frightened. Terrified. Have you ever seen a human face become a beast's—"

"*Mordieu*, you say it—"

"No, I don't mean that his features actually changed form; it was their expression. His eyes seemed positively gleaming in the dark and his lips snarled back from his teeth like those of a dog or cat, and he made the most horrifying noises in his throat. Not quite a growl, and yet—oh, I can't describe it, but it terrified me so—"

"And then?" de Grandin prompted softly as she paused and swallowed nervously.

"I hadn't noticed, but he'd drawn the glove from his right hand, and when he stretched it toward me *it had become a panther's paw!*"

"*Cordieu*, how do you say, *Mademoiselle*—*la patte d'une panthère?*"

"I mean just what I say, sir. Literally. It was black and furry, with great curving claws, and he swung it at me with a sort of dreadful playfulness—like a cat that torments a mouse with mock gentleness, you know. Each time he moved it, it came nearer, and suddenly I felt the claws rip through my dress, and in another moment I felt a quick pain in my chest. Then I seemed to come awake all of a sudden—I'd been positively paralyzed with fear—and jumped out of the car. Just like I told you in the Park, he didn't try to chase me, just sat there laughing and told me I'd not get far in the storm. Then I met you, and when we went back he was—"

Again she paused, and de Grandin supplied the ending. "Entirely dead, *parbleu*, with his neck most neatly broken."

"Yes, sir. You do believe me, don't you?" Her voice was piteous, but the big dark eyes she raised to his were even more so.

He tweaked the ends of his small wheat-blond mustache. "Perhaps I am a fool, *Mademoiselle*, but I believe you. However, it are more than barely possible the police would not share my *naïveté*. Accordingly, we shall say nothing to them of your part in this unfortunate affair. But since they must be apprised of the killing, I shall tend your hurts while Dr. Trowbridge calls them to impart the information." He handed me a slip of paper with a number scribbled on it. "That is the number of the dead man's car, Friend Trowbridge. Be kind enough to ask the good Costello to compare it with the license lists and tell us who the owner was and where he resided."

"Costello speakin'," came the well-known heavy voice when I had put my call through to headquarters. "That you, Dr. Trowbridge, sor? I wuz jist about to ring your house. What's cookin'?"

"I'm not quite certain," I replied. "Dr. de Grandin and I just ran across what seems to be a murder in Soldiers' Park—"

"Howly jumpin' Jehoshaphat, another? It's nuts I'm goin', sor; completely nuts, as th' felley says. That's the fourth one tonight, an' I'm gittin' so I dassen't pick th' tellyphone up for fear they'll tell me there's another. How'd your man git bumped off?"

"I'm not quite sure, but it looks like a broken neck—"

"It *looks* like it?" he roared. "Bedad, ye know right well 'tis nothin' else, sor! All their necks wuz broke. Everybody's neck is broke. I wish to Howly Patrick that me own wuz broke so's I didn't need to hear about these blokes wid broken necks, so I do! What'd ye say his number wuz? Thank ye. I'll be afther checkin' it wid th' files, an' be wid ye in ten minutes, more or less. Meantime I'll send a prowl car to pick up the auto an' th' body in th' Park."

I heard the surgery door close softly as I put the telephone down, and in a moment Jules de Grandin came into the office. "I painted her injuries with mercurochrome," he informed me. "They were superficial and showed no sign of sepsis, but I am puzzled. Yes, of course."

"Why 'of course'?" I demanded.

"Because they bore every evidence of large cat's claw-marks. Their edges were irregular, owing to the fact the skin had been forced back as the claws ripped through it, but a microscopic examination failed to disclose any foreign particles. This should not be. As you know, claws of animals, especially those of the cat family, are markedly concave on their under sides, and since the beast does not retract them completely when he walks a certain amount of foreign matter collects in the grooves. That is why a scratch-wound from a lion or leopard, or even a domestic pussy-cat, is always more or less septic. Hers were not. My friend, it was a most peculiar cat that gave her those scratches."

"Peculiar? I should say it was," I agreed. "I heard her tell you that his hand had changed into a panther's paw. You don't believe that gamine, do you? He probably made several passes at her with his bare hand, tore her dress and scratched her accidentally—"

"*Non*, that he did not, my friend. I did not begin to practice medicine last week, or even week before. I am too familiar with the marks of human nails to he mistaken. I do not say his hand turned to a paw; it is too early yet to affirm anything, but this I know. Those scratches on her thorax were not made by human nails. Moreover—"

"Where is she now?" I interrupted.

"Upon her homeward way, one hopes. I let her from the surgery door and went with her to the curb, where I stopped a taxi and put her into it—"

"But Costello will want to question her—"

"You did not tell him she was here?"

"No, but—"

"*Très bon*. That is good; that is entirely excellent. We shall not have her involved in the scandal. If it should transpire that we need her I know where to find her. Yes. I made her give me her address and verified it in the 'phone book before I released her. Meanwhile, what the good Costello does not know will do no harm to either him or Mademoiselle Upchurch. And so—"

The furious ringing of the front doorbell cut him short and in a minute Detective Lieutenant Costello stamped in, snow glinting on his overcoat and hat, and a most unhappy expression on his broad and usually good-natured face. "Good evenin', sors," he greeted as he hung his outside garments on the hall tree. "So it's another one o' those here broken neck murthers ye'd be afther tellin' me about?"

"It is, indeed, my old one," answered Jules de Grandin with a grin. "You have the name and address of the one we found all killed to death in the Park?"

"Here 'tis, sor. John Percy Singletary, 1652 Atwater Drive, an'—"

"One moment, if you please," de Grandin hurried to the library and came back with a copy of *Who's Who*. "Ah, here is his *dossier*: 'Singletary, John Percy. Born Fairfield County, Massachusetts, July 16, 1917. Son George Angus and

Martha Perry. Educated private schools and Harvard College; moved to Harrisonville, N.J., 1937; served in U. S. Army, CIB Theatre, 1943-44. Honorably discharged, CDD, 1945. Clubs, Lotus, Plumb Blossom, Explorers. Address, 1652 Atwater Drive, Harrisonville, N.J.' One sees, but dimly."

"What is it one sees, sor, dim or clear? From what ye've read I'd say this felley wuz one o' them rich willie-bhoys wid a lot more money than brains an' nothin' much to do but raise hell. His record shows he wuz run in a dozen times for speedin'. Why they didn't take his license up is more'n I can understand. I'm not weepin' any salty tears about his goin'. It's a dam' good riddance, if ye asks me, but—who kilt him? Who the' hell kilt him, an' why?"

De Grandin motioned toward the siphon and decanter. "Pour yourself a drink, my old and rare. The world will look much brighter when you have absorbed it. Meanwhile give me the names of those other three young men who were so unfortunate as to have their necks broken. Thank you," as Costello handed him the memorandum, "now, let us see—" He ruffled through the *Who's Who*, and, "*Dieu des porcs de Dieu des porcs de Dieu des cochons!*" he swore as he closed the book. *'Pas possible?"*

"What's that, sor?"

"The *dossiers* of these so unfortunate young men, they are almost identical. The young Monsieur Singletary, whom we found defunct in the Park, Messieurs George William Cherry, Francis Agnew Marlow and Jonathan Smith Goforth were all about the same age and went to the same schools. Most likely they were classmates. Three of them served in the United States Army, one with the British, but all in the same theatre of operations, China-Burma-India, and at the same time. The manner of their several deaths was identical, the time almost the same. *Très bon*. What does it mean?"

"O.K., sor. I'll bite—hard. What does it mean?"

The little Frenchman shrugged. "*Hélas*, I do not know. But there is more— much more—than meets the casual glance in this identity. Me, I shall think upon the matter, I shall make appropriate investigations. Already there begins to be a seeming pattern in the case. Consider, if you please. What do we know of them?" He leveled a forefinger like a pistol at Costello: "Were they killed because they were wealthy? Possibly, but not probably. Because they went to Harvard College? I have seen alumni of that institution I could gladly slay, but in this instance I doubt their *alma mater* has much bearing on the time and manner of their deaths. It might be possible they were killed because of military service, but that, I think, is merely incidental. *Très bon*. It would appear that there is still another factor. What is it?"

"I know th' answer to that one, sor. It's who kilt 'em, an' why?"

"It is, indeed, my friend. Tell me of their deaths if you will be so kind."

Costello checked the mortuary items off on thick fingers. "Young Cherry wuz found dead in th' front yard o' his house. He'd been out to a party an' come home 'bout ten o'clock. Logan, th' policeman on th' beat, seen 'im layin' in th' yard an' thought he wuz out cold until he took a closer look. Marlow lives at th' Lotus Club, to which, as ye wuz afther sayin', all of 'em belongs. He wuz found dead in bed when one o' his friends called for him shortly afther eight o'clock tonight. Goforth wuz kilt—leastwise he wuz found dead—in th' gents' wash-room o' th' Acme Theatre. All of 'em has broken necks, an' there's no marks on any of 'em. No finger bruises nor traces of a garrote. They hadn't got no business to be dead accordin' to th' book, but they're all dead as mutton, just th' same."

The Frenchman nodded. "Who was the friend who found young Monsieur Marlow murdered in his bed?"

"Felley be th' name o' Ambergrast. Lives on th' same floor o' th' clubhouse. Went to call 'im to go out to some brawl in New York, an' found him dead as yesterday's newspaper."

"One sees. Let us go all quickly and consult this Monsieur Ambergrast. It may be he can tell us something. It may be he, too, is among the list of those elected to have broken necks. Yes. Certainly."

WILFRED BAILEY AMBERGRAST, JR., seemed typical of his class. A rather pallid young person, not necessarily a vicious sort, but obviously the much-pampered son of a rich father. He was, as Jules de Grandin later said, "one of those persons of whom a false impression may be produced if you attempt to describe him at all."

He was plainly unnerved by his friend's death and not inclined to talk. "I can't imagine who killed Tubby, or why," he told us, staring moodily into his highball glass. "All I know I've told the police already. When I went to call him about eight o'clock this evening I found him lying half in, half out of bed." He paused, took a long swallow from his glass and finished, "He was dead. His mouth was open and his eyes staring—God, it was awful!"

"Monsieur," de Grandin looked at him with his unwinking cat-stare, "there would not be a possible connection between your friends' deaths and your mili-tary service—in India or Burma, by example?"

"Eh?"

"Précisément. One understands you were attached to the Air Corps, not as flyers, but as meteorologists. In such employment you had leisure to visit certain little-known and unfrequented places, to mingle with those better left alone—"

Young Ambergrast looked up quickly. "How'd you guess it?" he demanded.

"I do not guess, Monsieur. I am Jules de Grandin. My business is to know things, especially things which I am not supposed to know. Bien. Now, where was it you made the acquaintance of—" he paused with lifted brows, inviting the young man to complete the sentence.

The boy nodded sulkily. "Since you know so much already you might as well get filled in on the rest. Tubby Goforth, Bill Cherry and Jack Singletary were stationed with me near Gontur. Frank Marlow was with the British—his father was a Canadian—but stationed near enough to us so we could get together when we had a few days' leave. One day Jack told us there was something stirring at Stuartpuram. Sort o' camp meetin' of the Criminal Tribes who make their head-quarters there. We took a *garry* over and got there after dark. The natives were marchin' round and round a big mud-hut they called a temple, wavin' torches and singin' *mantras* to Bogiri, which is one of the avatars of Kali. While we were watchin' the procession an old goof came siddlin' up to us, and offered to sneak us into the temple for a rupee apiece. We took him up and he led us through a back way to a little room just back of a big mud image of the goddess.

"I don't know just what we'd expected to see, but what we saw was disap-pointing. We'd been certain there'd be women there—*nautchnis* and that sort o' thing; maybe some such goin's-on as are carved on the walls of the Black Pagoda at Kanarak. Instead they were all men, and a lousy lot of crow-bait, too. One of 'em who seemed to be some sort of priest got up and harangued the meetin' in Hindustani, which we couldn't understand, of course, and presently he passed out what looked like a lot o' black fur mittens to the congregation. After that the meetin' broke up and we were just about to leave when old Whiskers who had passed us into the temple showed up again. His English wasn't any too good, but finally we understood he was offerin' to sell us mittens like those we'd seen dis-tributed. 'What good are they?' Jack wanted to know, and the old sinner laughed until we thought he'd have a spell of asthma. 'You like make yum-yum love to brown gal?' he asked, and when Jack nodded he laughed even more wheezily. 'You wear theese glove an' show heem to brown gal, you not have trouble makin' yum-yum,' he promised. 'You geeve gal little scratch with heem and all is like you want.' So each of us bought a mitten for three rupees.

"When we examined 'em in the light we saw they were made of some sort of black fur and fitted with three claws made of bent horseshoe nails. How they'd operate as talismans in love-makin' we could not imagine, but next evenin' Tubby tried it, and it worked. He'd had a case on a Parsee girl for some time, but she'd stood him off. They're the aristocrats of India, those Parsees. Stand-offish as the devil. Most of 'em are rich and you can't buy or bribe 'em, and those who haven't money have enough pride to make up for it. So Tubby'd got just nowhere with the lady till the evenin' after we'd bought the mittens. He slipped the glove on his right hand and growled at her and scratched her lightly on the arm with it. It worked like magic, he told us. She was meek as Moses all evenin', and didn't seem to have a single 'No' in her vocabulary."

The little Frenchman nodded. "You have an explanation for this so strange phenomenon, *Monsieur?*"

"Well, sort of. In a few days we heard rumors of people—all sorts, men, women and children—bein' found in out of the way places and sometimes on the highway, all clawed up as if they'd been attacked by leopards. It had the police buffaloed, for nothing like it had been known before. The way we figured it was that the Crims had taken to these steel-clawed cat's-paws in place of their usual stranglin' towel, and had the population terrified, so when the girls saw our gloves and felt the scrape of the claws they figured we were members of the Criminal Tribes—you never know who is and who isn't mixed up with them, you know. They've got more disguises than Lon Chaney ever had; so the girls played safe by not antagonizin' us."

"One sees. And the estimable old scoundrel who sold you these cat's-paws?"

"Two days later he turned up strangled to death at the outskirts of his village. We assumed someone heard that he'd shown signs of sudden wealth—you know, he'd taken sixteen rupees from us, and that's a fortune to the average Indian peasant—and he'd been killed for it. I never heard of those birds turnin' on each other, though. Funny, ain't it?"

"Very funny. Very funny, indeed, *Monsieur*. But I doubt that the old gentleman or your four friends found much humor in the situation."

"My four friends? D'ye mean that Jack and Frank—"

"Precisely, *Monsieur*. Of those who visited the temple that night and bought the cat's-paws from the old man, only you survive."

"But, good Lord, man; that means that maybe they're on my trail, too!"

"Unless I am much more mistaken than I think, you have stated the equation most exactly, *Monsieur*. Now, will you be good enough to show us Monsieur Marlow's room?"

"Humph," Costello growled as we entered the small neat bedroom. "It's jist like I wuz afther tellin' ye, sor. Th' felley as did this must ha' been a bird or sumpin'." He flung the window up and pointed. "We're up two flights o' stairs, a good eighteen foot from th' ground. Anybody who went out that winder would ha' had to have a parryshoot or wings or sumpin', an' as for gittin' in—how'd he make it? There's no drain pipe near th' winder for him to climb, an he couldn't ha' stood a ladder up against th' wall. Ye don't take ladders through th' streets widout attractin' attention, ye know. O' course, he might ha' lowered hisself from th' roof wid a rope, but how'd he git up there to do it? Th' lobby downstairs is full o' flunkies, an' guests an' members are passin' back an' forth all th' time. Since there's no adjoinin' buildin' he couldn't ha' com across th' roofs—"

"It is, as you have said, a mystery, my friend," de Grandin agreed, "but we are presently more concerned with who did these so strange murders than how he managed ingress to or egress from this room. It might be that—*mordieu*, I have the thought, I have the inspiration, me!"

"Sure, have ye, now, sor?" asked Costello mildly. "Maybe, jist for old times' sake ye'd be afther lettin' us in on it?"

"Assuredly, *mon ami, pourquoi pas?* Let us consult our friend Ram Chitra Das. He can tell us more in half an hour than we can guess in twenty-four. Await me here. I rush, I fly to telephone him."

Five minutes later he returned and beckoned to us. "We are in luck, *mes amis* Monsieur and Madame Das have just returned from the opera and not yet gone to bed. They will wait up for us. Come let us hasten to them. Meanwhile," he took Costello by the arm, led him a little way apart and whispered to him earnestly.

"O.K., sor," I heard the detective agree. "I'll do it, but it's most irreg'lar. They'll spring him before daylight."

"That will be time enough," de Grandin answered. "Go telephone headquarters and make haste; we have little time to lose."

"What was all the whispering about?" I asked as we set out for New York. "What would be so irregular, and whom will they 'spring'?"

"The young Monsieur Ambergrast," de Grandin answered. "They get into locked rooms whose windows are entirely inaccessible, those ones. *Ha*, but I do not think that they can penetrate a jail. No, even they would find that difficult. So, since we cannot take the young man with us and dare not leave him in his room, we shall have him arrested as a material witness and lodge him safely in the *bastille* for a few hours. Of course he will obtain bail, but in the meantime we shall not have him on our conscience. No. Certainly. Quite not."

"HULLO, THERE, GLAD TO see you!" Ram Chitra Das greeted as we trooped up the stairs to his second story walkup apartment in East Eighty-Sixth Street. "How are you, Dr. Trowbridge? Glad to meet you, Lieutenant Costello." He shook hands cordially and ushered us into a room which might have served as setting for a more than usually elaborate presentation of the Arabian Nights. The walls were eggshell white and hung with rugs as gorgeous as the colors of a hashish eater's dreams, across the floor of polished yellow pine were strewn the pelts of leopards, mountain wolves with platinum-hued fur, and, by the couch against the farther wall a tiger skin of vivid ebony and gold was laid. The place was redolent with a mixture of exotic scents, the fragrance of flowers, applewood burning in the fireplace and cigarette smoke.

In his dinner clothes and spotless linen our host looked anything but Oriental. He might have been a Spaniard or Italian with his sleek black hair, alert dark eyes and small, regular features, and his accent was decidedly reminiscent of Oxford.

The woman who rose from the couch and came forward to greet us was positively breath-taking in her loveliness. Tall, slender, rather flat-chested, she moved with a grace that seemed more a flowing than a walk, as if she had been wafted by an unfelt, silent breeze. Her skin was an incredibly beautiful shade of pale gold, smooth and iridescent, her hair, demurely parted in the middle and gathered in a great loose knot at the nape of her neck, was a dull black cloud. But it was the strange, exotic molding of her features that held our gaze. Her high forehead continued downward to her nose without the faintest indication of a curve—the blood of Alexander's Grecian conquerors of India must have flowed in her veins—and beneath thin, highly arched brows her eyes were pools of deep moss-agate green. Her mouth was wide, her lips thin lines of scarlet. She wore an evening dress of dull white silk cut with classic Greek simplicity and girdled at the waist with a cord of silver. About her right arm just above the elbow was a wide bracelet of platinum set with emerald and rubies, and in her ears were emerald studs that picked up and accentuated the green of her eyes. Her whole appearance was one of superb, lithe grace.

"My dear," our host bowed formally as he presented us in turn, "Dr. de Grandin, Dr. Trowbridge, Lieutenant Costello. Gentlemen, my wife, Nairini, who but for a shockingly poor choice of husbands might now be Maharanee of Khandawah."

"*Tiens, Madame,*" de Grandin murmured, as he raised her slim jeweled fingers to his lips, "in India or Iceland, Nepal or New York, you would be nothing less than queen!"

Her great eyes dwelt on him in green abstraction for a moment, then a smile came into them, and teeth like pearls showed between scarlet lips: I never saw a woman who did not smile at Jules de Grandin. "*Merci, Monsieur,*" she murmured in a voice so deeply musical that it reminded me of the cooing of doves, "*vous me faites honneur!*"

"And now," Ram Chitra Das demanded as we seated ourselves, "what seems to be the matter? From your rather hurried message I gathered that you suspect Indian skullduggery of some sort?"

"Indeed, my friend, you have entirely right," de Grandin nodded solemnly. "Consider what we know and what we suspect, then see if you can add the keyword to our enigma."

The Indian made no comment as de Grandin outlined our problem, then, as the small Frenchman halted: "I think that your suspicions are well founded. These little stinkers stumbled onto something they had no business gettin' mixed up with, and the penalty they've been called upon to pay might have been foreseen by anybody who knows India and the Indians.

"You know, I suppose, that the Criminal Tribes of India number almost ten million members. They aren't just ordinary thieves and murderers and pickpockets; they're literally born criminals, just as you Americans are born Protestants or Catholics or Democrats or Republicans. Every child among them is hereditarily a criminal and is as such in the records of the Indian police. Stealin', murderin' and other criminal activity is as much a religious duty with them as giving alms to the poor is to the Jew, Christian or Moslem, and to fail in a career of crime is to lose caste.

"Loss of caste is serious to a Hindu. Something like excommunication to a medieval Christian—only more so. Spiritually it dooms him to countless reincarnations through unnumbered ages; physically it has drawbacks, too. If I were to return to my uncle's palace in Nepal I'd find myself a real nonentity. No servant would wait on me, no tradesman would sell me merchandise, no one but scavengers and street sweepers would dare speak to me. As for Nairini, who ran away from her princely father to marry a casteless vagabond, if she went back they'd probably sew her up in a sack and dump her in the most convenient river.

"So much for that. You know, of course, that Hindu workmen have gone nearly everywhere—China, the Dutch Indies, and, of course, the British colonies in Africa. It appears some of these 'Crims,' as they are familiarly but not affectionately known to the Indian police, gravitated to Sierra Leone some time ago, and picked up a few tricks from the Leopard Men of the Protectorate and adjacent Liberia. Some of them went back to Mother India and introduced the innovation of the 'cat's-paw'—a fur glove studded with steel claws—to their contemporaries. I heard that there had been an outbreak of killin's in which the victims had apparently been mauled by leopards in the Madras Presidency a couple of years ago. That seems to be where these young men fit in. Unquestionably they visited a gatherin' of the Criminal Tribesmen when 'cat's-paws' were bein' distributed, and the old scoundrel who conducted them decided to turn a dishonest rupee by sellin' them the devilish paraphernalia.

"You remember what happened to him. Young Ambergrast thought it odd that Criminal Tribesmen should have turned on one of their fellows. It was only to have been expected. The fellow had, to all intents sold a lodge secret, and secret societies resent that sort of thing, some more vigorously than others. It seems that this particular renegade didn't live long to enjoy his perfidious gains.

"The *roomal*—the Thugs' stranglin' towel, you know—did for him, but there remained the matter of the young outlanders to be settled. By buyin' these 'cat's-paws' and employin' them not for legitimate crimes, but to terrorize unwillin' native girls into compliance, these young white men had put an affront on the whole criminal clan. They'd made the Crims 'lose face.' Loss of face is almost as bad as loss of caste in the East, and something drastic had to be done about it. Accordingly—" He raised his hands as if he looped a cord, then drew them together with a snapping motion. "*Exeunt omnes*, as Shakespearian stage directions say."

"Then ye think, sor," Costello began, but Das forestalled him.

"I'm almost sure of it, Lieutenant. The man or men entrusted with the job of giving these youngsters the happy dispatch is probably some member of the Criminal Tribes who has lost caste, and must regain it by their murder. He or they will stop at nothing, and if there are several of them killing, some will not deter the others, for they believe implicitly that the surest, quickest route to Paradise is to be killed while in the commission of a crime, just as they lose caste by being caught."

"An' have ye anny idee how th' thafe o' th' wor-rld gained entrance to th' pore young felley's room, sir? It looked to me as if 'twould take a bir-rd to break into it, or git out; but as ye say, they are a clever lot and may know some tricks we ain't hep to."

"I have a very definite idea, Lieutenant," Ram Chitra Das replied. "Where's Ambergrast at present?"

"In jail, an' safe, we hope."

"He's safer there than anywhere, but if we want to catch our birds we'll have to bait our trap. D'ye think he's managed to raise bail by this time?"

"I dunno, sor, but I'll tellyphone if ye'd like."

"That might be a good idea. Tell them to detain him on any sort of pretext till they hear from you, then send him back to his rooms in a squad car."

R AM CHITRA DAS, DE Grandin and I crouched in an angle of the wall that ran along the alley back of the Lotus Club. The numbing cold gnawed at our bones like a starved dog, and as the sky began to lighten faintly in the east a sharp wind lent an extra sting to the air. "*Mille douleurs*," the little Frenchman murmured miserably, "one little hour more of this and Jules de Grandin is a stiffening corpse, *pardieu!*"

"Quiet, old thing!" Ram Chitra Das whispered. "We've invested so much time and discomfort already, it would be a shame to let him slip past us now. He's almost sure to come. Those johnnies waste no time and nearly always work in darkness. D'ye think Costello's on the job inside?"

"I left him and a plainclothes man in the room next to Ambergrast's," I answered. "They've left their door on a crack, and nothing bigger than a mouse can creep past them. If there's a squeak from Ambergrast's room they'll—"

"If the fellow we're expectin' gets into that room they'll hear no squeak," Ram Chitra Das broke in grimly. "Those Bagrees can clip an earring from a sleeping woman's head and never make her miss a snore, and when it comes to usin' the *roomal*—they can kill a man as quickly as a bullet, almost, and with no more noise than a fly walking on the ceiling. I've seen some of their work, and—by George, I think we're havin' company!"

Stepping noiselessly and sure-footedly as a cat on the frozen slush, a man was coming toward us. He was an undersized, emaciated fellow bundled in an overcoat much too large for him, and with a derby hat at least three sizes too big thrust incongruously down on his head. As nearly as I could determine he was dark-skinned, but I was certain that he was no Negro. For a moment he paused like a hound at fault, scanning the windows in the second story of the clubhouse, then walked unerringly to a spot beneath the partly opened window of the room where Ambergrast slept.

"Watch this," Ram Chitra Das commanded in an almost soundless whisper. "If it's what I think it'll be, it's goin' to be good."

The man came to a halt, drew a small flask from his pocket and uncorked it, letting some of its contents spill on the ground. "That's the libation," Das murmured. "They always pour a little out to Bhowanee as an offerin' before they drink the sacred *mhowa* as a part of ceremonial murder."

The fellow drained the contents of the flask and put the empty bottle in his pocket then, unconcernedly as a lad about to go swimming, stripped off his overcoat, his sweater, trousers and shoes, and stood in the raw winter wind unclothed save for a loin-cloth and his absurd derby. This was last of all to come off, and we saw he wore a close-wrapped turban of soiled white cloth under it.

"*Mordieu*, he mortifies the flesh, that one," de Grandin whispered, but checked on a sharp breath as the dark-skinned man unwound a length of rope from his waist, coiled it on the frozen snow at his feet and bent above it, making swift, cryptic passes with his hands.

I knew I did not see it—yet there it was. Slowly, like a snake that wakes from torpor, the rope seemed to come alive. Its end stirred, twitched, rose a few inches, fell back to the ground, then reared once more, this time remaining up. Then inch by stealthy inch it rose, seeming to feel its way cautiously, until it stood as straight and stiff as a pole, one end upon the frozen ground the other less than a foot from Ambergrast's window.

"*Grand Dieu des porcs*, it cannot be!" de Grandin whispered incredulously. "Me, I have heard of that rope trick a thousand times, but—"

"Seein' is believin', old chap," Ram Chitra Das cut in with a low chuckle. "You've heard old, seasoned travelers say the rope trick is a fake and can't really be done—but there it is, for you to make a note of in your diary."

The little dark man had begun to climb the upright rope. Agilely as a monkey he went up hand over hand, and it seemed to me his toes were as prehensile as a monkey's too, for instead of trying to twist his ankles in the cord to brace himself he grasped it with his feet.

He was opposite the partly opened window and was loosening the towel bound about his waist above the loin-cloth when Das stepped quickly forward, both hands raised and shouting, "*Darwaza bundo!*" in a strident voice.

The effect was electrical. The rope collapsed like a punctured balloon, and the man grasping it was hurled to the ice-covered bricks with crushing force. Half-way between the window and the ground he twisted in the air, both arms outspread, hands clutching futilely at nothingness, mouth squared in helpless, hopeless terror, turned end over end and struck the icy pavement shoulders first.

"Grab him!" Ram Chitra Das shouted as he leaped upon the fallen body, snatched the towel from the man's hand and began to knot it into a fetter. "Don't bother," he added disgustedly, as he rose and dusted snow from his knees. "He's out cold as yesterday's kipper."

"AND THAT IS MOST indubitably that," Ram Chitra Das informed us as we faced each other over coffee and sandwiches in the study. "I feared there might be several of 'em, but Sookdee Singh—our little Bagree playmate—tells me he did all those killin's by his naughty little self. Quite an enterprisin' young chap, I'd say."

"Can you put credence in his word?" de Grandin asked.

"Ordinarily, no. This time, yes. A Bagree thinks no more of lyin' than he does of breathin', but when he dips his hand in blood and says, 'May Bhowanee's wrath consume me utterly if I tell not the truth,' you can believe him. I borrowed a sponge from the hospital operatin' room and made the beggar smear his finger in the blood and swear to tell the truth before I'd make him any promises."

"But what could ye promise him, sor?" Costello demanded. "We've got dead wood on 'im. He'll take th' rap for murther, sure as shootin'—"

"I'm afraid not, Lieutenant. He was pretty badly smashed up in his fall, a fractured rib went through his lung, and the doctor at the hospital tells me he can't last the day. That gave me my hold on him."

"I don't see how—" Costello began, but the Indian continued with a smile.

"Those Criminal Tribesmen are devout Hindus, although the ethics of their devotion may be open to question. However, they share one thing with their more honest co-religionists. They feel it a disgrace to be buried, cremation bein' the only honorable method of disposin' of their bodies. If their ashes are committed to the Ganges they are just that much nearer heaven—somethin' like a Christian's bein' buried in consecrated ground, you know.

"That's where I got my leverage. I promised him that if he told the truth and the whole truth—if he 'came clean', I believe is the way you Americans would put it—I'd see his body was cremated and his ashes shipped to India to be thrown in the Ganges. I couldn't have offered him any greater inducement."

"If it's not a trade secret, would you mind telling me what it was you shouted to make that rope collapse?" I asked.

"Not at all. I said 'Darwaza bundo!' which means merely 'Shut the door!' in Hindustani. It didn't really matter what I said you know. In order to perform his tricks an adept has to concentrate his whole mind on them, and the slightest deviation—even for a second—breaks the charm. The shock of hearing himself suddenly addressed in his native tongue was so great that it diverted his attention. Only for a split-second, of course, but that was enough. Once the rope went soft, there was nothin' he could do about it till he had it coiled upon the ground once more and started his charm from the beginnin'."

"*Mon brave!*" de Grandin exclaimed delightedly. "My old and peerless one, *mon homme sensé. Parbleu,* I damn think next to Jules de Grandin you are the cleverest man alive! Come, let us drink to that!"

Lottë

"**L**ADIES AND GENTLEMEN," THE orchestra leader stepped to the edge of his dais, "Pablo and Francesca." On the heels of his announcement brass and woodwinds sounded a long chord, the hot erotic rhythm of a rumba started and a young man and woman glided out upon the dance floor of the Gold Room.

Jules de Grandin nibbled at a morsel of pink peppermint, washed it down with a sip of black coffee and wiped his lips with a quick brushing motion, taking care not to disturb a blond hair of his trimly-waxed mustache. "Come, Friend Trowbridge, if you are finished let us call for *l'addition* and depart," he suggested. "Me, I have dined most excellently well, but this—" he glanced at the dancers circling on the polished oak—"*cela m'ennuie*. I am bored, me."

I nodded sympathetically. When one is on the shadowed side of fifty and hasn't danced in almost thirty years the tortions of a dance team leave him rather cold. Besides, the curtain at the Cartaret would rise in twenty minutes and a decent respect for the comfort of others demanded we be in our seats when the house lights lowered. "Right with you," I agreed. "Soon as we can get that waiter's eye—"

"*Grand Dieu des petits porcs verts!*" his exclamation slashed through my words. Some small bright object, a prism from the chandelier above the dance floor, I thought, had flashed down like a minuscule meteor and crashed like a missile against the sleekly pomaded hair of the male dancer.

With me at his heels the small Frenchman wove his way between the tables and slipped across the polished oak boards of the dance floor. The blow had been surprisingly heavy for so small a projectile, and the young man was unconscious when we reached him. "Do not make yourself uneasy, *Mademoiselle*," de Grandin whispered to his distrait partner. "We are physicians. We shall give him the assistance. He cannot be hurt badly—

"*Hola, mon brave*," he sank to his knees beside the young man. "You are making the recovery, no? Ah, that is good. That is very good, indeed!" as the youngster's lids fluttered up and he attempted to rise. "*Non, restez tranquille*, you will be completely well in one small moment." As a waiter passed he raised a finger. "A little brandy, if you please, and some ice water."

"Lottë," the patient whispered, then, recovering his poise, "What happened? Did I fall—"

"You did, indeed, *Monsieur*," de Grandin assured as he held the pony of cognac to the young man's lips, then dipped the napkin in the bowl of ice water and laid the cold compress on the knot already forming over the boy's right temporal bone. "So, rest easily a moment." Methodically he took the patient's pulse, pursed his lips, then nodded shortly. "No bones are broken, nor is the skin ruptured. I would not suggest that you dance again tonight, but if you continue to improve—"

Mr. Melton, the hotel manager, had elbowed his way through the circling crowd. "What happened?" he demanded. "Was he drunk? I won't have drinkin' among the help on duty or off. Get your traps packed and get out!" he ordered the young dancer curtly.

"*Monsieur*, I should not be too hasty were I in your most undoubtlessly tight shoes," de Grandin advised coldly. "The young man was stricken by a pendant falling from the chandelier. Dr. Trowbridge and I both saw it, and if he should decide to take legal action—"

"Oh, there won't be any trouble," Melton interrupted hastily. "Everything will be all right. Feel up to finishing the act, Paul?"

"Yeh, I—I guess so," answered the young man as he got to his feet a little unsteadily, shook his head like a fighter who has taken a heavy punch, and smiled reassuringly at his partner.

"*Très bien*," de Grandin nodded. "I do not think that you have received much hurt, *Monsieur*, but if you are not well entirely in the morning you should see a physician. If—" he glanced coldly at Melton—"there should be complications with the hotel, do not hesitate to call on me for testimony."

He handed a card to the young man, bowed formally to the girl and led the way from the dining room.

"Friend Trowbridge, it is that I am puzzled," he confided as we drove toward the theatre.

"How's that?" I answered.

"That young man, Monsieur Pablo. You did observe his injury, *n'est-ce-pas?*"

"Of course, it was a simple bruise of the right temporal region with moderate ecchymosis. Nothing serious, I'd say, though it was surprising that so light an object as a pendant from the chandelier could have caused so much injury. I've seen bruises like that made by clubs or blackjacks—"

"*Précisément*. You have right there, my friend. But did you see him take his hurt?"

"Now that you mention it, no. I saw the missile hurtle through the air and saw him stagger and fall, but—"

"*Exactement*. But did you note the relative positions of Monsieur Pablo and the chandelier at the time?"

"No–o—"

"*Ah-ha!* That is enigma Number One. He was not under the fixture when he was struck. No. He was fifteen—possibly twenty—feet from it. The broken prism had to travel obliquely a distance of at least ten feet in order to strike him. What do you make from that, *hein?* Is it not against the laws of gravity?"

"You're sure?"

"But of course. Did not I see it?"

"It couldn't have been a strong draft—"

"*Mais non*. A wind sufficient to have hurled a bit of glass that distance, and with force enough to strike a man unconscious, would have to be of hurricane velocity."

"Ye-es. I suppose so."

"Indubitably. Moreover, when the so unfortunate young man revived from his swoon, what did he say?"

"I'm not sure, but it sounded like a woman's name—Lottë."

"You have entirely right, my old. And did it not seem to you he was frightened?"

"Well, now you speak of it, it did. But—"

"No buts, if you will be so kind. Now for enigma Number Two: The young man was unconscious from a sudden violent blow, *n'est-ce-pas?* That means he had sustained a shock, which as you know amounts to relaxation or abolition of the controlling influence the nervous system exercises over vital organic functions. Yes. Pulsation should have been slowed down, and respiration much retarded. But were they? Not at all, by damn it. *Au contraire*, they were very much accelerated. He was frightened, very badly frightened, that one."

"You may be right," I agreed as I jockeyed the car into the last remaining parking space before the theatre,—but it seems to me you're making an Alp out of an anthill."

"**N**ON," HE MUTTERED MOODILY as we paused in the kitchen for a goodnight snack, "I do not understand him, me."

"What the dickens are you maundering about?" I asked as I refilled his mug with beer. "At your confounded ghost-hunting again?"

"Not at all, by no means; quite the contrary," he denied, his mouth half full of cheese and biscuit, a foaming beer mug halfway to his lips. "This time I seek to dodge the specter, my friend. I wish to wipe my mind as blank as a dunce-school-boy's slate, to dismiss all thought of the matter from my memory. But *hèlas*, you know this Jules de Grandin. He annoys me. He is a very curious person. When a mystery presents itself it gnaws like a maggot at his brain, nor can he dislodge it till he has found its solution. *Ah bah*," he shrugged his shoulders irritably. "I shall think of it no more. Let the devil worry over it. Me, I have the craving for eight hours sleep, and if I wake before—"

The sharp, insistent clamor of the doorbell sawed through his words like an alarm clock shattering sleep, and I sighed in vexation as I glanced at my watch. "Half-past one, and some idiot with a bellyache comes for a dose of paregoric."

A girl was standing in the vestibule, a slim slip of a thing in lustrous furs with a pale face from which dark eyes looked, dilated and frightened. "Is Doctor—the French gentleman here?" she asked tremulously. "Étienne, the *maître d'hôtel* at the Gold Room said he knows about such things, and—"

"*Para servir á Vá. Señorita,*" broke in de Grandin in his best Spanish. In her changed costume, and with fright like a mask on her face, I had failed to recognize the girl, but as de Grandin spoke I realized she was the female member of the dance team we had seen at the Berkeley-York.

"Oh, sir," she knotted thin hands in a gesture of entreaty which somehow did not seem theatrical, "please help us! Étienne told us you know all about such things and—may I bring Paul in? He's waiting in the taxi."

For the first time I noticed a cab parked at the curb, and at de Grandin's nod she dashed across the porch and down the steps and front walk, the spool heels of her sling-back sandals clattering on the cement.

She leant into the cab's darkness a moment, then emerged slowly, helping a young man to climb from the machine, steadying him with both arms as he tottered drunkenly up the walk. "Let me," I offered, taking the unsteady man's free arm. "He must have had a greater shock than we'd supposed."

De Grandin seized the patient's other arm and motioned to the girl to precede us and open the consulting-room door. "So," he murmured as we eased the young man into an armchair. "That is good, *Señor*. Very good, indeed. Now, let us have a look—*que diable?*" With quick, practiced fingers he had felt the youngster's head, examining not only the discolored area on the right temple, but feeling for an evidence of skull-fracture or *contre-coup* lesion. "What is it, *Señor?* You seem in fair condition physically, yet—" Abruptly he lowered his hands, felt the boy's neck just below the hairline, then took the patient's right hand in his own. I noticed how the lad's slim fingers closed convulsively upon the Frenchman's, clinging to them as a drowning man might grasp at a twig. An interne could have diagnosed nervous exhaustion bordering on neurasthenia.

"Strychnine?" I suggested.

"Brandy," he corrected. "A large dose, if you please, at least four ounces, Friend Trowbridge. Five or six would be more better. Fear is gnawing at his nerves like a starved wolf. We must relax him, break his inhibitions down, before we can determine what our treatment should be."

I brought the cognac and de Grandin held the goblet to the patient's mouth. "A little, so small sip," he directed. "*Très bon*. Now another—and another. Let them prepare the way for that which follows. Now, all at once, *Señor*. Gulp him, swallow him. Down with him all!"

The patient made a face as if he had ingested raw quinine instead of old cognac, but his reaction to the liquor was almost instantaneous. The hands which had been tensely clasped on the chair arms relaxed gradually, color seeped into his pale cheeks, and the drawn lines round his mouth became a little slack.

De Grandin beamed with satisfaction. "*Esta mejor?*" he asked.

The young man looked at him and the ghost of a smile hovered on his lips. "You needn't use that Spig talk to me, sir. I'm an American," he answered.

"American? *Mon Dieu!* But your names—"

"Oh, that!" the girl broke in with the suspicion of a giggle. "Pablo and Francesca are just our stage names. We're really Paul and Frances Fogarty."

"Irish?"

"As Paddy's pig, sir. Our accent—when we use it—is assumed for strictly business purposes, and is as phony as our stage names."

The little Frenchman grinned delightedly. "*Parbleu*, you carry it off well, *mes amis*. One would swear you are from Argentina, or, perhaps Mexico." He glanced appreciatively from one of them to the other.

They were, as he had said, extremely "South of the Border" in appearance. Paul Fogarty wore dinner clothes of extreme cut, trousers fitted snugly at the waist and hips with a series of vertical tucks and flowing to bell bottoms like those of a sailor, satin waistcoat drawn so tightly as to suggest a corset, and a jacket with sloping, close-fitting shoulders. His hair, worn rather long, was trained down his cheeks in sideburns and brushed straight back from the brow, plastered sleekly with pomade till it fitted his head like a skullcap of black patent leather.

The girl, too, was perfectly in character. Her hair was so intensely black it seemed to give off blue lights like a grackle's throat and, defiant of the current fashion, it was cut short as a boy's. Like a boy's, too, it was parted far on the left side and plastered down with bandoline till it gleamed in the lamplight. Close-clipped mannish sideburns descended her cheeks before her ears and were rendered more conspicuous by the heavy pendants of green jade that dangled from the small pierced lobes almost to her shoulders. Her dull-black satin gown clung to her narrow figure with such sheath-tightness that it had to be slit at the sides to give her room to step—and incidentally display slim, silk-smooth legs and miniature feet in high-arched sandals. The dress was long-sleeved and high-necked at the front, but left her back exposed almost down to the coccyx. The jade earrings and the synthetic emerald buckles of her sandals were her only ornaments, the carmine of her painted lips and the green lacquer on her toe and fingernails were the sole spots of color in her ensemble. She was not beautiful or even pretty. Her features were too small and too irregular, but she was seductive in a strange way. She had little animal appeal, but her slender, almost boyish body, pale, thin face and scarlet lips had an appeal at once attractive and almost terrifying, like that of the fabled sirens—Circe in a Paris frock, Medea with Rue de la Paix accessories.

"You are perhaps *Monsieur* and *Madame* Fogarty?" de Grandin asked, "or is it *Monsieur* and *Mademoiselle?*"

"*Monsieur* and *Madame*, if you want it that way," the girl answered, as she gave him a languishing glance from dark eyes. Few women could resist de Grandin. "We're husband and wife. That's what's the matter."

"*Comment?*" he answered sharply. "'The matter,' *Madame*? Is it that you do not love each other?"

"No, sir, it's not that. We love each other till it hurts, but—"

"*Ah-ha!* That twenty-times-accursed but! What is it, Madame Fogarty? Perhaps I can help you—"

"Did I say anything when I came out of it at the Gold Room?" young Fogarty cut in.

De Grandin turned to face him almost fiercely. "You did, indeed, *Monsieur*. You said, if I do not make the mistake, 'Lottë.' I assumed at the time you called upon *Madame* your wife. A man does such things in the half light of returning consciousness sometimes."

"That's the answer," Fogarty returned dryly. "I know it sounds as nutty as a pecan roll, but I'm—we're both—convinced she's at the bottom of the trouble. Étienne told us—"

"One moment, if you please," de Grandin raised a slim white hand. "The estimable Étienne can wait. It is of yourselves I wish to know. Begin at the beginning if you please, *Monsieur*, and omit nothing. If we are to help you we must know all, and all does not imply a part, or even most, but everything. He dropped into a chair, lit a cigarette and crossed his knees, staring at our visitor like a cat at a rat-hole.

"Okay, sir, if you want my life history," young Fogarty took a deep breath and an Irish grin broke through his carefully cultivated Latin exterior. "I'm a dancer; always been a dancer; never did anything else and never wanted to. Grampaw Donnally said that I was born with jingle-boxes in both feet, and I guess he hit it right, for I've never seen the time when music didn't make me want to prance. Before I'd left kindergarten I could do an Irish jig as well as anyone, by the time I'd reached grade school I'd learned to imitate George M. Cohan, Frisco and Pat Rooney. I was on the program every time there was an entertainment at church or school, and by the time I'd reached fourteen I was copping prizes regularly at amateur nights in the vaudeville houses.

"But I was a lousy student, and nothing but the truant officers kept me in school till I was sixteen, then I ran away and shipped on a freighter for South America, jumped ship at Buenos Aires and hung around until I managed to get a job as bus boy in the Café 25 de Mayo. In six months I'd picked up enough Spanish to be promoted to waiter. One night I got the orchestra leader drunk and chiseled a dance job out of him.

"That started it. They billed me under the name of Pablo, as an exponent of *las Danzas de América del Norte*, and my act went over pretty well, especially my imitations of Frisco's soft-shoe routines. But I knew it couldn't last, so every *centavo* made above bare living expenses went into dancing lessons and I learned the works—tango, rumba, bolero, lulu-fardo, maxixe and seguidilla, as well as most of the folk dances. I even took some ballet instruction, but that, like fencing lessons, was more for poise than actual use. Within a year I spoke Argentine Spanish well enough to pass for a native—among foreigners—and had a spot in the floor show at El Centro. While I was working there a German vaudeville agent named Hanns Ewers saw me and offered me a job at the Café Zur Nekke in Berlin.

"It was there I met Lottë. I'd dropped into the Rixdorfer on my night off, thinking I might see some other act that would give me ideas, when she came on. I'd never seen anything like her. She was tall, tall as a tall man, slightly built, and with the small, cold, regular features that distinguish Saxon women from Prussians or Bavarians. In contrast to her cold, almost contemptuous face, her hair was flaming red. I don't mean russet or that shade of sepia we usually call red, but true flame-color, like molten copper in a crucible, and I knew instinctively that if she let it down it would reach to her knees. She had that white, almost transparent skin that sometimes goes with hair like that, and there was a bright, powdery dust of small gold freckles on her high cheekbones. Her eyes were a hot tortoise-shell, and in them I could see desire straining like a hound at the leash. There are people like that, you know. People to whom music, especially percussion, is intoxicating as an aphrodisiac, whose emotions almost burst the bounds of restraint when they dance. Lottë was one of them. She was drunk with the rhythm of the music, driven almost to frenzy by the movements of her own body.

"When she finished her turn, she saw me watching her and came over to my table. I don't know just how to describe it; it seemed as if we were two chemicals that needed only to be brought together to explode with a heat like a bursting atom bomb. A thrill that was as sharp as a pang of pain shot through me as she dropped into the chair opposite, it nearly lifted the hair on my head; I know it made me positively dizzy. It wasn't what you could call love at first sight; it wasn't love at all. It was something terrifying, like bewitchment, and I knew as I looked into her eyes she had it, too.

"For almost an hour we sat there drinking champagne mixed with cognac, and I don't believe in all that time either of us took his eyes off the other's. It was as if our gaze was magnetized. It wasn't that we didn't want to look away; we couldn't. When she finally rose to leave I followed her, walking like a drunken man, or one who has been hypnotized.

"Of course, we teamed up. Her contract at the Rixdorfer was about to finish the night I met her, and she joined me at the Café Zur Nekke."

Young Fogarty took a deep, trembling breath and shivered like a man on whom a sudden chilling wind has blown. "Have you ever been possessed, sir? I mean that literally. Most likely you haven't, so I can't hope to make you understand how utterly I became enslaved. Lottë dominated me as completely—more so—as she did her pet dachshund Fritz. To say that I had no more privacy than a goldfish would be understating it. I had to be with her constantly—every moment. Even when I went to shave or wash my hands I had to leave the bathroom door open that she might see me; I had to give up having my hair cut at the Adlon barber shop and have one of the male *coiffeurs* at the beauty shop she patronized cut it, so she could be with me, and watch me the whole time. If a woman, no matter how old, smiled at me or spoke she was vixenishly jealous; she even resented my exchanging a word with another man or a child, and had to be present while I talked our routines over with the bandleader.

"I couldn't stand it, no man could. It was worse than being in prison. It was like being sewn up in a strait-jacket and gradually strangled. I loved her—if you want to call the fierce, unreasoning enchantment I was under love—but at the same time I hated her, and the hate was growing stronger than the love.

"It wasn't long before she felt the same way about me. We'd be lying side by side, sometimes kissing, sometimes in each other's arms, sometimes only hand in hand, when suddenly she'd jump up, call me '*dumkopf*' or '*schlemmiel*' and give me a contemptuous kick, or spit on me and slap my face. And when I'd leap up in a rage she'd fairly fling herself on me, twine both arms about me so I was helpless—for she was strong as a man in spite of her slenderness—and smother me with kisses.

"One of us surely would have killed the other if it had gone on much longer, but in 1940 the draft came and my number was one of the first called. 'I have to go,' I told her. 'If I don't I'll be an outlaw.'

"She stormed and screamed hysterically, went to her knees before me. 'Do anything you want with me,' she begged. 'Do you want to beat me? I'll fetch the dog whip that I use on Fritz. Tear my skin with your teeth. Slash me with your razor—anything. Drink my blood; do whatever you care to, only don't leave me. Let them take the others to make war on the Führer. Stay with me. We can fly together to the mountains where no one will ever find us. I'll cook your food and wash your clothes and keep your house—be your servant, your slave—only don't leave me, *liebchen!*'

"But this was my chance for escape, and I wasn't letting it go by. 'I've got to go,' I repeated. 'This is more than either—or both—of us, Lottë. It's my country.'

"She threw her arms about my knees and pressed her cheeks against them, begging me to beat her, torture her, kill her, but not leave her, and when I finally managed to break free she fell face-forward on the floor and beat her forehead on it. The last I saw of her she lay full-length on the rug with her unbound red hair about her like a pool of blood, beating both fists on the carpet and screaming, 'You shall not leave me, I'll never let you go—never—never—*never!*'

"I was inducted as soon as I reached New York and went at once to training camp. Just before we sailed for England I met Frances at the USO. She was an entertainer, one of the best dancers I had ever seen, and when she heard I'd been a professional in civil life we were drawn together by our mutual interests.

"This time it was love, the real thing, not an unholy fascination.

"The entertainers weren't allowed to date with soldiers, but she gave me her address, and we corresponded regularly. We were married the day after my discharge and formed a team, using the Spanish form of our names—Pablo and Francesca. Fran hasn't been very well lately, and we're planning a vacation as soon as we've saved enough. I was stone-broke after almost six years in the army, and it cost my separation pay plus the few war bonds I'd managed to accumulate to outfit us. Costumes are expensive and don't wear very long."

De Grandin nodded smiling. "I congratulate you on the thoroughness of your report, Monsieur Paul, but what of Fraulein Lottë? You said that you suspected her."

"So I do, sir. Listen: I wanted to forget Lottë as I'd forget a bad dream, but she kept a constant stream of letters flowing to me till Pearl Harbor and our entrance into the war. They were all in the same tone, how she loved me, idolized me, worshiped me, how she counted every heartbeat till we were together again, and every one ended with, 'You are mine and mine alone. I shall never let you go!'

"After we got in the war I lost touch with her, thank the Lord, and when I next heard of her it was through the Army scuttlebutt. The British had swooped down on Geirstein and caught the Jerries in the act of trying to liquidate three hundred prisoners before they could be freed to testify. From all accounts Geirstein was worse than either Buchenwald or Dachau, but like them it had both he- and she-devils in charge. The leader of the female *schwartzstaffelkorps* was a tall, red-headed woman said to be as beautiful as Helen of Troy and crueler than Countess Bathory. They laid more than two hundred deaths of helpless Jews and Poles and Czechs to her, but none of them had died outright, all died under torture supervised or actually inflicted by her. I was shocked but not too much surprised when I heard her name was Lottë Dalberg. Her father had been a *scharfrichter* or headsman, and I supposed she took naturally to the bloody work.

"She was tried and found guilty with the other members of the Geirstein staff. Two months ago we read she had been hanged." Young Fogarty paused, swallowed twice and reached for the now-empty brandy glass.

"*Mais certainement*, but of course," de Grandin volunteered and poured out a fresh potion of cognac. "And then?"

"Then it began. Fran and I were practicing a new routine. Come to think of it, it was the very day they hanged Lottë, but, of course, we didn't know about that then. Suddenly the stool was jerked from under Tony. Anthony Nusbaum is pianist in the band at the Gold Room and plays for our rehearsals. It couldn't have slipped. It was standing on a rug, not the bare floor, and Tony weighs at least two hundred pounds. If anything would hold that stool down as if it had been nailed he would, but there it was, halfway across the room, with Tony sitting on his fanny and looking surprised as a kid who'd just sat down on a pin put in his school seat.

"In a moment every pane of glass in the windows began rattling as if a gale were blowing, though we could see the trees dead still outside, and the light bulbs in the chandelier all popped. They didn't go out, they burst and shattered, as if they'd been squeezed by an unseen hand.

"Fran was wearing rayon slacks with deep cuffs for practice, and had caught her heel in one of them, giving it a nasty rip. She'd had her sewing basket out to mend the tear and left a needle sticking in the spool of thread and there were half a dozen more in a paper packet. Not loose, but stuck in the black paper, the way they come, you know. Just as the light bulbs popped those needles detached themselves and came darting through the air, every one of 'em sticking in my face. Six of 'em stuck half an inch into my cheeks and the threaded one thrust itself into my nose, trailing half a yard of linen string. You won't believe that, I know, but it's absolutely true."

"*Monsieur*," de Grandin assured him, "I believe you implicitly. Proceed with your *précis*, if you please."

"We haven't had much peace since, sir. Several times a day, and most especially at night, something like that occurs. Chairs, books, tables and even such heavy pieces of furniture as a piano are moved about, sometimes slowly, sometimes fairly thrown, and jewelry and other small objects are hurled through the air. The blankets are jerked off our beds while we're sleeping, our clothes are snatched off hangers and wadded on the wardrobe floor or tossed into the corners of the room, food is snatched off the table before us. Only yesterday the whole tablecloth was jerked away as we were eating breakfast, spilling food and dishes over us and the floor."

"*Bien oui*," de Grandin murmured. "Thus far it runs entirely true to pattern. What else, if you please?"

"Last night I wakened at the sound of something scratching. When I got up and lit the light I saw a sentence taking form upon the wall of the bedroom.

There was no pencil—nothing that could make the letters visible—but the scratching kept up steadily as words were spelled out against the paint."

"You could read them? They were not cryptic, like those showing on the palace wall at the feast of Belshazzar?"

"Yes, sir, I could read them, all right," he said grimly. "I recognized the writing, too. I'd seen it often enough."

"Ah, and it said—"

"Just what I'd read in half a hundred letters from Lottë, the sentence with which she always ended: 'You are mine and mine alone. I shall never let you go.'"

"*Parbleu*," de Grandin began, but got no farther, for, apparently from the floor of the consulting room there came a deafening, clanging, banging racket, like a tin can bumping over cobbles at the tail of some luckless mongrel, and out of empty air, apparently some six feet overhead, burst a mocking, maniacal laugh.

The silence fairly beat upon our ears as the unholy racket stopped abruptly as it had begun, and Fogarty smiled bleakly. "You get used to it in time," he said wearily. "You saw that broken prism from the chandelier hit me tonight. You know it didn't fall on me; you know that it was thrown."

"I do, indeed, *Monsieur.*"

"Then look at this." The boy stripped back his jacket cuff and shirt sleeve. On his bared forearm, apparently scratched with some sharp instrument, was an intricately wrought, but easily decipherable, monogram: "L.D." "Tonight she put her brand on me. Now see this." From his jacket pocket he drew out a folded handkerchief and spread it on the table before us. Smeared on the linen, apparently with lipstick, was a seventeen-word message: "Pablo you are mine to torment and to kill. I shall do both in my good time." The writing was bold, ill-formed, angular, the sort of writing one accustomed to use German script might use to write English.

"And this came—?" de Grandin arched the slim black brows which were such a vivid contrast to his blond hair and mustache.

"Tonight, after we'd done our last turn. Fran was making up her mouth when the lipstick was snatched out of her hand and the handkerchief from my breast pocket. Next instant handkerchief and lipstick were flung into the far corner of the dressing room. When we picked 'em up we found this."

"*Tiens*," the little Frenchman began, then, "*Sacré nom!*" as he ducked his head. With a sharp click the key had turned in the lock of the instrument case that stood by the farther wall, the glass door swung open and from the upper shelf a lancet rose, shot like an arrow from a bow in low parabola and sped whirring past his head, missing his cheek by the bare fraction of a centimeter as it flashed across the room to bury itself a full inch in the wall.

"*Nom de nom de nom de nom de sacré nom!*" he swore savagely. "No twenty-times-accursed *fantôme*, no never-quite-to-be-sufficiently-anathematized *lutin* shall throw a knife at Jules de Grandin and boast of the exploit. *Mademoiselle la Revenante*, I am annoyed with you. I take your gauntlet up. I accept your challenge, me. *Parbleu*, but we shall see who makes a monkey out of whom before this business is finished!"

He looked from one of us to the other, the sharp vertical wrinkles of a frown of concentration etched between his brows. "My friends, I think I have the diagnosis, but as to treatment, *tenez*, that is another matter. Friend Trowbridge, have you not noted one constant factor in these so untoward happenings?"

"Why—" I temporized. "Why—"

"Not why, but what," he corrected with a quick grin. "Think, concentrate, meditate, if you will be so kind."

"H'm. The only condition common to all these occurrences as Mr. Fogarty has related them seems to be that he and his wife have been together—"

"*Bravo! Bravissimo!*"

"But of course, that could have no earthly bearing on—"

"Name of a small blue man, has it not so? I tell you it is diagnostic, my friend."

"I fail to see—"

"*Précisément, exactement*; quite so. Permit that I instruct you. Across the Rhine in that dark country which has spewed war twice upon the world in one generation they have some words which are most expressive. Among them is *poltergeist*, which signifies a pelting ghost, a ghost which flings things round the house and plays the stupid, childish tricks. More often he is not a ghost at all in the true sense, he is some evil entity which plagues a man or more often a woman. Not for nothing did the old ones call the Devil Prince of the Powers of the Air, for there are very many evil things in the air which we can no more see than we can see the micro-organisms of disease. Yes, it is so." He nodded solemn affirmation.

"This one, I damn think, however, are a true ghost, the earthbound spirit of a human creature tainted with the deadly sins of lust and murder. Also, it are a *poltergeist* of the first water.

"For why? Why should it not come back as an ordinary specter, sighing, weeping, wailing, crying, manifesting itself through the apperceptive senses rather than as a *poltergeist*, a pelter, a mover-around-of-furniture?

"You ask it? *Pardieu*, I shall tell you! The usual, ordinary haunting-ghost may make a noise, often a most unpleasant noise, and sometimes, with or without the aid of a medium, manifest itself visually. It may raise the hair upon the head of the beholder, frighten him until he is well-nigh witless, but that appears to be about the limit of its powers. It does not fling crockery, it does not move the furniture about, it does not exercise the physical force. The *poltergeist* does so. You apprehend? You follow me? Of course.

"This Lottë Dalberg was a very wicked woman. She was a bloodstained wanton who paid with her life for her crimes. And death has not reformed her. She would torment, injure, perhaps kill the man who had escaped her in life. And in order that she may have power to exercise the *violence physique* she comes back as a *poltergeist.* Yes, certainly; of course.

"Very well, then. Experience with such things shows some agent is essential for the *poltergeist's* activities. The agent, who may be, and usually is entirely innocent of all evil intent, is almost always one possessing some physical or mental abnormality. She are often a young girl in her teens, less often a boy of the same age, sometimes an old or sick person, perhaps a cripple whose vitality is low.

"You begin to comprehend? Monsieur Fogarty has told us that *Madame* his wife is unwell, that they wait only to accumulate a little money before they take a long vacation. *Madame,*" he bowed to the girl, "you have consulted a physician? He has diagnosed your illness?"

"Yes," tremulously, "he said I'm suffering from anemia. Things had gotten pretty bad for me before the war. Vaudeville had just about disappeared, there weren't enough floor shows to give employment to a tenth of the dancers 'at liberty.' I had to take what I could get. I was a taxi dancer at the Posieland Dance Hall—five cents a dance and a ten percent commission on the drinks I vamped the patrons into buying. For more than a year I ate ten-cent breakfasts and luncheons; if I had enough to dine at the steam table at the Automat I thought I was in luck. Something has to give way when you starve all day and dance all night, you know, sir."

"*Mordieu, tu parles, ma petite pauvre,*" he answered with a gleam of sympathy in his eyes. "You have said it, truly. But so it is. The so unpleasant workings of this naughty *poltergeist* undoubtedly are conditioned by your presence."

"You mean—" there was stark panic in the girl's cry—"you mean that I'm responsible—"

"Not at all, by no means, *Madame.* I mean the *poltergeist* works through, not with you. The movement of objects and the application of violence without the use of any physical force known to science is technically known as telekinesis. The *poltergeist* accomplishes it by means of in imponderable substance called teleplasm, which is akin to, though not the same as the ectoplasm or psychoplasm exuded by the medium at a spiritualistic séance. Now, neither the mind nor that discarnate entity we call a ghost for want of more exact terminology can affect matter without the influence of a human intermediary. You, *Madame,* are that. It is from you that this entirely detestable spirit-thing derives the necessary teleplasm. Yes.

"But should you blame yourself? *Bien non.* No more than the unfortunate householder whose home has been ravaged by a burglar. Indeed, the simile is apt. You have not given her the teleplasm; she has stolen it from you."

"Then what are we to do? Must Paul and I separate—"

He held a slim hand up for silence. "Permit me, *Madame*. I think, I concentrate; I cogitate."

At length: "I would suggest you spend the night apart, my friends. The farther the better. One of you should take the train for Philadelphia and stop at some hotel. The other should remain here. Tomorrow night, if all goes well, we shall attempt an experiment. I make no promises, but we shall see what we shall see. Yes. This Fraulein Lottë Dalberg has affronted me. She has thrown a knife at me. I am insulted, and I do not suffer insult placidly. If one thing fails we shall essay another, and another until we strike upon the proper one. Yes, I have said it, me."

IT WAS SHORTLY AFTER four o'clock next afternoon when we knocked at the door of the suite occupied by Paul and Frances Fogarty at the Berkeley-York. "And how were things last night?" de Grandin asked as Paul let us in.

"A little better, thank you," answered Fogarty. "I went to Philadelphia as you suggested. Fran stayed here, and aside from a bad dream I had no trouble."

"A bad dream? Like what, Monsieur Paul?"

"I dreamed I was some place, I don't quite know where, but it was probably a mountain top, for everything was shrouded in a heavy mist, and yet there was a wind blowing. It was intensely cold, and I felt very lonely. At last I couldn't stand it any longer and called for Fran."

"And then?"

"I got no answer, but when I called a second time I saw a figure coming slowly toward me through the fog. When it came closer I saw it was Lottë. She was wearing a long scarlet robe, and her hair, as red as the silk of her gown, hung down about her. Her arms were bare, so were her head and feet, and every time she took a step a flash of flame came from the ground where she had trod, and a little puff of yellow smoke accompanied it. It had an odd, nose-tickling smell, like that you get when you put a match to your cigarette before the sulphur has quite burned away."

"U'm," Jules de Grandin commented. "One need not be a Freud or Jung or Stekel to interpret the symbolism of that dream. What next, if you please?"

"I tried to run away, but had no power to move. It was as if I'd suddenly been turned to stone. No, not quite that, either. It was more as if I'd suddenly been paralyzed. I was entirely conscious, but powerless to move. I couldn't even shut my eyes, or take them off her as she walked toward me with a kind of gloating smile on her face. But I could feel my heart beating and the breath hissing in my throat. A bird must feel something like that when a snake creeps up on it.

"She came up to me and put both hands on my shoulders, while she looked straight in my eyes. 'I'm burning, Pablo,' she told me, 'burning for you. Soon I shall burn with you.' Then she kissed me.

"I felt her mouth against my mouth and the light nip of her sharp teeth on my lips, and a mist as red as blood—red as her robe and her hair—blinded me. I felt as if I were sinking into some dream-scented fog, half conscious, half unconscious, like a patient on the operating table when the ether is applied and the doctor tells him to begin counting: One-two-three. Then suddenly the fog caught fire, and I was burning, too. Flames leaped and roared and hissed about me, stripping the skin off my flesh and the flesh from my bones. The agony of it was almost past endurance, and yet—yet—"

"*Précisément. Monsieur,*" de Grandin supplied. "And yet you found the torment in a sense delightful. Even the damned in hell have some pleasures. One takes it that you awoke then?"

"I woke up in what seemed a raging fever, yet I was shaking as with a severe chill."

"And not one little minute too soon, either, *mon jeune.* Me, I think that was no ordinary dream you had. It was a vision, and one which might well have ended in disaster. Tell me," his face showed sudden concern, "you did not speak to her, you did not make her any promise, or declare your love or express rapture at the embrace?"

"No, sir."

"That is good. That is very fortunate, indeed. Poor, weak, finite human nature has its limitations, and the powers of hell are very strong. It seems that not content with doing you physical injury this vile one now would steal away your soul. She is a very naughty person, that one."

Abruptly he turned to Frances Fogarty. "*Madame!*"

"Yes, sir?"

"Attend me, if you please." From his waistcoat pocket he drew a short length of silken cord from which dangled a bright silver disc about the size of a dime. "See him," he ordered. "Is he not a pretty thing?"

Slowly, like a pendulum, he swung the bright disc back and forth. Frances watched it, fascinated. "Sleep, Madame Françoise," he commanded softly "Sleep. The clock is ticking; tick—tock; tick—tock. Slowly, very slowly, it is counting off the second, *ma petite.* Tick—tock. You are weary, very, very weary; you are tired, you long for sleep. Sleep is what you most desire, it is not? Tick—tock; tick—tock!"

The girl's eyes wavered back and forth following the arc of the bright disc, but as he droned his monotone they became heavy lidded, finally closed. Her slender bosom rose and fell convulsively a time or two, then regular soft breathing told us she was sleeping. He bent above her, pressing gentle fingers on her lids. "You are asleep, Madame Françoise?"

"I am asleep," she answered drowsily.

He turned from the girl to her husband "It is expedient that you join her, Monsieur Paul."

"You mean you want to hypnotize me?"

"Perfectly."

"O.K. I'll take a chance." He dropped into a chair beside his wife, settled his head comfortably and smiled tiredly. "Hope this works, sir," he muttered.

Once more de Grandin swung the shining silver disc, once more his soothing monotone commanded sleep. In something less than five minutes Paul was slumbering peacefully.

"Madame Françoise?" the Frenchman called softly. No answer came, and he repeated the summons. At last a sleepy little murmur like the whimper of a half-roused child responded. "The hypnosis is deep," he whispered, then aloud to the girl, "I am your master am I not, Madame Françoise?"

"You are my master."

"You will obey my command?"

"I will obey you."

"Then I command you to forget all thought of Lotté Dalberg. Dismiss her from your mind and memory, utterly, completely, wholly. As far as you are concerned there was never any such person. Her name if heard will evoke no memories pleasant or unpleasant. It will be the name of a stranger, never heard before. You understand?"

"I understand."

"You will obey?"

A long pause followed, then: "Madame Françoise, who is Lotté Dalberg?" he asked sharply.

"Lotté Dalberg?" she said sleepily. "I never heard of her. Should I know her?"

"No, emphatically no, my little."

He swung round to the sleeping Paul and repeated the commands he had given Frances. Then, five minutes later, "Who was Lotté Dalberg, Monsieur Paul?" he asked.

"She was—" the young man seemed to grope for an answer, then, slowly, like one trying to recall a half-forgotten snatch of poetry—"she was a German girl whom I met in Berlin. I loved her—hated her—"

"Non, par la barbe d'un bouc vert, you shall not say it!" de Grandin cut in savagely. "Attend me, Monsieur Paul: She was no one. She never had existence. There was never such a person. Do you understand?"

"I—I think so."

"Good. Now, who was Lotté Dalberg, Monsieur Paul?"

"I don't know."

"Think; think hard, my Paul. Who was she? Do not you recall your days and nights together in Berlin, the kisses and the vows of never-dying love?"

"No."

"You cannot recall her?"

"Who?"

"What was her name?"

"Whose name?"

"*Très bien.*" He turned to me, his little round blue eyes agleam. "I damn think that does it—"

"What's that?" I interrupted, seizing him by the elbow and spinning him around. "There, on the wall?"

Something like a water-stain was forming on the green-painted plaster. It grew, expanded, lengthened, widened till it was the silhouette of a female figure standing on tiptoe facing us. Tiny lines of red like veins began to show within the outline of the stain. Some were heavy, some lighter, and together they traced out a pattern like a line drawing crudely executed in red pigment.

The thing was like a five-pointed star, the widely outspread legs its lower points, the upstretched, outspread arms its upper ones, the head, thrust forward, the apex. Now we could see the snaky locks of red hair rippling unbound down the brow and neck and shoulders, reaching almost to the knees; the long and tapered arms uplifted as in evocation, the wide-opened and staring eyes, glaring at us in malevolent fury.

"*Hola,*" de Grandin greeted mockingly. "*Comment vous portez-vous, aujourd'hui,* Fraulein Lottë?—how are you?"

The red-etched picture seemed to struggle to free itself from the wall. Grotesquely, horribly, it was like some enormous beetle enmeshed on a sheet of fly-paper. He laughed sarcastically. "It is no use, *Fraulein.* Two dimensions are the most you can achieve; soon there will be none."

He dropped his bantering tone, and voice and eyes were hard as he proceeded: "Unquiet spirit of the unrepentant dead, go forth. You have said to the grave, 'Thou art my lover, in thy arms will I lie,' and to Death, 'Thou art my father and my mother.' The cord of memory and fear by which you held these ones is broken; your power over them is ended. Save in the memories of those who hate you and the records of the court that tried and sentenced you to death there is no thought or mention of your name. Oblivion has claimed you. You are swallowed up, wiped out; extinct. Now get you gone to that place prepared for you, and may your scarlet sins find pardon in the end. Avaunt, be gone; *te conjuro, abire ad tuum locum.*"

The simulacrum on the wall began to fade like a picture projected from a magic lantern when the light behind it dims, became a featureless shadow, a dull, amorphous stain—nothing.

"*Bien,*" de Grandin dusted one hand on the other. "That is indubitably that, Friend Trowbridge."

To the sleeping couple he called softly: "*Monsieur* and *Madame,* sleep until the time has come to rise and work, but forget all that has transpired. You never heard of Lottë Dalberg, have no recollection of the persecution with which she plagued you, never have you seen or heard of Jules de Grandin or his friend Dr. Samuel Trowbridge. All, all has been forgotten, *mes amis. Adieu.*"

He opened the door softly and we stepped out into the hall.

"No," HE DENIED AS we finished dinner that night, "I would not call it intuition, my friend. It was rather tentative and impractical. Consider, if you please:

"This thing which haunted Monsieur Fogarty was in the nature of a *poltergeist*, but it were not a true one. While it moved furniture and hurled light objects it had none of the droll mischievousness of the true *poltergeist*, who, while he often proves annoying, even dangerous, is a species of a ghostly clown who plays his Puckish tricks without much rhyme or reason. This naughty one had a very definite reason for everything she did; she was unquestionably bent on persecuting Monsieur Fogarty, perhaps eventually on killing him. Because she sought to do him physical injury by physical means she resorted to the form of *poltergeist*, and so the pattern of her actions—and her limitations—were those of that species of a ghost.

"Very well. We determined Madame Françoise was the agent through which the so wicked Fraulein Lottë operated, the reservoir of her supply of teleplasm without which she had no power for violence. *Très bien.* What then?

"It is an axiom of the occultist that this teleplasm is what you call ideoplastic, that is, it takes its appearance, its seeming, from the thoughts of those among whom it operates. Both Monsieur and Madame Fogarty knew and hated Lottë Dalberg, and with excellent reason. That gave her a hold on their minds. When she appeared to Monsieur Paul in Philadelphia last night she was knocking at the door of his subconscious, seeking to insinuate herself into his brain as well as do him bodily injury through external force.

"Now, I ask me, 'Jules de Grandin, are you afraid of the spirit of this most unpleasant young woman who has died upon the gallows for her murders and undoubtlessly is most uncomfortable at present for her other sins?' 'Damn no, Jules de Grandin,' I reply to me. 'I am ashamed of you that you should ask such a question.'

"Very well, suppose we hypnotize this poor, tormented couple, make them not afraid, even not aware, of Lottë Dalberg. What then?

"Hypnotism, in the last analysis, is nothing but the substitution of the operator's mind for that of the subject. In a measure, by fear and memory, the revenant had substituted her intelligence for that of Monsieur Paul and Madame Françoise. So what did I do? I thrust my mind into their brains, *pardieu*, and made them unafraid and even unaware of her. Thereafter, she had no place to go. She could not make them fear her, they had completely forgotten her. It was as if she had been trespassing in their brain-house when *pouf!* along comes Jules de Grandin and evicts her.

"But though they had forgotten her in their hypnotic sleep I had not. I thought of her, and there was still sufficient teleplasm to enable her to take feeble form as a picture on the wall. She was a fearsome, frightening sight, *n'est-ce-pas?* Ha, but she chose the wrong one for her frightening! Me, I told her which was what in no uncertain terms. I told her all her power was gone, that she was as forgotten as last year's bird's nest. Her last remaining ligamentary tie with earth was snapped. She had no place to go but outer darkness."

"You don't think she'll come back?"

"I do not, my friend. What was it that she said to Monsieur Paul in his vision? 'I burn'? *Parbleu*, I think that is exactly what she does.

"And me, I also burn. My throat is dry, my tongue is parched, my lips are all afire. Will you not have the goodness to refill my glass, Friend Trowbridge?"

Eyes in the Dark

"I AGREE ENTIRELY," JULES de Grandin nodded vigorously. "Too many of our profession wear blinders. This prejudice against Chiropractic is pig-ignorant as that shown against anesthesia when Simpson introduced it, or the abuse heaped on your own illustrious Holmes when he contended puerperal fever is infectious. Me, I think—*mordieu*, watch him! He will not live to grow old that one!"

Dodging drunkenly from the curb, a man had run into the roadway almost directly in the path of our car, and, as I clamped my brakes on frenziedly, fell sprawling to the pavement.

He lay face downward on the asphalt when we reached him, both arms extended to full length like those of a diver when he hits the water, and no clothing-dummy flung into the street could have been limper. "I'm sure we didn't hit him!" I exclaimed as we bent over the prostrate figure. "There was no jar—"

"You have right, my friend," de Grandin cut in. "I saw him fall a full three feet from the wheels but"—he looked up bleakly—"nevertheless, he is dead."

"Dead?" I echoed incredulously.

"*Comme un maquereau*," he agreed. "Completely; utterly."

"But—"

"I think that we had better save our buts for the inquest, Friend Trowbridge. It would be well if we called the police—"

"How? We can't just leave him lying here, nor can we move him, and where would we find a telephone?"

He rose and dusted the knees of his trousers. "I think I see a gleam of light on that doorway. Perhaps they have a 'phone."

The neighborhood was strange to me. We had been visiting the Westervelt Clinic to observe the effect of a course of chiropractic treatments on a neuras-thenic for whom potassium iodide and sodium salicylate had proved about as efficacious as so much distilled water. The old house occupied by the Clinic stood in what was little better than a slum and the old street through which we drove had seen better days, but not for a long time. Most of the houses were old brownstone fronts that had been elegant homes but now were shabby, run down at the heel, like gentlefolk in reduced circumstances. Signs announcing furnished rooms showed in most of the windows; on window-sills were half-filled milk bottles and the oddments common to "light housekeeping" apartments. Although it was but little after ten o'clock no lights showed in the blank-eyed windows. Either everyone had gone to bed or residents of the block economized on electricity.

However, as I followed the line of his pointed finger I saw a faint gleam seeping from the house before which we had stopped. A dull pattern of reds and blues lay on its white marble stoop where light shone dimly through the little panels of its stained-glass door, and though the place showed the air of decay that sat like a blight on the neighborhood it seemed a little better than its mates. None of its window lights had been broken and patched, it bore no card announcing rooms to let; the very curtains which obscured the light within seemed to announce it still maintained some sort of aloofness from the forthright poverty of the locality.

I started toward the dimly lighted door, but a sharp ejaculation from de Grandin halted me. "What is it?"

He had turned the dead man's face toward him and was staring at a small wound on the forehead with a look of fascination. "One cannot surely say," he answered softly, "but— What do you make of him, *hein?*"

"Why, when he fell he struck his brow—"

"On what, one asks to know? What is there in the street on which he could have cut himself?" As I bent to inspect the wound he added: "And if he cut himself when he fell, why should his injury take this form, *hein?*" With a wisp of paper napkin from the glove compartment of the car he wiped the corpse's brow, revealing not a straight or jagged cut, but three distinct incisions in the skin, clear-cut as if made with a needle or knife-point.

"Great Scott!" I exclaimed. "It looks like shorthand."

"It does, indeed," he agreed, "but it is not. Unless I miss my guess it is an Arabic inscription, perhaps Hindustani. I cannot be quite sure which."

"Arabic—Hindustani?" I echoed incredulously. "What would that be doing on a man's forehead—"

"*Tiens, mon vieux,* what would a man be doing falling dead in the street, with or without an inscription cut into his brow? *Le bon Dieu* knows, not I. Did not it seem to you he fled from something—"

"No, it didn't," I denied. "It seemed to me that he was drunk and didn't know what he was doing. Certainly, he wasn't watching his step—"

"Agreed," he nodded. "Most certainly he had not his wits about him, but few people *in extremis* do. However, let us wait the findings of the coroner. Our first concern is to find a telephone."

I JERKED THE SILVER-PLATED handle of the old-fashioned bell-pull vigorously, and from somewhere in the rear of the house came a responsive brassy tinkle, but no more. "*Grand Dieu des porcs*," de Grandin swore, "are we to be kept waiting while they rise and make a toilette like that of Marie Antoinette? *Hola dans la maison!*" he supplemented my ring with a vigorous thump upon the walnut panel of the door. "Awake, arouse yourselves within!" he shouted, and as he struck the door a second time a light click sounded and the portal swung back under the impact of his knuckles.

I hesitated on the threshold, but de Grandin had no scruples about violating the householders' privacy. "*Hola!*" he exclaimed again as he stepped over the sill. "Is there no one here to—*morbleu!*" he broke off, then, in a lower tone, "*Pas possible? In such a neighborhood? Regardez*, if you please, Friend Trowbridge."

We stood upon the entrance of a wide, long hall with frescoed ceiling and tall doors of massive walnut letting off to right and left. In the softly diffused light of a bronze-shaded Oriental lamp it seemed unreal as a stage setting—Persian, Indian and Chinese rugs almost hid the polished planking of the floor, more rugs, glowing with jewel-colors shading from pale jade to deepest ruby, draped along the walls. Where the white and mahogany balustrade of a wide staircase curved upward a peacock screen had been set, and immediately in front of it was a carved divan of inlaid blackwood. By the divan stood a tabouret of Indian cedar inlaid with copper, and on it, still emitting a thin plume of steam, a tiny cup of eggshell porcelain rested. Over everything there hung a heavy, heady, almost drugging perfume—ambergris.

"*Tenez*," de Grandin clicked his tongue against his teeth as he surveyed the apartment, "he is like a diamond set in brass or a pearl in a pig's snout, a room like this in such a neighborhood, *n'est-ce-pas?* One wonders—*ah-ha? Ah-ha-ha?*" His voice sank to a whisper as he nodded toward the stairway.

The blackwood divan just beneath the stairs was spread with leopard skin, and lying indolently on it was a woman, one arm extended toward us, wrist bent, hand drooping. Beneath her fingers coiled the brass stem of a *hookah* she had evidently let drop when she slipped off to sleep, and from the brass tobacco-cup that topped the cloisonné water-jar of the hubble-bubble the faintest coil of scented smoke ascended.

I had an odd feeling of unreality, a sort of this-can't-possibly-be-true sensation as I looked at her. She matched her surroundings as perfectly as if she had been made up for a part, and the big, gorgeous, dimly lighted room were the stage on which she played it. Small she was, almost childishly so, and dainty as a sweetly molded porcelain figurine. But her body was a woman's, not a child's.

The turn of her bare arms, the firm rondure of her breasts, spoke full maturity. Her skin was golden with the warm, glow of sun-ripened fruit, her nose was small and slightly hawk-beaked, her forehead low and wide. Her hair was black and sooty, without luster, parted smoothly in the middle and drawn down like wings above her ears, and the pandanus-red mouth was full-lipped, sensual and petulant, suggesting quick transitions from gay laughter to storms of anger, like that of a willful child.

A short, tight bodice of plum-colored satin like a zouave jacket covered but in nowise concealed the luscious fullness of her bosoms, from waist to ankles she was encased in exaggeratedly full pantaloons of saffron-yellow muslin drawn in tightly at the bottoms and ending in a triple row of fluffy ruffles. About her neck and wrists and ankles circled strands of gold discs almost large as pennies set with uncut rubies and off-color diamonds, and from each plate hung a tiny golden sleigh-bell. In her left nostril was a hoop of gold large and heavy as a wedding ring, and balanced on the tip of one small foot was a green-velvet heel-less slipper thickly worked with gold embroidery and seed-pearls. Its mate had fallen to the rug-strewn floor, baring a tiny blue-veined foot the heel and sole and toes of which were stained bright red with henna.

"*Pardonnez-moi, Madame,*" de Grandin began, speaking softly so as not to waken her abruptly. "We regret the intrusion, but—ah?" We had been walking toward the sleeping woman, our footsteps soundless on the rug-spread floor, now we stood beside her. Her heavy-lashed, kohl-shadowed lids were not quite closed. A little thread of white showed between them, and her petulantly sensuous mouth was lax and drooping at the corners, as though she was unutterably tired. "*Morbleu,*" he exclaimed, and his voice rasped as if his throat were sandy, "another?"

"How—" I began, but he shut me off impatiently. "*Par la barbe d'un bouc vert* do not you see it, my friend? There is something devilish here!" Scratched on the smooth, pale-amber skin of her forehead were the same shorthand-like characters we had found on the brow of the dead man in the street.

"What can it mean?" I wondered. "The wounds are fresh—the man, was still bleeding, this was probably made after death, for there's no evidence of hemorrhage, but she can't have been dead long. The coffee cup is still steaming, the *hookah* is smoking—"

"God and the devil know, not we, my friend," the little Frenchmen answered. "This case is not for the coroner alone. It is a matter for the police and the public prosecutor. Unless I am far more mistaken than I think, this is a matter of murder."

"YOU FELLERS DO SEND in the damnedest cases," complained Dr. Jason Parnell, the coroner's physician. "I don't mind 'em when they're messed up some, or even when they're ripe from bein' in the Bay too long, but when they're dead without a single, solitary reason—"

"How do you say?" de Grandin demanded. "Is it that you could not make a diagnosis?"

"That's a rough outline of the plot. A first-year student knows that death begins in one of three ways: Coma, starting at the brain; asphyxia, beginning at the lungs, or syncope, commencing at the heart. Those bodies you found have no right to be dead. There's absolutely nothing diagnostic. No trace of coma, syncope or asphyxia. The man had a slight touch of TB, but he'd have been good for another five years, anyway. The woman showed traces of drug-addiction, but nothing which could account for her death. Except for those dam', insignificant scratches on their foreheads neither of 'em had a thing wrong with him; certainly nothing that the wildest stretch of imagination could call fatal. Hearts, lungs, brains all intact, no trace of any known poison, nothing serious the matter with 'em, except that they're both dead as herrings."

"Ye say there wuzn't any trace o' poison, sor?" Lieutenant Costello of the Homicide Bureau asked in disappointment. "Sure, that's too bad entirely. I'd kind o' built me case around them scratches on their foreheads—"

"I didn't say there was no trace of poison," Parnell denied tartly. "I said there was no trace of known poison. Generally speaking, poisons fall into three categories: corrosives, such as phenol or carbolic acid, hydrocyanic acid, or oxalic acid; hypnotics and antipyretics, such as the derivatives of opium, alcohol, chloroform and the like; and alkaloidals, which affect the central nervous system, among which many snake venoms are to be found. Usually we suspect some class of poison from the physical appearance of the body. From a general classification we descend to particulars, gradually eliminating one suspected toxin, then another, till we've narrowed our investigation down to the particular poison causing death. Like you, when I found nothing radically wrong with these peoples' hearts or lungs or brains I suspected poison had been introduced into their systems through those scratches on their foreheads, but I drew a blank there, too.

"The area around the wounds should have been swollen, red and inflamed if snake venom had been introduced; these scratches seemed to have no effect on surrounding tissue, and specimens taken from them proved almost completely sterile. If one of the vegetable poisons such as curare had been injected symptoms similar to snake-bite would have been noticed, but as I said there were none. Furthermore, tests made on the blood and tissues yielded negative results. None of the familiar reactions was noted. All this, of course, does not preclude the possibility of poisoning. It merely means no poison known to me was used."

"Uh-huh," agreed Costello doubtfully. "What're ye goin' to tell the jury wuz the cause o' death, sor?"

Dr. Parnell drew out his wallet and extracted a ten-dollar bill which he laid on the desk before the policeman. "If you'll tell me what I should tell 'em that's yours, Lieutenant," he offered.

"*Tenez*, my friends, I think we waste the time," de Grandin broke in. "The key to this accursed mystery must lie under some doormat. Our task is to discover which one."

"True fer ye, sor," agreed Costello. "All we gotta do is find out why two people who didn't die from any known cause is dead, an' who kilt 'em, an' why. Afther that it's all simple. Where do we start turnin' up them doormats ye was spakin' of, I dunno?"

The little Frenchman took his narrow chin between his thumb and forefinger. "The markings on their brows are identical," he murmured. "It they had been different it might have meant something, or nothing. Their identity undoubtlessly means something, also, but what?" Abruptly he turned on us, small, round blue eyes blazing almost angrily. "Why do we stand here?" he demanded. "Why do we not go to consult the good Ram Chitra Das at once, right away, immediately?"

"WELL, WELL, THIS IS an unexpected pleasure!" our Hindu friend greeted as we trooped into his apartment in East Eighty-sixth Street. He and his charming wife were lunching on the tiny tiled terrace that let off of the dining room of their maisonette, a spot of grateful coolness in the sweltering city. A red-and-white striped awning kept the mid-September sun at bay, the tiled floor was a cool gray-green underfoot, at the terrace edge a row of scarlet geraniums nodded in the light breeze fanning in from the East River. The buhl table from which they ate was itself a museum piece, and the covered dishes of Georgian Sheffield plate were, I noted enviously, the kind about which antique dealers dream. Steam spiraled lazily from the swan's-neck spout of a teapot under which a spirit lamp burned, iced grapefruit, chops, scrambled eggs and buttered toast had just been set before them, and at the far side of the table, beaded like the forehead of a farmhand on a summer day, a tall, inviting bottle of Rhine wine waited.

"Had luncheon?" asked our host. "Yes? That's a pity. We'd love to have you join us, but perhaps you'd take a cup o' tea?"

He smiled at the woman who sat facing us. "You remember Drs. Trowbridge and de Grandin, and Lieutenant Costello, my dear?"

Nairini inclined her head in a bow that included us jointly, and there was something queenly in the movement. I knew that she had been an Indian prince's daughter who had eloped from her bridegroom's palace with Ram Chitra, Das, himself the grandson of a rajah and as engaging a scapegrace as ever backslid from the ancient Hindu faith and took service with His Britannic Majesty.

They were an oddly contrasting, yet completely complementary couple, these renegade children of Mother India. In his gray flannels with the bright stripes of his school tie in bold contrast, Ram Chitra Das looked anything but a Hindu. He might have been a Spaniard or Italian, perhaps a Basque or Portuguese, but there was nothing Oriental in his clear-olive complexion, his sleekly brushed black hair and humorous, alert dark eyes.

Nairini, on the contrary, could never have been mistaken for a Westerner. Her skin was an incredibly beautiful tan, as if it had been powdered with the finest gold, her eyes of deep, moss-agate green were set a trifle slantingly, and her hair, demurely parted in the middle and gathered in a great coil at the back was a dull black cloud. Her mouth was an extraordinary color, like the darker sort of strawberries. Her dress of block-printed linen, chocolate-brown on cocoa-tan, was sleeveless and reached to her ankles, about her waist was a girdle of amber beads as large as hazel nuts. There were bracelets of frail silver filigree on her wrists, jade-and-silver pendants hung in her ears; a soft, musical *cling-clong* sounded as she moved slightly, and we saw the slender bare ankles above her sandaled feet were ringed with heavy circlets of sand-molded silver.

With a grace that made the simple act seem like the art of a skilled dancer she poured tea for us, and Ram Chitra Das demanded, "I suppose you chaps are in trouble again? We never see you when the sailin's clear."

"Not so much in trouble as puzzled, my friend," de Grandin denied. "Last night Friend Trowbridge and I found two people dead without excuse."

Ram Chitra Das bent a mild frown upon the little Frenchman. "Let's see if I follow you. D'ye mean you'd no excuse for findin' 'em, or the late lamented had no adequate excuse for dyin'?"

"Both, *par les bois d'une huître!*" Briefly de Grandin sketched our adventure of the night before, ending with Parnell's failure to ascribe a cause of death.

"H'm." Ram Chitra Das helped himself to more scrambled egg and spread strawberry jam on his toast. "You say the scars on their foreheads looked like writin'? Sounds as if some o' my former fellow countrymen might have been up to tricks. Can you recall what the scars looked like?"

"By blue, I can, my friend. I have here an exact copy." The Frenchman drew a slip of paper from his pocket and handed it to Ram Chitra Das.

"*Sivanavama!*" For a moment our host's hand shook as he looked at the sketch, but in a moment it had steadied.

Nairini's delicately arched brows rose a trifle higher. "What is it?" she asked in her clear, smooth contralto that somehow reminded me of the cooing of doves.

"I fear, old dear, that this is it." Her husband's voice was so casual that we knew he held hysteria in check by an effort as he passed the slip of paper to her.

"*Oom Parvati!*" The superb gentility that comes from hundreds of generations of royal blood stood Nairini in good stead, but in the sudden widening of her pupils and the quick expansion of her narrow nostrils we read fear.

"Ah-ha!" de Grandin barked. "You know him? You recognize him, *hein?*"

Ram Chitra Das nodded grimly. "We know him very well indeed."

"And what, if one may ask, does he mean, this writing?"

"Oh, the writing? Literally translated it means 'The Afghan.'"

"*Vraiment?* And who would this so odious Afghan be?"

Ram Chitra Das' dark eyes were serious as he turned them on de Grandin. "You know something about me," he returned. "You know my father was a prince's son who made a misalliance with a *nautchni* and went into a not too onerous exile as a consequence, you know about my education. I was brought up as a high caste Brahmin lad and in addition had some trainin' under fakirs who, as the saying goes, could 'teach tricks to a fox.' They certainly taught me some things that have come in very handy. My English education was interrupted by the World War, but when I came back from France I took my degree at Oxford and topped it off with a year at the Sorbonne."

The grin with which he broke his recital had something of a small-boy-at-the-circus quality. "So there I was, schooled Orientally and Occidentally, restless with the restlessness of all demobbed soldiers, and with not a blessed thing to do. My caste had been completely smashed by my trip across the ocean and such indiscretions as eating beef, and after fourteen years of European life in peace and war Brahma, Vishnu and Siva meant no more to me than Pegasus or Apollo, nor had I filled this vacuum of disbelief by embracing Christianity, though several parsons and the Lord knows how many nice old ladies had labored manfully to bring me into the fold. I didn't need to work, my income was sufficient for my needs and almost equal to my wants, but I was bored. Bored stiff. I got so tired of being just Ram Chitra Das, idler, that I took service with the Intelligence Section of the Indian Police.

"I don't think that I'm boastin' when I say they got a bargain in me. I spoke every dialect that's used between Colombo and Kabul, and since I owed allegiance to no formal brand of religion and had no caste to be broken I could masquerade as a Hindu, Mohammedan, Jain, Buddhist, Sikh or Parsee without embarrassment. I gave 'em twenty-seven shillin's' worth for every pound they paid me. Besides, I had a lot of fun."

Then suddenly he drew his brows down and the whole aspect of his face changed. "They gave me an assignment to keep an eye on Karowlee Sahib, the *pershwa* of Bahadupore. He was a tricky old cuss, this Raja Karowlee, somewhere about fifty, more wives than any other possessions—though they said he used about ten pecks o' diamonds for playthings. When he's not thinkin' of women it's treason; makin' deals with Russia or the Afghans, anyone who'll play his game and give him a leg up with his schemes. That's how he got his nickname, The Afghan. He'd spent almost a year up north o' Kabul tryin' to sell one of those Afghan *amirs* the idea of comin' down and botherin' the Raja while he pulled off his local revolution, and when he came back he had a pack o' Afghan wolfhounds, a lot less money than he took away, and his beard dyed red with henna, Afghan fashion. He'd had no luck with the hillmen, though. Seems the *amir's* son had served with the British and seen the R.A.P. in action. He wasn't havin' any trouble with *those* babies.

"Well, as I was sayin', I was up Bahadupore way, posin' as a free-lance soldier and servin' as a lieutenant in Karowlee's guard when word comes that the Princess Mihri Nairini—that means Nairini the Beloved—was comin' up from Bhutanistan, where her father was in the king business in a small way, to marry this old reprobate Karowlee. Women didn't mean much to me in those days. I'd been petted by the English ladies and the French girls were nice to me, too, but I'd never seen one who could lure me into exchangin' ridin' boots and polo mallet for slippers and a pipe. Besides, I'd absorbed European ideas. This Princess Nairini was a 'native,' probably ate with her fingers and couldn't read or write. I'd seen her kind a thousand times, and the more I saw of 'em the more I thought my pater had the right idea when he married a *nautchni*. Then—" he paused with a slow, reminiscent smile, and Nairini cut in softly:

"Then I captured him."

"*Qu'est-ce donc?*" de Grandin demanded. "How do you say, *Madame?*"

She smiled at him and two deep dimples showed in her cheeks, a merrily incongruous combination with her exotic eyes. "There'd been every kind of merrymaking in the palace for three days, and I was almost tired to death. I'd slipped away from my attendants and gone down to the garden to sit by the lotus pool when I saw someone coming toward me in the moonlight. He wore the red tunic and gold-and-red turban of an officer in Karowlee's Guard, and was very beautiful. He carried a light cane with which he switched the heads off of the flowers bordering the path. Flowers always seemed like living, sentient things to me, not merely vegetables, and I couldn't bear to see him behead them. 'Stop that!' I ordered sharply, and he halted as if he had walked into a brick wall."

"Why not?" demanded Ram Chitra Das. "There I was, attendin' to my guardin', when a *houri* out o' the False Prophet's Paradise tells me to stop it. High caste Hindu women, like *Muslimmi*, observe *purdah*, you know—veil themselves before strange men. This girl wore no veil, but plainly she was neither a *nautchni* nor a palace servant. 'Who are you?' I asked and she told me, 'Your future queen who orders you to cease destroyin' her flowers.'

"That started it. The next night I was there, and the next night after that. So was she, and we had other things to talk about than flowers. I was windin' up my tour of duty, about ready to sneak back to headquarters, and when I left Nairini went with me.

"One understands," de Grandin grinned delightedly with a Frenchman's innate appreciation of romance. "And then?"

Ram Chitra Das grinned back. "Since then it's been a game o' tag. Karowlee's a revengeful old devil, and I rather think we made him lose face by elopin'. Two or three times his agents almost got us. Once I found a cobra in my bath in Calcutta where no cobra had a right to be; scorpions have appeared mysteriously in my boots, I nearly stopped a bullet one night when Nairini and I were ridin' outside Bombay. When they transferred me to duty in London, smellin' out sedition among Indian sailors in the neighborhood of East India Dock Road, I thought we'd shaken off pursuit, but one night—we were livin' in St. James' Park where you'd no more look for a Hindu than for a rich man in heaven—what should turn up in our bed but a krait, a little cousin to the cobra, less than a tenth his size and more than twenty times as deadly. Then we knew the heat was on again, as you say in America."

De Grandin nodded. "And you associate this brand upon the dead ones' foreheads with Karowlee Sahib?"

"Definitely. He's known as The Afghan from Cape Comorin to the Himalayas. Furthermore, elopements from his household ain't as rare as might be expected. His women are so numerous that he can't give 'em much attention. They get bored, and in India as in Ireland or Idaho there are always Boy Scouts ready to do their good deed by entertainin' bored wives. Sometimes these johnnies get serious and marry the gals—at least they run off with 'em.

"Usually Karowlee Sahib calls the turn on 'em before they get far. A year ago his agents killed a young Parsee who'd offered his protection to one of his runaway women, and disfigured the girl so that she committed suicide. That was in the outskirts of Benares, but instances of his revenge have been reported in Calcutta, Bombay and Madras. We know from personal experience he can reach across the ocean. I think it altogether likely the man who dropped dead before your car and the woman you found dead in the house were victims of his vengeance.

De Grandin stroked his little wheat-blond mustache gently, then gave its ends a sudden savage tug. "Would you come with us to inspect these defunct ones?" he asked. "It may be you might recognize them."

"Be glad to, old chap. I doubt I'll know 'em, but we might find out something, and I've more than a mere academic interest in this case. My dear," he turned to Nairini, "I think you'd better come along. With Karowlee's playmates on the loose I'd feel much safer if I had you in sight—"

"Why not pack a bag and stop at my house?" I suggested. "You'll be nearer to your base of operations there, and in no greater danger—"

"Thank you, Dr. Trowbridge," he accepted. "If Karowlee's agents are in Harrisonville we'll force their hand by movin' in on 'em. Might as well have a showdown now as later."

"AND DID YOU FIND out anything helpful?" de Grandin asked Ram Chitra Das that evening after dinner as Nairini, looking if possible more beautiful than ever in a white dinner dress embroidered at the hem with golden lotuses, poured coffee for us in the drawing room.

"Quite," answered the Indian. "I skipped down to the morgue as you suggested and had a look at the *corpora delicti*. I didn't recognize the woman, but the man was William Archer Thurmond, much better known to the Criminal Investigation Department as 'The Snapper,' from his playful little habit of snapping up any unconsidered trifle left lying about. I got in touch with a friend at New Delhi by radio telephone, and he tells me 'The Snapper' was last heard of in Bahadupore. That seems to match up. Evidently he was fascinated by the lady's charms, and quite as evidently she was one of Karowlee's women. They probably eloped, and if I know 'The Snapper' she took something more than herself from the palace when she kept the rendezvous. Probably a quart or two of pearls or diamonds. So Karowlee wrote two more names down in his black books, and it seems his agents scored a double first this time."

"I agree," Jules de Grandin nodded. "For our part Friend Costello and I ransacked the neighborhood of the strange deaths, ringing every doorbell in the street, and found out that a Hindu gentleman named Basanta Roy took a room not far from the house where the dead woman was found."

"Humph," grunted Ram Chitra Das, "Basanta Roy, eh? There are about three hundred and twenty million people in India, accordin' to latest reports, and not less than five million of 'em are named Basanta Roy. Might as well be John Smith in London or Sam Cohen in New York, as far as identification goes."

"Nevertheless," de Grandin persisted, "this Monsieur Roy took lodgings in Thornapple Street. He was by all accounts a very old gentleman who wore a long white beard and kept much to himself, going out only after dark. He spoke English very well, but with an accent. Last night he came back to his room a little before midnight, paid two weeks' rent in lieu of notice, and decamped with bag and baggage."

"Aye?" Ram Chitra Das replied. "That may mean one of several things. Either he's satisfied with his job and gone back to India, or he's shifted operations from New Jersey to New York, hopin' to catch us off guard—eh? Oh, yes, dear, quite!"

Nairini had slipped the cap from her lipstick and leaned across the coffee table as if to rearrange the cups, in reality to scrawl on the mahogany with the cosmetic pencil:

CAREFUL—ONE LISTENS AT THE WINDOW

"As I was sayin'," Ram Chitra Das recommenced, but de Grandin interrupted. "Why do we not have some music, my friends? We have all night to talk about the case, let us defer our discussion till later. Will not you play for us, *Madame*? Your music? But of course, I shall be delighted to fetch it."

He hurried from the room and Nairini crossed to the piano, seated herself before the instrument and began to play softly, a slow, haunting tune pitched in a minor key, the heart-broken lament of an Afridi lover. The notes sank till they were no more than a soft murmur under her fingers. She bent forward toward the keyboard as if listening, waiting for something violent and dramatic.

"Trowbridge, Costello, Ram Chitra Das—*à moi!*" the little Frenchman's hail came from the garden. "I have him, me!"

We rushed through the French windows, vaulted down into the garden from the veranda and saw what seemed a vague, amorphous shadow draw suddenly in two parts, and heard de Grandin's jubilant announcement, "*C'est fini, mes amis.* He was a slippery eel, this one, but Jules de Grandin knows the fisherman's tricks. Yes, certainly."

From the midst of my Paul Scarlets he dragged something which upon inspection proved to be a small, gray-bearded man in a bad state of disrepair. Scratches from rose-thorns criss-crossed his face, his neat white-linen suit was soiled with black earth from the rose bed, the beautiful pale-green turban which had covered his shaved head had been jerked off to form a fetter for his hands.

"Go forward, thou!" the Frenchman ordered as he gave his captive a shove. "By blue, the one who tries to drive a knife in Jules de Grandin's ribs must get up before sunrise!"

"Well, as I live and breathe, if it's not Ajeit Swami!" exclaimed Ram Chitra Das as he inspected our prisoner. "Salaam, most reverend *Guru.* We must apologize for your reception, but as this gentleman has said, it is not thought good taste to try to stab a person in America." He gave a quick look at the knife de Grandin had dropped on the surgery table, and, "He didn't scratch you with this thing, did he?" he asked anxiously.

"Scratch me—me, Jules de Grandin?" snapped back the small Frenchman. "*Mordieu,* if you and I were not such friends I should be made to be insulted! Have I not said that he who would stab me—"

"Yes, yes; of course. Quite so. I'm glad he didn't nick you, though. I've seen these toad-prickers in action up Darjeeling way. Look." Taking up the short, curve-bladed dagger he grasped its handle in a quick grip, and from the tip of the steel shot a needle-fine jet of almost colorless liquid which hardened into a jelly-like substance almost as soon as it struck the porcelain top of the examination table. "Ingenious little tool, eh, what?" he asked. "That's krait venom, my friend, if anyone should happen to ask you. One touch of it and you're a dead pigeon."

"Name of a small blue man, now I am angry!" exclaimed Jules de Grandin. "He has no sportsmanship, that one."

"I'll say he hasn't," agreed Ram Chitra Das. "The famous American formula of never giving a sucker an even break was developed by gentlemen of his profession several generations before Gautama Buddha came to spread the Light in Asia."

Abruptly he dropped his bantering manner. "The question is, what's to be done with him?"

"Why not let me run him in, sor?" volunteered Costello. "We can hold him on a charge of assault wid a dangerous weapon, an' suspicion o' murther—"

"No go," Ram Chitra Das shook his head. "It's true he tried to stab Dr. de Grandin, but it's also true Dr. de Grandin attacked him. As for the murder charge, no judge in the country would listen to it. The coroner's physician can't assign a cause of death. How'd we ever manage to connect him with those killin's in Thornapple Street?"

"Then ye're sure they wuz killin's, not natural deaths?" Costello responded.

"Sure?" The Indian grinned at him, then turned to the prisoner. "You polished off 'The Snapper' and his girl friend in great shape, didn't you, Swami?"

The old man smiled at him almost benignly. "The power of the eye, Nana Sahib—"

"No names!" cut in the other sharply. "I'm just Ram Chitra Das, if you please."

"So be it," acquiesced the old man. "I cast the power of the eye on them and they died."

"H'm."

"*Que diable?*" demanded de Grandin. "Is it that he claims to have the Evil Eye?"

"Something like that," answered the Indian. Then, to me. "Have you some safe place we can stow him temporarily, Dr. Trowbridge?"

I thought a moment, then, "The garage?" I hazarded. "The car's out front, and we could shut him up there for a while."

"How about the windows?"

"There's only one, and I had bars put on that during the tire shortage when burglaries became so numerous."

"Good enough. Would you mind staying with Nairini—just in case—while we put this bird in his cage? Be with you in a moment."

"BUT THAT CAN'T BE, sor," I heard Costello remonstrate as they returned from securing the prisoner in the garage. "It's agin the order o' nature!"

"*Non, mon Lieutenant*, it are entirely possible, I do assure you," Jules de Grandin answered. "Ask good Friend Trowbridge if you doubt us."

"Could it be, sor?" dutifully complied Costello. "They're afther tellin' me a man can hypnotize hisself to death."

"What?" I demanded incredulously. "Hypnotize—"

"Perfectly, my old one," broke in de Grandin. "It are entirely possible. Ram Chitra Das affirms it, and while I think it unlikely, I think it could be so."

I turned from one of them to the other in confusion. "What in heaven's name is all this about?"

"Just this, sir," answered Ram Chitra Das, "this Swami Ajeit Singh is one of Raja Karowlee's chief wonder-workers. He's a skilled fakir, an adept at every brand o' magic known in India, and, of course, an expert hypnotist. He probably never heard of Baird or Mesmer, and never studied even elementary psychology, but when it comes to practical ability as a hypnotist I doubt if any of your best professionals could hold a candle to him.

"I take it you've seen experiments in hypnotism performed in the psychological laboratory or on the stage?"

I nodded, wondering what was coming next.

"Very well, sir. You've seen the operator make the subject become rigid, so that if his head is placed on one chair and his feet on another weights can be piled on his stomach to a degree he could not possibly support in consciousness?"

"Yes, I've seen that."

"Have you seen an operator make the blood go from one arm and run into the other till the skin threatens to burst?"

"Yes."

"And blood come through the skin as if a wound had been inflicted?"

"Yes," I nodded.

"And have not you seen the operator tell the subject to decrease his pulse-beat?" interjected Jules de Grandin. "Have not you seen pulsation at the hypnotist's command sink from eighty beats a minute to sixty, fifty, or even forty?"

"Ye-es," I agreed doubtfully. "I seem to recall such a demonstration in Baltimore some years ago, but—"

"No buts, if you will be so kind. I ask you as a man of science, Friend Trowbridge, if it is possible to tell the human heart—which as we know is an involuntary muscle and takes no orders from the conscious mind—to beat more slowly, is it not possible to tell it to cease beating altogether?"

"Well, I—"

"Do not evade the logic of the question, if you please, my friend. You have admitted seeing pulsation slowed down, even though the action of the heart is altogether involuntary. If it can be slowed down by hypnotic suggestion, why can not it be stopped entirely?"

I saw the logical conclusion of his premises, but was not ready to capitulate. "How could the operator, by which I suppose you mean Ajeit Swami, gain control of his subjects?" I demanded. "We all agree that acquiescence is the prime factor in successful hypnotism. The subject must be willing—"

"*Non, dix mille fois, non!*" he disagreed. "Consent is not at all necessary. All that is required is a lack of opposition. That is why we use the lights, the mirrors, the upraised forefinger—anything to fix the subject's attention and divert him from a state of rebellion, from thinking 'I will not be hypnotized.'

"Consider, if you please: This Ajeit Singh Swami is a skilled hypnotist, as are all of his kind. He has a reputation as a wonder-worker throughout Northern India. Is it not so? Of course. Very well, then. The more his reputation grows the greater is his power. People fear him. They believe that he can do much more than he can in reality. They feel—by blue, they know—that it is useless to resist what they call his magic and we call his hypnotic power.

"*Très bon.* Where are we now? We are in the house in Thornapple Street occupied by Monsieur Snapper and his little pretty lady friend of unknown name. We see them sitting in that big, so lovely hall, in pleasant conversation. Perhaps they smoke the *hookah* together, it had more than one mouth-piece. Perhaps they drink the after dinner coffee. Perhaps they just make the love. She seemed to me the sort of person to whom it would not be difficult to whisper sweet nothings. *Ha,* they have fled across the ocean to America; they have buried themselves in a semi-slum. They fancy themselves immune from pursuit. They feel secure. Yes. And then, all suddenly, comes the Swami Ajeit Singh, the emissary of Karowlee Sahib, and tells them he is there to work his master's vengeance on them. Are they startled? *Parbleu,* they are what you call petrified. They know him, they fear him; they are powerless to resist him as the poor silly rabbit that sees the serpent slithering toward him. *Morbleu,* their chicken—*non,* their goose—is cooked! Yes, certainly; of course.

"The woman falls into a trance at once when Swami Ajeit bids her sleep. He bids her heart beat more slowly, miss a beat, cease beating altogether. Yes. So it is. Monsieur Snapper, being English and a little stronger in the will, does not succumb so quickly. He resists a so little moment, hears the Swami bid the woman die, sees her expire, and he feels the uselessness of struggling; yet he does struggle—a little. When the Swami puts the brand of The Afghan on his forehead it rouses him, he still has the vitality to rise and try to flee.

"But he runs poorly, weakly. We saw him run across the sidewalk, and thought that he was drunk because he staggered so. *Hélas,* it was not so. He ran to sure and certain death, that one. With each step that he ran his mind repeated, 'Die—die—die!' When he had reached the curb he was no better than a running corpse. We saw him fall into the street. We did not know it, but we saw him die. The command to his heart to stop had followed him from the house to the street, it was impossible for him to outrun it as it would be for a horse to outrun his tail. Yes, it are indubitably so. It are not strange the good Parnell could find no cause of death. Those so unfortunate ones did not die; they merely ceased to live."

"I'm not convinced," I told him, "but even if we grant your argument, what are you going to do about it? You don't think any jury would convict him on such testimony, do you?"

"I'm afraid he's got us in a forked stick," Ram Chitra Das admitted. "He couldn't work his hypnotism on Nairini or me, of course. We're too well versed in such things; but there are other little tricks he might try on us. I'd feel a lot more comfortable if he were out of the way. By Minakshi—"

The little Frenchman's short laugh broke through his sentence. "*Cordieu*, my friend, you have supplied the answer, I damn think!"

"What d'ye mean—"

"Your mention of Minakshi, the Fish-Eyed Goddess. Once when I was at Pondicherry I made the pilgrimage to Madura to witness the annual nuptials of Siva and Minakshi of the amethyst and emerald eyes—'The Fish-Eyed One' as she is known throughout India. I saw her image carried in a splendid bridal car, observed the great jeweled eyes in her serene face and said to me, 'Jules de Grandin, there is danger in those eyes of hers. A man might gaze too long at them and lose himself completely; become hypnotized. Does not the legend say even great Siva is enmeshed when he looks into them? There may be factual foundation for that legend, Jules de Grandin.' And so I looked away. I am a brave man, me, but I take no unnecessary chances. No."

Ram Chitra Das raised puzzled brows, but Costello was more forthright. "Is it completely daft ye've gone, sor?" he demanded.

"Daft—crazy?" answered Jules de Grandin with one of his quick elfin grins. "But yes, completely crazy, *mon Lieutenant*—crazy like the fox. Await me here, if you will be so kind." He hurried from the room and Costello turned to us with a Lord-save-my-sanity expression.

"What're ye goin' to do wid a leprechaun like that?" he asked helplessly. "Sometimes I think he's nutty as a fruitcake, then zowie! up he comes wid a idee that knocks ye for a loop."

THE PATTER OF DE Grandin's feet came from the hall and he bounced into the room with upraised hands. "Observe them, if you please, *mes enfants!*" he commanded. "Are they not superb?" Between the thumb and finger of each hand he held a disc of colored glass, its periphery marked by a zone of greenish-brown, its center by a dot of black. I recognized them as the glass eyes from a white bear rug that I had purchased in a thoughtless moment years before and relegated to the attic long since.

"What—" I began, but he cut me off with such a smug grin that I could have kicked him.

"*Regardez-moi*," he ordered. From his jacket pocket he produced a lead tube which I recognized as the container of some luminous paint with which I'd had the house number marked some time before in order that late-calling patients could see it more easily. Squeezing a bit of the paint paste on the tip of a match he proceeded to overlay the cornea of the glass eyes with it, working with that neat, swift precision which distinguished everything he did.

"Turn out the lights, if you please," he directed, and as I complied we were plunged in Stygian darkness, for the lamps had been extinguished in the dining room and no moonlight filtered through the windows. "Observe me, closely, if you please," his command came through the dark, and as we watched twin spots of luminance began to glow, at first faintly, then with sharper definition, finally with a greenish-toned infernal blaze that seemed to give off wisps of smoke as if its fire fed on itself and needed no other fuel.

"Howly Moses!" exclaimed Costello. "Who'd 'a' thought it?"

The lights blazed on again and I let my breath out with a jerk, nor was it till then that I realized I'd been holding it. "You see?" he asked. "Are they not truly fascinating?"

"Call it that if ye wish, sor," answered Costello: "I got another name for it."

"Precisely, *mon lieutenant*. So will he."

"He, sor? Who?"

"That wicked old man now incarcerated in Friend Trowbridge's garage. The one who tried to stab me with a poisoned dagger. Tonight we perform a most interesting experiment. We shall see how wickedness is turned against itself, how the power of suggestion may be made to rebound on him who exercises it for evil. Yes.

"Will you be kind enough to bring him from the garage?" he asked Costello and Ram Chitra Das.

"And now my old and very wicked one," he told the fakir when they had brought him into the drawing room, "you killed Monsieur the Snapper and his little pretty lady companion by the power of the eye. Is it not so?"

"It is so," replied the old man with a smile of such supreme self-satisfaction that it was little less than a smirk. "Moreover, I am safe from any harm your laws can do me. No judge sahib in your country would believe I have the power—"

"*Précisément, mon vieux et mangé des vers*, but we believe—and so do you. Anon we put you in a sure, safe place, and presently there comes another who will share the darkness with you. Think on her and be afraid. Remember into whose eyes even great Siva may not look without loss of his will. Bid the blood run slow and slower in your veins, the heart beat weak and weaker in your breast until it beats no more."

He turned abruptly on his heel and left the room, but in a moment he returned and whispered to Costello and Ram Chitra Das, "Take him all quickly into the garage, my friends, and bind him so his face is toward the window. I have fixed the eyes against the wall beneath the sill."

"S'pose he won't look at 'em, sor?" Costello asked when he and the Indian returned from securing the prisoner. "He might shut his eyes or turn his head away—"

"We need not make ourselves uneasy on that score," de Grandin replied. "Human nature being what it is, a man can no more help turning his eyes toward a point of light in a dark room than he can keep from snapping his lids shut when someone pokes a finger at his face. Also, you recall how you were fascinated by the glow of those eyes in the dark. You knew what they were, yet you felt fear; he has no warning. He was told only, 'Presently another comes.' When he has been in the dark a few moments the eyes will begin glowing, it will be as if one came from outside—whether from outside the garage or from another world he will not know.

"But do you seriously think a man can command himself to stop living?" I asked.

"Perfectly," de Grandin cut in "This Ajeit Swami may be a wise man, he may think he understands a great variety of things, but also he is very superstitious. He believes in magic. His is no coldly scientific mind. I planted the seed in his brain before they took him out. Fear—fear of the unknown, which is the greatest fear of all—will do the rest. We know the *ju-ju* of the African witch-doctor is powerless against the European because he does not believe in it, but even the educated native has active or latent superstitious dread of witchcraft, and in consequence, when he is told a spell has been put on him, he weakens, wastes away and dies, purely through the power of suggestion and the working of ingrained belief and fear. Yes, it is so."

Somewhat later he glanced at his watch and put down his glass. "An hour. It is time, I think, my friends. Come, let us go all quietly to the garage and observe what we shall observe."

SHORTLY AFTER NOON NEXT day we ran into Dr. Parnell. "Hey, you fellers been up to some more monkey-business?" he demanded.

"Business of the monkey?" Jules de Grandin's face was blank as a brick wall. "How do you mean, *cher collègue?*"

Parnell eyed us suspiciously. "Well, I wouldn't put it past you two. The police found a dead man in the street not far from Trowbridge's this morning about three o'clock, and—"

"Yes, and—" de Grandin prompted as Parnell came to a pause.

"And I'd say he died of heart failure except for one thing."

"And what is that one so small thing, if you please?"

"There's nothing wrong with his heart. It's sound as a dollar."

"*Tenez,*" de Grandin tweaked the ends o his mustache, "perhaps he auto-hypnotized himself to death, *cher collègue.* Will not you join us in a drink? You look as if you could use one, as *le bon Dieu* knows I can and shall."

Clair de Lune

M Y FRIEND DE GRANDIN turned to me, brows raised, lips pursed as if about to whistle. "*Comment?*" he demanded. "What is that you say?"

"You understand me perfectly," I grinned back. "I said that if I didn't know you for a case-hardened misogynist I'd think you contemplated an *affaire* with that woman. You've hardly taken your eyes off her since we came here."

The laugh lights gleamed in his small, round, blue eyes and he tweaked the ends of his diminutive wheat-blond mustache like a tomcat combing his whiskers after an especially toothsome meal. "*Eh, bien*, my old and rare, she interests me—"

"So I gathered—"

"And is she not one *bonne bouchée* to merit anybody's interest, I demand to know?"

"She is," I admitted. "She's utterly exquisite, but the way you've ogled her, like a moonstruck calf—"

"Oh, Dr. Trowbridge, Dr. de Grandin!" Miss Templeton, the resort's hostess and all 'round promoter of good times, came fairly dancing toward us across the hotel veranda, "I'm so thrilled!"

"Indeed, *Mademoiselle?*" de Grandin rose and gave her a particularly engaging smile. "One is rejoiced to hear it. What is the cause of your so happy quivering?"

"It's Madelon Leroy!" In ordinary conversation thrilled, delighted laughter seemed about to break through everything Dot Templeton said, and her sentences were punctuated exclusively with exclamation points. Now she positively talked in italics. "She's coming to our dance tonight! You know, she's been so *frightfully* exclusive since she came here—said she came down to the shore to rest and didn't want to meet a soul. But's she's relented, and will hold an informal reception just before the hop—"

"*Tiens*, but this is of the interest, truly," he cut in. "You may count upon our presence at the soirée, *Mademoiselle*. But of course."

As Dot danced off to spread glad tidings of great joy to other guests he glanced down at his wrist. "*Mon Dieu*, friend Trowbridge," he exclaimed, "it is almost one o'clock, and we have not yet lunched. Come, let us hasten to the dining room. Me, I am almost starved. I faint, I perish! I am vilely hungry."

TWO TABLES AWAY FROM us, where a gentle breeze fanned through a long window facing the ocean, Madelon Leroy sat at luncheon, cool, almost contemptuous of the looks leveled at her. She was, as Jules de Grandin had remarked, a *bonne bouchée* deserving anyone's attention. Her first performance in the name part of Eric Maxwell's *Clair de Lune* had set the critics raving, not only over her talent as an actress, but over her exquisite, faery beauty, her delicate fragility that seemed almost other-worldly. When, after a phenomenally long run on Broadway she refused flatly to consider Hollywood's most tempting offers, she stirred up a maelstrom of publicity that set theatrical press agents raving mad. Artists were permitted to sketch her, but she steadfastly refused to be photographed, and to thwart ambitious camera fiends and newsmen she went veiled demurely as a nun or odalisk when she appeared in public. *Clair de Lune* had closed for the summer, and its mysterious, lovely star was resting by the sea when Jules de Grandin and I checked in at the Adlon.

Covertly I studied her above the margin of my menu; de Grandin made no pretense of detachment, but stared at her as no one but a Frenchman can stare without giving offense. She was a lovely thing to look at, with her dead-white, almost transparent skin, her spun-gold hair, unbobbed, that made a halo of glory around her small head, and great, trustful-seeming eyes of soft, cerulean blue. There was a sort of fairylike, almost angelic fragility about her arching, slender neck and delicately cut profile, and though she was not really small she seemed so, for she was slender and small-boned, not like a Watteau shepherdess, but like a little girl, and every move she made was graceful and unhurried as grain bending in the wind. With her fragile fairness outlined against the window she was like some princess from a fairy tale come wondrously to life, the very spirit and epitome of all the fair, frail heroines of poetry.

"*Une belle créature, n'est-ce-pas?*" de Grandin asked as the waiter appeared to take our order, and he lost all interest in our fair neighbor. Women to him were blossoms brightening the pathway of life, but food—and drink—"*mon Dieu*," as he was wont to say, "they are that without which life is impossible!"

MISS LEROY HELD COURT like a princess at the reception preceding the ball that evening. If she had seemed captivating in the shadowed recess of the dining room, or on the wide veranda of the hotel, or emerging from the ocean in white satin bathing suit, dripping and lovely as a naiad, she was positively ravishing that night. More than ever she seemed like a being from another world in a sleeveless gown of clinging, white silk jersey that followed every curve and small roundness of her daintily moulded figure. It was belted at the waist with a gold cord whose tasselled ends hung almost to the floor, and as its hem swept back occasionally we caught fleeting glimpses of the little gilded sandals strapped to her bare feet.

Her pale-gold hair was done in a loose knot and tied with a fillet of narrow, white ribbon. About her left arm, just above the elbow, was a broad, gold bracelet chased with a Grecian motif, otherwise she wore no jewelry or ornaments.

She should have been completely charming, altogether lovely, but there was something vaguely repellent about her. Perhaps it was her slow and rather condescending smile that held no trace of warmth or human friendliness, perhaps it was the odd expression of her eyes—knowing, weary, rather sad, as if from their first opening they had seen people were a tiresome race, and hardly worth the effort of a second glance. Or possibly it might have been the eyes themselves, for despite her skillful makeup and the pains obviously taken with her by beauticians there was a fine lacework of wrinkles at their outer corners, and the lids were rubbed to the sheen of old silk with a faintly greenish eye-shadow; certainly not the lids of a woman in her twenties, or even in her middle thirties.

"Dr. Trowbridge," she extended a hand small and slender as a child's, rosy-tipped and fragile as a white iris, and, "Dr. de Grandin," as the little Frenchman clicked his heels before her.

"Enchanté, Mademoiselle," he bowed above the little hand and raised it to his lips, "mais je suis très heureux de vous voir!—but I am fortunate to meet you!"

There is no way of putting it in words, but as de Grandin straightened, he and Madelon Leroy looked squarely in each other's eyes, and while nothing moved in either of their faces something vague, intangible as air, yet perceptible as a chill, seemed forming round them like an envelope of cold vapor. For just an instant each took stock of the other, wary as a fencer measuring his opponent or a boxer feeling out his adversary, and I had the feeling they were like two chemicals that waited only the addition of a catalytic agent to explode them in a devastating detonation. Then the next guest was presented and we passed on, but I felt as if we had stepped back into normal summer temperature from a chilled refrigerator.

"Whatever—" I began, but the advent of Mazie Schaeffer interrupted my query.

"Oh, Dr. Trowbridge, isn't she adorable?" asked Mazie. "She's the most beautiful, the most wonderful actress in the world! There never was another like her. I've heard Dad and Mumsie talk about Maude Adams and Bernhardt and Duse, but Madelon Leroy—she's really tops! D'ye remember her in the last scene of Clair de Lune, where she says goodbye to her lover at the convent gate, then stands there—just stands there in the moonlight, saying nothing, but you can fairly see her heart breaking?"

De Grandin grinned engagingly at Mazie. "Perhaps it is that she has had much time to perfect her art, *Mademoiselle*—"

"Time?" Mazie echoed almost shrilly. "How could she have had time? She's just a girl—hardly more than a child. I'm twenty-one in August, and I'll bet she's two years my junior. It isn't time or talent, Dr. de Grandin, it's genius, sheer genius. Only one woman in a generation has it, and she has it—in spades!—for hers."

The little Frenchman studied her attentively. "You have perhaps met her?"

"Met her?" Mazie seemed upon the point of swooning, and her hands went to her bosom as if she would quiet a tumultuous heart. "Oh, *yes*. She was lovely to me—told me I might come to her suite for tea tomorrow—"

"*Mon Dieu!*" de Grandin exploded. "So soon? Do you mean it, *Mademoiselle?*"

"Yes, isn't it too wonderful? Much, much too fearfully wonderful to have happened to anyone like me!"

"You speak correctly," he agreed with a nod. "Fearfully wonderful is right. *Bon soir, Mademoiselle.*"

"Now," I demanded as we left the crowded ballroom and went out on the wide, breeze-swept veranda, "what's it all mean?"

"I only wish I knew," he answered somberly.

"Oh, for goodness' sake," I was nettled and made no attempt to hide it, "don't be so devilishly mysterious! I know there's something between you and that woman—I could fairly feel it when you met. But what—"

"I only wish I knew," he repeated almost morosely. "To suspect is one thing, to know is something else again, and I, *hélas!* have no more thin a naked suspicion. To say what gnaws my mind like a maggot might do a grave injustice to an innocent one. *Au contraire*, to keep silent may cause great and lasting injury to another. *Parbleu*, my friend, I know not what to do. I am entirely miserable."

I glanced at my watch. "We might try going to bed. It's after eleven, and we go back tomorrow morning. This will be our last sure chance of a night's sleep. No patients to rouse us at all sorts of unholy hours—"

"No babies to be ushered in, no *viellards* to be erased out of the world," he agreed with a chuckle. "I think you have right, my old one. Let us lose our troubles in our dreams."

N EXT MORNING AS, PRECEDED by two bellboys with our traps, we were about to leave the hotel, I stepped aside to make way for two women headed for the beach. The first was middle-aged, with long, sharp nose and small, sharp eyes, dark-haired, swarthy-skinned, with little strands of gray in her black hair and the white linen cap of a maid on her head. Her uniform was stiff, black bombazine and set off by a white apron and cuffs. Across her arm draped a huge, fluffy bath towel. She looked formidable to me, the sort of person who had seen much better days and had at last retired from a world that used her shabbily to commune secretly with ineffectual devils.

Behind her, muffled like an Arab woman in a hooded robe of white terry cloth, a smaller figure shuffled in wooden beach clogs. The fingers of one hand protruded from a fold of the robe as she clutched it about her, and I noted they were red-tipped, with long, sharp-pointed nails, and thin almost to the point of desiccation. Beneath the muffling hood of the robe we caught a glimpse of her face. It was Madelon Leroy's, but so altered that it bore hardly any semblance to that of the radiant being of the night before. She was pale as Mardi moonlight, and the delicate, small hollows underneath her cheekbones were accentuated till her countenance seemed positively ghastly. Her narrow lips, a little parted, seemed almost withered, and about her nose there was a pinched, drawn look, while her large sky-hued eyes seemed even larger, yet seemed to have receded in her head. Her whole face seemed instinct with longing, yet a longing that was impersonal. The only thing unchanged about her was her grace of movement, for she walked with an effortless, gliding step, turning her flat hips only slightly.

"*Grand Dieu!*" I heard de Grandin murmur, then, as she passed he bowed and raised his hand to his hat brim in salute. "*Mademoiselle!*"

She passed as if he had not been there, her deep-set, cavernous eyes fixed on the sunlit beach where little wavelets wove a line of lacy ruffles on the sand.

"Good heavens," I exclaimed as we proceeded to our waiting car, "she looks ten—twenty—years older. What do you make of it?"

He faced me somberly. "I do not quite know, Friend Trowbridge. List night I entertained suspicion. Today I have the almost-certainty. Tomorrow I may know exactly, but by tomorrow it may be too late."

"What are you driving at?" I demanded. "All this mystery about—"

"Do you remember this quotation?" he countered: "*Plus ça change, plus c'est la même chose?*"

I thought a moment. "Isn't that what Voltaire said about history—'the more it changes, the more it is the same'?"

"It is," he agreed with another sober nod, "and never did he state a greater truth. Once more I damn think history is about to repeat, and with what tragic consequences none can say."

"Tragic consequences? To whom?"

"*On ne sait pas?*" he raised his narrow shoulders in a shrug. "Who can say where lightning designs to strike, my old?"

WE HAD BEEN HOME from the shore a week or so, and I was just preparing to call it a day when the office telephone began to stutter. "Sam, this is Jane Schaeffer," came the troubled hail across the wire. "Can you come over right away?"

"What's wrong?" I temporized. The day had been a hot and tiring one, and Nora McGinnis had prepared veal with sweet and sour sauce. I was in no mood to drive two miles, miss my evening cocktail and sit down to a spoiled dinner.

"It's Mazie. She seems so much worse—"

"Worse?" I echoed. "She seemed all right when I saw her down at the shore. Lively as a cricket—"

"That's just it. She was well and healthy as a pony when she came home, but she's been acting so queerly, and getting weaker every day. I'm afraid it's consumption or leukemia, or something—"

"Now, take it easy," I advised. "Mazie can't dance every night till three o'clock and I play tennis every afternoon without something giving way. Give her some toast and tea for dinner, put her to bed, and see she stays there all night, then bring her round to see me in the morning—"

"Sam Trowbridge, listen to me! My child is dying—and not dying on her feet, either, and you tell me to give her toast and tea! You get right in your car this minute and come over, or—"

"All right," I placated. "Put her to bed, and I'll—"

"She's in bed now, you great booby. That's what I've been trying to tell you. She hasn't been up all day. She's too weak—"

"Why didn't you say so at first?" I interrupted rather unreasonably. "Hold everything. I'll be right over—"

"What presents itself, *mon vieux?*" de Grandin appeared at the office door, a beaded cocktail shaker in his hand. "Do not say that you must leave. The martinis are at the perfect state of chilliness—"

"Not now," I refused sadly. "Jane Schaeffer just called to say Mazie's in a bad way. So weak she couldn't rise this morning—"

"*Feu noir du diable*—black fire of Satan! Is it that small happy one who is selected as the victim? *Morbleu*, I should have apprehended it—"

"What's that?" I interrupted sharply. "What d'ye know—"

"*Hélas*, I know nothing. Not a thing, by blue! But if what I have good reason to damn suspect is true—come, let us hasten, let us fly, let us rush with all celerity to attend her! Dinner? Fie upon dinner! We have other things to think of, us."

H ER MOTHER HAD NOT overstated Mazie's condition. We found her in a state of semi-coma, with sharp concavities beneath her cheekbones and violet crescents underneath her eyes. The eyes themselves were bright as if with fever, but the hand I took in mine was cold as a dead thing, and when I read my clinical thermometer I saw it registered a scant eighty, while her pulse was thin and reedy, beating less than seventy slow, feeble strokes a minute. She rolled her head listlessly as I dropped into a chair beside the bed, and the smile she offered me was a thin ghost of her infectious grin which did no more than move her lips a little and never reached her eyes.

"What's going on here?" I demanded, noting how the epidermis of her hand seemed dry and roughened, almost as if it were chapped. "What have they been doing to my girl?"

The lids drooped sleepily above the feverishly bright eyes and she murmured in a voice so weak that I could not catch her reply. "What?" I asked.

"Le—let me go—I must—I have to—" she begged in a feeble whisper. "She'll be expecting me—she needs me—"

"Delirium?" I whispered, but de Grandin shook his head in negation.

"I do not think so, my friend. She is weak, yes; very weak, but not irrational. No, I would not say it. Cannot you read the symptoms?"

"If it weren't that we saw her horse-strong and well fed as an alderman less than two weeks ago, I'd say she is the victim of primary starvation. I saw cases showing all these symptoms after World War I when I was with the Belgian Relief—"

"Your wisdom and experience have not deserted you, my old one. It is that she starves—at least she is undernourished, and we would be advised to prescribe nux vomica for her, but first to see that she has strong beef tea with sherry in it, and after that some egg and milk with a little brandy—"

"But how could she possibly have developed such an advanced case of malnutrition in these few days—"

"Ha, yes, by damn it! That is for us to find out."

"What is it?" asked Jane Schaeffer as we came down the stairs. "Do you think she could have picked up an infection at the shore?"

De Grandin pursed his lips and took his chin between his thumb and forefinger. "Pas possible, Madame. How long has she been thus?"

"Almost since the day she came back. She met Madelon Leroy the actress at the shore, and developed one of those desperate girl-crushes on her. She's spent practically every waking moment with Miss Leroy, and—let's see, was it the second or the third day?—I think it was the third day she called on her since she came home almost exhausted and went right to bed. Next morning she seemed weak and listless, rose about noon, ate a big brunch, and went right back to Miss Leroy's. That night she came home almost in collapse and every day she's seemed to grow weaker."

He eyed her sharply. "You say her appetite is excellent?"

"Excellent? It's stupendous. You don't think she could have a malignant tapeworm, do you, or some such parasite—"

He nodded thoughtfully. "I think she might, indeed, Madame." Then, with what seemed to me like irrelevance: "This Miss Leroy, where is it that she lives, if you please?"

"She took a suite at the Zachary Taylor. Why she chose to stay here rather than New York I can't imagine—"

"Perhaps there are those who can, Madame Schaeffer. So. Very good. She took up quarters at the Hotel Taylor, and—"

"And Mazie's been to see her every day."

"*Très bon*. One understands, in part, at least. Your daughter's illness is not hopeless, but it is far more serious than we had at first suspected. We shall send her to the Sidewell Sanitorium at once, and there she is to have complete bed rest with a nurse constantly beside her. On no account are you to say where she has gone, *Madame*, and she must have no visitors. None. You comprehend?"

"Yes, sir. But—"

"Yes? But—"

"Miss Leroy has called her twice today, and seemed concerned when she heard Mazie could not get up. If she should call to see—"

"I said no visitors, *Madame*. It is an order, if you please."

"I HOPE YOU KNOW what you're doing," I grumbled as we left the Schaeffer house. "I can't find fault with your diagnosis or treatment, but why be so mysterious about it? If you know something—"

"Alas, my friend, that is just what I do not," he admitted. "It is not that I make the mystery purposely; it is that I am ignorant. Me, I am like a blind man teased by naughty little boys. I reach this way and that for my tormentors, but nothing can my reaching fingers grasp. You recall that we were speaking of the way that history repeats itself?"

"Yes, the morning we left the shore."

"Quite yes. Now, listen carefully, my friend. What I shall say may not make sense, but then, again, it may. Consider:

"More years ago than I like to remember I went to the *Théâtre Français* to see one called Madelon Larue. She was the toast of Paris, that one, for in an age when we were prim and prosy by today's standards she made bold to dance *au naturelle*. *Parbleu*, I thought myself a sad dog when I went to see her!" He nodded gravely. "She was very beautiful, her; not beautiful like Venus or Minerva, but like Hebe or Clytie, with a dainty, almost childlike loveliness, and an artlessness that made her nudity a thing of beauty rather than of passion. *Eh bien*, my *gran'père*—may the sod lie lightly on him!—had been a gay dog in his day, also. He was summering near Narbonne that year, and when I went to visit him and partake of his excellent Chateau Neuf and told him I had seen Larue he was amazed.

"For why? Because, *parbleu*, it seems that in the days of the Second Empire there had been an actress who was also the toast of Paris, one Madelon Larose. She, too, had danced *à découvert* before the gilded youth who flocked about the

Third Napoleon. He had seen her, worshiped her from afar, been willing to lay down his life for her. He told me of her fragile, childlike beauty that set men's hearts and brains ablaze and when he finished telling I knew Madelon Larose and Madelon Larue were either one and the same or mother and daughter. *Ha,* but he told me something else, my *gran'père.* Yes. He was a lawyer physician, that one, and as such connected with the *préfecture de police.*

"This Madelon Larose, her of the fragile, childlike beauty, began to age all suddenly. Within the space of one small month she grew ten—twenty—years older. In sixty days she was so old and feeble she could no longer appear on the stage. Then, I ask you, what happened?"

"She retired," I suggested ironically.

"Not she, by blue! She engaged a secretary and companion, a fine upstanding Breton girl and—attend me carefully, if you please—within two months the girl was dead, apparently of starvation, and Madelon Larose was once more dancing *sans chemise* to the infinite delight of the young men of Paris. Yes.

"There was a scandal, naturally. The police and the *Sûreté* made investigations. Of course. But when all had been pried into they were no wiser than before. The girl had been a strong and healthy wench. The girl was dead, apparently of inanition; Larose had seemed upon the point of dissolution from old age; now she was young and strong and lovelier than ever. That was all. One does not base a criminal prosecution on such evidence. *Enfin,* the girl was buried decently in *Père Lachaise,* and Larose—at the suggestion of the police—betook herself to Italy. What she did there is anybody's guess.

"Now, let us match my story with my *gran'père's:* It was in 1905 I saw Larue perform. Five years later, when I had become a member of *la faculté de médicine légale,* I learned she had been smitten with a strange disease, an illness that caused her to age a decade in a week; in two weeks she was no more able to appear upon the stage. Then, I ask to know, what happened? *Parbleu,* I shall tell you, me!

"She hired a *masseuse,* a strong and healthy young woman of robust physique. In two weeks that one died—apparently from starvation—and Larue, *mordieu,* she bloomed again, if not quite like the rose, at least like the lily.

"I was assigned as assistant to the *juge d'instruction* in the case. We did investigate most thoroughly. Oh, yes. And what did we discover, I damn ask? This, only this, *morbleu:* The girl had been a strong and healthy young person. Now she was dead, apparently of inanition. Larue had seemed upon the point of dissolution from some strange and nameless wasting disease. Now she was young and strong and very beautiful again. *C'est tout.* One does not base a criminal prosecution on such evidence. *Enfin,* the poor young *masseuse* was recently interred in Saint Supplice, and Larue—at the suggestion of the police—went to Buenos Aires. What she did there is anybody's guess.

"Now, let us see what we have. It may not amount to proof, but at least it is evidence: Larose, Larue, Leroy; the names are rather similar, although admittedly not identical. One Madelon Larose who is apparently about to die of some strange wasting malady—perhaps old age—makes contact with a vigorous young woman and regains health and apparent youth while the younger person perishes, sucked dry as an orange. That is in 1867. A generation later a woman called Madelon Larue who fits the description of Larose perfectly is stricken ill with precisely the same sort of sickness, and regains her health as Larose had done, leaving behind her the starved, worn-out remnant of a young, strong, vigorous woman with whom she had been associated. That is in 1910. Now in our time a woman named Madelon Leroy—"

"But this is utterly fantastic!" I objected. "You're assuming the whole thing. How can you possibly identify Madelon Leroy with those two—"

"Attend me for a little so small moment," he broke in. "You will recall that when Leroy first came under our notice I appeared interested?"

"You certainly did. You hardly took your eyes off her—"

"*Précisément*. Because of why? Because, *parbleu*, the moment I first saw her I said to me, 'Jules de Grandin, where have you seen that one before?' And, 'Jules de Grandin,' I reply to me, 'do not try to fool yourself. You know very well where you first saw her. She is Madelon Larue who thrilled you when she danced *nu comme la main* at the *Théâtre Français* when you were in your salad days. Again you saw her, and her charm and beauty had not faded, when you made inquiry of the so strange death of her young, healthy *masseuse*. Do not you remember, Jules de Grandin?'

"'I do,' I told me.

"'Very well, then, Jules de Grandin,' I continue cross-examining me, 'what are this so little pretty lady doing here today, apparently no older than she was in 1910—or 1905? You have grown older, all your friends have aged since then, is she alone in all the world a human evergreen, a creature ageless as the moonlight?'

"'The devil knows the answer, not I, Jules de Grandin,' I tell me.

"And so, what happens next, I ask you? There is a grand soirée, and Mademoiselle Leroy gives audience to her public. We meet, we look into each other's eyes, we recognize each other, *pardieu!* In me she sees the *juge d'instruction* who caused her much embarrassment so many years ago. In her I see—what shall I say? At any rate we recognize each other, nor are we happy in the mutual recognition. No. Of course."

NEXT AFTERNOON WHEN WE went to the sanitorium to see Mazie we found her much improved, but still weak and restless. "Please, when may I leave?" she asked. "I've an engagement that I really ought to keep, and I feel so marvelously better—"

"Precisely, *Mademoiselle*," de Grandin agreed. "You are much better. Presently you shall be all well if you remain here, soak up nourishment *comme une éponge* and—"

"But—"

"But?" he repeated, eyebrows raised in mild interrogation. "What is the 'but', if you please?"

"It's Madelon Leroy, sir. I was helping her—"

"One does not doubt it," he assented grimly. "How?"

"She said my youth and strength renewed her courage to go on—she's really on the verge of a breakdown, you know—and just having me visit her meant so much—"

The stern look on his face halted her. "Why, what's the matter?" she faltered.

"Attend me, *Mademoiselle*. Just what transpired on your visits to this person's suite at the hotel?"

"Why, nothing, really. *Madelon*—she lets me call her that—isn't it wonderful?—is so fatigued she hardly speaks. Just lies on a *chaise* lounge in the most fascinating *negligées* and has me hold her hand and read to her. Then we have tea and take a little nap with her cuddled in my arms like a baby. Sometimes she smiles in her sleep, and when she does she's like an angel having heavenly dreams."

"And you have joy in this friendship, *hein?*"

" Oh, *yes*, sir. It's the most wonderful thing that ever happened to me."

He smiled at her as he rose. "*Bien*. It will be a happy memory to you in the years to come, I am convinced. Meanwhile, we have others to attend, and if you gain in strength as you have done, in a few days—"

"But Madelon?"

"We shall see her and explain all, *ma petite*. Yes, of course."

"Oh, *will* you? How good of you!" Mazie gave him back an answering smile and nestled down to sleep as sweetly as a child.

"Miss Leroy's maid called three times today," Jane Schaeffer told us when we stopped at her house on our way from the sanitorium. "It seems her mistress is quite ill, and very anxious to see Mazie—"

"One can imagine," Jules de Grandin agreed dryly.

"So—she seems so fond of the dear child and asked for her so piteously—I finally gave in and told her where you'd sent Mazie—"

"You *what?*" De Grandin seemed to have some difficulty in swallowing, as if he'd taken a morsel of hot food in his mouth.

"Why, what's wrong about that? I thought—"

"There you make the mistake, *Madame*. If you had thought you would have remembered that we strictly forbade all visitors. We shall do what we can, and do it quickly as may be, but if we fail the fault is yours. *Bon jour, Madame!*" He clicked his heels together and bowed formally, his manner several degrees below freezing. "Come, Friend Trowbridge, we have duties to perform, duties that will not bear postponement."

Once on the pavement he exploded like a bursting rocket. "*Nom d'un chat de nom d'un chien de nom d'un coq!* We can defend ourselves against our ill-intentioned enemies; from chuckle-headed friends there is no refuge, *pardieu!* Come, my old one, speed is most essential."

"Where to?" I asked as I started the engine.

"To the sanitorium, by blue! If we make rushing-haste we may not be too late."

THE BLUE RIDGE OF the Orange Mountains drowsed in the distance through the heat-haze of the summer afternoon, and the gray highway reeled out behind us like a paid-out ribbon. "Faster, faster!" he urged. "It is that we must hasten, Friend Trowbridge."

Half a mile or so ahead a big black car, so elegant it might have belonged to a mortician, sped toward the sanitorium, and his small blue eyes lighted as he described it. "Hers!" he exclaimed. "If we can pass her all may yet be well. Cannot you squeeze more speed from the *moteur?*"

I bore down on the accelerator and the needle crawled across the dial of the speedometer. Sixty-five, seventy, seventy-five—the distance between us and our quarry melted with each revolution of the wheels.

The chauffeur of the other car must have seen us in his rear-view mirror, or perhaps his passenger espied us. At any rate he put on speed, drew steadily away from us and vanished round the turn of the road in a swirling cloud of dust and exhaust-smoke.

"*Parbleu, pardieu, par la barbe d'un porc vert!*" swore de Grandin. "It is that she outruns us; she makes a monkey of—"

The scream of futilely applied brakes and clash of splintering glass cut his complaint short, and as I braked to round the curve we saw the big black sedan sprawled upon its side, wheels spinning crazily, windshield and windows spider-webbed with cracks, and lenses smashed from its lights. Already a thin trail of smoke was spiraling from its motor. "*Triomphe!*" he cried as he leaped from my car and raced toward the wrecked vehicle. "Into our hands she has been delivered, my friend!"

The chauffeur was wedged in behind his wheel, unconscious but not bleeding, and in the tonneau two female forms huddled, a large woman in somber black whom I recognized as Miss Leroy's maid, and, swathed in veilings till she looked like a gray ghost, the diminutive form of Madelon Leroy. "Look to him, Friend Trowbridge," he ordered as he wrenched at the handle of the rear door. "I shall make it my affair to extricate the women." With a mighty heave he drew the fainting maid from the wreck, dragged her to a place of safety and dived back to lift Madelon Leroy out.

I had managed to drag the chauffeur to a cleared space in the roadside woodland, and not a moment too soon, for a broad sheet of flame whipped suddenly from the wrecked sedan, and in a moment its gas tank exploded like a bomb, strewing specks of fire and shattered glass and metal everywhere. "By George, that was a near thing!" I panted as I emerged from the shelter I had taken behind a tree. "If we'd been ten seconds later they would all have been cremated."

He nodded, almost absent-mindedly. "If you will watch beside them I shall seek a telephone to call an ambulance, my friend . . . they are in need of care, these ones, especially Mademoiselle Leroy. You have the weight at Mercy Hospital?"

"What d'ye mean—"

"The influence, the—how do you say him?—drag? If it can be arranged to have them given separate rooms it would be very beneficial to all parties concerned."

W E SAT BESIDE HER bed in Mercy Hospital. The chauffeur and maid had been given semi-private rooms, and under his direction Madelon Leroy had been assigned a private suite on the top floor. The sun was going down, a ball of crimson in a sea of swirling rose, and a little breeze played prankishly with the white curtains at the window. If we had not known her identity neither of us could have recognized the woman in the bed as lovely, glamorous Madelon Leroy.

Her face was livid, almost green, and the mortuary outlines of her skull were visible through her taut skin—the hollow temples, pitted eye-orbits, pinched, strangely shortened nose, projecting jawline, jutting superciliary ridges. Some azure veinlets in the bluish whiteness of her cheeks accentuated her pallor, giving her face a strange, waxen look, the ears were almost transparent, and all trace of fullness had gone from the lips that drew back from the small, white, even teeth as if she fought for breath. "Mazie," she called in a thin, weak whisper, "where are you, dear? Come, it is time for our nap. Take me in your arms, dear; hold me close to your strong, youthful body—"

De Grandin rose and leaned across the bed, looking down at her not as a doctor looks at his patient, nor even as a man may look at a suffering woman, but with the cold impersonality the executioner might show as he looks at the condemned. "Larose, Larue, Leroy—whatever name you choose to call yourself—you are at last at the end of the road. There are no victims to renew your pseudo-youth. By yourself you came into the world—*le bon Dieu* only knows how many years ago—and by yourself you leave it. Yes."

The woman looked at him with dull, lack-luster eyes, and gradual recognition came into her withered face. "You!" she exclaimed in a panic-stricken, small voice. "Hast thou found me, O mine enemy?"

"*Tu parles, ma vielle*," he replied nonchalantly. "You have said so, old woman. I have found thee. I was not there to keep thee from absorbing life from that poor one in 1910, nor could I stand between thee and that pitiful young girl in the days of the Third Napoleon, but this time I am here. Quite yes. Your time runs out; the end approaches."

"Be pitiful," she begged tremulously. "Have mercy, little cruel man. I am an *artiste*, a great actress. My art makes thousands happy. For years I have brought joy to those whose lives were *triste* and dull. Compared to me, what are those others—those farm women, those merchants' daughters, those offspring of the *bourgeoisie*? I am *Clair de Lune*—moonlight on soft-flowing water, the sweet promise of love unfulfilled—"

"*Tiens*, I think the moon is setting, *Mademoiselle*," he interrupted dryly. "If you would have a priest—"

"*Nigaud, bête, sot!*" she whispered, and her whisper was a muted scream. "O fool and son of imbecile parents, I want no priest to whine his lying promise of repentance and redemption in my ears. Give me my youth and beauty once again, bring me a fair, fresh maiden—"

She broke off as she saw the hard gleam in his eyes, and, so weak that she could scarcely find the breath to force the epithets between her graying lips, she cursed him with a nastiness that would have brought a blush to a Marseilles fishwife.

He took her tirade calmly, neither smiling nor angered, but with an air of detachment such as he might have shown while examining a new sort of germ-life through a microscope. "Thou beast, thou dog, thou swine! Thou species of a stinking camel—thou misbegotten offspring of an alley cat and a night-demon," she whispered stridently.

Physicians grow accustomed to the sight of death. At first it's hard to witness dissolution, but in our grim trade we become case-hardened. Yet even with the years of training and experience behind me I could not forebear a shudder at the change that came over her. The bluish whiteness of her skin turned mottled green, as if already putrefactive micro-organisms were at work there, wrinkles etched themselves across her face like cracks in shattering ice, the luster of her pale-gold hair faded to a muddy yellow, and the hands that plucked at the bed-clothes were like the withered talons of a dead and desiccated bird. She raised her head from the pillow, and we saw her eyes were red-rimmed and rheumy, empty of all sight as those of an old woman from whom age has stolen every faculty. Abruptly she sat up, bending at the waist like a hinged doll, pressed both shriveled hands against her withered bosom, gave a short, yelping cough like that of a hurt animal. Then she fell back and lay still.

There was no sound in the death chamber. No sound came through the opened windows. The world was still and breathless in the quiet of the sunset.

Nora McGinnis had done more than merely well by us, and dinner had been such a meal as gourmets love to dream of. Veal simmered in a sweet and sour sauce, tiny dumplings light as cirrus clouds, and for dessert small pancakes wrapped round cheese or apricot and prune jelly. De Grandin drained his coffee cup, grinned like a cherub playing truant from celestial school, and raised his glass of Chartreuse *vert* to savor its sharp, spicy aroma.

"Oh, no, my friend," he told me, "I have not an explanation for it. It is like electricity, one of those things about which we may understand a great deal, yet about which we actually know nothing. As I told you, I recognized her at first sight, yet was not willing to admit the evidence of my own eyes until she recognized me. Then I knew that we faced something evil, something altogether outside usual experience, but not necessarily what you would call supernatural. She was like a vampire, only different, that one. The vampire has a life-in-death, it is dead, yet undead. She were entirely alive, and likely to remain that way as long as she could find fresh victims. In some way—only the good God and the devil know how—she acquired the ability to absorb the vitality, the life-force, from young and vigorous women, taking from them all they had to give, leaving them but empty, sucked-out husks that perished from sheer weakness, while she went on with renewed youth and vigor."

He paused, lit a cigar, and: "You know it is quite generally believed that if a child sleeps with an aged person or an invalid he loses his vitality to his bedfellow. In the book of Kings we read how David, King of Israel, when he was old and very weak, was strengthened in that manner. The process she employed was something like that, only much accentuated.

"In 1867 she took sixty days to slip from seeming-youth to advanced age. In 1910 the process took but two weeks or ten days; this summer she was fair and seeming-young one night, next morning she seemed more than middle-aged. How many times between my *gran-père's* day and ours she did renew her youth and life by draining poor unfortunate young girls of theirs we cannot say. She was in Italy and South America and *le bon Dieu* only knows where else during that time. But one thing seems certain: With each succeeding renewal of her youth she became just a little weaker. Eventually she would have reached the point where old age struck her all at once, and there would not have been time to find a victim from whom she could absorb vitality. However, that is merely idle speculation. Mademoiselle Mazie had been selected as her victim this time, and if we had not been upon the scene—*eh bien*, I think there would have been another grave in the churchyard, and Mademoiselle Leroy would have reopened in her play this fall. Yes, certainly.

"You ask to know some more?" he added as I made no comment.

"One or two things puzzle me," I confessed. "First, I'm wondering if there were any connection between her unnatural ability to refresh herself at others' expense and her refusal to be photographed. Or do you think that was merely for the sake of publicity?"

He studied the question a moment, then: "I do not, my friend. The camera's eye is sharper than ours. Skilled makeup may deceive the human eye, the camera lens sees through it and shows every little so small imperfection. It may well be that she did fear to have her picture taken for that reason. You comprehend?"

I nodded. "One thing more. That afternoon you told Mazie that you were sure the memory of her friendship with the Leroy woman would always be a thing to cherish. You knew the cold and spider-like nature of the woman; how she sucked her victims dry so pitilessly, yet—"

"I knew it, yes," he broke in, "and so do you, now; but she did not. She was attached to this strange, beautiful freak; she adored her with the ardor no one but a young, impressionable girl can have for an older, more sophisticated woman. Had I told her the whole truth not only would she have refused to believe me, she would have had an ideal shattered. It is far, far better that she keep that ideal, that she remain in happy ignorance of the true quality of the person she called friend, and cherish her memory forever. Why take something beautiful away from her, when by merely keeping silence we can give her happy recollections?"

Once more I nodded. "It's hard to believe all this, even though I saw it," I confessed. "I'm willing to accept your thesis, but it did seem hard to let her die that way, even though—"

"Believe me, my friend," he cut in, "she was no really-truly woman. Did not you hear what she said of herself before she died, that she was *clair de lune*—moonlight—completely ageless and without passion? She was egotism carried to illogical conclusion, a being whose self-love transcended every other thought and purpose. A queer, strange thing she was, without a sense of right or wrong, or justice or injustice, like a faun or fairy or some grotesque creature out of an old book of magic."

He drained the last sip of his liqueur and passed the empty glass to me. "If you will be so kind, my friend."

Vampire Kith and Kin

"**A**ND I DON'T MIND admitting that the case has got my goat," young Dr. McCormick told me unhappily. "I've never seen another like it, and can't find anyone who has. Will you come have a look at her tomorrow, sir? Perhaps I'd better turn the case over to you entirely—"

"Oh, no, you don't!" I told him. "If you want to call me into consultation I'll be glad to help in any way I can, though I'm just a general practitioner, and this seems like a case for a specialist; but if you think it's hopeless—well, I'm hanged if I'll let you hand me the bag to hold. Signing death certificates for other doctors' patients isn't my idea of recreation—"

"Oh, no, sir!" McCormick's sharp denial bordered on hysteria. "It's not like that, at all. It's a matter of professional ethics. My personal interest—you see— oh, hang it, sir!—I'm in love with my patient. I can't observe her objectively any more, can't regard her illness as a case; can't even see her as a woman. She's *the* woman; the one woman in the world for me, and I'm afraid I might overlook a symptom that might lead me to a cure. When you begin to see a body that's functioning faultily not as a defective piece of physical mechanism, but as a beloved woman, your value as a scientist is impaired. When every indication of unfavorable prognosis throws you into panic—"

"I understand, my boy," I interrupted. "The rule that makes us call in other doctors for our families is a wise one. Sometimes I think the physician, like the priest, should remain celibate. I'll be glad to look in on your patient—"

"And so shall I, if you permit it," Jules de Grandin added as he stepped into the study. "Your pardon, *Monsieur*," he apologized to McCormick, "but I could not help hear what you said to Friend Trowbridge as I came down the hall. It was not that I eavesdropped, but"—he raised one shoulder in a Gallic shrug—"*je n'ai que faire de vous dire.*"

I made the necessary introductions and the little Frenchman dropped into a chair, then crossed his hands in his lap and stared fixedly at my visitor. "Say on, *Monsieur*," he ordered. "Tell me of this case which has deprived you of the goat."

"I'll try to be as clinical as possible," McCormick responded. "Her name is Anastasia Pappalukas; age twenty-three, unmarried. And"—his voice took on a sandy grittiness—"she's dying; dying for no earthly reason except that she is."

De Grandin nodded. "You have made the tentative diagnosis?"

"A dozen of 'em, sir, and they're all wrong. The only thing I'm certain of is that she's fading like a wilting flower, and nothing I can do seems any use."

"*Pardonnez-moi*, I do not mean to be too obvious, but sometimes we are blinded by our very nearness to a case. You have not discounted the possibility of latent TB?"

McCormick gave a short, chiding laugh. "I have not, sir; nor anemia nor any other likely ailment. Her sputum tests are all negative, so are her X-rays. Her temperature is nearly always normal; I've made repeated blood counts, and while she's just below the million mark the deficiency isn't great enough to cause concern. About her only objective symptoms are progressive loss of weight and increasing pallor; subjectively she complains of loss of appetite, slight headaches in the morning and profound lassitude. Lately she's been troubled by nightmares; says she's afraid to go to sleep for fear of 'em."

"U'm? One sees. And how long has this condition obtained?"

"I'm not quite sure, sir. I've had the case about three months, but how long she'd been ill before they called me I can't say. I don't know much about her background; you see, I'd never met her till they called me. It seems she's been in what we used to call 'a decline' for some time, but you know how vague lay-men are. She might have started downhill long before they called me, and not become aware of her condition till her illness had progressed beyond the hope of successful treatment."

He paused a moment, then, "Have you ever heard of a disease called *gusel vereni*?" he asked.

"*Mon Dieu!*" the Frenchman exploded. "Where did *you* hear of him, *Monsieur*, if you please?"

"I ran across the term for the first time last night, sir. I stopped at the County Medical Society library on my way from Anastasia's and happened to pick up a copy of Wolfgang Wholbrück's *Medicine in the Near East*. I don't know what made me consult the book, except that Anastasia is a Greek—her family came here in '21 as refugees from Smyrna after Greece had lost the war with Turkey—and I was fairly desperate for a clue—any kind of clue—to her condition."

"H'm'm'm'm," de Grandin made one of those odd noises, half grunt, half whinny, which no one but a Frenchman can produce. "And what did you learn of *gusel vereni*, if you please?"

McCormick answered like a schoolboy repeating a lesson: "According to

Wholbrück it is a disease of unknown origin to which Greeks, Turks, Armenians and kindred peoples seem peculiarly vulnerable, and which seldom or never attacks Western Europeans. All attempts to isolate its causative factor have failed. Objectively its symptoms parallel those of pulmonary tuberculosis, that is, there is progressive loss of weight and stamina, though there is neither fever nor a cough. It is sometimes called 'the Angels' Disease' because the patient loses nothing of his looks as it progresses, and women often seem to become more beautiful as the end approaches. It is painless, progressive and incurable—"

"And Jules de Grandin knows about him, by blue! Oh, yes. He has seen him at his dreadful worst, and better than the *Herr-doktor* Wholbrück he knows what causes him!

"Come, my friends, let us go see this Grecian lady who may be a victim of this so strange malady. Right away, all quickly, if you please."

"YOU SAID YOU KNOW the cause of this disease?" I whispered as we drove to our mystery patient's house.

He nodded somberly. "Perhaps I spoke with too much haste, my friend. In Greece and in the Turkish hospitals I have seen him and had him explained to me at great length, but—"

"But did you ever see a cure?" I persisted.

"*Hélas*, no," he admitted. "But perhaps that was because the patients' broth was spoiled by an excess of cooks."

"What d'ye mean? Too many doctors?"

"Perhaps; perhaps too few priests."

"Too few—whatever are you driving at?"

"I wish I had a ready answer, my old one. The best that I can do is guess, and though I am a very clever fellow I sometimes guess wrong."

"But what did you mean by 'too few priests'?"

"Just this: In Greece, as elsewhere in the Near and Middle East, the patina o' modernity is only a thin coating laid upon an ancient culture. For the most part their physicians have been trained at Vienna or Heidelberg, great scientific institutions where the god of words has been enthroned in the high place once sacred to the Word of God. Therefore they believe what they see, or what some *Herr-professor* tells them he has seen, and nothing else. The priesthood, on the contrary, have been nourished on the *vin du pais*, as one might say. They remember and to some extent give cedence to the ancient beliefs of the people."

"What's all that got to do with—"

"Just this: The priests contend the malady is spiritual in origin; the doctors hold that it, like all else, is completely physical. Left to themselves the *papas* would have attempted treatment by spiritual means, but they were not allowed to do so. And so the patients died. You see?"

"You mean it was another instance of conflict between science and religion?"

"*Mais non*; by no means. There is no conflict between true science and true religion. It is our faulty definition of the terms that breeds the conflict, my friend. All religions are things of the spirit, but all things of the spirit are not necessarily religious. All physical things are subject to the laws of science, but science may concern itself with things not wholly physical, and if it fails to do so it is not entirely scientific."

"I don't think I quite follow you," I admitted. "If you'd be a little more specific—"

"*Bien. Bon*," he broke in. "You do not understand. Neither, to tell the whole truth, do I. Let us start in mutual blindness and see who first discerns the light. Meanwhile, it seems, we are arrived."

THE SMALL HOUSE IN Van Amburg Street where Philammon Pappalukas lived with his motherless daughter was neat as the proverbial pin. It stood flush with the street, only three low marble steps topped by a narrow landing separating it from the sidewalk, and the front door led directly into a living room which occupied the entire width of the building. Mr. Pappalukas greeted us without enthusiasm. He was a small man, slim and attractive, with hair almost completely gray and a small white mustache. His face showed lines of worry and his shoulders sagged, not with defeat but with an angle that betokened resigned acquiescence.

"Good evening, Dr. Trowbridge, Dr. de Grandin," he acknowledged McCormick's introduction, then, in answer to our guide's inquiry, "No, there doesn't seem to be much change. I think the end is very near, now, Marshall. I've seen such cases before—"

"And so have I, *Monsieur*," de Grandin interrupted. "May we see this one, if you please?"

Our host gave him a rather weary look, as if to say, "Of course, if you insist, but it won't do any good," then led us to the bedroom where our patient lay.

She was a pretty little woman with a wealth of softly curling black hair, soft brown eyes almost disproportionately large, a rather small but very full-lipped mouth and a sweet, yielding chin cleft by a deep dimple. Except for her bright lipstick the only color in her face was centered round her eyes where violet shadows gathered in the hollows. "Thank you, Marshall;" she responded to young McCormick's inquiry, "I don't feel much better; I'm so tired, dear, so cruelly tired."

Our physical examination told us nothing, or, to be more exact, served only to confirm McCormick's report. Her temperature and pulse were normal and her skin was neither dry nor moist, but exactly as a healthy person's skin should be. Fremitus was no more than usual; upon percussion we could find no evidence of impaired resonance, and our stethoscopes disclosed no trace of mucous rales. Whatever her illness might be, I was prepared to stake my reputation it was not tuberculosis.

De Grandin showed no disappointment. He was cheerful, and with something more than the conventional "bedside manner," as he dropped into a chair and took her hand in his, his finger resting lightly on her pulse. "They tell me that you dream, *ma chère*," he announced. "Of what is it that you dream all unhappily?"

A thin wash of blood showed in her face, to be succeeded by a pallor even more pronounced than before. "I—I'd rather not discuss my dreams, sir," she answered, and it seemed to me a look of fear came in her eyes. "I—"

"No matter, my small one," he broke in with a quick, reassuring smile. "Some things are better left unsaid, even in the sick room or confessional."

He drew a notebook from his pocket and poised a silver pencil over it. "And when was it you first began to feel these spells of weakness, if you please?"

"I—" she began, then faltered, drew a long breath and fell silent.

"Yes?" he prompted. "You were saying—"

"I—I can't remember, sir."

His narrow black brows rose in Saracenic arches at her answer, but he made no comment. Instead, across his shoulder he asked me, "Will you be good enough to move the light, Friend Trowbridge? I find it difficult to see my notes."

Obediently I moved the bedside lamp until he nodded satisfaction with its place, and as I stepped back I noticed that the light fell directly on the silver pencil with which he appeared to be scribbling furiously, but with which he was actually making aimless circles.

"*Morbleu*, but he is bright, is he not, *Mademoiselle?*" he asked the girl as he held up the pencil. "Does he not shine like sunlight on clear water?"

She looked at the small shiny rod and as she did so he twirled it more quickly, then gradually decreased its speed until it revolved slowly, then swung back and forth like a pendulum. "Observe him closely, if you please," he ordered in a soft monotone. "Behold how he sways like a young tree in the wind, a tired, a very tired young tree that seeks to rest all quietly. It is a sleepy little tree, a very tired and sleepy little tree, almost as tired and sleepy as you, *ma petite*." His voice sank low and lower, and his words took on a slurred and almost singsong tone. It might have been a lullaby cradle-song to lure her into slumber, and as he kept repeating the slow, almost senseless phrases I saw her lids quiver for a moment, seem to fight to remain up, then slowly, almost reluctantly, fold across her big brown eyes.

"Ah, so!" he murmured as he rose and placed his thumbs upon her brow, stroking it toward the temples with a soft massaging motion. "So, my little poor one, you will rest, *n'est-ce-pas?*" For several moments he continued stroking her forehead, then, "Now, *Mademoiselle*, you are prepared to tell me when it was you first began to feel sensations of this tiredness, *hein?*"

"It was last autumn," she responded weakly. Her words came slowly, feebly, wearily, in a voice so tired that it might have been that of an old woman. "It was last autumn in November—All Souls' Day—"

"*Parbleu*, do you say so? And what had you been doing, if you please?"

"I'd been out to the cemetery to visit Timon's grave. Poor Timon! I could not love him, but he loved me—" Her voice sank lower and lower, like that of a radio when the rheostat is turned off slowly.

"Do you say so? And who was Timon, and why did you go to his grave?"

"Timon Kokinis," she began then stopped as a knock sounded from the ceiling just above her bed, as if a clenched fist had struck the plaster.

"Ah, yes, one sees; and this Monsieur Kokinis, he was—*grand Dieu*, my friends, look to her!"

"*Oh!*" The girl's sharp exclamation had been like the cry of a hurt animal and she caught her breath in a gasp as she began to tremble in a clonic spasm, quivering from throat to feet as if in the throes of a galvanic shock. Her hands, which had been meekly folded on her bosom, wreathed themselves together as if in mortal terror, her eyes forced open as if she were being throttled, then turned up underneath their lids till only a thin thread of white was visible. Her lips writhed back and her tongue thrust out.

"Good God!" cried McCormick. "Hold her. Dr. Trowbridge—watch her mouth; don't let her bite her tongue!" He snatched his kit up, hurried to the bathroom and came back with a filled hypo. "Easy! Easy does it," he soothed as he sponged her arm with alcohol, took up a fold of skin and thrust the needle in.

For something like a minute she continued struggling, then the morphine took effect and she subsided with a tired sigh.

"*Parbleu*, I thought it was *le petit mal* at first!" de Grandin murmured as he dropped the girl's quiescent hands.

"You *thought?*" McCormick shot back. "You know damn well it was, don't you? If that's not epilepsy I never saw a case—"

"Then you have never seen one, my friend," broke in the small Frenchman. "This seizure, if its origin were physical, was much more like hysteria than epilepsy. Consider, if you please: There was no epileptic cry or groan preceding the spasm, and while she ran her tongue out, there was no attempt to bite it." He looked down at the drugged girl pityingly. "*Ma pauvre*," he said in a low voice. "*Ma pauvre belle créature!*"

McCormick looked at him challengingly. "What d'ye mean, if the origin of her seizure were physical?" he demanded.

De Grandin fixed him with a long, unwinking stare, and nothing moved in his face. At last, "There are more things in heaven and earth, and most especially on earth, than medical philosophy is willing to admit, *mon jeune ami*," he answered in a level, toneless voice. "Attend her, if you please," he added as he moved toward the door. "I think that Friend Trowbridge and I have done all that we can at present, and further inquiries are necessary for our diagnosis. If anything untoward occurs do not delay to telephone us; we shall be in readiness."

"MAYBE YOU KNOW WHAT you're doing," I whispered as we went down the stairs, "but I'm completely at sea—"

"I, too, am tossed upon a chartless ocean of doubt," he confessed, "but in the distance I think that I see a small, clear light. Let us see if Monsieur Pappalukas can assist us in obtaining our bearings.

"Tell me, *Monsieur*," he demanded as we joined our patient's father in the downstairs room, "this Timon Kokinis, who was he?"

"Timon Kokinis?"

"*Précisément, Monsieur*, have I not said so?"

"He was a childhood friend of Anastasia's. His parents escaped from Smyrna with my wife and me when the American destroyers took us from the burning city. He and she were born in this country and grew up together. We Greeks are rather clannish, you know, and prefer to marry in our own nationality, so when the children showed a fondness for each other his father and I naturally assumed they'd marry."

"Perfectly, *Monsieur*. We make such arrangements in France, too; but the happy consummation of your plans was frustrated by the young man's death?"

"Not quite, Dr. de Grandin. Timon was a wild lad, rather too fond of the bottle, and with a hard streak of cruelty in him. He was two years Anna's senior, and almost from babyhood seemed to think he owned her. When they went to grammar school it was she who carried both their books, not the other way around, as usually happens, and if be did not feel like doing his homework, which he seldom did, he made her do it for him, then meet him at his house early enough for him to copy it. If she displeased him he would beat her. More than once she came home with a blackened eye where he had struck her in the face with his fist.

"By the time they reached high school he had become completely possessive. She was afraid to look at another boy or even have an intimate girl friend."

"Afraid, *Monsieur*?"

"Yes, sir; literally. Timon was an athlete, a four-letter man, and more than a match for any of his classmates. If he caught Anna at the soda fountain with another boy he did not hesitate to slap her face, then beat her escort unmercifully."

"*Mordieu*, and you permitted this?"

Mr. Pappalukas raised his brows and drew the corners of his mouth down. "The Levantine does not regard such things as Western Europeans and Americans do, sir. With us it is the woman's place to serve, the man's to command. Perhaps it is the relic of centuries of Turkish oppression, but—"

"And *Mademoiselle* your daughter? She was born here, grew up here. Surely she had no such Oriental ideas?"

Once more Mr. Pappalukas made that odd grimace that seemed almost a facial shrug. "Anna had been brought up in a Greek household, Dr. de Grandin, and Timon was conspicuously handsome—like one of our old demigods. From infancy she had been led to expect she would marry him—"

"But ultimately there was a break?"

"Yes, sir; ultimately. I don't think Anna ever loved Timon. She accepted the thought of their marriage as she might have accepted him as a brother, because there was no help for it, but notwithstanding her strict rearing and his possessive attitude she began to rebel before she was through high school. When war came and he joined the Army she broke away completely. We could not very well object to her engaging in Red Cross activities, and the contacts that she made in the work changed her attitude entirely. When Timon came back she told him she would not honor the engagement his father and I had made for them in infancy."

"And Monsieur Timon, how did he take her rebellion?"

"He flew into a rage and beat her so severely that she was in bed a week. Then I took sides with her, and the engagement was definitely broken. When I refused to force her to marry him he called a curse down on her, saying she should surely die a prey to a *vrykolakas*, which is to say—"

"One comprehends, *Monsieur*. And afterwards?"

"After that he shot himself."

De Grandin's little round blue eyes lit up with that sharp light I knew portended action. "One understands, in part, at least, *Monsieur*. You have been very helpful. It now remains for us to find a way to circumvent that curse."

"Then"—Mr. Pappalukas' voice trembled—"you think my daughter's illness is no natural thing?"

The little Frenchman gave a noncommittal shrug. "I would not go so far as that. We sometimes draw the limits of the natural too close. I am persuaded that she suffers from no infection known to biologists, and equally convinced her illness will not yield to ordinary medicine. *Eh bien*, since that is so we must resort to extraordinary means. The good young Dr. McCormick is with her, and will keep us posted as to her condition. Meantime, we shall do what we can—"

"Ah, but what can you do?" Mr. Pappalukas broke in. "You admit that medicine is powerless—"

"Perfectly, *Monsieur*, but did you hear me say that Jules de Grandin is helpless? *Mais non*, it is quite otherwise, I do assure you. I am of infinite resourcefulness, me, and if I do not find a way to aid your charming daughter I shall be astonished. Yes, certainly."

"I SUPPOSE YOU'VE WORKED out a theory?" I ventured as we drove toward home.

"Not quite a theory; let us rather say an hypothesis," he answered. "To begin, the young McCormick gave us a clue when he told us he had read Wholbrück. I know that one, me; I have read him carefully and cursed him roundly."

"Cursed him? Why?"

"Because he is a fool, by blue; because he will not believe what he sees. He is like the rustic who visited the zoo and on beholding a rhinoceros declared that notwithstanding he was looking at him there was no such animal. Consider, if you please: Time out of mind it has been believed in the Levant that *gusel vereni*, sometimes called 'the Angels' Disease,' sometimes 'the false consumption,' is not an illness in the usual sense of the term, but the result of demoniacal possession. In olden days it was more common, but in our time it is met often enough for Wholbrück to have made mention of it. And what does he say of it, I ask you? That its cause is unknown, and biochemistry is unable to isolate its infective agent. You see, he willfully shuts his eyes to the possibility of anything but physical causation. He will not even go so far as to say, 'It is believed by the peasants to be caused by demoniacal possession.' Not he! He says simply that its cause is unknown. *Parbleu*, a fool he is, a bigoted, blind fool."

"You mean you think that Anastasia is possessed by a demon?" I asked incredulously.

"Not necessarily. It would be sufficient if she thought herself possessed."

"If she thought—good Lord, man, what are you driving at?"

"Just this, my old one: Thoughts are very potent things. The African witch-doctor tells the native of the Congo, 'I have put a spell on you,' and straightway the poor fellow sickens, grows weak and dies. In Polynesia the same thing occurs. We have innumerable instances of natives being 'prayed to death' by pagan priests despite the efforts of the missionaries to prevent it. Have not our doctors borne repeated testimony of the potency of voodoo magic in Haiti, and does not the Pennsylvania farmer believe that a hex put on him can cause illness, even death? But of course.

"Very well, then. Let us assume Mademoiselle Anna believes herself possessed, believes that she, as the old saying has it, is 'called;' that she must surely fade away and die, and nothing can be done about it. Why should she not die in such circumstances? It is not difficult to think yourself into an illness, even a fatal one, as you know from experience with hypochondriacs in your practice."

"That's so," I admitted, "but why should she think herself possessed?"

"Because of Monsieur Timon the Deceased. He cursed her, then committed suicide. In many parts of Greece it is still thought that suicides become *vryko-lakas* at death, and you will recall he swore she should be destroyed by such an one."

"What the devil is a *vrykolakas?*"

"He is a species of vampire, not a true one, but something quite similar. The vampire is an animated corpse who steals forth from his grave to suck the blood of his victims. The *vrykolakas* is a disembodied spirit who subtly drains his victim of vitality, and he, my friend, is said to be the cause of *gusel vereni.*

"*Très bon*, let us review the evidence: First, we have a long and intimate association between a boy and girl. The boy is cruel and arrogant, almost, if not quite, sadistic in his attitude toward the girl. He dominates her completely, ordering her about as a harsh master might a dog. All this predisposes her to subservience and docility and makes her malleable to his will. At last she revolts, but her self-assertion is a shallow thing; deep down she feels that he is master. No matter, he hurls a curse at her, then destroys himself.

"She is extremely suggestible—did not you notice how quickly she sank into hypnosis this evening? *Bien. Bon.* The thought—the gnawing fear—of his curse has been planted in her mind like the seed of some malignant plant. Perhaps it does not germinate at once; perhaps it lies there in her mental soil awaiting circumstances favorable to gestation.

"Then what occurs, I ask to know? She visits his grave on All Souls' Day, she calls him to remembrance, perhaps she feels responsible for his self-murder, reproaches herself, thinks of him— How does she think of him, one wonders? Is it pityingly, as for one who died for love of her, or is it fearfully, as of one who placed a curse on her? A curse is very dreadful to the Greeks, my friend, and not a thing to be lightly regarded.

"And then what happens? Thinking of her almost-lifelong servitude to him she goes home, broods upon his tragic, violent death and on the curse he put upon her—that she should die a victim to a *vrykolakas. Barbe d'un poisson*, it has been said, 'As a man thinketh so is he;' it can be said with even greater truth of a woman. Our poor young Mademoiselle Anna goes to bed and slowly pines away, and nothing medicine can do will help her." He sat back, crossed his hands upon the knob of his stick and looked at me with the air of a man who has propounded an unanswerable proposition.

As always, I rose to the bait. "You say her case is hopeless—"

"*Non, non, mon vieux*, I said that nothing medicine can do will help her, not that Jules de Grandin is impotent."

"Then what do you propose doing—"

He glanced at his watch. "First I shall ask you to set me down here. I go to collect *matériel de siège*. In half an hour I shall join you, then"—he grinned one of his quick elfin grins—"we shall see what we shall see, if anything."

HE WAS PUNCTUAL TO the minute, and immensely pleased with himself as he laid a miscellany of packages on the study table. "These," he announced as he held up two small silver censers, "are for your use, and the young McCormick's, my old one."

"Our use?" I echoed. "What're we to do with 'em?"

"Swing them, *par la barbe d'un singe jaune*. I have filled them full of *Mandragora autumnalis*, which was esteemed a very potent drug by the old ones, for it is said that Solomon the Wise made use of it to compel djinn and devil to obey him. And Josephus Flavius declares that at the smell of it the demons which possess a man take flight—"

"Surely," I scoffed, "you don't believe such utter nonsense!"

From another parcel he drew a wide-mouthed bottle of what seemed like black or very dark amethyst glass, stoppered with a wax disc on which were impressed the letters I.X.N. "It is the prison into which I mean to drive him," he explained.

"Eh? The prison—"

"*Précisément. La Bastille.* In the Levant, where such things are, they believe evil spirits can be forced or lured into a bottle, and—"

"You're amazing!" I guffawed. "To think of grown men going through such mummery. I'll have trouble keeping a straight face—"

"Perhaps," he agreed, and the flatness of his voice might have betokened embarrassment or irony, "and then again, you may not. Are we ready? *Très bien, Allons-vous-en.*"

A NASTASIA WAS SLEEPING AS we tiptoed into her sick room. "How is she?" de Grandin whispered. "Is there any change, any indication of nightmare?"

"Not yet," McCormick answered. "I don't think the morphia has worn off yet."

"Good. Attend me, both of you, if you please." He drew the little silver censers from his portmanteau and laid them on the bedside table. "Anon the visitant will come, and we must be prepared for him. When I give the signal strike matches and ignite the incense in these thuribles, then march about the room while you swing them toward Mademoiselle Anna. Friend Trowbridge, you will march clockwise, from left to right; Friend McCormick, you will proceed counter-clockwise. It would be better if you maintained complete silence, but if you must speak do not raise your voices. *Comprenez-vous?*"

"You spoke of a visitant," I whispered. "D'ye mean when and if Anna has a nightmare?"

"*Peut-être que oui, peut-être que non*—perhaps yes; perhaps no," he responded. "In such a case as this—*tonnerre de Dieu*, regard her, if you please!"

The sleeping girl stirred restlessly and turned her head upon the pillow with a small protesting moan like that a sleepy child gives when wakened. "Quick, *mes amis*, set your censers glowing, commence the promenade!" he ordered.

Our matches bared in unison, and the powder in the censers took fire instantly, glowing redly and emitting pungent clouds of bitter-sweet smoke.

De Grandin laid the wide-mouthed bottle on the dressing table, set its wax cork beside it, and took his station near the girl's bed, gazing earnestly into her face.

She moaned again, made a small whimpering sound; then her lips parted and she raised her hands and thrust her head forward, as if she saw an ecstatic vision through her fast-closed lids. Her pale cheeks flushed, she moved her hands gently downward, as if stroking the face of one who bent above her, and a tremor shook her slender form as her slim bosom rose and fell with avid, quick breathing. Her lips opened and closed slowly, in a pantomime of blissful kissing, and a deep sigh issued from between her milk-white teeth; her breath came short and jerkily in quick exhausted gasps.

"*Grand Dieu, l'incube!*" de Grandin whispered almost wonderingly.

"Yes, it's an incubus, a nightmare!" I agreed. "Quick, waken her, de Grandin, this sort of thing can lead to erotomania!"

"Be silent!" he commanded sharply. "I did not say *an* incubus, but *the* incubus. This is no nightmare, my friend, no mere erotic boiling-up of the unconscious in a dream. It is *la séduction*—the wooing of a living woman by a thing from beyond—"

"Dr. de Grandin, look behind you, man, for God's sake!" McCormick's warning came in a thick, strangled voice. "It—it's—"

A ripping, tearing sound came from the window at the far end of the room, and from its rod one of the scrim curtains came fluttering, not as if falling of its own weight, nor yet as if wafted by a wind, but purposefully, sentiently, consciously, as if it were imbued with a life of its own.

We saw the flimsy fabric take on curves and form, as if it were a cerecloth draped loosely on a lich—there was the outline of the head, a sacklike rounded protuberance above the line of the shoulders, and from the right and left drooped fluttering wings of cloth as if they swayed downward from outspread arms, while as the thing came forward with a stealthy, creeping motion we saw its lower portion swirl and advance and retreat alternately, as if it fluttered against moving legs. Yet there was nothing—absolutely nothing—under it. Through the loosely-woven scrim we saw the light shine; when it moved between us and the dresser we could see the furniture through the meshes.

"*Grande cornes de Satan*, have you come to try conclusions with me, *Monsieur Sans Visage?*" asked Jules de Grandin in a hard, gritty voice. He stood upon his toes, his body bent as if he were about to take off in a run or spring upon the fluttering horror that came oscillating toward him, thrust a hand into his jacket pocket and drew out a small, shining object.

It was a little golden thing, a tiny reliquary of old hammered gold set with amethyst, so small a man could hide it like a coin in the hollow of his hand, and to it was attached a slender chain of golden links scarce thicker than a thread. He paid the gold chain out until the ikon hung from it like a pendulum, and with a quick move of his hand swung it toward the advancing form. "Accursed of God," his voice, though low, was harsh and strident as a battle-cry, "rejected of the earth, I bid thee stand, *in nomine Domini!*"

The ghastly, fluttering thing seemed to give back a step, as if it had encountered a quick blast of wind, and we could see its folds stretch tightly over something—though we knew that there was nothing there.

"*Conjuro, te,*" the little Frenchman whispered. "*Conjuro te, sclerastissime, retro—retro! Abire ad locum tuum!*"

The sheet-formed thing seemed hesitating, fluttered back a step, lost height and seeming-substance. As de Grandin advanced on it we could see it shrink. The curtain-hem which had been clear six inches from the floor when it first started forward now almost swept the broadloom carpet.

"Back, foul emanation from the tomb—back, revenant of the self-slain, into the place appointed for thee!" His command was harsh, inexorable, and the imponderable sheeted thing gave ground before him.

Perhaps it was a minute, perhaps ten—or an hour—that they dueled thus, but the little Frenchman's fiercely repeated injunction seemed resistless, inch by fractions of an inch the ceremented horror retreated, losing stature as it fled. By the time it reached the dressing table where the blackglass bottle lay it might have draped upon a two-year-old child instead of on a giant as at first.

There was a sudden swishing sound, like that made by a sword whipped through the air, and all at once the curtain fell upon the floor in an innocuous heap, while inside the darkly purple glass of the bottle showed something thicker than a vapor but less substantial than a liquid, something an obscene toad-belly gray that squirmed and writhed and pullulated like a knot of captive worms.

"*Misère de Dieu*, I have thee, naughty fellow!" Holding the small reliquary at the bottle's mouth with his left hand, de Grandin forced the wax stopper in place with his right, stepped back, restored the ikon to his pocket and mopped his brow with a silk handkerchief. "*Pardieu*, but it was touch and go, my friends," he told us with a relieved sigh. "I was not certain I could master him when we began our combat." He took a deep breath, wiped his forehead again, then grinned at us, a little wearily. "*Morbleu*, but I am tired, me," he confessed. "Like the horse of the plough at sunset. Yes." He leant against the dresser, and for a moment I thought he would fall, but he recovered himself with a visible effort and smiled at McCormick.

"Look to your sweetheart, *mon brave*," he ordered. "She will have need of you, both as a lover and physician, but—she will get well. Do not doubt it."

Anastasia lay upon her back, her arms outstretched to right and left as if she had been crucified upon the bed, her breath coming in hot, fevered gasps, tears welling from beneath her closed lids. "Go to her, *mon jeune*," the Frenchman bade. "Bend over her; *pardieu*, awaken her with kisses as the Prince did wake the Sleeping Beauty in the Wood! Yes, certainly. A man is young but once, and youth and love come back no more; you cannot hoard them as a miser does his gold."

He plucked me by the sleeve. "Come, let us go, my friend," he whispered. "What have we to do with such things? Besides, there is a final duty to perform."

With the dark-glass bottle underneath his arm he led the way down to the basement. "Will you be good enough to open the furnace?" he asked, and as I complied he heaved the bottle into the firebox. It landed on the bed of glowing coals and rolled an inch or so, then burst with a report like that of a smashed electric light bulb, and a sharp hissing followed while a cloud of milky vapor spiraled toward the flue. I sickened as the acrid odor of incinerating flesh assailed my nostrils.

"IT WAS THIS WAY, my friend," he told me some two hours later in the study. "I was of two minds concerning Mademoiselle Anna's illness; you of only one."

"Say that again," I ordered. "I don't think I quite understand."

He took a deep breath, swallowed once, and began again, speaking slowly "You were sure she suffered a psychoneurotic condition; I was not convinced of it. Undoubtlessly a good case could be made for either hypothesis, or both. She was neurotic, beyond question, she was extremely suggestible; she had been dominated since infancy by the naughty Kokinis person. Also, she had been brought up on Greek folklore, and knew the legends of the *vrykolakas* as English children know the rhymes of Mother Goose or French children their *contes de fées*. She might have scorned and derided them, but what we learn to believe in childhood we never quite succeed in disbelieving. *Bien. Très bon.* It were entirely plausible that she should have been impressed by his self-murder and the curse he put upon her, that she should be haunted and deprived of life by a *vrykolakas*. Yes, of course.

"In a neurasthenic state of hypochondria she might indeed have wasted away and finally perished. That she should have dreams of the lover she had spurned, dreams in which he wooed her and she had not power to withstand his importunities, is likewise possible. Even nice young people have erotic dreams, and a highly nervous state is conducive to them.

"You recall she would not tell us what she dreamed? How she blushed when questioned concerning her nightmares? That was clear proof that she did in dreamland what she would not think of doing in a conscious state.

"Very well. The spasm she suffered when she was about to tell us of this Kokinis person was another link in the chain of evidence. It was a nervous blocking of consciousness, a refusal to talk on a painful subject—what the psychiatrists refer to as a complex; a sort of mental traffic jam caused by a series of highly emotionally accented ideas in a repressed state.

"So far a good case for psychopathological illness has been made out; but as yet we lack complete proof. And what disproved it, or at least gave reason for suspecting that some super-physical agent—something you would call the supernatural—intervened?

"Listen, I shall tell you: When she was seized with that spasm there came a sound of knocking on the ceiling of her room. Her nerves—her disturbed psyche—could have caused the spasm, but not the knocking on the ceiling. Not at all, by no means. That was caused by something else, something outside her.

"What was the something that had caused it? *Qui sait*—who knows? Ghosts and spirits, all kinds of discarnate entities, are notoriously fond of announcing their presence by rappings on the walls and furniture. Hence the knocking might have been the visiting-card of such an one; again it might not.

"Accordingly I drew my line of battle up in two ranks. If what you assumed were true, and her illness was caused by psychic disturbance, we had a chance to master it by going through the show of exorcising the entity she thought possessed her, and making her believe she was cleansed of it.

"So far, so good. But what if it were a real ghostly thing that persecuted her? We should need more than a dumb-show to conquer that, *n'est-ce-pas?* So I prepared for him, also. I had a long talk with Father Zaimis, pastor of the Greek Church of St. Basil. He is a native-born Greek, and knew what I was talking of when I told him I suspected Mademoiselle Anna was the victim of a *vrykolakas*. He did not think I was outside my head when I requested that he lend me two small censers and a reliquary of St. Cyril, who was so justly famous for his conflicts with unholy spirits. Also, he prepared with his own hands the stopper for my bottle, and in it put a tiny filing from the reliquary. Thus armed, I was prepared for all eventualities."

"But whatever gave you the idea of imprisoning the *vry*—the whatever-you-call-it—in a bottle?" I demanded. "I never heard of that before."

"*Parbleu*, my friend, I fear that there are many things of which you have not heard," he grinned at me. "Have the goodness to attend me for one little so small minute."

From the bookshelf he drew a yellow-bound volume stamped in gold letters, *The Vampire, His Kith and Kin*, by Montague Summers. Leafing through it, he stopped at page 208 and began reading:

There is yet another method of abolishing a vampire—that of bottling him. There are certain persons who make a profession of this; and their mode of procedure is as follows: The sorcerer armed with a picture of some saint lies in ambush until he sees the vampire pass, when he pursues him with his ikon; the poor *Obour* takes refuge in a tree or on the roof of a house, but his persecutor follows him with the talisman, driving him from all shelter in the direction of a bottle specially prepared, in which is placed some of the vampire's favorite food. Having no other resource, he enters the prison, and is immediately fastened down with a cork, on the interior of which is a fragment of the ikon. The bottle is then thrown into the fire, and the vampire disappears for ever.

"You observed the color of that bottle?" he asked. "I had coated his interior with a mixture of gelatine and chicken's blood, of which all vampires are inordinately fond, if they can not obtain the blood of humans. *Eh bien*, I hope he enjoyed his last meal, though I did not give him much time to digest it."

"But see here," I persisted, "if you can pen an evil spirit in a bottle—"

"*Ah bah*, my friend, why continue harping on that single note? At present I am much more interested in releasing good spirits from their bottles." He poured himself a generous portion of cognac, drained it at a single gulp, then refilled his glass. "The first drink was for my great thirst," he told me solemnly. "Now that that has been assuaged, I drink for pleasure." He took a long, appreciative sip, and set the glass down on the coffee table, gazing at it fondly.

Conscience Maketh Cowards

Thus conscience does make cowards of us all.
— *Hamlet*, Act III, Scene 1.

LIEUTENANT JEREMIAH COSTELLO OF the homicide squad refilled his coffee cup, drained it in two gargantuan gulps, and tilted the silex pot over it again. "No, sor, Dr. de Grandin," he reported, "I'm not exactly satisfied with th' findin's. It *looks* like suicide, I'll grant, but there's many a wolf—four- or two-legged—as, looks as innocent as any lamb at first glance, too. Here's th' setup: This felly is supposed to have committed suicide by jumpin' out o' th' sixth storey winder, an' to make assurance doubly sure, as th' felly says, he tied th' cord o' his bathrobe round his neck before he jumped. But, says Dr. Parnell, th' coroner's physician, th' cord broke an' he was precipitated to th' courtyard. O.K., says I. Could be. But there's more here than meets th' eye; leastwise, Dr. Parnell's eye.

"You've seen throttlin' cases, I dunno?" he raised his almost copper-colored brows inquiringly.

De Grandin nodded. "Many of them, my old one."

"Just so, sor. An' ye'll be rememberin' that in most o' them th' hyoid bone is fractured an' th' larnyx cart'lages is broken, whereas in hangin' you don't often find this?"

"*Justement*," the little Frenchman nodded.

"Well, sor, every sign was present. If I ever seen a throttlin' case, this was one. I'm thinkin' that they choked him 'fore they swung him from th' winder, An' here's another thing: Th' cord by which he hung before he fell down to the cement o' th' courtyard hadn't frayed out gradual-like. It was clean-cut as if a knife or scissors snipped it off."

"*Vraiment?* And what does Dr. Parnell say to this, *mon lieutenant?*"

"He brushes it aside. Says th' fractures o' th' hyoid bone an' larynx could 'a' been made when th' felly hit th' ground—which I ain't disputin'—an' th' cord could just as well 'a' broken clean as frayed out, which is also possible, but"—he stabbed a thick, strong forefinger at de Grandin—"What gits me goat is that all these signs an' tokens manifestin' homicide 'stead o' suicide should be present, yet th' coroner's physician bulls th' jury into bringin' a verdict o' self-murder."

Jules de Grandin tapped a cigarette against his thumbnail, set it alight and blew smoke through his nostrils. "And what do you propose doing, my old and rare one?"

The Irishman raised ponderous shoulders in a gesture of futility. "What can I do, sor? Officially th' case is closed. Th' felly died by his own hand, an' that's th' end o' it. All th' same, I'll be afther doin' some gum-shoein' on me own. If someone's done a murder it's me job to find it out, an' afther that it's up to th' judge an' state's attorney—"

The cachinnation of the office telephone broke in, and I rose to answer it. "It's for you, Lieutenant." I said, and:

"Yes?" Costello challenged. "Oha? At 1515 Belvedere Street? An' th' name— glory be to God!"

In a moment he was back, a look that might have betokened anger or amaze-ment on his broad face. "I'll say there's sumpin' devilish in this business, sors," he told us. "That was th' Bureau callin' to report another suicidal hangin'. Right around th' corner from the one I'd just been afther tellin' ye about, an'—here's th' payoff!—'tis th' first man's brother who's supposed to 'a' bumped hisself off this time."

THE DAYS OF BLISTERING heat were done, and September had come in like a cool and gracious matron. Although there was a hint of fall in the clear air it was still warm enough to enjoy coffee on the veranda that overlooked the side yard where the dahlias bloomed, and after a late dinner we were sitting in low wicker chairs enjoying that delightful languor that accompanies the mingling of eupepsia and slow poisoning by nicotine, caffeine and alcohol when Nora McGinnis, my household factotum, came to us wearing that peculiarly forbid-ding expression she assumes when anybody obtrudes on "her doctors'" post-pran-dial period. "If ye plaze, sors," she announced with something more than a thin rime of frost upon her voice, "there's two people askin' for ye; a man an' woman."

"Patients?" I asked, stifling a groan. I'd had five T. and A.'s at Mercy Hospital that day, and performed an emergency paracentesis on an aging woman—nec-essarily without anesthesia—and the fatigue of strained nerves had left me in a state of near-exhaustion.

Nora raised her shoulders in a shrug—a trick she'd caught from Jules de Grandin—and gave me a look that announced complete nescience. "I wouldn't know, sor. They says as how they'd like to see yerself *an'* Dr. de Grandin. Shall I go back an' say it's afther hours?"

I was about to nod assent, but de Grandin intervened. "By no means, *ma petite*. If they desire to see Friend Trowbridge solely it is obviously a medical matter; but if they also wish to consult me that is another pair of sleeves. Tell them we will see them, if you please."

The couple who awaited us in the consulting room were not entirely prepossessing. The man was middle-aged, balding, heavy-shouldered, rather puffy at the waistline. He wore a neat, dark, formally-cut suit with narrow piqué edging at the V of his waistcoat. From his black-rimmed pince-nez trailed a rather wide black ribbon, and through their lenses he was studying my excellent copy of Renoir's "Boating Party" with evident disapproval. (In passing I might state I studiously avoid "professional pictures" such as "The Doctor," "The Study in Anatomy," or even the slightly humorous cartoons of Hogarth and Hans Holbein.)

His companion was more difficult to catalogue. She was just an average female of indeterminate age with undistinguished features and an undistinguished hat and hairdo. Her dress, though well made and of good material, seemed somehow not urban. A man might find some difficulty saying what was wrong with her, but a woman would have known at once. She had, as Jules de Grandin would have put it, a total lack of *le chic*.

"Dr. Trowbridge? Dr. de Grandin?" the man asked as we entered.

"I am Dr. Trowbridge," I answered, "and this is Dr. de Grandin." I paused, awaiting an exchange of confidences.

Our caller cleared his throat and looked at us, rather expectantly, it seemed to me. "You know me, of course." He did not ask it as a question, but made the announcement as a statement of fact.

De Grandin shook his head and looked distressed. "*Je suis désolé, Monsieur*, but I do not. I have lived in this so splendid country but a little quarter-century, and have not met all its celebrities. You are not George Washington, or *Général* Pershing—"

"I am Pastor Rodney Roggenbuck of the Complete Scriptures Congregation."

The smile that hovered underneath the waxed tips of de Grandin's small blond mustache gave way to something like a sneer. The shepherd of the flourishing new congregation was known to both of us by reputation. With calculating shrewdness he had filched doctrinal bits from such divergent sects as Whiteism, Christian Science, Russellism, fundamental Calvinism and the Eutychian heresy, spiced them highly with intolerance, and with this potpourri for creed and doctrine had begun crusading against the theatre and movies, medicine and Sunday papers, vivisection, vaccination, newspaper comics, liquor, coffee, tea and tobacco, the teaching of elementary geology in public schools and "graven images"—in connection with which latter he had attempted to enjoin the May processions of local Catholic churches and statuary in the city's parks. That one professing such beliefs should consult a physician was, to speak conservatively, amazing.

"And which of us do you desire to consult, *Monsieur?*" de Grandin asked. "Is it that you are *indisposé?*"

"I've come because Lieutenant Costello suggested it."

"Ah?"

"He tells me you are skilled in magic, witchcraft, and such things."

"A-ah?" de Grandin repeated, and there was something like cold-lightning flashes in his small blue eyes. I braced myself for an atomic explosion.

"Precisely, sir. He's no more satisfied that Fred and Theobald committed suicide than I am. "

"And just exactly who, if one may ask, were Fred and Théobald, *Monsieur*, and why should they not have destroyed themselves, and what concern of mine is it if they did so? Were they, perhaps, your brothers—"

"They were."

De Grandin sucked in a quick mouthful of air, but his look of angry suspicion did not soften. "Say on, *Monsieur*," he ordered. "I am listening."

"Frederick Roggenbuck was my younger brother. He lived at 1213 Quincy Street. Night before last he was supposed to have hanged himself from the window of his apartment. The coroner says it was suicide.

"Early this morning, or very late last night, my elder brother Theobald who lived with us at 1515 Belvedere Street, just around the corner from my brother Fred's, is supposed to have hanged himself from a pipe in the basement. None of us heard him rise from bed, or heard him in the cellar, but when Lucinda, the maid who gets our meals and looks after the house, let herself in this morning she found him hanging by a length of clothesline.

"Both my brothers were good, religious men, sir, and well aware of the enormity of the crime of self-murder. Neither would have thought of doing such a thing. Besides, they both had everything to live for—they were well fixed financially, and were engaged in work they loved with holy zeal—"

"Were they, by any chance, associated with you in your labors, monsieur?" de Grandin interrupted.

"They were. Theo was a presbyter and Fred a deacon."

"U'm?"

"What are you implying, sir? Why do you say 'u'm' in that manner?"

"*Pardieu, Monsieur*, why should I not say 'u'm' in any manner that I choose?" de Grandin shot back testily. "I shall say 'u'm' or '*hĕ*' or '*sacré bleu*' or anything I wish to say in any manner I desire, and if you do not like it there is neither lock nor bolt upon our door. You are at liberty to leave forthwith."

"Oh, no offense, sir, I assure you," Mr. Roggenbuck soothed. "Perhaps we do not understand each other. I wish you'd let me tell you—"

"Your wish is granted, *Monsieur*." De Grandin dropped into a chair and lit a cigarette. "Begin at the beginning, if you please, and tell me why it is that you suspect your estimable brothers did not give themselves the happy dispatch. Have you, perhaps, physical as well as moral reasons for your supposition?"

"Lieutenant Costello tells me he informed you of his reasons for suspecting Brother Fred did not do away with himself. In Brother Theo's case his suspicions are even more firmly founded.

"Theobald was portly, somewhat stouter than I, and just a little shorter, say about five foot six or seven. The pipe from which he is supposed to have hanged himself is eight feet from the floor, the rope by which he was suspended was just a little over two feet long from knot to noose. Theo's feet swung four or five inches from the floor, and there was no stool or chair or other object which he could have stood on near them. It would have been physically impossible for him to have looped the rope around his neck while standing on the floor, and equally impossible for him to have hanged himself without standing on something, yet there was nothing underneath him, and no object on which he could have stood anywhere within such distance as he could have kicked it from under him while he struggled as he hung."

"U'm?" Jules de Grandin put his fingers tip to tip and pondered. "And how was Monsieur Théobald arrayed? In his *chemise de nuit*—"

"No, sir. The night-shirt is a garment feminine in form, and Holy Scripture says explicitly a man shall not put on a woman's garment. He was wearing pajamas and a cotton bathrobe. His straw slippers had fallen from his feet as he hung from the pipe."

De Grandin lit another cigarette and blew smoke from his nose. "Perhaps you have a point there, *Monsieur*. I could not say until I've reconnoitered the terrain. Have you other grounds for suspicion, or is there any person you suspect?"

"Yes, sir; I suspect one Amos Frye, my sister-in-law's husband. I believe he drove them to self-murder by vindictive witchcraft—in fine, that he 'put a hex upon them,' as they say in the part of the country from which I come."

"But this is of the utmost interest, *Monsieur*. Where may one find *Monsieur* your *belle-soeur's* husband?"

"He is dead."

"Hein? *Feu noir du diable*, do you say so? Proceed, *Monsieur*. Tell more; tell all. Like Baalam's ass, I am all ears!"

"My wife has an afflicted sister named Eulalia," our caller answered. "For some years she has had the impression of tuberculosis, but stubbornly refuses to drink of the healing waters of faith, preferring to entrust herself to the worldly aid of physicians."

De Grandin pursed his lips as if to whistle, but made no comment. His features gave no indication of his thoughts; his eyes were absolutely void of expression.

"She was a wilful, headstrong girl," continued Mr. Roggenbuck, "and when the war came on as punishment for the sins of the world she insisted on becoming involved in canteen work. Strictly against our wishes, I may add. The Scriptures say specifically, 'Thou shalt not kill,' and every soldier is potentially a murderer. However, she insisted on consorting with these men of blood, and finally she married one of them.

"We offered her a home while he was overseas, and would have made him welcome when he returned, although he was a Gentile—that is, not of our faith—but he insisted on her living with him in an apartment he provided. Then he secured employment as a traveling salesman, and was forced to be away from home much of the time. Eulalia's impression of disease became stronger, and at last we took her to our house, where she could receive treatment in accordance with the tenets of true religion. When he returned from his trip we refused to let her go to him, or let him come to her. My wife Rosita is her sister, and I am like a brother to her, aye, more than a brother, since I have her spiritual welfare at heart—what's that, sir?" he broke off as de Grandin murmured something *sotto voce*.

"*Pardonnez-moi, monsieur*, it is that I seem to recall a passage in the Bible that says a man shall leave his father and mother and cleave unto his wife, since the twain are one flesh—"

"My dear sir! If you understood such things you'd know that Holy Scripture is to be received seriously, but not literally. Besides, the reference is to a man's cleaving to his wife, not a wife's cleaving to her husband; and in addition we are not Eulalia's father and mother, but her sister and brother-in-law. I challenge you to find a passage in the Bible which says a woman shall desert her brother-in-law to follow her husband!"

De Grandin's expression would have done credit to a cynical, blond Mephistopheles, but he answered with astonishing mildness, "You have me fairly there, *Monsieur*. I do not think that I can cite you such a verse. And now, as you were saying—"

"Amos made several attempts to see Eulalia, and was on the brink of bringing legal action when he was unfortunately killed in a highway accident. Most fortunately my brothers happened by while he lay dying by the roadside, and Theobald, who as a presbyter has power to loose or retain sins, gave him absolution. We thought, at least we hoped, that he was saved, but it appears his vengeful, earthbound spirit has pursued my poor, dear brothers, hounded them to suicide; made them self-murderers."

"What makes you think so, *Monsieur*?"

"Almost a year ago, shortly after Amos's fatal accident, my brother Fred began to have strange feelings. Have you ever had the feeling you were watched intently by some evilly-disposed person, sir? That is the feeling Fred complained of—as if someone who wished him ill were looking at him from the back continually, waiting opportunity to pounce. Sometimes the feeling grew so strong that he would turn around to see if he were actually being stared at; but there was never anybody visible.

"Three months later Theobald began to suffer the same eerie sensations. They had no privacy. When they disrobed for bed or for the bath that feeling of surveillance was on them; when they walked along the street or drove their cars they felt another walked behind them or was sitting at their sides; when they wrote a letter or perused a book there was always the impression that another looked across their shoulders, watching every move they made, never taking their eyes off them, never ceasing to hate them with poisonous, suppurating hatred. It must have been a terrible sensation, and one calculated to drive them to madness and self-murder."

De Grandin's eyes had lifted as our caller spoke. Now they were fixed in an unwinking cat-stare on a point a little beyond Mr. Roggenbuck's shoulder. For the first time the other seemed aware of the Frenchman's intent gaze, and a tremor ran through his hard-shaven, rather fleshy face. His jaws seemed suddenly to sag flaccidly like the dewlaps of a hound, and his mouth began to twist convulsively. "What—who—is it?" he demanded in a voice that seemed to come from a clogged throat.

The little Frenchman shrugged his shoulders. "Who can say, *Monsieur?* Perhaps it was no more than a shadow."

"What sort of shadow—what did it look like?"

"*On ne sait pas?* Perhaps it was like that of a man, perhaps that of a curtain shaken in the wind, perhaps a trick of the lamplight. *N'en parlons plus.* At any rate, it is gone now."

"You're sure?"

"Oh, quite sure, *Monsieur.*"

"Then"—Mr. Roggenbuck drew a silk handkerchief and wiped his brow—"what would you advise, Dr. de Grandin? Are you willing—can you help?"

"I am willing, and I think that I can help the cause of justice, Monsieur Roggenbuck. My fee will be a thousand dollars, in advance."

"A thousand dollars!"

"Perfectly. In fifteen minutes it will be increased to fifteen hundred. In half an hour I am not for hire at any price."

He pocketed the check, and, "Now, *Monsieur,*" he suggested, "suppose we go to your house and inspect the scene of your late brother's *déces.*"

THE HOUSE IN BELVEDERE Street was a substantial frame dwelling, neither opulent nor unpretentious, with a wide portico behind the tall, white pillars of which shadows seemed to be imprisoned. No lights showed anywhere in it, and Mr. Roggenbuck had to feel for the keyhole before he was able to admit us. Inside the place was quite as uninspiring as it was outwardly. It seemed to have been ordered, straighted into complete impersonality. The furniture was of good quality and obviously expensive, and just as obviously chosen without taste. Mahogany of no particular period stood cheek-by-jowl with golden oak and maple patently of neo-Grand Rapids design. The floors were waxed and highly polished, and on them were some simulated Kashan rugs arranged without regard to pattern or color. Such pictures as adorned the walls were of the Landseer-Rosa Bonheur school. I almost expected to see "The Stag at Bay" or "Pharaoh's Horses," or an enlarged sepia print of the Colosseum.

"The basement first, if you will be so kind," de Grandin asked, and led by our host we descended a flight of narrow stairs. The room ran under the entire house and was in nowise remarkable. In one corner was the gas furnace, flanked by the hot water tank, with stationary washtubs and a mechanical washer beside them. Odds and ends of cast-off furniture, rolled-up summer matting rugs and similar lumber lay around the walls.

"Here was where my brother was found," Mr. Roggenbuck told us, pointing to an iron pipe that snaked between the joists supporting the first floor. "He hung, as I told you, with his feet almost on the ground, and there was nothing under or near him which he could have stood on while adjusting the noose—"

"Did you observe him before he was cut down?" de Grandin interrupted.

"Why, yes—"

"He wore no slippers, I believe?"

"They had dropped from his feet, I assume—"

"One does not make assumptions in such cases, Monsieur. Have you any reason to believe that they had fallen, rather than been slipped off?"

"No-o; I can't say I have."

"Bien. Bon. We begin to make the progress. Now, what, exactly, was his position?"

Roggenbuck was silent for a moment, then dropped to one knee. "I'd say he hung just about here, with his feet clear of the floor."

"U'm. And he was five feet and a half in height, the rope by which he hung was approximately two feet long, his feet lacked four or so inches of contact with the floor?"

"That is correct, sir."

"H'm. Then something less than a foot high—something perhaps no more than six or seven inches would have been sufficient for him to mount as a scaffold—"

"But there was nothing there, I tell you—"

"Not even this, perhaps?" Wheeling as if on a pivot, the little Frenchman walked to the wall opposite the place where we stood, stooped and retrieved an object lying in the shadow.

It was a bowling ball of some eight inches diameter, black and highly polished,

but overlaid with a thin film of dust. As he held it daintily, with thumb and forefinger in the grip-holes, we saw the dust upon its surface had been wiped away
in two parallel patches roughly oblong in shape, and that a wavering diagonal of
cleared space ran down one side. "Unless I am far more mistaken than I think,"
he told us, "*Monsieur le Suicide* stood on this globe while he adjusted the loop to
his neck, then kicked it from him so it rolled to the spot where I spied it. That
we can readily determine. Your brother balanced barefoot on this ball, *Monsieur*.
The slippery soles of his straw shoes would not have afforded a purchase on its
smooth surface. *Alors*, he left the prints of his feet on the polished wood. See
them?" He indicated the two spots where the dust was disturbed. "The ridges
on the friction skin of hands and feet are as highly individual as the prints of
the fingers. Your brother has not yet been buried. It is necessary only that we
bring the prints on this ball out, make an impression of the pattern of the soles
of his feet, and *voilà*, we can be sure that he stood upon the sphere before he did
la danse macabre. Yes, certainly." He wrapped his salvage in a newspaper taken
from the pile that stood in readiness for the trash-collector, then:

"If you will be so kind as to conduct us to *Madame* your sister-in-law, we shall
be obliged," he said.

"I'm sorry, but I can't permit her to be disturbed," Mr. Roggenbuck refused.

"*Très bien*; just as you say," de Grandin agreed. "I think that we have gleaned
sufficient data for one call already. If you will be so good as to give me an order
on the mortician permitting me to make prints of your brother's feet we need not
trouble you further at this time, *Monsieur*."

"WHERE'VE YOU BEEN?" I demanded as he came in sometime after eleven
the next evening and began attacking the snack of turkey sandwiches,
champagne, lemon pie and coffee Nora had left for him with a ferocity that
would have made a famished wolf seem daintily abstemious by comparison.

"*Mon Dieu, mon Dieu*, where have I not been, my old one?" he answered
between mouthfuls. "Me, I have been up hill and down dale, and completely
round the barn of Monsieur Robin Hood. I have visited the excellent mortician,
the newspaper office, the office of the county clerk, the house of Monsieur Roggenbuck—*grand Dieu*, what a name!—and a dozen other places, also.

"And has my search been vain? *Par la barbe d'une pieuvre*, I shall say otherwise!" He finished the last morsel of sandwich, washed it down with the last sip
of champagne, poured a cup of steaming coffee, and prepared to demolish a great
wedge of lemon meringue. "My friend," he leveled his fork at me like a weapon,
"my old and fare one, I learned a number of most interesting things today. Some
of them may have a bearing on *l'affaire* Roggenbuck, although at present I cannot make out their pattern. Consider, if you please:

"The Brothers Roggenbuck appear to have worked as a team for years, the estimable Rodney furnishing the invention, his less talented kinsmen attending to the details. Before the 1929 debacle their specialty was peddling securities, stock of goldless gold mines, oilless oil wells, real estate entirely under water, and the like. Their favorite clients were bereaved ladies left some small insurance, or, failing those, old couples who had laid away a little for their final years. Frédéric, the younger brother, went to jail, Théobald was fined, but not incarcerated; Rodney went free for lack of evidence.

"Let us, like surveyors, drive a peg down there, and proceed with our examination of the terrain. The present Madame Roggenbuck is not the first, nor second, nor third spouse of this *manqué* evangelist. He has, it seems, been married three times previously. It seems she was the elder of two orphan daughters of a *viellard* named Stretfuse."

"Old Henry Stretfuse?" I asked. "I remember him. He had a farm out on the Andover Road—"

"*Précisément.* A very old, worked-out farm which was considered worthless when he left it to his daughters. But with the coming of the war, when the city commenced expanding like a blown-up bladder, it became most valuable for building sites. The boom in building had just begun when Monsieur Roggenbuck married Mademoiselle Stretfuse.

"She was, as I have said, the elder of two sisters, and much flattered to receive attention from the reverend gentleman. Eulalia, her younger sister, was already suffering from incipient tuberculosis." He paused, swallowed the last crumb of pie, and added, "According to the terms of the will, the sisters were named joint tenants in the land. Does that mean anything to you?"

I shook my head.

"Nor did it signify to me until I had consulted Monsieur Mitchell the *avoué.* Then I began to scent a little so small mouse. Joint tenancy, the lawyer told me, means that tenants hold the land in equal, undivided shares, but at the death of one the whole estate passes to the other instead of going partly to the heirs of him who dies. *Et puis?* No one will buy the share of one joint tenant unless the other also signs the deed, since he who buys is subrogated only to the rights of his grantor, and liable to have his heirs' inheritance defeated if he dies before the other joint tenant. Do you also begin to smell the rodent?"

"H'm; can't say that I do."

"*Très bien.* Regard me: If Monsieur Roggenbuck married Mademoiselle Eulalia the chances are that she, the victim of an often fatal malady, would predecease her elder sister; but if he married Mademoiselle Sara, as he did, the chances are that she, though older, will survive and become sole owner of a valuable property. For that reason, and no other, I am convinced, he chose the elder of the sisters for his bride.

"However, complications rose when Mademoiselle the younger sister married

Monsieur Frye. Under his loving care and cherishment she might outlive her elder sister, then *pouf!* where would the reverend gentleman be?

"Not to be caught napping, *pardieu!* Not he! When Monsieur Frye goes to the war he takes his sister-in-law to his house, sees that she has no medical attention, and hopes for the best.

"*Hélas*, the soldier-husband comes home from the battlefields, so stronger measures must be taken. He takes the young wife from her home and holds her virtually a prisoner, *incommunicado*.

"Now, listen carefully. *Monsieur* the husband is about to ask the court to give him back his wife when he meets death upon the highway. The accident occurs on a steep hill, and, quite fortuitously, two of the firm of Roggenbuck *Frères* are there at or about the time it happens."

"Are you implying—"

"I am implying nothing. I am merely marshalling the facts for our review. Two days before this fatal accident Monsieur Frédéric buys a motor car, a swift vehicle fitted with a driving searchlight, such as police cars carry. Moreover, he goes to garageman and has an even more powerful light installed. He is a city-dweller and not given to much driving on the country roads. Why should he desire so powerful a search light?"

"I haven't the remotest idea."

"Well spoken, my good, trusting friend. You would be the last to entertain unworthy suspicions. Me, I am otherwise."

"What d'ye mean?"

"Not anything at present. This is just another peg we drive down in our surveying tour. But listen further, if you please:

"This afternoon I made it my business to watch Monsieur Roggenbuck's house. By a 'phone call I ascertained that he was at his office. I saw *Madame* his wife go out; I telephoned his house and got no answer. '*Bien,*' I tell me. 'The house are empty; the domestic is not there.' So, like the robber in the night, I break into that house. *Parbleu*, I tell you a most excellent burglar was lost when Jules de Grandin decided to be comparatively honest.

"I went through that house carefully. And in an upper room, a little so small sunless room set high beneath the roof, I find poor Madame Frye. She are locked in like any *félone*. She lies upon a narrow, unkempt bed, her *robe de nuit* is far from clean, she coughs almost incessantly.

"I speak to her, me. She answers feebly, between coughings. She tells me that her brother-in-law keeps at her constantly to deed her share of the farm to her sister. He tells her that her husband is dead, but she will not believe him. She stubbornly withholds her signature, for he, her husband had told her to sign nothing. Until he comes she will not sign. *Parbleu*, unless we intervene all soon she will assuredly succumb, and Madame Roggenbuck will be sole heiress. When that occurs, *cordieu*, I do not think that she will be a good risk for insurance. No. I ask to know if it is not a pretty pan of fish I have discovered?"

"It's infamous!" I exclaimed. "We must do something—"

"*Précisément, mon vieux*, we must, indeed. Come, let us go."

"Go? Where?"

"About a little piece of business that I have in mind."

P ETEROS, READ THE SMALL bronze tablet on the red-brick house before which we stopped half an hour later. As far as I could see it was the only thing distinguishing it from the other houses in the eminently respectable block. When de Grandin pressed the bell a neatly uniformed maid answered and led us to a parlor.

I glanced about me curiously. The place was rather elegant. A Chinese rug of the Kien-lung period lay on the floor, against the farther wall hung a Ghiordes prayer-cloth, the furniture was clearly of French manufacture, gilt wood upholstered in an apple-green brocade. The only picture in the room was a life-sized portrait of a blond woman with wide, brooding eyes and a sad mouth. A latch clicked, and a small, neat gentleman entered.

He was perhaps fifty, his hair was slightly gray at the temples, his rather long face was clean-shaven, the dark eyes behind the tortoise-shell spectacles were serious and thoughtful. His dinner clothes were impeccable, but of a slightly foreign cut. He might have been a lawyer or a banker, or perhaps the curator of an art gallery, but I recognized him as Gregor Peteros who, though professionally a medium and clairvoyant, was so highly thought of that psychologists of reputable standing did not hesitate to consult him, and whose monographs on extrasensory perception had been printed in a dozen scientific magazines. "Good evening, gentlemen," he greeted. "I'll be with you in a moment. If you don't mind I'll take a topcoat; I'm rather sensitive to chill."

" A S NEAR AS I could determine from studying the newspapers and police reports, this is the spot," de Grandin told us as we drew up at a curve that twisted down a steep hill above Harrison Creek. The roadway had been widened recently, and where a hundred-foot drop led to the rock-studded, bawling waters of the stream a breast-high wall of stone and reinforced concrete had been erected. The spot had been a famous—or infamous—one for fatal accidents until this safeguard had been put up, I recalled.

"Can you put yourself *en rapport* with the past, Monsieur Peteros?" de Grandin asked. "I realize it may be difficult, for much traffic has passed since—"

"Do not tell me the details!" Mr. Peteros broke in. "When did the accident occur?"

"September eighteenth, two years ago."

"I see." The medium made a note on a slip of paper, did a quick calculation, and tapped his teeth with his pencil. "That would have been under the sign of Virgo in the decanus of Mercury." He settled himself back on the cushions, closed his eyes, and seemed about to take a nap. For several minutes there was complete silence, and we could hear the ticking of our watches beating out a fugue; from the distance came the dismal wailing of a freight train's locomotive, somewhere nearer a dog barked, and the mounting sound was slender as a strand of spider-web.

Abruptly Mr. Peteros sat up. His eyes were closed, but his face worked excitedly. "I see him!" he exclaimed. "He has swung around the curve at the hilltop and commenced the descent. He seems distrait; he is not watching the road. He should not rely on his brakes, he ought to put his engine into low gear."

He swallowed with excitement, then turned his closed eyes down the road. "There is another car coming," he announced. "It's a small, open car, with two men in it. One drives, the other leans out. He is watching . . . watching. He has his hand upon a driving searchlight set upon a rod beside the windshield. It is covered with some kind of cloth, a bag or sack of heavy felt through which no light can pass. The two cars are not more than fifty feet apart now. The man descending the hill swerves to the right, toward the guardrail. The other car swings to the left. They are approaching head-on. Ah! The man beside the driver of the second car has turned his hooded spotlight squarely on the driver of the first vehicle. Now he snatches the hood off. A-a-ah! There is a beam of dazzling light shining full into the other driver's eyes. It blinds him. He—his car is out of control! He will crash against the barrier. He has crashed through it! His car is turning over and over as it tumbles down the bank. *Kyrie eleïson!* The glass of his windshield has shattered. He is pierced by a great splinter of it. He is bleeding, dying. . . ."

He paused a moment, breathing hard, like an exhausted runner, then, more calmly: "The other car has stopped and its passengers have gotten out. They are slipping, sliding down the steep bank. They have reached the wreck, but they make no move to take its occupant out. One of them reaches in and feels his pulse, shakes his head, and steps back. They wait . . . wait. Now they feel the wreck victim's pulse again, and still they make no move to lift him out. Now they seem satisfied. They reach into the wreck and lift the victim out. He is dead. I see them nod to each other, then turn to scramble up the bank again. . . ."

"*Yes, yes, monsieur?* What next?" de Grandin rasped as Mr. Peteros ceased speaking. "*Pour le chapeau d'un cochon vert,* what else is it you see, I ask to know?"

"Eh?" Mr. Peteros looked at him with the blank stare of a wakened sleeper. "What's that?"

"*Mordieu,* what else was it you saw?"

"I don't remember. I can never recall what I've seen in the trance."

The little Frenchman looked as if he were about to spring on him, then raised his narrow shoulders in a shrug of resignation. "*Tenez*, it is of no real importance. I damn think you have told us quite enough."

"**J**E SUIS AFFAMÉ, I am hungry, like a wolf, me," he told me as we reached the house. "Let us see what Madame Nora has concealed in the ice box."

We rummaged in the frigidaire and brought out some cold roast lamb, some lettuce and a jar of mayonnaise. Also several bottles of beer.

"Now," he asked, seating himself on the kitchen table with a sandwich in one hand and beer mug in the other, "what is it that we have? It seems that in the matter of eliminating Monsieur Frye the middle Roggenbuck brother was, as usual, the master mind. He planned the so clever assassination, his henchmen-brothers executed it,

"I am persuaded that they died self-hanged, and that they richly deserved hanging. Of Monsieur Théobald's suicide there is no doubt. The prints upon the bowling ball exactly match the lines of his feet. That he stood on it, then kicked it away when he had draped the noose around his neck, there is no question. Concerning Monsieur Frédéric I cannot say with certainty, but I incline to think that Dr. Parnell is for once right, and the good Costello once unfortunately wrong.

"Why did they do it? Who can say? Perhaps it was their guilty conscience, though I do not think so, for *fripons* such as they have little conscience. Perhaps it was the vengeful spirit of their victim seeking justice—forcing them to do that which the law could not. It could be so. At any rate, they are eliminated. Our problem now is Monsieur Rodney."

"There's nothing we can do about him," I rejoined. "There's no way we can bring the crime home to him. No court and jury in New Jersey would listen to such testimony as Peteros gave us tonight, and even if they did we can't Prove Rodney planned the murder."

"I agree with you, *mon vieux*, but we may do what the law cannot. His conscience—granting that he has one—is not clean. His brothers' statements that they had a feeling of being watched troubled him. He is persuaded that his murdered brother-in-law has the power to bewitch him—to 'hex' him, as he puts it. When, to test his sensibility to suggestion, I pretended to see someone standing behind him last night, did not you see how frightened he was? I think that there we shall find the chink in his armor, and I shall work industriously to enlarge it. Yes, certainly. Of course."

IT WAS SHORTLY BEFORE noon next day when he entered Mr. Roggenbuck's office. The place swarmed with activity. A battery of typewriters, operated by singularly photogenic young women, filled in spaces in processed form letters and addressed envelopes; a boy and girl were busy at a multi-graphing machine, several curvaceous females stuffed the filled-in forms into envelopes.

"Yes, sirs?" challenged the young woman at the switchboard, who also evidently acted as receptionist. Advised of our errand she whispered something into an inter-office communicator, and in a moment looked up with a smile. "Straight ahead, please," she directed. "The Bishop's office is at the end of the corridor."

"*Parbleu*," de Grandin chuckled as we walked down the hall, "when he first came to see us he was a simple pastor. Today he is a bishop. We must hurry to take care of him, my friend, or he will assuredly become pope.

"*Monseigneur*," he announced as we entered Roggenbuck's dimly-lighted, softly carpeted sanctum, "I have the proof that both your brothers died by their own hands, and—*mon Dieu*, who is that!" he stepped back, both hands raised as if to ward away some horror.

"Who—where?" the other turned half round in his swivel chair.

"The one who stands behind you with his face all smeared in blood and points at you accusingly—"

"No!" Roggenbuck exclaimed. "It can't be—he can't say—"

"Friend Trowbridge, do not you see him?" de Grandin turned to me. "Do not you see him standing there?"

I knit my brows and tried to sound as convincing as possible. "Yes, there's someone there. He seems to have met with an accident. Shall we call an ambulance—"

"No! No!" Roggenbuck broke in hoarsely. "You're lying, both of you!" He pressed a button on his desk, and in a moment there came the click of high heels on the floor outside.

"Did you ring, Bishop?" asked a young woman as she entered. "I—oh! who is it—what's happened?" She stared across her employer's shoulder, apparently wide-eyed with horror, then put her hands up to her face and dropped back a step, shuddering. "Oh, o-oh!" she moaned. "The blood—the blood!"

Sweat was streaming down Roggenbuck's face, his full-lipped mouth began to work convulsively, and at its corners little flecks of foam showed. His eyes were bright and dilated as if under the influence of a drug. "Do you see it, too, Elsie?" he choked.

She made no answer, but nodded, her face still cupped in her hands, her shoulders shaking with repressed sobs.

"Oh, my God!" the frightened man rose from his desk and stumbled toward the rear door. "He's come for me, too. He came for Fred and Theo, now it's my turn—leave me alone, Amos Frye, I didn't—I didn't—" The door banged to behind him, and de Grandin patted the girl's shoulder.

"Bravo, *Mademoiselle*," he applauded. "The great Bernhardt at her greatest could not have done better. Here is what I promised you." From his wallet he drew several bills and pressed them into her hand.

The girl giggled. "I wouldn't 'a' done it if he hadn't been such a heel," she confessed. "But he was always makin' passes at us girls, an' threatenin' to fire us if we squawked. The pious old hypocrite!"

The Frenchman grinned delightedly. "You have given me a new word for my vocabulary, *ma chère*. It are entirely as you say. He was an eel of the first water, him."

From the driveway beside the office we heard the rasp of gears and the roaring of a motor being started. In a moment, from the corner came the shrill, hysterical scream of a police whistle, the crash of metal smashing into metal and the ring of breaking glass.

We rushed into the street and raced toward the corner, with the shriek of the policeman's whistle and a chorus of hoarse cries still sounding.

Telescoped until it was foreshortened by at least a third its length, Roggenbuck's convertible stood at the intersection of the street and boulevard, while towering above it, like a bulldog straddling a luckless cat, was a ten-ton truck.

"Hullo, Dr. de Grandin," greeted the policeman. "Good mornin', Dr. Trowbridge. Gimme a hand with him, will you? He was comin' hell-bent-for-election down the street, payin' no more attention to the red light than if it wasn't there, when *zingo!* he barged into this here now truck, like he'd knock it outa his way. Yeah, the cemeteries is full o' birds that drive like that. He didn't have no more chance than a rabbit."

"One sees," returned de Grandin as, assisting the policeman, we lifted what was left of Roggenbuck from his car. Death must have been instantaneous. Certainly, it had been messy. His whole face was bashed in as if it had been struck by a battering-ram. His skull, from frontal bone to occiput, had been smashed like an egg and almost denuded of scalp. "*Mort*," pronounced de Grandin. "*Mort comme un mouton*—he is dead like a herring, this one." He nodded to the policeman. "This is for the coroner, *mon brave*. Do not disturb the internes at the hospital. They hate to have their poker playing interrupted by such fruitless calls."

The Body-Snatchers

S TREET LIGHTS WERE COMING on and the afterglow was faint in the west under the first cold stars as I let myself in at the front door. I'd had a hard day at the hospital, two T and A's in the morning and a cholitonotomy in the afternoon, and at my age surgery is almost as hard on the physician as the patient. "Thank heaven, no calls this evening," I murmured as I shrugged out of my overcoat and started toward the study where I knew Nora McGinnis would have a preprandial cocktail iced and waiting for me.

My heart sank like a plummet as the voices came to me from the consulting room. "I realize this is more a case for a lawyer than a physician, but I've known Dr. Trowbridge since I was thirty seconds old, and I *have* to talk it over with somebody. Just going to an attorney seems so sort of—well, common, if you understand, Dr. de Grandin. There's never been a divorce in our family, but—"

"Hullo, there young 'un!" I greeted with wholly meretricious cordiality as I paused at the door. "What's all this talk about divorce—"

"Oh, Dr. Trowbridge, I'm *so* glad you've come!" Nancy Northrop fairly leaped from her chair and threw her arms about me. "I—I've been so miserable, Doctor!" The held-back tears broke through her eyelids and in a moment she was sobbing like a little girl whose doll is broken.

"There, there," I soothed, patting her shoulder. "A dry Martini won't cure the trouble, but it'll help. Come into the study, both of you."

Nancy Northrop was a small, pretty woman with bright hair, a straight little nose and wide-set amber eyes "put in with a smutty finger," as the Irish say. For a long moment she was calm, immovable as the embalmed bride of a Pharoah, staring broodingly into the tawny depths of her cocktail. "I just don't seem to have the proper words to tell it," she murmured finally. "You've known Norman and me all our lives, Doctor; you know we went together even in grammar school days, and when we married it was no more a surprise to anyone—including us— than setting down the sum beneath a column of figures would have been."

"That's so," I agreed. "You were childhood sweethearts, I remember. A lot of people thought it just one of those boy-and-girl affairs, but—"

"I said it was no more surprising than the sum arrived at when you add a line of figures," she broke in. "Well, someone made a mistake in addition, Doctor. Norman's left me."

"Eh? What d'ye mean, child?"

"Just what I said. He's—as the old song had it—'gone with a handsomer girl.'"

"*Tenez, Madame,*" de Grandin interrupted, "suppose we start at the beginning and work forward. How was it that *Monsieur* your husband left you, and when?"

"Last Monday, sir. There was a party at the Lakerim Country Club that evening, and Norman and I went. We had the first few dances together, then Norman went somewhere—he was on the committee, you know—and the next I saw of him he was dancing with a strange girl."

"A stranger?" I prompted as she fell into a thoughtful silence, turning the stem of her glass between her fingers, biting her lower lip to hold it steady.

"Yes, sir, a stranger. No one seemed to know who she was—just how she came to be at the party, or who brought her is a mystery—but there she was in his arms, and"—she offered us a pitiful, small smile—"I must admit she was attractive and danced extraordinarily well."

"Can you perhaps describe her, *Madame?*" de Grandin asked as the silence lengthened again.

"Can I? Was there ever a woman who couldn't describe her successful rival down to the last hair of her plucked eyebrows and final hook and eye of her gown? She was tall, as tall as a tall man, and built exquisitely—no, not exquisitely, grandly built is more nearly correct. She was more of a Minerva than a Venus. Her hair was dark, either black or very dark brown, and her eyes an intense blue, like the sea off Ogunquit or Hamilton. She must have just come back from Cuba or Bermuda, for her neck and arms and shoulders all seemed carved of smoky amber, and she wore an evening gown of red brocade, sleeveless, of course, and belted at the waist with a gold cord, Grecian fashion. Her sandals were gold, too, and the lovely sun-tan on her feet made them look gilded, except for the red-lacquered nails. Oh"—once more she gave a rueful little smile—"I couldn't any more compete with her than Hera or Pallas could with Aphrodite! I'd never felt a pang of jealousy before, but when I saw my husband dancing with that gorgeous hussy I was positively green-eyed.

"They were playing 'Tales From the Vienna Woods,' and she and Norm were waltzing to it like a pair of ballroom professionals when a man came from the conservatory and cut in. As she danced away with her new partner I could see her signalling Norman, positively teasing him with her eyes.

"The strange couple circled round the floor once then danced into the conservatory, and I felt everything inside me coming loose as I saw Norman follow them.

"I hadn't any business doing it, I know, it was a cheap, unworthy way to act, but I went in after them. Just as I reached the entrance to the greenhouse I heard voices raised in angry argument, then a crash, and Norman and the strange girl brushed past me. 'Brushed' is the verb, too. I might have been just one of the potted plants for all the notice they took of me. As they passed she linked her fingers round his arm and laughed. I heard her say, 'How handsome you are—'"

Nancy paused in her recital, and a puzzled frown formed on her face, as if she were endeavoring to see something just beyond her vision.

"Yes?" I prompted.

"That's what's worrying me, Doctor. What she called him. It wasn't Norm or Norman nor even Mr. Northrop. It was some other name, some strange name I had never heard."

Her preoccupation with the trifle annoyed me. "What happened next?" I asked a little acidly.

"I went into the conservatory, and as I staggered between the plants I knew just how an injured animal that crawls away to die must feel. I was so blinded by my tears that I didn't see the other man until I stumbled over him. He was lying on his back, both arms flung out as if he had been crucified against the floor, and blood was running from a cut in his head where he'd struck it against a *jardinière* as he fell.

"The first thing I thought was, 'He's dead. Norman's killed him!' but when I bent down I could hear him breathing hoarsely, and knew that he was only unconscious. I don't know how long I waited beside him. You see, I wanted to make sure that Norman had a chance to get away before I gave the alarm, but finally I ran back to the ballroom and told Ed Pennybacker what I'd found. Of course, I didn't tell him anything about the struggle I'd heard, or even about seeing Norman and the strange woman in the greenhouse. Dr. Ferris was at the dance, and went to give the man first aid, but in a moment he came back looking serious and muttering something about concussion. They called an ambulance and took him to Mercy Hospital."

"And where was Norman all this time?" I asked as she lapsed into brooding silence once more.

"I don't know, Doctor. I haven't seen him since."

"Wh—what?"

"That's correct, sir. He didn't come to take me home. Our car was gone from the parking lot, and I had to ride back with Joe and Louise Tralor. He didn't come home that night. He hasn't been home since, nor has he been to the office. O-oh!"

Her cry was a small sad sound that heightened and grew thinner, finally ravelled out to nothingness like a pulled woolen thread. "He's gone, Doctor; left me; deserted me!"

There are times when nothing we can say seems adequate. This was one of them, and so I had to content myself with patting her shoulder and murmuring, "There, there!"

She turned on me, eyes blazing with a sudden heat that fairly burned the tears away as she put her forefinger to her dimpled chin, made me a bobbing little curtsy and, like a little girl reciting, repeated:

There, little girl; don't cry!
They have broken your heart, I know—

Her voice cracked like a shattering glass, and her laughter was a ghastly thing to hear as she ran from the study and out the front door.

"THERE'S A MISTHER NORTHROP to see yez, gentlemen," Nora McGinnis told us as de Grandin and I sat over brandy, coffee and cigars in the drawing room after dinner that evening. "He says as how it's most important."

"*Tiens*," de Grandin murmured. "Is it that the errant husband comes to tell us his side of the story, one wonders?"

"Humph, it had better be a good tale he's cooked up," I answered. "The unconscionable young pup, treating Nancy that way—"

"Misther Northrop," Nora interrupted from the doorway.

He was a very ugly little man, some sixty-five years old, I judged, for his face was criss-crossed by a network of deep wrinkles and his small mustache was quite white. His eyes were small, black and deep-set, and what we could see of his hair was also white, though for the most part it was covered by a Sayer's occipital bandage. His clothes were well cut and of good material, very neatly pressed, but obviously not new. "Good evening, Dr. Trowbridge," he greeted as he paused at the door.

"Mr. Northrop?" I asked inquiringly. "I don't think that I've had the pleasure—"

The laugh that interrupted me was mirthless as the bark of a teased dog. "Oh, yes, we've met before, Doctor," he corrected. "It was thirty-two years ago, on the seventeenth of January, to be exact, in Mercy Hospital. I'm Norman Northrop."

I could feel a wash of angry blood in my cheeks. "If this is a joke—" I began, but once more his eerie, bitter laugh broke in.

"If it's a joke it's on me, Doctor. I don't understand it any more than you do, but I'm Norman Northrop."

"*Grand Dieu des porcs!*" I heard de Grandin murmur almost soundlessly, then aloud, "Come in, *Monsieur*; come in and tell us how it comes that you are strange to Dr. Trowbridge, and, I damn suspect, to yourself also."

"Thank you, Doctor," the caller bowed acknowledgement of de Grandin's invitation and came into the drawing room. I noticed that he limped a little, as if he had suffered a slight stroke some time before, for his right foot dragged and turned in as he stepped.

"And now, *Monsieur*?" de Grandin poured an ounce or so of brandy into an inhaler, filled a demi-tasse and placed them at the stranger's elbow, motioning toward the cigars as he did so. "You are, one takes it, the husband of Madame Northrop who called on us this after—"

"Nancy's been here?" Our caller's face, already nearly colorless, went absolutely corpse-gray, and the hand that held his brandy glass shook with something more than the slight senile tremor I had noticed. "What did she tell you?"

"*Tiens*, the story was not pretty, *Monsieur*. She told us that you had deserted her; that you fought with some strange man for the favors of a strange woman; that then you went with your new charmer without so much as one small backward look by way of valedictory."

The caller seemed to shrink in on himself. The wrinkled skin around his mouth and on his neck seemed trembling like the dewlaps of a hound, and tears came in his small black eyes. "Please, gentlemen," he begged, "be kind enough to hear me through. Before I'm half done you'll call me a damned liar, and when I've finished you will think I'm drunk or crazy, maybe both; but what I have to say is true, every word of it.

"Nancy must have told you how we went to Lakerim Monday night. We had the first three dances together, and just as the band began playing for the fourth I saw Bob Eastman beckoning. Bob was on the committee, though why they put him there Lord only knows. If there's any way of snafuing a deal he'll find it. We'd gone all out on the refreshments, and Braunstein's were to furnish baked Alaskas for dessert. They hadn't come, and Bob was in a hissy. He'd called the caterer's, and they'd told him their wagon had left half an hour before. What should we do about it?

"I got Braunstein's on the 'phone and found that Bob had given orders for the desserts to be delivered to the Lake View Club instead of the Lakerim. Lake View is over by Morristown, you know, and Bob had belonged there before transferring to Lakerim. I suppose it was a pardonable slip of the tongue, but it had certainly snarled our party up. After several minutes' conversation I got 'em to promise to send another wagon out to Lakerim, and was hurrying to rejoin Nancy when I bumped into a girl.

"I mean that literally. The floor outside the steward's office was slippery. She was hurrying one way! I was barging through the door, and we collided like a pair of kids on roller skates. Both our feet went out from under us, and there we sat on our respective fannies, not hurt but with the wind knocked out of us. For a moment we grinned at each other, then I helped her up and apologized.

"She seemed to be taking inventory. 'I'm not hurt,' she told me, 'but I seem to have broken something. Will you take me to the powder room where I can make a few repairs, please?'

"The quickest way to the powder room was across the dance floor, and the quickest way to cross the dance floor was to dance rather than trying to dodge between the couples. So we danced.

"She was a superb dancer; you'd have thought the music ran through her nerves like wind through an Æolian harp.

"Just as we reached the far side of the ballroom her hand tightened on mine 'Don't look now,' she whispered, 'but I'm being pursued by the Big Bad Wolf. He's been trailing me all evening.' She didn't seem frightened, just a little nervous and annoyed, and I didn't think much of it.

"'Let's circle round the floor again,' she suggested. 'Maybe he'll get discouraged and go back to the bar.' So we waltzed around the floor again, and she went on 'He's an old friend of my father's, a widower who's looking for a replacement. Honestly, he persecutes me! If he catches us he'll want to cut in, and I suppose you'll have to let him, but if you want to do your Boy Scout's daily good deed please follow us. He'll head for the conservatory—that's his technique—and all you'll have to do is wait a moment, then come barging in and say, "This is our dance, I believe," or something similarly original. Can do?'

"'Can do,' I promised, and, as she predicted, there was her aged Lothario lying in ambush by the entrance to the conservatory.

"'May I cut in?' he asked as he tapped me on the shoulder, and as I resigned my partner to him she whispered, 'Remember, Perseus, Andromeda'll be waiting to be rescued!'

"I watched them circle the ballroom and noticed that though he danced quite well he dragged his right foot. Sure enough, he guided her into the greenhouse, and in a moment I followed.

"I don't know just what I'd expected to find, but I was certainly unprepared for the tableau on which I stumbled. The little man had backed her up against the wall, and stood threatening her with one of those case-knives—those things that snap an eight-inch blade out when you press a spring, you know. 'If I can't have you, no one else shall,' I heard him say as I entered the conservatory.

"I knew I had to do something, and do it in a hurry. The man was little, scarcely larger than a half-grown boy, but a crazy man armed with an eight-inch dirk is not a pleasant customer to deal with, and for a moment I was at a loss. Then the girl's appeal sparked me to action. 'Please, please!' she begged. 'He's crazy—mad as a hatter—'

"'Put that knife up,' I told him. 'You're acting like a—'

"He turned from her and came at me, and I knew I really had a maniac to deal with, for there was no light of sanity in his eyes, and at the corners of his mouth I could see little flecks of foam. 'So you're the favored swain tonight?' he rasped in a hard, gritty voice.

"'Hit him; knock him senseless!' the girl begged. 'He'll kill us if you don't—'

"I hit as hard as I could, bringing my fist up from the hip and pivoting on my right foot to put my weight behind the blow. He went down like a pole-axed ox, but something seemed to go wrong with me at the same time. A paralyzing tingling, like the pins and needles we feel when a foot has gone to sleep, went up my arm as my fist struck his chin, and in a moment every nerve in my body seemed shrieking in agony.

"The pain was almost unendurable, but I couldn't make a move, just stood there, trembling as with a galvanic shock and saw the girl go up to him, take his left hand in her right, then felt her grasp my right in her left. The man got up and put his free hand over mine, so in a moment we had formed a circle, and they were moving slowly round and round, dragging me after them.

"I don't know what it was they said, or rather sang in a monotonous crooning tune, the words seemed meaningless—perhaps they were in some foreign tongue, perhaps they were just doggerel—but they kept repeating over and over, as near as I can remember:

"'*Aristeas, Kartaphilos, Ahasverus, Buttadaeus.*'"

"*Morbleu!*" ejaculated Jules de Grandin. "Are you sure that is what they said, *Monsieur?*"

"No, sir, I'm not. But that's as near as can come to it."

"*Très bon*, my friend. Continue." The little Frenchman had leant forward, his small blue eyes fixed on our caller's face intently as a cat pins its gaze on a rat-hole. "Say on, *Monsieur*," he ordered. "We are listening."

"Well, in a moment it seemed that the greenhouse was in motion, too; turning in reverse to the way we moved. That is, we moved from right to left, counter-clockwise, while it seemed to revolve from left to right, and somehow I was being twisted mentally.

"It's hard to put in words, but somehow—don't ask me how, I don't know!—I seemed to be becoming someone else. The first thing that I noticed was that my right foot was dragging, and somehow I seemed smaller. I had to look up at the tall girl holding my right hand, and in a moment I seemed looking at myself—as if I saw my own reflection in a mirror, yet held the hand of the man in the looking-glass. All images were rather blurred, like things seen under water. Then suddenly I felt a dull ache at the back of my head as my knees sagged under me."

The caller stopped his narrative and looked at us in turn, as though expecting us to finish the story.

"And then, *Monsieur*?" de Grandin prompted when the silence had lasted at least a minute.

"The next thing I knew I was lying in a bed. The bed was white, the walls of the room were white, everything around me was white and sterile. It was a hospital bedroom, I realized, but how I'd gotten there I had no idea. For a moment I lay there, trying to gather my wits, then I put out my hand for the call-bell. That was the first shock I got. The hand I moved *wasn't mine*. I'm thirty-two years old, as you know, Dr. Trowbridge. The hand that moved when I reached for the bell was that of an old man, thin, bony, high-veined, speckled with liver-spots.

"I lay there for a moment, wondering if I were delirious, then called, 'Anybody around?' and that was the second shock. The voice that sounded when I formed the words in my mind wasn't mine. It was the thin, rasping treble of an old man. I recognized it! I had heard it in the conservatory when I found the old man threatening the girl.

"I don't know how long I lay there after that, and the more I tried to make sense of the senseless business the less sense it seemed to make. At last a nurse came in and greeted me with that false cheeriness they always use on patients. 'Good morning! Feeling better? That was a nasty crack on the head you had.'

"'Nurse,' I begged, and my fear grew into absolute panic as I heard the senile piping of the voice with which I spoke, 'Please get me a mirror.'

"'Oh, you're not disfigured, gran'paw,' she assured me as she took a hand-glass from the dresser and gave it to me. 'You'll be right as rain in a day or two.'

"There's not much use in trying to describe my feelings as I looked into the glass. The face that gazed back at me was not mine, but that of the old man whom I had knocked out in the conservatory.

"'That's not—that isn't I!' I screamed. 'That's not my face—'

"The nurse took the mirror away. 'Take it easy, gran'paw,' she advised. 'Who'd you expect to see, Charles Boyer, or maybe Mickey Mouse?' She stepped out to the corridor and in a moment a young interne hurried in.

"'Still pretty bad, eh?' I heard him whisper. He swabbed my arm with alcohol and drove a hypo into it. The anesthetic acted almost immediately, and I was out almost before I had a chance to protest.

"When I woke up the sun was slanting in the window and there were shadows in the corners of the room that hadn't been there when I first regained consciousness. My first thought was to ring the bell and ask to see the superintendent. Then I reconsidered. How I came to be in this old body I had no idea. It was like one of those dreadful things you read about in fairy-story books—or books of witchcraft and black magic—but one thing was sure: If I attempted to disclaim the body into which I seemed to have been thrust I'd get nowhere, except into the psychopathic ward. They'd given me a shot of dope that morning when they thought that I was still delirious from the blow on the head. Now, when I'd regained full consciousness, if I still insisted I was someone else—what would you have done if a patient acted that way, Dr. Trowbridge?"

"I'd be inclined to certify him—" I began, but he cut in sharply:

"Exactly. And you, Dr. de Grandin?"

Jules de Grandin pursed his lips as if he were about to whistle, and tweaked the ends of his small blond mustache. "I do not know, my friend," he answered. "What you have told us sounds incredible. Such things just do not happen, as Dr. Trowbridge—or any jury of a lunacy commission—will assure you; but I withhold the judgment. Will you proceed?"

Our caller drew a deep, quick breath, whether of relief or excitement I could not determine. Then: "I realized that I had to 'go along with the gag,' so to speak," he said. "If I continued to deny my body I was headed straight for the padded cell; the only chance I had to gain my liberty was to keep silent, get out of the hospital as quickly as I could, and get in touch with Nancy. I wasn't sure that I could make her believe me, or that I could convince anybody, but it was worth a trial, while I was sure to be incarcerated if I fought against the form that had been thrust on me.

"So when the house physician came to see me I was meek as the proverbial Moses, making up a name and address for myself, answering all questions that he asked as promptly and with as much show of reason as I could. At four o'clock this afternoon they signed my release and I left Mercy Hospital.

"The only clothes I had were those I wore when I came to the hospital, of course, and they were a dinner kit. I couldn't very well go marching round in that, but fortunately there had been considerable money in the pockets, so when all charges had been paid at the hospital I still had better than a hundred dollars left. I called a cab and had him drive me to South Second Street, where the second-hand clothing stores are, you know. In one of those I got a pretty good outfit for fifty dollars, and the dealer allowed me twenty in trade for the clothes I wore, so I was not completely destitute.

"Next, I tried to get in touch with Nancy. I 'phoned her several times and got no answer, and when I went to the house it was closed and dark. I waited outside for a while, then when no one came, I thought of you and Dr. de Grandin, and—here I am."

The look he turned on us was that sick, apprehensive, slightly hopeful glance I'd seen so many patients wear when they were waiting for a diagnosis in suspected carcinoma. Despite myself I felt a pang of pity. This was a clean-cut case of organic dementia, probably consequent upon a head injury. What the hospital authorities were thinking of to turn a man in his condition out of doors was more than I could imagine. The patient seemed in a bland humor, but—

De Grandin's level voice broke through my thoughts. "I do not understand your case, *Monsieur,*" he told the caller, "but I believe what you have said. What we can do about it I am not certain, but what we can do will be done, I assure you. You say you have sufficient money to provide for your immediate wants?"

"Yes, sir."

"Very good. I would suggest that you find yourself lodgings and let us know where we can get in touch with you. Meantime, I shall make such investigations as seem necessary at the moment, and consult with you when I have completed them. Shall we say tomorrow afternoon at half-past four? Very well. Till then, *Monsieur*."

"That was the cruelest thing I've ever seen you do," I accused as the door closed behind the caller. "You know as well as I that he's a dement, probably suffering organic dementia as the result of a head wound, possibly complicated by senile dementia. To pretend belief in his delusions—"

"Can you remember what it was he said the man and woman chanted in the conservatory?" he broke in irrelevantly.

"Remember what they chanted—what in the world—"

"There are so many things in the world, my friend, not all of them to be found in the medical textbooks. Attend me. Did he not say they repeated:

"*Aristeas, Kartaphilos, Ahasverus, Buttadaeus*'?

"Do those words mean anything to you?"

"No more than hickory, dickory, dock, or eenie, meenie, mini mo," I answered rather tartly.

"U'm? Are you familiar with the legend of the Wandering Jew."

"You mean the character of whom Eugene Sue wrote?"

"*Monsieur le Général*, among others. In Greek tradition he is known as Aristeas, the Jewish folklore calls him Kartaphilos, another legend names him Ahasverus, while in the German lore he is called John Buttadaeus.

"*Le bon Dieu* only knows where the old legend started. It has been current throughout Europe for almost two thousand years, and has gathered many accretions in retelling, but one thing all the folk-tales have in common, whether they be Greek or Jewish, German, French or Italian: At the end of every century, or a cycle of approximately that length of time, the wretched man, accursed with immortality, falls into a stupor of some kind and wakes up as a young man of somewhere in the vicinity of thirty."

"Are you suggesting that this man who calls himself Norman Northrop might be—"

"I am suggesting nothing, my old one. What I have tried to point out is the possible connection between the names of one who had his youth miraculously restored and this species of possession which we seem to have here. It is not likely, I admit, but it is possible that by some kind of black magic the man who wore the body of the one who just left us was able to exchange his aging frame for the young, vigorous body worn by Monsieur Northrop, much as a tramp might steal the garments of a swimmer and leave his own rags in their place. You comprehend?"

"I should say not!" I jerked back. "This is the most fantastic, incredible sort of nonsense—"

"Forrester!" he exclaimed. "*Morbleu*, I do remember now! *Pour la barbe d'un bouc vert*, that is it!"

"Whatever are you raving about?" I demanded.

"Her name, *pardieu*; I had forgotten it, now it is that I remember!"

SHORTLY AFTER LUNCHEON THE next day he came into the office, pleased as Punch with himself. "Observe, peruse, read him, if you will be so kind, my friend," he ordered, holding out a paper. "Does he not answer some, at least, of our so vexing, questions?"

AGED WOMAN COMMITTED

the headline read, and under it:

A jury in Judge Anslem's court today ruled that an unidentified old woman was insane. The respondent in the lunacy inquiry had claimed to be Margaret Forrester, nationally known swimming champion, who disappeared near Port of Spain, Trinidad, while bathing in the sea some time ago. The respondent had a fixed delusion that the missing young woman's soul had entered her body at the moment she was lost in the sea, and insisted that she be addressed as Miss Forrester, that the bank in which the missing swimmer's account was honor her checks, and that all property of the vanished young woman was hers.

Miss Forrester, it will be remembered, was an orphan without near kin, and her estate has been in the hands of a conservator since her disappearance.

"Well?" I asked as I laid down the photostat.

He shook his head. "I do not think that it is well, Friend Trowbridge. That one person should suffer such obsessions is no matter for remark, but when two—a man and woman—suffer from identical delusions there is a smell of fish upon the business. Nor is that all. Not by any means. On my way from the office of *le journal* I called at Madame Northrop's and showed her a newspaper picture of the missing Margaret Forrester. What do you think she said?"

I drew bow at a venture, making as absurd a guess as seemed possible. "That the picture of Miss Forrester was that of the young woman with whom Norman went away?"

"*Mon Dieu!*" he almost shouted. "How did you know it, my friend? Has Madame Northrop been here?"

"Of course not. I was merely trying to be as crazy as you seem."

"Crazy or not, I am convinced," he answered in a level voice. "Me, I shall investigate this business of the monkey, and see what is to be seen."

"I don't doubt it," I replied as I rose. "Run along and see what's to be seen. I've got some calls to make."

H E WAS ALMOST AS ebullient as a freshly mixed Seidlitz powder when he came bouncing in a few minutes before dinner. "*Pardieu*, my old, we make the progress!" he told me as he sipped his third Martini. "That Madame Nancy, she is superb, so is her brother, Monsieur Wilfred. They are most cooperative."

"How's that?" I asked as we went in to dinner.

He sampled the pottage Bellevue approvingly took a sip of sherry before he replied. "It seems that Monsieur Norman's watch was in a state of disrepair last Monday night, and so he borrowed Monsieur Wilfred's for the evening. It was a fine timepiece, that; a fine Swiss watch which cost four hundred dollars."

I looked at him in amazement. "I fail to see what connection there is between the value of a watch and—"

"Of course, you do, *mon ami*. I should have fallen in a swoon if you had. But listen, pay attention, regard me: When Monsieur Norman's body walked off with the strange young woman it wore Monsieur Wilfred's watch upon its wrist. To take away another's property without so much as by-your-leave is larceny, at least such actions will support a charge of theft. And so we have a police lookout broadcast for them, the one as principal, the other as accessory. I do not doubt that they will be arrested, and when they are I shall be ready for them with the party of surprise. Yes, of course."

"You speak of Norman's body as if it were a thing apart from him," I said. "Am I to understand that you believe that crazy man's story—the dement who was here last night and claimed to be Norman? Is it your theory that both Norman and the aging man are victims of some sort of possession?"

He gave me a long, serious look. "It are entirely possible, Friend Trowbridge. Today we make fun of the old belief in demoniacal possession, and of the possibility of spirit-transference. But can we say with certainty that the old ones were wrong and we are right? We call it epilepsy, or manic-depressive insanity, or sometimes dementia. They called conditions which exhibited the same symptoms possession. The Biblical accounts are far from complete, but any modern psychiatrist examining a patient having symptoms similar to those of King Saul would have no hesitancy in pronouncing him a manic-depressive. Remember how Saul brooded in black melancholy, then flew into a sudden rage and flung a spear at David? Or take the story of the Gadarene demoniac who flew into such frenzies that no chain could restrain him. Has not that the earmarks of what we call acute mania? It may be that the old ones were not foolish, after all."

"But that all happened long ago—"

"*Et puis?* The ancients died of carcinoma and tuberculosis and nephritis, just as we do, why should not we be subject to possession just as they were? Do not mistake me, my friend. I do not say possession explains every case of so-called mental aberration, or even many of them. But in a proper case what we call lunacy might be possession in the strict Biblical meaning of the term. Remember, if you please, possession was no common thing, even in those days. The instances of it that have come down to us have been preserved in the records precisely because they are so unusual. Why should it not be met with occasionally today? Every psychiatrist will tell you he's had cases which defied both diagnosis and treatment, cases not to be explained by anything but the modernly rejected belief in demoniacal possession."

"Well—er—" I temporized, "I suppose it's barely possible, but hardly probable—"

"*Précisément, exactement*, quite so," he nodded vigorously. "It is possibilities, not probabilities, with which we must deal here, my friend. Now—"

"Excuse me, sor, but Lieutenant Costello's on th' 'phone," Nora McGinnis interrupted. "He says as how th' pair ye wanted has been took up near Lake Owassa, an' th' sthate troopers is bringin' 'em down. They should be here in half a hour or so."

"*Morbleu*, but it is magnificent, it is superb!" he exclaimed jubilantly. "Come, Friend Trowbridge, let us hasten dinner, even at the peril to digestion. Either I am more mistaken than I think, or I shall show you something, me!"

L IEUTENANT COSTELLO HAD ASSIGNED a room to de Grandin, one of those bare, ascetic cells that characterize police headquarters, and implemented it according to the little Frenchman's orders. Two comfortable chairs had been placed in the center of the floor, and above them hung a powerful electric bulb whose coned-down light was enhanced by a powerful reflector-shade. The rest of the apartment seemed pitch-dark in contrast to the almost dazzling pyramid of light. At the far end of the room, hidden in the shadows, was a large metal clock that ticked with a sound like the beating of a hammer on an anvil and a deliberation like the surging of the surf upon the beach. *Tick*—tock; *tick*—tock, it told the seconds off slowly, and somehow, as absurd things sometimes pop into our minds, I was reminded of the clock inside the crocodile which followed Captain Hook in *Peter Pan*.

De Grandin looked about the bleak apartment with a smile of grim satisfaction. "All is in readiness, I damn think," he told us. "Bring them to me as soon as they arrive, *mon lieutenant*."

It might have been fifteen minutes later when the errant pair were ushered in by a patrolman and seated in the chairs beneath the light.

I recognized young Northrop at a glance, and saw the woman with him fitted Nancy's description exactly. A "gorgeous hussy," Nancy had called her, and she lived up to the term in every particular. Boldly but beautifully formed, she was, with long slim legs, a flat back, high, firm breasts, and a proud head set superbly on a full round throat.

"*Bon soir, Monsieur, Mademoiselle*," de Grandin greeted pleasantly. "I take it that you know why you have been made arrested?"

Norman Northrop cleared his throat a little nervously. "Some absurd charge of larceny! Bring the complainant here; I'll make good any loss he claims to have suffered—"

"*Monsieur!*" de Grandin's urbane voice had just the proper tone of incredulity. "Are you so utterly *naïf*? Could you not guess the charge of larceny was but an *attrape*, a hoax?"

"Then what—" Norman began, seemed to think better of the question, and lapsed into silence.

De Grandin made no answer, and the metal clock in its corner ticked loudly, deliberately. *Tick*—tock; *tick*—tock!

The little Frenchman reached into his waistcoat pocket, and took out his slim gold watch and swung it by its chain. Back and forth, pendulum-like, in perfect accord to the clock's deliberate ticking the watch swung, its brightly polished surface shining like a dazzling disc of radiance in the cruel white light from the electric bulb.

Tick—tock—swing—swing! I felt my head begin to move from side to side in rhythm with the ticking clock and swaying watch. There was an almost overwhelming fascination in the synchronized sound and movement. I saw Norman and the girl look away, turn their gaze upon the floor, even close their eyes, but in a moment they again looked at the blindingly-bright watch as it swayed in time to the clock's slow tick.

"Would it astonish you to learn that the statute against witchcraft has never been repealed in this state?" de Grandin asked in an almost gentle voice. "It was an oversight on the part of the legislature, of course, but"—the watch swayed slowly and the clock ticked loudly—"but it is still entirely possible for one—or two—to be convicted of the crime today, and made to undergo the ancient penalty. The stake, the fire—" His soft voice paused, but still the clock ticked loudly, slowly; still the blindingly-bright watch swung in long, sweeping arcs.

The prisoners watched the swaying golden disc in fascination. First their heads turned slowly as it swung before them, then only their eyes moved in their motionless faces, finally the woman's chin fell downward to her chest. The man held out a few minutes longer, but finally his eyes closed and his head inclined toward one shoulder.

"Quickly, my friend," de Grandin thrust the watch back in his pocket as he rose. "Bid Costello have the cots brought in."

The lieutenant was ready, and as I opened the door two policemen trundled in a pair of wheeled stretchers of the kind used for emergency cases, lifted the unconscious man and woman on them and stood awaiting further orders.

"*Non*, not that way, *mes braves*," de Grandin told them. "Their heads should be to the west and their feet to the east, that the magnetic currents of the earth may flow through them. Ah, so! *Très bon*."

For a minute or so he stood at the foot of the cots, then, "Aristeas, Kartaphilos, Ahasverus, Buttadaeus, or by whatever name you are known, I order you to quit these bodies!" he whispered sharply. "Go, seek thy proper place, wherever that may be, but trouble Norman Northrop and Margaret Forrester no more! Begone!" He struck the unconscious man a sharp blow in the face, then to the woman he ordered, "Go thou, too, female counterpart of yon male wanderer. Go, get thee hence, ere I call down the ancient judgments on thee—the rack, the thumbscrews, the stake, the fire—" A sharp slap sounded. He had struck the woman in the face.

A silence we could fairly hear succeeded, for he had stopped the clock, and even the street noises outside were insulated from the little basement cell. There came a faint moan from the man on the wheeled litter. "Nancy!" he whimpered. "Nancy, dear, please try to believe me. I know you cannot recognize me, but this is I, your husband Norman—"

"Who says you are not recognizable, Monsieur," de Grandin cut in jubilantly. "Come, rise; get on thy feet"—he held his hand out to Norman. *Madame* your wife is waiting in the corridor outside. She has been told much of your story, and while she does not understand—*eh bien*, did not the good St. Paul say it? 'Love believeth all things.' Go to her, take her in your arms and tell her that you love her, and her only."

He fairly pushed the young man from the room and tiptoed to the bier on which the woman lay. "*Mademoiselle*, Mademoiselle Forrester!" he called softly.

"Wh—what?" The girl half rose, dropped back upon the litter and gave a small mewling cry. "Oh, don't—I tell you I *am* Margaret Forrester—"

"Of course you are, and who says otherwise is an unconscionable liar!" the little Frenchman chuckled. "You are indeed none other. *Mademoiselle*, and you are in proper person, too!"

The girl sat up and looked about the barren room half fearfully. Then she looked down at her hands. "O-o-oh!" the exclamation was a squeal of ecstasy. "They are my hands—my hands; my very own!" She raised her long, slim feet and looked at them and at the shapely legs and ankles to which they were attached as if she'd never seen anything so beautiful. "My feet my legs—"

"And very pretty feet and legs they are, too," Jules de Grandin broke in gallantly. "Come, there is one outside who will be much surprised to see you. Monsieur Horace Hendry from the bank, who has been nursing your estate in your absence." He smiled and put a finger to his lips. "We shall not tell him everything we know, shall we? When he asks where you were—*tenez*, is it not woman's right to be mysterious?"

"Oh," the girl exclaimed, as she put both feet to the floor, took de Grandin's face between her large and well formed hands and kissed him first on one cheek, then on the other, and finally on the mouth. "Oh, you wonderful, wonderful little man! It's as if you'd brought me back from the dead! When you told me that you'd try this afternoon I hadn't any faith, but—"

"*Mademoiselle!*" his voice was filled with shocked reproof. "Remember, I am Jules de Grandin!"

"No, I SHALL NOT try to tell you it was simple," he assured me as we drove home. "It was most damnably complicated, and I was not at all certain of the outcome till the end. Two and two is always four, but what if one mistakes a 3 for a 2? *Pardieu*, the sum will not meet the requirements, *n'est-ce-pas?*

"I went about my adding thus: When Monsieur Norman came to us last night I thought at first as you did. 'We have here a dement, bursting with delusions,' I tell me. But as he talked and I observed the youthful ardor of his speech in such strange contrast to his aged body, I began to wonder. And then all of a suddenly a memory came to me. The journal's story of the strange old woman who insisted she was Mademoiselle Forrester, and kept insisting what was obviously not so till they clapped her into durance in the lunatic asylum.

"'Jules de Grandin,' I ask me, 'are it not odd that a man and a woman should have the same delusions, and at approximately the same time?'

"'It are entirely extraordinary, Jules de Grandin,' I agree with me.

"So I go to the newspaper to refresh my memory, and there I borrow a picture of the disappeared young lady. I take it to Madame Nancy for her inspection, and without a moment's hesitation she identifies it as that of the woman who had gone away with her husband.

"Then, I ask you, what was it I did? *Parbleu*, I went to the asylum where they had that aged woman in confinement and talked with her. *Nom d'une barbe d'un chameau vert*, the story that she tells is strangely like that told by the old man who claims to be Monsieur Northrop!"

"She had been swimming in the sea near Port of Spain in Trinidad when she was accosted by an aged woman who met her as she emerged from the water and heaped insults and abuse on her. At last she could endure no more and struck her tormentor, whereat her whole arm seemed to be paralyzed, and she stood helpless on the sand.

"Then up there came a man, a man of sixty years or more, who took the woman by the hand and raised her, then seized the helpless young woman's hand and started to move round and round. And as they circled round upon the sand they crooned a song about Aristeas, and Kartaphilos and the rest of those queer names by which *le juif errant* has been known in different lands.

"Now I was sure that it was two and two and not some other figures that I added, and the answer must be four!

"Apparently their technique was unvarying. They induced someone previously chosen for his physical appearance to strike one of them, rendering him unconscious for a moment. Then they began their chant, their dance, their witches' incantation, and when the chant and dance were ended the stricken one had moved into the victim's body, leaving his old form to house the victim's soul or spirit or ego—whatever you may care to call it.

"Mademoiselle Forrester had been chosen as the new 'house' for the female of the pair; they left her in the old body and came to this country, where they settled on Monsieur Northrop as a suitable dwelling-place for the male member of this pair of body-snatchers.

"You know the rest, or nearly all of it. You know how we sent out police alarms, how we had them arrested and brought here, how I induced hypnosis by the ticking of the clock and swinging of my watch, having put the fear of prosecution for witchcraft in them, thereby focusing their attention—forcing it into a single channel, as one might say.

"Apparently unconsciousness was a prerequisite to their leaving the bodies they occupied. I induced it by hypnosis, then, since they were unable to work their charm, they took their flight to *le bon Dieu* only knows where when I ordered them to depart. And when they left, the spirits of Monsieur Norman and Mademoiselle Margaret returned to their proper bodies."

"What became of the—er—old bodies?" I asked as we turned into my driveway.

He chuckled. "They will not be used again, my friend. I called the Avondale asylum before we left police headquarters, and was told the aged woman who had claimed to be Miss Forrester had died at just 8:55, which was the moment when I called *la Forrester* from her swoon. Another call I made also. To the rooming house to which Monsieur Northrop went when he left us. The landlady informed me she had found her latest lodger dead in bed a few minutes before. *Voilà tout.*"

"But see here," I demanded, "who were these things, or demons, or whatever they were, who went around snatching bodies, living in them till they'd passed the climacteric, then trading them for others?"

He raised his shoulders in a shrug. "Who knows? Perhaps they were a wicked witch and wizard who had learned to make those vile exchanges, and thus acquire a pseudo-immortality. Perhaps they were a pair of elementals, that is, preadamite spirits who had never lived in human bodies, but somehow managed to get into them and liked them so well that they continued to tenant them, moving from one to another as a man may change his rented residence as it deteriorates or as he finds a more desirable dwelling.

"Who can say with certainty? Not I, the problem is too much for me."

He paused with a quick elfin grin as we entered the hall. "Is it not possible the ice box contains apple pie and beer to which we can give a more fitting home before we go to bed, Friend Trowbridge?"

The Ring of Bastet

I T HAD SNOWED EARLIER, then rained until the snow had melted into muddy slush; now a shrewish wind came scolding up from the Bay, and the sad black puddles that were the dregs of the storm began to glaze and shine with a thin film of ice beneath the street lamps' glare. Walking became hazardous, with the outcome of each step in doubt.

"*Parbleu, mon ami*," Jules de Grandin muttered as he dug his pointed chin two inches deeper into the fur collar of his coat, "I do not like this weather. *Nom d'un poisson!*" his feet slipped on the icy pavement and he caromed into me. "Let us seek the shelter. I do not wish to nurse a broken arm; also I am villainously hungry."

I nodded agreement. I'd treated half a dozen fractures due to falls on ice-glazed streets that winter, and had no wish to spend the next six weeks or so encased in splints and bandages. "Here's the Squire Grill. They have good steaks, if you'd care to try—"

"*Morbleu*, I would attack a dead raw horse without seasoning!" he interjected. "My friend, it is that I am hungry like a lady-wolf with sixteen pups."

The Squire Grill was warm and cozy. Windsor chairs of dark oak were drawn up to the tables, shaded lamplight fell on red-checked tablecloths, behind the bar a man in a white jacket polished glasses and at the far end of the room there blazed an open fire quite large enough to have burnt a Mediæval heretic.

"*Une eau-de-vie, pour l'amour de Dieu*," de Grandin told the waitress, then as she looked blank, "A brandy, if you please, and bring her with the speed of an antelope, *Mademoiselle*."

The girl gave him a friendly smile—women always smiled at Jules de Grandin—then, to me, "And yours, sir?"

"Oh, an old fashioned without too much fruit, if you please, then two steaks, medium, French fries, lettuce and tomato salad—"

"And mugs of beer and apple tart and copious pots of coffee, *s'il vous plaît*," the little Frenchman completed the order.

The look of pleased anticipation on his face became an expression of ecstasy as he cut into his steak, black as charcoal on the outside, and pale watermelon pink within. He raised his eyes and seemed to contemplate some vision of supernal joy. "Ah," he murmured, "Ah, *mon Dieu*—"

The door swung open and a blast of frigid air came rowdying in, and with it came a party of young folks, healthy, obviously ravenously hungry, riotous with gaiety. They made a noisy entrance, moved with more than necessary noise to the long table set before the fireplace, and began calling loudly for service. Evidently they were expected, for a waitress hurried up with a tray of Martinis, and was back with another before the first round was finished.

A young man who had plainly had more than a modest quantum of *pot-valiency* already, rose and held his glass up. "Lad-eez: an' gen'men," he announced a bit unsteadily, "to—to th' bride'n groom; may all their troubles be little ones, an'—"

"Hold on, there, Freddy, hold it!" warned a blonde girl whose pink cheeks glowed with something more than the cold. "They aren't married yet—"

The young man seemed to take this under advisement. "U'm," he drew his hand across his face. "Tha's so, they ain't. Very well, then: Lad-eez an' gen'men, *les fiancés*. May they live long an' prosper!"

"Speech! Speech!" the youngsters chorused, pounding on the table with their cutlery. "You tell 'em, Scotty!"

A tall young man in a crew cut, tweed jacket and tan slacks rose in response to the demand. He was a good-looking youngster, blond, high-colored, with a casual not-long-out-of-college look that labeled him a junior executive in some advertising agency or slickpaper magazine's editorial staff. "My friends," he began, but:

"The ring, Scott—put your brand on her!" his tablemates clamored. "Stand up, Bina, it won't hurt—much!"

The laughing girl who rose in response to the summons was small and delicate and looked as if she had been molded in fragile, daintily tinted porcelain. Her nose and brow and chin were aquiline but delicately proportioned, her skin exquisite. Framed by hair of almost startling blackness that fell to her shoulders and was cut across the forehead in straight bangs, her face had the look of one of those stylized pictures of a Renaissance saint. Coupled with the blush that washed up her pale cheeks her smile gave her a look of almost pious embarrassment. Demurely as a nun about to take the veil of a bride at her wedding ceremony, she held out a slim, fragile hand and the young man slipped a heavy ring on its third finger.

"Seal the bargain! Seal the bargain!" the demand rose like a rhythmed chant, and in obedience to it the girl lifted her face for his kiss. The flush deepened in her checks, and she sat down quickly as two waitresses came up with trays of steaming food and in their wake the *cellérier* with an ice bucket and a magnum of champagne.

De Grandin grinned delightedly at me above the rim of his beer mug. "*C'est très joli, n'est-ce-pas?*" he asked. "*Dites*, youth is marvelous, my friend; it is a pity that it must be wasted on those too young to appreciate it. If—"

A shout came from the merrymakers' table. "Look at Bina! She's passing out!"

I glanced across the room. The girl on whose hand we had seen the ring placed had fallen back in her chair, but the look on her face was not one of alcoholic stupor. Her scarlet lipstick—the sole makeup on her face—seemed suddenly to stand out, vivid as a fresh wound, as if what little color she possessed had retreated behind it, changing the whole aspect of her countenance. Her lips hung open slackly, tried to move and failed, and in her eyes was a look of fascination such as might have been there if she saw a viper crawling toward her. "That girl's ill!" I exclaimed.

"*Pardieu*, my friend, you are so right!" de Grandin agreed. "*C'est—*"

The girl rose slowly, like one who makes as little noise as possible before she takes to panic flight, and walked toward the door of the restaurant. Her patellar reflexes seemed to weaken as she stepped; her knees flexed and her feet kicked aimlessly, as if she suffered motor ataxia. Then suddenly her knees buckled and her legs twisted under her. She fell as limply, as flaccidly, as a filled sack from which the grain had run out, or a rag doll emptied of its sawdust. We saw the shape of total fear form on her face as we reached her. She turned wide, frightened eyes on us, and I noted that although her pupils were large and black they were rimmed by dark green irises. "My legs," she whimpered in a voice that seemed to shake with chill. "I can't move them—there's no feeling in them; but they're cold. Cold!"

"I am Dr. Jules de Grandin, this is Dr. Samuel Trowbridge," the little Frenchman introduced us as we knelt beside the fallen girl. Then, "You have no pain, *Mademoiselle*? No feeling of—"

"No feeling in my legs at all, sir. They're numb—and cold."

"U'm?" he raised the hem of her full, pleated brown wool-jersey dress and took the calf of one slim leg between his thumb and forefinger. "You do not feel?" he pinched the firm flesh till it showed white with pressure.

"No, sir."

I noted that she wore no stockings and shook my head in disapproval.

De Grandin nodded. "Cold," he pronounced. "*Froid comme une grenouille.*"

"No wonder," I shot back. "You'd be cold as a frog, too, if you went traipsing out in sub-freezing weather with no more stockings than a—"

"*Ah bah*," he cut me off. "Do not let Madame Grundy sway your judgment, Friend Trowbridge. It may be cold outside, but it is warm in here, and she sat almost within arm's length of that great fire. She should not have the chill."

I knelt beside him and laid a hand on the girl's leg. It was cold as a dead woman's, though the skin was smooth and sleek, without a sign of goose-flesh.

"You're sure you have no pain, Mademoiselle?" de Grandin asked again, leaning close to look into her eyes and nostrils. "No headache, no pains in back or sides or limbs—"

"No, sir. Nothing, till just now when my legs gave way under me."

He took his clinical thermometer from his waistcoat, shook it and thrust it into her mouth, then placed his fingers on her wrist. At length. "Pulse and temperature are normal," he reported. " It is not anterior polio-myelitis. Except for this localized chill and inability to walk—"

"Berger's paresthesia?" I hazarded.

He nodded doubtfully. "Perhaps. At any rate, she cannot lie here. Let us take her home and see what we can do."

JOBINA HOUSTON LIVED IN one of those cubicles known as "efficiency apartments"—a single fairly large room with furnishings designed to lead a double life. The small round dining table could be made into a bench by tilting up its top, a minuscule kitchenette, complete with porcelain sink and electric grill, lay in ambush behind a mirrored door the divan opened out to form a bed, the chest of drawers did duty both as china closet and clothes press.

With the help of the blonde girl who had been ringleader at the party we got our patient into bed with hot water bottles at her feet and an electric pad under her.

De Grandin looked more puzzled than alarmed. "When did you first begin to notice this sensation of numbness, Mademoiselle?" he asked when we had made the girl as comfortable as possible.

She wrinkled her smooth brow. "I—I don't quite know," she answered. "It must have been—oh, no, that's silly!"

"Permit me to be judge of silliness and sense, if you please," he returned. "When was it that you first began to feel this chilly numbness?"

"We-ell, I think I first felt it just as Scott put the ring on my finger. You see," she hurried on, as if an autobiographical sketch would help us, "Scott Driggs and I both work at Bartlett, Babson, Butler and Breckenridge's advertising agency. He's in copy, I'm in production."

"Of course," he agreed as if he understood her perfectly. "And then, if you please?"

"Well, we sort of drifted together, and—and suddenly we both realized this is it, and so decided to get married, and—" One hand crept from the shrouding blankets as she spoke, and began to smooth the bedclothes gently. "So tonight we gave an engagement party, and—"

"Mademoiselle, where did that ring come from, if you please?" he interrupted.

"Why, from Scott of course. He gave it to me tonight—"

"*Bien oui*, one understands all that, but what I most desire to know is where did he get it—where did it come from originally?"

"Why, I really don't know, sir. Scott and I don't really know much about each other. All we know is we're in love—that's plenty, isn't it?"

He nodded, but I noticed that his eyes were on the ring with a long, speculative stare. "You do not know who was his father?" he asked at length.

"Not really, sir. I understand he was some sort of scientist, an explorer or something; but he's been dead a long time. Scott hasn't any family. He finished college on his G.I. money and came to work at B.B.B.&B. about the same time I did. So, as I said, our work threw us together, and we—"

A small frown of annoyance gathered between de Grandin's brows as he stared in fascination at the ring. It was a heavy golden circlet, heavy as a man's seal ring, and set with some sort of green stone which might have been peridot or zircon, or even a ceramic cartouche. Certainly it could not have been more than semi-precious, for it had no luster, although its color was peculiarly lovely. The gem was deeply incised with what appeared to be a human figure swathed like an Egyptian mummy, but having a peculiarly malformed head. "You recognize him?" he asked as I completed my inspection. I shook my head. To the best of my knowledge I had never seen such a figure before.

"Tell me, *Mademoiselle*," he demanded, "just what did you mean when you said you began to feel this so strange numbness at the moment your fiancé put this ring on your hand?"

"I don't quite know how to put it, sir, but I'll try. Scott had just put the ring on my finger when the dinner came, and as I took the cover off my *coq au vin* I happened to look toward the fireplace and saw—" she halted with a little shudder of revulsion.

"Yeah, what was it you saw?" he prompted.

"A cat."

"A cat? *Grand Dieu des porcs*, you mean a puss? Why not? Most restaurants have one."

"Ye-es, sir; I know. That's why I chose the Squire Grill for our party. They haven't one."

He raised his slim black brows. "*Qu'est-ce que c'est, Mademoiselle?*"

"You see, I'm one of those people who can't abide the sight of a cat. It terrifies me just to have one in the same room with me. There's a technical name for it. I forget—"

"Ailurophobia," he supplied. "*Bien*, my little, you are one of those who cannot stand the sight of a puss-cat. What next?"

"At first I thought I must have been mistaken, but there it was, coming right at me, snarling, and getting bigger with each step it took. When I first saw it, it was just an ordinary-sized cat, but by the time it had advanced three feet it was big as a large dog, and by the time it almost reached the table it seemed big as a lion."

"U'm? That is what terrified you?"

"Oh, you noticed how frightened I was?"

"But naturally. And then?"

"Then I began to feel all funny inside—as if everything had come loose, you know—and at the same time I felt my feet growing numb and cold, then my ankles, then my legs. I knew that if I didn't get away that awful thing would pounce on me as if I were a mouse, so I got up and started for the door, and then—" Her narrow shoulders moved in the suggestion of a shrug. "That's where you came in, sir."

He tweaked the needle points of his small blond mustache. "One sees." Turning to the girl who had come with us from the restaurant, he asked, "Will you be kind enough to stay with her tonight? She has sustained a shock, but seems to be progressing well. I do not think that you will need do more than keep her covered, but if by any chance you should need us—" He scribbled our phone number on a card and handed it to her.

"O.K., sir," the girl answered. "I'll ring you if I need you, but I don't expect I shall."

"THE TROUBLE WITH TODAY'S young folks is that they don't know how to drink," I complained as we left Jobina's apartment. "That gang of kids had been pub crawling—stopping at every bar between their office and the Squire, probably—and Jobina thought she had to match Scott glass for glass. No wonder she thought she saw a monstrous cat. The only wonder is she didn't see a pink elephant or crocodile."

De Grandin chuckled. "*La, la,* to hear you talk one might suspect you wear long underwear and drive a horse instead of a car, Friend Trowbridge. I fear, however"—he sobered abruptly—"that her trouble stems from something more than too much *gaieté*—"

"D'ye mean to tell me that you think she saw that great cat?" I demanded.

"I think perhaps she did," he answered levelly.

"Nobody else did—"

"Notwithstanding that, it is entirely possible she saw what she claimed—"

"Humph, when people see things that aren't there—"

"Perhaps it was there, spiritually, if not corporeally."

"Spiritually? What the devil—"

"Something not so far from that, my old," he agreed. "Suppose we call on young Driggs. He may be able to tell us something."

I expelled a long, annoyed breath. When he was in one of these secretive moods it was useless to question him, I knew from experience.

"How's Bina?" young Driggs greeted as he let us into his apartment something like a quarter-hour later.

"She seems recovering," the Frenchman answered non-committally. "Meanwhile—"

"What was it? What was wrong with her?"

"One cannot say with certainty at this time. Perhaps you can enlighten us."

"I?"

"*Précisément.* You can, by example, tell us something of the history of the ring you put upon her finger just before her seizure."

The young man looked at him blankly. "I don't see what connection there could be between the ring and Bina's illness."

"Neither do I?" de Grandin confessed, "but if there is, what you can tell us may prove helpful. Where did it come from, if you know?"

"It belonged to my father, Dad was assistant curator of Egyptology at the Adelphi Museum in Brooklyn."

"Ah?" de Grandin bent a little forward in his chair. "It may be you can help us, after all, *Monsieur.* What of your father, if you please?"

"In 1898 or '99 the Museum sent him to Egypt, and while there he went up the Nile to Tel Basta, where—"

"Where the worship of Ubasti and Pasht, the cat-headed goddesses, was centered in the olden days," de Grandin interjected.

"Just so, sir. While Dad was poking round the old ruins he unearthed several little balls of what seemed like amber, except that it was much clearer, almost transparent. The Egyptian government had begun to clamp down on the exportation of relics, but Dad managed to smuggle three of the small spheres out with him. Two he gave to the Museum, the other one be kept.

"That little amber ball is among my earliest recollections. I used to look at it in awe, for buried in it was a gold ring with a green set, and when you held it to the light the stone seemed almost alive, as if it were an eye—a big green cat's eye—that looked at you.

"I don't know much about Egyptian antiques, my tastes all ran to other things, but I remember Dad once told me the ring had once belonged to a priest of Bastet, the cat-headed goddess who personified the beneficent principle of fire."

De Grandin nodded eagerly. "Quite yes *Monsieur.* And then?"

"My father died while I was still in the Army, and Mother left the old house in Gates Avenue and went to live with some cousins out at Patchogue, and when she died that little amber envelope containing the old priest's ring was about all she left me."

He grinned a little self-consciously. "Any man can give his girl a diamond— if he has the price—but nobody but I could give Jobina such a ring as that I put on her finger tonight."

De Grandin tugged at his mustache until I feared that he would wrench it loose from his lip. "How did you get the ring from its envelope, *Monsieur?*" he asked.

"I had a jeweler cut it out. He had the devil of a time doing it, too. I'd always thought the capsule that enclosed it was amber, or perhaps resin, but it proved so hard that he broke several drills before he could succeed in cutting it away from the ring."

The Frenchman rose and held out his hand. "Thank you, my friend," he told our host. "I think that you have been most helpful."

"You're sure Jobina'll be all right?" the young man asked.

"Her progress has been satisfactory so far," de Grandin took refuge in that vagueness which physicians have used since the days of Hippocrates. "I see no reason why she should not make a quick, complete recovery."

"What's it all about?" I demanded as we reached the street. "You seem to see some connection between that ring and Jobina Houston's seizure, but—"

"Your guess is good as mine, perhaps a little better," he admitted as he held his stick up to signal a taxi. "My recollections of the cults of Bastet and Pasht are somewhat hazy. I must put on the *toque de pensée*—the how do you call him—thinking-hat?—before I can give you an opinion. At present I am stumbling in the dark like a blind man in a strange neighborhood."

I T MUST HAVE BEEN sometime past midnight, for the moon which had come out with the cessation of the storm had nearly set, when the ringing of the bedside telephone woke me. "Dr. Trowbridge speaking," I announced as I lifted the instrument.

The voice that answered me was high and thin with incipient hysteria. "This is Hazel Armstrong, Doctor—the girl you left with Jobina Houston, you know."

"Oh?"

"I'll say it's, Oh! She's gone."

"Eh? How's that?"

"She's gone, I tell you. Walked right out in her nightgown, and in this cold, too." Her voice broke like a smashing cup, and I could hear the sound of high-pitched sobbing over the wire.

"Stop crying!" I commanded sharply. "Stop it at once and tell me just what happened."

"I—I don't know, sir. I think she's gone crazy, and I'm scared. I did just as you told me, kept her covered up and kept the water bottles hot, but after a while I fell asleep. About ten minutes ago—maybe fifteen—I heard a noise and when I woke up I saw her standing by the door, about to go out. She'd pulled her night-gown down off the shoulders, and had a perfectly terrible look on her face. I said, 'Jobina, what in the world are you doing?' and then I stopped talking, for she looked at me and growled—growled like an animal, sir. I thought she was going to spring at me, and held a pillow up for a shield, but finally she turned away and went out the door. I didn't try to stop her—I was afraid!"

"Do not be frightened, *Mademoiselle*," de Grandin's voice came soothingly over the extension. "We shall go seeking her at once. Be good enough to leave the door unlocked."

"Unlocked? With a crazy woman on the rampage? Not me, sir. If you find her you knock three times on the door like this"—three sharp taps sounded as she struck the telephone with her nail—"I'll let you in, but—"

"Very well," he agreed. "Have it that way, if you wish, *Mademoiselle*. We go in search of her at once."

"She can't have gone far in her night-clothes in such weather as this," I volunteered as we set out. "I only hope she doesn't develop pneumonia—"

"I greatly doubt she will," he comforted. "The inward fire—"

"The what—"

"No matter, I was only thinking aloud. To the right, if you please."

"But she lives in Raleigh Street, down that way—"

"We shall not find her there, my friend. She will be at Monsieur Driggs' unless I am far more mistaken than I think. When the cat goes mousing one goes to the mousehole to find her, *n'est-ce-pas?*"

I shook my head. This talk of cats and mice seemed utterly irrelevant.

THE AUTOMATIC ELEVATOR TOOK us up to the floor where Scott Driggs lived, and the heavy carpets on the hall floor made our footsteps noiseless as we hurried down the corridor. "*Ah?*" de Grandin murmured as we turned the corner and came in view of his apartment entrance. "*Ah-ha?*" The door hung open and a little stream of pallid lamplight dribbled out into the corridor.

Through the door leading to Scott's bedroom, which stood ajar, we saw them like the figures in a tableau. Scott lay motionless upon the bed, and standing by him, seeming more a phantom than a person, stood Jobina Houston.

But how changed! She wore a night-gown of sheer silver-blue crêpe, knife-pleated from the bosom, and flaring like an inverted lily-cup from the waist, but she had torn the bodice of the robe, or turned it down, so bust and shoulders were exposed, and she was clothed only from waist to insteps. Her straight-cut uncurled black hair hung about her face like that of some Egyptian woman pictured on the frescoes of a Pharaoh's tomb, and as we stepped across the sill she turned her face toward us.

Involuntarily I shrank back, for never on a human countenance had I seen such a look of savage hatred. Although her lids were lowered it seemed her eyes glared through the palpebrae, and the muscles round her mouth had stretched until the very contours of her face were altered. There was something feline—bestial—about it, and bestial was the humming, growling sound that issued from her throat through tight-closed lips.

The glance—if you could call it that—she threw in our direction lasted but a second, then she turned toward the man on the bed. She moved with a peculiar gliding step, so silently, so furtively that it seemed that she hardly stepped at all, but rather as if she were drawn along by some force outside herself. I'd seen a cat move that way as it rushed in for the kill when it had finished stalking a bird.

I opened my mouth to shout a warning—or a protest, I don't know which—and de Grandin clapped his hand across my lips. "Be silent, species of an elephant!" he hissed, then stepped across the room as silently as the form moving toward the bed.

"Jobina Houston," he called softly, yet in a voice so cold and distinct it might have been the tinkle of a breaking icicle. "Jobina Houston, attend me! Do not be deceived, Jobina, God is not mocked. The Lord God overcame Osiris, threw down Memnon's altars and made desolate the temples of Bastet and Sechmet. Those Olden Ones, they have no being; they are but myths. The fires upon their altars have been cold a thousand years and more; no worshippers bow at their shrines, their priests and priestesses have shuddered into dust—"

The woman faltered, half turned toward him, seemed uncertain of her next step, and he walked quickly up to her, holding out his hand imperatively. "The ring!" he ordered sharply. "Give me the ring thou wearest without right, O maiden of the latter world!"

Slowly, like a subject under hypnosis, or a sleep-walker making an unconscious gesture, she raised her left hand, and I could have sworn the green stone of her ring glowed in the lamplight as if it were the living eye of a cat.

He drew the heavy circlet from the girl's slim finger and dropped it into his pocket. "Quick, Friend Trowbridge," he ordered, "take a blanket from the bed, envelope her in it as in a *camisole de force*—what you call the strait-jacket! Quickly, while her indecision lasts!"

I obeyed him mechanically, expecting every moment she would resist me ferociously, but to my astonishment she stood quiescent as a well trained horse when the groom puts the harness on it.

"*Bien*," he ordered, "let us take her home and see that she is rendered docile with an opiate."

Half an hour later Jobina lay tucked in bed, sleeping under an injection of a half-grain of morphine. Hazel Armstrong had gone home, the city's noises had sunk to a low, muted hum, and in the east the stars were paling in the light of coming day.

"NOW MAYBE YOU'LL CONDESCEND to tell me what it's all about?" I asked sarcastically as we drove home after turning Jobina over to the nurse for whom we'd telephoned the agency.

He raised his narrow shoulders in the sort of shrug that no one but a Frenchman can achieve and made one of those half-grunting, half-whinnying noises no one but a Frenchman can make. "To tell the plain, ungilded truth, I am not sure I know, myself," he confessed.

"But you must have had some idea—some relevant clue to it all," I protested.

"Yes and no. When Mademoiselle Jobina first showed signs of being over-come last night I thought as you did, that she had been taken ill, but the more I examined her the farther from a diagnosis I found myself. The sudden onset of her symptoms did not seem to match any disease I knew. Then when she told us about seeing the cat-thing almost at the moment Monsieur Scott put the ring on her finger I was till more puzzled. As you were at such pains to point out, no one else had seen the thing; the vision, if it may be called such, had been entirely subjective, something visible to her alone. It did not seem to me that she had drunk enough to see nonexistent animals, yet. . . . Then I observed the ring, and suddenly, something clicked in my memory. 'Where have you seen a ring like that, Jules de Grandin?' I asked me, and, 'At *Le Musée des Antiques* in Cairo,' I replied to me.

"'*Bien*, and what about that ring, Jules de Grandin?' I asked me.

"I searched my memory, trying to recall all that I knew about it as one strug-gles to recall the tune of a forgotten song.

"*Eh*, then I had it! It had been a priest's ring from Bubastis, the city of Ubasti or Bastet, the cat-headed goddess!

"Now Bastet, or Ubasti, was the sister and the wife of Ptah, who shaped the world and had his shrine at Memphis. She typified the benign influence of heat, the warming sun that made the grain to grow, the fire that gave men com-fort. She was a mild and rather playful goddess, and therefore was depicted as a woman with a cat's head—the kind, affectionate and gentle pussy-cat we like to have about the house.

"*Eh bien*, she had a sister variously known as Sechmet and Merienptha who was her antithesis. That one represented the cruel principle of heat—the blazing sun that parched the fields and threw men down with sunstroke, the fire that ravaged and consumed, more, the blazing heat of savage, maddened passion. Now, strangely, though they represented bane and blessing to be had from the same thing, the sisters were depicted exactly alike—a woman swathed in mum-my-clothes with a cat's head and wearing an uræus topped by the sun's disc. Their temples stood nearby each other in the city of Bubastis, on the site of which the modern mud-village of Tel Basta stands.

"Good. When the Persians under Cambyses swarmed over Egypt in 525 B.C., the city of Bubastis was among the first they took. *Parbleu*, they were the *boches* of their day, those Persians; all that they could not steal they destroyed. So when the priests of Bastet and Sechmet heard they were about to come they hid their temples' treasures. Some they sunk in the Nile, some they buried, some few they took with them.

"As part of his ecclesiastical vesture the priest of Bastet and Sechmet wore a gold ring set with a green stone like a cat's eye. Many of these they enclosed in capsules of balsam resin, which was also an ingredient of their embalming. The rings thus held in their protective envelopes were buried in the earth—it was much easier to find a sphere larger than a golf ball than to hunt for a ring buried in the shifting sand.

"And then what happened I ask you? *Mordieu*, the Persians came, they pulled the city's walls down, razed the temples to the ground, killed all the people they could find, then went upon their way of conquest.

"The years went by, the Romans came, and after them the Arabs, and still those priestly rings lay buried in their envelopes of hardened balsam. Explorers delved among the ruins of the once great temple-city and dug these rings up and took them to museums. Young Driggs's father was one such. He brought back three rings of Bastet, two for his museum, one for himself, remember?"

"Yes," I nodded, "but what connection is there between the ring and Jobina's seizure, and—"

"Be patient, if you please," he interrupted. "I shall explain if you will give me time. Like priests of every cult and faith, the priests of ancient Egypt were a class apart. They were vowed to their gods, none others might serve at the altar, none others invoke divine aid, none others wear the priestly vestments. You comprehend?"

"I can't say that I do."

"*Eh*, then I must make the blueprint for you. As far as can be ascertained, such priestly rings as came to light were either melted down for their gold or taken to museums; none were ever worn. Jobina Houston seems to be the first one not initiated into the priesthood to wear a ring of Bastet on her finger.

"*Tiens*, those olden gods were jealous. They took offense at her wearing that ring. Bastet, or possibly Sechmet, appeared to her as in a vision, paralyzed her with fright, and finally took possession of her mind and body, driving her to make a makeshift imitation of an Egyptian priestess's costume and go to young Drigg's house to wreak vengeance on him for the sacrilege he had committed when he put the sacerdotal ring on a profane finger."

"Oh, pshaw!" I scoffed. "You really believe that?"

"I do, indeed, my friend. Jobina Houston had a morbid fear of cats, therefore she was doubly sensitive to the influence of the cat-headed goddess. In ancient days that ring had soaked up influences of the old temples when it adorned the finger of some priest of Bastet or Sechmet; it had lain sealed in resin for a full thousand years and more. Those influences could not be dissipated because of the hermetic sealing of the balsam envelope that held them. Then when they had been released from their integument those forces—those psychic influences with which the ring was saturated—were released from it as water is released from a squeezed sponge. The malefic forces took possession of Jobina like a tangible mephitic vapor. She was helpless under their influence."

"U'm-h'm," I agreed doubtfully. "I've heard of such things, but how was it you managed to arrest their working? When you called to her in Scott Driggs' flat she seemed like a sleep-walker and made no effort to resist when you demanded the ring. How was that?"

"Ah, there I took the chance, my friend. I played the hunch, as you would say. I knew that girl had been brought up religiously. She believed firmly in the power of God—of good. She was like a person in light hypnosis, unable to control herself or her movements, but able to hear outside voices. So I called to her, reminding her of the great power of God—reminded her how He had overcome the heathen world and made a mock of all the pantheon of heathen gods and goddesses. In effect I said to her, 'What are you, a Christian woman, doing when you listen to the blandishments of heathen deities? Don't you know that they are powerless before the might of the Lord God?' A child may dread its shadow, but when its father tells it that the shadow has no substance, *pouf!* that fear is gone. I told her that the forces that enthralled her had no being, that they were but myths and memories—just the shadows of old dreams that vanished in the brightness of the face of God. And so it was. For just a little moment she rebelled against their malign power, and in that moment I took off the ring. Then *paf!* the charm was broken, the spell dissolved, the powerhouse of their influence put out of commission. *Voilà.*"

"What about the ring?" I asked. "Will you give it back to Scott?"

"Of course," he answered, "but only when he promises to give it to some museum. That thing is far too dangerous to be left where unwary young women may slip it on their fingers. Yes."

Dawn came, heralded by an ever-widening crimson glow, as we turned into the driveway. "*Tiens,*" he raised a hand to pat back a great yawn. "I am a tired old man, me. I think I need a tonic before I climb into bed. Yes, certainly; of course."

"A tonic?" I echoed.

"But yes. I prescribe him. Four ounces of brandy, the dose to be repeated at five-minute intervals for the next quarter-hour."

The Complete Tales of Jules de Grandin by Seabury Quinn
is collected by Night Shade Books in the following volumes:

The Horror on the Links
The Devil's Rosary
The Dark Angel
A Rival from the Grave
Black Moon